THE OUTLANDERS

Tor Books by David B. Coe

THE LONTOBYN CHRONICLE
Children of Amarid
The Outlanders

THE OUTLANDERS

BOOK II

of

The LonTobyn Chronicle

DAVID B. COE

TOR®

A Tom Doherty Associates Book / *New York*

THE OUTLANDERS

Copyright © 1998 by David B. Coe

This book is printed on acid-free paper.

Edited by James Frenkel

Maps by Ellisa H. Mitchell

A Tor Book
Published by Tom Doherty Associates, Inc.
175 Fifth Avenue
New York, NY 10010

Tor Books on the World Wide Web:
http://www.tor.com

Tor® is a registered trademark of Tom Doherty Associates, Inc.

Library of Congress Cataloging-in-Publication Data

Coe, David B.
        The outlanders / David B. Coe; maps by Ellisa H. Mitchell.—1st ed.
            p.   cm.—(The LonTobyn chronicle; bk. 2)
        "A Tom Doherty Associates book."
        ISBN 0-312-86447-7
        I. Title.   II. Series: Coe, David B.   LonTobyn chronicle; bk. 2.
PS3553.034308   1998
813'.54—dc21   98-23672
                                                                CIP

First Edition: October 1998

Printed in the United States of America

0 9 8 7 6 5 4 3 2 1

In memory of my parents,
Sylvia W. Coe (1922–1995)
and
Jacques Coe, Jr. (1919–1997),
who taught me to love, encouraged me to dream,
and allowed me to become who I am.

Acknowledgments

Once again, I have many people I wish to thank: Harold Roth, my agent and good friend; Tom Doherty, for his continued faith in me; James Frenkel, my editor, whose friendship and guidance have improved my writing and enhanced the entire process; Karen Lovell, Jim Minz, Jennifer Hogan, and all the other wonderful people at Tor; my friends Alan Goldberg and Chris Meeker, who again read early drafts of the novel and offered helpful comments and suggestions; and my siblings, Bill, Liz, and Jim, who, as always, gave me their love and support.

Finally, my deepest thanks go once more to my wife, Nancy Berner, and to our daughter, Alex. Nancy's astute comments on the manuscript and her constant love and encouragement made this book possible. And Alex's joyful spirit and tireless exploration and discovery of the world around her reminded me that there are other wonders in this life besides mages and cerylls.

—D.B.C.

Dhaalmar
Shallows

the Boreal Stand

Dhaalmar Mts.

MOUNTSEA R.

Dhaalmar Spur

Three Fools Lakes

Oerellan Harbor

DEEP CANYON R.

VRUDAN R.

VRUDAN R. EAST FORK

Oerellan
Peninsula

Oerella-Nal

Lake of the
Matrons

Point of the
Sovereigns

Ari

GLACIER GAP R.

Gold Inlet

Bay of Storms

Oerellan
Green

Lake of the Clouds

S

DARKWATER R.

Western
Ocean

Median Range

THREE NALS R.

Bragory
Wood

REIVDRAH R.

THE RIVER WANDERER

Bragor-
Nal

Gold
Palace

Gu

Lake
Merrie

BRAGORY R.

Cape of Stars

Gulf of Dalrek

Einar's Fen

Greenwater Range

VIHIR R.

Guarde
Swam

Stony Harbor

Stib
Grove

Cape Lon

LITTLE GREEUR

Gulf of the Gods

Stib-
Nal

Stib Bay

Isthmus
Point

Lon-Ser

Duch

Abborij

Tobyn-Ser

Forests of Leora

Abborij Strait

Hawksfind Wood

Brisalli

Accalia

Taima

Dacias Lake

Amarid

Northern Plain

Upper Horn

Tobyn's Wood

DHAALISMIN R.

Wood's Mist Lake

Arick's Wrath

Seaside Mts

North Shelter

South Shelter

Riversmeet Traverse

Emerald Hills

Phelan Spur

Lower Horn

Lake of the Dunes

Kaera

Sunsfury Harbor

Sern

Great Desert

Tobyn's Plain

Watersbend

LonTobyn Isthmus

TONG R.

MORANDRAL R.

Southern Swamp

Duclea's Tears

Firegrass Lake

the Shadow Forest

Therons' Grove

Riversend Harbor

Gulf of Ceryllon

Necklace

the Sawblade

Ceryl Cavern

Ceryllon

Southern Archipelago

Bragor-Nal

Arick's Sea

North

Gold Inlet

Median Range

Lake of the Clouds

3rd

2nd

4th

1st

CEDRYCH'S

23rd 22nd

TRESTOR-PROPER

DOMINION

Bragory Wood

24th

BRAGOR-
PROPER

5th Gold
Palace

8th

26th

THE RIVER WANDERED

25th

The Farm

6th

CEDRYCH'S
DOMINION

10th

28th

27th

NEWELL'S
DOMINION

29th

THREE NALS R.

9th

MERNE-PROPER

7th

11th

30th

Gulf of Dalrek

13th

BRAGORY R.

15th

17th

20th

Lake
Merne

Einar's Fen

12th

WILDON'S
DOMINION

14th

16th

VIHIR R.

18th

21st

19th

Greenwater Range

Guardian
Swamp

'97 ©Lisa Mitchell

1

In considering the sum of my interrogations of the outlander Baram, I am forced to conclude that future encounters with invaders from Lon-Ser are inevitable. The conditions in Lon-Ser that prompted this first attempt to destroy the Order and seize control of Tobyn-Ser have plagued that land for more than two centuries, steadily growing worse with the passage of time. They will not have disappeared. Indeed it seems likely that the intervening four years have served only to heighten the urgency felt by those who initiated the plot against us. It is up to us, therefore, to choose the circumstances of our next encounter: Do we wait for them to make their next move, and risk that this time we will be unable to withstand their assault? Or do we act first, and set the terms of the confrontation ourselves? Certainly, no one who knows me will be surprised to learn that I would advocate the latter.

—From Section Nine of "The Report of Owl-Master Baden on his Interrogation of the Outlander Baram," Submitted to the 1,014th Gathering of the Order of Mages and Masters. Spring, Gods' Year 4625.

The paper itself was a message. Immaculately white, its edges were as straight as sunbeams, its corners so sharp that they seemed capable of drawing blood. It had arrived with first light at Amarid's Great Hall, Sonel had been informed, delivered by an Abboriji merchant who sailed with it across Arick's Sea, through the Abborij Strait, and around the northeast tip of Tobyn-Ser into Duclea's vast ocean. Yet, despite the distance it had travelled, it still came rolled in a precise, narrow cylinder and tied with a shining, golden ribbon of silk. Indeed, it looked so elegant, so unnaturally perfect, that Sonel had known, even before she read the infuriatingly terse response to her own letter of several months before, what the flawless, ornate lettering would say. She thought now of her own note and she felt embarrassed. She had used the finest parchment in the land; she had employed the most skilled scribe in Amarid, and

had tied her letter with the fine, blue satin used for all of the Order's communications. But when compared with this missive from Lon-Ser, the image of that
first letter seemed to wither and fade. In her memory the parchment now
looked dingy and rough-edged, the lettering coarse and uneven, the blue satin
crude and inadequate. The letter from Lon-Ser's leaders made a mockery of her
effort.

Which, of course, was the point. The words printed so finely beneath the
gold seal of Lon-Ser's Council of Sovereigns made that much clear:

Owl-Sage Sonel:
Regarding your note of this past winter: We have no knowledge of the
events you describe, nor do we have any desire to become entangled in what
are most likely internal disturbances endemic to Tobyn-Ser.

That was all, except for the date, given in a notation that Sonel did not recognize, and a second seal pressed in gold wax beneath the message.

She leaned back in her chair and closed her eyes, smelling the sweet breads
and *shan* tea that sat on the low table before her, still untouched, no doubt cold
by now. Nearly half the morning was gone, and still she could not bring herself
to stir. Twice already, Basya had come to the door, urging her to eat and offering to help her make preparations for tomorrow's opening of the Gathering,
and twice Sonel had put her off. The third time could not be far away. Again
she read the note, as she had perhaps a dozen times already. It was a dismissal,
cold and disdainful. Little more, and certainly nothing less. She wasn't sure
what she had expected, although she knew that it hadn't been much. More
than this, though; she needed more than this.

The idea of writing the letter had first come to her late in the fall, during one of
Baden's frequent visits to Amarid. Once more, he had come to the First Mage's
city to continue his conversations with Baram, the outlander. But each of
Baden's visits had seen the Owl-Master and the Owl-Sage spending greater
amounts of time together, and Sonel's recollection of this particular occasion
remained vivid and brought a smile to her lips, even as she continued to stare at
the note from Lon-Ser. Before that visit, it had been several years since she had
lain with any man, and several more since she had passed a night with Baden.
Her smile deepened, then faded as the memory moved past their lovemaking to
what had followed. Lying together in these very quarters, as the glow of the
moon seeped through the translucent white windows and illuminated the tangle of sheets and bare limbs, Sonel had shared with the Owl-Master her frustration with the Order's inaction over the last four years. Ever since Sartol, the
renegade Owl-Master, was destroyed by the combined might of the Order in
the Great Hall, and the band of outlanders with which the renegade had allied
himself was defeated at Phelan Spur, she had tried to compel the Order to address the threat posed by Lon-Ser. But every proposed plan of action had
drawn fierce opposition from a small but outspoken clique of older mages and

masters, and, though a majority of the Order agreed that some action was war-ranted, Sonel had been unable to win support for any specific plan. The prob-lem persisted even after Owl-Master Odinan's death, just before last summer's Gathering, robbed the older mages of their most impassioned voice. Indeed, if anything, Odinan's passing appeared to reinvigorate his allies, giving them a symbol around which to rally. With the venerable Owl-Master gone, a new leader emerged, Erland, who, though revered less than Odinan, had proven himself an energetic and persuasive spokesman.

"We haven't done a thing," Sonel concluded on that autumn night, lying with Baden. She had been unable to keep the desperation from her voice as she passed a hand through her wheat-colored hair. "For all we know, there's al-ready another group of outlanders in Tobyn-Ser, and we've done nothing."

Baden cleared his throat awkwardly before astonishing her with a confidence of his own. "They may be planning something," he told her, taking her hand. "They may even be on their way. But they're not here yet. That much we do know." And in this way, Sonel first learned of the psychic link that Baden and his friends had formed in western Tobyn-Ser. It was an old magic, first devel-oped by Amarid himself after the death of Theron, his friend and rival, and the departure from Tobyn-Ser of Theron's followers. The First Mage had feared that the Owl-Master's disciples would return and seek to avenge their leader, and he had established a mind link among all the land's remaining mages, a web of consciousness that monitored the land's borders. Even after the First Mage died several decades later, the Order continued to maintain it. For nearly three hundred years, Amarid's psychic link guarded the land. But the link de-manded a tremendous expenditure of power that drained both mage and famil-iar, and eventually, it was allowed to slacken, until it ceased to exist altogether.

Now Baden and his allies had created a similar link in western Tobyn-Ser, smaller to be sure, but, if formed correctly, no less effective than Amarid's. And they had done so without any proper authority. The Order had rejected the reestablishment of the psychic link as an option several times over the past few years, though the issue continued to be a point of bitter contention within the Order. For a time, before the mages learned that outlanders had been responsi-ble for the attacks on Tobyn-Ser, Baden himself had spoken against the link. Later, he switched sides in the debate, but those against the link still prevailed. And now Baden and his friends had gone against the will of the Order. He had no right to do this. Sonel should have been indignant. But her immediate sense of relief and gratitude at learning of what he had done would not allow it.

"You have every right to be angry with us," Baden told her, concern etched in his thin face, his bright blue eyes locked on hers. "With me really; it was my idea. But if Erland and his followers learn of this, it won't matter to them that you weren't involved. You're the one they'll blame."

She allowed herself a smile in response to his earnestness, his dismay at expos-ing her to this risk when his impulse had always been, had remained even to this day, to protect her. Then she felt her expression harden. "If they learn of your link," she assured him in a tone that would brook no contradiction, "I'll tell them that I knew of it from its inception, and that you had my blessing. Because if I had known, you would have." She paused, gratified to see him smiling at her with equal measures of surprise and pride. "So you'd best fill me in on the details," she added a moment later. "I'll want to be as convincing as possible."

That Trahn and Radomil were involved came as no shock to her. The dark mage from the Great Desert was Baden's closest friend in the world, and Radomil, the portly, goateed Hawk-Mage who served Leora's Forest was, in his own quiet way, as courageous and steadfast in his devotion to the land as any mage she knew. Nor was the Owl-Sage surprised to learn that Jaryd and Alayna had joined them. Jaryd, Baden's nephew, had been the Owl-Master's apprentice. But more than that, both he and Alayna, who had once been Mage-Attend to Sartol, had played a pivotal role in thwarting the traitorous mage's plot and defeating the outlanders. Now Sonel fully understood the young mages' decision to serve the Lower Horn rather than returning to Alayna's home near the Abborij Strait or Jaryd's home in Leora's wood.

Sonel was surprised to hear that Orris, Ursel, and Mered had also joined Baden's little conspiracy. Mered tended to avoid political entanglements of any sort, and Ursel, though she had battled the outlanders at Phelan Spur and was closely allied with Orris and the other younger mages, had never seemed to Sonel the type to take such a bold step. And then there was Orris himself. True, the burly mage travelled with Baden, Trahn, Jaryd, and Alayna to Theron's Grove, and stood with Baden and Trahn against Sartol when the renegade accused the three of them of treason and murder. But Orris and Baden had never gotten along, and they often found themselves on opposing sides of the Order's most acrimonious debates. Even after all that had happened during the struggle against Sartol and the outlanders, Sonel found it difficult to think of them as allies.

"It's an uneasy alliance," Baden admitted when she asked him about the burly Hawk-Mage, "but Orris has grown quite close to Jaryd and Alayna, and he and Trahn have always had a good rapport."

"So that's why he agreed to work with you," Sonel ventured.

Baden shook his head in response. "He's doing it because he believes it's the right thing to do. I've never met anyone who takes his oath to serve this land more seriously than Orris."

Sonel considered this in silence for several moments, glancing at the two owls that sat perched together on the window sill across the room. She still had not gotten used to seeing Baden with his new familiar, though he had been bound to the creature for over three years. His owl resembled the bird to which Jessamyn, Sonel's predecessor as Owl-Sage, had been bound. She was an imposing bird, a good deal larger than Sonel's familiar, with feathers as white as snow, and bright, yellow eyes in a round face. After some time Sonel looked back at Baden, her mind turning once more to the Lon-Ser threat. "You've seen nothing, then? No sign of the outlanders?"

"No sign."

Yet. He didn't actually say it, but he didn't have to. It was manifest in his tone, in the shadows lurking in his eyes. They would be coming.

The Owl-Master seemed to read her thoughts. "We're keeping watch, but that's all. Certainly we've done nothing to prevent the next attack."

Sonel let out a long breath. "I know. I've been considering calling the Order back to Amarid."

"Why?"

The question caught her off guard. "To discuss our options; to come up with a plan for dealing with Lon-Ser."

"What makes you think that we'll have any more success than we did at Midsummer?"

"What are you saying?" she demanded irritably. "That we should continue to do nothing? That we should just wait for them to come after us again?"

"I'm just wondering," the Owl-Master countered in a quiet, even tone, "why you need to convene another Gathering. You're the Owl-Sage; you lead the Order. I don't think you need to get prior approval for every thing you do in that capacity." He smiled, the dazzling, disarming smile she had come to know so well over the years. "It's just a thought."

Sitting now in her chamber, with the tea and breads before her, she allowed herself a smile of her own at the memory of that last comment. *Just a thought.* Nothing Baden ever said could be dismissed so easily, and this particular thought stayed with her for the next several days, tugging at the corner of her mind like an insistent child, demanding attention. It was not until a week later, however, when a second visitor came to her chambers bearing news, that Baden's suggestion and her own frustration with the Order's inaction crystallized into a decision to draft her letter.

It was one of those grey, cold autumn days that presages winter's approach, and Sonel had been wrapped tightly in her forest green cloak, with her chair set before the hearth and her long legs folded beneath her, when Basya knocked on the chamber door and announced the caller. Twice the Owl-Sage had to ask her servant to repeat the name of her guest, and even after hearing it for a third time, Sonel was not sure she believed it. But a moment later, Linnea, the highest authority among the Keepers of Arick's Temple in all the land, Eldest of the Gods, as she was properly addressed, swept into the Owl-Sage's chambers, her silver-grey robe swirling impressively around her bulky frame.

As a young girl, Sonel had trained briefly as an acolyte in the Temple near her home, and, as she often did in the presence of the Keepers, she found herself having to resist an immediate impulse to fall to her knees in obeisance. Instead she rose from her chair, smiling broadly, her arms open in welcome. As the Eldest stopped before her, she bowed just slightly, enough to show proper respect for the Temple and Linnea's position within it, but not so much that Sonel compromised the standing of the Order and her own status as its leader. Such was the delicate balance that leaders of the Order had been striking in their interaction with the Children of the Gods for nearly a millennium. Ever since Amarid's emergence as a powerful figure in Tobyn-Ser, relations between the two institutions had not been easy. From the beginning, the Temples had distrusted the wild magic of Amarid's Children and had seen the mages and masters as threats to their authority. Where the Order could offer Tobyn-Ser's people healing from disease and injury, and protection from the land's enemies, the Temples could offer only lore and faith. The Sons and Daughters of the Gods had found themselves unable to compete with the wielders of the Mage-Craft, and their influence had waned. And though the Order had done nothing overt to confirm their suspicions or undermine their power, neither had the mages gone out of their way to cultivate an alliance with the Keepers, an oversight the God's children had taken as an affront.

Over the last several years, the Order had paid the price of that provocation. With the attacks on Tobyn-Ser by outlanders posing as mages, and the Order's slow response to that threat, the people of Tobyn-Ser had grown increasingly disenchanted with the Mage-Craft and had begun to turn back to the Temples for leadership. Bloodied and humiliated, the mages had hoped that their victory over the attackers at Phelan Spur would help them win back the people's esteem. But it had not. Indeed, any good will that might have been garnered from this success was more than offset by Baden's legitimate but unpopular insistence that Baram, the surviving outlander, be imprisoned and interrogated, rather than executed as the people had demanded. Not surprisingly, the Temples had revelled in the mages' fall from favor and had hastened their own resurgence by leading both the criticism of the Order's response to the attacks and the calls for Baram's death. The relationship between the Children of Amarid and the Children of the Gods had never been so strained; Sonel had not believed that it could possibly get any worse.

And yet it had. Soon after Sonel's ascension to the position of Sage, Raina, Tobyn-Ser's Eldest for more than a decade, died, and the Keepers chose Linnea to take her place. Where Raina had been as accommodating and cordial as one could hope, Linnea had a reputation for confrontation and hostility toward the Order. Because she was relatively young, the "Eldest" in title only, Baden and Trahn speculated that she had been selected for just this reason. And in the months and years that followed, Linnea proved them right, taking advantage of every opportunity to remind the people of the land of the Order's failures.

Even as she greeted the Eldest on that grey afternoon, with all the graciousness she could muster, Sonel could not help but wonder why Linnea had come. "Eldest," the Sage had said, still smiling, "be welcome in the Great Hall. You honor me with this unexpected visit." The Owl-Sage turned toward the doorway where her attendant still stood, staring at the two women with unconcealed curiosity. "Basya," she called in a commanding tone, forcing the young woman to mind her duties, "please bring us some fresh tea and something to eat."

Basya flushed slightly and nodded. "Right away, Owl-Sage."

Linnea watched the attendant withdraw, a sardonic grin on her broad, pale face. "Impertinent, isn't she?" the Eldest remarked when Basya was gone, a breezy arrogance in her voice.

"I wouldn't call her impertinent," Sonel replied, fighting to keep the anger from her voice. She motioned for Linnea to sit in the chair nearest her own. "She's just young, and easily impressed."

Still lowering herself into the chair, the Eldest stiffened and opened her mouth to fling back a retort of her own. But then, surprisingly, she appeared to think better of it. And as she settled herself into the seat, awkwardly smoothing her robe with a meaty hand and nervously shifting her gaze around the chamber, Sonel wondered again why she had come. "You are well, I presume?" Linnea asked perfunctorily, her pale, blue eyes finally coming to rest on Sonel's face.

"Yes, Eldest, thank you. And you?"

"Yes, fine." And then, as an afterthought, "Thank you." The large woman continued to fidget with her shimmering robe for several moments until, at last, she seemed to gather her resolve with a deep, slow breath. "Owl-Sage," she began, surprising Sonel with the use of her formal title, "I have come today seeking your—"

A knock on the door stopped her, and Basya entered the chamber carrying a crystal tray of fruits, cheeses, and dry breads, and a pot of steaming shan tea. With quick, economical movements the young woman placed the tray on the low table between the Sage and the Eldest and poured out two cups of tea, seemingly unaware that Linnea was following her every move with manifest impatience.

"Thank you, Basya," Sonel said when the girl was done. "That will be all."

Basya nodded and left, quietly closing the chamber door behind her.

The Eldest appeared to consider offering another comment on Basya's manners. But instead she took another breath in an attempt to regain her composure, and began once more, her tone somewhat less subdued than it had been a minute before, and her eyes fixed on her hands. "As I was saying, I've come seeking your . . . advice," she said, with obvious discomfort, "on a matter of some sensitivity." Linnea was full of surprises this day.

"Of course, Eldest," Sonel replied. "Whatever guidance I can offer is yours, and with it, a pledge of my discretion."

The Keeper looked up at that and inclined her head slightly in acknowledgement. "You remember Cailin?"

"Of course," Sonel answered, her tone suddenly flat. An image of the young girl flashed into the Sage's mind. Her straight, dark hair; the beautiful open face; the pale, blue eyes, much like those of the woman who now sat with Sonel in her quarters. And the sadness that had resided in those eyes. For Cailin was the lone survivor of the massacre at Kaera.

During one night of blood and flame and terror, this child had seen her village utterly destroyed, and her parents, her friends, every person she knew in the world slaughtered by two men posing as mages. She had been quite literally, the only shred of Kaera that they had left intact. And she had lived only because the outlanders had chosen her to be their messenger, so that she might be an agent of their campaign to destroy the Order.

In the aftermath of all this, the girl had been brought back to Amarid where the Order assumed responsibility for her upbringing. But Cailin continued to blame the Children of Amarid for her parents' deaths, even after it had been explained to her several times that the men who destroyed her town had only been pretending to be mages. When several of the Keepers came from Arick's Temple demanding that Cailin be placed in their care, Sonel refused. But she could not refuse Cailin's own request that she be allowed to leave the Great Hall. In the end, Sonel found herself forced to give the girl over to the Keepers, who wasted no time in making Cailin a symbol of both their own redemption and the Order's inability to protect Tobyn-Ser.

"Of course I remember her," Sonel said again. "How old is she now? Ten?"

Linnea nodded absently. "I think so. Yes, ten."

"Is she all right?"

"Naturally she's all right!" the Eldest snapped, her eyes flashing, and her round face growing red. "The Keepers vowed that we would care for her! Do you doubt our word? Or do you think perhaps that we lack the compassion necessary to raise a child?"

"Neither, Eldest," Sonel responded soothingly. "I meant no offense. You have come here seeking my advice and asking if I remember Cailin. In what way was my inquiry inappropriate?"

Linnea closed her eyes and said nothing. After some time she managed a slight grin and shook her head. "There was nothing wrong with your question, Owl-Sage. This is . . . difficult for me." She opened her eyes. "Please accept my apology."

"Of course," Sonel assured her, returning the smile. "Now, please, tell me about Cailin."

"She is a fine child: still beautiful, as you no doubt recall her being, and clever. She excels in her studies. She loves to read, but she's good with numbers as well. And she's as strong and nimble as any of the boys in the Temple." Linnea wore a wistful smile as she spoke, and it occurred to Sonel in that moment that the Eldest genuinely cared for the girl. In the next instant, however, Linnea's smile fled from her lips, and her gaze turned inward. "There is, as one might expect, a sadness to her. But it's strange—it can materialize almost instantly, under any circumstances. One minute she will be laughing, or speaking with passion of the latest story she's read, and the next she'll grow silent and a darkness will come into her eyes." The Keeper shook her head slowly and took a sip of tea. "More recently, these bouts of melancholy have been accompanied by a rebelliousness that we hadn't seen before."

"And this is why you've come," Sonel guessed, brushing a wisp of light hair from her smooth brow.

Linnea smiled wanly and shook her head again. "I've dealt with a child's temper tantrums before, Owl-Sage," she said evenly. "If it were just that, I wouldn't be here."

"So there's more."

"Yes." The Eldest hesitated, but only for a second. "There's no delicate way to approach this, so I'll just say it: for more than a year now Cailin has shown signs of possessing the Sight. We considered coming to you then, but thought better of it. Last month, though, she bound to a falcon. She's a mage."

Sonel couldn't have been more shocked if Linnea had said that she herself had bound to a hawk. But the Sage's astonishment gave way almost instantly to rage and indignation. *For more than a year? Last month?* "The Order should have been informed immediately!" she stormed, hurling it at the Eldest like an accusation.

"I'm informing you now!" Linnea returned hotly.

Sonel propelled her lanky frame out of the chair and began pacing in front of the hearth. "I want her returned to the Great Hall at once!"

Linnea glared at the Owl-Sage defiantly. "I won't allow it!"

"You must!"

"I won't! And neither will Cailin!"

"You don't know that," Sonel replied, less sure of herself.

"Yes, I do," the large woman told her, seeming to sense the Owl-Sage's uncertainty. "You still haven't heard everything, Sonel."

The Sage halted in front of the Eldest and crossed her arms in front of her chest as if to shield her heart from a blow. "Tell me," she demanded.

Linnea swallowed. "Whatever you might think of us, know this: we are not stupid, and we do not underestimate the power that you wield. While we will not give Cailin over to your custody, neither would we allow her to use the Mage-Craft as she would a toy. We have instructed her in the ways of the Order and explained Amarid's Laws to her." Another pause, and then: "She has refused to submit herself to them."

"What?" Sonel hissed. "You can't be serious!"

"I'm afraid I am. She still blames the Order for the death of her parents—"

"Yes!" Sonel spat, "I'm sure you saw to that a long time ago!"

Linnea shot to her feet, her round cheeks flushed with anger once more, and she leveled a rigid finger at the Owl-Sage. "You can't place this on me, Sonel! The Order brought this poor girl's hatred upon itself!"

"We didn't kill her parents or destroy her town! You know we didn't, and yet you perpetuate these lies!"

"We never accused the Order of attacking Kaera," the Eldest countered, her voice suddenly low, her choler under control for the moment. "We would never have said such a thing." Sonel started to protest, but Linnea stopped her with an abrupt gesture. "Let me finish! We never accused you of murdering Cailin's parents, but we have held you responsible for the promises you failed to keep. You mages have pledged yourselves to guarding this land, and you've enjoyed a thousand years of reverence due in large part to the success of your forebears in honoring that pledge. But the Order as we know it now, the Order that Cailin has come to know in her few years upon this earth, has proven itself incapable of protecting the people of Tobyn-Ser. Cailin doesn't think you killed her parents—oh, she did for a time, but she's understood for several years now that it was the outlanders posing as mages—but she blames you for allowing this to happen. And, quite frankly, so do I." Linnea started to say more, but then she stopped herself. She was breathing hard. The fierce anger in her pale eyes was gone, leaving something else, something unexpected. Not self-righteousness, or exultation at the Owl-Sage's discomfort, but pain.

Sonel had no answer, either for the Eldest's words or for the look in the heavy woman's eyes. She and Baden had been saying much the same thing about the Order for nearly four years; she could hardly fault Linnea for speaking the truth. There was a dryness in her mouth, like dust or ashes, and she took a long drink of tea. She felt spent, and, when finally she spoke, it was in a voice scraped raw by the emotions of the afternoon. "So you want to know what you can do about Cailin?" she asked. "How you can control her power?"

"Yes."

"Actually," the Sage began, again brushing the strands of hair from her forehead, "there's very little that you can do. We police our own; the collective power of all the mages in the Order keeps the individual in line—that, and the oath we take upon earning our cloaks. There's nothing really magical about Amarid's Laws; there's no power in the words themselves beyond the honor and scruples that each mage brings to them. From what you've told me of her, I would expect Cailin to be bound to the spirit of the Laws by her strength of character, even without taking the oath."

"I would hope so," Linnea agreed thoughtfully.

"The danger lies in her age, and the rebelliousness of which you spoke. So young a child, regardless of her normal disposition, might be subject to fits of anger. That's where you'll have to be careful—you'll have to teach her to control her temper. And I don't even want to think of what you'll face as she enters her adolescence." The Sage shook her head slowly and stroked the chin of her owl, which sat perched above the hearth. The bird opened its eyes and began to preen itself. "I've never heard of anyone binding so young," Sonel murmured, as much to herself as to the Eldest. "You say it was to a falcon?"

"A small one, yes. A kestrel, I believe."

Again, the Sage shook her head. "Remarkable."

"Is there anything more that you can tell me, Owl-Sage?" Linnea asked, rising from her chair with a rustle of cloth.

"Not much, I'm afraid. Frankly, I would feel much better with Cailin in the Great Hall, under our supervision, but I will accept what you say: that she would not agree to such an arrangement. Short of that, I would just tell you to raise her as you have been. To the extent that it's possible, you should treat her just as you would the other children. She shouldn't feel overly special, nor should she be given reason to believe that she's feared." Sonel took a slow breath and offered Linnea a thin smile. "I don't envy you this task, Eldest. But if there's anything more you need from me, don't hesitate to ask."

The Keeper gazed at her for a moment. Then she nodded once. "Thank you, Sonel. I'll keep you apprised of Cailin's progress." She began to leave, but, as she reached the door, she paused. At last she turned and faced Sonel again. "I don't know if you'll believe this, Sonel, particularly coming from me. But we in the Temple didn't wish for the Order to fail. Certainly, we've taken advantage of your loss of prestige, and I make no apology for that. But we know that, ultimately, Tobyn-Ser will be served best by a strong Temple and a strong Order working side by side. I personally look forward to a day when that will be possible."

Caught off guard by the Eldest's admission, Sonel stared at her for several seconds. Linnea seemed sincere in what she had said, but still the Owl-Sage found it difficult to accept that such sentiments could come from this woman. In the end, she merely nodded in acknowledgement and said, with as much feeling as she could muster, "I look forward to such a day as well, Eldest."

Without another word, the Keeper departed. Listening to the sound of Linnea's footsteps retreating across the Gathering Chamber, Sonel came to a decision. Notwithstanding the accommodating words with which Sonel and the Eldest had concluded their encounter, the frayed relations between the Order and the Temples would not be easy to repair, nor would the reputation of Amarid's Children be rehabilitated overnight. But the Order had done nothing for too long. And now, in Arick's Temple just a few miles outside this city, a ten year-old girl was mastering the Mage-Craft with no mage to guide her. The time had come.

Moving to the folding wooden desk by her bed, Sonel took up parchment and writing lead, and began composing an unauthorized letter to Lon-Ser's Council of Sovereigns. Since her conversation with Baden, the Owl-Sage had given a good deal of thought to what she would say in such a correspondence, and the words came to her easily.

> *To the Council of Sovereigns:*
>
> *I write to you as a representative of the people of Tobyn-Ser and as the leader of this land's Order of Mages and Masters.*
>
> *Nearly four years ago a band of Lon-Ser's citizens entered our land and, in the guise of mages, began a campaign of vandalism and violence against our people. Although we eventually succeeded in defeating these invaders, killing all but one of them, their actions resulted in considerable loss of property and life.*
>
> *We seek no compensation for the crimes committed against us, but we do wish to avoid future hostilities. To this end, I propose a meeting, at a place and time of mutual satisfaction, to discuss the events I have described and any outstanding conflicts that may exist between our peoples.*
>
> *We did not seek this conflict, nor do we wish to prolong it. But know this: our desire for peace is matched by our determination to remain free.*
>
> *In friendship I am yours,*
> *Sonel,*
> *Owl-Sage of Tobyn-Ser*

By the end of the following day, the letter had been scribed and sent. Sonel told no one, not even Baden, who, having said what he needed to say that night in her bed, never broached the subject again. Nor did she speak with anyone of her conversation with Linnea. Cailin's binding, she decided on that autumn evening, was a matter to be broached at a Gathering of the whole Order.

And so, silently bearing the burden of her secrets, she waited. Through the cold snows and wind of winter, and the grey, damp chill of the rainy season, she struggled to control both her fears and her hopes, all the while watching for acolytes of the Temple, who occasionally brought her news of Cailin, and anxiously anticipating a response from Lon-Ser. As the last of the rains blew off to

the east, however, and the warmth of the growing spring gave way to summer,
Sonel's anticipation gave way to a dark foreboding. In the winter she had
looked forward to the arrival of each new merchant ship, thinking that perhaps
this one would bare the Council's reply, but she now came to dread the dock-
ages and the grim vigils she found herself keeping for several hours after each
ship began to unload.

Thus it seemed an irony that on this, the day before midsummer, the reply
should arrive at dawn, coming from a vessel that had docked late in the night,
as she slept. It was small consolation, given what the letter contained. Or, more
exactly, what it didn't contain. Smoothing the radiant white paper with a careful hand, Sonel read the message one last time. Such a letter was worse than no
reply at all, she realized despairingly, because now she had no idea what to do.

For the third time that morning, Basya tapped lightly on the door, and, for a
moment, the Sage gave no answer. Then, reluctantly, she rose. There would be
visitors soon, she knew: mages and masters arriving in Amarid and making their
way to the Great Hall to offer greetings and to try to divine her mind on their
dearest issues. It was a ritual of sorts; as much a part of the Gathering as the
Opening Procession, as much a part of her duties as calling the mages to order.
She still recalled with fondness her own audiences with Jessamyn, when she had
been just another mage and Jessamyn led the Order, and she found herself
wondering if the diminutive, white-haired woman's cordial hospitality had served
as but a cover for burdens as great as her own. "Of course it did," Sonel said
out loud as she raised an arm for her dark owl. "Why should I think that I'm
any different?" The bird flew to her, hopped up to her shoulder, and regarded
her in silence.

Another knock, a bit louder this time.

"Yes, Basya," Sonel called, with forced brightness. "You may enter."

The young woman opened the door tentatively and seemed surprised to see
that Sonel had risen from her chair. "I'm sorry to disturb you, Owl-Sage, but
you have visitors."

Sonel smiled reassuringly. The girl was, after all, merely doing her job.
"You're not disturbing me, Basya. Please show them in."

"Right away, Owl-Sage."

Sonel saw the girl turn and motion, heard voices drawing near, and, as she
did, she remembered the piece of immaculate paper that she still held in her
hand. Quickly, unobtrusively, she concealed the Council of Sovereign's letter
within the folds of her cloak. There would be plenty of time for such matters
over the course of the Gathering. This was a day for welcomes, and friendships
renewed. As her first guests reached her door, however, a thought occurred to
her: if sending a letter did not get the attention of Lon-Ser's leaders, perhaps
sending a group of envoys would.

2

Not surprisingly, the governing structure of Bragor-Nal is far more complex than anything that exists here in Tobyn-Ser. Indeed, the only suitable comparison I can find is to the land tenantry system that has developed under the Potentates of Abborij. In Bragor-Nal, as in Abborij, a single ruler, whom Baram calls the Sovereign, presides over a complex hierarchy of Overlords, Lords, subordinates, and hirelings. Moreover, like the Potentates, Bragor-Nal's Sovereign, and presumably the Sovereigns of the other two Nals, encourage and profit from competition among their underlings. This, however, is where the similarities end. For while the Abboriji tenantry structure creates wealth through husbandry, and maintains its stability through homage and tribute, the leaders of the Nals gather their spoils through corruption and extortion, and guard their status with a violent campaign of intimidation and retribution.

—From Section Five of "The Report of Owl-Master Baden on his Interrogation of the Outlander Baram," Submitted to the 1,014th Gathering of the Order of Mages and Masters. Spring, Gods' Year 4625.

Melyor surveyed the bar, her casual bearing and indifferent expression masking the keenness of her gaze. In another part of the Nal, not too many quads from here, her dissembling would have fooled no one, and every man and woman she encountered would have quailed at the merest touch of her glance. But in this place, where no one knew her, Melyor blended into her surroundings, as much a part of the bar as the drunks slumped in the corners, or the glowing signs, aged and dingy, that hung above the drinks-counter at which she sat. It helped, of course, that she was wearing the sheer, brightly colored body scarves of an *uestra* girl—purple and blue, to offset the amethyst studs she wore in her ears and the sapphire lenses with which she had altered the color of her eyes from their usual bright green.

The crowd seemed a typical one—she might just as easily have found the same assortment of uestras, break-laws, and sots in a bar in the Fourth Realm of the Nal. Except that she would not have looked for Savil in her domain. Any more than he would be looking for her in his. Melyor suppressed a smile and took stock of what she saw around her. The drunks, of course, would not be a problem, and most of the break-laws appeared to be absorbed in their own affairs. There was one group, however, at an adjacent table who had been drinking and carrying on loudly for the better part of an hour, and they had begun, a short while ago, to eye her and the other girls with an expression she knew quite well. But, for now, there was nothing she could do about that. Savil had not arrived yet.

"Ale," she said to the tarnished chrome dispenser beside her.

"Pale or dark?" came the metallic voice in reply.

"Dark. And not chilled," she added anticipating the machine's next question.

"Cash or credit?"

She almost slipped. Almost. Normally, she did everything by credit, because normally, back in the Fourth, no one ever tried to collect. Nal-Lords were afforded certain privileges, even by the barkeeps. But here, in Savil's Realm, it wouldn't do for anyone to overhear her announcing herself as Melyor i Lakin, even to a dispenser. She had planned for too long, and gotten herself too close, to give herself away in that manner. "Cash," she answered, pulling two silvers from the small purse that hung from her sash and depositing them in the slot beside the speaker. An instant later, she heard the clang of the metal tankard and the soft hiss of the ale being pumped into it.

Taking the mug from the machine Melyor grinned in spite of herself. Only three-quarters full, even with the head. *Some things are the same everywhere,* she observed silently. She sipped the ale and looked around the bar again. And, as she did, she caught a glimpse of herself in a mirror on the far side of the counter. The heavy makeup gave her normally soft features a sharpness to which she was not accustomed, and, despite all her preparation, she was momentarily surprised to see the gentle waves of her amber hair teased into soft ringlets and lightened nearly to blond. Actually, it was a look she liked, she thought with the flicker of a smile, as she passed an absent hand through the curls. Her expression sobered quickly. More importantly, she looked the part.

Perhaps too much so, she amended with an inward grimace. Her eyes still fixed on the mirror, she watched one of the men at the nearby table pull himself to his feet, drain his glass, and saunter over to where she sat. Slowly, she placed her ale on the counter and took a deep breath. *Carefully,* she cautioned herself.

"You're new here," the man said to her, leaning against the counter so close to where she sat that she could feel his breath of the side of her neck. He stank of whiskey.

"Am I?" she asked in reply, not bothering to look at him, but shifting her position slightly to create some space between them.

"Yes," he told her, moving with her to close the distance once more. "I make it my business to know the uestras in this part of the Nal, particularly the good-looking ones. I'm certain that I would have noticed you. I'm Dob, and I'm very pleased to meet you."

She glanced at him briefly, looking him up and down with an appraising eye before facing forward again. He was a big man, a full head taller than she and broad in the shoulders and chest. His hair was black and he wore it long and unkempt so that it fell down over his shoulders and in front of his cold, blue eyes. Like most of the break-laws in the Nal, his beard was rough, but not quite full, as if he hadn't shaved in several days. It was, she had concluded long ago, an appearance that the break-laws cultivated. On the other hand, unlike the other men of his kind, most of whom had managed to have their noses broken at least once, this one had a straight, aristocratic nose, indicating to Melyor that he was either very good at what he did, or very new at it. Given the man's swagger, she assumed the former.

All this Melyor gathered from her brief look in his direction. All this, and two other things that were, under the circumstances, far more significant. First, the man was well armed. He wore a thrower on his belt, a long-handled dagger in a sheath that was strapped to his thigh, and sharpened spikes on the toes of his black boots and on the stiff wrist cuffs of his long, black coat. And second, judging from the position of his thrower and blade, she guessed that he was better with his left hand.

"I'm Kellyn," Melyor said at last, her tone cool even as her mind wandered to the long, thin blade of the dirk that lay hidden within her boot, nestled comfortably against her calf. It was, thanks to the body scarves, the only weapon she had dared carry with her, the only weapon she could conceal. Uestras didn't normally arm themselves; they usually had no need. Not that she doubted that the blade would be enough, but she hoped it would not come to that, at least not with this one. She sipped her ale, quickly scanning the bar again. Where is Savil? she thought impatiently.

"Where are you from, Kellyn?"

"I used to work a series of bars up in Trestor-Proper," she told him, absently tracing her finger around the rim of her mug.

"Twenty-Sixth Realm?" Dob asked, rubbing a hand across his coarse beard.

"Twenty-Fourth, actually. But it got too crowded—too many girls walking the same quad. And I was looking for a change."

"Twenty-Fourth Realm," he repeated. "That's Bren's territory isn't it?"

She nodded.

"You ever meet a break-law in the Twenty-Fourth named Lavrik?"

She turned toward Dob, sneering with disgust. "Yeah, I know Lavrik. The man's a pig. He still owes me for two times; and, to be honest, neither was any good."

Dob stared at her for a moment as if unsure of what he had heard. And then he began to laugh, harder and harder, until tears poured from his eyes. Melyor noticed that his friends at the nearby table had also fallen into hysterics. Apparently they had an audience. This would make what she knew was coming next that much more difficult.

After some time, his laughter subsiding, Dob laid a rough hand on her bare shoulder. "I like you, Kellyn," he told her, his blue eyes straying from her face down to her breasts. "I like you a lot. And seeing as you're new to the Second, you may not realize how lucky you are to have met me. I'm an important man in this part of the Nal—I have many friends, some of them powerful." He moved closer to her, his hand still on her shoulder and his gaze traveling her body. "I'd like for us to be friends, too," he added pointedly.

"As far as I'm concerned we already are, Dob," she replied, smiling disarmingly and removing his hand from her shoulder. "I'm very glad to have met you. I feel at home in the Second already." She turned away from him, back toward the counter, and she reached for her ale.

Dob stopped her with a hand on her wrist. One of the men at the adjoining table snickered. "You misunderstand." The break-law's tone had grown colder, though a thin smile remained on his lips. "I'd like for us to be friends. But friendship as valuable as mine is never given freely; it must be earned."

Once again, more deliberately this time, she removed his hand. Then she looked at him. "I don't like games, Dob," she said, not bothering to mask the ice in her voice. "If you want something, ask for it. Otherwise, go away."

More titters from the break-law's friends, but Dob had grown deadly serious. For a moment, Melyor thought that he might strike her and she braced herself for the blow. But then he grinned broadly and allowed himself to laugh. "As I said, Kellyn: I like you." He glanced back at his companions and winked. "Very well; you value candor, as do I." He hesitated, running a hand through his long, dark hair. "I propose a deal," he went on after another glance at his comrades. "My friendship and all the benefits that come with it, in exchange for your . . . services for the evening."

She gave him a coy smile. "That's a very attractive proposition, Dob—"

"One you would do well to accept." All traces of mirth had left his face, leaving only the grimly set, unshaved jaw, and the severity of his cold eyes.

Melyor straightened, and her expression grew solemn. "I'm afraid I can't."

"Why not?" Dob demanded, his tone low and dangerous.

"Because I'm waiting for someone," she explained matter-of-factly. "I'll be offering my services to him this evening."

The break-law narrowed his eyes. "Who?"

"Nal-Lord Savil."

Dob raised his eyebrows in unfeigned surprise. And then, once more, he began to laugh. "Savil?" he asked incredulously. His companions began to chuckle as well and he turned toward them. "She's waiting for Nal-Lord Savil," he repeated, his voice colored in equal shades with amusement and derision. The other men's laughter mounted, and Dob turned back toward Melyor shaking his head slowly. "You may be pretty, Kellyn," he told her. "Perhaps even beautiful. But you have much to learn about the workings of this part of the Nal. Savil is the most important person in the Realm; he answers to no one save his Overlord and the Sovereign, and he certainly doesn't allow himself to be chosen by the likes of you. He can have any uestra he wants. And here you come, new to the Realm, thinking you can just select him as you would an ale from a dispenser." He shook his head again. "It would be funny if it wasn't so pathetic. You'll be lucky if he even notices you."

Melyor regarded the break-law coolly. "You seem jealous, Dob. Am I stepping on toes here? Perhaps you had planned on taking Savil back to your flat tonight."

She was an accomplished street fighter—she had to be to have gotten as far as she had—and, slight as she was, she was exceptionally strong. Even so, and despite the fact that she had been prepared for Dob's reaction, the large man surprised her with his swiftness. Before the last word passed her lips, Dob had twisted a brawny hand into her hair, and jerked her toward him so that the gleaming spikes on the wrist of his coat rested menacingly against her temple. "I have killed for far less!" he hissed, wrapping his other hand around her throat.

"I'm sure you have," she answered evenly. "But, in this case, you might wish to temper your response a bit."

"What?" he snorted contemptuously.

And, by way of reply, Melyor trapped the blade of her dirk, which she already had in hand, lightly against his groin. She felt him look down, heard him gasp with fear and disbelief.

"Tell your men to back off," she commanded under her breath, sensing that the break-law's friends had formed a semicircle around them, "and then let go of me. Slowly, Dob—you wouldn't want to do anything to make me nervous."

For a moment he did nothing, and Melyor pressed the blade just a bit harder against his britches. "All right!" he whispered fervently. "All right!"

"Tell them, Dob," she instructed quietly, "not me."

"It's all right," he said, pitching his voice to carry. "Everything's all right." And then, cautiously, he relaxed his grip on her hair.

As soon as he released her, Melyor stepped away and turned to face him, a thin smile on her lips. The break-law was breathing hard and glaring at her in chagrined silence, his lips pressed thin, and his eyes filled with outrage and injured pride. His friends stood motionless, looking nervously from Dob to her, unsure of what Dob wanted them to do.

"You handle that thing well," the big man said at last, indicating Melyor's dirk with a motion of his head as she slipped it back into her boot. A note of suspicion had crept into his voice. "Uestras aren't usually so skilled with a blade."

"I learned to take care of myself in Trestor-Proper," she replied casually, although she remained watchful lest Dob or his friends attempt something else. "People up there aren't as friendly as they are around here."

He seemed to accept this, and if he sensed the irony in her tone, he showed no sign of it. "I hope you realize that you've made an enemy today," he said in a flat tone.

For the first time since Dob had approached her, Melyor allowed herself to laugh. And though she did so gently and quietly, she saw from the break-law's expression that this infuriated him more than anything else she had done to him thus far. "Forgive me for laughing, Dob—I mean no offense—but, to be honest, I expected that from the first." This failed to mollify him, and she pressed on. "It may be small consolation now, but I never stay in one place very long; I'll be gone soon, and you'll be free to forget that this evening ever happened." There was some truth in her assurances. More, in fact, than there had been in most of what she had said since the beginning of their encounter. But this last Melyor knew to be the biggest lie of all: she was certain that Dob and his comrades would remember this night for the rest of their lives.

His face reddening with anger, the break-law started to reply. But, at that moment, the door to the bar swung open and another group of men walked in.

Turning to look in that direction, Melyor understood immediately that her waiting was over. She knew it from the sudden attentiveness of Dob and the other break-laws; she knew it from the fact that every other conversation in the bar ceased as soon as the door opened; she knew it from the odd array of uestras, break-laws, and bodyguards that accompanied the one figure who seemed to guide the throng through the doorway and into the tavern; and, even had she not seen still shots of Savil on several occasions, she would have known it from the striking resemblance that this man bore to Calbyr, the former Nal-Lord of the Second Realm, and Savil's cousin. Like Calbyr, this man's hair and beard were the color of sand, and, despite his loose fitting trousers and the dark, long coat he wore over his ivory shirt, she could see that he had the wiry, muscular frame of a skilled fighter. His eyes were dark and impenetrable, and he carried himself with the arrogance of a man accustomed to power. All of this he had in common with Calbyr, whom he had succeeded as Nal-Lord. And, if the reports gathered for Melyor by her intelligence aides were accurate, Savil also shared his cousin's ambition and ruthlessness, not to mention his proficiency as a killer. Melyor also noticed that, like Dob, Savil carried a thrower and a blade.

Stopping just inside the doorway, Savil scanned the bar as one might peruse a dispenser menu. Little of what he saw appeared to interest him until his eyes came to rest on Melyor and Dob, at which point a hungry smile lit his sharp features. Striding purposefully toward the two of them, the Nal-Lord called out Dob's name and extended an arm in greeting. His eyes, however, flicked repeatedly in Melyor's direction.

"Well met, Nal-Lord," Dob intoned, glancing sidelong at Melyor, and unable to keep the residue of hurt and humiliation from his tone.

"Hello, Dob," Savil returned as he halted in front of them. He was closer in height to Melyor than to Dob, but he seemed larger than the break-law somehow, or perhaps Dob just looked smaller when the Nal-Lord was nearby; it was hard to say which. Melyor knew, though, that whatever danger Dob had represented was magnified a dozen times in the lithe figure of the Nal-Lord.

"We're honored by your presence here, Nal-Lord. How may we serve you?" She could hear the strain in Dob's voice. She could only imagine how the dishonor she had brought him a few minutes ago would affect his standing in Savil's Realm.

Savil smiled generously. The expression looked oddly incongruous on his face. "Relax, Dob. Everything's all right." *Dob's words from before*—Melyor smiled inwardly. Savil turned his gaze in her direction, his grin deepening. "But I will allow you to introduce me to your friend."

"She's not my friend," the break-law said a bit too vehemently. Savil looked at him sharply, and Melyor could see that Dob instantly regretted using such a tone.

"I see," Savil commented. He looked at Melyor again. "What's your name?"

"Kellyn, Nal-Lord. I've been waiting for you."

"She claims to be from the Twenty-Fourth Realm, Nal-Lord," Dob added quickly. "But I don't trust her. I think she's an assassin; she carries a dagger in her right boot."

Savil raised an eyebrow inquisitively. "Is this true, Kellyn?"

Melyor smiled warmly. "It's true that I carry a blade. As for the rest, you must know that no matter what the truth, I can only give one answer."

The Nal-Lord stared at her for another moment, his features giving away nothing. Then he nodded and gave a small laugh before turning back to the break-law. "Thank you, Dob. Your concern is noted." It was a dismissal. The big man's face began to redden, and he looked like he might say more, but a second glance from Savil silenced him. With one last glare at Melyor, Dob stalked off toward the back of the bar, his men following wordlessly.

"May I see your dagger?" Savil asked, the grin lingering on his lips, even as the expression in his dark eyes hardened.

"You may," Melyor responded, deftly retrieving the dirk from her boot and handing it to him hilt first. "Indeed, you're welcome to keep it."

"That won't be necessary," he told her, examining the weapon, "although I will hold on to it for the remainder of the evening." He looked up, smiling again. "Merely as a precaution."

Melyor returned the smile, lightly tracing a finger down the man's bearded jawline. "Does that mean we'll be leaving together?"

He looked her up and down, drinking her in with his eyes. "The sooner the better." He glanced back at his entourage. "Wait just a minute," he told her. "Then we can go." He approached one of his bodyguards, a burly man with a large gold ring in one ear and an equally large thrower strapped conspicuously to his belt. Savil whispered something to the man, who gazed at Melyor impassively before nodding once. Then Savil returned and, taking her by the hand, led her out into the street.

After the din of the bar, the warm, sour air of the street seemed unnaturally still and quiet. It had rained earlier, a rare midsummer downpour, fleeting but intense, like a memory of spring. Steam rose from the darkened pavement like smoke from a dying fire, and water ran silently down the smooth, metallic faces of the towering buildings that loomed on both sides of the avenue. A carrier hummed past, the faces of its passengers framed by the small windows, staring out at the night like portraits in a moving gallery. Even after it had passed, the acrid smell of its discharge stung Melyor's nostrils and made her eyes water. But otherwise the street was empty. It was early yet.

Savil started toward one of the byways leading off of the quad's main concourse and Melyor followed. She guessed they were headed back to the Nal-Lord's flat.

"I don't know what happened back there, Kellyn," Savil began in an easy tone, "but Dob doesn't like you very much."

Melyor looked at him sidelong and grinned. "I know. But it's his own fault: he doesn't handle rejection very well."

"None of my men do; they learned that from me. Tell me though," he went on, "what role did your dagger play in all of this?"

She glanced at him a second time. "Let's just say that Dob doesn't like to be bested either."

Savil smiled coldly. "Another product of my leadership. My men don't easily accept defeat because they know that I have never been defeated. That is something you would be well advised to keep in mind . . . Melyor i Lakin."

At that, for the first time that night, Melyor felt a rush of fear. And though she quashed it an instant later, she knew that Savil had noticed. He had, after all, been looking for it.

"What are you doing in my Realm, Melyor?" The light-haired man had been walking all this time with his hands thrust in the deep pockets of his overcoat, and he did not remove them now. But the tone of his voice made Melyor feel as if he had a thrower aimed at her heart.

"When did you know?" she asked, hoping to put him off for a few moments.

"When you gave me the blade. Even taking it out of your boot and handing it to me, you seemed too skilled for an uestra."

Melyor gave a small laugh. "Dob said the same thing."

"I'll have to remember to commend him for his insight."

"But why didn't you have me taken as an assassin?" she persisted. "How did you know it was me?"

Savil hesitated. "Calbyr told me about you once," he explained at last. "I wasn't certain why until tonight. He said that he had once seen you win a knife fight against a much larger, stronger opponent, despite having been slashed across the back of your blade hand. He told me that it was one of the most remarkable displays of fighting craft that he had ever seen. I believe he was offering the story as a warning." He paused again as they turned a second time into a more narrow passage. Then the Nal-Lord indicated her hand with a bob of his head. "I noticed the two parallel scars across your hand."

Melyor looked down at the back of her right hand and grinned ruefully. "Serves me right for not being vain enough to cover it up. I guess I wouldn't make much of an uestra."

Savil halted and turned to face her. Once more he looked her up and down, not bothering to mask the desire in his dark eyes. Melyor noticed that they had reached the end of the byway.

"You are very beautiful, Melyor," he said huskily. "More beautiful even than I was led to believe, and certainly more lovely than any uestra I've ever had the pleasure of knowing." Melyor could not help but catch the double meaning in Savil's words, and she suddenly felt herself growing self-conscious. As a disguise, the sheer body scarves were a necessity. But now they made her feel weak; they placed her at a disadvantage. Savil seemed to sense this, and he grinned, as if relishing her discomfort. A moment later though, his expression changed. "Before such diversions can be contemplated, however," he added, the ice returning to his voice, and his eyes boring into hers, *"I must know why you are in my Realm!"*

She held his gaze for several moments before responding, and neither one of them looked away. "It's no secret that Cedrych is considering giving you command of the next force that will be sent to Tobyn-Ser," she said at last, her tone crisp and businesslike. "I came here hoping to convince you that you need a partner."

Savil laughed. "A partner? Why would I want a partner?"

"It's a big job. Too big for most people."

"Too big for me?" he asked testily.

"I believe it was too big for Calbyr," she told him, sidestepping the question. "I wouldn't want to see you lost as well."

Her reply did not seem to satisfy him. He stood staring at her, his eyes smoldering and his mouth set in a hard line. "And what was the rest of your plan?" he asked at last. "If you failed to convince me, what then?"

She shrugged. "Failing that, I suppose I planned to kill you."

He bared his teeth in a humorless grin and shook his head. "I don't believe you," he said. "There were other ways for you to convey this message. But you came to me, disguised and armed. I think you planned to kill me all along, hoping that Cedrych would then turn to you. I think you hoped to lure me to bed, render me defenseless, and then slit my throat with that dagger of yours."

"You may be right," Melyor conceded with an enigmatic smile and a toss of the blond curls she had given herself earlier that day. "But what's important now is that we're here, together, and I'm proposing a partnership."

"You're proposing that we share something that you've admitted is probably already mine. What would I have to gain?"

"I already told you: it's too big a job. By joining with me, you ensure your own success."

For a second time, Savil shook his head, the same harsh grin still stretched across his face. "No," he said with finality. "I don't need anyone's help. And frankly, Melyor, I don't trust you. I don't think you'd be a very good partner. I think eventually, I'd wind up with that dagger in my back."

Melyor gazed at him for several seconds without speaking, and then she shrugged again. "Very well." She cocked her head to the side and smiled at him. "It's too bad though, Savil. I think we would have had fun together. If you change your mind," she added, starting to turn away, "you know where to find me."

"Hold it, Melyor!" he commanded in a tone that stopped her cold. "I'm afraid I can't let you go." She turned to face him again. He had drawn his thrower. "I wouldn't trust you as a partner, but, after tonight, after seeing you here and knowing that you bested one of my most talented men, I can't risk having you as an adversary either." His expression had grown somber. "You understand, I have to kill you."

Melyor nodded. "I understand, Savil. I'd do the same, were I in your position." But even as she spoke, even as she assented to her own death, she felt the familiar tranquility coming over her, taking her to the still point within her that she had come to know so well over the years. Savil was speaking again, saying something about how disappointed he was that they wouldn't be going up to his flat after all. But she barely heard him. And by the time he raised his thrower to fire, she had already started to move.

Ducking her head as the spurt of red flame hissed from his weapon and passed harmlessly over her shoulder, she pivoted on her right foot and spun, swinging her left foot in a wide, violently swift arc. Savil had begun to move as well, twisting his body, as she knew he would, to shield what would have been Melyor's most obvious target. And so, in mid-turn, she adjusted her attack slightly—just enough to catch him full in the kidney with the hard point of her toe. The Nal-Lord crumpled to his knees with a retching gasp, his eyes squeezed shut as his weapon flew from his hand and clattered on the wet pavement. Barely able to remain upright, he struggled desperately to free his knife from the sheath on his thigh. But before he could, Melyor struck him again, this time driving her fist into his throat, shattering his larynx with the blow. The light-haired man toppled onto his back, laboring for each breath with a terrible, rasping sound, and staring at her now with wide, terrified eyes.

"You were right, Savil," Melyor told him as she retrieved his thrower. "I had every intention of killing you tonight. Cedrych would have been foolish to send you to Tobyn-Ser; you were bound to fail, just as your cousin did. It's not your fault, really. It's just that this job calls for a subtlety of mind that you don't possess." She smiled. "I am sorry." The Nal-Lord was struggling vainly to climb to his feet, and she moved closer, looking down at him with pity and just a shade of contempt. "I have one other thing to share with you before I kill you: it's a secret. I've told people before, but only just before they die—that way it remains a secret. Think of it as a tradition." She paused, taking a deep breath, and then she spoke the words, just as she had so many times before. And she was gratified to see his eyes widen at what she said, so gratified in fact, that she killed him quickly, with a single burst of thrower fire to the heart, rather than prolonging his death as she sometimes did to those who had angered her.

After that it was but a simple matter to find her way out of Savil's Realm and back to the safety of her flat. There, she removed the blue lenses, slipped out of the body scarves, and washed the curls and the color out of her hair before falling into bed, exhausted, but pleased with the way her evening had gone. *I should hear from Cedrych tomorrow,* she thought with anticipation. *The day after at the latest.* She smiled in the darkness, and, closing her eyes, allowed herself to drift toward sleep. Only then did she realize, with a small pang of regret, that she had forgotten to reclaim her dagger.

3

My conversations with the outlander have covered a wide range of topics and have taught me a good deal about Lon-Ser, its huge cities, or Nals, as Baram calls them, and its striking mechanical advances. I have even begun to learn the outlander's language, although, I must admit, not as thoroughly as he has mastered ours. While I have been forced to gather much of this informa-

*tion through the use of prolonged probings of the outlander's mind, I did suc-
ceed, early on, in convincing him to share some of what he knows voluntarily.
These discussions, it seems to me, were by far the most productive and satisfying for both of us. With the passage of time, however, he has grown more resistant, and the frequency of these free conversations has diminished. Still, I
continue to believe that we have too much to gain from the outlander, and I
am not yet willing to accede to persistent demands for his execution.*

—From Section Three of "The Report
of Owl-Master Baden on his Interrogation of the Outlander Baram," Submitted to the 1,014th Gathering of the
Order of Mages and Masters. Spring,
Gods' Year 4625.

There had been times, more recently than he would have admitted to
anyone in this chamber, when Baden had considered what it might be
like to become Owl-Sage. He had a vision for the future of the Order—he had
given a great deal of thought to how and where the Mage-Craft fit into the fab-
ric of Tobyn-Ser's culture. He had watched two of his dearest friends, Jessamyn
and Sonel, grapple with the challenges and strains of leadership, and while he
never underestimated the difficulties they faced, neither did he find himself
shrinking from the idea of carrying this weight himself. And perhaps most significantly, he knew that four years ago, when the Owl-Masters selected Sonel to
lead the Order, they did so with some reluctance, for he, Baden, had been their
first choice. He was one of the few masters who had earned the trust of both
the older and younger mages; many felt that he alone could mend the rifts that
had come to divide the Order so deeply. Only the death of his familiar at Phelan
Spur had prevented the Masters from formally offering him the position. Sonel
seemed to know this as well. She had alluded to it, obliquely to be sure, during
a conversation less than a year after her ascension, and Baden took it as proof of
the power of their bond that this circumstance had not affected their relationship.

At the time, he had not allowed himself the luxury of feeling disappointed.
Indeed, he had been too wrapped in his grief at losing Anla to focus on this lost
opportunity. For she had not simply died; he himself had killed her. To be sure
it had been an act of mercy. In the next moment, she would have been torn
apart by the huge, mechanical creature that gripped her in its razor claws. And
in the aftermath of Phelan Spur, as the circumstances of her death became general knowledge and the inevitable questions arose regarding the provision in
Amarid's Law that prohibited mages from harming their familiars, the Order
agreed unanimously that Baden's actions had been justified. Still, the pain of
losing her ran deep. The fact that he could not be named Owl-Sage seemed a
matter of small consequence.

In the months that followed, he convinced himself that he could do more for the Order, and for the people of the land, as a simple mage, unconstrained by the political and ceremonial duties that came with being Sage. And he focused his energies on establishing the clandestine psychic link in eastern Tobyn-Ser, something he could never have done as leader of the Order. But he consoled himself with another thought as well, one that he shared with no one: he would have another chance. Obviously, he wished no ill fortune for Sonel, but he was a practical man—someday her familiar would die, and the Order would need a new leader. Perhaps then he would be ready. This, at least, was what he had told himself at the time.

Only four years had passed, but now, on the first afternoon of the Gathering, as Baden stood at the council table in Amarid's Great Hall, with Golivas, his large, white owl, perched on the chair behind him, it felt so long ago that it might as well have been another lifetime. Every mage in the Order was watching him, waiting for him to speak, some with expressions of open hostility, others with a cool detachment. There was little warmth here. Scanning the faces, feeling their eyes upon him, Baden marveled that all the good will he had once enjoyed could have evaporated so quickly. Certainly he still had a few friends in the Order: Jaryd, Alayna, and Trahn, of course, as well as Sonel. And he had earned the trust of the other mages with whom he had created the link, including Orris, oddly enough. But that was all. He had driven the rest away. By pushing for an aggressive response to the Lon-Ser threat, he had angered the older mages, who perceived great peril in deviating too far from the rather limited role they believed that the Mage-Craft should play in governing Tobyn-Ser. At the same time, he had alienated many of the younger, more quick-tempered members of the Order by blocking their preparations for what would have amounted to total war with Lon-Ser.

His efforts to forge a compromise that he hoped would bridge the gap between one faction and the other, had instead won him the resentment of both. Add to that the animosity engendered by his successful effort to keep Baram alive, and it was little wonder that he was now hated by most of those in the Gathering Chamber.

"You are recognized, Owl-Master," Sonel said for a second time, prodding him gently. "You may speak."

Baden forced a smile, and tried to infuse his voice with as much confidence as he could. "Of course, Owl-Sage. Thank you." He glanced around the table. "My fellow mages, I present to you today my report on my conversations with the outlander Baram, in the hope that it will further our discussion of how best to face the threat from Lon-Ser." He dropped the report on the table, allowing it to land with an emphatic thud. It had been scribed and bound in dark leather by a bookbinder Baden knew in the city, a man who owed him a favor. He had done a fine job; the report looked quite impressive. "I apologize for its length," the Owl-Master went on, looking over at Trahn, who had raised an eyebrow at its appearance. "I don't expect anyone to read all of it—I've summarized my findings in the opening section, and I will just take a few moments now to go over my conclusions and recommendations."

"That hardly seems necessary, Baden," came an all-too-familiar voice. On the far side of the table, only a few seats removed from Sonel's place of honor, Erland rose smoothly from his chair. His hair was as white as Baden's owl, and he wore a trim, silver beard, but, though his position at the table marked him as one of the Order's senior members, these were the only signs of age upon him. He was hale and tall, with a ruddy complexion and dark, piercing blue eyes. He stood now with casual ease, his fingers resting lightly on the table, and a sardonic smile on his lips.

No one in this chamber had taken greater pleasure than Erland in Baden's fall from power. A few years ago, he had been just another Owl-Master; not particularly influential, and certainly no one whom Baden thought of as ambitious. But in the wake of Odinan's death, Erland had established himself as the primary spokesman for the older masters, and he had quickly proven himself a formidable advocate for their positions. His success lay not in his style, as, for example, Sartol's had—Erland's speaking voice was rather ordinary and he lacked the grace and elegance with which the dead Owl-Master had carried himself. Rather it was the older man's caustic wit and his audacity that made him so effective; his reliance on innuendo and hyperbole, his willingness to say almost anything to advance his point of view. Baden thought him the most dangerous person in the Order, and he had no doubt that Erland hoped and expected to succeed Sonel as Owl-Sage. Which explained, perhaps, why the white-haired mage had focused so much of his vitriol on Baden. As a master himself, Erland knew how close Baden had come to being named Sage four years ago, and, with Baden's reputation now sullied, he seemed determined to keep his rival down. He used Baden as a foil for his own aggrandizement whenever he could. And Baden had come to hate him for it—the mere sight of the man caused him to flush with anger. It didn't help that Erland's familiar, a dark, round-headed bird with wide, yellow eyes, looked almost exactly like Baden's beloved Anla. Baden had long since recovered from the pain of losing her, and he had come to love Golivas as much as he had his first owl. But he still found it galling that such a man should be bound to so beautiful a bird.

In light of all of this, it was not surprising that Erland should begin to belittle the report before Baden had even submitted it. "I think you can give us your little work of fiction without comment," the mage was saying now, dismissing the document with a gesture. "We all know what conclusions you've reached."

"Really, Erland," Baden returned with heavy sarcasm, "I'm flattered. You've already read my report?"

"Hardly," the older mage scoffed, his grin broadening, and his arms opening expansively. "That's the beauty of it, Baden: I didn't have to." He stepped away from the table and began pacing its length as he spoke. And the irony in his tone made Baden's comment of a moment before sound sincere. "Without even looking at it I know that your 'report' finds us faced with a dire threat from Lon-Ser, one which we fully understand only now, because you, in your wisdom and foresight, demanded that we keep the outlander alive. From him," Erland continued, his voice rising and falling with melodramatic flourish, "from this innocent boy who was corrupted by a harsh society, we have learned of

Lon-Ser's government, of its culture, and of its miraculous mechanical break-throughs. Now we must take action, you tell us; we must put to use all that we have learned before we are attacked again. And," the mage concluded, his tone turning bitter and derisive, "we must do so precisely as you say, or all will be lost. For only you—"

"That's enough, Erland!" Sonel commanded angrily, cutting him off.

The Owl-Master looked at her, grinning once more. Then, with a slight bow of his head toward the Sage, he returned to his place at the council table and calmly lowered himself into his chair.

"Please go on, Baden," Sonel added, turning back in his direction.

The Owl-Master hesitated. Notwithstanding the Sage's rebuke, Erland had accomplished precisely what he had set out to do. His parody of the report came just close enough to the broad-stroke summary that Baden had planned to give to prove his point. If Baden went ahead with what he had intended to say, he would make himself appear as pompous and self-righteous as Erland had implied. And if he declined to comment on the report at all, it would look like he had backed away from a conflict with the older master. He did not find either option especially attractive. Once again, the mages were watching him, waiting. "It seems that Erland finds humor in all this," he began harshly. "It seems that he is willing to make a mockery of the tragedies at Taima, Kaera, and Watersbend. He believes that he can laugh away the murder of Niall and the deaths of Orris's familiar and my own—"

"*That is a lie!*" Erland thundered, leaping out of his chair.

But it was too late. The mages were still looking at Baden, and, while they remained cool and skeptical, they were at least listening to him. "But the rest of us know better," he continued, ignoring Erland's outburst. "The rest of us realize that, one way or another, we must eventually deal with Lon-Ser." That was a stretch, he knew: there were many gathered around the council table who did not share this view. But he pressed on. "It is true, as Erland said, that I advocate in my report that we take action. It has been four years since Phelan Spur; we've waited long enough. However, I do not stand before you with any notion of what form that action should take. That is a decision for all of us to make, not me alone.

"It is also true that my report offers a good deal of information on Lon-Ser's people, its leadership, and its advanced mechanical knowledge. But most importantly—and this," the Owl-Master added pointedly, "is something Erland failed to mention—it describes the circumstances that led to Lon-Ser's first attack on our people. Lon-Ser's vast cities are alarmingly overcrowded; nearly all its forests have been destroyed; its air and water have grown foul. For these reasons, Baram tells us, he and his cohort were sent to Tobyn-Ser. And we have no reason to believe that Lon-Ser's problems have solved themselves in Baram's absence. So Erland can laugh all he likes—he can belittle this threat in the hope that it will just go away." Baden shook his head. "But it will not. They will be coming again."

"Let them come!" one of the younger mages cried out. "We defeated them once, we'll defeat them again!"

Several of the other Hawk-Mages nodded their agreement. But Orris stood and silenced them with a sweeping glare. With his broad, muscular frame, bristling beard, and long, thick, golden hair, Orris was still an imposing physical presence. And he remained a leader among the younger mages, able to command their attention with little more than a gesture. "Brave words, Arslan," the burly Hawk-Mage said grimly, his brown eyes coming to rest on the man who had spoken, "but foolish ones."

The other mage stood as well, as if to meet Orris's challenge. He was young, with a boyish face beneath unruly red hair. "You doubt our ability to fight them?"

Orris gave a sad grin. "Not at all. But I fear the cost of this war you're so anxious to wage. Last time it was Kaera and Watersbend. Who'll pay the price this time?"

"But this time we'll be ready!" another mage shouted confidently. And once more, nods and murmurs of approval greeted the words.

"Perhaps," Trahn said, entering the fray, his dark features solemn. "But do you doubt that they will be equally prepared? Last time it was sixteen men with mechanical birds and what Baram calls throwers. What if this time it's fifty men, or a hundred, or a thousand, armed with weapons we can't even imagine?"

"They wouldn't dare try anything so brazen!" Arslan countered. "Theron told Jaryd and Alayna that they fear the Mage-Craft—why else would they have used the tactic they did? As long as the Mage-Craft guards Tobyn-Ser, we're safe."

"Theron also told us that the Order would have to change," Alayna broke in. "That it could no longer afford to limit its vision to Tobyn-Ser's borders." Every pair of eyes in the Gathering Chamber turned in her direction, and all the mages who were standing sat back down. Even as he settled himself back into his chair, Baden marvelled at the respect that Alayna and Jaryd now commanded from the entire Order. Ever since their encounter with Theron and their heroics at Phelan Spur the young mages had been treated with a reverence normally reserved for the most senior of Owl-Masters, as if everyone, despite their differing opinions on other issues, acknowledged the fact that these two would someday lead the Order. For their part, Jaryd and Alayna acted as though they did not notice. Which, of course, was entirely appropriate.

"So what would you suggest we do, Alayna?" Arslan asked.

"Do you mean after we all read Baden's report?" she replied, giving a small smile. Several mages allowed themselves a chuckle, and Baden grinned at her appreciatively. In the next instant, however, the mood in the Great Hall sobered. Alayna shrugged uncertainly, passing a nervous hand through her long, dark hair in a gesture that Baden had come to know quite well over the past few years. "I don't know," she said in a low voice. And then, her tone growing bolder once more, she added, "but we must act—and soon. We've been idle for too long."

Jaryd rose to stand beside her, and, as he did, Baden noted, not for the first time, how much his nephew had matured over the past four years. Physically, his lean frame had filled out, his shoulders broadening and the muscles in his arms growing more defined. His face, though still youthful, had also matured. His chin was squarer than it had been, more like his father's, although with his grey eyes and straight brown hair, which he wore long now, and tied back, he still favored Drina more than he did Bernel. But the growth Baden had seen in the young mage went far deeper than these changes in his appearance. He possessed a self-confidence now that he had lacked when Baden first led him away from Accalia four years ago; an inner strength and sense of purpose that seemed to have brought some perspective and control to the unbridled passion Baden remembered from the mage's younger days. And, Baden realized, these changes were due in large part to the life he now shared with the beautiful, dark-eyed woman standing beside him. "Alayna's right," Jaryd said, in a voice deeper than Baden remembered. "The longer we wait, the greater our peril." Several other mages, most of them sitting near Jaryd and Alayna, at the younger end of the table, signalled their agreement.

"With all due respect to my young colleagues," Erland countered, an unnatural smile stretching across his features, "taking action for its own sake is neither logical nor wise. Without a clear course to take, prudence, I believe, would be our best choice."

"With all due respect, Erland," Jaryd shot back, in a passable imitation of the older mage, "you'd say the same thing if the entire Lon-Ser army was camped out in Hawksfind Wood!"

A number of mages laughed, including Baden. Erland, for his part, fought to maintain his grin, keeping his teeth bared and producing something that most resembled a sneer. "I see that you get your manners from your uncle, Hawk-Mage. It's a shame really: such comments do all of us a disservice." He paused, allowing the last ripples of laughter to die away and then prolonging the ensuing silence until several of the younger mages who had laughed at Jaryd's remark began to fidget uncomfortably in their seats. "Let me remind all of you once more why I have resisted most of the proposed responses to this so-called threat, and why, in the end, my view in these matters has prevailed again and again." He glanced coldly at Baden. "While some may claim to understand what goes on in the minds of Lon-Ser's leaders, the fact remains that we have no idea what they plan to do next, or even if they plan to do anything at all. For all we know, the outlanders' failure at Phelan Spur ended the threat. If so, any action we take in the name of prevention may in fact serve as provocation for a new, broader assault." He took a breath. "We must also keep in mind that our land has prospered for better than a thousand years without any outside interference. Yes," he said, gesturing toward Jaryd and Alayna, "I have heard the warnings from Theron conveyed to us by our young friends. But, the Owl-Master gave them no indication that he meant for us to seek a confrontation with the people of Lon-Ser." He looked down the length of the table at the two Hawk-Mages. "Did he?"

Jaryd glanced at Alayna and then shook his head reluctantly. "No," he admitted, "he didn't."

"Of course not," Erland responded. "It is one thing to pay attention to the world around us, but it is quite another to abandon a thousand year's worth of common sense in some foolhardy adventure across Arick's Sea." He smiled and nodded, as if struck by the wisdom of his own argument. "And this brings me to the most important point of all: we are not the government of Tobyn-Ser. We are its guardians and its servants, but we are not its leaders. Amarid made that clear when he first created this Order, and despite the rehabilitation of Theron's reputation, I am not ready to embrace the Owl-Master's vision of our proper role. If we are to end our land's long tradition of self-sufficiency and independence, it should be because the people of Tobyn-Ser choose to do so, not because we do. It is not our decision to make."

"On that last point I must disagree," Orris commented, standing once more. "I've been thinking about this since the last Gathering: Amarid's Law states not only that we are to be the land's guardians, but also that we are to be the arbiters of its disputes. It may be true, as some have argued in this Hall, that war with Lon-Ser is inevitable. But we're not at war yet, and, until we are, we ought to be looking for a peaceful end to this conflict. Amarid would have seen this as the Order's responsibility—his Law makes that clear. I believe that it falls to us to make peace with the people of Lon-Ser."

Baden turned toward Trahn, only to find the dark mage already gazing in his direction, a thoughtful expression in his vivid green eyes. Orris had advanced an intriguing interpretation of Amarid's First Law, one which, if it withstood the test of scrutiny, might go a long way toward negating Erland's previously successful arguments.

Apparently, Erland sensed the same possibility. "That's preposterous, Orris, and you know it!" he argued hotly, "Amarid's Law refers to disputes among the people of this land, not conflicts between Tobyn-Ser and her neighbors!"

"You know this, Erland?" Trahn inquired, his voice even, a slight grin tugging at the corners of his wide mouth. "You've glimpsed the inner workings of the First Mage's mind?"

"No, Trahn," the older mage replied severely, "but I've studied his words and teachings for more years than you've been alive. I've seen nothing to support Orris's interpretation of Amarid's First Law."

"Have you seen anything that would directly contradict it?" Trahn persisted. Erland hesitated, and the Hawk-Mage pressed his advantage. "It would surprise me if you had. The wording of the Law itself is ambiguous: 'Mages shall serve the people of the land. They shall be the arbiters of disputes.' I take this to mean any and all disputes relating to the safety of Tobyn-Ser; I don't think that Amarid would have intended anything less."

"That's preposterous," Erland said again, but he seemed far less sure of himself than he had a few minutes earlier.

"Assuming for a moment that you and Orris are right, Trahn," Arslan broke in, disregarding Erland's protest, "what would you have us do?"

Trahn pressed his lips together and shrugged slightly. "I'm not sure. Orris?"

The barrel-chested mage took a long breath. "I'm at a loss as well."

"I have some thoughts on that."

It took them all by surprise, even Baden. Especially Baden. He looked at Sonel, who had just spoken, and who was now staring back at him, an inscrutable smile on her lips.

"You, Owl-Sage?" Radomil asked with genuine surprise, stroking his neat goatee.

"Yes," she replied, her eyes still holding Baden's. "But before I share them with you, I should inform you all of a recent correspondence I have had with the leaders of Lon-Ser."

A strained silence engulfed the Hall, to be broken at length by Erland's incredulous voice. "Would you repeat that please, Owl-Sage?"

"Of course, Erland," she responded calmly. "I said that I should like to tell you all about my recent correspondence with Lon-Ser's Council of Sovereigns. I sent them a letter late last fall in which I described for them the crimes committed by the outlanders and requested a meeting at which we might discuss the conflict between our two lands." Silence again. Every face in the chamber wore an expression of genuine shock; the degree to which this was mixed with fear and dismay seemed to depend upon where the individual sat. The older mages, those sitting nearest the Sage, appeared most disturbed by her revelation, none more so than Erland.

"On whose authority did you do this?" he demanded.

"My own!" Sonel snapped, her green eyes flashing. "I am the leader of this Order, Erland, duly selected by you and the rest of the Masters! Do you now wish to contest that choice?"

"Not at all, Owl-Sage," the Owl-Master answered quickly, glancing nervously about the chamber. "I'm just surprised that you would send such a message without consulting the rest of us."

"I wasn't aware that I had to!" the Sage returned, driving each word into the older mage. "I felt that it was time for us to contact Lon-Ser's leaders, and, as Sage, I saw this not only as my prerogative, but also as my responsibility!"

"Have they responded?" Baden asked.

Sonel continued to glare at Erland for a moment longer, before turning to answer. "Yes, as of this morning." Baden saw her pull a piece of snow white parchment from her cloak and unroll it. " 'Owl-Sage Sonel,' " she read, " 'Regarding your note of this past winter: We have no knowledge of the events you describe, nor do we have any desire to become entangled in what are most likely internal disturbances endemic to Tobyn-Ser.' " She looked up, allowing the paper to curl back into a cylinder.

They all stared at her for several seconds without speaking. "That's it?" Baden finally asked. "That's all they wrote?"

"I'm afraid so."

"They're lying!" one of the young mages shouted. Several others voiced their agreement.

Baden nodded slowly. "At least one of them is," he commented, more to himself than to the rest of the chamber.

Sonel narrowed her eyes. "What do you mean?"

"Just that we shouldn't lose sight of what we've learned about Lon-Ser and its government." He stood again, feeling their eyes upon him once more. And they were heeding his every word. Regardless of what they thought of him, none doubted that Baden knew more about their enemy than anyone else in Tobyn-Ser. "The ruling body is known as the Council of Sovereigns, and in that name lies a great truth: each of the three Nals, the huge cities of which I spoke before, is an independent entity, with its own ruler, its own customs and culture, and its own concerns. Their leaders come together in the Council to make policy for the land as a whole, but they represent different and, at times, competing interests. From what Baram has told me, I would guess that they don't always get along. They won't willingly share information about their mechanical advances, because each one views the other two as economic rivals. In the past, they have even fought wars against one another."

"So," Trahn ventured, "you think that one of the Nals could have carried out the attacks on Tobyn-Ser without the consent of the other two."

Baden nodded again. "I think it's possible. Baram comes from Bragor-Nal, the largest of the three, and according to him, the most powerful." He turned to Sonel. "That message you read to us may have been signed in good faith by two of the three Sovereigns."

"In which case," the Sage observed, completing Baden's thought, "our dispute lies not with all of Lon-Ser, but with a single Nal."

"Yes. Probably Bragor-Nal."

"You're just speculating now," Erland protested. "You can't be certain of any of this."

"True," Baden admitted placidly.

"And yet you expect us to decide upon some course of action, based solely on your guesswork?"

"I must say, Baden," Arslan chimed in, "I'm inclined to agree with Erland in this instance."

A number of mages, both young and old, voiced their agreement, and heated arguments erupted all around the table.

After several moments, Erland opened his arms and shrugged, a smug grin on his face. "You see? We simply do not have enough information to endorse any plan right now."

"Don't presume to speak for me, Erland!" Trahn called out above the growing din. "I'd like to hear the Owl-Sage's proposal before we dismiss all our options out of hand."

"So would I," Orris echoed.

"Well, when I first thought of it," Sonel began, as the other discussions died away, "I hadn't considered the possibility that one of Lon-Ser's Nals might be responsible for all that transpired four years ago. But I'm not sure that it matters." She paused, as if bracing herself for the Order's reaction to what she was about to say. "I would like to send a group of envoys to meet with the Council of Sovereigns."

Silence. Followed by an explosion of protest and incredulity, led, naturally, by Erland. "Why, Owl-Sage?" the white-haired mage implored. "What could be gained by such a venture? What could be worth the lives of those you would send?"

"We have no reason to believe that these envoys would be killed!" Orris argued.

"On the contrary!" the Owl-Master insisted. "We have every reason to believe it! Think of Kaera! Think of Watersbend! And then tell me that such a mission could end in anything but bloodshed!"

"Erland is right!" another master cried out. "There is nothing to be gained, and everything to be lost!"

"That's not true!" Baden countered, trying to make himself heard over the commotion Sonel's proposal had sparked. "There's a great deal to be gained! Dismissing a letter from a distant land is one thing; ignoring a delegation of mages is quite another!" He regretted the use of the word "delegation" as soon as he spoke, and he hoped no one would notice. He should have known better.

"A *delegation*, Baden?" Erland mocked, his tone laden with bitter irony. "Do you remember the last time you coaxed us into sending delegations to do your bidding? The rest of us certainly do. We never saw Jessamyn, Peredur, or Niall again."

"That's uncalled for, Erland!" Jaryd shot back. "If you want to blame someone, blame Sartol! Baden wasn't responsible!"

"Perhaps not," the Owl-Master acceded grudgingly, "but the fact remains that these things always seem to end in tragedy."

Jaryd opened his mouth to respond, but there was nothing he could say, nothing any of them could say. Regardless of who was to blame, Jessamyn was dead, as were the others. And over the last four years, Erland and his allies had repeatedly used the white-haired Sage's death as a justification for inaction.

From that point on, the debate followed a predictable course, one that Baden had watched with dismay several times before. The same tired arguments chased each other around the council table again and again, until the session came to resemble one of Cearbhall's farces, with each player reciting well-rehearsed lines, and no one listening to what anyone else had to say. Long after he had removed himself from the discussion, Baden found himself watching Sonel as she presided over the debate, compelled by her standing within the Order to listen to all those who wished to speak, and denied the luxury of Baden's aloofness. She was still beautiful, sitting straight-backed and tall at the end of the table, her light hair pulled back from her smooth brow, and her green eyes nearly a match for the cloak she wore. But Baden, who knew her so well, could see a sadness in her now, as if she recognized the futility of the Gathering she had convened that morning. At one point, she glanced in his direction and when their eyes met, she smiled wanly and shook her head, as if to say, *can you believe my proposal caused all this?* He tried to summon a smile in return, but he couldn't. There was too much at stake, and not enough people in the chamber seemed to realize it. Once again, as he had so many times over the past four years, Baden wondered if the Order had stopped the outlanders in time, or if Tobyn-Ser's enemies had already achieved what they sought: the elimination of the Mage-Craft as a threat to their plans. Yes, the Order still survived, but it was paralyzed by indecision and riven with conflict.

And if the collapse of the Order came, as he feared it soon might, this woman before him, the one woman he had ever loved in his life, would be remembered by history as having presided over its demise. The idea of it was more than he could bear. On several occasions in the months leading up to this Gathering, he had sworn to himself that he would not allow such a thing to happen. Silently, he did so again now. But he feared that oaths and good intentions would not be sufficient to save the Order from its own weaknesses. Not this time; not against this enemy. There was something coming. He had sensed it as he wandered through the land, as he walked the streets of Amarid, even as he sat here in the First Mage's Great Hall. He could taste it in the air. He didn't know what form it would take, or whence it would come, but he could already hear the first rumblings, as of a distant storm on a warm summer afternoon. They wouldn't have to wait very long.

4

Baram himself is a man of contradictions and dichotomies. Indeed, referring to him as a man at all seems, at times, a misnomer. He was but eighteen when captured, and, when speaking of his home or his parents, he still sounds very much like a boy. And yet, when he describes, dispassionately and in chilling detail, the violent acts he committed as a "break-law" in Bragor-Nal, and, later, as a willing participant in the attacks carried out against the people of our land, the youth and innocence vanish, leaving only a killer, a man to be feared. . . . Unfortunately, as I have observed him over the course of his incarceration, I have seen less and less of the boy, and more and more of the killer.

> —From Section Four of "The Report of Owl-Master Baden on his Interrogation of the Outlander Baram," Submitted to the 1,014th Gathering of the Order of Mages and Masters. Spring, Gods' Year 4625.

Orris was seething. He sat in the Aerie, at a dimly lit corner table drinking Amari Ale with Jaryd, Alayna, Baden, Trahn, and Ursel. It was dark outside; the Gathering had adjourned for the day several hours before. But his mind was still in the Great Hall, revisiting the so-called debate that had taken place there that afternoon. Listening to the posturing of Erland and his allies, the elaborate arguments that sought to justify inaction and excuse cowardice, had alternately saddened and sickened him. But mostly, it had infuriated him. They had taken an oath to guard Tobyn-Ser! They had devoted their lives to following the teachings of the First Mage! And yet, faced with the greatest threat this land had seen in a thousand years, they did nothing! Didn't they see the danger? Didn't their vows mean anything to them?

As it happened, Arslan and his bunch were nearly as bad, with their hunger for retribution and their belief in the invincibility of the Mage-Craft. Several years ago, Orris might have been one of them: belligerent, reckless, willful. But he was older now, more mature. He had been at Theron's Grove when Sartol murdered Jessamyn and Peredur; he had felt the sudden, consuming anguish of losing his first familiar, Pordath, who had been killed by Sartol's owl as Orris tried to save Jaryd and Alayna from the renegade; and he had seen the carnage at Watersbend, the charred remains of homes and people left there by the outlanders and their terrible weapons. Such experiences could not help but temper a man, even one such as he had been. He actually liked Arslan; the young mage had a passion that Orris admired, one that could be harnessed some day. But right now, that zeal was gravely misdirected. Indeed, either faction—the young or the old—appeared perfectly capable of leading the Order and all of Tobyn-Ser to ruin, be it with a blind leap into war, or the slow decay of torpor.

Orris found this all particularly galling because the Sage finally seemed willing to act. Sonel's proposal to send envoys to Lon-Ser made sense to him. It struck the proper balance between appeasement and provocation. And, in the past, the creation of such a group—even Orris, who no longer blamed Baden for what had happened four years ago, and who had travelled with Jessamyn and the others to the Shadow Forest, could not bring himself to use the word "delegation"—would have been approved by the moderate majority that once controlled the Order. Those days were gone, however. Adversity and tragedy had driven rival factions even farther apart. The problem, Orris believed, was not that the proper compromise had yet to be found, but rather that the Order was no longer capable of reaching an amicable agreement on anything. And while the day's debate had made him angry, Orris knew himself well enough to recognize what lay behind his ire: he was frightened.

"We've got the support of the Owl-Sage this time," Jaryd was saying, his pale eyes intent as he gently stroked the chin of his fierce, grey hawk. "That's got to count for something."

"Perhaps," Baden replied doubtfully. He took a sip of the dark ale. "But I'm not even certain that Sonel has enough influence anymore."

Notwithstanding the psychic link he had created with the lean mage and the others, and the four years he had spent working with Baden toward the same goals, Orris was still surprised, and just a bit uncomfortable, each time he found himself agreeing with the Owl-Master. Old animosities were not easily forgotten. "I fear Baden is right," he said staring into his tankard. "Erland won't give in, and I have little confidence in our ability to win Arslan's support. He's spoiling for a fight; I don't think he'll be satisfied with negotiations."

Trahn shook his head slowly. "That's unfortunate. I think Sonel's plan has merit."

"It has more than that," Baden observed. "If my interpretation of that letter she received is correct—if only one of the Nals is responsible for the attacks—then her plan may offer us a chance to enlist the help of Lon-Ser's other two Nals."

"Do you really think they'd help us against one of their own?" Jaryd asked.

Baden shook his head at the Hawk-Mage's question. "The leaders of the other two Nals wouldn't look at it that way. They'd see Bragor-Nal's attack on us as an attempt by a military and economic rival to gain a huge advantage at their expense. They'd look to stop them any way they could. But first they'd have to be convinced that we were telling them the truth. That's why sending a delegation makes so much sense: it would give us the opportunity to present proof of our allegations to the leaders of all three Nals."

"What proof?" Alayna demanded. "The remnants of the mechanical birds? I don't think that would do it."

She was right, Orris knew. They still had the outlanders' weapons, and the carcasses of several of the outlanders' deadly, mechanical hawks. But as Orris's friend Crob, an Abboriji merchant, had told him several years ago, items like these were becoming increasingly common among the mercenaries hired to fight in the wars that raged continually among Abborij's Potentates. That the mages had taken them from Tobyn-Ser's invaders offered no proof that these men had come from Lon-Ser. The world was changing more rapidly than Orris cared to contemplate, and Tobyn-Ser was no longer immune to those changes.

"I don't think the weapons and birds would be enough either," Baden agreed, a roguish grin creeping across his face. "No, I had something else in mind."

"What?" Ursel asked, rising to the bait.

"Baram, of course."

"*Baram?*" Trahn exploded, his green eyes wide with shock. "You can't believe that Sonel would agree to such a thing!"

"No," Baden conceded mildly, "I don't expect she would, at least not at present. But," he added with certainty, "eventually she'll reach the same conclusion I have: the outlander represents our only hope of convincing the Council of Sovereigns. Otherwise it's our word against that of Bragor-Nal's leader. And, while I do think that the other Nals would help us against one of their own, I wouldn't expect them to believe us under those circumstances."

"Regardless of what the Sage says," Orris asserted, more fervently than he had intended, "the Order will never allow this!"

"They must!" Baden returned. "It's the only—"

"I'm not arguing with your logic, Baden," the burly mage interrupted. "I think you're probably right. I'm just stating what I know to be true: the Order will never allow it. Erland will oppose you on this, and so will Arslan and rest of the young mages. They wanted Baram executed four years ago, and, while they've resigned themselves to his incarceration, they won't agree to grant him his freedom." Baden started to protest, but Orris held up a hand to silence him. "That may not be how you intend it," the Hawk-Mage added, "but that would be the effect."

The Owl-Master stared at him for several moments, his bright blue eyes smoldering, but then, looking away, he sighed wearily and nodded. "It would be difficult to prevent," he admitted.

"Do you think that Sonel's plan can succeed without Baram?" Ursel asked, looking first at Baden, but then addressing the others as well.

"It's so short-sighted," Baden said sadly, as if he hadn't heard Ursel speak. "We're allowing vengeance to keep us from protecting the land. It makes no sense."

No one spoke for some time, as Baden, looking frail and beaten, gazed blindly at the flagon in front of him.

"It may be possible," Trahn suggested with some uncertainty, responding at last to the Hawk-Mage's question. "I thought the Sage's proposal reasonable when I first heard it this afternoon, and I never considered sending Baram with the envoys. So I must believe that there are other paths to success." He shrugged. "Perhaps, with the physical evidence we do have, the mages we send can make a strong enough case to convince them."

"Perhaps," Alayna echoed. "But I must say, having heard Baden's argument, I'm far less hopeful than I was earlier today."

Once again, silence descended on their table. Alayna, it seemed, had spoken for all of them. For his part, Orris viewed Sonel's proposal as the Order's best hope for peace, but he also recognized that, without Baram, the Order's envoys would probably accomplish very little. And, as he himself had told Baden, the Order would never agree to send the outlander home. Which brought them right back to the original problem. They could do nothing, no doubt just as Erland hoped. As long as the white-haired Owl-Master could confound their efforts to decide upon a course of action, he won. And the thought of that rekindled the fury that had burned in Orris just a short while ago. But with this renewal of his anger came another notion as well, and, outrageous as it was, it did offer him an option. Not one that he relished, to be sure, but an option nonetheless; one that he would keep to himself until he had exhausted all other possibilities.

"It's getting late," Jaryd observed, draining his tankard and pushing his chair back from the table. "And tomorrow's discussion won't be any easier than today's." He stood, as did Alayna, who took his hand.

"Rest well, you two," Baden said, shaking off his dark mood and forcing a smile. "Maybe tomorrow holds an answer to all this."

Alayna smiled at him, the radiant smile they had all come to know so well. "I hope so, Baden," she returned softly, momentarily placing her free hand on his shoulder. And, with a "good night" to the others, the young mages made their way upstairs to their room.

"I think I'll try to get some sleep, too," Trahn said, forcing the words through a yawn.

Orris laughed in spite of himself. "That would appear to be a good idea," he commented drily.

In the end, Ursel departed as well, leaving Orris and Baden alone together at the dark table.

Orris was about to make an excuse and leave the Owl-Master to his musings when Baden surprised him. "Another ale?" the lean mage asked, signalling one of the barmaids.

Orris hesitated.

"I'd welcome the company," Baden added.

After a moment, the Hawk-Mage nodded, drawing a smile from the older man.

"Good," Baden said, turning to the serving girl once more and holding up two fingers.

They sat without speaking for some time, their awkward silence interrupted only by the arrival of their ales. Orris mostly stared at his hands, his eyes flicking up to Baden's face every so often. The Owl-Master, however, did not appear to notice, absorbed as he was in his own thoughts. And so when, at length, Baden finally spoke, it took Orris by surprise.

"You said before that many of the younger mages wanted Baram killed," he began without preamble. "Did you as well?"

Orris stared at the Master for several seconds before responding. "Yes," he answered matter-of-factly. "I was angry," he explained after a brief pause. "And Pordath was gone." He started to say more, then stopped, stung by the memory of his beautiful pale hawk. Despite the intervening years, and the magnificent dark falcon that sat now on his shoulder—the same type of falcon, Jaryd and Alayna had told him just after his binding, that Theron carried—Orris could not help but still grieve the loss of that first familiar.

"The first is always the hardest," Baden offered, as if reading his thoughts.

"I suppose." This was not a subject on which Orris wished to linger. "In any case," he continued, returning to Baden's original question, "I was wrong."

The Owl-Master shrugged noncommittally. "Maybe. I don't know how much good has come of keeping him alive." He was gazing into his ale again, but even so, Orris could read the unspoken emotions that flickered in the Owl-Master's bright eyes. *And the cost of not allowing his death has been great.*

"But your report: we wouldn't have any of that information without Baram."

Baden looked up at that, the dimness of the tavern giving his gaunt features a sharp, hawklike appearance. "What good is knowledge if no one will heed it?"

The bearded mage could make no reply, and, an instant later, the intensity in Baden's face disappeared, leaving only the weariness Orris had seen there before.

"It's still possible that the Order will make use of what you've learned," Orris ventured. But even as he spoke, the Hawk-Mage could hear the hollowness in his words. "I may also be wrong about Arslan—perhaps I can convince him at least to consider allowing Baram to accompany the envoys."

Baden shook his head. "No. You were right in what you said before. They won't agree. I should have known better; I could have saved myself a good deal of grief."

Orris narrowed his eyes. "Should have known—? Did you foresee this circumstance back then?" he asked, suddenly marvelling at the possibility. "Is this the real reason you fought to keep Baram alive?"

Baden managed a thin, rueful smile. "I'm not that wise," he said, "nor am I so blessed with the Sight that I could trace the potential paths of history with such certainty." He hesitated. "I saw possibilities, no more. I believed—and, on some level I still believe—that Baram holds the key to our survival. And I always felt that he would be of more value to us alive than dead, even if just for what he could tell us of Lon-Ser. That's why I argued for his life, and prevailed upon the Sage to spare him even after a majority of the Order opposed me."

Orris considered this, sipping idly at his ale. In that moment, despite Baden's protestations, the burly mage thought him as wise and courageous a man as he had ever known. The magnitude of what the Owl-Master had done four years ago, and the memory of his own passionate resistance to Baden's reasoning left him feeling terribly young and just a bit foolish. "If you could have explained it to us. . . ." Orris began, knowing again how ridiculous he sounded.

Baden laughed gently. "Explained what?" he asked. "That I had a vague premonition that we might need Baram to help us make peace with the leaders of Lon-Ser? That I not only wished to keep him alive, but I also expected someday to send him back to Bragor-Nal?" He passed a hand through his thin red and grey hair and chuckled again. "I'm not sure that would have changed too many votes."

Orris laughed. "I guess not," he conceded. Again he drank from the pewter tankard. "So now what? How do we handle the rest of the Gathering?"

The Owl-Master made a small, helpless gesture with his hands. "I don't see that we have many choices. We continue to argue our point of view and hope that, somehow, we can convince a majority that we're right."

"And if we fail?"

"If we fail, we return to western Tobyn-Ser and reestablish the psychic link, just as we did after last year's Gathering, and the one before that."

"But is that enough?" Orris demanded with fervor.

Maybe too much fervor. Baden looked at him, and the Owl-Master's eyes seemed to pierce his own. Orris felt exposed, as if all his thoughts suddenly lay bared before Baden's gaze, including the one that he dared not share with anyone: the notion that had struck him just a bit earlier, the one that he had set aside as a last resort. "I'm not sure what you're getting at, Orris," the lean mage told him in a low, strained voice, "and I don't think I want to know. This may sound strange coming from me, given my role in creating our psychic link, but I do not enjoy defying the decrees of the Order. I'll only do so if I believe that I must to honor my oath to serve and guard the land, and I'll only go so far; I'm afraid that the link is about my limit. But every mage has to find that point for himself, and then he has to choose his path accordingly. Do you understand?"

Orris nodded, but said nothing. His mouth had gone dry.

"Whatever you decide," the master went on, "think it through carefully. I would never presume to judge you, nor would Trahn, or Jaryd and Alayna. But others will. I've paid a price for saving Baram's life, and the eight of us may yet pay a price for the link we've created. This thing you're considering, whatever it is, will carry a cost as well. Keep that in mind. I'm not trying to talk you out of it; I just want you to be prepared."

Again, the Hawk-Mage nodded. "How did you know?" he asked his voice tinged with both fear and wonder.

Baden grinned darkly. "I know nothing." He got up from the table and raised an arm as his large, white owl flew to him from a nearby window sill. "I think it's time I went to sleep," he said, "but let me leave you with this: don't give up on your fellow mages just yet. I share your frustration, but maybe they'll surprise us. At least allow them another day before you do anything that you might regret."

"I'll consider it," Orris answered. "Good night, Baden."

"Until tomorrow."

Orris watched the lean mage climb the steps to his room. Theirs was a strange relationship. They had a long history of mutual suspicion and hostility, and yet, in many ways, the Owl-Master appeared to understand him better than anyone in Tobyn-Ser. How else could Orris explain what had just passed between them? Friendships had never come easily to him; even with Jaryd and Alayna, whom he now considered his closest friends, he had first had to overcome his resentment of the apparent ease with which the young mages had established themselves as influential members of the Order. He had always been a bit of a loner; he had struggled for many years to establish himself as a leader among the Hawk-Mages. And these two, it had seemed to Orris, merely showed up at the Great Hall with Amarid's Hawk on their shoulders, and in no time at all they had been included in the Theron's Grove delegation, arguably the most important mission in the history of the Order. True, they had quickly justified the faith placed in them by Jessamyn and the rest of the Order. Not only had they faced the unsettled ghost of Theron, they had convinced the Owl-Master's spirit to aid the Order. Nonetheless, Orris's resentment had been slow to fade. The friendship he shared with them was the product of a good deal of work, on both sides. And now, it seemed, Baden was becoming a friend as well. This was no less unexpected, and Orris was surprised to find that it pleased him.

But there was another, more critical matter to consider. While Baden's warnings had sobered him, forcing him to face the magnitude of what he was contemplating, they had also crystallized things for him. He had made his decision; now he needed a plan. He signalled the barmaid for another ale and moved to a smaller table in the farthest recesses of the tavern. He had much to ponder.

Sixteen deep, twenty across. Sixteen deep, twenty across. Sixteen deep, twenty across. Rocking gently, his knees drawn up to his chest, the small of his back against the cold, rough stone wall, and his eyes open wide in the absolute darkness, he repeats the words again and again, chanting them, as if he were a cleric reciting his litany in one of Lon's sanctuaries. He can hear the monotony of crickets from outside, descending to him with the cool, sweet summer air from the lone, high window directly above him. Occasionally, he hears an owl call from nearby, to be answered by another one, more distant. But no human sounds reach him. None at all, save his own voice. *Sixteen deep, twenty across. Sixteen deep, twenty across.*

He chants at night. Every night. He has for a long time now. And, for all this time, the chant has never changed. But that's only because he started his night-time ritual too late. He knows that now, and yet he dares not give up the practice. If he were to stop, even for one night, they would surely come for the stones again, just as they did before. He's not certain how they did it, although he knows that they used sorcery and that they waited until he was asleep. But he still remembers the morning when he woke up and realized that his cell was smaller than it had been. He remembers trying to convince himself that he was wrong, that he had imagined it. But he knows better. It happened again the next night and the one after that. Every morning he woke up to find that the walls were closer together. So, finally, on a grey, cold morning, he counted the stones, crawling over the length and breadth of the cell floor like an insect. It took him some time; he kept on losing count. But, after a while, he got it right, and, so he wouldn't forget, he did it over and over, until his knees were raw and bloody.

There are three hundred and eighteen of them left, plus the drain in the far corner, which takes up a space the size of two. It's easier, though, to remember the dimensions: sixteen deep, twenty across.

That same day he resolved that he would not sleep anymore, at least not at night; that's when they come for the stones. He can keep himself awake by reciting the measurements of the cell, just as he is doing now in the blackness. Counting, his eyes open, maintaining his vigil on the stones that remain. He's determined that they won't get any more of them.

He allows himself to nap during the day, although never for very long—if they figure out that he's sleeping during the day, they'll come for the stones then.

He continues his incantation until the first glimmer of dawn appears high on the wall before him, silver and spectral, very much like the ghosts of the wolf lord—Phelan, Baden called him—and his great animal, which Baram still remembers from the night he was captured. Then he stops. Or at least he tries. Recently, he's tried to make himself stop, only to realize some time later, long after the cell has begun to brighten, that he's still speaking. On this morning, though, he does stop. He's fairly certain—the problem is he can still hear the chant in his head, even when he's not saying it aloud—and, like he does every morning, he watches the wall and he waits. If the silver light turns to gold, he knows that the sun is shining, and he stands slowly, stretching the stiffness out of his legs, before moving to lean against the other wall so that, eventually, as the sun rises into Tobyn-Ser's deep blue sky and the broken rectangle of light from the barred window creeps down the wall of his cell, stone by stone, rays of light will touch his face like warm, tender fingers of the Goddess.

If the silver light turns grey, keeping its cool, somber quality, he'll remain where he is and hope for rain, so that the drops that splatter on the window sill or that are blown against the lattice of steel bars will fall on him. The best days come late in the summer, when the sun shines most mornings, and thunderstorms cool off the afternoons. Winters, on the other hand, are very bad. The nights are long, the days are mostly grey, and even the extra blanket they give him can't ward off the cold entirely.

But this is midsummer, and, he soon learns, the skies are clear. Gingerly, he climbs to his feet and shuffles across the cell to rest his back against the other wall. He remains standing, his eyes raised toward the window, his long ragged beard and longer hair hanging down to his waist. And he waits for the sun to reach him.

Perhaps today they'll let him out of the cell for a brief walk around the inner court of the prison. Perhaps they'll even let him bathe. There's a timetable for all of this he knows, a rhythm of sorts to his prison life. But he's forgotten it, and he's long since lost track of the days and weeks. It's easier this way actually: waiting for daylight is bad enough. Waiting for bath days is excruciating. But now he doesn't wait for them; they just happen.

He hears a latch thrown and the creaking of a steel door. A guard's boots click on the stone floor of the corridor outside the cell. Breakfast.

"Talking to yourself again, you crazy bastard?" the guard calls to him in Tobynmir through the small opening at the top of the door.

Chagrined, he stops the chant. This time, he's sure.

The guard's pale, scarred face disappears from the opening as he bends down. A moment later, the small, steel grating at the bottom of the door is pulled open and a tray slides into the cell. "There's your food, Outlander. You'll get a walk today, later."

The grating closes, and the guard's footsteps retreat down the corridor. Soon he hears the outside door being shut and locked. He's alone again. He doesn't move toward the food—he won't until after he's felt the sun on his skin—but he glances at it. Moldy cheese, stale bread, a morsel of smoked meat, several pieces of dried fruit, and some water. It's pretty much the same every day. Still, his stomach growls loudly at the sight of it.

You'll get a walk today, the guard said. He didn't say anything about a bath, but maybe they'll give him that, too. Sometimes they do both. That would be very good. Even without the bath, though, he'll enjoy a walk. At first, after they started stealing the stones from his cell, he had been afraid during the walks and baths and had rushed back to his cell afterwards and immediately started counting. But, so far, they haven't tried anything during the days. Perhaps they know that he's onto them. Whatever the reason, he doesn't worry during his time out of the cell anymore.

A good thing, too: he'd be hard pressed to choose between protecting his stones and enjoying his walks and baths. The only other thing he has to look forward to are his talks with Baden. And even these have begun to grow tedious. The questions don't interest him anymore. In his mind, Lon-Ser has grown dim and distant—he finds it more and more difficult to call up images of the Nal or of his life there. It sometimes seems to him that the sorcerer knows more about Lon-Ser than he does. He still remembers the killing, although even with this, the memories have grown confused. The faces of the people he killed here in Tobyn-Ser seem to blur and blend into the faces of his victims in the Nal. His other recollections are even cloudier. Perhaps because of this, Baden has been resorting with ever-increasing frequency to what he calls "probings." Baram hates them. Not that they hurt—they don't cause him any discomfort at all, and they do bring a welcome clarity to his memories. But he resents them as he would an invasion of his home, or the theft of the stones from his cell.

The sorcerer seems to sense this. He apologizes after he uses the probing, and he often brings gifts: food, or, in the winter, heavier clothing. The two of them have also managed to teach each other something of the other's language, and, occasionally, after asking Baram a battery of questions, Baden will linger a while, offering tales of Tobyn-Ser's past, and the history of what the sorcerer calls the "Mage-Craft." These are the visits that Baram enjoys the most.

He feels sunshine touch the top of his head, warm and gentle, and he closes his eyes, allowing the heat to creep like honey down over his brow and onto the bridge of his nose. He sees bright orange through his eyelids and he allows his eyes to flutter open slightly, so that the brilliant light can leave traces on his mind. The sunshine reaches his lips, and he opens his mouth as if he can taste it. Raising his chin, he allows the warmth to flow through his beard to his neck and chest. It continues down his torso, like a lover, warming his stomach and his waist. And, as he does every sunny morning, he feels the beginning of an erection pressing against his tattered britches. His arms are hanging by his sides and he turns his palms outward so that he can feel the warmth with his finger-tips. He is immersed in it; light and warmth are everything. He sees them through closed eyes, he tastes and smells them, he feels them as a caress. And then he senses them bending around to his side. At the same time, cool shade begins to envelop his face: the top of the window. It's ending.

After another moment, with a sigh, he moves to the tray of food. The pressure in his britches subsides.

He eats absently, trying to hold on to the sensations he has just experienced, and thinking about the walk he will have later. Chewing some fruit, he imagines the sun and the wind massaging his whole body; he visualizes the dark trees on the nearby foothills and the snow-peaked mountains towering beyond them. A walk will do him good. And maybe a bath, too. Later, after his breakfast and a nap. All in all, not a bad day.

5

It is now five years to the day since Calbyr and his men departed for Tobyn-Ser, and I am forced to conclude that their mission has ended in failure. Even the most liberal time allowance for additional training, gradual escalation of the attacks on Tobyn-Ser, and erosion of popular support for that land's Order of Mages and Masters cannot account for Calbyr's prolonged silence. He is, I must assume, either dead or imprisoned. This result is regrettable. The Initiative represents a sizable investment of time and resources, and, of course, Calbyr was a talented and productive Nal-Lord.

I am not yet ready, however, to abandon the Initiative. Clearly, certain aspects of the plan require revision, and, in hindsight, I can see that some of our personnel choices were flawed. But provided I can find an intelligent leader and a competent crew, I remain convinced that Tobyn-Ser can be conquered.

> —Personal journal of Cedrych i Vran, Overlord of the First Dominion of Bragor-Nal, Day 5, Week 2, Winter, Year 3059.

The summons came even earlier than Melyor had expected, the soft beeping of the speak-screen rousing her from her slumber even before the streets below her flat began to bustle and drone with the early morning sounds of people and carriers. Swinging herself smoothly out of the large bed and wrapping herself in a silk robe, she padded lightly across the wooden floor to the screen, which rested on a marble table on the far side of her spacious bedchamber. And as she did, she felt her heart hammering within her chest. This is what I wanted, she reminded herself, trying to calm her nerves. This is why I went to the Second last night.

Reaching the table, she switched on the unit and watched as the severe face of one of Cedrych's guardsmen came into focus. He was clean shaven with squared, granite-like features, wintry grey eyes, and closely cropped blond hair. His neck and shoulders were massive, and the muscles of his arms bulged within his impeccable black uniform.

Belatedly aware of how she must have looked, Melyor passed a hand through the tangled waves of her hair. The guardsman smirked.

"Melyor i Lakin?" he asked coolly.

"Yes."

"Overlord Cedrych wishes to see you."

She nodded once. "When?"

"Now of course," he answered in a tone that made her feel foolish. "You are to come to his quarters immediately."

An instant later, the guardsman was gone and Melyor found herself staring at the soft blue glow of a blank screen. She stood motionless for several moments, imagining what it would be like to bury her dagger in the throat of the impertinent guardsman. Then she remembered that her dagger was gone, and she felt her fear returning, like a single drop of frigid water creeping down her spine.

"This is what I wanted," she told herself again, speaking the words aloud, as if hearing them might ease her mind. *Overlord Cedrych wishes to see you.* She nodded, just as she had to Cedrych's henchman. *Yes, I'll bet he does.*

She turned off the screen and, moving to the closet beside her bed, quickly put on a loose-fitting tunic, a pair of britches, and her boots. She strapped on her hand thrower, and then, as an afterthought, just before leaving her chamber, she tied back her hair. Cedrych, she knew, liked her hair unbound, but on this day she wanted him to see her as more than his "beautiful Nal-Lord," as he often called her.

Stepping out of the bedchamber and into the common room of her flat, Melyor was greeted by the imposing figure of Jibb, her chief of security. She couldn't help but smile at the sight of him sitting on the silk covered sofa on the far side of the room. He was good-looking in an odd way. He was not elegant like Savil or ruggedly handsome like Dob. But he had kind brown eyes and youthful, round features beneath a head full of shaggy black curls. Though indoors, and though it was midsummer, he still wore a long black coat over his black pants, ivory tunic, and spike-adorned black boots. The uniform of a break-law, Melyor thought with gentle amusement. Even without the neat black uniform, he seemed to her a physical match for Cedrych's impressive guardsman. And though Jibb no doubt had far less formal training than the Overlord's man, in a fight between the two—be it with throwers, or knives, or just bare hands—she would have wagered all the gold pieces she had on Jibb.

She still remembered the first time she saw him fight. It had been nearly four years ago, less than a half year after her installation as Nal-Lord of the Fourth. She and several of her men had been drinking in one of her favorite pubs when Jibb walked in. He had been an independent then, confident to the point of brashness, and, new to her Realm that night, he had not known who she was. Hence, in fairness, his proposition, though somewhat crude, had not been meant disrespectfully. But Melyor had been too new to her authority to let it pass, and she had ordered her men to kill him. There had been seven of them, well armed, and, she thought at the time, well-trained. Three of them died in the first rush at this brawny stranger without giving Jibb so much as a scratch. Two more fell before she called the survivors back, and still, Jibb hadn't even drawn his thrower. He had done it all with two dirks and the sharpened spikes on his boots.

She knew at that moment that she had found the perfect bodyguard. But first she had to win his respect. She approached him, holding her own dagger casually in her hand.

"You handle yourself well," she told him. "I could use a man like you."

"And, as I started to say before you sent your goons after me, I could use a woman like you."

She smiled darkly. "First though, you're going to have to learn a thing or two about this part of the Nal." She motioned toward his knives with a nod of her head. "Why don't you and I give it a try."

"Me and you?" Jibb asked with disbelief. And then he laughed, giving her the opening she needed. Pivoting swiftly on her right foot, she knocked both knives out of Jibb's hands with a widely arcing kick, much like the one she had used just last night against Savil. Without pause, the motion so fluid she felt like one of the decorative fountains in front of the Sovereign's estate, she spun again, this time smashing the hilt of her dagger into the break-law's temple. Jibb toppled to the dirty tavern floor and she pounced on him, grabbing a handful of his black curls with her free hand, and laying the razor edge of her blade against the side of his neck.

"My name is Melyor i Lakin," she told him in a level tone. She wasn't even breathing hard. "I am Nal-Lord here in the Fourth Realm, and you have a choice. You can die right here, or you can swear your loyalty to me and serve me as my bodyguard."

There was astonishment in the big man's brown eyes, and perhaps a touch of fear, but his reply, given in a steady voice, surprised her. "I guess this means that bedding you is out of the question."

Melyor laughed out loud, but her dagger remained pressed against his skin. "You have a sense of humor," she observed. "I like that. But I also like the men who work for me to show me the proper amount of respect." She tightened her grip on his hair. "I'm still waiting for an answer."

His expression growing sober, Jibb regarded her for several moments. All other conversations in the bar had stopped. "I pledge my loyalty to you, and I'll serve you in whatever capacity you ask, but under one condition."

The Nal-Lord raised her eyebrows. "Do you often bargain with a knife at your throat?" Jibb said nothing, and after a brief pause, Melyor nodded. "Tell me."

"I'm responsible for all the men in my charge. I choose them, train them, and discipline them as I see fit, with no interference from anyone, including you."

Melyor considered this briefly. "All right," she agreed, releasing her hold on the break-law. "We'll give it a try."

Though skeptical, she had been prepared to give Jibb a month or two to succeed on his terms. But in the months stretching to years that followed, the big man proved himself more than capable, and the arrangement remained just as they had agreed that first night in the bar. Assassinations were commonplace among the lords of Bragor-Nal, and in his first year as Melyor's security chief, Jibb thwarted five attempts on her life. In the second year, he stopped two more. There had been none since, and Melyor's security force—Jibb's security force really—had gained a reputation as being the best of any Nal-Lord's in all Bragor-Nal. Some said it was even better than Cedrych's and those of the other two Overlords; second only to the Sovereign's, they said. And while Melyor did nothing to encourage such talk, she did nothing to stop it either.

She chafed sometimes at the precautions he took, even as she recognized their necessity. And occasionally, as she had the night before when she ventured alone into Savil's Realm, she defied him. But for the most part she gave Jibb a wide latitude, allowing him to make security arrangements as he saw fit.

The break-law rose as she entered the common room. "Good morning, Nal-Lord," he said briskly. "You slept well?"

Melyor grinned inwardly. He remained so formal, even after all these years. Several times she had told him to call her Melyor, but he had never allowed himself that familiarity. "Yes, Jibb. Thank you."

She saw him glance at her thrower. "Are we going somewhere, Nal-Lord?"

"Yes. Cedrych would like a word with me."

Jibb looked at her intently. "Does this have something to do with last night?" Melyor hesitated, and Jibb took a step forward. "Nal-Lord," he began earnestly, "I can't protect you if I don't know what kind of danger you might be in. I can understand that last night's . . . endeavors demanded a certain level of circumspection, but surely you can tell me now. You have to let me do my job."

"Why, Jibb," she returned lightly, "I didn't know you cared so much."

He looked away, his face reddening. "I have a reputation to worry about," he said gruffly. "And I don't want your recklessness ruining it." Melyor laughed, and they stood there without speaking for some time. Then Jibb looked at her once more, a look of concern in his eyes. "Please, Nal-Lord. You hired me for a reason."

Melyor pressed her lips together. They had been through this before, many times. And, as usual he was right. After some time, she nodded. "Very well," she said, taking a breath. "Cedrych wants to see me because Savil was murdered in his Realm last night, and because he's probably figured out by now that I killed him."

Jibb exhaled slowly, making a low hissing noise through his teeth, but his expression remained neutral and he said nothing. After several moments, he nodded curtly, as if acknowledging what she had told him.

"You wanted to know," Melyor commented with a shrug.

"You planned this?" he finally asked her.

"Yes," she replied breezily. "He was about to get something that I want for myself."

Again the break-law nodded, and then immediately he began to shake his head.

"You look like you're talking to yourself, Jibb," Melyor joked. "People will think the pressure of your job is getting to you."

The big man grimaced. "Let them try protecting you for a day. They'll understand."

Melyor laughed. "We should get going," she told him. "It wouldn't do to keep Cedrych waiting."

Jibb moved his hand to his thrower, as if to reassure himself that it was still there. It was a gesture Melyor had seen him make a thousand times before. "I'm ready," he said.

Still smiling, Melyor winked at him. "I never had any doubt."

The two of them stepped out of the common room and into the largest of three antechambers that stood at the entrance to Melyor's flat. These rooms housed Jibb's security personnel during their time on duty, and the central room was filled now with armed, muscular men all of them dressed exactly like Jibb.

"We're moving!" Jibb announced as he and Melyor entered the antechamber. "I want units one and two with the Nal-Lord and me! The rest of you stay here, but be ready for my signal!"

A flurry of activity greeted the break-law's command, and in an instant, a large contingent of men fell in behind Jibb and Melyor, who never even had to break stride. Two units, Melyor commented to herself. A dozen men. Twice the usual entourage. This could have been because of where they were going; a visit to the Overlord's quarters was enough to unnerve even the most confident security man. But Melyor thought it more likely that Jibb had chosen to take an extra unit in response to what she had done the night before. It was quite possible, even likely, that one of Savil's men, perhaps Dob, would seek to avenge his Nal-Lord and place himself in a position to assume control of the Second Realm. Jibb's doubling of the security contingent merely acknowledged the obvious; Melyor had made a number of enemies last night.

Melyor, Jibb, and the twelve security men went through another door, down a long hallway, and into a large lifter that carried them down to the subfloor where the Nal-Lord's armored private carrier waited for them.

"Overlord Cedrych's quarters," Melyor told her driver as she climbed into the vehicle. Jibb sat down beside her and two of the break-law's men sat in the seats across from them. The rest of the security force got into a second, larger carrier that sat behind Melyor's, and the two vehicles started forward with a low hum. They climbed a steep ramp out of the subfloor, emerging onto a narrow byway that fed into the main concourse of Melyor's quad, which was beginning to fill up with the usual collection of break-laws, peddlers, and laborers as well as private and mass carriers. From there, weaving through the morning congestion, they steered onto a second ramp that carried them to the Upper, the elevated roadway that allowed them to avoid the endless lattice of quads and byways below.

From above, the Nal resembled a great honeycomb, like those kept in the Farm. Looking to the southwest, Melyor could see the huge glass structures of the agricultural sector rising into the dingy brown air that hung like a fog over Bragor-Nal. She had been in the Farm once, as a young girl, taken there by her father, an Overlord at the time, who was given a tour of the complex by the Sovereign himself. She still remembered the vast enclosed expanses of grain that swayed in a gentle artificial wind beneath bright warm lights, and the towering forests of pines, firs, spruce, maples, and oaks that reached endlessly toward a lofty glass sky. There had been other buildings as well, some of them fragrant with the scent of flowers and fruit-bearing trees, others rank with the smells of cow, sheep, and pig dung. She had even seen the beehives and she recalled having to shout to her father over the drone of millions upon millions of honey bees.

Most of all, however, she remembered the guards, for they were everywhere singly or in groups, all of them with dour expressions, wearing the stiff blue uniforms of SovSec, the Sovereign's Security Force, and carrying the largest throwers Melyor had ever seen. She had asked her father about the guards that night, after they had returned to their home.

"The Farm is the most important part of Bragor-Nal," he had explained, sitting on the edge of her bed as light from the hallway outside her room spilled across his handsome angular features and made his prematurely grey hair look even whiter than usual. "It needs to be protected."

"From who?" she persisted. She had enjoyed her day alone with him—such days were a rare treat—and she was not yet ready for it to end.

"Oh, a number of people. The Sovereign has enemies in Oerella-Nal and Stib-Nal who might want to destroy Bragor-Nal's food supply and conquer us. Or one of the other Overlords might try to threaten the Farm as a means to getting greater power or more territory."

"Would you do that?"

"No," her father had answered with a smile and a shake of his head. "I'm happy with what I've got."

He had kissed her forehead then, smoothed her blankets, and bid her goodnight, telling her that he had an early meeting the next day, but that he would join her for dinner. She never saw him again. That next morning, an assassin's bomb obliterated her father's carrier, killing him instantly, and elevating the man who had hired the assassin to the position of Overlord. This man, as it happened, would die in a similar manner several years later, the victim of an assassin hired by Cedrych, who became Overlord in turn. In the meantime, Melyor went to live with her father's sister in another part of the Nal. Melyor's mother had been killed in a failed attempt on her husband's life when Melyor was but an infant, leaving this aunt as Melyor's closest living relative.

So it went in Bragor-Nal, Melyor mused, staring out the smoke-colored windows of her carrier at the glass towers of the Farm. Here she was, a woman orphaned by assassins, going to see a man who had gained power through assassination, to discuss the fact that she had assassinated a rival the night before. At another time, under different circumstances, the situation might have struck her as comical.

She glanced up at the timepiece mounted above the window. It had been over half an hour since she had spoken with Cedrych's guardsman, and it would be at least another half-hour before they reached the Overlord's quarters, even traveling on the Upper. Cedrych's Realm, the First, bordered her own to the south, and her flat actually lay in the southern half of the Fourth, but Bragor-Nal was vast, and they had a considerable distance to cover this morning. She felt her pulse quickening once more; Cedrych had never been known for his patience.

"It's still early," Jibb told her reassuringly, perhaps sensing her tension, "and Cedrych knows how long it takes to get from your Realm to his."

Melyor nodded in response and essayed a thin smile, before gazing out the window again. *This is what I wanted,* she told herself once more, feeling like a cleric repeating her litany.

The journey to the Overlord's quarters passed slowly for Melyor, and when the two carriers finally halted in front of the impressive marble structure, with its mirrored windows, steel doors, and finely carved edgings, the Nal-Lord practically hurled herself out of the lead vehicle and toward the building's entrance. Jibb and his men rushed to keep up with her, but there was no need. One of Cedrych's guardsmen stopped her at the top of the marble stairs.

"Nal-Lord," he said crisply. "He's been expecting you. I'm afraid, though, that I can only allow three of your men to accompany you; the rest will have to wait out here."

"Of course," Melyor replied, "I should have remembered." She glanced back at Jibb and gave a single nod. The break-law, in turn, spoke in low tones to the other men. A moment later he returned her nod, and she faced the guardsman again. "We're ready."

Cedrych's man spoke into a transmitter on the shoulder of his black uniform. Instantly, the lock of the polished metal door was unlocked with a soft clicking sound. The guard pushed it open and motioned Melyor inside. Taking a breath, the Nal-Lord stepped through the doorway. Jibb followed, with the two men who had ridden in Melyor's carrier. The four of them were met inside by a contingent of six guardsmen who conducted them to a spacious lifter, the inside of which was decorated tastefully with brass, mirrors, and dark wood. One of Cedrych's men touched an unmarked red circle at the top of the lifter control panel. Immediately, the door slid shut and the lifter began to rise. No one spoke, and Melyor stared at the polished wood of the door, keeping her expression neutral and, as the chamber continued to climb higher, swallowing once or twice to unclog her ears.

After some time she felt the lifter slow to a halt and the door glided open. Yet another contingent of guardsmen stood waiting for her—again there were six of them—and she recognized their leader as the man with whom she had spoken that morning.

"Nal-Lord," he said, smiling at her as if they were old friends. "The Overlord is pleased you could come on such short notice."

"How could I refuse such a gracious invitation?" Melyor asked smoothly, stepping out of the lifter. "I'll have to commend the Overlord on the impeccable manners of his guardsmen."

The man appeared to catch the irony in her tone, for his smile vanished, and the color seemed to drain from his square face. "This way, Nal-Lord," he offered, gesturing to the left with a hand that might have trembled.

Melyor gave him a frosty glare and brushed past him. "Yes," she said over her shoulder, "I know the way." She strode purposefully down the broad corridor toward Cedrych's quarters. Glancing behind her at one point, she was gratified to see the guard hurrying to keep up with her. She smiled inwardly, and quickened her pace.

Six more guards waited for her at the end of the hallway. In the back of her mind Melyor wondered how many men Cedrych had working for him. The count had to reach well into the tens of thousands; with an army this size she could have marched into Savil's Realm at midday rather than bothering with her disguise. She grinned at the thought. Someday, she promised herself. Someday.

She halted in front of the guardsmen, eyeing the booth that stood behind them. It was over eight feet tall and two across—easily large enough to accommodate even the tallest and brawniest of Cedrych's guards. It was glossy black all around and unmarked save for a readout console on the left side, and two lights above the entrance that faced Melyor, one of them red and the other, which was lit now, blue.

"You're familiar with the weapons chamber, Nal-Lord?" asked one of the guards, a somber looking man who was somewhat older than the others, though no less muscular.

Of course she was, and not simply because she had been here before. Every person who lived in the Nal knew about Cedrych and his weapons chamber. A number of years ago, an assassin managed to smuggle an explosive into the Overlord's quarters and detonate it within five or six feet of where Cedrych stood. The man died, of course, but he nearly succeeded in taking Cedrych with him: the Overlord lost his right eye and spent months recovering from his other injuries. Indeed, he never fully regained the use of his right leg.

Cedrych responded to the incident in a number of ways, some of them predictable, others terrifyingly unpredictable. The assassin, a break-law who had been given powerful, mind-mastering drugs, had been sent by a renegade Nal-Lord named Vanniver, and not surprisingly, Cedrych had Vanniver captured and brought to him while he was still recovering from his wounds. But no one could have anticipated what the Overlord would do next. Rather than simply killing the man, Cedrych had him stripped naked and hung by his wrists from the roof of the Overlord's headquarters. And that was all. Vanniver hung there for months. It was midsummer when the punishment was first carried out, so despite the strain on his body, the lack of food or water, and his exposure to the heat and sudden storms of summer in the Nal, Vanniver actually lingered for over a week before finally dying. Still, he hung there. His body started to rot, carrion eating crows ravaged his corpse for days on end. And still he hung there. Cedrych forbade anyone to cut him down. Weakened by the elements, the bones in his wrists finally gave out early the following spring and his skeleton fell to the street below, shattering into thousands of pieces when it hit. Still, Cedrych prohibited his men from cleaning up the mess. Carriers continued to drive along the avenue, grinding the Nal-Lord's bones into the pavement until Vanniver was little more than dust and a soaking rain washed him away. The ropes were never removed from the roof, and, according to some, they still hung there to this day.

But Cedrych's punishment for the Nal-Lord was only the beginning. As far as he was concerned, the two dozen guards who had been on duty that day were as much to blame for his injuries as Vanniver. While still recuperating, he had the guardsmen brought to him one at a time. And he killed each one of them, blasting them through the right eye with his thrower. The last two, realizing what had happened to their comrades, tried to escape. Cedrych's other guards, fearing for their lives, caught these two and took them to the Overlord. And Cedrych found a suitable penalty for their incompetence and their cowardice: he had the two men blinded, had their right legs cut off at the knee, and had their right arms cut off at the elbow. And then he allowed them to live.

Even with these measures of vengeance, however, Cedrych knew that he could not prevent future attempts on his life or failures by his guards. So he set about trying to create the perfect security system. The weapons chamber was the result. It was the most effective tool for detecting concealed weapons in Lon-Ser, and the most envied. When the Sovereign heard of it, he ordered

Cedrych to have a second one built and brought to the Sovereign's estate. It did not make assassination impossible—how could this single booth in the corridor outside his door protect him on the streets of the Nal? But it did ensure that Cedrych would always be the only armed person in his own quarters. As far as anyone knew there wasn't a weapon or an explosive in Lon-Ser that could escape detection by the chamber. Of course no one knew this for certain. In the eight years since its construction, no assassin had ever dared test it.

"Yes, I'm familiar with the chamber," Melyor told the guard, handing him her thrower with a wry smirk.

The older guardsman took her weapon and motioned toward the entrance to the black cubicle. "Then please step inside."

Melyor glanced back at Jibb and his men who, she knew, would not be allowed to accompany her into her meeting with the Overlord. "It's all right," she told them, her eyes meeting Jibb's. "I'll be fine."

Melyor saw Jibb take a breath and nod. Then she stepped into the booth. Immediately, a door slid into place behind her, blotting out all light and locking her inside. But as far as she could tell, nothing else happened. A few moments later the door in front of her glided open. The older guard was there, standing between Melyor and another door that led into Cedrych's quarters.

"There is an empty sheath in your right boot!" he said accusingly. "Where is the blade that goes with it?"

"I've lost it," she answered.

The guardsman regarded her skeptically.

She opened her arms wide. "It's true," she insisted. "Your machine couldn't find it, right? How could I hide it from the weapons chamber?"

He seemed to consider this. After some time, he gave a small shrug. "Very well." He glanced down at her feet. "You will have to remove your boots, Nal-Lord." He held out a pair of soft shoes made entirely of black elastic cloth. "You may wear these instead."

Melyor stared at the shoes for a moment and then nodded, taking them from the guard. This was new; Cedrych was taking even fewer chances than usual. And suddenly, feeling a surge of apprehension, she remembered that she had been wearing these boots the night before, and that she had used a spinning kick to disable Savil. Did Cedrych know what had happened to that level of detail? Was that possible? Trying desperately now to slow her heartbeat, she pulled off her boots and replaced them with the cloth shoes.

"She's ready," the guard said quietly into the transmitter on his uniform.

Melyor heard the lock click within the door behind the guard. The man turned and pushed the door open before moving to the side and gesturing for Melyor to enter the Overlord's chambers. The Nal-Lord stepped through the doorway cautiously, as if uncertain of what awaited her inside. She started when the door closed behind her, paused to take a steadying breath, and then surveyed her surroundings. The outer room of the Overlord's quarters hadn't changed much since her last visit. A long sofa and three large, opulent chairs, all upholstered in a pale silver-grey, sat around a low round table of glass that rested on a simple silver frame. Tasteful pen and ink drawings of scenes from the Nal adorned the white walls. Thick carpet, which felt soft beneath her feet, and which matched perfectly the color of the chairs and sofa, covered the floor. The far wall of the room was made entirely of glass and offered a spectacular view of the entire southern half of the Nal and, far in the distance, almost completely obscured by the brown air that hung over the metropolis, the lofty peaks of the Greenwater Range.

It was all impeccably clean, as if no one had set foot in the place for days or weeks, and, Melyor remarked to herself, not for the first time, that it could have been anyone's home. In light of what she knew of Cedrych, it always struck her as odd that he shouldn't have daggers and throwers hanging from the ceiling, and pictures of firefights on the walls. Then again, people in the Fourth would probably have responded the same way to seeing her flat, modest though it was compared to this one.

"Come in!" came a voice from another room. Cedrych's voice: clear and warm, much the way Melyor remembered her father's. "I'm back in the reading room! Come join me!"

She made her way back to the Overlord's office, thinking as she did that she had never seen Cedrych in any other part of his quarters. Not that he hadn't invited her on several occasions to join him in his bedroom, but, after her delicate refusal of his initial advances, these invitations had been offered with a certain jocularity that had allowed her to laugh them off without giving offense. Melyor wondered at times what lay behind Cedrych's flippancy, but she had not pushed the matter, and, thus far, much to her relief, neither had he.

Reaching the reading room, Melyor tapped lightly on the wooden door frame, even though the door was already open. Cedrych sat at his desk, in a black leather chair that creaked softly as the Overlord leaned back in it. The desk was quite old—several hundred years old he had once told her—and it was made of a dark wood with a wide, curving grain. Papers sat in neat piles on its surface along with a low desk lamp of polished brass and a speak-screen much like Melyor's. The elegant carpeting that covered the rest of the Overlord's flat ended at the door to his office, replaced in this one room by polished wooden floors that were slightly lighter in color than the desk. Like the far wall in the outer room, the wall behind Cedrych was made entirely of glass, and it looked out over eastern Bragor-Nal and the nearby Median Mountains. Wooden bookshelves, filled with volumes from floor to ceiling, stood along the other three walls.

Cedrych looked up at Melyor when he heard her knock, his one good eye looking her over quickly before coming to rest on her face, and a smile stretching across his features.

"Melyor, my dear!" he said expansively, standing to greet her. He wore black pants and a loose-fitting black shirt, and he had a thrower strapped to his thigh. She came forward so that he could take her hand in his and kiss the back of it. Cedrych's nod to chivalry, she said to herself, amused by the thought despite the pounding of her pulse. "I'm delighted that you could come," he added, returning to his seat, and indicating with a wave of his hand that she should sit in one of the dark wooden chairs that stood between the doorway and the desk.

"It's my pleasure, Overlord," she returned, lowering herself into one of the chairs. "I'm honored by the invitation."

Again Cedrych smiled, although this time there seemed to be a strange gleam in his left eye. "Surely, though, you expected it."

It wasn't offered as a question. "I knew that you'd contact me," she admitted, "although I didn't expect the summons to come quite so soon."

The grin lingered on the Overlord's scarred face. "I'm glad to know that I can still surprise you." He glanced at the papers on his desk. "I received your latest tribute," he said. "On time as usual. Your payments are increasing every month, my dear. I'm very pleased."

"Thank you, Overlord."

"As to your request for additional funds for repairs on the Upper and quad maintenance, I'll have to speak with Durell of course, but I don't anticipate any problem." He looked at her and smiled. "Dealing with the desk men, naturally, is your responsibility."

Melyor nodded. The most difficult part of getting work of this sort accomplished lay not in securing approval and funds from Cedrych, but rather in having the money she received spent as she intended. There were papers to be filled out and workers to be deployed. It was the worst part of her job. She knew that it drove many of her fellow Nal-Lords to distraction. Yet it was also something at which she had grown quite adept. While other Nal-Lords used the threat of violence to compel the paper handlers, or desk men as they were often called, to do their jobs, Melyor used a subtle mix of bribery and cajolery. It had worked quite well over the years, helped no doubt by Jibb's reputation and the threat implied by his mere presence by her side.

"Do you need anything else?" Cedrych asked her. "Perhaps tunnel repairs?"

Melyor took a breath, wishing Cedrych would just dispense with the trivialities and move on to what they both knew really mattered. "No, thank you, Overlord. Just the road repairs and maintenance."

"Very well, my dear," he said, his smile deepening as if he enjoyed making her wait. A moment later he swivelled his high-backed chair so that he faced the glass wall and all Melyor could see of him was the top of his clean-shaven head. "I lost a good man last night, Melyor," he told her. He turned his chair just a bit so that he could see her. "Perhaps you heard?" He faced the window again. "I hate to lose a man of Savil's talents, although I understand that these things happen in the Nal. It's the nature of the world in which we live. But I would find it especially disturbing to lose such a man were I to learn that his death resulted from some frivolous dispute that could easily have been settled had cooler heads prevailed."

Melyor opened her mouth to say something, but Cedrych, without turning around, held up a single finger to stop her, as if he sensed that she was about to speak. "Allow me to finish," he commanded.

She fell silent, and dropped her gaze momentarily to the desk in front of her. And doing so, she saw something that she had missed before, something that made her head spin with bewilderment and fear. Her dagger. Incredibly, it was her dagger. It sat beside the desk lamp, its worn black handle pointing accusingly in her direction.

Cedrych was speaking again, saying something about the pernicious effect assassination could have on the ruling structure that he was trying to maintain in this portion of Bragor-Nal. She knew that she should be listening to what he said, that it was important that she at least appear to be paying attention. But she couldn't stop staring at the blade, pondering its possible implications.

He must have known that it was hers, although she wasn't certain how he could know. She couldn't remember if he had ever seen her holding it. Did he expect her to reclaim it? Or would taking it confirm for him that she had killed Savil? On the other hand, if he had proof that she had killed Savil, would leaving without the dagger make it seem that she was trying to deceive him? And had she not come here expecting Cedrych to know that she had killed Savil, and prepared to tell him as much if he didn't know?

Cedrych liked to play games, particularly those that made his adversaries, or, in this case, his underlings uncomfortable. No doubt he already sensed Melyor's discomfort, and delighted in it. But that worked to Melyor's advantage as well. For she had her secret, the one she had told Savil just before killing him. And if ever Cedrych learned of it . . . She shuddered. That was more than she cared to imagine. The point was, however, that the games Cedrych played—the dagger left on his desk, the sexual innuendo that always seemed to creep into his conversations with her, and the dozens of other ways in which the Overlord liked to tease and torment his Nal-Lords—allowed her to mask her real fear of being discovered with the uneasiness that Cedrych himself inflicted.

So she tore her attention away from the blade, forcing herself to listen to the Overlord. The dagger was a game, a diversion that the Overlord had set up for his own amusement. She would deal with it before she left, somehow. For now, though, she had more important things on which to focus.

"With Savil dead, there promises to be a protracted, bloody struggle among those who seek to take his place as Nal-Lord," Cedrych was telling her, as he continued to stare out the window. "There are at least six of them who feel they've earned the position. That was part of Savil's talent, and Calbyr's before him: they knew how to inspire their men, how to make them believe that they had a chance to advance themselves. All these men believed that Savil would become Overlord after me, and that he would then name them to take his place. It made them loyal, eager to please, and ambitious enough to take pride in what they did. It also made Savil's Realm my most lucrative." Cedrych glanced back at Melyor again. "Even more lucrative than yours, my dear. Although, admittedly, not by much." He swivelled his chair so that it faced her fully. "Now that flow of wealth into my pocket has been interrupted. I'll have to break in a new man. Or woman," he added with a mirthless grin that lasted but a moment. "That can take some time, and time costs me money." He was looking at her intently now, the single blue eye, piercing and alert, watching for anything her expression might give away. "So," the Overlord concluded, "you can see why, as I said before, I would be disturbed to learn that whatever conflict led to Savil's death could have been averted."

Cedrych fell silent and regarded Melyor expectantly, as if what he had just said demanded a response. The Nal-Lord's heart was racing again, her fear at what she was about to do tinged with the exhilaration she felt as two years of planning came, at last, to fruition. *This is what I wanted.* And so, taking a slow breath, and hoping her voice would remain steady, she took the next step. "There are other reasons why Savil was important, aren't there?"

"I'm not sure what you mean" the Overlord replied innocently.

She suppressed a smile. She should have known that he wouldn't make this easy for her. "He was going to lead the next mission to Tobyn-Ser. You chose him to replace Calbyr. Hence, losing him complicates that as well. Isn't that so?"

Cedrych grinned. "So word of this has reached the Fourth Realm, has it?"

"Word reached me," Melyor told him, holding his gaze.

The Overlord nodded. "I see." He stood and moved to the window, his back turned toward her once more. "Yes, what you say is true. Savil's death has left me in need of a new leader for the Tobyn-Ser Initiative."

Melyor drew another breath. Her heart was like a power-hammer in her chest. "Perhaps I can be of some help."

He turned at that, a grin tugging at the corners of his mouth. They were playing a game, Melyor knew: yet another game in what sometimes seemed an endless series of them. "You?" he asked, his tone betraying both amusement and interest.

"I'm not certain that Savil was the best choice for the job," she chanced. "He was a competent Nal-Lord, but he lacked imagination."

The Overlord's expression hardened. "Are you questioning my judgement, Melyor?"

"Not at all," she assured him quickly. "I'm certain that Savil would have handled the assignment adequately. I just wonder if such an important mission doesn't call for someone with a bit more resourcefulness. Savil may have been ruthless, and he may have driven his men to perform well for him, but this job requires even more than that. The person you choose should also be creative, daring, and shrewd; he or she should be adaptable enough to deal with any contingency. In other words, Overlord," she went on, eyeing Cedrych closely, "he or she should be someone whom you could trust implicitly to lead this mission just as you would, were you able to go yourself. In my opinion, Savil didn't possess these qualities. I do."

"You may be right, Melyor," Cedrych returned, his tone neutral. "Such qualities would be useful, and I agree that you possess them in good measure. But this assignment also calls for delicacy and discretion. Whoever leads the mission can't be leaving clues lying around as if they were candy wrappers."

Before she could help it, Melyor's eyes flew to the dagger lying on Cedrych's desk. Perhaps it wasn't just a game piece after all.

Cedrych gave no indication that he had noticed the direction of her gaze. "He or she can't behave rashly, or allow emotion and ambition to obscure sound judgement," he went on, his tone becoming increasingly strident. "Violence for the sake of violence may work all right out there," he waved a hand dismissively toward the window overlooking the Nal. "But this job calls for subtlety."

Melyor gritted her teeth. She had said essentially the same thing to Savil. And then she had left her dagger lying in the street by the Nal-Lord's crumpled body. She hadn't done anything this stupid in years, until now of course; naturally, she had to do it now. She shook her head at the irony. She wasn't sure what Cedrych expected of her, and her own meticulously laid plans for this meeting had been ruined by the appearance of her dirk. But she had come too far to give up what she had earned the night before. So she took the only path left to her.

"Whether you believe it or not, Overlord," she said, heedless of her tone, "I can be discreet and subtle and all the things you're looking for! I wouldn't have gotten as far as I have if I couldn't! I want this job, and you ought to want me for it! I'm the best Nal-Lord you've got, and that was as true yesterday as it is this morning! Certainly, I would never have allowed myself to be murdered in my own Realm!" She stopped herself.

Cedrych was glaring at her, his jaw clenched and his hands fisted and white-knuckled. Melyor knew that she had gone too far. She was indeed questioning the Overlord's judgement; she had just said as much. For an instant, no more really, for she knew Cedrych well, she wondered if she was about to die for her presumption.

But then the Overlord appeared to relax; he might even have smiled, albeit briefly. "I'm glad you feel that way, Melyor. I'd like all my Nal-Lords to believe so strongly in their own abilities." He sat back down in the leather chair and folded his large, though delicate hands on the desk. "The truth of the matter is, I agree with much of what you've said about yourself. And I'll grant that the way Savil died has forced me to question the faith I placed in him." He paused, his gaze fixed on his hands, and he said nothing for what seemed to Melyor a very long time. When finally he did speak, what he had to say caught her off guard.

"You'll need to designate an interim Nal-Lord," he told her, still staring at his hands. "Someone who can get results, and keep your Realm running at the standards to which I've grown accustomed." He grinned, looking up at her. Again, though, the smile was fleeting. "But it must also be someone you can trust," he continued, a moment later. "Someone who'll run the Realm as you would, and who'll relinquish control without a fight if and when you return. Is there anyone in the Fourth who meets those criteria?"

Melyor's immediate reaction was one of relief, rather than exhilaration, but that would follow she knew. She had planned for so long. Forcing her mind past these emotions, she considered the Overlord's question. Jibb, of course. Who else was there? She nodded. "Yes, I have someone in mind."

"I thought as much," Cedrych replied. "How soon can you be ready to begin the training?"

"I need a day or two to settle some affairs and prepare my men," she told him. "Is that soon enough?"

"Take three," the Overlord told her. "We're pressed for time, but I'd rather you were able to come to this completely focused on the task at hand, and not worrying about your Realm." He rose from his chair, and Melyor took it as a signal that she should stand as well. Their meeting was over. "I want to see you back here first thing in the morning three days hence," Cedrych instructed. "We'll talk in detail about the Initiative, and then I'll take you to the training area. My sponsors and I will supply weapons, clothes, and food, but when you come here next, you should bring anything else you think you'll need for the journey. You won't be returning to your Realm for some time. Don't tell anyone where you're going to be, or what you'll be doing. Just tell them you're on a special assignment for me. Do you understand?"

"Yes, Overlord."

"Good." He smiled. "I'm looking forward to working more closely with you, my dear. I believe we'll make a fine team." She suffered his look, which lingered on her body longer than it should have, and, fighting to quell an involuntary shudder, she managed to smile in return. "I'm looking forward to that as well, Overlord."

"Please, my dear. Call me Cedrych."

She nodded.

The Overlord said nothing more, but he continued to watch her, as if waiting for something. There was really nothing she could do. So she reached down casually and picked up the dagger from the desk. Then, without another word, she turned and left Cedrych's quarters.

6

The communication devices Calbyr and his crew carried with them to Tobyn-Ser were primitive though inconspicuous, allowing Calbyr to communicate with his men and with me only by code. This was by design—Calbyr and I believed that each additional piece of equipment his men carried further jeopardized the deception they hoped to maintain. I realize now, however, that this was a mistake, for I learned little from his cryptic messages. I know no more of Tobyn-Ser now than I did before he left. I have only a vague sense of how far their mission had progressed before his communications abruptly ceased. I don't even know for certain the degree to which the initial stages of our plan succeeded in damaging the Order's standing.

What I do know is that Calbyr and his men were in Tobyn-Ser for more than a year, and that Calbyr's communications did indicate that, for the most part, he and his crew were following the schedule upon which we had agreed. Beyond that I can be sure of nothing. And yet, even this meager bit of

information, combined with my abiding faith in the soundness of our strate-
gy, convinces me that the second crew I send to Tobyn-Ser will have far less
work to do than did the first.

—Personal journal of Cedrych i Vran,
Overlord of the First Dominion of
Bragor-Nal, Day 6, Week 9, Spring,
Year 3060.

Jaryd had been looking forward to this Gathering, just as he had awaited with anxious anticipation the previous three Gatherings, and almost as much as he had looked forward to his first, which he had attended as Baden's apprentice four years ago. Almost. It was not that he ignored or even underestimated the magnitude of the problems facing the Order, nor that he was unaware of the deep rift that divided mage from mage, and master from master. He had come with no illusions, just a deep reverence for the splendor and tradition embodied in these three days of processions, debates, and feasts. It was a feeling he had harbored and nourished ever since that first Gathering. He had been just a Mage-Attend then, drawn to the great city by the bright future Baden had predicted for him, and by his own fervent wish that the Owl-Master's vision should carry the weight of prophesy. But those three days in Amarid transformed him. He discovered his power during an encounter with bandits in Hawksfind Wood, and the following morning he bound to Ishalla, thus becoming a mage. At the closing ceremony, he received his cloak, signifying his admission to the Order, and he swore an oath to serve the people of Tobyn-Ser. And, most importantly, he met the people who would become his closest, most trusted friends: Trahn, Orris, Ursel, and, of course, Alayna, with whom he had been in love since the harrowing night they passed together in Theron's Grove, and to whom he had been married the day after the Feast of Leora, nearly four years ago. The Gatherings since had been rife with contention; there could be no masking the divisions within the Order. And yet, for Jaryd, they had also been times to renew old friendships and acquaintances, and to reaffirm his faith in the Order's ability to overcome the challenges it faced.

Until this year. Perhaps the Order's troubles had worsened. Perhaps Jaryd's patience had run out. Whatever the reason, the rituals and celebrations of this Gathering struck him as hollow, and even the sight of familiar faces could not lighten his mood. The debates had suddenly become too bitter to be constructive; the schisms had widened beyond the mages' ability to bridge them. Everyone seemed more interested in recriminations than they did in results. The first day of this Gathering had been terrible; that night, lying together in their room at the Aerie, Jaryd and Alayna had agreed that it had been as rancorous and senseless as any discussion they had ever witnessed in the Great Hall. And yet, neither of them harbored much hope that matters would improve.

As soon as the mages reconvened in the morning, the argument over Sonel's proposal resumed, with Erland once more leading the opposition, characterizing any overtures to Lon-Ser's leaders as an undue risk of life and an overreaching of the Order's authority. Initially, however, there did appear to be a glimmer of hope: Arslan and several of the other younger mages, after taking the night to consider the idea of sending a delegation, expressed tentative support for the Owl-Sage's plan, contingent on a more precise explanation of just what she had in mind. As Baden had anticipated, however, it quickly became clear that the success or failure of the delegates' mission would turn on their ability to offer proof that invaders from Lon-Ser had been responsible for the attacks that had occurred four years earlier. The gathered mages were almost unanimous in their agreement that the remains of the outlanders' weapons and mechanical birds would not be enough to convince the Council of Sovereigns, and for several hours, the mages weighed a number of other options, including, most promisingly, a suggestion from Trahn that witnesses from the attack on Watersbend be included in the delegation. Eventually, though, following a relentless attack on the idea by Erland and his allies, who claimed that the Order had no right to ask these people to assume such a grave risk, the plan was rejected.

Jaryd kept silent through much of this discussion. Although he was loath to admit it, in this case he found himself swayed by Erland's reasoning. The journey into Lon-Ser would have been dangerous enough for a group of mages; bringing others who could not call upon the Mage-Craft in times of trouble would increase the peril for every member of the delegation. But, while he could not honestly say anything in support of Trahn's idea, he was not about to ally himself with Erland, even on this one issue. Instead, he found himself watching Baden, who also said nothing on the matter. From the expression on the Owl-Master's lean face—the inward focus of his sharp, blue eyes, the deep furrows in his brow, the involuntary clenching of the muscles in his jaw—Jaryd could see that a war raged inside Baden's mind. And he knew what was at stake. The gaunt Owl-Master understood that sending Baram with the delegation represented the Order's only hope of convincing the Council of Sovereigns that the outlanders had come from Lon-Ser. He had told Jaryd and the others as much the night before, in the Aerie. But Baden had already suffered greatly for his efforts to keep Baram alive—he had been ridiculed repeatedly within these walls, and he had been burned in effigy in the streets of the city. For him to suggest now that the outlander be sent home would subject him to even more abuse from Erland and Arslan, and from the people of Amarid, who did not appear to grasp the magnitude of the threat Tobyn-Ser faced. It struck Jaryd as so utterly unjust: no one had given more of himself to serving and protecting the land than his uncle, and no one had paid a greater price.

So, although he recognized the futility of the gesture, Jaryd did the only thing he could. He waited until his uncle appeared to reach a decision—and, recognizing the look of resignation in the Owl-Master's eyes, Jaryd knew what Baden had resolved to do—and then, before Sonel could recognize the Owl-Master, Jaryd leapt to his feet.

"Owl-Sage!" he cried out. "There is one piece of evidence we can offer the Council of Sovereigns that they can neither dismiss nor refute!"

The Hall fell silent.

"Jaryd, don't do this," Baden pleaded. "This is my burden, not yours."

But Jaryd kept his gaze fixed on the Owl-Sage, who stared back at him with unconcealed curiosity. "Tell us," she demanded. "What evidence could possibly carry such weight?"

"The outlander. Baram."

Jaryd had been struck the day before by the fervor of the reaction that met Sonel's proposal to send mages to Lon-Ser, and he had, in past years, witnessed similarly violent outbursts from the gathered mages. But none of these previous displays matched in vehemence or power the eruption that his words provoked on this day. Mages and masters shouted obscenities at him and called him a traitor; two of the younger mages had to be physically restrained from coming after him; and one of Erland's older allies worked himself into such a frenzy that he actually collapsed at his seat, giving everyone in the chamber a momentary scare, but doing little to ease the passions set loose by Jaryd's suggestion. When Orris and Trahn attempted to speak in support of the idea, they were shouted down, and Orris and Arslan nearly came to blows. Even Sonel could not restore order. In the end, it was Alayna who imposed an abrupt silence on the Gathering with a bright, twisting arc of purple mage-fire that flew from the crystal mounted atop her staff, across the length of the council table, to the far end of the chamber, where it crashed harmlessly into the dark, brooding mass of the Summoning Stone.

"Stop it!" she commanded, in a voice edged with steel. "All of you! Just stop it!" Everyone in the hall stared at her. The stillness she had shaped seemed alien and awkward after the tumult of a moment before. "Is this what we've become? Are we incapable of even speaking to each other anymore? By the Gods, we're mages! All of Tobyn-Ser is looking to us for guidance and protection, and we can't even discuss our problems without trying to tear each other apart!" She paused, sweeping the hall with her glare, daring them to speak. "I never thought I'd say this," she went on, her voice steady despite the single tear that rolled down her cheek, "but I'm ashamed to be a member of this Order." Without another word, she raised her arm for Fylimar, her majestic, grey hawk, and began walking toward the door.

"Alayna, please don't leave," Sonel called after her. "Not like this."

The Hawk-Mage stopped, and after a moment, she turned back toward the gathered mages. The tears were flowing freely now, but, once more, her voice remained strong. "I'm sorry Owl-Sage, but I see no reason to stay. We're doing no good here. And I won't just sit and watch something I love being destroyed by petty bickering."

"But if you leave, won't you be dealing this body an even more devastating blow?" It was Trahn, and the desperate plea in his tone echoed the sadness and fear that lay in his green eyes.

"I know that you and I disagree in this instance, Alayna," Arslan added. "No doubt we will again on other matters. But Trahn's right: if even one of us leaves—especially now—the damage might be irrevocable."

Alayna stood motionless for what seemed a long time, her dark eyes wandering the room, as if she were searching for something in the faces of her fellow mages. Finally, casting a brief, almost wistful glance back over her shoulder toward the door, she took a slow breath and walked back to her place at the table.

"We can't continue like this," she said, addressing all of them as her hawk hopped back onto the wooden perch mounted on her chair. "Fighting like this isn't getting us anywhere." She took Jaryd's hand. "This man is no more a traitor than I am. Neither is Baden, nor Orris, nor Trahn. We have to be able to disagree without questioning each other's motives all the time."

"You're right," Arslan conceded. He turned to Orris and then Jaryd. "I offer apologies to both of you. Some of the things I said were . . . inappropriate."

Jaryd nodded in acknowledgement, as did Orris. But an instant later, looking at Alayna once more, Arslan began again, and there was no compromise in his tone. "Nonetheless, I will not surrender on this point: Baram cannot be sent back to Lon-Ser, no matter what the purpose. I can accept that he will live out his full life, although I still wish to see him executed. But as long as I have any say in the matter, he will not set foot outside of that prison!"

"I feel the same way," Erland broke in, glaring sidelong in Baden's direction, as if to tell the Owl-Master that he knew whose idea this really had been. "Regardless of what this body decides to do with respect to sending a delegation to Lon-Ser—and I sincerely hope that we don't send one—I will not stand by and watch as that butcher is allowed to return to his home!"

"How many of the rest of you feel the same way?" Sonel asked, looking up and down the table.

Almost every mage in the chamber raised a hand.

"Then this part of our discussion is over," the Owl-Sage announced grimly.

Orris stood. "May I just say something, Owl-Sage?" he requested.

"On the topic of Baram going to Lon-Ser?"

The Hawk-Mage nodded.

Sonel sighed. "I don't normally like to do this, Orris," she replied after a brief hesitation. "As you know, I seldom place any constraints at all on our discussions. But in this instance, in the interests of keeping our discussion civil and constructive, I feel that I must. It would be best if we simply move on. I'm sorry."

Orris made no reply, but he remained standing for several more seconds, his dark eyes smoldering, his lips pressed in a thin, hard line, and his hands clenched in white-knuckled fists. And when finally he lowered himself into his chair, he did so slowly, as if fearing that any sudden movement would unleash the rage he had worked so hard to control.

"Well, this has certainly been a most extraordinary day!" Baden commented, his voice heavy with sarcasm and scorn. "We've seen one mage so disgusted by the tone of this body's deliberations that she had to be convinced to remain with us; we've seen another mage denied permission to speak, something I had never witnessed before," he added, casting a disapproving glance at Sonel. "And we've seen mages attempting to inflict physical harm on their colleagues." He shook his head. "What could be next? What could we possibly do for an encore?"

"You forgot something, Baden," Erland threw back at him with equal disdain. "We also witnessed a supreme act of cowardice today: we saw an

Owl-Master, one of the most powerful men in this Order, allow a Hawk-Mage to take the blame for a repugnant idea, and, I might add, a dangerous one, that obviously came from the older man."

Jaryd jumped out of his chair, a searing retort on his lips. But Baden stopped him.

"Not this time, Jaryd," the Owl-Master told him, his blue eyes locked on Erland, and his gaunt features fixed in a malevolent grin. "From now on I'll fight my own battles."

"Not in this Hall you won't!" Sonel interrupted. "Not during this Gathering!" She glared at Baden and then at Erland. "Have the two of you learned nothing today? Perhaps you feel that you can just ignore everything that Alayna said a few moments ago, but I cannot! And I will not allow this Gathering to degenerate any further than it already has! Yes," she went on, turning back to Baden, her emerald eyes flashing, "I kept Orris from speaking—I hope he will forgive me. But I will do it again, to anyone I choose, if I feel it necessary in order to maintain the integrity of these proceedings!" She swept the room with her gaze. "I hope that's clear to all of you!"

Her words echoed loudly off the domed ceiling with its portrait of Amarid binding to his first hawk, and settled over the table as if they had come from the First Mage himself. The Gathered mages said nothing for what felt to Jaryd like a very long time. No one looked at anyone else, although Alayna took Jaryd's hand again and held it tightly in hers.

"I think we need a break," Sonel finally told them, ringing the crystal bell that sat before her on the council table. Instantly, the blue-robed attendants of the Great Hall appeared, carrying trays of shan tea and sweet breads to the mages. Slowly, conversations began again, although in hushed tones.

For the rest of that day, Sonel presided over an acceptably placid discussion. Unfortunately, it accomplished little. With Baden, Orris, and Erland brooding silently, and several other members of the Order, including Alayna and Jaryd, too drained by the day's events to say much of value, the debate over the Owl-Sage's proposal to send a group of mages to Lon-Ser foundered. Those who usually looked to Orris or Erland for guidance seemed reluctant to step into the void created by their leaders' reticence. For a second day, the Order adjourned in late afternoon without having reached any decision.

That night's observance of the Feast of Duclea was an unusually somber affair. The ceremonial toasts sounded forced and insincere, and, though the musicians were as fine as they were every year, the bawdy songs that were a tradition at the midsummer festival, which celebrated the fertility of both the soil and the people, evoked little response from the gathered mages. The evening ended early, and Jaryd and Alayna walked without speaking back to the Aerie. They had not been in their room for more than a few minutes, however, when they heard a single emphatic knock on the door.

Alayna glanced quickly in Jaryd's direction, a look of concern in her eyes, a look he understood. Even before Erland called Baden a coward, no one in the chamber could have doubted whose idea it had been to send Baram with the delegation. Still, by offering the suggestion as his own, Jaryd might very well have made an enemy this day, or several. And after all that had transpired, anything was possible.

"Who's there?" Alayna called cautiously.

"Let me in!" came a familiar growl.

They both smiled, and Alayna opened the door and ushered Orris into the small room.

"We didn't see you at the Feast," Alayna commented, closing the door behind the burly mage. "We figured you were observing some fertility rites of your own."

Jaryd could see that Orris still carried much of the fury that he had fought so hard to control earlier in the day. Nonetheless, his friend could not help but laugh at Alayna's remark, even as his face reddened. She had a knack for doing that to people—making them laugh in spite of themselves, forcing them to take things just a bit less seriously. Jaryd had fallen in love with her because of it. And, knowing how that love was returned, it did not trouble him that, on some level, Orris might have as well.

"Actually, I was out walking," Orris explained, his dour mood returning as he sat on the bed beside Jaryd. "I needed to clear my head after today's session."

Alayna lowered herself into a chair by the window and flipped her long, dark hair off her shoulder with a toss of her head. "Did it help?"

The mage shook his head and made a sour face. "No. I think it's going to take a lot more than just a walk."

"I don't think that Sonel meant any disrespect," she assured him.

Again, Orris shook his head. "I'm sure she didn't," he agreed. "That's not really what's bothering me." He looked at Jaryd, as if anticipating what the younger man was going to say. "Yes, it bothered me at the time, but I understand why she didn't want me to speak." He managed a rueful grin. "What I had planned to say wouldn't have been very constructive."

Jaryd and Alayna both chuckled, but they said nothing, and after a brief pause, Orris went on.

"It occurred to me last night, while the six of us were talking downstairs, that I'd lost faith in the Order's ability to reach any sort of compromise," he told them, his dark eyes focused on the floor in front of him, as he gently stroked the chin of the dark falcon on his shoulder. "What I saw today only served to deepen my doubts. The factions are too far apart; and nobody's even trying to bridge the gap."

"Alayna and I reached the same conclusion last night," Jaryd offered, "after we left the rest of you in the tavern. But what can we do about it?"

Orris looked up at that, his eyes meeting Jaryd's momentarily before flicking away again. "I'm not sure," he replied. "I wish I had an answer, but I don't." But the strain in his voice, and the brief look they had shared, told Jaryd that Orris had given the question more thought than he was letting on.

"Then what are you doing here?" Jaryd asked, taking a chance.

Orris gazed at him again, thoughtfully this time. "How is it that you and your uncle understand me so well?"

"My uncle? What's he got to do with this?"

The brawny man shook his head. "It doesn't matter." He took a breath. "I'm here because I needed to be with friends. And the two of you are the best I have."

"How sad," Alayna said. "we don't even like you."

The three of them began to laugh, and Orris picked up one of the pillows from the bed and threw it in Alayna's direction.

"I could use an ale," Orris said after their laughter had died away. "And I wouldn't mind some company."

It ended up being a very late evening. Trahn and Baden arrived at the tavern just as Jaryd, Alayna, and Orris descended the stairs, and the five mages drank a good deal of ale and, for the first time in what seemed like years, spent a night joking and telling stories, rather than dwelling on the problems facing Tobyn-Ser and the Order. It had the feeling of a party, Jaryd reflected as he and Alayna finally—for a second time—made their way up to their room. It certainly seemed to do Orris a world of good. And Baden, too. This had been a difficult Gathering for him, and Jaryd was gratified to see his uncle laughing and relaxing for a change. But when Jaryd lay down next to Alayna, who fell into a deep sleep almost immediately, he found himself dwelling not on the joviality of the time they had just spent in the tavern, but rather on the brief exchange with Orris that had come before it, specifically on the burly mage's strange comment about how Baden and he understood Orris so well. Jaryd knew that it was somehow significant; that it had something to do with the pensive mood Orris had been in when he first arrived at Jaryd and Alayna's room. But he was tired, and Amari Ale had a way of clouding his thoughts. He fell asleep before he could make any sense of Orris's comment.

The next day's session, the last of the Gathering, opened, predictably, with renewed argument over the merits and dangers of sending mages to Lon-Ser. The strained courtesy with which the debate had ended the day before, lasted but a short while before giving way once more to the animosity that had prevailed up until Alayna's outburst. By the end of the morning, it had grown obvious to everyone that the mages would not be able to agree on a plan for sending Sonel's delegation, and, after a midday meal, the Owl-Sage admitted as much, effectively ending the discussion.

At any normal Gathering, this would have brought an end to the turmoil that had characterized the proceedings since the first morning. But this was no ordinary Gathering, and the Order, it seemed, was beset by crises.

"There is another matter of some urgency of which I must inform you," the Sage announced, barely giving them time to recover from the battle over the delegation. An expectant hush settled over the chamber. Jaryd glanced at Baden, who was staring with grave interest at Sonel. Apparently he didn't know what was coming either.

"Linnea, Eldest of the Gods, came to see me some time ago with news of Cailin, the young girl who survived the outlanders' attack on Kaera."

Jaryd remembered Cailin quite well, as much for her striking beauty and quiet strength as for the tragedy visited upon her by the invaders from Lon-Ser.

Alayna and he had met her only once, but they had spoken of her many times since, and she had been in his thoughts quite often over the past four years.

"Cailin is growing up well," Sonel continued. "To the extent that can be expected, her scars are healing." She hesitated, taking a deep breath. "But something has happened, something none of us could have foreseen: Cailin has bound to a hawk."

Perhaps because it was so unexpected—she was, after all, just a young girl—or perhaps because the mages had expended all their energy with three days of bitter debate, the response to this news struck Jaryd as remarkably muted. For several moments no one spoke; they all just sat, silent and motionless, as if unsure of what they had just heard.

"She can't be much more than ten," Baden observed at last, his voice subdued, his eyes trained on the Sage.

"She recently turned eleven," Sonel corrected, "but your point is well taken. She is exceptionally young to be bound already."

"Who is supervising her mastery of the Mage-Craft?" Erland inquired. "You, I hope, Owl-Sage," he added obsequiously.

Once more, Sonel hesitated.

"Someone is supervising her?" Erland persisted.

"Yes, Erland," the Sage replied at last, "but no one from this body."

"What?" the white-haired Owl-Master rasped. "She must have guidance from someone with knowledge of the Mage-Craft!"

"I'm inclined to agree with Erland in this instance," Baden added.

"Don't you think I am as well?" Sonel stormed. She paused, trembling with anger and frustration. "I had this same conversation with Linnea several months ago," she began again, more quietly this time, "and believe me: I did all I could to impress upon her the importance of providing Cailin with an experienced instructor. But the Eldest has charge of her care until Cailin comes of age, and there's really very little we can do."

"We can demand that she ask Cailin!" Baden argued. "Let the child decide if she wants guidance from a mage!"

"Yes, we could do that," the Sage answered. "But, frankly, I don't believe that Cailin wants anything to do with this Order. She won't even take an oath to observe Amarid's Laws."

"You—you can't be serious!" Erland stammered, speaking now for all of them.

"I'm afraid I am, though I'm also reasonably certain that her refusal stems from her hostility toward the Order rather than from any intent to violate the substance of the Laws. I've been in touch almost constantly with either Linnea or her representatives; the Eldest has been surprisingly forthcoming on this matter—"

"Well, she's probably frightened," Baden interjected. "Even she must realize that she's beyond her depth."

Sonel nodded. "I think she does. She came to me for advice—that's how I first learned of this—and she has continued to consult with me on a regular basis. And as I began to say a moment ago: Cailin is not an evil child by any means. From all I've been told, she seems to be bright, kind, and respectful of those in charge of her upbringing. She holds us responsible for the death of her parents and the destruction of her village; this is what keeps her from formally submitting herself to Amarid's Laws. But I don't think she poses too great a threat to the people of this land."

"You don't *think* she poses *too* great a threat?" Baden repeated. "I'd feel better if you could be a bit more certain."

Sonel gave a small laugh. "As would I. Even the best behaved eleven-year-old is still an eleven-year-old. Therein lies the greatest danger."

"Does she have a ceryll, Owl-Sage?" Trahn asked, a look of concern on his dark features.

Jaryd glanced at his own ceryll, the sapphire blue stone glowing atop his wooden staff. A ceryll allowed a mage to focus his or her power, to both control it and augment it. Cailin was likely to be far more powerful with a stone than without one.

Sonel considered Trahn's question briefly. "I don't believe so, no," she finally replied. "At least no one has mentioned a ceryll to me. Why?"

Trahn shrugged. "Curiosity mostly. I'm trying to decide which frightens me more: the notion of a child with power and no way to control it, or the notion of a child with power and the ability to make it do whatever she wants. Neither image is terribly reassuring."

"Indeed," Radomil concurred. "Nor am I comforted by the thought of the Keepers having access to the Mage-Craft. Cailin could easily become a pawn in a very old conflict."

"I share your concerns, Radomil," Sonel admitted, "and Trahn's as well, although I must say it hadn't occurred to me before. But again, I don't see that we have many options. I felt you should know—I was, to be honest, tired of bearing this burden alone. But I don't think that we can do anything to affect this situation, at least not at this time."

"Perhaps if you had told us earlier," Baden offered gently, "it might have persuaded some of our colleagues to support your proposal to negotiate with Lon-Ser's leaders."

"Don't be ridiculous, Baden!" Erland countered. "This changes nothing! Sending mages to Lon-Ser was a bad idea yesterday; it's a bad idea today; and it will be a bad idea tomorrow! The binding of one child does nothing to alter that fact!"

Baden shook his head wearily. "Then again, perhaps not," he said in a quiet voice.

Sonel adjourned the gathered mages a short time later, leaving them the remainder of the afternoon to do as they pleased before the Procession of Light and the feast that marked the closing of the Gathering. Jaryd and Alayna used the time to wander through the markets of Amarid's old town center, as they liked to do each time they visited the city. They invited Orris to join them, but the barrel-chested mage's dark mood had returned, and he mumbled something about having other things to do before stalking off on his own. And, in truth, neither Jaryd nor Alayna enjoyed their time in the town center as much as they usually did. It had been too difficult a Gathering, and their concerns about the Order's inability to act left both of them preoccupied and weary.

They returned to the Great Hall just as dusk was beginning to color the western sky with shades of pink and orange. Moving inside immediately, they saw that most of the mages and masters had already taken their places around the perimeter of the Gathering Chamber, in front of the tall, cast-iron candle holders that the blue-robed stewards of the Great Hall had put in place during the mages' absence that afternoon. They quickly positioned themselves as the others had done, and awaited the return of the stewards with the thin, blue candles that they would light and place in the holders.

It was quiet in the chamber, strangely so. Usually the mages and masters would speak among themselves as they waited for this final ceremony of the Gathering to begin, but this year they merely stood in awkward silence. Jaryd tried to cheer himself by calling up memories from his first Procession of Light, when he and Alayna were the newest members of the Order. No one, not even Baden, had prepared him for the beauty of the ritual: all the candles and fires in the city had been extinguished or shaded, so that the moon overhead and the line of glowing cerylls carried by the mages as they made their way through the city streets were the only sources of light in all of Amarid. But that had been only part of what made his first Procession so special. Just before the ceremony had begun, he and Alayna had been given baskets to carry, and, as they had followed the older mages through the streets of Amarid, the crowds lining the Procession's route had filled the baskets with feathers, welcoming the young mages to the Order. It had been a glorious night.

But now, four years later, even these images did little to lift Jaryd's spirits. For this year, as had been the case last year, the Order had no new members to welcome. It seemed to Jaryd a dark omen, made worse by the fact that the last mage to earn her cloak, a young woman named Rhonwen, who entered the Order two summers ago, had fallen ill and died the following winter, after having been rendered unbound that autumn when a stray arrow from a hunter's bow struck her familiar. He shook his head at the thought. Less than a year after her first binding, she had become one of the Unsettled, doomed to walk the land in eternal unrest. And not a single new mage since. Except Cailin. He couldn't begin to fathom what it all might mean.

"Orris isn't here," Alayna whispered to him, unable to mask the tension in her voice.

Instinctively, Jaryd's eyes flew to where his friend should have been standing. It was growing late; the Hall had begun to grow dark. As if on cue, the first of the stewards emerged from a room at the back of the Hall and started lighting candles and placing them in the holders. And at the same time, finally, Jaryd remembered Orris's remark from the night before. *How is it that you and your uncle understand me so well?* he had asked. What could he have meant?

"I'll be right back," Jaryd told Alayna, crossing the chamber to where Baden stood before she could ask him where he was going.

"Have you seen Orris?" he asked the Owl-Master without preamble.

Despite the poor light, Jaryd could see Baden's features blanch at the question, and, as he himself had done an instant before, the Owl-Master shot a look toward Orris's customary place in the Procession. "I had hoped that he would speak with me again before doing anything," he mumbled, more to himself than to Jaryd.

"What do you mean?" Jaryd demanded. He could feel himself growing more agitated by the moment. "Speak with you about what? What's going on, Baden?"

Baden hesitated, as if unsure of how much he should reveal. "In truth, I'm not certain," he confided at last, his voice low, his bright blue eyes gleaming in the flickering light that had begun to fill the Chamber. "Orris has been very frustrated by the Order's inaction."

"We all have!" Jaryd returned, more sharply than he had intended. "What's that—" He halted, his thoughts racing ahead to catch up with Baden's implication. "We all have," he repeated, more speculatively this time, "but Orris is more likely than the rest of us to do something about it."

The Owl-Master nodded. "Yes. But I have no idea what he has in mind. I was hoping you or Alayna might."

"He hasn't said anything to either of us, except for asking me how you and I had come to understand him so well. Do you know what he meant?"

"Not really." Baden opened his mouth to say more, but then he stopped, his face breaking into a broad grin at something he saw over Jaryd's shoulder. "Why don't you ask him yourself."

Jaryd spun in time to see the bearded mage striding across the marble floor of the Chamber to take his place in the Procession. The mage and his uncle went to greet him, confronting Orris just as the Hawk-Mage reached his spot along the Hall's perimeter.

The burly mage inclined his head slightly and managed a thin smile, but he said nothing.

"We're glad to see you," Jaryd told him with genuine relief. "We were worried that you might have done something rash."

Orris wet his lips. "Well, as you can see," he replied, his tone muted but taut, "you had nothing to be concerned about."

Baden narrowed his eyes. "Didn't we?"

Orris averted his gaze, refusing to look directly at either of them. "The Procession will be starting soon. We can talk about this later."

Jaryd glanced at his uncle, who returned the look and shrugged. Jaryd could feel his stomach starting to knot with tension. "All right," he said turning back to Orris. "You're still sitting with Alayna and me at the feast, aren't you?" he asked, reminding the mage of plans they had made the night before.

Orris nodded, still not meeting Jaryd's gaze. "If the seating works out, yes."

Jaryd stood before the mage for another moment, and then turned away and moved back toward Alayna. Baden followed him for part of the way.

"I'm afraid of what he might do, Jaryd," the Owl-Master whispered. "Keep an eye on him."

Jaryd nodded and Baden continued toward the front of the Procession.

"What's going on?" Alayna asked as Jaryd took his place beside her.

"We're not sure. Orris is behaving strangely. He may be planning something."

"Like what?"

Jaryd shook his head.

The candles had all been lit and placed in the holders. The gathered mages stood silently, waiting for Sonel to commence the ceremony by extinguishing the candle behind her and simultaneously raising her glowing ceryll above her head. This was Jaryd's favorite part of every Gathering, but he could not stop thinking about Orris, and the ominous expression that had been lurking in the Hawk-Mage's eyes. Baden was frightened, and Jaryd knew that he should have been as well. But instead, he felt something else, something unexpected.

And just as Sonel raised her ceryll, beginning the Procession of Light, Alayna gave voice to his thoughts.

"I wouldn't want anything to happen to him," she said softly, but with certainty and perhaps—dare he think it—a touch of hope, "but somebody has to act."

7

The most difficult aspect of preparing Savil's men for their mission in Tobyn-Ser will not be the physical conditioning, although certainly they will find that the rigors of this training surpasses anything they have experienced before. Nor does it lie in the challenge of getting break-laws—men who are violent by nature and accustomed to relying solely on their instincts—to focus on the intellectual elements of their preparation: the language, the memorization of maps, etc.

By far the most difficult of my tasks will be impressing upon these men that they are about to enter an alien culture. They must understand that this is not like mercenary work in Abborij. When they arrive in Tobyn-Ser, they must immediately blend into their surroundings. They must appear no more out of place in the raw wilds of that land than a drunk does in a quad bar. Even the slightest deviation on their part from what the people of Tobyn-Ser consider "normal," will result in disaster.

—Personal journal of Cedrych i Vran, Overlord of the First Dominion of Bragor-Nal, Day 4, Week 1, Summer, Year 3060.

He had made his decision the other night, during the course of his unexpected conversation with Baden in the Aerie. But he had not made peace with that decision until earlier today, during the interval between the adjournment of the Gathering and the commencement of the Procession of Light.

He still wasn't sure why he had gone out to see the prison. He had simply known at the time that he needed to, that somehow seeing it would help. And he was right.

It was smaller than he had expected, standing incongruously amid the warm grasses and bright flowers of a meadow, with the dark foothills and brilliant peaks of the Parneshome Range rising behind it. But even in this setting, in the bright sunshine, it had appeared dark and austere, its ponderous slabs of coarse stone and disturbingly small barred windows causing him to shudder involuntarily.

And yet, it was not sympathy that had finally brought him the surety he sought, nor was it overconfidence, for the structure was as impressive as it was forbidding. There was a single steel door on one side, large enough for a horse and cart to pass through, with a massive iron lock that could only be opened by key from the inside, and two heavy bolts that could only be operated by the guards on duty outside the door. Six archers stood on the battlements atop the prison, and the smaller stone guardhouse located a short distance from the door looked capable of housing several dozen men. Escape from such a place, whether planned from within or by allies on the outside, would be impossible.

In the end, what reassured him was merely the reality of it. Within this prison sat Baram. And because of him, and others who had come to Tobyn-Ser with him, "Taima" and "Watersbend" and "Kaera," which had once merely been the names of towns, had become synonyms for "devastation" and "savagery" and "bloodbath." Regardless of the certain risks, notwithstanding the possible consequences, Orris understood, staring at the prison, seeing in his mind the face of the outlander, that he had reached the right decision, the only decision. One way or another, he would be leaving for Lon-Ser tonight. And Baram would be going with him.

Since leaving the prison and commencing the long walk back to the Great Hall, he had been preparing himself for the problems he would face winning Baram's release from the jail, and, more importantly, the difficulty he might have convincing the outlander to make the journey with him, in good faith, as his guide. He had not anticipated, however, that the most troublesome aspect of his plan would be slipping away unnoticed from the feast being served at the First Mage's home.

Jaryd and Alayna found him as soon as the Procession of Light completed its winding passage through the streets of Amarid, and guided him to a section of the large horseshoe-shaped table at which all the mages were seated. There, he sat not only with Jaryd and Alayna, but also with Trahn, Ursel, Baden, Mered, and Radomil—the people with whom he had forged the psychic link that had been guarding the western borders of Tobyn-Ser for the last four years; the people who knew him better than any others in the world. Keeping his intentions a secret would be hard enough; leaving early without arousing their suspicions would be next to impossible.

So he sat, eating little, saying even less, and meticulously avoiding any of the dark wine that was flowing so freely on either side of him. At one point Sonel rose to speak, briefly observing that, despite the lack of new mages, the Order remained strong and vibrant, with a favorable mix of experienced older members and energetic younger ones. She also urged the mages not to allow differences of opinion to undermine the Order's tradition of cohesiveness and camaraderie. The remarks struck Orris as well-meaning, and certainly appropriate to the occasion. But they were received rather coolly. Perhaps at some point they would all be ready to begin a process of healing, but that time had not yet come, and it occurred to Orris that he might never see it. He was going far; he had no idea how long he would be gone. His friends deserved more from him than he was giving, and yet he found that he had nothing to offer them.

"The last few days have left me pretty tired," he said abruptly, as Sonel finished her remarks and a group of musicians started to tune their instruments. "I think I'll head off to bed."

Jaryd and Baden exchanged a look.

"All right," Alayna said with a kind smile. "We'll see you in the morning before we leave, right?"

"Of course," he murmured, standing and holding out an arm for his dark falcon. "Good night."

He made his way slowly through the trees and torches, and past table after table of the city people who had followed the Procession to the grounds of Amarid's home to feast with the mages, and who now called out greetings to him that he acknowledged with waves and nods. He didn't look back, but he sensed that Jaryd was following, and he dreaded the confrontation that he knew was coming.

As he reached the edge of the trees and stepped onto the cobblestone street, he quickened his pace, ducking into the first alleyway he could find and muting the light of his ceryll. But it was no use.

"Orris!" he heard from behind him. Jaryd's voice.

He kept moving, taking a second, narrower passage.

"Orris!" Jaryd called again, more insistent this time, and closer.

Reluctantly, the burly mage stopped, turning to face his pursuer. "Don't try to stop me, Jaryd!" he warned, raising his staff as the young mage approached him.

"What are you going to do, Orris?" Jaryd asked, his face looking lean and boyish in the mage-light. "Blast me with mage-fire? Send your hawk after mine?" He shook his head, a lock of straight brown hair falling across his brow. "I don't think so."

"I'll do whatever I have to do," Orris replied grimly, although, in truth, he wasn't certain that he could match the younger man in a battle of magic if it came to that. Four years ago he had watched Jaryd do battle with Sartol in the Great Hall when the renegade Owl-Master, his power channeled through the Summoning Stone, had tried to kill Baden. Other mages had come to Jaryd's aid, but not before the shimmering sapphire shield of magic that the youth created had blocked Sartol's initial blast. Few mages could have withstood such a blow, and Jaryd had been little more than a boy then, new to the ways of the Mage-Craft. There was no telling how strong he had grown over the intervening years, or how much more powerful he would become.

"I didn't come to fight you, Orris," Jaryd offered.

"How else did you think you were going to stop me?"

"I didn't come to stop you either."

"What?" Orris demanded skeptically.

"I didn't come to stop you," Jaryd repeated. "That's the truth." He grinned. "I'm not foolish enough to think that you'd listen to reason."

Orris gave a small laugh in spite of himself. "So why are you following me?"

"Because one of us should know what you're planning."

"In case it doesn't work?"

Jaryd shrugged slightly, suddenly looking uncomfortable.

"If it doesn't work, my friend," Orris went on with a wry smile, "I'm a dead man. And it won't matter who knows what my plans were."

The younger man said nothing, but his pale eyes held Orris's gaze, and, after some time, Orris relented. "I'm going to Lon-Ser. But I think you already knew that."

Jaryd nodded and offered a wan smile.

"Beyond that, I really haven't thought things through. It's a long journey; there'll be time along the way."

"Do you know anything about where you're going?"

"Only what Baden has told us, and what little I could get from the first section of his report. That's all I had time to read."

"That's unfortunate."

"I guess. He's managed to tell us a good deal; certainly more than I ever thought I wanted to know." They both chuckled. "In any case," Orris concluded, "maybe some of it stuck."

There was a brief pause. And then Jaryd asked the one question Orris had been fearing the most. "How about the evidence? Do you have their weapons and the mechanical birds?"

Orris shook his head, averting his eyes. "No," he replied quietly. "I won't need them."

"What do you mean? Of course you will. How else—?" Jaryd stopped, comprehension breaking over him like a wave.

Orris looked at him again, and almost laughed. Under different circumstances, the look on the young mage's face would have been comical.

"How are you going to get—?"

"No, Jaryd," Orris told him, shaking his head again. "The less you know about this part of it the better."

His friend took a slow breath. "You're probably right."

They stood a moment without speaking, and then Jaryd stepped forward and pulled Orris to him like a brother. "Arick guard you," he said hoarsely, "and guide you back to us."

Orris held him tightly for several seconds, blinking back tears, and then stepped back. "You and Alayna take care of each other."

"We will."

"I'll need some time, Jaryd," he said, a plea in his tone. "Don't tell anyone, other than Alayna. At least not until you get back to the Lower Horn, and you and the rest reestablish the link. That should be enough. All right?"

Jaryd nodded, and Orris turned to go.

"Orris."

He turned back again and waited.

"Theron told us—Alayna and me—that the Order would not defeat this enemy through conventional means." The young mage hesitated, as if trying to remember the Owl-Master's exact words. And as he did, Orris could not help but stare at the staff his friend carried. Theron's staff, charred at the top from the evil curse the Unsettled Master had conjured a thousand years ago, and crowned now with Jaryd's deep blue ceryll. " 'The Order will have to adapt,' " Jaryd went on, quoting the Owl-Master. " 'It will have to change.' That's what he said. And I think he'd approve of what you're doing. I think he had something like this in mind. Carry that with you on your journey."

Orris nodded. "I will. Arick guard you." He turned again, leaving Jaryd in the narrow alley, and taking the quickest route he could out of the city.

The walk to the prison seemed to take longer in the darkness, and, at one point, Orris feared that he had taken a wrong turn off one of the paths leading through the forest. Eventually, though, he found the clearing. The moon was up, and, bathed in the silvery light, the stone structure loomed larger and more menacing than it had during the day. Orange torchlight seeped through some of the windows, ghostly and faint, and a bright fire burned next to the guard-house. Orris approached the steel door.

"Who's there?" a guard called out, his voice young and not quite steady.

"A friend," Orris replied soothingly. "Hawk-Mage Orris. I've been sent by Owl-Sage Sonel to get the outlander."

"Hawk-Mage?" the guard repeated. He watched Orris approach the prison, wide-eyed and obviously impressed, his gaze darting briefly to Orris's falcon and staff before returning to Orris himself. His face was as youthful as his voice, but he was a large man, broad-chested, with muscular arms. He had unsheathed his broadsword, and he held it now in his right hand.

"Yes. You can put away your sword."

"Oh! Oh! Of course!" the man stammered, struggling to slip the weapon back into its scabbard. "I'm sorry Hawk-Mage," he managed, still trying to put his sword away. "My watch commander said nothing about this. Otherwise I would have been—"

"No one knew," Orris said, keeping his voice calm. "It wasn't planned. But the Owl-Sage has decided that the prisoner should be moved back to the Great Hall, so that the interrogations can be conducted with greater ease."

"But so late at night?"

"There are still those in the city who would like to see the man dead," Orris told him, thinking the explanation plausible. "Moving him at this hour seemed prudent."

The guard nodded, as if considering this.

"The door?" Orris said after several moments, allowing a hint of impatience to creep into his voice.

The guard practically jumped. "Of course, Hawk-Mage!" He stepped quickly to the door and threw the two bolts before pounding on the door with a meaty fist. "Sefton! Open the door!" he called urgently. "Hurry up!"

"All right!" came a faint voice from inside. "No need to get all bothered about it!" The clicking of boots on stone echoed within the prison, growing gradually louder until they stopped. A narrow, eye-level grate in the door slid open and a pair of dark eyes stared out at the young guard. "What's going on? What's all the noise?"

"Open the door, Sefton!" The guard said again, a little desperately this time. "There's a Child of Amarid come to get the outlander!"

"A Child of Amarid you say?," the voice asked, the eyes shifting toward Orris and widening a bit.

"Yes! Now open the door before you make him mad!"

Sefton backed away from the opening in the door, leaving the grate open. Orris heard the jangling of keys, and then, finally, the loud, metallic clinking of the lock opening.

Sefton stepped out of the building and looked Orris up and down. He was an older man with light hair that might have been blond or silver—it was difficult to tell in the darkness. His face was pale, and a white scar ran down one side from the corner of his eye to the top of his lip. He was considerably smaller than the other guard, but he carried an equally large sword, and Orris had no doubt that he knew how to use it.

"You've come for the outlander, eh?" he asked, his tone respectful but cautious.

"Yes. The Owl-Sage wants him moved back to the Great Hall for a time, so that she might continue his questioning herself."

"The watch commander didn't say you'd be coming."

Orris smiled disarmingly. "As I told your friend here, no one knew about it. Sonel made her decision this evening."

The man nodded, but said nothing for several moments, as he continued to regard Orris appraisingly. Orris could feel his heart pounding within his chest. His throat was dry and he felt the muscle in his cheek starting to jump. He found it hard to imagine that Sefton would defy him, but the man certainly did not act as though he was intimidated, nor did he seem to be entirely convinced. At last, however, he glanced at the young guard. "Wait here," he commanded. Then he turned, gesturing for Orris to follow. "This way, Hawk-Mage."

Sefton led Orris through the door and into a large torch-lit entrance hall with a high ceiling. Along the length of the room on either side, there were tall, narrow slits in the rough stone walls, and Orris could see that there were archers stationed in small rooms behind them.

"I'll have to leave word of this with my commander," Sefton told him, looking back over his shoulder. "And I'll need to tell him who took the outlander. Your name, I mean."

The mage hesitated. He'd already given the younger guard his name; he couldn't use an alias. "Of course," he responded, forcing himself to smile. "My name is Orris."

Sefton nodded. "This way," he said again, moving to a narrow corridor at the end of the hallway.

The ceiling was far lower in the passageway, and the sound of Sefton's footsteps reverberated loudly off the stone.

"I'm one who thinks they ought to have killed him, if you want to know," Sefton volunteered.

"That decision was made a long time ago," Orris answered grimly.

The guard stopped in front of another locked, steel door. "Yes, Hawk-Mage, I know that. I just don't see what use there is in keeping him alive, seeing as—"

"Are we almost there?" Orris asked impatiently.

"Yes, Hawk-Mage," the man replied, fumbling for his keys again. "Just through here."

The door opened onto a second, equally cramped corridor which was unlit, save for Orris's amber ceryll.

"Should I get a torch, Hawk-Mage?"

"No," Orris told him, increasing the brightness from his crystal with little more than a thought. "Just take me to the prisoner."

The man nodded again and continued on to the end of the dark hallway. There, he unlocked a third door and pushed it open. The stench of urine, feces, sweat, rotting food, and Arick knew what else hit Orris like a fist in the face, causing him to stagger backwards momentarily.

The guard grinned. "Pretty rank, eh?"

Orris ignored him. From inside the cell, along with the fetor, came the sound of a man's voice repeating a phrase again and again. Orris didn't understand a word of it.

"What's he saying?"

Sefton shrugged. "Who knows? He doesn't talk like us. We call it Outland Speak, but none of us knows what any of it means."

Orris stepped forward again, steeling himself against the foul air, and raising his ceryll so that it would light the cell. Sitting on the floor against the far wall, his arms hugging his knees to his chest, was a man whom he only vaguely recognized as Baram. His hair and beard, both of them matted with filth, hung to the floor. He had open sores on his hands and face, and his clothes were in tatters. He glanced briefly toward Orris, apparently drawn by the light. But his chanting continued, and his eyes appeared vacant and without focus.

"This man needs a bath and new clothes before we go."

"But Hawk-Mage, it's the middle of the night."

Orris spun toward the guard. "You'd have him sent to the Owl-Sage like this!"

"No, of course not, but—"

"*Now!*" Orris thundered.

The guard nodded and hurried away, leaving Orris to retrieve Baram.

Hesitantly, the Hawk-Mage approached the prisoner and extended his hand. "Come on, Outlander. It's time to go."

The man looked up at him without interrupting his litany. Orris wondered if it was a religious practice.

"You're coming with me," he said, trying again. He glanced back over his shoulder. They were alone; he could hear Sefton far off, barking commands at the guard outside. "I'm taking you away from here. I'm taking you back home, to Lon-Ser."

The chanting stopped. "Baden?" the man croaked.

"No. My name is Orris. I'm a friend of Baden's." He offered his hand again. "Come on; we're going."

Baram shook his head and said something, gesturing at his surroundings.

Orris grabbed him by the shoulder and hoisted him onto his feet. "I said come on!" he commanded, trying to pull the outlander with him.

The man was surprisingly strong, given his bedraggled appearance, and he wrenched himself out of Orris's grip, repeating whatever it was he had said a moment before, but shouting it this time. Orris tried to seize him again, but Baram jumped away. His eyes had a wild look to them, like those of a horse caught in a lightning storm.

Baram said something else, angrily this time, and he shook a rigid finger at the mage. Orris held out his hands in a placating gesture, and for a moment the two of them, mage and outlander, stood glaring at one another, both of them breathing hard. Then Orris heard boots on the stone corridor again. Someone was running back to the cell. An instant later Sefton appeared in the doorway.

"I'm sorry to have left you, Hawk-Mage. I had to get things ready."

"He won't come with me," Orris told him. The mage was trembling. This was one thing he hadn't expected at all.

"He's a weird one sometimes," the guard explained. "But he loves his baths. That should get him to follow."

"A bath?' the outlander asked the guard.

"Yes, Baram," Orris answered, drawing the pale eyes back his way. "A bath, and after that a journey. Do you understand?"

Baram stared at him for a few seconds more before turning his gaze back to Sefton. "A bath," he repeated.

The guard nodded, glancing briefly at Orris, who gestured for him to lead the prisoner away.

The two of them started down the dark hallway, but Orris lingered briefly, looking around the small, filthy cell. Four years he's been here, he thought, shaking his head. Four years.

The interrogations were over by and large; he had written his report. And yet Baden felt compelled to visit Baram once more before heading back to western Tobyn-Ser; somehow he felt that he owed the outlander that much. He had said his farewells to Jaryd and Alayna, Trahn, and Ursel first thing that morning. He knew that he would be reestablishing the psychic link with them within a few weeks, but it wasn't the same as seeing them. In spite of everything, he still treasured these Gatherings.

He had been alarmed last night when Orris retired early, and even more so this morning when Jaryd told him that the burly mage had departed for Duclea's Tears with first light. But Jaryd had assured him that everything was fine, that Orris had decided against taking any rash action, at least for now, which, Baden supposed, was as much as they could hope for under the circumstances.

The Owl-Master reached the prison near midday, and the watch commander, a stout man named Sean, greeted him as he strode toward the large, steel door.

"Owl-Master!" the guard called out, a broad smile on his tanned face. He was, Baden had often remarked to himself, an exceptionally cheerful man, considering what he did for a living.

"Hello, Sean. It's good to see you."

"And you, sir. Though I can't say as I expected to see you here again."

It seemed to Baden that a shadow passed over him, although the sky was a cloudless, deep blue. "I don't understand," the Owl-Master said tentatively.

"Well, with Baram gone back to the Great Hall, I assumed you'd be done with us. Not that I'm sorry to see you. Children of Amarid are always welcome here."

Baden felt as if he had been kicked in the stomach. He needed desperately to sit down and catch his breath, and he feared he might be ill.

"Are you all right, Owl-Master?" Sean asked, concern creeping into his voice. "You don't look so good."

"I'm fine," Baden replied, fighting to smile. "I'm fine."

"You knew about Baram going back to the Hall, didn't you?" This time Baden heard fear in the guard's voice. "It wasn't me that let him go. It was last night and I was off duty. But I was surprised when they told me that someone other than you had come for him. Everything's all right, isn't it?"

"Of course," Baden assured him. "Everything's fine." He had to think. It must have been Orris. Better Orris than Arslan or one of his allies. "You say someone came last night?" he asked, trying to keep his voice even.

"Yes, sir. A mage. You're sure it's all right?"

"Yes, Sean. I'm sure. I didn't think the transfer was going to occur until next week. I was a bit confused, that's all."

The guard smiled with relief. "Of course, sir. Happens to me all the time."

"I wonder, do you remember the mage's name?"

"Yes, sir." He hesitated. "I think I do, sir."

"Was it Hawk-Mage Orris?" Baden asked.

Sean smiled. "Orris! Yes, that's the name, sir."

Baden took a breath. Last night, the guard had said. And yet Jaryd claimed to have said goodbye to Orris this morning. "Thank you, Sean. Sorry to have troubled you."

"No trouble at all, sir. I'm sorry you walked out all this way for nothing."

The Owl-Master made himself smile and patted the man's shoulder, before starting down the path that led back into the forest. He moved casually, not wanting to give anything away. But once he entered the wood and convinced himself that the guards at the prison could no longer see him, he hurried off the main path and sat down on a log. His chest was heaving with every breath, and he was shaking violently with fear, anger, and the effort it had taken to keep his composure while speaking with the guard.

He rested for some time, for what he was about to do required a great effort. He usually tried to avoid using the *Ceryll-Var*. It involved an enormous expenditure of power, draining both mage and familiar. But, in this case, he had little choice. He briefly considered reaching for Orris, but he was uncertain of which direction the mage had taken, and he was too angry right now. Orris wouldn't respond well to rage. So he reached for Jaryd instead.

Closing his eyes, he felt the power from Golivas rushing into him like a cool wind sweeping down the side of a mountain, filling him until he could contain it no longer. And when he had held it within him as long as he could, he raised his ceryll over his head and sent the magic westward, into the foothills of the Parneshome Range, to the trail that he knew Alayna and Jaryd would take over the mountains. And with this magic went his awareness and his mind-sight, so that he might search for the bright blue of Jaryd's ceryll. In his mind he saw nothing—only blackness, and after some time he began to wonder if they had taken a different route after all.

And then he saw them. Not the mages, or their identical grey birds, or the mountain path on which they walked. Just their cerylls; Alayna's purple and Jaryd's blue. Honing in on the latter, Baden forced his orange fire into the blue, momentarily changing the appearance of Jaryd's stone.

After that, he waited, his eyes still closed. It didn't take very long, but still it startled him to hear Jaryd's voice in his head, so vivid and strong that the young mage could easily have been standing beside him in the forest.

Baden?

You lied to me! Baden sent, conveying as much anger as he could.

A pause, and then: *Yes.*

How could you do something so foolish!

Orris asked me not to tell anyone, not until we reestablish the link. I felt I owed it to him to honor that request.

"Owed" it to him? Baden raged. *This isn't a game Jaryd; we're not operating under some schoolyard code of honor here! Orris's life is in danger! And you just let him go?*

Are you through? Jaryd sent, his tone icy.

Yes, Baden returned after a brief pause.

Good. Then let me ask you this: How was I supposed to stop him? With magefire? With brute strength? Should I have told you? Do you think you could have dissuaded him? Or should I have gone right to Sonel? Or Erland?

Baden kept still; in truth, he had no idea what Jaryd could have done. That is, other than what he did.

Don't you think, the young mage went on, *that he would have found a way to do this no matter what any of us thought or said or did? And given that, don't you think that he deserves a chance to succeed? It might work, Baden. He might make it work. Isn't it worth that chance?*

Perhaps, Baden answered, his tone more subdued now. *But there's so much that he doesn't know, that none of you know.*

You've taught us a great deal. And he read some of your report before he left.

Baden shook his head, even though he knew Jaryd couldn't see. *I'm not talking about the report,* he sent, conveying his concern and his frustration. *Not everything is in the report.*

Not everything about Lon-Ser, you mean?

About Lon-Ser, yes. But more importantly about Baram.

What about Baram? Jaryd demanded, and for the first time Baden sensed fear in the Hawk-Mage's thoughts.

The Owl-Master hesitated, gathering himself.

Baden? Jaryd called to him. *What about Baram?*

Baden took a breath. There was no way to cushion it. *He's lost his mind, Jaryd. Baram is insane.*

8

I had hoped to learn something from Baram of Lon-Ser's history, believing that such information would prove useful as we search for a solution to our present crisis. Unfortunately, however, the outlander knows little about his homeland's past. He has referred on several occasions to an era known as "The Consolidation," which was, as far as I can tell, a time of civil war, lasting well over one hundred years, that resulted in the conquest of several smaller cities by the three remaining Nals. This "Consolidation" ended more than two centuries ago, and in the time since, an uneasy peace has been maintained by the surviving Nals. But that, I am sad to report, represents the sum of Baram's historical knowledge.

There is, however, one related matter that bears mentioning: Baram has spoken of a group of people known in his land as "the Gildriites," or more popularly, "the Oracles." He says that little is known about them, but based upon what he has told me, I suspect that their history may offer an unexpected and intriguing glimpse into our own past.

—From Section Six of "The Report of Owl-Master Baden on his Interrogation of the Outlander Baram," Submitted to the 1,014th Gathering of the Order of Mages and Masters. Spring, Gods' Year 4625.

 The winds had turned cold early this year, whipping through the Dhaalmar passes with a high keening that sounded like the death cry of a mountain cat. Gwilym was warm enough, lying on his pallet beneath the heavy blankets, but listening to the frenzied ruffling of the cloth shelter, he could not sleep. He could hear Hertha sleeping beside him, her calm, steady breathing seeming to defy the elements outside. And for a moment he thought about waking her, gently, with caresses and kisses, the way he had in the early years of their joining, when Nelya and Idwal were still children, and intimate moments had to be stolen in the quiet hours before dawn. But there was much preying on his mind this night, and, instead, he rose silently from the bed, put on his cloak, and wandered out into the wind and cold.

The sky was clear, save for a few small clouds that raced overhead like hawks riding the wind. Duclea's moon, a few days past full, shone brightly on the snowy peaks that surrounded the settlement, and lit the sky so that all but the brightest stars were obscured by its silvery glow. Gwilym had forgotten his staff, he realized, and he considered going back for it. Not that he needed it for anything—it was a symbol, nothing more—but he felt incomplete without it. Hertha would have thought his vanity amusing.

"Behold Gwilym, Bearer of the Stone!" she would have said, her tone mocking, but her eyes proud, "who will go nowhere without the tokens of his power!"

He smiled inwardly at his own foolishness. It was late; he was the only one up. No one would see him without it. And besides, he might wake Hertha.

So he remained where he was, on the small promontory in front of his shelter, overlooking the Gildriite settlement that he governed. The rest of the shelters nestled among the low, twisted trees and stone outcroppings of the cirque were much like his own: small, made of cloth and wood, but strong enough to withstand even the fiercest of the storms that roared through the mountains each winter. In the middle of the cirque stood the common buildings—the meeting hall and smokehouse, which were constructed of wood, and the armory, which was built entirely of stone. Along the rim of the valley, also made of stone, stood a series of guard towers, which, in all probability, housed the only other people within miles of where Gwilym stood who were awake at this hour. And below the shelters, at the base of the valley, the herd animals stood and sat in tight clusters, shielding each other from the cold.

Gwilym hadn't slept well in several days. This, in and of itself, was not that unusual for him. He had a tendency, during difficult times, to brood. Often he would forget to eat—not a bad thing given his girth—and always he would spend his nights lying awake on the pallet beside Hertha, or wandering alone through the community.

What made this night strange was that these were not especially difficult times. The weather, though cold, had been good. The summer had been bountiful, leaving them with ample food stores for the winter. His people were healthy, his family was thriving. Within the last fortnight he had received messages from Veina, Oswin, and the leaders of the other two Gildriite settlements in the Dhaalmar. All reported pretty much the same thing: the people were well, the summer had been generous, and they had heard of no ominous Seeings among those in their communities.

Gwilym himself had not had a Seeing in weeks. None at all, good or bad. That was a bit strange, but certainly not enough to cause him any alarm, not enough to explain his recent restlessness.

Hertha had sensed it in him tonight at supper. They had been alone; Nelya, of course, was in her own shelter now, hers and Quim's, and this was Idwal's night on the rim. Gwilym and Hertha had sat in silence for some time, although Gwilym had been oblivious, picking absently at his smoked meat and steamed ram's-root.

"The food's dead," Hertha finally told him, after watching him play with it for Arick-knew-how-long. "I made sure before I gave it to you."

"I know that," he had replied quickly, looking up at her. And then, seeing the wry grin on her soft, round features, he had laughed. "I'm sorry. I'm a bit preoccupied."

"You hide it well," she said, her brown eyes dancing. A moment later, though, her expression grew serious. "Have you had a Seeing?" she asked, concern in her voice. He understood. In a community populated by people who had the Sight, behavior such as his could be a troubling sign.

Gwilym had shaken his head. "No. No Seeings. Not for weeks now."

"Then what?"

He made a small helpless gesture with his fleshy hands. "I'm not certain." He hesitated. "It's a feeling really, nothing more."

She gazed at him intently. She had put down her knife and fork, and folded her hands tightly on the table. "Like something bad's going to happen?"

"Not necessarily something bad," he explained, knowing how silly it all sounded, and how frustrating his answers must have been for her. "But something important." *Something that could change our lives,* he had wanted to say. But how does one say such a thing, even when one is Bearer of the Stone? It sounded ridiculous, Gwilym knew, like the worst kind of melodrama. And yet, there it was, unspoken, but reverberating within his mind like thunder off the mountainside. Something was coming that had the potential to change their lives, and the life of every Gildriite living in Lon-Ser. Finally, after a millennium. And Gwilym couldn't even tell his wife what it was.

For as long as Gwilym had been alive, indeed, since well before the birth of his grandfather's grandfather, the Gildriites had lived in the Dhaalmar Range, far away from the violent persecution they had faced in the Nals below. Gwilym still remembered the tales his father told him, soon after his fourteenth birthday, about how Gildriite families had been hunted down by the assassins and mercenaries of Bragor and Stib Nals, and how the survivors had been forced to flee, first into the Median and Greenwater ranges, and then finally, when even those regions were not remote enough to afford them safety, into the high reaches of the Dhaalmar.

His father told him other stories as well, stories that had been passed down from generation to generation for hundreds of years. For the history of Gwilym's people consisted of more than just grief and oppression. Once, there had also been glory and power.

According to legend, Gildri led his people into Lon-Ser a thousand years ago, after they were exiled from Tobyn-Ser. Little was known about the circumstances of their banishment, but it was said that the Gildriites had mastered the Magic of the Hawk, which the sorcerers of Tobyn-Ser were purported still to wield. Some speculated that they may have been the first to do so, and that their exile resulted from Tobyn-Ser's fear of the black arts. Certainly the Gildriites met with such fear upon their arrival in Lon-Ser. When Gildri and his followers attempted to find a place for themselves in Lon-Ser, they were confronted by a hostile, suspicious people who distrusted strangers and who condemned the sorcerers' abilities as evil. So the Gildriites wandered the land, coming, eventually, to the court of the Monarch, who encouraged his Sovereigns and Overlords to hire the sorcerers as healers and advisors. The Gildriites accepted this arrangement, and so it was that their company was fractured, with at least a few sorcerers going to each of the six Nals that existed then.

For a time, they enjoyed great prestige, valued as they were by Lon-Ser's ruling elite for their powers and their ability to divine the future. But, perhaps predictably, their status and influence proved to be short-lived. The Magic of the Hawk did not exist in Lon-Ser, and after a few years, the Gildriites' powers began to diminish. All their powers, that is, except for the Sight. A few of the sorcerers, those whose employers had come to rely on their wisdom or their prescience, held on to their status for a while longer. But most of the others, Gildri among them, were cast out, and a small number, those in the service of the land's most ruthless leaders, were executed for what was seen as their betrayal. Expelled from the chambers of Lon-Ser's leaders, unwelcome in the villages they encountered, the Gildriites roamed the land once more, settling down eventually where they could, and trying, with varying degrees of success, to blend into Lon-Ser's society. For several hundred years, their story disappeared from the pages of Lon-Ser's history.

During this period, the Nals grew from loosely bound communities to large urban areas that sprawled across the land like giants. At the same time, Lon-Ser's unremitting technological advances took hold of the land's economy and culture, bringing healthy trade and riches to many across the land. But with the success and prosperity brought on by the mechanization of Lon-Ser, came as well fierce competition among the Nals that threatened on many occasions to plunge Lon-Ser into civil war. Always, though, the Monarchs managed to bring the Council of Sovereigns together and mediate an agreement that would preserve the peace. Always, that is, until a few hundred years ago.

In the year 2614, dated from the formal division of Lon-Ser into the six original Nals, Grayson, the last of the monarchs, died. Unable to agree upon a replacement, the Council of Sovereigns decided instead to do away with the Monarchy entirely. The turmoil and civil strife that followed, had come to be known euphemistically as the Consolidation. In reality, it was little more than one-hundred and sixty years of bloody, ruinous warfare.

Without a Monarch to keep their conflicts in check, the Sovereigns allowed the bickering, petty jealousies, and struggles for preeminence that had marked Council meetings, to spill over into armed confrontations that quickly spread through the land. As the violence intensified, and the Sovereigns began to realize that the very existence of their Nals might be at stake, they began to look for any advantage over their rivals that they could find. Perhaps it was inevitable then that they should seek out those people within Lon-Ser who were known to have the Sight.

Most came to believe that the men and women who manifested the Sight were descendants of the Gildriites. No one could prove it, of course, and indeed it was unlikely considering how many Gildriites there were now, and how few followers Gildri brought with him from Tobyn-Ser. But by his mere existence, Gildri had given a name to a phenomenon once thought to be rooted in the black arts. Following the lead of their superiors, Overlords, and even Nal-Lords, also sought out the Gildriites as they too struggled for power and economic gain. Thus, for the first time in over five hundred years, those people blessed with the Sight reassumed their places of influence within Lon-Ser. But as they were drawn into the intrigue and savagery of the Consolidation, the Gildriites could not hope to avoid falling prey to its excesses. They became popular assassination targets, particularly those within Bragor-Nal or in the employ of Bragor-Nal's strongest rivals. As the danger they faced grew, many Gildriites sought an escape from the Consolidation and from the downward spiral into chaos and brutality in which they found themselves. They retreated into the safety of the nearby mountains where they attempted to create their own independent societies. They maintained relations solely with the Oerella Matriarchy, which was the only one of the Nal governments that did not have a hand in the assassinations. The Gildriites did not serve Oerella-Nal, for the Matriarchy did participate fully in other atrocities of the Consolidation, and the danger of assassination still existed from the other Nals, but their ties to Oerella-Nal persisted. As a result, the leaders of the other Nals, again led by those in Bragor-Nal, grew suspicious and stepped up their persecution of those showing signs of having the Sight. Eventually, the Gilriites migrated northward, away from the southern and central mountains, to the remote high country of the Dhaalmar Range north of Oerella-Nal. There, they founded their five settlements, and carved out an existence for themselves in sheltered isolation from the cruelty and depravity of the Nals.

A cold gust of wind swirled around Gwilym, causing his cloak to flutter and snap. He had not given so much thought to the Nals and the history of his people in some time. And yet, he considered with a smile, even just now, as he had listened to the tale in his mind, he had heard the words spoken in his father's voice.

Why tonight? he wondered. And then, looking into the night sky and finding the bright stars of Arick's constellation just above the eastern horizon, Gwilym opened his arms in supplication.

"What is it that you want?" he asked. "What is it that you're trying to tell me?" Another gust of wind swept through the cirque, driving the cold air through Gwilym's cloak and causing him to shiver suddenly. The cloth of his shelter flapped in the gale, beckoning to him. Gwilym sighed. He did not always enjoy the power he had been given. Knowledge of the future was, quite often, as much a burden as a gift, and Seeings, whether promising or ominous, always left him physically and mentally drained. They came to him unbidden; he rarely went to sleep hoping for a vision. But tonight he would. He grinned in the moonlight. *If I ever go to sleep.* Taking one last glance around the settlement, Gwilym retreated into the warmth of the shelter, seeking sleep, and the knowledge that sleep sometimes brought him.

As it happened, no vision came to him that night, or the next. But on the third night, finally, Gwilym had his Seeing.

It began, as did all his Seeings, with an image of his mother and father, their hair white and thin, their faces, lined with age, but smiling. They stood before him in the cirque, and they handed him the staff that bore the stone. As always, as soon as Gwilym placed his hand on the staff, the stone changed color from the dark forest green of his father, to his own golden brown, the color of sun-dried grasses on the mountainside. And Gwilym moved the stone close to his face, staring at it until its pale glow was all that he saw. And in that moment, as usual, he was transported to the site of his vision. Sometimes he was taken to another of the settlements or to a remote region of the mountains. At other times the vision merely carried him to another part of the cirque; sometimes, he remained where he was, but the time of day shifted. On this occasion, though, he was taken somewhere he had never been before: Bragor-Nal.

He knew it was a Nal because no other place could smell as rank or feel as threatening and alien. He wasn't sure how he knew it was Bragor-Nal; he just did. He stood in a narrow passage between two immense buildings, shielding the glow of his stone from view. It was raining, and he was cold; the cloak he wore, which usually provided so much warmth in the highlands of the Dhaal-mar, seemed to do little against the damp chill of the Nal. Water from one of the buildings dripped on his bald head, each drop as hard and cold as a chip of ice. More than anything in the world, he wanted to leave, to make his way out of the Nal and back to his home in the mountains. But he was waiting for someone. A man was coming who would need his help, who would die without it.

So he huddled in the alleyway, and he waited. A nearby streetlamp, its covering cracked and partially discolored, cast a dim yellow light that glistened on the wet pavement. Gwilym heard a woman laughing in the distance and, from another direction, an angry exchange between two men.

Then he heard footsteps, light, nimble, but unmistakable. Turning toward the sound he saw a figure approaching, and he gasped in disbelief, his heart vaulting into his throat. For this could be none other than Gildri himself. Or so Gwilym thought at first. The man was wearing a cloak of forest green, finer than those worn by the Gildriites, and more elaborately detailed. He was carrying a magnificent, dark falcon on his shoulder and, in his hand, he bore a staff, similar in appearance to Gwilym's own, with an amber stone that resembled the Bearer's golden brown crystal. The stranger was muscular, broad in the chest and shoulders, and he moved with grace, as would one who believed strongly in himself and in his abilities. He had a closely cropped beard and long golden hair that he wore tied back. His eyes were dark, and they surveyed his surroundings warily, though seemingly without fear.

Surely, Gwilym told himself, this must be Gildri. But another voice within the Gildriite's head, the one that was watching the vision from the pallet in his Dhaalmar shelter, said no. This was a Seeing, and so it must have been true. And as much as Gwilym would have relished the chance to meet the legend, the namesake of his people, he knew that this could not be. Besides, the old tales spoke of Gildri as being dark-haired and wiry, with a pale bird.

No, this was a living man, a stranger to Lon-Ser. Like Gildri before him, he wielded the Magic of the Hawk, but there the similarities ended. Again, the sleeping Gwilym corrected himself. There was another similarity as well, one that he recognized several nights ago as he ate supper with Hertha, although at the time he didn't fully understand. This man, like Gildri, carried within him the power to remake Lon-Ser's history, and to change forever the lives of Gildri's followers. Realizing this, watching the man move toward him through the passageway, Gwilym felt hope flower within his chest like aster and lupine blooming in the Dhaalmar meadows beneath a summer sun.

In the very next instant, however, he felt terror grip his heart as though it were death's hand ripping the blossoms from the earth. Two men suddenly appeared in the alley, seeming to materialize out of the night itself. And in perfect unison, with an elegance so frightening and deadly that it was almost beautiful, each pulled a weapon from his long overcoat, aimed it at the stranger, and fired.

Gwilym awoke with a violent start, his face soaked with sweat, and his limbs trembling. A single candle illuminated the shelter, and Hertha sat on the pallet beside him, stroking his brow tenderly. He tried to sit up, but she shook her head and gently held him down.

"Rest," she whispered. "Don't try to move yet. You were dreaming for a long time."

Gwilym closed his eyes, swallowed, and nodded. "Some water?" he managed in a choked voice.

A moment later, Hertha helped him sit up slightly and held a cup of cool water to his lips. He drank deeply and then settled back onto the pallet. Opening his eyes again, Gwilym saw that she was watching him closely, her soft features etched uncharacteristically with worry.

"This was the Seeing you've been waiting for." She offered it as a statement.

"Yes."

"Do you know what it means?" She was keeping a tight hold on her emotions, as if she feared her reactions to what he was about to say. He was not used to seeing her so troubled, and it heightened his own apprehension.

"I think so," he replied carefully.

"And is it good, this future you've seen?"

Gwilym said nothing, but he took her hand and laced his fingers through hers. For a long time, neither of them said anything.

"There's a man coming," he finally told her. "I think he's from Tobyn-Ser." Her eyes widened. "Tobyn-Ser? You're certain?"

"He carries a bird, and a staff like mine."

"A sorcerer!" she breathed.

"Yes," Gwilym agreed. "I don't know why he's coming—I didn't see that— but I believe his arrival portends great things for our people."

Hertha nodded, a look of wonder still in her eyes. "A sorcerer!" she repeated. "And he's coming here!"

Gwilym took a breath. This would be the hard part. "No, Hertha. Not here."

She stared at him. "But you said—"

"I said a man was coming from Tobyn-Ser, but I didn't say that he was coming here." He hesitated. There was no easy way to tell her. "I saw him in Bragor-Nal."

Her face blanched. "You were there as well?"

"I have to be, Hertha. I saw two men trying to kill him." Gwilym sat up abruptly. Too abruptly. His head spun sickeningly, but he forced himself to go on. "I don't know if they succeed or not. I woke up too soon. But I know that I have to be there, to help him if I can."

Hertha stood and turned away from him. He guessed that she was crying; she always turned away when she did. "How can you be sure that this man is so important?" she demanded, her voice quavering. "Maybe you're wrong about him! Maybe he means nothing to us!" She faced him again. There were tears on her cheeks. "Or maybe he will change our lives, but for the worse! Maybe he's meant to die! Did you consider that?"

"Hertha," he said, as gently as he could, holding out a hand to her. Reluctantly, she stepped forward and took it. "He's a sorcerer," Gwilym reminded her, "like Gildri was. He's coming to Lon-Ser, and two men are going to try to kill him. Don't you think the gods have shown me this for a reason?"

She would not meet his gaze, but after a moment she nodded once. "How soon?" she asked.

"I don't know. Soon. It was still cold, although it seemed that the worst of the winter had passed." He still surprised himself with the things he learned from his Seeings. He hadn't given the time of year much thought, except to note that he was cold and the pavement was wet. But somehow he knew that what he had seen took place in early spring. Which meant that he had to leave very soon indeed. He had many hundreds of miles to cover.

"You should begin preparing in the morning," she told him, her dark eyes meeting his. "With winter coming you'll be hard pressed to reach the Nal by early spring."

"You're probably right."

Again, silence descended on the shelter and they gazed at each other in the candlelight. *How can I leave her?* he asked himself. And then, remembering his vision and all that it might mean, he answered his own question. *I am Bearer of the Stone. How can I not?*

"We should sleep," Hertha offered, "but suddenly I'm not very tired."

He smiled at her and raised an eyebrow. "You're not?"

She grinned shyly, and then laughed, although tears were falling from her eyes again. "No," she said softly, blowing out the candle, "I'm not."

Gwilym and Hertha remained in bed late into the morning, unwilling to leave the comfort of each other's arms. Even after they rose, as they made their preparations for Gwilym's departure the following day, they remained together, refusing to be separated for any more time than was absolutely necessary. They gathered food for his journey—cheeses, smoked meats, dried roots and fruit, and dry breads—and placed them in his shoulder pack along with five or six lengths of rope, several flints, a few water skins, extra clothing, and a sturdy sleeping roll. Gwilym also helped Hertha bring in the last of the autumn harvest from their plot at the base of the valley. It was a bit early still for some of the roots, but it would have been a difficult task for Hertha to do alone. Late in the day, they went with Idwal to find Nelya and Quim, and the five of them enjoyed one last family meal together.

Just before dusk, Gwilym walked to the meeting hall and rang the bell that was mounted outside, summoning the entire settlement. No one who had seen him during the course of the day could have any doubt that he was preparing to leave the cirque, and news traveled swiftly through the settlement. But he still felt it necessary to announce formally that he would be leaving, and to offer as much explanation as he could. He also knew that in his absence, the settlement would need an interim leader, and that his departure would raise a somewhat sensitive issue, one that he would have to deal with carefully, but firmly.

With the sound of the bell still echoing off the mountainside, Gwilym entered the hall, took his customary place at the front of the room, and waited. Within a few moments those who lived closest to the center of the village began to arrive. They came in wordlessly, eyeing Gwilym with unconcealed curiosity. Usually meetings were preceded by laughter and conversations about the day's events. But not tonight. No one had left the settlement in years, except for the messengers who travelled to the other encampments, and those who watched over the herds in the warmer months. No Bearer of the Stone had left the village in Gwilym's lifetime. So he watched them enter the room, and he allowed them their silence and their stares.

Hertha, Nelya, and Idwal were among the last to arrive, and as they came in, Gwilym saw that Hertha had been crying again. That was all right, he told himself. It was understandable, and it eased his mind to know that Idwal and Nelya would be here to take care of her.

"I believe we're all here, Gwilym," came a voice from the back of the room. Urias's voice. Gwilym spotted the young man leaning against the back wall, his height allowing him to see over the rest, his pale green eyes fixed on Gwilym's face. Urias had been speaking for the younger Gildriites for some time now. He would make a good leader someday. Gwilym smiled to himself. Perhaps sooner than that; perhaps tonight if the settlement chose him.

"Thank you, Urias," Gwilym said aloud. He let out a slow breath, and surveyed the familiar faces arrayed before him. On the front bench, he saw old Emlyn watching him with rheumy eyes, her mouth opened in what he might have taken for a toothless grin had he not known that she always looked like that now. She had been with Gwilym's mother when Gwilym was born, and had attended the birth of just about every other person in the room. Next to her sat Hertha, and with her Nelya, Quim, and Idwal. Farther back he saw Siarl, his childhood friend, who stood with Gwilym at his joining to Hertha, and who, a few years later, risked his own life to save Nelya's when she wandered too far from the settlement just before the onset of a sudden, violent storm. These were his people, the only people he had ever really known. He had celebrated their joinings and the births of their children. He had grieved with them at the loss of their parents and spouses and siblings. Every day of his life had been inextricably bound with every day of theirs. And now he was going to leave them? Gwilym shrunk from the very idea of it. He felt a wave of nausea pass over him.

"I'm not sure where to begin," he told them candidly.

"Tell us why, Gwilym," Siarl suggested gently. "Why are you leaving us?"

"Yes," someone else called out. "What have you Seen?"

Gwilym nodded. That was as good a place as any. "There is a man who has come to Bragor-Nal—or rather who will be coming. His life is in danger."

"Isn't that true of every man in Bragor-Nal?" Urias asked. "And every woman and child, too?"

Gwilym smiled briefly. "Yes, of course. But this is a man of great importance to us. He is a sorcerer from Tobyn-Ser." Widened eyes and whispers of amazement met his words, but Gwilym was gazing at Hertha, wondering if this really was important enough to justify what he was doing.

Urias took a step away from the wall, the curiosity manifest on his sharp, bony features giving him a hawklike appearance. "Why is he coming?" he asked.

"I wish I knew," Gwilym replied. "But I'm certain that his arrival in Lon-Ser presages great changes for our people. That's why I can't just allow him to be killed. I have to do something."

"But Bragor-Nal, Gwilym," Siarl said. "Isn't there some other way you can help this man without going there?" Several of the others nodded their agreement.

"I wish there was, my friend. Believe me, I wish there was. But I don't know what it might be, so this is the only course left to me."

"In that case," Quim demanded, "will you at least allow some of us to go with you?" Again, several of the others signalled their agreement and offered to make the journey with him.

Gwilym found himself fighting to hold back tears. These were his people. Not for the first time, he remarked to himself that Nelya had found a good man in Quim. He smiled at her, hoping she would understand.

He held up his hands to quiet the room. "Thank you, friends. It would be an easier journey and a far more pleasant one were I to take even one of you with me. But I cannot."

Several people began to protest, Urias and Siarl most vehemently. "We had a good summer, Gwilym," Quim argued, drawing nods from the others. "A few of us can be spared to make the journey."

Once more Gwilym raised his hands. "We did have a good summer," he agreed, raising his voice to force them to listen, "and, thus far, the autumn harvest has gone well. But winter has a way of deciding on its own what we will need and what we won't. I needn't tell any of you that a good summer carries no promise of an easy winter, and the winds have already begun to turn cold."

He shook his head. "No," he told them with finality. "I am still Bearer of the Stone, and this is still my decision. We would risk too much by sending a group. I have to go alone; that way we risk only me." This last, he knew, was not entirely true.

Naturally, it was Urias who broached the issue. "Will you be taking the stone, Gwilym?"

"Of course he will!" Hertha broke in before Gwilym could respond. "We selected him to be Bearer! It's his to take if he chooses!"

The younger man held up his hands in a placating gesture. "I meant no disrespect, Hertha," he told her, and then looking at Gwilym, he added, "Honestly."

"I know that, Urias," Gwilym assured him. He glanced at Hertha with an expression that told her to behave herself. She had never liked Urias. She saw him as impertinent, and she often felt that he was too quick to challenge the decisions Gwilym made in his capacity as leader of the settlement. In truth, she may have been right. But Gwilym chose to view these traits in a more favorable light. Urias might someday bear the stone himself, and a future leader needed to have strong opinions. Siarl once told him that some of the older Gildriites thought Gwilym arrogant in the years before he became Bearer, and though Gwilym was hurt when Siarl first told him, he soon realized that the elders had probably been justified in their feelings.

Moreover, on this particular matter, Urias's concerns were probably warranted. Gwilym would be traveling a long way to a very dangerous place. The chances of his returning, he knew, were no better than even. And the stone was the single most valuable and important item in the settlement. It was, Gwilym had to admit, more important to the village than any one person, even its Bearer. After all, it was one of the original stones carried from Tobyn-Ser by Gildri and his followers. There were only five of them left. Each settlement had one, mounted still on the staves that Gildri and his fellow sorcerers had handled. As leader of the settlement, as Bearer of the Stone, Gwilym was responsible for its care. For much of the day he had grappled with the question of whether he had the right to take it with him. True, they had chosen him to be Bearer, but it belonged to the village, not to him.

Which was exactly the point that Urias was trying to make at that very moment. "The stone has been in this cirque since before any of our grandparents were born," the young man was saying. "Its Bearers have brought to it more colors than we can even imagine. It's part of who we are. I don't mean to question your judgement, Gwilym, or your authority. But—and I'm sorry to say this so bluntly, Hertha—you might not return, and then the stone would be lost forever."

Several of the others shouted for Urias to be quiet. "You're tempting the gods!" Siarl told him angrily, his dark eyes flashing beneath thick silver hair. "Gwilym will be fine, and so will your precious stone!"

"May your words find their way into your dreams, my friend," Gwilym said, looking at Siarl with an appreciative grin. "But Urias is right: I might not return, and the stone might be lost." A tense stillness spread through the hall as the others fell silent and regarded him expectantly. "I've thought about this quite a bit," he went on. "And I believe one could make a case either way. On the one hand, the stone belongs to all of us; it belongs to this settlement. But it also belongs with its Bearer, and I may need it to convince the sorcerer that I'm a friend, and that I can help him."

Urias nodded curtly. "So you've decided to take it," he said accusingly.

Gwilym tightened his jaw. Enough was enough. "Yes," he replied with finality, "I've decided to take it, as is my right as leader of this settlement. But if you must know, Urias, this was not a decision I came to alone. In the vision sent to me by the gods, I was carrying the stone. Apparently they deem it important that I take it with me."

"That's all the convincing I need," Siarl commented quickly. Most of the others voiced their agreement as well, and Urias, seeming to realize that he was badly outnumbered, backed down.

"Well, with that decided," Gwilym began again a few moments later, reasserting his control over the meeting, "the only question left before us is who will lead you while I'm gone?"

"Who do you suggest?" Quim asked.

Gwilym shook his head and grinned. "Oh, no," he said. "I'm not going down that path."

"Coward!" Hertha called out to general laughter. She stood. "What about Siarl?" she suggested. "I think he'd do very nicely."

Siarl's face reddened, and he smiled somewhat sheepishly. But he said nothing to discourage the idea and, though two other names were mentioned by others as possible candidates, in the end, the villagers chose Siarl.

"This is not a position I want for any length of time," he told Gwilym later, after the meeting was over, as the two of them stepped out of the meeting hall and into the chill wind of another clear night. The others were already gone. Hertha had returned to the shelter. She'd be waiting up for him, Gwilym knew. But he had wanted a bit of time to say good-bye to Siarl. "I'm very happy with things as they are right now," Siarl added.

"I know," Gwilym returned, pulling his cloak tight around himself as they walked. He could not remember a colder autumn. Or perhaps he was just growing older, and less inured to the elements. *Am I up to this journey?* he asked himself, not for the first time.

Siarl, Gwilym realized, was speaking again. He had no idea what his friend had said. Siarl reached out and took hold of Gwilym's arm, stopping him. "Gwilym, are you all right?"

Gwilym nodded and tried to smile. "I'm fine. This is difficult for me. Leaving Hertha, leaving the settlement. I'm sorry what were you saying?"

Siarl dismissed the apology with a wave of his hand. "Never mind that." He paused. "Are you frightened?"

"Very," Gwilym answered honestly. "Look at me, Siarl," he went on, indicating his ample waistline with a wave of his chubby hand. "I'm no adventurer; I'm certainly no fighter. And yet I'm going down to the most dangerous place in Lon-Ser to save the life of a man who wields a power that I can scarcely fathom. Am I crazy?"

His friend allowed himself a small laugh. "You're a lot of things, Gwilym, but crazy isn't one of them. In all the years I've known you, you've never done anything reckless. And given that you seem to be dreading what you're about to do, I'd guess that deep down you don't feel that you have a choice."

Gwilym passed a hand over his bare head. "No, I don't."

"On the other hand, though," Siarl added, looking at Gwilym closely, the wind ruffling his silver hair, "you still have time to change your mind about taking someone with you."

"I can't do that," Gwilym said.

"Why not?"

"I told you before, during the meeting."

Siarl shook his head fiercely. "That's not good enough, Gwilym! It might be a hard winter? We'll need everyone here?" He shook his head a second time. "That may satisfy the others, but it's not enough for me!"

"I'm afraid it will have to be!" Gwilym replied sharply.

He started to walk away, but Siarl grabbed his arm again and pulled him around so that they stood facing each other again. "Take me with you!" Siarl insisted. "Or if not me, Quim or Urias! Take Emlyn for all I care! But don't do this alone!"

Gwilym closed his eyes and took a breath. "I have to," he replied, the energy sapped from his voice.

"Why?"

He opened his eyes again. Siarl's expression was pained.

"In my Seeing, I was alone," Gwilym said. This was true, but it was meant only to postpone telling Siarl the truth. Siarl knew him too well.

"But that's not the reason."

"No, it's not." He took a breath. "I dreamed of the sorcerer and I saw two men trying to kill him. But I awoke too soon. I don't know if I can save him." He swallowed. "And I don't know if I'm going to survive the attempt."

"All the more reason to take one of us with you!" Siarl said.

Gwilym shook his head slowly. "I don't think another Gildriite or two will make a difference, and I'm not willing to risk your life or Quim's." He grinned. "Or even Urias's."

Siarl gave a small laugh, but quickly grew serious again. "Don't you think that's a decision we should make?" he asked.

"No, my friend. I think it's a decision a Bearer must make. And I would ask you to respect that."

Siarl looked at Gwilym for a long time, saying nothing. Finally he let out a long breath. "All right," he said. "But isn't there anything I can do?"

Gwilym nodded. "Yes, there is." He hesitated, but only for a moment. "Take care of her for me, Siarl," he whispered. "Take care of Hertha." And suddenly, finally, he was crying, letting go of all the fear and sadness that he had kept under tight control since his Seeing.

"I will," his friend managed to say, his voice unsteady. "All of us will."

They stood there in awkward silence for several moments. Then Gwilym pulled Siarl to his chest in a hard embrace, and held him there for a long time. Finally, reluctantly, he released his hold on his friend, and without another word, he turned and made his way back to the shelter where Hertha waited for him.

Gwilym departed the next morning, just as the sun appeared from behind the jagged, ice-covered peaks to the east. He and Hertha had not slept at all, and after a night of lovemaking and tears, both of them were too exhausted and numb to expend much emotion on their farewell.

"Do whatever it is that you have to do," she said quietly, as he held her in the cold morning air, "and then come home to me. Don't try to change history yourself. Leave that to the sorcerer."

"Aren't I allowed any heroics at all?" he asked, trying to keep his tone light.

"No," she answered, pulling back so that he could see her face. Her brown eyes, red from crying and lack of sleep, showed no hint of mirth. "No heroics. I don't want a hero, I just want you."

He nodded, feeling the tears fall from his own eyes again, but he said nothing. There was nothing really that he could say. So he kissed her deeply one last time, and then he left her and began his long journey to Bragor-Nal.

Gwilym had planned originally to follow the small brook that flowed out of the cirque all the way down to the bottom of the valley. From there, he would have followed the larger stream into which it flowed to West Fools Lake, and the beginning of the west fork of the mighty Vrudan River. But given how tired he was from his sleepless night, he decided instead to make his way to Oswin's settlement, which lay just a day's walk to the southeast of his own village. There, he might get one final home-cooked meal and a night in a comfortable bed. He would also be able to stick to the high country for a few days longer and follow a series of passes down to Middle Fools Lake and the Vrudan's main branch. It was a slightly more strenuous route, but a more direct one. And, for a number of reasons, he felt that he should speak with Oswin before he left the Dhaalmar.

The skies remained clear throughout the day, and, with just a light wind blowing cold from the north, Gwilym was able to make good time, arriving at Oswin's village more than an hour before dusk. The young guard who greeted him at the outer wall recognized him immediately, aided no doubt by the glowing stone mounted atop Gwilym's staff, and he led him to Oswin's shelter, which like Gwilym's, sat at the top of the cirque. The guard went to inform Oswin that he had a visitor, leaving Gwilym to survey his surroundings. In most respects this settlement resembled his own. Its cloth shelters and common buildings lay in a large cirque that faced south, to maximize the amount of sun it received in the colder months. Guard towers stood at regular intervals along the rim of the basin, and herd animals grazed among the deep grasses at its base.

Indeed, the only significant difference between this settlement and Gwilym's was their relative sizes. Oswin's village was by far the largest of the five Gildriite settlements. Or, more accurately, it was the most populous. It was home to nearly twice as many people as lived in Gwilym's village, and, though this cirque was larger than the one Gwilym had left that morning, it was not that much larger. Everything seemed more crowded here: the shelters were closer together; smoke from the many cooking fires mingled into an unrecognizable amalgam of aromas; and the sounds of children shouting and parents calling for their offspring filled the cirque. It was not, Gwilym thought to himself, the kind of lifestyle he would of chosen for himself. An irony, given where he was going.

"Gwilym!" came a voice from behind him. "To what do I owe this unexpected pleasure?"

Gwilym turned in time to see Oswin emerging from his shelter carrying his turquoise stone and a cup of mulled wine. Oswin was a tall man, and solidly built, but though his face retained its familiar ruddy complexion, he seemed to have aged a good deal in the year since Gwilym had last seen him. Of the five Bearers who currently led the Gildriite settlements, Oswin had carried his stone the longest, making him, in a sense, the leader of all the Gildriites. Though he didn't know for certain, Gwilym guessed that Oswin was at least fifteen years his senior. Perhaps more. It should have come as no surprise then that Oswin stood more stooped than Gwilym remembered, and that his hair had thinned and grown white. The older man was still quick to smile though, and his bright blue eyes still looked clear and alert.

"It's good to see you, Oswin," Gwilym said, stepping forward and grasping the Bearer's shoulders in greeting. Gwilym indicated Oswin's cup of wine with a nod of his head. "I hope I'm not interrupting your supper."

"Not at all," Oswin replied with a grin. "Breatta and I were just celebrating the completion of our autumn harvest. Can I offer you a cup?"

"Yes, thank you. I'd like that."

"Breatta, my love!" Oswin called to the shelter. "We have a visitor! Could you bring out another cup of wine?"

"Right away!" came a musical voice from within.

"Shouldn't you be home, doing some harvesting of your own?" the Bearer asked, turning back to Gwilym. "Or have you left all the hard work for Hertha?"

Gwilym tried to muster a smile, although he felt a painful twisting in his heart at the mention of Hertha's name. Oswin seemed to notice, for his smile vanished, and a look of concern crept into his eyes. Before he could ask any questions, however, Breatta came out of the shelter with the wine, and seeing Gwilym, she grinned broadly.

"Gwilym! What a lovely surprise!" she said, coming forward to embrace him lightly before handing him the steaming cup of wine. Like Oswin, Breatta had aged some in the past year. She had always been petite, but she looked almost frail now, and her auburn hair was streaked with silver. Still, she remained an attractive woman, with delicate features and pale green eyes. She glanced around briefly, before looking at Gwilym again. "Is Hertha with you?"

Gwilym looked away. "No, I'm afraid not. She sends her regards to both of you though." A half-truth: she would have had she known Gwilym intended to stop here.

The three of them stood without speaking for several moments, sipping their wine and looking around the cirque until their silence began to grow awkward.

"Perhaps I should leave you two alone for a time," Breatta offered at last. "I'll see if I can conjure up some supper out of all those lovely roots and greens that we brought in today." She smiled at Gwilym. "You will stay for supper, won't you?"

"I'd be honored, Breatta," he replied.

"We may want to pull out the spare pallet as well, my dear," Oswin chimed in. "I expect our friend here would like a place to sleep tonight. Am I right?"

Gwilym laughed in spite of himself. "I'm afraid so. I guess traveling friends tend to be burdens, don't they?"

"Nonsense!" Breatta scoffed, starting back toward the shelter. "It's our pleasure, Gwilym. And don't let my grouch of a husband tell you anything different!"

An instant later, the two Bearers were alone.

"Thank you, Oswin," Gwilym said taking another sip of wine. "You and Breatta have always been kind to me."

Oswin smiled, although the look in his bright eyes remained serious. "She's right: it is our pleasure. But you've piqued my curiosity. Where are you headed with such a full pack this close to winter?"

Gwilym had forgotten about the pack he carried, but at its mention, he became aware again of its weight. Handing his cup to Oswin, he swung the pack off his shoulders, and immediately felt the cold air reach his sweat-soaked back. "It's not quite as heavy as it looks," Gwilym commented, glancing at the older man who was waiting patiently for an answer to his question. "But it feels good to take it off."

"I don't doubt it," Oswin returned, giving Gwilym his cup once more.

Gwilym took a long breath. "I'm on my way to Bragor-Nal," he said. "I've had a Seeing that leads me to believe that I have no other choice."

To his credit, Oswin gave no outward reaction other than a slight raising of his eyebrows. "Tell me what you saw."

Relieved in a way to be discussing his vision with someone who had little emotional stake in his decision to leave the Dhaalmar, Gwilym described his Seeing in extensive detail. Again, Oswin offered little reaction as he listened, other than to ask an occasional question or request that Gwilym repeat something. They walked as they spoke, making a small circle around the upper portion of the settlement and returning to Oswin's shelter just as Gwilym completed his account.

"I thought that you should know where I was going and why," Gwilym concluded as they stopped again in front of the shelter. "I didn't have time before leaving to dispatch messengers to you and the other Bearers. Perhaps you could inform them for me?"

Oswin nodded. "Certainly. I agree that such a Seeing demands action," he remarked. "And, given what you saw, I can't see that you have much choice either. If I were in your position—and if I were a few years younger—I'd be going, too."

Gwilym gave a small smile. "I'm relieved to hear you say that," he answered sincerely. "If you were in my position, would you be taking the stone?"

Oswin inclined his head slightly. "A more difficult matter." He paused for several moments, as if turning the question over in his mind. "Probably," he said at last, "since it appeared in the Seeing. But I'd have some qualms about it, just as you seem to."

"Some in my settlement thought it an unnecessary risk," Gwilym explained. "I'd been unsure even before that, but it didn't help."

"Let me guess," Oswin said with a smirk. "Urias?"

Gwilym laughed and nodded.

"I thought so." They laughed for a few seconds longer. Then the tall Bearer's mirth subsided and he regarded the younger man closely. "It is a risk, Gwilym. I don't need to tell you that. I think you're right to take it, but if you want to change your mind, you can leave it here. I'll take it back to your people personally."

"Thank you," Gwilym told him, "but I'll stick with my original decision."

Oswin nodded. "Good for you." He paused, as if considering something. "Have you ever heard of the Network?" he finally asked.

"The Network," Gwilym repeated. "No."

"I hadn't either," the tall man admitted with a grin. "At least not until early this summer. Come with me," he added, starting down toward the center of the cirque. "There's someone I think you should meet."

Gwilym followed the Bearer through the center of the village to the lower fringe of the settlement, just above the herd animals' grazing land. There they found a small, new-looking shelter and, sitting beside it, tending a cooking fire, a large, muscular man with long, unruly blond hair. He smiled when he saw Oswin approaching, although the warmth on his features never reached his hard blue eyes. He glanced briefly at Gwilym, but his expression revealed nothing.

"Hello, Kham!" Oswin called out as the two Bearers drew nearer to the big man's home. "I hope we're not intruding."

"Not at all, Oswin," the man returned. He did not seem to raise his voice, but the words carried clearly in the open air. "I was just preparing my supper. Join me?"

"Thank you, no," Oswin replied. "Breatta's expecting us." He indicated Gwilym with a gesture. "Kham, this is Gwilym. He's the Bearer at the nearest settlement."

The stranger stood and grasped Gwilym's hand in a powerful grip although he reached across his body with his left hand to do so. His right hand was scarred and badly mangled. He did not appear to have use of it.

"Kham came to us earlier this summer," Oswin explained as the man sat back down. "Prior to that, he had lived all his life in Bragor-Nal. He had been passing as what they call a break-law, but he has demonstrated beyond anyone's doubt that he has the Sight. From what he says, there are many like him down there." Oswin turned to Kham. "Gwilym here is on his way to Bragor-Nal, and I was hoping that you might give him some information about the Network."

Kham looked at Gwilym again, more intently this time, as if he was gauging what he saw against some invisible standard. "Have you ever been to the Nal before?" he demanded.

Gwilym shook his head.

"I take it you have good reasons for doing this."

"Yes, he does," Oswin broke in before Gwilym could respond. "I'd appreciate any help that you could give him, Kham."

The big man hesitated, seeming to consider this. After a moment he nodded. "The Network operates in all the Nals," he began, turning to Gwilym. "But it's most active in Bragor-Nal, because the hatred of us Oracles is the greatest there. Mostly it offers us a place where we're welcome, and where we don't have to hide who we are. But it also offers protection to those who have been exposed, and aid to those, like me, who want to get out of the Nal altogether."

"How many Gildriites are in Bragor-Nal?" Gwilym asked him.

Kham shrugged. "There are lots of us. Tens of thousands, I'd guess." Gwilym's eyes widened, and the man gave a smirk. "It sounds more impressive than it is," he said. "Here it would be a lot, but in the Nal that's not many."

Gwilym swallowed and nodded. It occurred to him that he probably wasn't prepared for what he was going to encounter once he left the Dhaalmar.

"How will Gwilym find the Network?" Oswin asked.

Kham regarded Gwilym again. "You going dressed like that?"

"Yes."

"Then don't worry: they'll find you. That is if SovSec doesn't first."

"SovSec?"

"The Sovereign's Security Force." Kham stared into the fire, a haunted look in his eyes. And Gwilym noticed that he absently massaged his maimed hand. "They're not very good at keeping the peace," he said bitterly, "but they excel at torture. And they seem to take special pleasure in hurting Gildriites."

"We'd like to keep that from happening to Gwilym," Oswin said gently. "Can you help us?"

Again, Kham hesitated. Then, abruptly, he stood and went into his shelter. He emerged a moment later carrying some maps, printed on the most refined paper Gwilym had ever seen. He knelt, and spread them out on the ground in front of the two Bearers.

"The first thing you'll want to do," Kham told Gwilym, "is contact the Network in Oerella-Nal. Things are quieter there, safer, but you'll still be better off crossing through under their cover." He pointed to a spot he had marked on the map of Oerella-Nal near where the Deep Canyon River first entered the Nal. "That's where you'll be most likely to find them. They'll get you to the Median Range, tell you which of the passes to take through the mountains, and where to go once you reach Bragor-Nal. Understand?"

Gwilym nodded. "Yes," he said, realizing that Kham was still surveying the maps.

"You can take these if you like," Kham added. "I've got others, and I don't think I'll be needing them again anyway."

He looked over his shoulder and smiled briefly at Oswin, before fixing his gaze on Gwilym once more. "I'm not going to lie to you: You're going to a dangerous place. I was happy to get out of there alive. You sure you want to do this?"

Gwilym smiled grimly. "Actually, I'm sure I don't. But I've had a Seeing that tells me I must. As one who's also blessed with the Sight, I'm sure you understand."

"Actually, I haven't learned to trust my Sight yet," Kham admitted. "At least not that much."

"It takes time," Gwilym assured him. "I wouldn't have done this when I was your age. Which is too bad since I'm probably too old to be doing it now."

Kham laughed, as did Oswin.

"Is there anything else you can tell us, Kham?" the older Bearer asked. "Anything else Gwilym should know?"

The big man shook his head. "The maps should help some, but other than that you'll have to trust the people from the Network. We used to change our routes and meeting sites several times each season to keep the security goons guessing. Chances are, nothing I can tell you will be worth anything. Except for the Deep Canyon location. That stays relatively stable in case people like me decide they want to go back in. If you make it to there, you should be all right."

Gwilym nodded. "I'll try. Thank you, Kham."

Kham folded the maps, rose, and handed them to Gwilym. "You're welcome. Travel safely, Bearer. Arick guard you."

Oswin grasped the big man's arm momentarily, and then the Bearers turned and made their back up the cirque to Oswin and Breatta's shelter.

They found Breatta waiting for them with dinner already prepared. It was a pleasant meal, although, Gwilym remarked to himself, not nearly as flavorful as the suppers he and Hertha used to cook together. This thought, naturally, brought on a profound bout of homesickness, and, soon after the three of them finished eating, Gwilym made some excuse about his need to get an early start, and went off to bed.

Once there though, the Bearer lay awake for some time. And despite the fact that he missed Hertha terribly, he found himself thinking mostly about his conversation with Kham. Notwithstanding the big man's words of caution, Gwilym was heartened to learn of the Network and relieved to have a better knowledge of the Nals. For the first time since having his vision, Gwilym truly believed that he could survive the journey and find the stranger in time. There were Gildriites down there, men and women like him, who might understand the importance of what he had seen in his dream, and the urgency of his mission to save the life of the yellow-haired sorcerer.

9

Many times have I presented my arguments against an overly ambitious response to the atrocities committed by Lon-Ser's invaders. I need not repeat them here. That they have prevailed time and time again is proof enough of their cogency. I do feel compelled, however, to comment on the disturbing suggestion, offered at this summer's Gathering, that Baram might somehow serve as a credential to be offered to the leaders of Lon-Ser by our envoys, should we be foolish enough to send any. I should not have to remind those who support this appalling idea that the outlander committed the most heinous crimes against this land and its people. To suggest that he be allowed to go free and return to his homeland dishonors the memory of Jessamyn, Peredur, Niall, and every other man, woman, and child who died as a direct or indirect result of his villainy. The citizens of Tobyn-Ser rest easier at night knowing that the outlander is imprisoned, and they will rest easier still when he is finally put to death, as he should have been long ago.

> —From "A Response to the Report of Owl-Master Baden on his Interrogation of the Outlander Baram," Submitted by Owl-Master Erland, Autumn, God's Year 4625.

He was in over his head. Way over.

It hadn't taken him very long to figure it out, although for the first week or two he had been loath to admit it to himself. There was, after all, nothing he could do about it; there was no one he could turn to for help, and there was no way he could think of to undo what he had done. Certainly he couldn't go back; he couldn't just return Baram to the prison and say, "Sorry, I shouldn't have taken him, but I really didn't know how mad he was." As Orris saw it he had only two alternatives: he could kill the outlander and continue on to Lon-Ser alone, or he could do everything in his power to keep Baram from hurting himself, or Orris, or anyone else, and hope that, with time, Baram's freedom would begin to heal his mind. He chose the latter, though only after a good deal of deliberation.

He should have known what he was getting into that first night at the prison. He should have seen it in the way the guards flinched at any sudden movements that Baram made; he should have heard it in the tension that lay behind the jokes they made about the outlander's erratic behavior. And maybe he should have given more thought to the meaning behind Baram's strange repetitive chanting. On some level, he realized, he had known, but he had convinced himself that he could handle it. *It's just from being in that cell for so long,* he had told himself, and he probably was right. But that didn't make it any less of a problem.

Things went fairly smoothly for the first day and a half. Even after his bath, Baram had been somewhat reluctant to leave the prison—this, too, should have told Orris something—but once they got moving, the novelty of traveling outdoors by night seemed to distract him. True, their pace was much too slow as far as Orris was concerned. He had never been a patient man and, on this night, he had reason to be nervous. But after four years in a tiny prison cell, the outlander was in terrible physical shape. Not only did he lack the strength and endurance necessary for prolonged travel, but he also was hampered by the ugly sores that covered the soles of his feet. Orris would have healed these, but the outlander would not allow the Hawk-Mage to touch him, or even to get close to him. Nonetheless, they did manage to put some distance between themselves and the prison, beginning the slow ascent through Hawksfind Wood into the foothills of the Parneshome Mountains.

As the eastern sky began to brighten, however, Baram insisted that they stop. Or, more accurately, he simply halted and resisted the Hawk-Mage's every attempt to make him move again. Instead, the man stood facing the rising sun, his eyes closed and his arms held rigid by his side, his palms turned toward the light. Orris tried to convince him to move, initially with reason and then, when that failed, with shouted threats. But railing at him did no good. The mage attempted to carry him, but Baram wrenched himself out of the burly man's grip, just as he had the night before in the prison cell, and then assumed his stance once again. Finally Orris gave up, hoping that whatever it was the outlander was doing would pass quickly, and taking the opportunity to eat a small meal.

Hearing the rustling of Orris's food pack, Baram seemed suddenly less single-minded than he had a moment before. He stared longingly at the dried meat and cheese that the Hawk-Mage was eating, and even took a hesitant step in Orris's direction. An instant later, though, he turned his attention back to the climbing sun, raising his head slightly and thrusting out his chest as if trying to absorb the warmth and light through every part of his body. Baram stood that way for several minutes as the sun rose higher into the sky, until abruptly he opened his eyes, shook his body slightly, like an animal shaking out his fur after a swim, and approached Orris, his hand outstretched and his eyes wide.

"Now you're hungry, eh?" the mage said with a smirk.

The outlander nodded earnestly and Orris handed him the pouches of food. Immediately the man sat down on the ground and began digging frantically into the bags, shoving handfuls of meat, cheese, and dried fruit into his mouth.

"Hey!," Orris shouted, grabbing the bags away from him. "Slow down, Outlander! You'll eat everything we've got!"

Baram glared at him angrily, as he continued to chew what he had managed to take, but he made no effort to get the pouches back as Orris put them into his cloak pockets.

"Let's go," the mage commanded, indicating with a curt gesture that Baram should stand up. "We've wasted too much time as it is."

Baram stood slowly and began shambling down the path as Orris fell in behind him. And for the rest of the day they continued their slow but steady climb into the mountains. Fortunately, despite their frustratingly slow pace, the outlander did seem genuinely grateful to be out of the prison. He spent most of the day gazing avidly at the sky and the landscape, drinking in the vistas the way parched soil soaks up a midsummer rain. When they rested, he lay on the ground, his eyes closed, and his face lifted toward the sun. Late in the afternoon, when a passing rainstorm doused the trail, he did not bother to seek shelter, appearing instead to savor each drop of water that fell on him. Orris thought it ironic that a man who came to Tobyn-Ser intent upon destroying it could now draw so much pleasure from the land. More to the point, however, Baram's contentment at his new-found freedom made him at least somewhat pliant. Although he couldn't move quickly, he was, during that first day, more than willing to move.

That night, however, Orris's troubles began in earnest. After eating a light dinner, Orris indicated to the outlander as well as he could that it was time for them to sleep. But rather than following Orris's example and lying down beside the fire, Baram remained seated, his knees drawn up against his chest. And a moment later, he began rocking gently back and forth and chanting under his breath. It wasn't as loud as it had been the night before in the cell, but even without understanding the words, Orris recognized them. It was the same chant. Again, the mage wondered if this was some sort of religious practice, but having observed the man all day long, and seeing now, by the light of the fire, how Baram's eyes darted nervously from side to side, Orris doubted it. This, he realized suddenly, feeling a cold clenching in his stomach, was no rite, but rather a compulsion born of captivity and isolation. And in that moment he also understood that it wasn't likely to end any time soon. It had been pitch black in the cell the night before when Orris and the guard found Baram fully awake and chanting, and Orris could only assume that the outlander had expected to repeat his litany until dawn. Just as he planned tonight.

And therein lay the problem, the mage realized, lying on the ground by the fire. As long as the outsider remained awake, Orris really couldn't let himself sleep. And with neither of them sleeping during the nights, their progress during the days would come even slower than it had on this day. That was something Orris could not tolerate. They had great need of haste. If they were discovered Orris would be accused of treason—again—expelled from the Order, and, in all likelihood, executed. And, of course, Baram would be executed as well. Orris had to get them to the LonTobyn Isthmus, a distance of nearly four hundred leagues, as quickly as possible.

Unfortunately, he couldn't force Baram to sleep. The mage's powers went deep, but not that deep. Short of beating the man into unconsciousness, which, after only a few minutes of the incessant chanting, had already become tempting, Orris was powerless to do anything but bear it and hope that eventually Baram's exhaustion would overcome his obsession.

In the end, the Hawk-Mage got some sleep, although not very much, and not intentionally. He managed to keep himself awake for much of the night, dosing off shortly before dawn, and waking with a start only when he realized, through a thin shroud of sleep, that Baram's litany had stopped. He nearly leapt to his feet with alarm, but he realized immediately that the outlander was still sitting in the same place, in the same position even, by the dark remains of the fire. The man said nothing when Orris gaped at him, but his pale eyes regarded the mage with cool amusement. They broke camp and resumed their journey a short time later, stopping once again as the sun rose so that the outlander could repeat his strange ritual from the morning before. But even with an early start and this brief rest, their pace did not improve from the day before. Indeed, in the days that followed, their progress remained disturbingly slow. More than once Orris wished that they were on horseback, but even if Baram knew how to ride, which Orris doubted, he was in no condition to do so.

It didn't help that they were forced to travel like fugitives, leaving the trail whenever other travelers approached, journeying at night rather than during the day when the terrain allowed, and avoiding villages and towns. In all likelihood, no one would have recognized Baram or figured out that he was an outlander. But all it would have taken was one inquisitive stranger to raise suspicions. That first night at the prison, Orris had ordered the guards to cut the outlander's wild hair and trim his beard. But even bathed and in clean clothes, Baram did not look quite right. A frightening savagery lurked in his grey eyes, and he carried himself awkwardly, like a man unaccustomed to his own frame. Add to that the fact that the Hawk-Mage could not tell how much of Tobyn-Ser's language the man understood or spoke, and it seemed obvious to Orris that there would be too much danger in allowing the outlander to have any contact with the land's people.

Nor did it help that even on those nights when they did not attempt to travel, they still did not rest. Even as he allowed himself to sleep a few hours each night, trusting Anizir to watch the outlander for a time, Orris felt himself growing dangerously fatigued. He had no idea how the outlander could continue to travel and function on no sleep at all. Each day as he watched Baram walking in front of him, noting the heaviness of the man's steps and the drooping of his shoulders, Orris would tell himself that Baram couldn't go on like this for another day. And each night the outlander would prove him wrong. He would eat whatever food Orris put in front of him, position himself by the fire in his usual way—knees drawn up to his chest, arms wrapped tightly around his shins—and begin to rock himself and chant, his pale eyes fixed warily on Orris.

It occurred to the Hawk-Mage in the middle of one of these endless nights that Baram might keep himself awake for the same reason Orris did. Certainly there was little in their interaction on which to build a trusting relationship. According to Baden, the outlander understood Tobyn-Ser's language, but Orris had seen no direct evidence of this. Aside from his litany, Baram rarely said anything, and, when he did, it was invariably in his own language, of which the mage had no knowledge at all. Mostly, their communication consisted of gestures, head shakes, and nods. When they did speak, the tone of their voices usually conveyed much more meaning than their words. Orris, who had never been much of a talker himself, found that he actually missed having conversations, not only because of the troubling direction his relationship with Baram had taken, but also because he simply felt lonely. A part of him knew that Jaryd and Alayna would have found this amusing; they frequently complained about his reticence. But he didn't see much humor in the situation.

Even if he could not bring himself to laugh at his current circumstance, Orris could not help but see the ironies of it, bitter as they were. He had been at Watersbend. He had seen what the invaders from Lon-Ser had done to the town and its people. The searing images of ruined homes, decimated crops, and charred bodies would remain with him, he knew, for as long as he lived. Baram, of course, had not been there—the two who destroyed Watersbend were dead, killed by the traitor Sartol to cover his deception. But Baram had done similar things in other towns, and were it not for the intervention of Theron, Phelan, and the other Unsettled, he would probably have done worse.

Despite all that Orris had learned from Baden, notwithstanding the Owl-Master's valid reasons for wanting to keep the outlander alive, there was still a part of Orris that wanted Baram to die a prolonged and painful death. And instead, here he was conducting the outlander back to Lon-Ser, providing him with food, and shielding him from any harm that might come to him at the hands of those seeking vengeance for his crimes. "May the gods forgive me," Orris muttered under his breath on a number of occasions during the first several days of their journey.

On the twelfth night after they left the prison, Baram finally fell asleep. The evening had begun just like any other, but this time the outlander drifted into a deep slumber in the midst of his litany, his head falling forward onto his chest, and then, eventually, his whole body slumping over to the side. He remained that way for the rest of the night, and did not wake until well past sunrise the following morning. Orris slept that night as well, and, from that night forward, Baram's litany became a prelude to sleep rather than a substitute for it.

Seven days later the two travelers finally made their way out of the Parneshome mountains and into the brooding shadows of Tobyn's Wood. Once they did, their speed increased, and not simply because of the more level terrain. Now that he was getting a decent amount of sleep, Baram began to grow stronger. Orris could see it in the way he carried himself on the trail, and he could measure it in the distance they covered each day. The improvement came slowly, but it was unmistakable, but though Baram still kept the Hawk-Mage from the pace he would have set for himself had he been alone, Orris found his frustration and impatience ebbing. But only slightly. Even with the improvement in their speed, at the end of two fortnights they were still in Tobyn's Wood. Had he been traveling alone, Orris could have reached the Seaside Range in that much time.

Moreover, while the sleep problem had resolved itself, other difficulties soon emerged. As the novelty of his freedom faded, Baram became more intractable. It started slowly, during their passage through the God's wood, when the outlander began to resist Orris's efforts to get them moving in the morning by refusing to rise, or by eating slowly. Soon he also began attempting to prolong their rest stops during the day. And as the summer progressed, and they completed their passage through Tobyn's Wood and climbed into the Emerald Hills, Baram's defiance escalated. Even knowing that Orris could start and restart their cooking fires with ease, the outlander went out of his way to douse the flames with water or kicked dirt. He purposely spilled their water rations and overturned spits that held cooking meat.

Throughout this rash of incidents, which continued as they crossed the grasslands separating the hills from the Great Desert, the mage managed to keep his temper in check. Realizing that the outlander was trying to provoke a response, Orris resolved not to react at all.

During their first night in the desert, however, Baram went too far. It had been a long, hot day, made longer and more difficult by the repeated delays contrived by the outlander. They had covered a good deal of ground, but not as much as Orris would have liked. Finally, reluctantly, with the last vestiges of daylight disappearing, Orris signalled to Baram that they should stop and make camp beside the slow-moving waters of the Long River. He sent Anizir to hunt for their dinner and started a fire. Baram seemed unusually quiet, and Orris guessed that he was exhausted from their travels. Anizir soon returned with a large duck that Orris quickly prepared and placed on a spit over the flames. Turning his back on the fire to gather some more of the scrub pine branches that he was burning, Orris didn't see Baram rush toward the flames until it was too late. Orris screamed at him to stop, but Baram paid no attention. Instead he kicked the spit away from the fire, picked up the half-cooked duck and threw it into the river.

On any other day Orris might have taken the loss of their supper in stride, but on this occasion his anger exploded so suddenly that he couldn't control it. Without thinking, he grabbed Baram by the shoulder, spun him around, and smashed his fist into the man's face. The outlander staggered backwards and collapsed onto his back, blood pouring from his nose.

"Bastard!" Orris spat, standing over him and breathing hard. His hand was throbbing, but he didn't let the outlander see that. "I've had enough of your mischief, Outlander! Do you hear me? Enough! Next time you'll get worse! I swear it in Arick's name!"

Baram held a hand to his nose and then stared at the blood that gushed over his fingers. Muttering something angrily in his own language, the outlander scrambled to his feet and took a menacing step toward Orris. Anizir spread her wings and hissed, and Orris leveled his staff at Baram's chest. The outlander faltered.

Orris grinned darkly. "You've seen what mage-fire can do to a man, haven't you, Outlander?"

Baram glared at him, his pale eyes hard and angry, the blood continuing to flow from his nose into his moustache and beard. But he did nothing more.

They stood staring at each other for several moments before Baram finally turned away, grumbling under his breath once again, but appearing to recognize that he was beaten.

The rest of the night seemed interminable. Orris sent Anizir to hunt for a meal to replace the one Baram had ruined. She returned with a hare, and, once it was cooked, the mage offered some to the outlander, uncertain as to whether he would accept. He did, and the two of them ate in silence, avoiding each other's gaze even as they watched each other across the firelight. They continued to keep an eye on one another after they had finished eating, much as they had every night during the first several weeks of their journey. But on this night, Orris sensed something different in their mutual vigil. For one thing, Baram wasn't chanting. He was just sitting there. But more than that, Orris understood that their relationship had changed; he had changed it. Certainly they had never been friends, perhaps they had never even been companions except in the most literal sense. But neither had there been any overt acts of hostility between them. Until today. By striking the outlander, Orris had crossed some invisible barrier; he had made them enemies. And he realized now that Baram was waiting for him to fall asleep, probably so that the outlander could kill him.

The night became a contest of endurance and will, both of them struggling to stay awake, each waiting for the other to doze off. Of course Orris trusted Anizir to watch the outlander, but he didn't trust himself to react fast enough to her warning if it came while he slept. In the end, neither of them slept. They barely even moved. Occasionally Orris reached for another scrap of wood to keep their small fire alive, but he didn't dare search for more and give the outlander a chance to escape or attack. The two of them merely watched each other. And when the eastern sky began at last to brighten, they both turned to gaze at the sun coming up over the sage and juniper.

Stiffly and silently the two men climbed to their feet. Orris pulled out his pouch of food, took a few pieces of dried fruit, and offered the pouch to the outlander. Baram regarded him sullenly, but he took some food and handed the bag back.

"I don't know how much you understand of what I tell you, Outlander," Orris said between mouthfuls, "but I'd guess it's more than you let on. So listen closely: I won't tolerate any of your antics today. We need to make up some time; we've taken too long to get this far. So I don't care what it takes. I don't care if I have to beat you senseless and carry you. When I say move, you're going to move. No delays, no games. You're just going to do as I say. Is that clear?"

Baram merely stared at him, giving no indication that he had understood. But a few moments later they set off southward along the eastern bank of the river, and throughout the day the outlander did just as Orris had instructed. He wasn't happy about it; that much was clear. The expression in his wild, grey eyes remained defiant and bitter, and, after breakfast, he refused to eat anything more. But they did manage to cover close to six leagues, far more than they had during any previous day. Indeed, Orris was so pleased with their progress that late in the day, as the deeply slanting rays of the sun fell across the sagebrush and the torpid waters of the river, he began to question his perceptions of what had happened the night before. True, by striking the outlander Orris had changed their relationship, but perhaps he had changed it for the better. From all that Baden had told him he knew that Baram came from a violent society. Perhaps, the mage speculated, it had taken a violent act to get Baram to recognize his authority over him. Orris grinned inwardly. He might not understand our language, he told himself, but he certainly seems to understand a bloodied nose.

They stopped for the day just before dusk, camping once more on the riverbank. As he had the previous evening, Orris sent Anizir in search of some game and gathered old scraps of wood for a small fire, keeping a close eye on Baram as he did. And a short time later, when his falcon returned bearing a plump grouse, Orris prepared the bird the same way he had the duck that Baram threw into the river the previous night. This time Baram kept to himself. He sat beside the fire watching everything that the Hawk-Mage did, but he did nothing to disrupt the preparation of the meal. When Orris offered him half of the fowl, the outlander ate it eagerly. Once again the mage considered the possibility that his confrontation with the outlander had actually improved their situation.

They finished their meal and continued to sit by the fire, much as they had every night for weeks and weeks, with the exception of the night before. Neither of them spoke. Orris absently stirred the coals of the fire with a long stick, thinking about his friends in the Order and wondering if Baden had found someone to take his place in the psychic link.

After some time, however, it occurred to the mage that Baram had yet to begin his chanting. Glancing up, he saw that the outlander was watching him again, just the way he had the night before. Their eyes met for but an instant before Baram looked away. But that was enough. The expression in the outlander's pale eyes had been shockingly cold, not unlike the look Orris sometimes saw in his familiar's eyes as she prepared to hunt. The mage let out a long, shuddering breath. Striking the outlander had accomplished nothing, he realized, feeling foolish for having believed otherwise. Baram was every bit as determined to kill him as he had been the night before. Once again, he was just waiting for Orris to fall asleep.

"No," the mage said aloud. Baram glared at him. "No," Orris repeated shaking his head this time. "We're not playing that game again, Outlander." He stood, drawing a low growl from Baram, who started to scramble away. "Stay where you are!" the mage commanded, pointing his staff at the outlander and making the amber stone glow malevolently.

Baram halted and cringed slightly, his eyes smoldering.

Orris pulled a long piece of cord from within his cloak, cut it in half with his dagger, and took a step toward the outlander. Again Baram tried to stand and flee, this time ignoring Orris's warnings. With little more than a thought, Orris sent a burst of mage-fire hurtling just past the man's head, feeling the power flow through him like wind across Tobyn's Plain. Immediately Baram dropped to the ground, his arms covering his head and his legs drawn up to his chest.

Orris rushed to where the outlander lay and quickly tied his wrists behind his back. Baram kicked violently, his feet flailing in all directions. Several times he caught Orris in the legs and torso, until finally the mage pounded his fist into Baram's stomach. The outlander gave a retching gasp, but he stopped kicking long enough for Orris to tie his ankles together. Baram let out an inarticulate howl of protest and struggled against the bindings, but the cord held.

"Tonight we sleep," Orris said with satisfaction, standing again and catching his breath.

He walked back to his side of the fire and lay down. Baram kept up his howls and struggles for what seemed a long time, but Orris found them easy to ignore. The outlander, he knew, wasn't going anywhere. After a while Baram appeared to recognize this as well, and he fell silent and lay still. Soon Orris heard the outlander's breathing settle into a slow, regular rhythm and he smiled to himself. *Tonight we sleep.*

Orris woke well after sunrise, feeling rested and refreshed. He couldn't remember the last time he had slept so well. Baram was already awake. Somehow he had managed to raise himself into a sitting position and he watched with brooding eyes and a scowl on his bearded face as the mage sat up.

"Sleep well, Outlander?" Orris asked cheerily.

Baram turned his head and spat.

Orris watched him for another moment before looking away, chagrined. "I deserved that," he told the outlander honestly. "But the ropes were necessary. We can't make any progress without sleep. And you might as well accept the fact that I'm going to do the same thing tonight, and tomorrow night, and every night after that until I'm convinced that I can trust you." He stood and walked over to Baram. Squatting behind him he untied the cord that held the outlander's wrists and slipped the cord back into his cloak. Baram quickly untied his ankles, balled up the cord and threw it into the river.

Shaking his head, Orris conveyed a thought to Anizir who was perched on a low rock a few feet away. The falcon leaped into the air, circled once over the river, and swooped down, plucking the cord out of the water. Then she wheeled back toward Orris, carrying the cord in her talons. The mage held his arm aloft for her.

"Nice tr—" Before he could finish, Orris was sent sprawling to the ground by a full body blow from Baram. The outlander rolled once and then was on his feet again racing down the riverbank and plunging into the water.

"Fist of the God!" Orris snarled, jumping to his feet and rushing after the man. Reaching the edge of the water, he threw off his cloak and dove in.

The river hadn't appeared to be flowing very swiftly, but as soon as Orris hit the water he realized that the current was far stronger than it had looked. Already Baram was several yards downstream, and though Orris was being swept along quickly as well, the river's eddies and cross currents made it difficult for him to control where he was going. Fortunately, he had learned to swim in the waters of the Moriandral when he was just a boy. He had done this before. Baram, on the other hand, did not seem at all comfortable in the water. He was thrashing wildly, allowing Orris to catch up with him.

It was only when Orris got to within a few feet of the outlander that he realized Baram was not trying to swim. He was trying to keep from drowning. And he was failing.

"Take my hand!" Orris cried out, reaching for the outlander.

Baram turned at the sound of Orris's voice and began flailing at the mage so furiously that Orris couldn't tell if the man was trying to drive him away or save himself. Orris tried to get close enough to subdue Baram, but the outlander pushed him down under the water. Orris wrenched himself away and came up sputtering for breath. He thought about giving up then. Baram had been nothing but trouble since their departure from Amarid. Orris could leave him to drown and complete his mission without him. But at that moment he thought of Baden, and of how much the Owl-Master had sacrificed in his personal flight to keep the outlander alive. And he knew that he had to save Baram regardless of whether that outlander wanted to be saved. Swimming toward the man again, Orris ducked under the water, circled behind the outlander, and grabbed him, wrapping his arm around the outlander's chest and under his arms. Baram continued to fight, blindly lashing out with his arms and legs. But Orris had him now, and he slowly pulled the man back toward the riverbank.

After a short time, Baram abruptly stopped struggling, which made the going a bit easier. But with the strong, swirling current, it still took Orris some time to reach land. When he finally did, he heaved Baram up onto the sandy shore and then collapsed, exhausted and gasping for breath. If Baram had attempted to run away the mage would have been helpless to stop him. But the outlander had worn himself out and he lay beside Orris, gasping as well and coughing up mouthfuls of water. Anizir swooped down and landed on the sand next to them, still clutching the cord in her claws. *I'm all right,* Orris sent to her, sensing her concern. *Tired, but all right.* In return she conveyed an image of his staff and cloak which lay on the ground nearly a mile upstream. *I know. We'll have to go back.*

He sat up and looked at Baram. The outlander hadn't moved. His eyes were closed and he was breathing deeply. He looked even more bedraggled than usual.

Orris stood, though it took an effort to do so. "We need to get going, Outlander," he said.

Baram opened one eye and squinted up at him.

"Now!" Orris commanded.

The man sat up slowly and took a long breath. "Why?" he asked.

Orris froze, unsure that he had heard correctly. "What did you just say?" he asked, his voice barely more than an whisper.

"Why?" Baram repeated. "Why did you bring me out of the water?"

He had a strange accent, and it took Orris a moment to figure out what he had asked. "You mean why did I keep you from drowning?"

The outlander nodded, eyeing him closely.

Orris hesitated. The question, so unexpected and sudden, struck a bit too close to home. He almost hadn't. "I'm not sure," he replied at last. "I couldn't just let you die." The man continued to stare at him, as if not satisfied. "I guess

I need you," Orris told him at last. "I need you to help me with what I've got to do in Lon-Ser."

Baram nodded once, seeming to accept this.

Orris narrowed his eyes, feeling as though he was seeing the outlander for the first time. "You speak our language!" he said. "Do you understand everything I've been saying to you?"

"Yes."

"And you have since we left the prison?"

"Yes."

Orris shook his head in bewilderment and shock. "So you've known all along that I was taking you home. And you're still fighting me?"

"I do not believe you," the man said. "Until maybe today."

Orris let out a mirthless laugh. "You didn't believe me? That's what all this has been about?"

"No," Baram said, the expression in his grey eyes hardening. "I am prisoner. I am out of cell, but I am prisoner. This is why I fight you."

The mage regarded him closely. It made sense really. He would have done the same thing if he had been in Baram's place. "Fair enough," he conceded at last. "But you believe me now, right? You believe that I'm taking you home."

"I believe you want me alive," Baram answered cautiously. "Maybe I believe you take me home. I do not know. Maybe. But I want to know why."

Again the mage hesitated. He felt as though his world was balanced on the edge of a blade. "You came here to make war," he began, choosing his words with great care, "you and the rest of the outlanders. I'm taking you back so that I can make peace. I want you to take me to the people who govern your land so that I can keep all this from happening again." He considered saying more, but then he stopped himself. "Do you understand?" he asked instead.

The outlander seemed to weigh what Orris had said, passing a hand over his mouth in a gesture oddly reminiscent of Baden. Finally he nodded.

"Will you stop fighting me?" Orris asked, hoping it didn't sound too much like a plea. "Can we do this in peace?"

Baram looked up at the mage solemnly and rubbed his wrist. "No more rope."

"I promise you," Orris told him, "if you don't fight me, I won't use the rope." He paused, looking closely at the outlander. "Truce?"

"What is 'truce?' "

Orris grinned. "Truce means we don't fight anymore."

Baram glanced briefly at the river. "Truce," he agreed, meeting Orris's gaze once more.

The mage exhaled slowly through his teeth. He wanted desperately to believe the man. They had wasted too much time battling each other. Autumn was not far off and they still had nearly two hundred leagues to travel before they reached the Isthmus. If they didn't cross the Seaside Range before the snows began. . . .

"Truce," he repeated quietly, trying to smile. He held out a hand to help the man to his feet. "Come on, Outlander. We need to get going."

The outlander didn't move. "Baram," he corrected. "I am called Baram."

"All right," Orris said after a brief pause. "Baram it is."

The outlander took Orris's hand and pulled himself up, and the two of them began the long walk back upstream to where Orris's staff and cloak lay.

It was almost midday by the time they returned to their campsite. After retrieving Orris's belongings they ate a quick meal and then resumed their journey. Again they followed the river southward and, despite their late start, they walked nearly four leagues before nightfall. The next day they turned westward, crossing the river at a relatively shallow spot, and then cutting across the dry terrain to a cluster of cottonwood trees that Orris had spotted from the riverbank. There, as the mage had hoped, they found a fresh water spring to replenish their supply of water, which Orris carried in an old wineskin. And during the days that followed, the travelers followed an erratic, but generally southwestward path across the desert, walking from oasis to oasis. When they could find none on the horizon they traveled due west, rationing their water and constantly searching for the telltale copses of cottonwoods.

They came within sight of the southern Seaside Mountains late in the afternoon of the eighth day after the incident by the river. Once they entered the foothills water became more plentiful. Though the eastern slope of the Seaside Range tended to be more arid than the western slope, enough streams flowed out of the mountains to keep Orris's wineskin full.

Upon reaching the foothills, the travelers turned south, following the contour of the range. Orris was anxious to cross the mountains before the weather turned cold, but he preferred to do so farther south, below South Shelter and the Lower Horn which were among the most heavily populated regions of Tobyn-Ser. Since their conversation by the Long River, Baram's behavior had been less erratic. Perhaps they could have moved among the land's people without drawing undue attention to themselves. They would have to soon; they needed more food, and Baram's clothes looked too threadbare and tattered to protect the outlander once winter arrived. They needed to find a village, or at least a peddlar, and once they were beyond Duclea's Tears there would be few opportunities. But Orris was not yet ready to take that chance.

They remained on the western slope of the foothills for ten days, making steady progress southward until Orris was convinced that they were far enough from the lower shore of South Shelter. Only then did they turn west once more and begin the steep ascent into the Seaside Range. As they climbed higher into the mountains, searching for a pass to take through the maze of glaciated peaks, the air grew colder. The meadows still bloomed with lupine and paintbrush, but a few of the aspens and maples had already started to turn golden and orange with the fall. A fortnight later, Orris thought to himself, and we might have been caught in the snows. As it was, the winds blowing down from the northwest seemed to Orris uncommonly cold for this time of year. It was going to be a hard winter.

It snowed on the travelers during their ninth day in the highlands, but by that time they had passed through the most difficult stretches of mountain terrain and had started the slow descent into Duclea's Tears, the cluster of rivers and streams that coursed out of the mountains and into Riversend Harbor. They were making good time now, almost as good as Orris would have made on his own. It had taken the entire summer and more effort than he had ever dreamed would be necessary, but they had finally settled into a rhythm of sorts, one that got them through the days with a minimum of conflict and delay. More importantly, Orris reflected as they walked in the light snow, he now believed that they would reach the jungles of the LonTobyn Isthmus before the onset of winter. Just barely perhaps, but they would make it.

They had covered nearly four hundred leagues and he guessed that they had at least that far left to go before they reached the great Nals of Lon-Ser. But in a sense Orris felt as though his journey was just beginning. Traversing Tobyn-Ser was one thing, but now they were about to leave the mage's homeland. He had never ventured beyond the Tears and he had heard only vague stories about the Isthmus and its jungles. And of course he knew nothing of Lon-Ser beyond what he had learned from Baden. Up until now, he had been Baram's guide and protector. But that was about to change. Soon, every mile they traveled would force him to rely more and more on the outlander and the tenuous partnership they had forged in the desert.

Thinking this, Orris gazed to the west as if he might see beyond the clouds and the thin haze of snow. He could not even imagine the place to which he was going. A land made up of cities the size of Tobyn's Plain. A land without farms or forests. He shook his head. What could such a place look like? He faced forward again. Baram was walking in front of him, silent and withdrawn as usual, his arms crossed in front of his chest and his shoulders shivering slightly with the cold. The mage let out a slow breath. The outlander, he thought, feeling fear settle like a stone in his stomach. I guess it'll be my turn soon enough.

10

With the possible exception of Lon-Ser's advanced goods, no aspect of Baram's homeland has been more difficult for me to grasp than the workings of its commerce and production. It is so alien in so many different ways, that I can find few parallels in my own experience to help me make sense of it. Part of the problem is that, in Lon-Ser, commerce and production are inextricably bound with governance. Like the Potentates of Abborij, the lords of Bragor-Nal collect tribute from their underlings. A portion of this they, in turn, pass on to their Sovereign, again, as tribute. Some of it they keep for themselves, and the rest they distribute back to their underlings so that these lesser lords may see to the maintenance of their portions of the Nal. To this point, the similarities between the Nal system and the Abboriji land tenentry structure are obvious. Unfortunately, the comparison cannot be carried beyond this elementary point, for the complexity of the Nal's commerce is breathtaking.

—From Section Five of "The Report of Owl-Master Baden on his Interrogation of the Outlander Baram," Submitted to the 1,014th Gathering of the Order of Mages and Masters. Spring, Gods' Year 4625.

He sat on a large stone outcropping, staring into the darkness and listening to the small waves that lapped gently at the rocky shore below. A cool, damp breeze blew in off Arick's sea, carrying the scent of brine and seaweed. A few bright stars sparkled overhead, but most were obscured by the thin mist that hung over the coast between North and South Shelters.

You still with us, Baden? Jaryd sent, a hint of amusement in the thought.

The Owl-Master smiled in the darkness. *Yes,* he returned, closing his eyes and extending his awareness outward once more. *I'm here. I was just trying to enjoy a moment of solitude. But I guess that's too much to ask with all you people in my head.*

No need to be rude, Trahn returned. *After all, this was your idea.*

Personally, I'm sick to death of solitude, Jaryd added.

Me too, Love, Alayna told him.

That's enough, you two, Mered chimed in. *I'm getting all teary-eyed.*

Baden laughed aloud, and he felt laughter coming from the others as well. In truth, though he was tired from maintaining the connection with the other mages and longed for sleep, he enjoyed sharing his friends' thoughts. He was used to wandering, rather than being settled in one part of the land. He enjoyed journeying from village to village and meeting people in the course of his travels. He was a migrant not a nester in the parlance of the Order. But for the purposes of the psychic link, he had given up his wanderings. He remained by the shores of Arick's Sea throughout the year now, serving a few of the local fishing villages, but otherwise keeping to himself. In a sense, he saw the connection he maintained with the others as a sort of compensation for this small sacrifice.

In many respects, the link was similar to his bond with Golivas and the familiars that had come before her. He had access to the thoughts and emotions of the other mages, just as he had access to those of the great white owl on his shoulder. Indeed, he even shared, in a superficial sense, their bonds to their familiars, and he often found himself sifting through the random thoughts and images that came not only from Golivas and the mages, but also the other birds. The link greatly complicated the task of keeping a firm hold on one's own consciousness. This was one of the reasons it was so exhausting to maintain. But it also afforded a level of intimacy that mages often achieved with their birds, but seldom with other people. And, just as Baden's bond with Golivas enhanced his awareness of his surroundings, the link allowed him and the others to keep watch over the entire length of Tobyn-Ser's western coast. Each mage reached with his or her mind to the two nearest mages. For Baden this meant that he reached for Mered, who was at the southern tip of the Upper Horn to the north, and for Jaryd who was on the shore of South Shelter to the south. They in turn reached back toward Baden and also in the opposite direction, Mered toward Radomil in Leora's Forest and Jaryd toward Alayna in the southern half of the Lower Horn. In this way the mages created a web of consciousness that watched over the land's western border.

They were looking for anything that struck them as being alien to the land. Four years ago, the company of mages sent by the Order to Phelan Spur learned from the unsettled spirit of the Wolf-Master that he and the other Unsettled were able to track the outlanders by their strange weapons and mechanical birds.

"They are alien to this land," Phelan had explained at the time, "far more so than the people themselves. And, so, we are tuned to them in a way. We can sense them."

A few days later, as he first began to formulate his plan for establishing this link, it occurred to Baden that since the Unsettled were, in Theron's words, "walking incarnations of the Mage-Craft," it might follow that mages could perceive these alien objects just as the spirits did. To test his theory, Baden hid one of the destroyed mechanical creatures in a deserted alleyway in Amarid. He then positioned Radomil and Trahn at opposite ends of the great city and had them create their own psychic link. As Baden had expected, the two Hawk-Mages found that, like the Unsettled, they could sense the creature and determine its location within a few dozen yards. No doubt, if another contingent of outlanders came to Tobyn-Ser intent upon conquering the land, they too would bear weapons constructed in Lon-Ser. And if they did, Baden and his friends would find them.

Sitting above the rocky beach in the darkness and the mist, however, the Owl-Master felt reasonably certain that, for this night at least, Tobyn-Ser was safe. *I don't sense anything unusual,* he finally sent. *Maybe we should stop for the night.* The other mages conveyed their agreement and a moment later the presences in his mind began to vanish one by one. Jaryd and Alayna were the last, of course. *Good night, you two,* he said before leaving them to themselves.

Good night, Baden, they sent simultaneously.

Of all of them, Baden knew, Jaryd and Alayna had forfeited the most for the sake of the psychic link. Following Orris's departure Baden had been unable to recruit another mage to take the burly man's place. In truth, he hadn't even tried. Once the Gathering was over, it would have been hard to approach someone. And he didn't know who he would have asked. So instead the seven of them who remained, Baden, Trahn, Radomil, Ursel, Mered, and the two young mages, stretched their awarenesses even farther than they had before, taxing themselves and their familiars to their limits.

To ease the burden on the others, Jaryd and Alayna agreed to leave their new home on the shores of South Shelter, one of them traveling several leagues north along the coast and the other taking a position on the Lower Horn. In return, the older mages agreed to give them a few days rest every fortnight so that they could spend some time together. It was not an ideal arrangement but, under the circumstances it seemed the logical solution. At least it had gotten them through the summer. But Baden often found himself wishing that Orris had never left.

As usual, thoughts of the golden-haired mage sent Baden's thoughts southward. By now, if all had gone favorably, he and Baram should have been on the Isthmus. But Baden knew Baram well enough to understand how unlikely that was. During the four years of interrogations Baden had seen frightening changes in the outlander's personality. For the most part, their rapport had remained civil, although Baram appeared to grow more and more suspicious of the Owl-Master with each visit to the prison. But there had been no mistaking the man's hostility toward the guards. And when Baram started to make vague references to a plot to steal stones from his cell, the Owl-Master realized just how far his mind had slipped. Baden's conversations with the outlander had yielded little useful information for over a year. Baram had forgotten so much that at times it seemed to Baden that he knew more about Bragor-Nal than the outlander did.

Baden hadn't mentioned this to anyone because he feared that if Erland and his allies learned that his conversations with the outlander had ceased to be productive, they would push even harder for the man's execution. He never dreamed that Orris would try to take the outlander back to Lon-Ser. Even when they spoke in the Aerie during the Gathering, and Orris hinted at taking action on his own, Baden assumed that at worst he would steal what was left of the outlanders' mechanical birds and take them to Lon-Ser's Council of Sovereigns. Baden shook his head.

"Arick guard you, Orris," he said to the night, as he had so many times since the Gathering.

The Owl-Master rose stiffly and turned to start back toward the village in which he was staying. He rarely took shelter before winter, preferring to sleep on his own in the forests or on the plains. But the air had turned cold early this year, and he was unaccustomed to the damp climate here by the sea. He grinned ruefully. "Or maybe I'm just getting old," he commented, glancing at Golivas.

The white owl blinked once, but offered no other response.

The mage had only taken a few steps, however, when he noticed a flicker of green light in the otherwise steady orange glow of his ceryll. Again he smiled, recognizing the color. It was late, and he was tired, but he stopped, and he gladly reached back to answer Sonel's summons.

You should be asleep, he sent, chiding her gently.

I can't sleep, and I figured you'd be awake.

He felt tension in her thoughts. *What's the matter?*

Erland was here today.

That would be enough to ruin anyone's day, he replied. He sensed her smiling in response. *But he serves the forests north of the Larian,* he continued a moment later. *I'd imagine he visits you a lot.*

He does. But he came today to submit his formal response to your report on Baram. I haven't had a chance to read it thoroughly, but just skimming through it I can see that it's little more than an attack on you and a renewal of his call for Baram's execution.

Baden gave a small laugh. *Did you expect anything different?*

No, Sonel answered. *I suppose not.* But there was something in the way she replied, a catch in her mind's voice, that stopped him cold.

What is it, Sonel? he demanded. *What aren't you telling me?*

The Owl-Sage hesitated. *You did the right thing keeping Baram alive, Baden. We learned so much from him. Even with the price you paid, it was the right thing.*

But? Baden prodded, feeling his pulse quicken at the mention of the outlander's name. Again Sonel hesitated. *Just tell me,* he sent, a plea in the thought.

It's just that he's given you all the information he can. You yourself told me during the Gathering that you were worried about him; that he was forgetting things and behaving strangely—

You didn't tell Erland that, did you? Baden broke in.

Of course not! she fired back. He felt her anger and knew that he had hurt her with the question. For a long time neither of them conveyed anything to the other.

I'm sorry, Baden finally sent. *Please go on.* Still she did not respond. Baden could imagine the expression in her bright green eyes, and he cursed his thoughtlessness and his temper. *Please, Sonel,* he sent again.

I don't know, she finally began, the pain still in her thoughts. *He's not telling us anything new, and I can't see Erland, Arslan, and the others ever allowing him to be taken back to Lon-Ser. So I'm starting to wonder if there's any sense in keeping him alive any longer.*

What?

Well it's not as though he'll ever have a decent life here. He's in prison, Baden. I know that you want to protect him, that you had hoped he'd come to trust us and help us. But it hasn't happened. She paused. There was more, he knew. *I also have a responsibility as Owl-Sage to do what's best for the land and the Mage-Craft. I'm worried about all the divisions I see forming within the Order.*

And you think that killing Baram will bring us all together again? Baden flung at her savagely. *That doesn't say much for us as a body, does it?*

That's not fair and you know it! she returned with equal intensity. *You of all people understand just how difficult an issue this has been for us! It's not a matter of killing him! It's a matter of closure and, yes, revenge! Can't you understand that? Can't you see why so many people want to see him dead?*

Baden started to argue, but then he stopped himself. It was, of course, a moot point. He had intended to tell Sonel what Orris had done the next time he saw her. With the burly mage gone though, and the link stretched to its limits, that wasn't going to be for some time, perhaps until the next Gathering. And, he now realized, he couldn't wait that long.

I know this is hard for you, she sent, apparently misinterpreting his silence, *but I think I'm going to allow Baram to be executed.*

You can't, he told her.

I understand wh—

No, you don't. He exhaled slowly. *You don't understand at all. And it's my fault.*

What do you mean?

He tried to think of an easy way to tell her, but there was none. *Baram's gone. Orris got him released from the prison the night of the Procession of Light. He's taking him to Lon-Ser. I don't know where they are right now. I don't even know if they're still in Tobyn-Ser. But even if they are, there's nothing we can do.*

The ensuing silence stretched for so long that Baden began to wonder if Sonel had simply broken their connection. He should have been so lucky.

You let this happen! she accused at last, her words buffeting his mind like a cold winter wind. *You just stood by and let him go!*

Yes, Baden replied, trying to keep his thoughts calm. *That's essentially what happened.*

"Essentially what happened?" she threw back at him. *What's that supposed to mean?*

Just that you've obviously made up your mind as to what happened that night, and your notion is close enough to the truth that I won't bother correcting you. I stood by and let Orris take Baram to Lon-Ser. I didn't do anything to stop him. That's all you need to know.

Again Sonel sent nothing for some time. *I'm sorry,* she finally conveyed to him, the tone of her thoughts more subdued this time. *Why don't you tell me what happened.*

Baden took a long breath and sat down on the ground. He was growing tired, as was Golivas. Between the link and this merging with Sonel, he had been reaching for other mages for several hours now. *It's not important,* he told her wearily. *I didn't find out that Baram was gone until the next day, but I still might have been able to stop them. Certainly I could have warned Orris.*

Warned him of what? the Owl-Sage asked, the thought tinged with alarm.

Baram is in even worse shape than I told you, Baden explained. *At least he was when I saw him last. I think his captivity drove him mad.*

By the Gods! Have you heard from Orris? Have you tried to contact him?

No. Baden felt a dull pain behind his eyes. He couldn't keep this up much longer. *You're going to have to find some way to keep this from Erland,* he sent. *There's no telling what he might do if he finds out. And Orris deserves a chance to succeed.*

I'm not sure what Orris deserves, she returned. *Your link was one thing. Yes, you defied the Order, but you did so in a way that does no harm to anyone else. But this . . .* She left the thought unfinished. Baden could almost see her shaking her head.

What will you tell Erland? he asked, trying to ignore the throbbing in his head. Golivas let out a small mewing sound. She was tiring as well.

I don't know. Don't worry, I'll come up with something. But you must realize that you won't be able to keep this a secret for much longer. Someone's bound to notice that one of them is missing.

Yes, Baden managed.

He felt her concern. *Are you all right?* she asked.

Just tired.

Of course: the link. I should have realized, Baden. I'll let you rest.

His head was pounding now. With every beat of his heart, with every surge of blood to his brain, the pain grew worse. But still he held on for one moment more. *Sonel, I'm sorry. I was going to tell you. I swear. The timing—* He faltered, it was so hard to keep his thoughts clear. *I'm sorry,* he repeated.

I know, she replied. *I think I understand.* He sensed so much sadness coming from her. He should have known what to say, but he could barely maintain their connection enough to listen. *Be well, Baden. Get some rest.*

An instant later she was gone and Baden allowed himself to lay back on the cold damp ground, although even that much movement amplified the pain. He sensed Golivas sitting beside him and he reached out gingerly to stroke her chin. Then he let his arm drop to his side and lay utterly still, waiting for the pounding in his skull to subside.

He awoke some time later. It was dark still, but he had no sense of how much of the night had passed. The mist had grown denser, blocking out all of the stars. He sat up slowly. The pain in his head had subsided somewhat, settling in his temples, a persistent, dull throbbing. Looking at his owl in the orange light of his ceryll he saw that she was awake as well, staring at him alertly, her bright yellow eyes wide.

"I'd guess that you look better than I do," he said, his voice sounding loud in the still air. "You certainly look better than I feel." She continued to stare at him.

The mage stood gingerly, noting thankfully that his headache did not worsen. He held out his arm for Golivas, and as she hopped to her familiar place on his shoulder, he turned and started back toward the village. He tried not to think about Sonel or Orris, choosing instead to think about the warm bed that waited for him at the small inn. But one thing that the Owl-Sage had told him kept repeating itself in his mind. *You won't be able to keep this a secret much longer,* she had warned. *Someone's bound to notice that one of them is missing.* She was right, of course. Orris would be missed at the next Gathering. But somehow he knew that it would happen sooner than that. And once it did, Tobyn-Ser would never be the same.

They stand on the outskirts of the village like statues, grimly surveying the jumble of low roofs, smoking chimneys, and patchwork garden plots. A small stream rolls past the village, its water sparkling in the sunshine. The air is cold, although not as cold as it had been in the mountains, and the sky is so blue it hurts his eyes. He doesn't see many people; most, he assumes, have yet to rise. Of those who have emerged from their homes, only two or three have noticed them standing there.

"This shouldn't take too long," the Child of Amarid says with quiet intensity. He has left his cloak, staff, and bird in the forest. He looks strange without them. In their place he carries five birds that his hawk has killed, tied together with a piece of cord. He places his free hand on Baram's shoulder and turns to face him. "Remember what I told you: stay close to me and don't say anything."

Baram nods. He opens his mouth to ask a question, but then he closes it. He nods again.

The Child of Amarid frowns.

A little boy is running in their direction, pointing at them and shouting something over his shoulder to a woman standing beside one of the houses.

"Are you trappers?" the little boy asks breathlessly, kicking up dust as he stops in front of them.

The mage hesitates, but only for a moment. "Yes," he answers, smiling. "We've been trapping up in the Seasides and we came down for some supplies. What's your name?"

"Rodri."

"It's nice to meet you Rodri. My name is Orris and this is my friend Baram."

Orris. Baram realizes that he has never heard the mage's name before. He wonders if this is really it.

"I knew you were trappers when I saw those quail," the boy boasts, gesturing toward the birds Orris carries. "I told my mom." He turns and waves to the woman. Then he nods emphatically.

"What town are we in, Rodri?" the mage asks, pulling the boy's gaze back in his direction.

"Cloudsden. Are you trapping wildcat?" he asks excitedly. "I bet you're trapping wildcat."

Orris nods. "Wildcat, beaver, marmot. Everything you can imagine."

The boy's eyes widen. "Have you ever caught bear?"

"No," the mage answers, shaking his head. "No bear."

The boy twists his mouth disapprovingly. "Oh."

The mage squats down to look the boy in the eye. "Rodri, is there a peddler in your town?"

The boy shakes his head. "No."

The mage's expression betrays nothing, but Baram sees a look in his dark brown eyes that he recognizes. Baram flinches involuntarily. *Sixteen deep, twenty across. Sixteen deep, twenty across.* He doesn't say it out loud anymore, but he finds that the words still comfort him, and he repeats them in his mind as he eyes the mage.

"Is there anyone in town who might sell us some food and an overshirt?" Orris asks the boy.

"Why would you need food?" the boy asks skeptically. "Don't you eat what you trap?"

Orris smiles, though not with his eyes. "Of course. But it's nice to have some cheese and dried fruit for a change. Don't you think? Or do you eat the same thing every day?"

The boy shrugs. "I guess you're right," he murmurs. Baram gets the impression that Orris is not what the boy thought a trapper would be like.

"Is there anyone, Rodri?"

"There's old Alban," he says, turning to point at a small house near the stream. "He sometimes trades with the peddlers who come through in the spring." The boy's eyes widen again. "I once heard of a trapper who caught a bear using nothing but a snare and his knife!" he tells them excitedly.

"Really!" Orris answers with false brightness.

The boy nods again and looks at them expectantly, as if waiting for a similar tale from them.

"You say Alban lives over there?" Orris asks pointing at the small house.

"Yes," the boy replies with disappointment.

Orris stands again, ruffles the boy's hair, and gestures for Baram to follow him toward the house.

"Can I see your other pelts?" the boy calls after them.

"The rest are curing back at our camp," Orris answers over his shoulder, not bothering to stop. He holds up the birds. "This is all we have with us."

"That will be enough?" Baram asks quietly.

The mage shrugs slightly. "It better be."

In the end, the five birds are enough only for a rough wool overshirt and a small block of cheese. Orris tries to get Alban, a gnarled old man with a bald head and a toothless grin to part with a pouch of dried fruit as well. But the old trader holds firm and Orris eventually gives in, anxious as he is to be out of the village and on their way again. Alban is full of questions about the fur trade with Abborij and it takes Orris some time to extract himself from the conversation.

Baram and the mage leave the trader's house and take the most direct route out of the village, even though it means that they must circle back through the forest to retrieve the mage's cloak and staff. The hawk finds them immediately, flying to Orris's shoulder and holding out its neck so that Orris can caress its chin.

"Orris," Baram says.

The mage looks at him, puzzled.

"Your name. Orris."

Orris nods and gives a small smile. "Yes."

As they walk back to where Orris left his things, Baram puts on his woolen shirt. It itches, but it's warm and he's grateful for it.

The cold air reminds him of winters in the Nal, standing beside fires that burn in large trash holders, or stepping out of his favorite bar in the Second Realm with an uestra on his arm and hurrying through the chilled air back to the warmth of his flat. He remembers more and more these days. Ever since the river, the images have been clearer, easier to read. He doesn't know why. Perhaps the shock of almost drowning has triggered something, or maybe hearing from the mage that he is going home has made the Nal real again. But whatever the reason, he can picture it again in his mind, the way he could before they put him in the prison. He can see the sleek perfection of the buildings rising above the streets and the precise curve of the Upper soaring over the Realm. He can feel the soft vibration of a thrower in his hand. If he tries hard enough he can even hear the hiss of a dispenser and taste the musty sweetness of a dark ale.

He remembers other things as well. Names. Faces. The things he did before Calbyr chose him for the mission to Tobyn-Ser. And he is beginning to understand what these things mean and what he will do when he is home again.

The mage needs him, he knows. The mage has told him this. But Baram realizes now that the mage has told him only half. *I need you to help me with what I've got to do in Lon-Ser,* the mage has said. *I'm taking you back so that I can make peace.* Yes. But he also needs Baram as a guide. Without him the mage will be lost in the Nal. Baram grins darkly at the thought.

The mage has fed him and guarded him, and now, Baram realizes, glancing at the woolen shirt he wears, the mage has clothed him as well. He has even saved Baram's life. But he has done these things for one reason only: he needs Baram's help. And though Baram has accepted that they must work together for now, he has not forgotten being threatened and beaten and tied up. Time and again the mage has used his knowledge of this land and the threat of his sorcery to press his advantage and keep Baram as his captive. But soon they will be in Baram's land; they will be in Bragor-Nal. He allows himself another smile, knowing that Orris is behind him and cannot see. Let's see how you do on my terms, Child of Amarid, he says to himself. Let's see how you survive alone in the Nal.

11

There were so many disturbing facets to the attacks carried out by the out-landers that it is difficult to single out one as being more frightening than the others. The power of their weapons, the uncanny ability of their "birds" to behave like living creatures, the cunning revealed by their tactics—one cannot help but be unnerved by any and all of these things. And yet for myself, and for many of those with whom I have spoken, one element of their campaign of violence stands out above even these: their preparation. They knew precisely how to mimic the dress, traditions, and migration patterns of mages. They moved about our land with an ease that bespoke a startling familiarity with Tobyn-Ser's terrain. To be sure, they may have had help from the traitor Sartol. But according to Baram they only joined forces with Sartol after their arrival in Tobyn-Ser. They brought their birds, staffs, and cloaks with them from Lon-Ser, and the basic outlines of their plot were formulated before they left their homeland. Baram could not tell me how his superiors came to have such accurate information about the Order and Tobyn-Ser, but it is clear from his description of the extensive training he went through prior to coming here, that our enemies know far more about us than we do about them.

—From Section Seven of "The Report of Owl-Master Baden on his Interrogation of the Outlander Baram," Submitted to the 1,014th Gathering of the Order of Mages and Masters. Spring, Gods' Year 4625.

She awoke with a shuddering gasp, emerging from the light of her vision into the waking darkness of night. She was trembling and she could feel her dampened hair clinging to the sweat that covered her face. She felt a dry aching in her throat and mouth. She forced herself into a sitting position and groped for the cup of water that she kept beside her bed. Finding it, she drank deeply before leaning back against the wall and taking a long, calming breath.

It was always this way after a Seeing. Not that she needed any confirmation that her dream had been prophecy. She had known as soon as it began. She was a Gildriite; she had been having such visions all her life. After a while you learned to recognize them.

She glanced at the glowing face of the clock on her night table. The sun would not be up for several more hours. She knew that she needed sleep: the training was exhausting, mentally and physically, and it wouldn't do for the commander to be dragging behind while her men set the pace. But this vision required careful consideration and she knew herself well enough to understand that until she gave it some thought she would be unable to focus thoroughly on anything else. Fatigue could be overcome, but distractions were dangerous.

So Melyor switched on her light, swung herself out of bed, and put on her robe. Moving to the stark room's lone window, she stared out at the lights of the Nal and began to sift through her memory of the dream.

There had been a man, powerfully built with long yellow hair, dark brooding eyes, and a rough beard. He carried a bird on his shoulder, a great, dark hawk, and he bore a staff with a bright amber stone. The cloak he wore was green, much like the ones Melyor and her men wore during their training sessions. A year ago, such a vision would have startled her, but considering where she expected to go in the near future it should not have been surprising at all. Except that in this dream, rather than encountering the sorcerer in the forests or mountains of Tobyn-Ser, she saw him here in the Nal, although not a section that she recognized. And rather than seeing the man as her enemy, she saw herself fighting by his side, her thrower and his staff spewing forth deadly torrents of red and amber fire at some unseen enemy.

She couldn't imagine what it might mean, but she was certain that the sorcerer's presence in Tobyn-Ser could only serve to undermine her plans. Even if they were fighting together for some reason, it couldn't bode well for her standing in the Nal. And if the stranger was coming to Lon-Ser on a mission of peace, which seemed likely in light of recent events and the fact that she saw him coming to the Nal alone, the Tobyn-Ser Initiative would be endangered. She couldn't let that happen. The Initiative was the cornerstone of her ambitions, the foundation of everything for which she had prepared and worked.

If the Initiative succeeded—and she fully expected that it would—power and riches would be hers for the asking. Cedrych would almost certainly be named Sovereign when Durell relinquished the position or died, and she would take his place as Overlord. And eventually, when Cedrych's time as Sovereign ended, she would be the natural choice to take his place. She would rule Bragor-Nal. But more than that, she would, in effect, rule all of Lon-Ser.

Anyone with any sense at all understood the balance of power within the Council of Sovereigns. Marar, Sovereign of Stib-Nal, followed Durell's lead on all matters of importance, giving Bragor-Nal effective control over Council policy. Indeed, this had been true long before Durell, Marar, and Oerella-Nal's leader, Shivohn ever came to power. It dated back to the Consolidation. When Dalrek, Sovereign of Bragor-Nal at that time, realized that he would be unable to defeat Oerella-Nal, he decided to hold off on annexing Stib-Nal as well. Instead he offered the leader of Bragor-Nal's diminutive neighbor a deal: Stib-Nal's continued independence in return for its full support within the Council. Stib-Nal's Sovereign accepted—how could he refuse?—and ever since, Oerella-Nal's Sovereigns had stood alone on all issues. And so long as Stib-Nal's autonomy remained dependent on the pitifully small string of mountains separating that tiny metropolis from Bragor-Nal, the Matriarchy would continue to be outnumbered.

Thus, the success of the Initiative might very well set her on the path to supreme power within Lon-Ser. In recent days, however, Melyor had begun to consider another possibility. The success of the Initiative would give Lon-Ser control over Tobyn-Ser and would require the establishment of a provisional government there. Or so she expected. Cedrych had said nothing to her about this, but it made sense. And who better to lead this provisional government than the person responsible for Tobyn-Ser's conquest? From such an office she might find a quicker route to the Council of Sovereigns. Eventually, Lon-Ser's territory across Arick's Sea might even earn its own seat within the Council. That seat could be hers.

Regardless of how she came to possess the status and influence she so desperately desired, however, she knew that her mission to Tobyn-Ser was the first step. And she was equally sure that the sorcerer who had appeared in her dream carried with him the power to destroy the Initiative before it even began. He had to die. But how?

She could not tell anyone that he was coming without giving away the fact that she was a Gildriite. No living person knew, not even Jibb. The only people she had ever told were those, like Savil, who she intended to kill in the next instant. She had learned enough of the Gildriites' history to understand the dangers of telling anyone else. The Oracles had been persecuted for a thousand years, and here in the Nal, where everyone was either a potential rival or an informant for SovSec, the knowledge of her ancestry would place her in grave peril.

She gave a small laugh and leaned her forehead against the cool glass of the window. *Knowledge of her ancestry.* Even she didn't have that. She wasn't certain which of her parents carried the Gildriite blood, although she believed that it was her mother. She had known her father pretty well, even though she was rather young when he died, and she could remember no indications that he had the Sight or harbored a secret of such import. She'd never know for certain, however, and really it didn't matter. No matter whose secret it once had been, now it was hers, and she had to find a way to kill the sorcerer without giving it away, a task that would be greatly complicated by her current mission.

Cedrych's enormous training center was located in the center of the First Realm. Actually, in terms of quads, she wasn't all that far from the Fourth. But mere distance was the least of her concerns. Cedrych had made it clear from the outset that once she reached the training center she was to remain there until she and her men left for Tobyn-Ser. No one was to know where she was or what she was doing. The Fourth belonged to Jibb now. She could have no hand in running it. To contact her bodyguard for any reason at all was to defy Cedrych's orders and risk incurring the Overlord's wrath.

Melyor shivered suddenly, as if a gust of cold air had swept through the room. She would have to be very careful and she would have to create an opportunity. But when? Her days were full. They rose each day at dawn and commenced the morning by running forty times around the perimeter of the center—the equivalent of ten quads. After a quick, light breakfast, they spent two hours in briefings. Here they committed to memory Tobyn-Ser's terrain, working from the maps pieced together by Cedrych's cartographers from information given to them by Abboriji merchants, and the Bragory spies posing as merchants who had been sailing Duclea's waters for several decades. Here too they were drilled on Tobyn-Ser's language, the practices of the sorcerers, and the customs and traits of the populace they intended to vanquish, all of which they were expected to learn on their own time.

After the briefings, they moved to the combat grounds where, for two hours, they worked with the long throwers they would carry with them in Tobyn-Ser, and they took turns working with the twenty mechanical hawks that had been developed for this mission. From what Cedrych had told her, Melyor gathered that these birds and weapons represented a vast improvement over those used by Calbyr and his ill-fated crew. For one thing, the stones on these weapons were different colors, like the stones carried by Tobyn-Ser's sorcerers. Each member of Calbyr's group had carried a red stone. Similarly, where Calbyr's birds had all been large and black, these birds came in a variety of shapes and plumages. But all of them were remarkable creatures, regardless of their sizes or appearances. They responded to commands instantaneously, flying with as much grace and precisions as any hawk Melyor had ever seen in the Nal's aviary.

At midday, Melyor and her men paused for lunch, their largest meal of the day. Afterwards they returned to the briefing room for another hour, and then to the combat grounds for another three hours. Finally, after twenty more laps around the center, they were given dinner and sent back to their quarters for two hours of private study before all the main lights in the building were turned off.

To call the days grueling hardly did them justice. Cedrych had started her with seventy break-laws. That had been in the middle of the summer. It was winter now, and she was down to twenty-six. Many of those who were gone had simply been overcome by exhaustion. Several had been dismissed because of physical or mental failings, and just as many had quit because they couldn't take it, or they didn't like the idea of being pushed so hard without knowing what the mission was about, or because they wanted to bed an uestra more than they wanted to make money. Six had been maimed during combat drills. Three had been killed.

As the number of mechanical birds implied, Cedrych wanted to send a party of twenty to Tobyn-Ser: Melyor and the best nineteen break-laws. But Melyor had serious doubts as to whether there would be that many left come spring, when the Overlord expected them to depart. Calbyr had gone with only fifteen, and at this point she wasn't sure that her band would be that big.

"The rate of attrition slows after the first several weeks," Cedrych had assured her some time ago. "Soon we'll have winnowed out the fools and the incompetents and we'll be able to select a fine crew from what's left. You'll see," he added, sensing her skepticism, "there are some good men here."

But the losses had continued. In recent days, even Cedrych had begun to show concern. His temper seemed even shorter and more violent than usual, and he had little tolerance for any sort of lapse. She could only imagine what he'd do to her if he caught her contacting Jibb so that she could tell the break-law to kill the sorcerer. Again she smiled. Actually, Cedrych couldn't do much to her at all; with the number of available break-laws dwindling, he could scarcely afford to lose his commander as well.

She shook her head and turned away from the window. It was a moot point. When it came time to her to speak with Jibb, she'd find a way to do so without Cedrych learning of it. She wasn't certain how, but she would. She had some time yet to figure it out. Not much, judging from what she had seen in her vision, but enough.

She shrugged off her robe and climbed back into bed, switching off the light, and curling up beneath the blankets. The appearance of the stranger and his hawk was a complication, nothing more. Jibb might think it odd that she knew of the sorcerer, but he was loyal and discreet. He would not push the issue. Contacting her security chief would be difficult, but no more so than slipping in and out of Savil's Realm had been. From what she had learned of the Hawk-Magic, she knew that killing the sorcerer would not be easy, but that was Jibb's concern not hers. She had complete confidence in his ability to carry out an assignment of this sort. The sorcerer would not be a problem for long.

Melyor closed her eyes, waiting for sleep to take hold of her again. But instead she found herself beset by a swarm of troublesome questions. What if Jibb failed? Didn't her vision imply that he would? How else could she explain

seeing herself fighting side by side with the sorcerer? And how could such a
thing come to pass? Why would she ally herself with him? Who could they have
been fighting against? She sat up and turned on her light again.

"I need sleep!" she said aloud, as if telling the sorcerer to leave her alone.
She rubbed her forehead and spat a curse under her breath. Then, for a second
time she got out of bed, threw on her robe, and moved to the window.

Notwithstanding her faith in Jibb, she needed to prepare herself for the possibility that he might fail. She had seen herself with the sorcerer, and though
her visions could not always be taken literally, they were, for the most part, fairly
accurate. There was a good chance that she would meet the sorcerer. Which, of
course, led to the next question: why would she join forces with him? Again,
though she might never actually fight beside him as she had seen, Melyor could
not ignore the implications of her dream. They would be allies. Somehow, for
some reason, she would help him with whatever he was coming here to do. She
faltered, a cold surge of fear rushing through her body. Or perhaps he would
help her, maybe he would even save her life. In which case sending Jibb to kill
him . . .

"Stop it!" she snapped, disgusted with herself for thinking this way. "Just
stop it!'

If Jibb failed, she'd deal with the sorcerer herself, but she was going to give
the bodyguard a chance to succeed. She had worked too long and hard to get
this far. She let out a slow breath and glanced back longingly at her bed. "I
need to sleep," she said again. But still something bothered her.

And closing her eyes, and recalling her vision once more, she realized that it
was the sorcerer himself, or rather, what he represented.

She was a Gildriite. She had never thought much about it really, other than
to recognize how dangerous it would be to let anyone know. She had heard rumors of an underground organization of Oracles that existed in the Nals. The
Network, they called it. And she had wondered what it might be like to meet
others who also possessed the Sight. But she had never felt sufficiently compelled by her curiosity to act on it. For though she was a Gildriite, she was a
Nal-Lord first. And while the one identity carried with it the threat of persecution and death, the other held the promise of power and gold. It had never
been a difficult choice. Until now.

Because when she closed her eyes and saw again the severe though handsome face of the sorcerer, she saw someone else as well. She saw her mother.
Melyor had always been her father's child: a Nal-Lord, skilled with a knife or
thrower, and shrewd when it came to business matters. She and her father had
been alone together for so long that it had seemed the natural way to grow up.
But as a woman in Lon-Ser she carried her mother's name, rather than her father's. She was Melyor i Lakin. And even though she barely remembered her
mother—or perhaps because of it—she bore that name with pride and love. It
was one of the few things she had from her mother: her name, her green eyes
and amber hair, and the Sight.

She had been only nine at the time of her first vision, and as overwhelmed as
she had been by the dream's vividness, she had been even more disturbed when

the images that had come to her that night turned real the next day. Her first prophecy, however had concerned just a small matter—the burning of a nearby bar. As she grew older, her visions began to focus on more weighty matters: firefights between rival Nal-Lords within her father's dominion, unexpected visits by the Sovereign, and, finally, too late for her to do anything about it except await the news, the bombing of her father's carrier. She grew to dread the exhausting visions and the agonizing vigils she kept, waiting for them to come to fruition. And in the wake of her father's death, unable to cope with her grief and guilt, she made an unsuccessful attempt at suicide.

But even if she wasn't able to kill herself, she did manage, perhaps through sheer force of will, to keep herself from having any more visions. For several years, her ability to foresee the future vanished. The memory of her dreams faded and she began to wonder if her power had ever even been real, or if she had just imagined it all, a child fooled by vivid nightmares and tragic coincidences.

In the interim, she ran away from her aunt's home, returned to the Nal, and, at the age of fifteen, became a break-law. Staring out at the Nal, she grinned at the memory. Becoming a break-law entailed little more than wearing black, talking tough, and doing something illegal, preferably violent in nature. Melyor's first crime was a simple bash-and-rob. She picked out a wealthy-looking, middle-aged stranger, beat him into unconsciousness, and stole his money. And suddenly she was a break-law.

But her father had been an Overlord, and she wasn't satisfied with the petty crimes and marginal existence of an independent. Sure, independents could make it big, but the ones who did tended to be like Jibb: intelligent, exceptionally strong, and excellent fighters. At fifteen years of age, Melyor was none of those things. For most break-laws, the good money and opportunities for advancement lay in gang work, in finding a leader who worked directly under a Nal-Lord, and getting him or her to hire you on. For several months she wandered the Nal, living from hand to mouth, hiding from SovSec, which was much more diligent in upholding the laws when independents were the ones breaking them, and looking for the right situation. She found it in the Fourth Realm with a gang leader named Mirk. Or so she thought.

She met Mirk in a bar, boldly introducing herself and telling him, over the taunting laughter of his men, that she wished to join his gang. Mirk seemed to take her seriously. He nodded a lot and looked her over appraisingly before explaining to her that he and his men had business to take care of that night, but that he would be more than happy to discuss her future the next evening at his flat. Amazed at her own success and confident that she was on her way to gang work, Melyor returned to the boarding house at which she was staying and went to sleep.

But that night, for the first time in nearly four years, Melyor had a vision. Mirk had her pinned on the hard gritty floor of a cheap, dimly lit flat, and he was raping her. She woke up shaking and soaked with perspiration, and she cried at how stupid she had been to trust the gang leader. Unsure of what to do, afraid to go, but equally frightened of raising suspicions by not showing up for their meeting, Melyor finally did the only thing she could: she kept her appointment, but she carried an extra blade hidden in her boot. When Mirk attacked her, as she knew he would, she surprised him, spinning away before he could overpower her, and plunging the hidden dagger into his heart.

"How—?" he gasped, sinking to the floor, his eyes wide with shock.

"How did I know you were going to rape me?" she flung back at him, kicking him in the side with the toe of her boot. "I'm a Gildriite, you shit! That's how!"

And hearing that, his eyes growing wider still, Mirk died.

Melyor fled the flat, but Mirk's men had heard their conversation the night before. It took less than twelve hours for the break-laws to find her. But rather than killing her, as she had expected, they took her to Yumel, Nal-Lord of the Fourth. He was impressed that so slight a girl had killed one of his best men, and, perhaps sensing her potential, he made her a gang leader. It was the break she had needed. Six years later, when Yumel was assassinated—no one ever figured out who was responsible—Cedrych chose Melyor to take his place.

But just as importantly, her experience with Mirk taught Melyor that the Sight could be her ally; that it could, in fact, save her life. She began to take a certain pride in her secret and, following up on the precedent she had set with the gang leader, she made a kind of ritual of sharing it with those she killed. And the more she learned of the Gildriites and their history, the closer she felt to her mother. She wondered if her father ever knew of Lakin's abilities. As a girl, Melyor had gone to great lengths to hide her own powers from him, but as she grew older she began to wonder if that had been necessary, or if she and her mother had, in a sense, shared a secret. She chose to believe the latter. She had so much in common with her father already, and her mother had been gone for so long. This was theirs, Melyor's and Lakin's. Her father wouldn't mind.

That connection to her mother had been a source of strength and comfort for her ever since. It made the visions easier to accept; it made her feel that she wasn't alone, even though she had decided not to join the Network. It allowed her to believe that her success as a Nal-Lord came from both her parents—from Fissar who had taught her how to run a Realm and a Dominion, and from Lakin, who had given her the Sight. But never before had it threatened to get in the way of what she had to do.

Still gazing out the window at the lights of the Nal, Melyor shook her head. There was a sorcerer coming to Lon-Ser, the first to do so since Gildri himself. And within her, the part of her that was Fissar warred with the part of her that was Lakin. The sorcerer threatened to destroy everything. He had to die. But he carried a bird and wielded the Hawk-Magic. Melyor's Sight and this man's power originated from the same source. The connection between them was ancient and tenuous, but it was real nonetheless. Melyor could feel it.

She spun away from the window and began pacing impatiently. *This is ridiculous!* she railed at herself. *I've spent the last two years of my life working for the chance to go to Tobyn-Ser and destroy the Hawk-Magic! And now I'm getting squeamish about killing one sorcerer?* She stopped her pacing abruptly and let loose with a lengthy string of curses. She didn't have time for this. Somehow she would have to contact Jibb tomorrow night or the next and tell him that a sorcerer was on his way to the Nal. Let the bodyguard raise an eye-brow at the information; she trusted him enough to take that small risk. But at least this way it would be out of her hands. When the time came, Jibb would have the stranger killed and that would be the end of it.

She yanked off her robe and tossed it to the floor, fell back into bed, and turned off the light so roughly that she almost knocked it off the night table. She closed her eyes again, but she knew that it was futile. She'd be awake for the rest of the night. So she began to practice her Tobynmir. That way at least, the time wouldn't be a complete waste, and she wouldn't have to think about anything else. Not even the sorcerer.

12

I will concede that the report submitted this past summer by Owl-Master Baden offers some interesting information on the governing structure of Lon-Ser and the problems facing that distant land. It is not this aspect of the report with which I take issue. Rather it is the prescriptive elements of Baden's treatise that I find troubling. . . .

Perhaps someday, when the people of Tobyn-Ser deem it appropriate, we shall be ready to venture beyond our shores as Baden suggests. But we are not ready. Our land faces a host of problems that must be solved first, not the least of which is the recent troubling development regarding the child currently in the care of the Keepers of Arick's Temple.

> —From "A Response to the Report of Owl-Master Baden on his Interrogation of the Outlander Baram," Submitted by Owl-Master Erland, Autumn, God's Year 4625.

Winter came swiftly and harshly to Hawksfind Wood and the hills above Amarid. Day after day, a cruel wind swept down from the icy peaks of the Parneshome Range, carrying frigid air and a dry stinging snow. Even the sturdy stone walls of the God's Temple groaned under the strain of the gale and failed to keep out the cold. Extra tapestries were hung throughout the sanctuary, their resplendent depictions of the four gods and the creation of Tobyn-Ser a last line of defense against winter's assault. But this year, not even the additional protection afforded by the heavy wall hangings could help.

Cailin sat close to the hearth in her small room, huddled in a heavy woolen blanket, trying to keep her mind on the play she was reading. It was not one of Cearbhall's best. She had read all of those already: *The Crown of Abborij*, *Tears for Leora*, *Gods in the Valley*, and the rest. Those had been easy to get through. But this one, an early work called, appropriately enough, *A Child's Folly*, lacked the humor and excitement of the others. Frequently during the course of the morning, Cailin had found herself daydreaming, her eyes fixed on the fire, and the heavy volume, a special gift from Linnea, Eldest of the Gods, resting in her lap, still open, but forgotten. She longed to be outside, flying Marcran in the clearing above the temple, watching him ride the wind or stoop to strike at some unsuspecting sparrow.

She glanced over at the headboard of her bed where the small falcon sat, his large eyes closed, and his colorful feathers slightly ruffled. He was barely larger than a jay, far smaller than the impressive birds she remembered from her brief stay at the Great Hall. And, she knew, most mages bound to females rather than tiercels. But none of that mattered to her. He was the most beautiful bird she had ever seen, with his cinnamon colored back and breast, his blue-grey wings, and his red and black tail. His belly and sides were speckled with black, and he had two dark lines on his face, below his blue and russet crown. He looked like the musicians and dancers who performed each year at Arick's Feast wearing multicolored garb and face paint. Except when he flew. Then he looked like a rainbow-hued comet streaking across the sky.

They had been bound to each other for just over a year, although it seemed much longer. Cailin had trouble remembering what her life had been like before Marcran. Or more accurately, she had trouble remembering what her life *here* had been like. She still remembered Kaera like it was yesterday. But after that, after the night of fire and terror that ended her life there, everything was a blur. Until her binding.

She had been in the clearing. She went there often, even before Marcran. It was ringed by trees, and it wasn't very big, but here in the forests near Amarid, it was the closest thing she could find to the vast plain on which she had spent her earliest years. It was the one place she could go where thinking of her parents didn't make her want to cry. On this particular day though, she hadn't been thinking of home. It was fall, and she was sitting at the edge of the clearing watching as a cool wind liberated leaves of orange, gold, and brown from the trees around her and carried them to the ground in meandering, circular flights.

After some time she became aware of another presence in the clearing. She wasn't certain how; she simply knew that something else was there. And turning her gaze, she saw the falcon. He was perched on a low branch just a few feet from where she sat, staring at her with his large dark eyes. Startled and enthralled, afraid that any movement on her part might frighten him off, she sat perfectly still and stared back.

An instant later, a tidal wave of random images and emotions crashed down upon her mind, obliterating her own consciousness. She was a falcon, hovering over a meadow, drawing in her wings to dive at a field mouse, tearing at the fur and flesh with her hooked beak. Then she was flying again, riding wind currents in ever climbing circles until she was closer to the clouds than to the ground

below; diving at a larger hawk, her talons outstretched, her beak open in an enraged scream, ripping hungrily into the still-warm carcass of a finch; fighting
with another small falcon.

The images came to her so swiftly that she could barely comprehend them
beyond the primal emotions they stirred within her breast. At one point she
even saw herself and she cried out in recognition. But she was gone so quickly
that it might have been an illusion. She could do nothing to stem the tide. She
was losing herself. She sensed the world slipping away from her, as if she was
the falcon rising into the sky again, never to return. There was nothing she
could do. She felt herself on the verge of passing out.

And then she heard a voice calling her name, tugging insistently at the last
sliver of her sanity. For just a moment she thought it was her mother, and her
mind reeled at the notion. But she quickly realized that it was Irrian, the
acolyte who had become her closest friend in the Temple.

Cailin tried to answer her, but she couldn't speak. She couldn't even look
away from the falcon. But as the young woman drew nearer, the bird looked
away, interrupting for just a split second the flow of images. That was all the time
Cailin needed. Suddenly she was herself again, sitting in the clearing looking at a
small, colorful hawk. And when the bird turned its gaze toward her again, she
was ready. Rather than sending the images again, however, the falcon flew, leaping into the air, circling overhead once and then disappearing over the trees.

"Cailin!" Irrian called from the edge of the forest. "Why didn't you answer me?"

Cailin stared after the hawk for a moment longer, and then she turned to
look at the acolyte. She felt dizzy, and she was trembling.

Irrian's cheeks were flushed with the exertion of climbing up the wooded
slope to the clearing and her close-cropped yellow hair stirred slightly in the
wind. "Are you all right?" the young woman asked, concern on her round features as she stepped forward into the clearing.

Cailin nodded. It was still difficult to speak.

"Then why are you just sitting there?"

The girl shrugged. "I'm just watching the leaves fall," she finally managed to
say, not quite certain why she was lying.

Irrian cocked her head to the side. "The leaves," she repeated skeptically,
eyeing Cailin closely.

Cailin kept silent and returned her friend's gaze.

The acolyte slowly surveyed the clearing, breathing in deeply. "I can see why
you like it here," she said quietly, her brown eyes coming to rest once again on
Cailin. "But it's time for your afternoon lessons." She held out her hand.

Cailin rose a bit unsteadily and clasped the offered hand in her own.

"Are you sure you're feeling all right?" Irrian asked.

Again the girl nodded.

They left the clearing and started to make their way back down to the Temple. Still trembling slightly, Cailin searched the trees for the falcon, but she didn't
see him again.

"You're shivering," Irrian said, her brow creased with worry. "Are you cold?"

"No." Cailin tried to stop herself from shaking, but she couldn't. The more she thought about her encounter with the hawk, the more frightened she became. She had read about Amarid. Even in the Temple they taught her about the Mage-Craft, and despite what had happened to her parents and her village, or perhaps because of it, she had been fascinated by stories of the First Mage. She had even started to read the tedious life story he himself had written. She hadn't finished it, but she had read the part about his first binding. So she knew that there was really only one explanation for what had happened, especially after the visions that had come to her during the past year.

The previous fall she had dreamed of crackling lightning and torrents of rain, and the next day a powerful storm, highly unusual for that time of the year, had touched off fires in the forest and caused flooding along the Larian. Early in the spring, she had dreamed of strange foods and exotic fabrics, and the following afternoon a peddler had shown up at the Temple unexpectedly, bearing fine cloths and delicacies from Abborij. And finally, most recently, she had dreamed of the attack on Kaera, as she often did. But this time she had seen herself fighting the men who had attacked her home. She had been wearing a cloak similar to those worn by members of the Order, although it had been blue rather than green. An enormous brown bird had been perched on her shoulder, and a brilliant golden fire had poured from the staff she carried, killing the men and destroying their strange, lethal birds.

After this dream, Cailin had finally told Irrian about the first two visions, and the acolyte, in turn, had informed the Sons and Daughters of the Gods. Since then, no one had spoken to her about the visions; no one had bothered to tell her what they said about her. No one had to. The third vision, the one she kept to herself, made it all too obvious.

The very idea of it terrified her, made her sick to her stomach. She hated them. She hated all of them. And yet now, she thought, walking with Irrian, because of what had just happened in the clearing, she might be one of them. She felt tears welling in her eyes, and she fought them back.

"Actually, I guess I don't feel that well," she told the acolyte as she caught a glimpse of the Temple through the trees.

"I had a feeling you weren't being honest with me." Irrian stopped her and squatted down, placing a hand on Cailin's forehead. "You feel a little feverish," she said, the crease in her forehead growing more pronounced. "When we get back to the Temple I want you to go to your room. I'll send for one of the Keepers."

"All right," Cailin agreed.

They reached the sanctuary a few minutes later and Cailin hurried to her room. Closing the door behind her, she flung herself on her bed and started to sob uncontrollably. How could the gods do this to her? What kind of a cruel joke was this? Because of the Children of Amarid her mother and father were dead. Everyone in Kaera was dead. Except her of course. Somehow she had been spared. In the years since, she had become a living symbol of the Order's failure to protect the land, of their broken promises and their betrayals. But now she was one of them.

After several minutes, someone knocked on the door. Cailin sat up quickly and wiped the tears from her face.

"Come in," she called, wincing at the quavering of her voice.

The door swung open and Zira, one of the younger Daughters of the Gods, stuck her head in the room.

"Hello, Cailin," the petite woman said with a sympathetic smile. "I hear you're not feeling well."

Cailin felt herself blushing. "I'm—I'm all right," she stammered. "Irrian said I have a fever."

Zira held out a cup of steaming liquid. "I brought you some tea. May I come in?"

When Cailin nodded, Zira closed the door behind her and sat down on the bed beside Cailin. She handed the girl the cup of tea and then placed the back of her hand on Cailin's cheek. "You do seem a bit warm," she confirmed. "Tell me how you feel."

Cailin opened her mouth to speak, but the next thing she knew she was crying again, her whole body shaking with her sobs. Zira placed an awkward arm around her shoulders and tried to comfort her, but Cailin barely heard her. She was in Kaera again, reliving once more that final, horrible night. But now, as in her dream from the summer, she saw herself wielding mage-fire and hurling it at the outlanders. It was more than she could bear.

"Leave me alone," she said between sobs, her voice thick with grief. "I just want to be alone."

Zira lingered for another moment, but then she did as Cailin had asked, rising silently and slipping out of the room. Hearing the door close, Cailin lay down again, and allowed her tears to flow freely until finally, mercifully, they carried her into a fitful slumber.

She awoke to the sound of the dinner bell tolling in the Temple courtyard. The last vestiges of daylight seeped through her window, illuminating the little room with a ghostly silver light. She sat up slowly and yawned before padding across the cold stone floor to the wash basin that rested in the far corner. She splashed the water on her face, shuddering slightly with the cold as she dried herself with a cloth that hung nearby.

Taking a deep breath, she realized that she felt better. And she understood that she had come to a decision. She would return to the clearing the next day. If she had learned anything from the Children of Arick, it was that she could not hide from the future chosen for her by the gods, regardless of where that future might lead. But while she could not avoid it, she could make of it what she wanted. That, it seemed, was all that was left for her. So she would bind to the hawk, as Amarid had done. She would become a mage, but only on her own terms. She would never join the Order, or wear a cloak, or even take the oath to obey Amarid's Laws.

She remained in her room for the rest of the night. Irrian brought her some food, but Cailin was not very hungry. She went to sleep early and rose with the sun, slipping out of the sanctuary in silence and making her way back to the clearing while the morning dew still sparkled on the tall grass and scattered leaves.

As she had expected, the falcon found her almost immediately. It flew to her from the far side of the small meadow, gliding low over the ground and alighting on a nearby stump.

With her heart pounding like a fist within her chest, Cailin averted her eyes for several moments, bracing herself for what she knew would happen when her gaze met the hawk's. Faced now with the reality of what she had decided to do, she was beset by doubts. They had let Kaera burn. They had let her parents die. And somehow the gods expected her to join them. Her entire life's experience told her to run, to leave the clearing while she still had the chance. And yet, the mere presence of the hawk held her there. Finally, she took a steadying breath and looked at the bird.

Even having prepared herself, she was almost lost again in the tumult of memories and emotions that the creature poured into her mind. Instantly she was flying again, hunting, soaring, fighting. She felt as though her mind was under assault, although she sensed no malice from the bird, and she struggled to hold on to her own thoughts and identity. But as the whirlwind of images continued to flash through her brain, she began to recognize some of them from the day before. There was a pattern here, she realized. The bird was conveying something to her, something specific.

As if on cue, the hawk began to send her a different set of images. And these Cailin recognized. She saw Irrian and Zira. She saw the other children who lived in the Temple. She saw the Great Hall in Amarid. She saw Tobyn's Plain and the shops and farms of Kaera. And finally, with such agonizing clarity that she felt herself begin to weep, she saw her home and her parents. This was her life, offered to her by the bird, just as it—just as he, she suddenly understood, just as Marcran had offered her a vision of his life. Once more the images came. Flying, hunting, soaring, fighting. And now it made sense to her.

Gradually the flow of images slowed and Cailin found that she could see and move. But she knew that she had changed: she felt his presence in her mind; she was conscious of his thoughts; she sensed that her awareness of her surroundings was sharper somehow, enhanced by the perceptions of her hawk. She sighed deeply, feeling herself overwhelmed once more by a flurry of emotions. They were hers this time, not the bird's. And they were deeply conflicted, battling within her like armies in a Abboriji war. She was a mage. For better or worse, she was a mage.

She thought at the time that she understood what it meant to become a mage, but she soon discovered that she had been wrong. Certainly she hadn't realized that Marcran's appearance in her life would finally end the loneliness and grief that had darkened her days since her parents died. He was with her all the time, on her shoulder and in her mind. And though she still thought of her parents often and missed them terribly, she no longer felt homeless and alone. She belonged with Marcran and he with her. He was her family now.

Nor had she understood the extent to which her binding would change her life within the Temple. She had learned enough of Tobyn-Ser's history to know that the Children of Amarid and the Children of the Gods had been rivals since Amarid's discovery of the Mage-Craft. So while she had expected the Keepers of the Temple to disapprove of what she had done, she had thought that they would commend her for her refusal to submit herself to Amarid's Laws. She had never imagined that they would be afraid of her, or that they would attempt to force her to abide by the laws governing the Order.

Linnea, Eldest of the Gods, whom Cailin had met only two or three times during her first three years in the Temple, began to visit her daily, supposedly in order to check on the progress of her studies. Cailin knew better. She couldn't help but notice how nervous the Sons and Daughters of the Gods were around her, particularly when she lost her temper. Even the other children treated her differently. They didn't act frightened the way the adults did, but neither did they play with her anymore. They barely even talked to her except to ask if they could hold Marcran or stroke his feathers. At first, eager to please them, she let them. But when she saw that they still would not let her play their games, she started to refuse. She and Marcran spent more and more time by themselves. Except that the more isolated Cailin became, the more time Linnea spent with her.

For the most part Cailin liked the Eldest. The heavy woman treated her kindly, and, unlike the others, she did not seem afraid when they were together. But she was always asking Cailin questions. Sometimes the Eldest would just ask about her studies and how she felt about the other children. But often her questions were more personal and intrusive. "Tell me about your relationship with your hawk," she'd say. Or she'd ask, "Have you learned to use any of your powers yet?" On a few occasions she even offered to bring a mage to the Temple. "They can teach you how to control to the Mage-Craft," she'd explain. "None of us can help you with that." Linnea might act calm, Cailin came to understand, but the Eldest was as afraid as the rest.

Actually, Cailin had done little to develop her powers, or even to explore what abilities she had. She was happy just having Marcran, and she was wary of the Mage-Craft. She felt that using it would be wrong. Only when the Eldest persisted in inquiring about her powers did Cailin start to wonder about them herself. She wasn't entirely sure how her magic worked. It came from Marcran she knew, or, more precisely, from the bond she had forged with the falcon. But she lacked a mage's staff and she didn't know if she had access to her power without one.

After several months of wondering, of lying awake at night thinking about what it would be like to wield such magic, Cailin finally resolved to find out. The next day, after her lessons, she stole away to the clearing. It was a glorious afternoon, sunny and breezy, yet uncommonly warm for so early in the spring. But as she sat in the meadow, with a pile of sticks and dried leaves before her, she was shivering with excitement and apprehension. Unsure of what she was supposed to do, Cailin stared intently at the kindling, thinking that perhaps if she just waited long enough, it would light. Nothing happened. She closed her eyes and formed a picture of fire in her mind. Again, nothing happened.

She frowned, opening her eyes. "Maybe I need a staff after all," she said aloud.

Marcran let out a soft cry in response.

And in that moment, a thought came to her. Closing her eyes again, and forming the image of fire in her mind once more, she reached for Marcran the way she did when she wanted him to fly to her or soar up into the sky. Immediately she felt something surge through her body, so warm and potent that it might have been shafts of sunlight streaming through her. She heard a crackling sound and, opening her eyes, saw that the wood and leaves were burning.

She jumped to her feet and stamped out the fire. Breathing hard, she looked around her, feeling ashamed of what she had done and of the racing of her pulse. She was still alone. No one had seen. Repulsed and fascinated, abashed and thrilled, she gathered more kindling and did it again. It came easier this time, although she started to grow dizzy with the effort. Again, she quickly extinguished the flames.

"That's enough," she said, as if telling Marcran that they should stop. "We should go home."

She returned to the clearing the next day, and the one after that. And soon she was going every day in order to practice, even when it rained. Though she had no staff, she found that, in addition to lighting fires, she could also shape wood and heal her own cuts and bruises. It was difficult at first. She tired easily, often growing so dizzy with fatigue that she had to rest for several minutes before she could try again or start back toward the Temple. Moreover, she had little control over her power. Her attempts to sculpt wood often turned out so poorly that she felt compelled to burn the pieces on which she had worked rather than leave them lying about where someone might see them. And once, while trying to start a small fire, she actually burned an entire tree. It was only by sheerest luck that the blaze burned itself out before destroying the forest itself.

The more she practiced, however, the more adept she became, and the more she enjoyed it. She came to anticipate the sensation of power flowing through her. She felt as though she was a prism, channeling light through her body, altering it, making it hers. She felt closer to Marcran in those moments than she had to any person or creature she had ever known. And every day she felt her power increasing.

Her shame at what she had become never left her, but it did lessen with time. The others might have been afraid of her, but they showed no sign that they thought she was bad for binding to Marcran. And when Cailin finally admitted to Linnea that she had used her abilities once or twice, the Eldest, of all people, seemed genuinely pleased. She asked Cailin a number of questions about how it felt to use the Mage-Craft and how the honing of her skills was progressing. If the Eldest disapproved at all, she kept it to herself.

*   *   *

Sitting in her room, wrapped in the warm blankets as she stared at Marcran, Cailin smiled at the memory of her binding and her early explorations of her powers. It all seemed so long ago. She had gotten used to the fact that she was a mage. She had even started to think of herself that way. Some of her old ambivalence remained, but very little. That she had power, it seemed to Cailin, mattered less than what she did with that power. In and of itself, her binding to Marcran had not been a betrayal of her parents. Joining the Order would have been, but she was never going to do that. Instead she would find her own way to serve the land and honor the gift given to her by the gods.

Even when her father believed that the Order had betrayed Tobyn-Ser, he maintained his faith in Amarid and all that the First Mage had done. "Amarid was still the greatest man who ever lived in Tobyn-Ser," he told her the night he died, trying to explain to her how gifts from Amarid could still be good luck even though Amarid's Children had forsaken their oath to serve the land. At the time she hadn't understood, and she never had the chance to ask him about it. But since her binding she had slowly come to realize what her father had been saying. The First Mage's vision for the Mage-Craft remained valid, despite what the Order had done. The Order did not own Leora's Gift, and no matter what they did with it or failed to do with it, they could not change its essence. It belonged to the land. And now that Cailin had found it for herself, now that she had felt it coursing through her, she knew that it was good. Provided that the person wielding it had good intentions.

She closed the volume of plays that rested in her lap and put it aside. She stood, keeping the blanket around her shoulders as she stretched and sighed. She felt restless. Glancing at Marcran who was still asleep on the headboard, she knew a brief moment of envy. If only she could doze off as easily as he, these dreary winter afternoons might pass more quickly. She didn't really want to sleep though. What she really wanted was to go to the clearing. But she could still hear the wind keening outside and the dry flakes of snow bouncing off her window. Resignedly she shook her head, sat back down by the hearth, and picked up the volume once more.

Before she had a chance to open it, however, someone knocked lightly on her door.

"Come in," she called, laying down the book again.

The door swung open and Linnea stuck her head in the room. "Am I disturbing you, Cailin?"

"Eldest!" Cailin said, jumping to her feet and allowing the blanket to fall to the floor. "No, not at all. I was just reading. Won't you come in?"

Linnea smiled, although she seemed preoccupied, and she remained at the door. "Please sit, child," she said absently. She looked back over her shoulder at something Cailin couldn't see. Then she faced the girl again. "I've brought someone to see you, Cailin. She's travelled a long way and I'd like you speak with her."

Cailin shrugged. "Of course, Eldest. Who is it?"

By way of reply, Linnea stepped farther into the room, gesturing for the visitor to follow her. A moment later Cailin saw a woman walk through the doorway. Her first impressions of the stranger were vague at best. She was tall and slender and she carried herself with an air of importance. But Cailin was much more interested in what the woman wore and carried: the forest green cloak, the long wooden staff with its glowing green crystal, and, of course, the large, round-headed owl that sat on her shoulder. Only with an effort did Cailin manage to tear her eyes from the impressive bird so that she could look at the visitor's face. She appeared to be about Linnea's age. Her features were sharper than those of the Eldest, though her expression was kind. She had bright green eyes, and wheat-colored hair that she wore tied back, and she smiled at Cailin as she stood by Linnea.

"This is Owl-Sage Sonel," the Eldest said, her pale blue eyes darting uncomfortable from the mage to the girl. "Owl-Sage, this is Cailin."

The Sage took a step forward, the smile still on her lips. "Hello, Cailin."

Cailin said nothing. *Owl-Sage Sonel.* She had known all along that her refusal to join the Order or take an oath to abide by Amarid's Laws would trouble the mages. Indeed, she had expected a visitor from the Great Hall long before this. But she hadn't expected that the Owl-Sage herself would come.

Sonel glanced back over her shoulder at the Eldest.

"Oh!" Linnea said abruptly, her discomfort still manifest in her expression. "I suppose I should leave you."

"If you would, Eldest," Sonel answered politely.

Cailin wanted to ask Linnea to stay, but she didn't dare.

With a rustle of her silver robe and one last concerned look at Cailin and the Owl-Sage, Linnea left, closing the door behind her.

Sonel surveyed the small room. "May I sit?" she asked, indicating Cailin's bed with a gesture.

The girl shrugged, sitting down again herself next to the fire.

Smiling once more, although thinly this time, the Sage sat, laying her staff across the bed with the bright stone resting on Cailin's pillow. Noticing Marcran, she stroked his chin. The falcon awoke with a start and, seeing Sonel's owl, let out a soft, frightened cry.

"Your hawk is lovely," Sonel said quietly. "What's his name?"

Cailin hesitated. She had expected the Owl-Sage to tell her how important it was that she join the Order and follow their rules. Surely that was why Sonel had come. And Cailin had made up her mind that she wouldn't say anything at all. But she wasn't prepared for such a direct and harmless question. "Marcran," she finally replied, her voice barely more than a whisper.

"Marcran," the mage repeated. "I like that." She caressed the bird's chin again, and this time he stretched out his neck and closed his eyes, much the way he did when Cailin petted him. "It's fun, isn't it?" she asked after a brief silence.

"What is?"

"Being bound to a hawk," Sonel answered, a smile lighting her face. "Flying him. Watching him hunt. I love it. Don't you?"

Cailin nodded, unable to suppress a slight grin.

"I find that I can use the Hawk-Sight for hours at a time without getting tired," the Sage went on, growing more animated as she spoke. "Expending my power for that long in any other way would exhaust me, but not the Hawk-Sight." She shook her head wistfully and gazed at her owl.

"What's the Hawk-Sight?" Cailin asked after a moment, feeling embarrassed that she didn't know.

"The Hawk-Sight is a power that lets a mage see things through her familiar's eyes. It's a way of using your bond with Marcran to enhance your own ability to see."

Cailin frowned. "I don't understand."

"It's not an easy thing to grasp until you've tried it," Sonel told her. "Say you want to see something that's on the top of the Temple. You could strain your eyes trying to look at it, or you could climb up onto the roof. Or you could reach for your connection with Marcran and see it as he does."

"I still don't get it."

Sonel smiled. "Well, why don't we try it now," she suggested. "Close your eyes and reach for Marcran with your mind."

Cailin did as she was told, experiencing the now familiar rush of images and emotions that always came when she focused her mind on her connection with the falcon.

"Now reach further," Sonel instructed a few moments later. "Go beyond the normal bond until you actually see what he sees."

Unsure of just what the Owl-Sage meant, Cailin tried as best she could to delve further into the myriad thoughts and feelings that flowed to her from Marcran. At first they seemed a jumble, nearly as confusing as they had been in the early days of their binding. But then, it almost seemed that the bird sensed what she was after. Cailin felt herself being guided through the tangle of images until suddenly she saw herself sitting on the floor by the fire.

"I did it!" she cried out, her outburst so startling Marcran that the vision vanished. But now she knew how to find it, and an instant later she was looking at herself again. "I did it," she repeated in a softer voice.

"Good for you!"

Cailin turned toward the Owl-Sage. Or rather, Marcran did. The Sage looked strange through the bird's eyes: distorted somehow, though unnaturally vivid. Even the colors looked different. Marcran turned his head back toward Cailin, who felt herself starting to grow dizzy. She found it hard to maintain the connection, and harder still to keep her bearings as she viewed things through the bird's eyes. After a few more seconds, Cailin opened her eyes, breaking the intensified link with her familiar.

"It's hard," she said, looking at Sonel. "I got dizzy."

The Sage nodded. "It takes time to get used to it, but once you do, you'll love it. Imagine flying with your hawk!"

"Can you do that?" Cailin asked, scarcely able to comprehend such a thing.

"You certainly can! And it's as glorious as you'd expect!" Sonel glanced at the window. "If it was warmer I'd take you outside right now and show you."

"Can you show me in the spring?"

"It would be my pleasure."

But even as the Owl-Sage responded to her request, Cailin felt a sudden surge of anger, at Sonel to be sure, but mostly at herself. She had planned to remain silent during the Sage's entire visit; she had intended to deny Sonel the satisfaction of hearing a single word come out of her mouth. And instead she had just invited the woman back to the Temple.

Cailin glared at the Sage. "I know what you're trying to do!"

Sonel's smile slowly melted away. "I'm merely trying to be your friend, Cailin."

"You only want to be my friend so you can make me join the Order!"

The woman shook her head, a somber expression in her green eyes. "I want to be your friend because the Eldest has told me that you're a remarkable girl, and because I thought maybe you'd enjoy having a friend who understands what it's like to be bound to a hawk."

Cailin faltered, but only for an instant. "I don't need any friends!" she said, looking away. "I don't need you!"

"I didn't say that you did," Sonel returned soothingly. "I'm sure that Marcran gives you more than any human friend ever could. But having a mage as your friend can have its advantages. I can teach you things," she concluded gently, "like the Hawk-Sight."

A single tear rolled down Cailin's cheek and she brushed it away impatiently, unsure of why she was crying, and angry with herself for letting the Owl-Sage see that she was upset. "So you teach me things and I repay you by joining the Order, right?"

"No one can force you to join the order, Cailin," the Owl-Sage told her. "Mages who accept their cloaks must first take an oath to obey Amarid's Laws, and they must do so freely."

"I'll never do that!"

"Yes, I know."

Cailin looked at her sharply.

"Linnea told me," the Sage explained. "She said that you'd made that quite clear. To be honest, I think I understand."

"I don't believe you," Cailin muttered, looking away again.

"If you do become my friend, child!" Sonel shot back, a trace of anger in her voice, "you'll quickly learn that I don't lie!" Cailin offered no response, and a moment later Sonel continued, her tone calm once more. "I can't make you join the Order, and I won't try. But I have a responsibility to oversee your mastery of the Mage-Craft, regardless of whether I have your consent."

"Even if I'm not in the Order?"

"Especially if you're not in the Order. As Owl-Sage I'm supposed to ensure that Amarid's Laws are followed and enforced."

Cailin started to protest, but Sonel silenced her with a gesture and a severe look.

"I don't care if you take the oath or not. I'll make certain that you obey the spirit of the Laws—Linnea has sworn her aid to me in this." The Sage must have noticed Cailin's surprise, for she paused and smiled. "Yes, Cailin. Despite our differences, Linnea and I agree on this. It's too important a matter for us to let petty squabbling get in the way. If we find that you're violating any of the First Mage's laws," she promised, her smile vanishing and her voice growing cold, "we'll have Marcran taken from you and we'll do everything in our power to keep you from ever binding again. Do you understand?"

It suddenly seemed to Cailin that a cold hand had seized her heart, its fingers tightening until she wondered if her blood would stop flowing entirely. *We'll have Marcran taken from you.* Her mouth was dry and she could not take her eyes off the Owl-Sage. For all she knew of Amarid's Laws, she had already violated them, giving them cause to take her beloved falcon.

Sonel gazed at her thoughtfully. "Do you know Amarid's Laws, Cailin?" she asked, seeming to read the girl's thoughts. "Do you know what they say?"

Cailin felt herself blush. "No," she whispered.

She had expected that the mage would get angry with her again, but instead the woman gave a slight smile. "That's all right. They're very simple, and very reasonable. I don't think you'll have any trouble obeying them, even if you don't take the oath. They just say that we'll use our powers to help people, that we'll never use them to take advantage of people who aren't as strong as us. We'll never use them to fight against one another, and we'll never do anything to hurt our familiars."

"That's all?" Cailin asked.

Sonel grinned. "That's all. Those are Amarid's Laws. Do you think you can obey them?"

Cailin looked at her skeptically. "I'm not stupid you know."

"I'm not trying to trick you into taking the oath," the Owl-Sage assured her. "To take the oath, you have to recite the laws out loud, word for word. I just want to know if you think you can live by those rules."

"I guess so," Cailin answered after thinking about it for a moment. "I wouldn't do those things anyway."

Sonel regarded her soberly. "I didn't think you would."

They both fell silent. Sonel stared out the window at the swirling snow, and Cailin glanced at the fire, which had burned itself down to a pile of red embers and grey ash. It was well past time for lunch, and her stomach felt empty and unsettled. Their conversation had drained her and she wished the Owl-Sage would leave.

"What have you learned to do?" Sonel asked abruptly, looking at Cailin again.

It was far too late to retreat into silence. Sonel had taken care of that option a long time ago. "I can light fires and shape wood," Cailin answered dully. "And I can heal myself when I need to."

The Sage nodded and gazed out the window again. "Good," she commented in a faraway voice. "That's very good."

Another silence ensued, to be broken this time by the rustling of Sonel's cloak as she rose. "I should leave you," she said, picking up her staff and stepping to the door. She reached for the handle, but then stopped herself. "Regardless of what you may think, Cailin," she began, turning to face the girl once more, "I would like to be your friend."

Cailin stared at the Owl-Sage, saying nothing. It would have been easier if she hadn't believed her. After several moments, she nodded.

Sonel smiled, though the look in her eyes remained sad, and she opened the door to leave.

"Why did you come today?" Cailin asked impulsively.

The Sage halted.

"The Eldest has known about my powers for a long time," Cailin went on. "Why didn't you come sooner?"

The woman stood motionless, her hand still clutching the door handle. "I was afraid to," she said at last.

Cailin blinked. "Afraid?"

That brought a smile to the mage's lips, and she closed the door. "Yes, Cailin," she replied, facing the girl. "I was afraid of meeting you. I know what you've been through, and I know how you feel about the Order. And there was a part of me that was afraid to face you."

"So why did you come at all?"

The Owl-Sage shrugged. "As I told you, I have a responsibility to keep track of how your powers are developing." She hesitated. "And I have other . . . concerns that made me feel that I should see to this now."

"The outlanders?" Cailin whispered, knowing a moment of genuine terror.

"No," Sonel told her quickly, shaking her head vehemently. "You needn't be afraid of that. We won't let them take us by surprise again. Other things. Nothing you need to worry about."

But something in Sonel's tone told Cailin that the Owl-Sage was worried, and she felt her own fears growing.

Sonel sighed. "I've frightened you," she observed, an apology in the words. "It's really nothing, child. I promise. It's Order politics, nothing more." She held Cailin's gaze, her eyes wide. "I promise," she repeated.

Hearing the truth in the mage's words, seeing it in the woman's green eyes, Cailin felt something loosen in her chest. She nodded slowly.

The Sage opened the door again. "Be well, Cailin," she said with a gentle smile. "Arick guard you."

Cailin offered no response, but she continued to meet the Owl-Sage's gaze. Finally Sonel looked away, the smile lingering on her lips, but the look in her eyes growing sad again. Without another word, she turned and left.

Cailin remained where she was for a long time, watching her falcon sleep and bundling herself in the blanket. Eventually though, her stomach began to growl again and she rose, shrugged off the blanket, and called Marcran to her arm. Her conversation with the Owl-Sage hadn't gone as she had planned, she mused, leaving her room and making her way to the Temple kitchen, but she was certain that it hadn't gone as Sonel had intended either. She was surprised by how much that pleased her.

*   *   *

On days like these, when the wind howled at the door like a wild dog, and the snow and ice gathered in the window frames, pressing against the glass as if anxious to come inside, Erland appreciated his small house even more than usual. A few years ago on a day like this he would have been seeking shelter in some stale-smelling inn in one of the local villages, or imposing himself on well-meaning friends. But today he could enjoy the warmth of his own fire, in his own common room, as he watered and pruned the flowers and shrubs that he had brought inside for the winter from his own garden. Three summers ago, when the people of Pinehaven first offered to build the house for him as a token of thanks for his years of service to their village and the rest of Hawksfind Wood, he had refused. He had been embarrassed by the offer, and he had worried that accepting it would violate Amarid's First Law. But they had insisted, promising him that their gift was offered freely, in a spirit of gratitude and friendship.

Reassured as to the propriety of their offer, the Owl-Master had been forced to acknowledge its attractiveness. In recent years he had grown tired of the rootlessness of his life. He was an old man after all, and he had been without a proper home for more than thirty years. And a house within a few miles of Pinehaven would allow him to settle down without having to abandon the fine people he had served for so long. He had seen what happened to those Masters who gave up their lives of active service to settle in Amarid: they shrivelled up like dried apples. They grew lazy and apathetic, drifting through their final days without purpose or passion. That was not how Erland planned to go. He had too much yet to do. In the end, he relented and allowed the villagers to build him his house.

It was a modest dwelling, although more than adequate for his needs. It had a small common room, a similarly sized eating room with a cooking hearth, and a comfortable bedroom. Like the homes of Pinehaven and most of the other surrounding villages, it was constructed of peeled logs and packed clay. The chimney was fashioned out of mortar bricks, and the roof consisted of wood shingles. The only extravagance in the home's design was the preponderance of glass windows. While most of Pinehaven's homes had only one or two for the entire structure, Erland's home had at least two in each room. Perhaps, the mage often mused, the villagers believed that by giving him more windows through which to see his surroundings, they were ensuring their own safety. Whatever the reason for the windows, however, they had in no way compromised the sturdiness of the structure. Already the house had withstood a number of ferocious storms, and it seemed to Erland that it had been tested daily by this winter's winds. Through it all, the house had survived.

The irony was, however, that while Erland had no intention of wasting away in Amarid as so many other Masters had done, neither did he expect to live out his remaining days in this house. Oh, he had once, when he first moved in. He still remembered his first night in the house, when he had wandered wistfully from room to room, thinking, This is my home, the last one I'll ever know. I will die here.

Erland grinned, shaking his head at the memory as he pinched the dying blooms off his columbines. It was hard to believe that he had ever entertained such maudlin, self-pitying sentiments. But that had been before Odinan died, leaving Erland as the leader of the older Owl-Masters, and, he sometimes believed, the sole voice of reason among those willing to make themselves heard in the Gathering Chamber. And that had been before Erland realized that the only way to prevent Baden from becoming Owl-Sage and leading the Order and Tobyn-Ser into a disastrous conflict with Lon-Ser would be for him to become Sage himself. No, he did not plan to waste away, nor did he plan to die in this wonderful house. He would die in the Great Hall, probably in the Sage's quarters. What choice did he really have?

But that ending was a long time away. He had much to do in the intervening years. Granted, most of it would have to wait. Sonel was a competent leader, but not a bold one. She would take no dramatic action of any sort. If she had been inclined to do so, she would have long ago. Erland knew that Baden was her lover—considering how obvious it was, he was surprised that no one else seemed to have noticed—and he was certain that the Owl-Master had taken advantage of their relationship by encouraging her to follow through on the recommendations in his accursed report. And yet, to Sonel's credit, she had not. Yes, she did surprise Erland and the rest of the Order by contacting Lon-Ser's Council of Sovereigns. But she did nothing to follow up on that gesture. The turmoil of the last Gathering had disturbed her, perhaps even frightened her, and she had quickly retreated into compromise and conciliation.

But while Sonel was not inclined to do anything unexpected or remarkable, Erland did believe that she could be prodded to take small steps. No doubt Baden had a hand in her decision to send that ill-conceived letter to Lon-Ser. So maybe Erland could prevail upon her to do a few things as well. He had chosen to begin with Baram.

That the outlander was still alive struck Erland as an affront to the memory of every person who died at Kaera and Watersbend. Each breath Baram took dishonored the sacrifices made by Peredur, Jessamyn, and Niall. How could Baden fail to see this? The Owl-Master and Jessamyn had been close friends. Baden had lost his familiar at Phelan Spur. And still he fought for the outlander's life, forfeiting his own standing within the Order in the process. Erland couldn't understand it.

But if Baram's mere imprisonment was an affront, the idea of returning him to Lon-Ser was an abomination. Just the thought of it filled him with rage. He would never allow it; he would die first, if it came to that. He would tear apart the Order if he had to. And indeed, he sensed that this issue carried such potential. It was the most dangerous matter to have come before the gathered mages in his lifetime.

And so, as a way of mitigating that threat, Erland had resolved to devote all his energies to having Baram executed. It was the Order's only choice, but more than that, it was the proper thing to do. By this one simple action the mages could exact a measure of revenge for the deaths of the Owl-Masters and the attacks on the land; they could reclaim the trust and respect of Tobyn-Ser's people; and they could rid themselves of the greatest existing threat to unity within the Great Hall. It seemed so clear, so logical, that Erland could hardly believe that it hadn't been done already. Baden, he had to admit, had been quite persuasive. And, more recently, even when the lean Owl-Master's arguments failed to convince a majority of the Order they continued to hold sway over Sonel. When the Order voted to execute Baram, she intervened, giving the outlander clemency as was her prerogative as Owl-Sage.

But Erland could be persuasive as well. And on this matter he could say with confidence that he spoke for a majority of the Order. Hence, during his recent visit to Amarid, undertaken ostensibly to submit his response to Baden's report, Erland had begun the slow, careful process of turning the Sage to his point of view.

"This has nothing to do with my past differences with Baden," he had told her, as they sat in the Sage's quarters sipping shan tea. "I'll even allow that I may have been wrong initially; that there was some merit in Baden's efforts to keep the outlander alive for a time. But that time has past, Sonel. You know it has. Baram has become a millstone around our necks. As long as he lives the people will never trust us, and we will continue to fight amongst ourselves."

Standing in the cozy warmth of his house, Erland paused over a rosebush, remembering the look of indecision and disquiet that had flickered briefly in the Owl-Sage's eyes. She had recovered quickly, turning their conversation in a new direction before he could press the matter. But she herself had returned to the topic later in the day. "I will consider your recommendation concerning Baram, Erland," she said as she saw him to the massive wooden doors of the Great Hall. "I promise nothing, but I will consider it."

Her expression, however, had told him much more than that. He no longer thought it a question of if she would allow Baram to be killed. Now it was a question of when.

Sometime this summer, I expect, he thought, reaching for a shriveled flower that had fallen to the middle of the bush. Perhaps earlier, with a few more visits to Amarid. He had even begun to consider organizing vigils at the prison where Baram was kept. He glanced out the nearest window at the windblown snow and the grey sky. Not now certainly, but in the spring. Such demonstrations could expedite the process quite nicely. With the people of Amarid clamoring for Baram's death, his own arguments would be far more compelling. Yes, a vigil at the prison struck him as a marvelous idea.

He cut off a dead rose with his pruning knife and doing so, cut his finger as well. He pulled his hand back and saw a drop of dark blood rising from the wound. Putting the finger in his mouth, he smiled at his carelessness. A lesson, he mused. Don't allow yourself to be distracted from the task at hand, be it pruning roses or fighting for a just cause. His smile deepened. There was something to be said for spilling a little blood now and then.

13

*In light of our experience with the outlanders and the information I have of-
fered in other sections of this report, it is tempting to assume that Bragor-
Nal is populated by thieves and murderers and nothing more. In fact, this is
far from the truth. According to Baram, his fellow break-laws and their
lords comprise a minute segment of the population. The vast majority of
Bragor-Nal's people participate in a complex, multifarious system of commerce and production that is responsible for the creation of so many of Lon-
Ser's advanced goods. These people rise each day, work hard to feed their
families and themselves, and abide by the laws of their land. In this way, as
in so many other ways that are not immediately apparent, Lon-Ser is very
much like Tobyn-Ser. What makes Bragor-Nal so strange and so dangerous,
is that while the vast majority of its people are peaceful and honest, its rulers
are not.*

—From Section Eight of "The Report of
Owl-Master Baden on his Interrogation
of the Outlander Baram," Submitted to
the 1,014th Gathering of the Order of
Mages and Masters. Spring, Gods' Year
4625.

"It is time, Bearer," the lean man told him, the whispered words
barely audible over the drone of carriers and the whistling of the cold
wind as it swirled among the supports of the elevated roadway. Gwilym glanced
around cautiously, but he could see little. With his feet still resting on the steep
stairs leading up out of the underground passages, and his head just barely at
street level, he could tell only that it was night. But he had trusted the men and
women of the Network to get him this far, he wasn't going to start questioning
their judgement now.

The lean man began to run across a wide expanse of road toward a tall sheet
metal fence on the far side. Taking a deep breath, adjusting his pack slightly,
and checking once more to make certain that his stone was completely covered,
Gwilym ascended the remaining steps and followed, keeping low to the ground
as the man in front of him had. By the time the Bearer reached the fence his
guide had already peeled back a narrow section, creating an opening—or, more
likely revealing one that had been there all along. His dark eyes darting watch-
fully from side to side, the lean man motioned for Gwilym to go through. It
was as tight fit, although far more so for Gwilym than for his guide. Once on
the other side, the lean man pulled the fence back into place.

Gwilym sighed deeply, feeling, he guessed, as a man might upon being released from a prison. He was out of Oerella-Nal. It had taken better than half the winter from the time Gwilym entered the Nal at Deep Canyon and first made contact with the Network, but he was finally out. He had traveled by foot and by carrier, above ground and below, sometimes in disguise, other times in sacks or crates or half-filled tanks of liquid. He had been guided and protected by scores of men and women, none of whom had ever asked for anything in return. He didn't even know their names. Indeed, that was their first rule.

He had gone to the place described for him by Kham, and uncovered his stone, just as the big man had instructed. Within minutes an attractive fair-haired woman approached him, her expression neutral save for the eager look in her brown eyes.

"May I help you, Bearer?" she asked politely, unable to take her eyes off the glowing brown crystal.

"Yes, thank you," he replied. "I am—"

"No names!" she broke in, looking up sharply. "We'll always address you as Bearer, and you'll call us Sister or Brother. It's safer that way."

Gwilym nodded before going on. "I was sent here by . . ." He hesitated, swallowed. "By a friend. I need to get to Bragor-Nal by early spring. There is a man coming—"

But she raised a finger to her lips and shook her head. "That's all I need to know: Bragor-Nal by early spring. Come," she added, turning and leading him to a passageway that he hadn't noticed before, "we have food and a place where you can sleep."

It had been that way ever since. One after another they had fed him, guarded him, conducted him to the next meeting point, and passed him on to another. There were so many of them that, after a while, their features began to blur. Young and old, fair-skinned and dark, they moved through his life like the anonymous faces looking out through the windows of the great carriers he had seen on the streets of the Nal. The only faces that he remembered clearly at any given time were those of his current guide, whoever that might be, and that young woman who first met him at Deep Canyon. And yet, like him, all of these people were Gildriites; for all Gwilym knew, he was related to some of them. Which, perhaps, was the point.

"This way, Bearer," the lean man said quietly, the tension gone from his voice.

They started to walk across a barren plain of stunted brush and brittle soil. There was no moon, but the light from the Nal reflected off the dirty haze that hung overhead, giving them enough light to navigate around the bushes and thick bunches of dry grass. Ahead of them, shrouded in haze and clouds, loomed the sheer cliffs and glaciated peaks of the Median Range.

"We're safe here?" Gwilym asked, slightly breathless. His guide walked with long, graceful strides, and the Bearer had to work hard to keep pace with him.

"Relatively, yes," the man answered, his voice just barely carrying over the wind. "Oerella-Nal's security force is far less concerned with people leaving the Nal than with people entering it. They won't bother us."

"But how will you get back?"

The man grinned darkly. "Carefully."

Gwilym nodded, remembering the Network's credo: The less said, the better.

"Bragor-Nal's security is another matter," the guide continued a moment later. "They are renowned throughout Lon-Ser for their vigilance and their . . . zeal. They're concerned with everything that goes on at their borders as well as all that happens within them. Watch yourself." The man's tone was casual, but this too Gwilym had come to understand about the men and women of the Network: their entire existence was based upon affecting an air of nonchalance. Their lives depended upon their ability to blend into society. They always assumed that they were being watched, and so they never gave anything away with their tone of voice or their facial expressions. Even when they knew that they were safe and alone, they spoke of secret meetings and security raids the same way they spoke of the weather.

"I'll be careful," Gwilym said, hoping that he sounded as composed as the lean man. "Thank you."

They continued on in silence for perhaps an hour, reaching the end of the plain and beginning the gradual climb into the foothills. The low shrubs and grasses gave way to gnarled pines and junipers, and the terrain grew rocky and uneven. Gwilym could see no landmarks or guideposts indicating that they were following a set route, but his guide seemed certain of their way. And when finally they reached a narrow but distinct path that led further into the hills, Gwilym felt pride swell in his chest as it had time and time again during the course of his journey through Oerella-Nal. He was a long way from his friends and family in the Dhaalmar, but in a way, these were his people too.

The guide stopped, his gaze following the path up into the mountains. "This is as far as I go, Bearer. You must cross the mountains yourself. I'm sorry."

You're sorry? Gwilym thought, both humbled and proud. "It's all right," he managed. "You've all done so much. . . ." He shook his head. Whatever he might think of to say couldn't possible do justice to all they had given him. Better to follow their example and say nothing.

"The path will fork three times before you reach the first summit and twice more after you start down toward Bragor-Nal," the guide explained, his eyes looking intently into Gwilym's as if he could will the Bearer to remember. "Always take the left fork. This lengthens your journey somewhat, but it will allow you to avoid the mining camps that lie to the west."

Gwilym nodded.

"Starting here, and continuing until you reach the river on the far side of the mountains," the lean man went on, "you can use your stone to light your way. You have little to fear in this part of the mountains. Once you reach Three Nals River, however, you will have to be more careful."

"I understand. How will I find my next contact?"

"He or she will find you. This path eventually ends at a sharp bend in the river. By then you should be able to see Bragor-Nal to the south. There will be a huge decaying tree stump on the river bank—it's unmistakable; there are other stumps, but none come close to this one in size. Nearby there is a rock pile. Place one rock in the center of the stump and then walk two hundred paces back up the trail. Someone will come to you."

Again Gwilym nodded. There was really nothing left to say.

"Goodbye, Bearer," the man said grasping Gwilym's shoulder. "Arick guard you."

"And you," Gwilym returned.

Without another word, the guide turned and started back toward Oerella-Nal. Gwilym watched him for several moments and then he uncovered his stone and followed the path into the foothills. It was a steep climb and Gwilym's day had been long and taxing. He stopped after less than an hour and swung his pack off. He still carried the equipment that he had taken from his settlement in the Dhaalmar, and the Network had given him ample food for this next leg of his journey, making the pack every bit as heavy as it had been the day he left his home. He was stronger now and more accustomed to bearing the weight, but he wasn't getting any younger.

He unpacked his sleeping roll and pulled out something to eat. The food in the Nal was strange, and not very pleasant. It lacked flavor and substance, although his guides had assured him repeatedly that it was quite nourishing. And it all came covered by a thin, clear wrapping which, he had been told, was capable of preserving it indefinitely. Still, he would have given anything for some hard cheese and dried meat, or, better yet, a bowl of Hertha's ram's-root and mutton stew.

It still hurt when he thought of her. Not as it had just after he left the settlement, when the pain of wanting her had slashed at his heart like a blade. It was duller now, but constant, as if the blade had been removed, but the wound had refused to heal. The ache had become a part of him, a reminder of love and the life he had left behind. And he clung to it as if it were a keepsake. If he couldn't have Hertha, he would, at least, carry the grief that had come to replace love and passion.

He ate only a few bites of the alien food before shoving it back into his pack. He couldn't remember the last time he had actually been hungry. His stomach grew empty and he filled it, but he hadn't enjoyed eating since leaving home. On the other hand, it seemed to Gwilym that he was exhausted all the time. He woke up tired every day and grew more fatigued with each passing hour. Yet he rarely slept well: the soreness in his heart seemed to worsen at night. He dreamed often of Hertha—occasionally he found that he could will himself to dream of her. In most of these dreams they just spoke or walked together in the meadow above the cirque. Sometimes they made love among the flowers and grass. But in the morning when he awoke it was always the same. He was alone and in pain, and so tired that he just wanted to close his eyes again. And still, come nightfall, he would try once more to call her to his dreams.

Gwilym lay down on the sleeping roll and stared up at the night. Even here in the foothills, the haze from Oerella-Nal obscured most of the stars. He could make out Arick's fist and arm high in the western sky, but that was all. It was just as well. He needed sleep. He had a great distance left to cover, and he was running out of time. He closed his eyes, wondering if Hertha would come to him again tonight.

But when finally he did dream, it was not of his love. Rather, he found himself on a crowded thoroughfare, alone amid thousands of unfamiliar faces. He held his staff before him, parting the mass of people as he slowly walked forward. The street was broad, and its walkways were covered with decorative tiles of blue and gold. Enormous trees, their limbs covered with young, bright green leaves, lined the avenue as far as the eye could see, and in the distance, the tall buildings of central Oerella-Nal gleamed in the sunlight.

At first, the people did not appear to take notice of him. No one met his gaze; conversations buzzed around him like flies on a summer afternoon, but no one said a word to him. But then, all at once, everything around him stopped, and every pair of eyes on the street swung toward him. And the dream-Gwilym, as if waiting for this moment, raised his staff over his head and stabbed it into the roadway.

Somehow, the shaft of wood pierced the pavement and instantly the color of the stone changed from Gwilym's golden brown to scarlet. Otherwise the staff appeared unharmed, jutting out of the avenue, slightly aslant and still vibrating from the force of Gwilym's thrust. Inexplicably, the dream-Gwilym then turned and walked away leaving the staff there, abandoning the stone of his father, and his grandfather, and all the Bearers who came before him, to the streets of the Nal.

He woke up shaking, as much from the chill wind that sliced through his sweat-soaked clothes as from the dream. He gathered his cloak snugly around his body, but it didn't help much. Sitting up, he retrieved a dry tunic from his carry sack, and quickly changed out of the wet one. He briefly considered building a fire, but he didn't have the energy. Instead, he merely lay back down again, curling himself into a tight ball and staring absently at the glowing stone that rested on the ground beside him.

He hadn't had a Seeing since his vision of the sorcerer before he left the settlement. And as strange and unsettling as this dream had been, he could at least reassure himself with the knowledge that this dream hadn't been prophetic either. His parents hadn't come to him as they did at the beginning of every vision. They hadn't given him the staff. This dream had been fantasy, nothing more. Or so he told himself.

For, even though his mother and father hadn't appeared before him, this dream had felt very much like a true Seeing. The images had been as vivid as they were in his visions. He felt physically and emotionally drained, just as he did after glimpsing the future. And somehow Gwilym sensed that what he had dreamed would prove to be accurate.

Which, of course, was impossible. He had seen his staff penetrate the paved avenue as if the street was soil. He had seen his stone change color as soon as it touched the street, as if the Nal itself was a Gildriite. And he had seen himself walk away from the staff, discarding the most important token of his heritage as if it were a piece of trash. He couldn't explain any of these things; he certainly couldn't imagine how they could come to pass.

He shook his head, frustrated by the ambiguities of his dream and his inability to divine their meaning. I am Bearer of the Stone, he told himself angrily. I should know my own visions.

In response he heard another voice within his mind—his father's voice. *Perhaps,* it said, *but you are too far from home; too far from your woman, and your bed, and the people who remind you of who and what you are. Your Sight comes from them as much as it does from within.*

And lying on the cold ground, feeling the wind moving over him like water rushing over a stone, Gwilym smiled ruefully. At least he still recognized the truth when he heard it. Rolling onto his back and staring up at the haze and the dim stars, he forced his mind past still another wave of homesickness and wondered where the yellow-haired sorcerer was at that moment. Was he in Bragor-Nal yet? Was he alone, like Gwilym? Had he left a wife and children in Tobyn-Ser, or had he been chosen for his journey because he had no family?

"Do you understand what I've sacrificed for you?" Gwilym asked aloud, as if the stranger could hear him.

A bird called from a nearby tree and, in the distance, an owl hooted.

You're not doing this for him, the voice in his head corrected. *And you're not doing it for yourself either. You would do well to remember that.*

Gwilym frowned at the night. His father had always been unnervingly insightful.

He was wide awake now; sleep seemed as distant as the Dhaalmar. Coming to a decision abruptly, he climbed to his feet, rolled up his sleeping roll, and shouldered his carry sack. If he wasn't going to sleep, there was no sense in just lying there. With his stone held close to the ground, and the hazy sky above him still reflecting some light from the Nal, he could see well enough to chance the mountain path. Besides, walking would give him an opportunity to think more about his dream. And at least for one morning, he wouldn't have to wake up lonely.

Even before he was fully awake, he knew that he was not alone, that somehow someone had slipped into his bedchamber. Willing his pulse to stop racing and opening his eyes slowly, Jibb saw that the room was still dark. It gave him an advantage, albeit a small one. His thrower was at the foot of his bed, and, as always, his dagger lay hidden beneath his pillow. If he could figure out exactly where the intruder was standing, he might have a chance to use both weapons before diving for cover.

He was lying on his right side, covered only by a silk sheet and a light blanket. Slowly, silently, he moved his left foot until he felt the weight of his thrower through the bed coverings. At the same time, he slipped his hand under his pillow and gripped the tip of his dagger's blade between his thumb and forefinger. One fluid motion, he told himself, taking a noiseless, calming breath. One fluid—

"If I had come to kill you," he heard an all-too-familiar voice whisper in his ear, as a thrower was pressed against his bare back, "you'd be dead already. How many times have I told you to keep the thrower under your pillow with the dagger?"

A moment later a slender arm reached across his body to switch on the lamp by his bed. He turned over and saw Melyor sitting on the edge of the bed, a smirk on her flawlessly beautiful features. "Hello, Jibb," she said quietly.

"Nal-Lord!" he said, sitting up quickly. Realizing that he had nothing on beneath the sheets, he blushed and pulled the blanket tight around his waist. "What are you doing here?"

"What's the matter, Jibb?" she asked teasingly, tugging lightly at the blanket. "Are you hiding something from me?" Jibb felt his color deepen as Melyor laughed.

"What are you doing here?" he asked again, more pointedly this time.

The Nal-Lord stood and began wandering around his bedroom. Even in the baggy black britches and the loose-fitting white tunic she looked lissome and muscular, her movements as graceful and economical as a cat's. She stopped to play idly with a small glass figurine that sat on his desk. "I was homesick," she finally said, glancing at him over her shoulder with a toss of her amber hair. "I missed the Fourth."

Jibb continued to stare at her, but he said nothing. A moment later Melyor gave a small tense laugh and walked back to the bed. As she drew nearer, Jibb noticed that there were dark rings under her bright green eyes, and her face, though still exquisite, had a slightly pinched look.

"I need a favor, Jibb."

"Of course, Nal-Lord," he replied without hesitation. "Anything."

She smiled at him. "I'm not the Nal-Lord anymore, Jibb, you are. I think it's time you started calling me 'Melyor.' "

He nodded. "All right. You look exhausted. You should be asleep in your bed—wherever that may be."

Melyor made a sour face. "I told you to call me by my name, not to tell me I look like shit."

Jibb shrugged, a sheepish grin tugging at the corners of his mouth. "Sorry. What's the favor?"

She shook her head. "First, I need you to promise me a few things: no questions, absolute discretion, and only your best men can know."

"You have my word," Jibb told her. He narrowed his eyes. "You've got me curious."

"I've received intelligence reports of a stranger making his way to the Nal," she began. "He may be here already, I'm not sure. He's a sorcerer from Tobyn-Ser."

Jibb raised an eyebrow, but he kept silent, waiting.

"I don't know why he's coming here, but his presence in Lon-Ser could create . . . complications for the project I'm working on right now." She paused, a flicker of uncertainty in her eyes. But only a flicker. "I want him dead, Jibb. I want it to happen quietly and quickly. No mess, no traces. Understood?"

"Yes."

"He's bearded, with yellow hair. Stocky build. He wears a green cloak and is accompanied by a large dark hawk."

"That was some intelligence report," Jibb commented.

She blushed slightly and raised a finger in warning. "I said no questions." She looked away briefly, before meeting his gaze again. "I'm sorry, Jibb. I just can't tell you any more."

"There's no need to apologize, Nal—Melyor." He glanced at the clock by his speak-screen. It was the middle of the night. "I'll have me best men on it beginning first thing in the morning. Is that satisfactory?"

Melyor nodded, a ghost of a smile touching her lips. "Of course. I'm sure I don't need to tell you this, but the Hawk-Magic is nothing to be taken lightly. Watch yourself."

"I will. Don't worry; I'll take care of this."

"I know you will. Thank you, Jibb." She looked as if she might say more, but then she stopped herself and looked away again. "I should get back before I'm missed."

"Get back where? What is it you're doing?"

She smiled, although the expression in her eyes seemed almost sad. "I can't tell you that either. I'm sorry. I want to, but . . ." She trailed off.

Jibb waved off her apology. "I shouldn't have asked. Is there anything I can do to help you get back? Do you need a carrier, or a driver?"

"No," she said with a shake of her head. "I'm better off doing this alone." She stood and walked to the open door that led to the rest of his flat. But reaching the threshold she halted. "You're a good friend, Jibb," she said without turning around. "Don't think I don't realize that."

"I never would," he replied. "Take care of yourself, Melyor. And don't concern yourself with this anymore; I'll see to it."

She nodded once and then left his bedchamber.

Jibb switched off his light and lay back down listening for the opening and closing of the door to his flat.

There's a sorcerer coming to the Nal, he mused. He had heard stories about the Magic of the Hawk since his childhood, and, more recently, he had heard talk of an initiative aimed at conquering Tobyn-Ser. But he hadn't given the rumors much credence until now. In light of what Melyor had said about the stranger endangering her current project, what else could she have been working on? No wonder she had given up the Fourth. If the Initiative succeeded, she'd be first in line for control over Cedrych's Dominion when the Overlord became Sovereign, which he surely would eventually. And if the sorcerer's presence in Bragor-Nal threatened the Initiative, then Melyor was right: he did have to die.

Jibb had never entertained the notion that he might someday see a sorcerer; certainly he had never expected that he'd have to kill one. But what he had said to Melyor was true: he'd have done anything she asked of him. Never mind the fact that she was beautiful and that he was half in love with her. She was the best lord in Bragor-Nal. Even before tonight Jibb expected that she would eventually become Overlord. And if she really was going to conquer Tobyn-Ser she might even become Sovereign someday. Whatever she accomplished, Jibb planned to be right there with her. He had tied his future to hers a long time ago, and he had never regretted it. She could have asked him to take on Cedrych himself and he would have done it. Although for the Overlord, he would have recruited seven or eight men to help him. For the sorcerer, he'd only need two. Darel and Chev were probably the best choices. They were smart and discreet, and they were as deadly with their throwers as any of his men. Yes, they'd do very nicely. Jibb grinned in the dark. "I'm going to kill a sorcerer," he said out loud.

He gave up listening for the door; it had been several minutes. She was gone, he knew. He hadn't heard a sound.

You should have known better, Cedrych wanted to tell her, looking out his window at the Nal, which was bathed in the golden light of early morning. *You should have known that I'd be watching: that I'd see you leave, that I'd have you followed, that I'd watch you sneak back into the training center just as the sky was beginning to lighten. You should have known.* He wanted to rail at her for her stupidity and her recklessness. She was about to embark on a mission that called for patience and precision, and here she was running around the Nal like an overgrown child. He wanted to hurt her, to punish her. He wanted to slap her face until it was bloody; he wanted to teach her a lesson that she wouldn't forget any time soon. He wanted to do a lot of things. Only Arick knew how much he wanted to feel himself moving inside her.

But more than anything else, he wanted to know what she was up to. In truth, Cedrych had expected that Melyor would try something like this before she departed for Tobyn-Ser. Everything that the Overlord knew about her told him she would. Yes, she was a bit reckless, but that was an outgrowth of her courage and resourcefulness. Though he would never have admitted it to her, she was right when she said that Savil had been a bad choice for this job. He was too predictable. Cedrych had learned to anticipate Melyor's actions only through careful observation; he understood everything he needed to know about Savil within five minutes of meeting him.

He had known that Melyor would try to leave the training center only because he had practically dared her to. He had gone on at length about the efficiency of his security, and about how important it was that she remain here throughout her training. A woman like Melyor couldn't help but see this as a challenge. In a sense, she *had* to sneak out. And in fairness, the finesse with which she had done so was quite impressive.

But that didn't alter the fact that she had defied him. Cedrych had little tolerance for disobedience. As a younger man, still making a name for himself as a Nal-Lord, he had routinely killed break-laws for deviating even slightly from his instructions. And even after becoming Overlord, he had responded swiftly and violently to any hint of defiance by his subordinates. Calbyr, who had been Cedrych's favorite Nal-Lord before his ill-fated journey to Tobyn-Ser, had once argued with him over a matter so trivial that Cedrych could not even remember what it was. And as a result, the Nal-Lord bore a white scar, running from his left temple to the corner of his mouth, for the rest of his life.

As he grew older, Cedrych learned to control his temper; chances are that Melyor would never know how angry he was at this moment. The fact was that had he been in her position—locked up in this center for months, facing the pressure of a lengthy mission in a strange land that carried unknown risks—he would have attempted to leave as well. Just for a night, so that he could have a few drinks, or bed someone, or just enjoy the taste of freedom in the Nal one more time.

What alarmed him was that Melyor hadn't done any of these things. According to the man who followed her, a man Cedrych trusted, she had gone to the flat of her bodyguard, where she stayed for only a few minutes. Not long enough to get drunk, certainly not long enough for any satisfying sexual encounter, but easily long enough to convey a command, or to give or receive information.

The Overlord wasn't sure what to make of this. He rarely allowed himself to be caught off guard; surprises, as he had learned from a would-be assassin a few years back, could be deadly. And yet tonight, despite all his preparations and all that he had learned about Melyor over the years, the Nal-Lord had surprised him.

He frowned, but only briefly. There was little that went on in Bragor-Nal without his knowledge. Whatever Melyor was plotting, he would learn of it. She had surprised him once, but he wouldn't let it happen again.

14

While the size of Lon-Ser's Nals almost defies comprehension, their physical layout, according to Baram, is fairly simple. They are arranged like giant honeycombs and partitioned into individual units called "quads." Each quad consists of an open square, surrounded by exceptionally tall structures that contain living quarters and businesses, and connected to other quads by broad avenues that radiate from all four corners. Smaller roads wind among the structures, creating a network of alleyways that is repeated in each quad. Because of the exact symmetry of these partitions, the term "quad" is also used as a unit of measurement. In this case it refers not just to a single square, but to the entire honeycomb formed by the square and its avenues. Although I have been unable to determine the precise length of a quad, it does seem, from what Baram has described to me, to be close to one of our miles. Based upon this estimate, I have determined, with the outlander's help, that Bragor-Nal alone covers approximately two hundred thousand square miles.

> —From Section Five of "The Report of
> Owl-Master Baden on his Interrogation
> of the Outlander Baram," Submitted to
> the 1,014th Gathering of the Order of
> Mages and Masters. Spring, Gods' Year
> 4625.

Winter in the jungles of the LonTobyn Isthmus tended to be mild, but wet. With Arick's Sea to the north and the temperate waters of Riversend Harbor and the Southern Ocean to the south, the isthmus was battered throughout the colder months by heavy storms. But while the powerful warm winds that roared in off the water swept torrents of rain across the narrow strip of land, they also kept the air warm and comfortable.

This, at least, is what Orris had heard in the past from Abboriji merchants and sea captains. But this year the northern winds that had brought early snows to the southern reaches of the Seaside Range carried winter all the way down to the jungles. Baram and the Hawk-Mage encountered no snow once they commenced their journey across the bridge of land connecting Tobyn-Ser and Lon-Ser, but the rains that fell on them almost every day were cold and stinging, and the chill winds carved through their clothes like daggers. For periods of several days, the sky remained overcast and grey, until Orris could barely remember what it was like to see blue sky peeking through the dense tree cover, or feel the warmth of the sun on his face and back. On those few days when it was clear, the wind still blew fiercely, sending wisps of clouds racing overhead, and driving the next storm toward them with disconcerting speed.

The dense cover provided by the huge, strange plants that overran the isthmus offered a measure of protection from the weather, but not nearly enough. The same could be said of Orris's cloak and Baram's woolen overshirt: they provided the travelers with some comfort—without them the men would surely have died—but both men were cold nearly all the time. Orris sometimes felt that their clothes and hair and food would never again be dry, and late in the afternoons, as soon as they stopped their traveling, he would light a fire and urge his companion to sit close to the flames. He knew that he could heal Baram if the outlander grew feverish from exposure, but he worried that if he himself fell ill, or if, Arick forbid, something happened to Anizir, they might both perish.

The one advantage of crossing the isthmus during a harsh winter was that they did not have to face some of the jungle's more dangerous inhabitants. The tales Orris had heard about the swarming bugs of the isthmus made the insects he had encountered in the Southern Swamp with the Theron's Grove delegation seem innocuous by comparison. And the jungle was renowned for its large and diverse population of venomous snakes. Yet, no doubt due to the cold, Baram and Orris encountered few bugs and no serpents. One afternoon early in the winter, Baram did stumble into the thorns of a poisonous plant. But after carefully removing the barbed spurs from the outlander's arm, and sucking the venom from his wounds, Orris had no trouble healing the injuries. And aside from this single incident, the two men managed to elude the perils normally associated with the jungle.

In spite of the foul weather and the maddening tangle of roots, vines, and undergrowth that continually blocked their way, the travellers also made fairly good time. Standing on the sandy southern coast of the isthmus on the morning of the Feast of Tobyn, Tobyn-Ser's celebration of midwinter, Orris guessed that they were more than halfway to Lon-Ser. The mage wouldn't have tolerated their current pace in Tobyn's Wood or the Great Desert, but he accepted it as the best they were likely to do in the jungle.

They could find nothing on the overgrown isthmus that even resembled a path and were forced to follow a tortuous route around thick clusters of trees, sodden patches of mud and sand, and tangles of the poisonous plants Baram had encountered. On clear days they followed the coastline to make better time, savoring the directness of their path and their ability to see what lay more than just a few feet in front of them. But when the rain returned, as it invariably did, they were compelled to return to the relative shelter afforded by the jungle. That they made any progress at all sometimes struck Orris as nothing short of miraculous. Considering how exhausted they were at the end of each day, he certainly couldn't complain about their speed.

He was troubled, however, by his interaction with the outlander. For a brief time after the incident in the Great Desert, Orris convinced himself that their relationship was improving and indeed, the mere fact that Baram allowed the Hawk-Mage to heal his wounds offered some evidence of this. But as the winter progressed, Orris found elements of their interaction increasingly disturbing. Whenever they spoke, they used Tobyn-Ser's language. Even after Orris made it clear that he wished to learn Baram's native tongue, the outlander balked at teaching him. Similarly, Baram told Orris little about Lon-Ser. The outlander responded to most of Orris's questions about his homeland or language by claiming to have forgotten everything about his former life, an answer he belied every time he began mumbling to himself in his own language, which he did with alarming frequency. Orris would have been a fool not to see the pattern that was emerging. Baram eagerly accepted the food that Anizir killed, and he partook of the warmth given off by Orris's fires. He even was willing to be healed by the Mage-Craft. But he steadfastly refused to tell Orris anything that might help the mage make his way through Bragor-Nal.

Initially the mage had chosen to believe that Baram's reluctance to speak of Lon-Ser was no more than a symptom of his madness, which had grown less severe, but had not vanished entirely. As midwinter came and went, however, and the days began to lengthen again, Orris was forced to consider the possibility that a more sinister purpose lay at the root of Baram's persistent reticence. And slowly—day by day, mile by mile—Orris's faith in the outlander, which the mage had nurtured with such care since the incident in the desert, began to die. For months, the mage had been impatient to reach Lon-Ser. The sooner he met with the Council of Sovereigns and reached some sort of agreement that would guard Tobyn-Ser from further attacks, the sooner he could return to his home and friends. But now, as the two men drew closer to Lon-Ser, Orris's fears intensified, until the mage came to dread their arrival in Baram's Nal. He had no idea what he would face there, but he was more and more certain that whatever it was, he would have to face it alone.

Two fortnights after Tobyn's Feast, winter showed its first sign of relenting. The morning dawned sunny and warm, and the travelers walked along the shoreline, enjoying the novelty of a mild breeze. For the first time in weeks, Orris felt his spirits lifting. They weren't through with the storms, he knew. Already he could see the next line of billowing dark clouds massing on the horizon beyond the islands of Duclea's Necklace, which lay to the south. But the winds had shifted; this next storm was coming from the south, carrying with it the promise of warmer air and, eventually, spring.

Still looking across the water, but farther to the west, Orris saw something else that made his heart stop for just an instant: another land mass, this one paler than the wooded islands, but substantially closer.

The outlander appeared to notice the direction of his gaze. Pointing to the pale green spur he said something that Orris didn't understand. It took the mage a moment to realize that Baram had spoken in his own language.

"What?" the mage asked.

Baram repeated the phrase. Then he smiled. "You would say it as Isthmus Point."

Orris's mouth was suddenly dry. "You know that place?"

"Yes. That is Lon-Ser."

The mage nodded. "What did you call it?"

"Isthmus Point."

"No, before then. What did you call it the first time?"

The outlander shook his head and began walking again. "It is not important."

Orris hurried after him and, grabbing his arm, pulled Baram to a halt. "Yes it is important!" he said pointedly. "I need to know your language!"

The outlander eyed him placidly for a moment and then deliberately removed Orris's hand from his arm. "You are planning on taking me with you to Lon-Ser, yes?"

The mage blinked. "Yes."

"Then why is it so important that you learn Lonmir?"

"Lonmir?" Orris demanded, pouncing on the word like a hawk.

Baram's face reddened slightly. "That is what we call our language," he finally admitted, looking away. After a few seconds he faced Orris once more, his wild hair stirring in the breeze. "Answer. Why is it so important?"

The Hawk-Mage hesitated. He could not respond truthfully without revealing his suspicions of the outlander. "It's important," he said cautiously, "because even if something happens to you, I still need to be able to finish what I've come here to do."

"What is going to happen to me?" Baram asked, his pale eyes narrowing.

"Hopefully, nothing!" Orris replied with exasperation. "But the Nal is a dangerous place, right?" The outlander offered no response. "I just want to be prepared," the mage said wearily.

"I am prepared," the outlander said, turning away and continuing up the beach. "That is all that matters."

Orris stared after the man for several moments before following him. He was aware suddenly of Anizir's weight on his shoulder, of her talons gripping his padded cloak, and of her consciousness touching his mind. As always, her presence reassured him. But today the comfort she brought him was tinged with something else. He looked down at his cloak and at the staff he carried. We're not exactly going to blend in with our surroundings, he thought ruefully. If he and Anizir did end up alone in the Nal, as he still suspected they would, it would be impossible for him to do anything without drawing attention to himself.

Anizir abruptly leaped off his shoulder toward the jungle and disappeared among the trees.

Another concern, the mage mused, watching her fly off: would there be food in the Nal for Anizir? Or for himself, for that matter. He carried no currency; he didn't even know what kind of currency they used in Lon-Ser. He let out a long breath. "I guess I didn't plan this so well," he muttered aloud. He thought suddenly of Baden, imagining the lean Owl-Master's expression as he shook his head at Orris's lack of foresight. In spite of everything, Orris chuckled. I'll find a way, he told himself. I always do. Besides, it's far too late to turn back.

The storms returned the following day, and though the air remained warm, just as Orris had expected, the rain seemed to fall even harder than it had earlier in the winter. Driven back into the jungle for shelter from the torrent, the two men traveled for nearly a fortnight before the vegetation began at last to thin out, the strange trees and vines of the jungle giving way to woodland that at least resembled the forests of Tobyn-Ser. They were able to increase their speed as the terrain grew more hospitable, and they were in the forest for only four days before they reached the edge of an enormous swamp. By then, according to Tobyn-Ser's calendar, it was early spring.

Stopping at the fringe of the woodland late in the morning, Orris stared out at the mud and grasses that lay before him. Perhaps during the summer months, baked by a sweltering sun and infested with bugs, this fen would have looked and smelled as menacing as Tobyn-Ser's Southern Swamp. But as Orris and Baram had put some distance between themselves and the isthmus, the air had turned cold again. There were no bugs yet, and the odor emanating from the mud was unpleasant but not overwhelming. Crossing the swamp would be difficult and slow, but it would not be an ordeal.

Standing beside him, Baram pointed toward the horizon. The air appeared brown and heavy, as if something was burning in the distance.

Orris glanced at the outlander. "What is it?" he asked.

Baram grinned. "Bragor-Nal." He turned to the mage. "Not far now; this is the Guardian Swamp. After this we are in the Nal."

"How wide is the swamp?"

The outlander shrugged. "Twenty of your leagues maybe. No more."

Orris swallowed and nodded. "Well then let's go," he said grimly, starting forward into the swamp.

For the first two days, traveling through the fen proved even easier than Orris had feared. The vast plain of dark mud was firm enough to bear their weight, and it was interrupted frequently by broad islands of waist-high grass on which they were able to make good time. With few trees except for hollowed stumps, the swamp offered little protection from the wind, which blew cold from the north, carrying with it the acrid smells of the Nal. But while the sky remained overcast, no rain fell on them and as long as they kept moving, they managed to keep warm.

On the third day, however, the mire began to grown increasingly rank, not because of any change in the weather or the wind, Orris realized, but rather because of the proximity of the Nal. The mud stank of human waste, and what little water there was appeared slick with oils and discolored with strange, fetid algae. As they continued to draw closer to the enormous metropolis, the stench worsened, mingling with other pungent odors that Orris did not recognize. Unnatural colors began to appear in the mud: pinks, blues, yellows, and oranges that were so bright they appeared to glow. There were still grasses sticking out of the muck, but they were stunted and brown, as if choked by the putrid air. Orris had the feeling that even in the summer, no bugs lived here. The brown haze that they had seen from a distance a few days earlier now hung overhead, so thick and dark that Orris could not have said if the sky were clear or cloudy; it no longer seemed to matter. At night, the hazy overcast glowed balefully with the light given off by the city, creating a grotesque palette of yellows, reds, blues, and, of course, the omnipresent brown.

By the morning of the fifth day they could see the Nal itself, looming above the horizon, its dark, massive structures, partially obscured by the murky air like mountains shrouded in mist. A paler structure, higher and thinner, and supported by what looked to be narrow legs, curved over the buildings with a strange sort of grace, as if someone had decorated the Nal with a white ribbon. *We'll be there by nightfall,* Orris thought, shivering slightly in the wind. *It can't be more than three or four leagues now.*

Standing on a small island of stunted grass gazing at the dark haze that covered the Nal like an old blanket, and then at the defiled swamp that lay all around him, Orris could not help but think back to what Baden had once told him about the reasons for Lon-Ser's infiltration of Tobyn-Ser. They had been in the Aerie in Amarid, sitting at a corner table with Jaryd, Alayna, and Trahn. Baden had just completed his very first interrogation of Baram, and the lean mage had appeared shaken by what he had learned.

"The Nals are overcrowded," he had explained. "They've befouled the air they breathe and the water they drink. In short, they seek a new home, or at least an additional home. And we have exactly what they need."

Orris had never doubted the truth in what Baden had said, but neither had he truly understood what the Owl-Master described that night. Indeed, he now realized, feeling his senses battered by his surroundings, sensing Anizir's uneasiness and the way she shrunk from all she saw, he hadn't been capable of understanding. Nothing in Tobyn-Ser could have prepared him for this. More than anything in the world, he wished to turn away from the Nal and go home. Yet, hearing Baden's words again and again, he felt anew the urgency of his mission. Clearly, the denizens of Bragor-Nal had not solved their problems—they still needed Tobyn-Ser. The thought of his beloved homeland being turned into this enraged him and strengthened his resolve.

He glanced at Baram and found that the outlander was already watching him, an expectant look in his wild, pale eyes. He looked like he might say something, but he remained silent.

"You're almost home," Orris said, looking at the Nal once more. "Does it look like you remembered?"

Baram swung his eyes from the mage to the distant buildings. He almost seemed to be flinching, as if the very sight of the Nal might hurt him, but for some time he said nothing "It looks big," he finally answered. "I remember it smaller."

Orris pointed at the ribbonlike structure. "What's the white thing?" he asked.

The outlander said something in his own language and then facing Orris again he added, "It is a road."

"A road," the mage repeated, wondering what kind of road rose up into the air like that. Somehow he knew that he would find more on this road than just horses and merchant carts. "A road," he said again, shaking his head.

Baram grinned, his features wearing an expression that made Orris vaguely uncomfortable.

They lingered a few moments longer and then resumed their advance on the enormous city. Orris allowed the outlander to walk in front of him. Baram was behaving strangely, looking back at him repeatedly, muttering under his breath, and occasionally laughing aloud. Orris did not trust the outlander to walk behind him just now; he preferred having Baram where he could see him. In truth though, the mage was more concerned with Anizir, who sat on his shoulder. The anxiety that he had sensed in her late the previous evening, even before they had actually seen the Nal, had mounted throughout the morning until it began to cloud his perceptions. The falcon seemed to be turning in upon herself, as if unwilling to face this alien land.

I need you, Orris sent, trying to coax her out of her isolation. *I can't do this without you.*

In return she conveyed an image of a rocky shoreline. Breakers pounded the coast, sending sea foam high into the air, and a dark forest of firs and hemlocks stood nearby. It was the place of their binding.

Orris smiled sadly. *I know. I miss it, too. We'll get back there, I promise. But we have to do this first.*

A second image entered his mind: Anizir tearing into the warm carcass of a quail.

Orris felt panic rising in his chest and he moved instantly to quell it. It wouldn't do to let Anizir know just how frightened he was. As the fen had grown increasingly defiled, the amount of animal life had fallen off dramatically. Orris had seen no birds in over a day, and Anizir had not eaten in nearly two. And Orris was not at all certain that the situation would improve once they left the swamp and entered Bragor-Nal. He sensed the falcon waiting for some reassurance, and he didn't know what to tell her. Dissembling with one's familiar was never easy.

I'll do everything I can, he finally sent. *If there's food to be found, we'll find it.*

By way of reply, the bird nuzzled the side of his head. The mage smiled again, his eyes misting slightly. *You are the bravest soul I know,* he told her truthfully. *We'll get through this.*

Late in the afternoon, hard, dry dirt began to replace the rank swamp mud. A wide, slow-moving river carried the Nal's refuse toward the fen, but the rest of the landscape, though stark, grew far less foul. At the same time, an enormous wall appeared in the distance, just in front of the imposing buildings and roadways of the Nal. Seeing it, Baram halted.

"What is it?" Orris asked. "What's the matter?"

Again, as he seemed to do all the time now, the outlander said something in his own language before answering Orris in words the Hawk-Mage could understand. "Guards," he said at last. "The Sovereign's guards."

"I don't see anyone," Orris replied, scanning the length of the wall.

Baram looked at him. "That means nothing here."

The mage stared back at him. It was more information about the Nal than Baram had given him all winter. He said nothing, hoping that the outlander might say more.

Instead, Baram gestured for Orris to follow him and started to walk westward, parallel to the Nal's southern boundary, his eyes never leaving the wall.

"Where are we going?" Orris asked, suddenly unable to take his own eyes off the wall.

"There is a better place."

"For what?"

Baram glanced at Orris as if the mage were an idiot. "For getting in."

"How do you know?" the Hawk-Mage demanded. "You've been gone for years! Don't things ever change in the Nal?"

Baram stopped, his pale eyes flicking doubtfully from Orris to the giant city. After a moment he continue on this new route.

"Wait a minute!" Orris called, forcing the outlander to stop again. "I'm trying to get to the Council of Sovereigns; why should I be afraid of the Sovereign's guards?"

"You tell me that you want me to be your guide!" Baram returned hotly. "You want me to take you to Sovereigns, right?"

Taken aback, Orris merely nodded.

"Then we do this my way!"

After several moments, Orris nodded a second time. "You're right," he said. "Get us into the Nal. I'll follow you."

"Come then," Baram commanded, turning and starting westward once more.

They walked that way for perhaps two hours, watching the sun, huge and rust-colored, dip below the horizon in front of them. Then they turned a bit so that they were angling toward the Nal again, specifically toward a bend in the wall. And as night fell, it occurred to Orris that part of Baram's goal had been to delay their approach to the Nal until after dusk. The Nal itself shone brightly at night, but the wall was not lit, nor was the land outside the confines of the city. Their chances of reaching the wall undetected were far greater now than they had been a few hours earlier.

As if to confirm this, Baram glanced at Orris over his shoulder. "Can you make your stone less bright?" he asked, his voice barely more than a whisper.

"Yes," Orris answered.

"Then do it. The guards might see."

The Hawk-Mage did as Baram had instructed. The mage didn't believe that he had anything to fear from the Sovereign's guards, but clearly Baram did. And for now at least, Orris sensed that he was better off trusting the outlander's instincts on this matter, even if he didn't fully trust the outlander. Better to stay with the enemy he knew than to risk being captured by one who might be even more dangerous.

Orris had expected that they would scale the wall, but when they reached it, he saw that this was impossible. The barrier was even taller than it had appeared from a distance, and its face was as smooth as glass.

"Rope?" Orris asked quietly, as the two of them stood in the shadows at the base of the structure.

Baram shook his head. He hesitated, as if searching for the proper words. "The top is . . . sharp," he said at last.

Orris stared at him. "What?"

The outlander frowned and then pointed upward.

Taking several steps back and gazing at the top of the wall, the mage saw several objects that resembled blades glinting in the light emitted by the Nal. "I understand," he said, looking at Baram again. "So how?"

"Follow me."

The outlander stepped closer to the wall and began to walk beside it slowly, staring at the ground as if he were searching for something. After several minutes of this he stopped and looked at the mage, a triumphant smile on his face. He bent to pick up what looked to be a stone resting at the base of the wall. It turned out to be the handle of a small door that covered a hole in the ground.

Orris's eyes widened and he stared at the outlander. "The guards don't know about this?"

"It is used only by gangmen," Baram replied, as if this answered the mage's question. He stepped onto a ladder and climbed down into the ground. "Quickly!" he urged, waving Orris toward the hole.

Orris followed the outlander, descending into what turned out to be a dark, narrow passageway.

"Your stone," Baram whispered.

Orris brightened his ceryll until he could see what lay ahead of them. The passage went straight for several yards, no doubt far enough to clear the wall. But then it widened and forked. Hurrying forward with the outlander to where the passage split, Orris saw that these two paths also divided into tunnels that, he guessed, soon divided themselves. He was on the edge of a tremendous labyrinth, he realized, one that probably stretched from one end of the Nal to the other. It wouldn't take much to get lost in a place like this, he thought, shuddering.

Baram led him to the left at the first junction and then to the right at the next. A few seconds later they came to a dark stairway. "This way," the outlander whispered.

Ascending a short flight of steps, they came to another small doorway. Orris could see light seeping through around the edges. I'm about to enter Bragor-Na, he told himself.

Baram looked back at him. "Your stone," he said again.

Orris muted the ceryll until it was almost completely dark.

Nodding with satisfaction, Baram slowly pushed open the door and the two travelers stepped out into the Nal.

They emerged into a small alley between two massive buildings that were constructed of glass and some sort of lustrous metal. At either end of the alley, light shone from a small glass ball mounted atop a tall pole. These he had been prepared for. But beyond one of the lights there was a smooth black roadway on which glass and metal objects, far larger than a merchant's street cart and mounted on wheels, sped past with a low humming sound. Orris could see people sitting inside of them.

"What were those?" he asked breathlessly, pointing toward the street.

Baram was glancing nervously from side to side. He did not appear to have heard Orris's question.

On the far side of the roadway loomed more buildings, all of them just as huge as those that towered above the alleyway.

Orris hadn't taken a step and he already felt overwhelmed. Anizir eyed the buildings warily and cried out softly as another of the wheeled objects raced by the entrance to the alley. The mage sent comforting thoughts to her and reached up to stroke her chin, but in that instant several things happened.

A flock of grey doves wheeled into view at the end of the alley and then continued up the main roadway. Seeing them, Anizir leaped off Orris's shoulder so forcefully that her talons gouged his shoulder through the padding in his cloak. He winced and grabbed at his shoulder. And doing so, he inadvertently blocked Baram's fist, which had been heading for his jaw. The outlander shouted something that might have been a curse, and tried to snatch Orris's staff out of the mage's hand.

But Orris was ready for him. He tightened his grip just in time, and the two men fell to the ground, wrestling for the staff. Baram was on top of him and had the advantage, but Orris was the stronger man. A moment later, the mage heard Anizir cry out from behind him and he knew that she had returned to help. Baram saw this as well. Pushing away from the mage, and throwing one more punch that caught Orris flush in the mouth, the outlander scrambled to his feet and sprinted out of the alley. Orris jumped up as well and started to give chase, but then he stopped himself. Even if he caught Baram now, it would just be a matter of time before the outlander tried to get away again. And next time he might succeed in inflicting a more serious injury. Orris touched his lip gently and realized that he was bleeding.

"Bastard!" he spat under his breath. Anizir sat on the ground in front of him, staring at him with her dark, intelligent eyes. "Go find those doves," he said gently. "I'm fine."

The falcon gazed at him for another moment and then flew off to find herself a meal. Orris leaned heavily against one of the buildings and took a long, slow breath. For several weeks now he had suspected that something like this might happen. Indeed, on some level he had known all along. But that didn't make it any easier. He and Anizir were alone in Bragor-Nal.

15

I fully expect that the contents of this report will draw criticism from many of my colleagues within the Order. And I also realize that no feature of my discussion is likely to be more controversial than my insistence that the people of Tobyn-Ser have much in common with the people of Lon-Ser. But we must remember that our two lands share a common origin. Before Arick, in his rage, smote the land he had given to his sons, Tobyn-Ser and Lon-Ser were one. It should come as no surprise then that their language resembles ours in certain ways, or that, except for honoring Lon rather than Tobyn, they worship the same gods we do. Clearly, based upon our experience with the outlanders, we must conclude that our two lands have followed markedly different paths since Arick sundered our land from theirs. But if we are to find a peaceful solution to the conflict that recently has developed between us, we must stress not our differences, but our commonalities.

> —From Section One of "The Report of Owl-Master Baden on his Interrogation of the Outlander Baram," Submitted to the 1,014th Gathering of the Order of Mages and Masters. Spring, Gods' Year 4625.

It was early morning, and he was still asleep when his speak-screen woke him with its soft beeping. He rose slowly and sauntered to the device, wondering with some annoyance who could be bothering him so early in the day. For several weeks after Melyor's visit the beeping of his screen sent him hurrying to his desk, his heart racing and his mouth suddenly dry. But as the memory of his conversation with the Nal-Lord faded, so too did the urgency he felt about the sorcerer's impending arrival in Bragor-Nal. "I've received intelligence reports of a stranger making his way to the Nal," she had said. And Jibb had not doubted her. After all, this was Melyor, and her description of the man had been remarkably detailed.

Too detailed, he had come to realize as the weeks passed; far more specific than any intelligence report he had ever seen. She had a tendency toward superstition he knew, and despite the fact that the decisions she based upon her strange beliefs had, over the years, been extraordinarily fortuitous, he had always considered her superstitious nature her one significant flaw as a leader. Certainly it had seemed to get the better of her on this occasion. It seemed that she had risked a great deal coming to see him, and for what? To discuss a concern that was, in all probability, based upon a dream, or some false intuition.

Or so Jibb had come to believe. But when he switched on his speak-screen and saw Chev's round, scarred face staring back at him, he realized that Melyor had been right after all. Again.

"Good morning, Nal-Lord," the break-law said, a crooked grin on his face. "I'm sorry if I woke you."

"Not at all, Chev," Jibb replied. *Nal-Lord*. He still wasn't used to being addressed that way. "Report."

"I received word about an hour ago, sir: the sorcerer has been seen in the Nal."

Jibb took a breath. *Extraordinary*. "Where?" he asked.

"Twenty-First Realm. Just a short distance north of the wall."

Jibb nodded. "Good. That must mean he hasn't been here long."

"Probably no more than two days, sir. He's still outside of Cedrych's Dominion. Should we wait—"

"No," Jibb cut in. "That may actually work to our advantage. I worked that part of the Nal as an independent a long time ago. I'm familiar with it. And for this particular assignment it might be to our advantage to be a good distance from the Overlord."

Chev looked into his screen quizzically. "Sir?"

Jibb had been thinking out loud, a habit, he now realized, that he would have to break if he was to be a successful Nal-Lord. "Never mind, Chev. I'll meet you and Darel in the Twenty-First late this afternoon. There's a bar in southeast quad twenty with a glowing likeness of a carrier in the front window. I forget the name."

"The Hummer, sir. I know it well." Chev grinned again in response to Jibb's raised eyebrow. "I've spent some time in the Twenty-First as well," the break-law explained.

"Apparently," Jibb said with a smirk. "I expect you to know precisely where we can find the sorcerer by then," he continued after a moment, his tone crisp once more. "Understood?"

Chev nodded. "Of course, Nal-Lord. Darel is tracking him right now."

"Glad to hear it."

"This afternoon then, sir."

"This afternoon. And Chev."

"Yes, sir?"

Jibb allowed himself a smile. "Well done."

"Thank you, sir."

An instant later, Jibb's speak-screen went blank. The Nal-Lord moved from his desk to the window and, opening the blinds, saw that it was another grey day. Rain fell on the street below, and carriers hummed past the flat, sending a fine mist of water into the air. All in all a typical early spring day in the Nal.

Except that today—tonight really—Jibb was going to kill a sorcerer. He shook his head, marvelling once more at the unfailing accuracy of Melyor's intelligence reports. If that really was where she got her information. It was hard for him to reconcile her susceptibility to superstitions with the precision of her intelligence network. Indeed, Jibb had often speculated that there might be some other explanation for why she was always so prepared for everything that happened in the Nal. But he had never come up with any that made sense. There was one possibility that stood out above all the rest in Jibb's mind, but it struck Jibb as so far-fetched as to be fanciful. Even Melyor, with her subtle mind and keen instincts could not have kept a secret of that magnitude for so long. Not from every other lord in the Nal; certainly not from Cedrych.

He shook his head for a second time. It didn't matter, and he had more important things to think about. Once more Melyor had been proven correct on a matter of enormous consequence. And as a result, Jibb had business to attend to in the Twenty-First Realm.

He knew the moment he awoke that this was the day, that before he slept again, he would either save the life of the yellow-haired sorcerer or die trying. He was in a small underground chamber in southeastern Bragor-Nal, still under the protection of the Network. But while all the people he had met on this side of the Median Range had been Gildriites, they had been as different from the Oracles of Oerella-Nal as their vast city was from its northern neighbor. The reserved warmth of Oerella-Nal's Gildriites seemed positively effusive next to the brooding silence that permeated the network of Bragor-Nal. The Gildriites here barely spoke at all, other than to give instructions or information. And even when they offered these, they did so in a clipped monotone that masked all emotion. The watchfulness that Gwilym had seen in the Gildriites of Oerella-Nal was replaced here by a perpetual state of panic that soon had Gwilym jumping at every unexpected noise. Oerella-Nal's Oracles lived their lives cautiously; Bragor-Nal's Oracles, Gwilym had come to believe, lived theirs with a dark oppressive terror.

Most disturbing of all was the fact that after only a few days in Bragor-Nal, Gwilym had understood. Even after the time he spent in Oerella-Nal, he had been thoroughly unprepared for what he found on this side of the Medians. The foul brown air, the squalor in the streets, the constant threat of violence that he sensed during even the briefest time spent above ground; all of these things combined to make Bragor-Nal more like a prison than a city. The sprawling system of passages and chambers that existed beneath the streets of the Nal offered only a modicum of safety for the Gildriites, for they shared it with the Nal's break-laws who, it appeared to Gwilym, had far more freedom here than ordinary law-abiding citizens.

On several occasions the Bearer and his taciturn guides were almost discovered by gangs of armed men. Twice he witnessed killings from dangerously conspicuous hiding places, and once he and a companion were fired upon by two men with large hand weapons that spewed out torrents of red flame. Only by sheerest luck had Gwilym found his way through the Nal safely. And yet, for all the danger he had faced, and the apparent indifference of the Network's members, he had gotten this far swiftly. He had been well-fed; he had never lacked for a place to sleep. *I have no right to complain,* he told himself. *For all the distance I have traveled, the sorcerer has come farther.*

This last thought impelled him off of the narrow canvas cot. He picked up his staff and pack, and stepped out of the chamber into a dimly lit passageway that smelled of urine and stale ale. A woman he did not recognize stood leaning against the wall. Her hair was short and dark save for a few wisps of silver. Her face was lined and pale, but her light blue eyes were surprisingly youthful.

"Are you hungry, Bearer?" she asked in a flat voice, holding out a large piece of dark bread, a block of hard cheese, and a sealed container of water.

"Yes, thank you." He took the offered food and began eating as they walked through the underground tunnels. "I need to be on the street tonight," he told her between mouthfuls.

She looked back at him, her expression revealing nothing. "Is that wise, Bearer?" she asked, facing forward again.

"Probably not, no," he said with a smile. The woman did not react and Gwilym pressed on. "Wise or not though, I don't have a choice. Tonight, the vision that brought me here will come to fruition."

She glanced at him again and nodded. The Oracles here might not be as friendly as those in Oerella-Nal, but they understood the Sight. "Very well. Where?"

Gwilym shook his head. "I'm not sure. South, in the part of the Nal that lies closest to the LonTobyn Isthmus. An alley between two large buildings. There was a yellow streetlamp nearby."

The woman grimaced. It took Gwilym a moment to realize that she was trying to smile. "That could be any quad in southeastern Bragor-Nal, Bearer. You'll need to do better than that."

"Just get me onto the street," he said. "The gods will do the rest."

She stared at him for a few seconds, saying nothing. Then she shrugged slightly.

They continued walking for what felt to Gwilym like a very long time, although it was hard to judge in the unchanging darkness of the tunnels. Perhaps an hour after they commenced their journey, they passed one of the small blue beacons which, Gwilym had learned, marked the boundary between one of Bragor-Nal's Realms and another. But if this was significant for them in some way, Gwilym's companion gave no indication of it other than to glance up at the light without breaking stride. The woman guided him through the twists and turns of the passageways with a surety that the Bearer found daunting, taking fork after fork without any visible hesitation. Gwilym assumed that they were headed in the proper direction, but he had no way of knowing for certain. Once again, as he had so many times since leaving the Dhaalmar, he found himself relying entirely on the good will and competence of others. As one who had been the leader of his settlement he was accustomed to having people look to him for guidance and protection. This new role still did not come to him easily.

After a time, Gwilym found himself paying little attention to the woman in front of him or the route she took through the underground maze. Once more, he had slept poorly the night before, and he was weary from months of uninterrupted travel. Here he was on the verge of meeting the man whose presence in a dream had driven him to leave his wife and home, and it was all he could do to shuffle along behind his guide, and keep from tripping over his own feet. And he was supposed to save the sorcerer's life? He shook his head, cursing his own stupidity. He couldn't do this on his own, and yet neither could he ask any of these people for help. They were doing all they could. For all Gildriites, but especially those living in Bragor-Nal, concealing their ancestry and their membership in the Network was a matter of survival. "We carry a poison tablet in the seams of our clothing," one unusually talkative woman had told him just over a week ago, "just in case we are captured. It is said that the Sovereign's security forces are so proficient at torture because they enjoy it so much. The capture of one of us could mean death for all of us." It was one thing to transport Gwilym through the Nal. It was quite another to help him save the life of the sorcerer. No, this was his task alone. And not for the first time, Gwilym railed at himself for ever thinking that he could succeed.

He was still berating himself, his eyes fixed on his feet, when the woman finally stopped. He nearly bumped into her. He did not notice the slight young man standing in the middle of the corridor in front of them until the stranger spoke.

"You're late," the man said quietly, his dark eyes fixed on Gwilym's guide.

"I know," she replied. "There was nothing to be done." She gestured back at Gwilym with a small movement of her head, as if to say that it was his fault. Which, after a moment's consideration, Gwilym accepted as true; she had been ready to go as soon as he awoke.

"Very well," the man said after a moment. He swung his dark gaze to Gwilym. "Come, Bearer. I'll take you to your next meeting point."

"He has need of haste," the woman said as Gwilym stepped past her to join his new guide. "And he wants to be on the street tonight."

The man looked at the Bearer sharply. "Why?"

"I'm just supposed to be," Gwilym answered, smiling inwardly. *See, I can be enigmatic, too.*

"Where?" the new guide asked.

Gwilym glanced sheepishly at the woman. "The southeastern corner of the Nal. Beyond that I don't know."

"That would be the Twenty-First Realm," the man said, as if thinking aloud.

"We're in the Twentieth now, so that shouldn't be too great a problem." He looked at Gwilym again. "I can get us a carrier, but you'll have to wait here for a short while."

The Bearer nodded. "All right."

The man disappeared down a narrow corridor that Gwilym hadn't noticed before, leaving Gwilym alone with the woman who had guided him throughout the morning. There was nowhere to sit, and so the two of them simply stood in the dim passageway, silent and awkward, waiting for the dark-eyed man to return. The time passed slowly, but even so, the man was not gone for very long.

"I have a carrier," he announced, as he stepped back into the passageway carrying a dark, studded overcoat. "It's waiting on the street above. Are you ready, Bearer?"

"Yes."

"Good," the man said, handing Gwilym the coat. "Put this on and cover your stone."

The Bearer slipped on the coat, tucked his staff against his side beneath it, and picked up his pack. The man slipped back into the narrow corridor, beckoning for Gwilym to follow.

"Goodbye," Gwilym said to the woman. "Thank you."

She nodded once before turning and walking back the way she and Gwilym had come.

"Quickly, Bearer!" the man whispered from down the corridor. "We have a good deal of distance to travel."

Gwilym hurried after the man and followed him up a flight of stairs. The guide waited for him at the top, his fingers gripping the handle of a small door. He looked Gwilym over once, as if to satisfy himself that the Bearer wouldn't attract too much attention. Then he pushed the door open.

After spending so much time underground, Gwilym was unprepared for the painfully bright daylight that greeted them. It took his eyes several moments to adjust. When they finally did, he saw that he and the man were in an alley between two large buildings. The road was wet, but it was no longer raining. Looking more closely at the alley, Gwilym realized that it looked very much like the narrow street he had seen in his dream. Too much like it. The Bearer's heart sank. According to his guide they weren't even in the right Realm yet, and already he had found an alley that matched the meager details he remembered from his vision. The woman had been right: he couldn't possibly find the correct alleyway based on what he had seen. *Just get me onto the street,* he had said. *The gods will do the rest.* He had believed the words when he spoke them, but now they sounded arrogant and foolish.

"Get in," the man said, opening the doors of a small, dilapidated carrier. Gwilym hurried after him, trying to mask his skepticism as he examined the vehicle.

As bad as it looked though, the carrier started up immediately and before Gwilym had managed to close his door, they were speeding out of the alley and onto the main avenue. From there they made their way to an elevated roadway that the guide called the Upper and which would, he explained, allow them to reach the southeastern end of the Twenty-first Realm in a fraction of the time it would have taken had they gone through the quads.

High as it was, the Upper afforded a striking view of the Nal. From this perspective, Gwilym could see the precise symmetry and mind-numbing sameness of the quads that stretched endlessly in all directions below. Looking up he also saw that they were quite close to the thick brown cloud that hung perpetually over the Nal. Oddly, it reminded him of the heavy grey storm clouds that settled over the Dhaalmar during the winter. He smiled to himself, though sadly, wondering why this mass of filthy air should be the most familiar thing about the Nal.

They remained on the Upper for well over an hour, until they came within sight of a broad muddy plain that extended far to the south.

"That's the Guardian Swamp," the dark-eyed guide said when Gwilym asked him about it. "We're over the Twenty-First now, but I want to get us a bit closer to the edge of the Nal before leaving the Upper."

Gwilym nodded, although he was no longer listening very closely to what the man said. His heart was suddenly pounding heavily within his chest—no faster than usual, but harder, as if his blood had thickened. He found it hard to focus his eyes on anything and he wondered for just a moment if he was ill. But he knew better. For while his vision was blurred, his senses felt heightened. Somehow he knew that the yellow-haired sorcerer was here, close now, wandering through the lattice of roads and squares that lay below them. And despite the tightness in his chest, and the dryness in his throat, Gwilym smiled. It seemed the gods were with him after all.

"You don't have to go much farther," Gwilym said quietly, still staring out the window. He felt the carrier slow slightly.

"What?" the man asked.

Even without turning, Gwilym knew the man was looking at him. "He's close," Gwilym said. "We need to get down to the street soon."

"Who's close?" the guide demanded. "How do you know this all of a sudden?"

Gwilym faced him. "I just do. The man I've come to meet is down there in the Nal. We need to get off the Upper." He hadn't raised his voice at all, but something in Gwilym's tone seemed to reach the man, because after a moment he nodded, and at the next opportunity, he steered the carrier off the Upper and down toward the quads.

At the bottom of the ramp, the man stopped the carrier and looked at Gwilym once more. "Which way, Bearer?"

Again, Gwilym grinned inwardly. For the first time today, the man had addressed him with a note of respect in his voice. "That way," Gwilym answered, pointing. "But not far."

"That's north," the man said.

"North then."

The small vehicle started forward again, slipping into the stream of carriers that flowed slowly through the avenues of the Twenty-First Realm. Gwilym gazed out the window at the faces of the people on the walkways. The sorcerer wouldn't be there, he knew. By now the man would have realized that he was better off in the alleys and byways than he was on the main roads. But Gwilym looked anyway, seeking anything at all that might tell him where to find the sorcerer.

They drove for a long time, circling each quad so that Gwilym could examine every alley. The confidence the Bearer had felt as they descended from the Upper gradually diminished, giving way to an uncertainty and fear that had become all too familiar in recent weeks. He was searching—desperately now, as the grey daylight began to fade—for a single man in a place that was so impossibly large Gwilym could not have imagined it prior to leaving his home. He felt despair seeping into his heart like ice water. An image of Hertha entered his mind and he thought he might cry.

As they entered yet another quad, the Nal's streetlamps switched on, and something both strange and familiar caught Gwilym's eye. On the far side of the quad, one of the lights shone unevenly. Looking more closely, Gwilym saw why. Its covering was cracked and stained on one side, just like the lamp he had seen in his dream of the sorcerer.

"There!" he shouted so suddenly that the guide flinched, causing the carrier to swerve dangerously close to another vehicle.

"You see him?" the man asked, his eyes scanning the avenue.

"No!" Gwilym could barely contain himself. "That broken streetlamp over there," he said pointing to the broken light. "That's where I'm supposed to be."

The man stared at him, skepticism manifest in his thin face. "You're sure of this?" he asked.

Before the Bearer could answer it began to rain again in small drops that streaked the carrier's windows. This is my vision, Gwilym thought. It's all coming to pass. "Yes," he said simply. He reached for the door handle. "I'll get out here."

"Do you know how to reach us again?"

Gwilym hesitated.

"You see that alley?" the man asked, pointing to a passageway that lay about halfway between the carrier and Gwilym's streetlight. "Go to the corresponding alley three quads west and two north of here," he instructed, his eyes flicking repeatedly to the road as he spoke. "There will be a small door in the precise middle of the alley. Knock once, then twice more. I'll let you in."

Gwilym nodded, repeating the directions quietly so as to commit them to memory. He glanced at the alley the guide had indicated and let out a slow breath. The quads were all so similar and symmetrical; he found it difficult to keep his bearings. He wasn't at all certain that he could find the corresponding alley in the next quad, much less one several quads away. "I'll find it," he said, hoping he sounded convincing. "Thank you for everything."

The man faced forward again, as if embarrassed by Gwilym's gratitude. "Go, Bearer," he said, slowing the carrier. "Keep your stone covered and watch yourself."

Gwilym put his staff within the folds of the overcoat that he still wore, gripped the straps of his pack, and climbed out of the carrier into the cold Nal rain. Hurrying to the walkway, he watched the dilapidated carrier pull away. Then he started toward the broken streetlamp. The sky was darkening rapidly and Gwilym realized that he had no idea when to expect the sorcerer. It had been night in his vision, but it could have been any time between dusk and dawn. He quickened his pace.

Reaching the entrance to the alley, Gwilym glanced around him to be sure that no one was watching. Then he stepped into the passageway, suddenly alert, his pulse quickening. The assassins might already be here. Of course they have no reason to pay any attention to you, he told himself, unless you give them one. Doing his best to appear casual, Gwilym walked the length of the alley to where it ended at one of the quad's internal byways, then turned and walked back to the alley's entrance. Convinced that he was alone, he looked for a place to hide and wait. The sound of dripping water drew his attention. Walking to its source Gwilym found the place where he had seen himself in the dream, huddled against the cold, waiting for the sorcerer. It didn't look terribly comfortable, and he considered searching for another spot.

But at that moment he heard voices behind him and he dove down out of sight. Three men entered the alley, two of whom Gwilym recognized immediately as the men who had fired their weapons at the stranger in his vision. One of them was of medium height and build, with a round, scarred face and dark hair. The other was taller, leaner, with light hair, and deep-set, angry eyes. But it was to the third man that the Bearer's eyes were continually drawn. In his vision he had seen only two men, and he would have remembered this one. He was enormous and muscular, although he carried himself with a lightness and grace that belied his size. He had dark eyes and his hair was unkempt and curly. Gwilym knew just from looking at him that he was by far the most dangerous of the three men. And yet, he had a disarmingly pleasant face and a kind smile that he flashed at his companions now, even as he spoke to them of killing the sorcerer.

Gwilym shook his head at his own foolishness. He had assumed from the start that there would be two men lying in wait for the stranger, that everything he needed to know had been presented to him in his vision. But obviously he had been wrong. There were three armed assassins, not two. What else had he failed to see? And here was Gwilym, trapped in the alley, squatting in the shadows between a trash holder and a building's drainage pipe, unable to do anything at all except wait for the terrifying scene to play itself out before him once again.

The three men spoke for another few moments and then took their positions in the alley, the two men Gwilym recognized from his vision walking together to the far end of the alley, and the large man finding a spot alarmingly close to where Gwilym was hiding. He heard the men moving for a short while, settling in to wait for the sorcerer. Soon though, the alley grew eerily still save for the rain and the water dripping off the buildings. The muscles in the Bearer's legs and back began to ache, and despite the overcoat he wore, he was growing cold. He longed to stretch out his legs or at least shift his position slightly, but he was afraid to move at all lest he alert the big man to his presence. Time crawled forward, measured by the sound of his own breathing, which sounded terribly loud just now, and by the painful stiffening of his limbs.

After a while the rain intensified, and the water from the building beside him began to drip on his head, cold and hard, triggering a memory. He heard a woman laugh. In the distance two men argued. It seemed to Gwilym that his heart stopped beating, that the entire world paused in anticipation of what was coming. He knew what he would hear next, but even so, when the sound finally reached him, he started so violently that he nearly lost his balance: footsteps, light, nimble, but unmistakable. Gwilym waited for the sound to draw nearer; he had to be certain. He heard the big assassin shift his position slightly, as if readying himself for the attack. The time had come. He took a deep breath, closed his eyes, and formed an image of Hertha's face in his mind one last time. Then he leaped out into the open, shouting a warning to the sorcerer, and fully expecting to die in the next instant.

For a while, as he stood in the alley waiting for Anizir to return to him, his lip still bleeding from Baram's blow, Orris wasn't certain what to do next. He had no idea where he was or where he needed to go to find the Council of Sovereigns. And though he hadn't seen any people other than those in the strange wheeled objects that sped past the entrance to the alley, he assumed that daybreak would bring hordes of people onto the streets. He didn't care to find out how they might react to seeing a stranger dressed in a mage's cloak and carrying a bird like Anizir. He could always return to the underground tunnels, he considered, glancing back at the small door through which he and Baram had entered the alley, but he knew that he would have even less of a chance of finding his way through the passageways than he would of navigating Bragor-Nal's streets.

Anizir flew into view clutching a dove in her talons. She landed at Orris's feet and immediately began ripping at the bird with her beak. Orris smiled. At least one of his concerns had been taken care of: his familiar wouldn't starve in the Nal. The mage looked toward the street again as another of the wheeled objects rolled by. He should have been tired. He had been traveling for the better part of a year, and he had fought with Baram just a short while ago. But he felt strangely alert and energetic. The more he thought about it, the more he realized that there was only one thing to do.

"Eventually, someone's going to see us," he said aloud. "There's really nothing we can do about it."

Anizir looked up at him briefly before returning to her meal.

Orris gave a small laugh. "I'll take that as a sign of your agreement."

A few minutes later, the falcon finished eating and flew to his shoulder. The mage took one last look around him and then started in the direction Baram had run. Reaching the end of the alley and gazing down the avenue, Orris gasped. There were so many enormous buildings on both sides of the street and in both directions, that he had to resist an urge to retreat back into the alley. Several wheeled objects of varying sizes sped by. Orris noticed that several of the people inside them stared at him as they went past. He also saw that on the far side of the street another alley began. Hurrying across the broad avenue, he followed this passageway until it ended at a narrow street lined with still more buildings. Here he turned right, following this street until it too ended. Left to the next street, right again, and then left again.

As he made this last turn he finally spotted another main avenue in the distance and he ran toward it. But when he reached it and looked first one way and then the other, he couldn't believe what he saw. It appeared to be the same street he had seen as he stepped out of the first alley. For a moment he thought that he was imagining things, and then glancing back toward the narrow road he had just taken, he wondered if he had managed somehow to go around in a circle. Examining the avenue again, he saw that there was another alley on the far side of the road. Careful to keep track this time of exactly what he did, Orris repeated the turns he had taken through the last maze of streets and passages until he reached the next main avenue. Once again, he found that this road was identical to the previous two.

He stepped back into this last alley to catch his breath. There was no way he had gone in a circle this time. He was certain. Which meant that all the buildings and roads looked the same. Orris shook his head. How did these people find their way to and from their homes every day? Venturing onto the main avenue again, Orris spotted a sign mounted on one of the tall lights. The sign read simply "ES—27." Moved as much by sheer curiosity as by his need to make some sense of the Nal, Orris entered the next alley and repeated the pattern a third time. Coming to yet another avenue, he immediately located another sign. This one said, "ES—26."

"There's a pattern here after all," he said aloud, eliciting a soft cry from Anizir. He stroked her chin, whispering to her reassuringly, and then he crossed the avenue to the next alley and continued in whatever direction it was he had been going.

He altered his direction slightly at daybreak, when the light of morning allowed him to orient himself. He had been going due west, and now he changed the pattern he followed through the smaller roads so that it carried him north and west. He wasn't certain that this was where he wanted to go; he was going on instinct mostly. But it stood to reason that he should travel away from the swamp, farther into Bragor-Nal. It was certainly better than standing still.

As the sky brightened he encountered more and more people. They stared at him with unconcealed curiosity, some even shouted things at him in their language, but he didn't care. He still had his powers; he could protect himself. And now that he had started to grasp the layout of the Nal, he felt his confidence returning. Near midday, however, his sleepless night began to catch up with him. Finding one of the small doors that led to the tunnels, he went underground, found a dark corner, and fell immediately into a deep, dreamless slumber.

He woke up ravenous and ate the last of the food he had been rationing for the final several days of his journey through the swamp. He'd have to find more food soon, but for now at least, he was sated. Emerging onto the street again, he found that it was already dark—he had no idea how long he had slept. Anizir conveyed an image to him of the grey doves and flew off to hunt, leaving Orris to get his bearings again. It only took him a minute or two, and after the falcon returned and ate her meal, they resumed their journey through the city, once more keeping to the alleys and narrow roads that connected the broader avenues. They kept moving throughout the night, stopping to sleep midway through the following day, and emerging from the tunnels again just at dusk.

Plunging into the alleys once more, Orris rushed through the narrow streets with a grim singlemindedness. He still hadn't eaten, and he had begun to contemplate building a small fire so that he could cook one of the grey doves. It was not an appealing thought—not only because the birds looked scrawny and unappetizing, but also because he did not like the idea of drawing attention to himself in that way. He was growing desperate, however.

He was still weighing that possibility as he crossed another avenue and stepped into the next alley. He had lost track of the numbers printed on the signs, and he briefly considered going back to check this one. But instead he resolved to check the sign at the next avenue and he continued through the alley.

He had only gone a short distance, however, when suddenly a person jumped out just in front of him. He was an older man, portly. He wore a dark overcoat over something that resembled a mage's cloak and, amazing though it seemed, he carried a staff crowned by a ceryll that was quite similar in color to Orris's. He was shouting something frantically at Orris, but the mage didn't understand a word of it. An instant later though, two other men appeared several yards behind this one, and both of them had weapons.

Orris leveled his staff at them, intending to blast them with mage-fire, but before he could, the heavy man cried out again and Orris heard a noise behind him. A trap, he had time to think, before red flame burst from the weapons of the two men in front of him. The mage leaped forward, knocking the older man to the ground. At the same time, he sheathed himself in an armor of shimmering amber power that blocked the fire from the two men in front of him, as well as the one behind him.

Orris heard the men cry out in astonishment, and using that opportunity, he dove for cover behind a large metal box that smelled of rotting food. He reached for Anizir, who was circling overhead, screaming, and he instructed her to fly at the lone attacker who had been behind him. A few seconds later he heard the man snarl with anger and then shout something to his accomplices. One of them started to respond. But before he could, Orris sprang out into the open again, pointed his staff at the two men and sent a stream of amber fire in their direction, making it fork at the last minute. One of the men managed to duck under the blast, but the other did not react fast enough. The mage-fire caught him full in the chest, smashing him to the ground like a giant, glowing fist.

By this time the lone attacker had recovered from Anizir's initial assault, which had left him with an angry gash on his forehead, and he was firing his weapon repeatedly at the falcon. She was darting and swooping from side to side to evade the beams of red flame, but her cries were growing increasingly strident.

"Hey!" Orris shouted, spinning toward the man and in the same motion hurling a ball of flame at him. The attacker jumped to the side, rolled, and came up firing at Orris. The mage blocked the salvo with another curtain of power, but he sensed that Anizir was starting to tire, and he knew that the other assailant had probably recovered from the shock of seeing his friend die. The mage and his bird were running out of time.

He heard something hiss behind him and in the next instant saw red flame smash into the wall of the building just above where the man who had helped him was now hiding. A second later he was forced to block another blast from the lone attacker. Orris threw another burst of power at him, but the man flung himself to the side. Without hesitating, Orris whirled toward the one who remained behind him. The timing was perfect, as the mage had guessed it would be. The man was just coming out into the open. Orris saw his eyes widen, saw him try to duck back down. But by then the mage-fire was on its way. Still the man almost managed to elude it. The burst of power hit him just above the chin with such force that Orris looked away immediately, unwilling to see the damage he had inflicted.

The remaining assassin had seen it, however, and rather than stay to continue the fight, he sprinted out of the alley and disappeared around a corner, leaving Orris alone with the man who had saved his life.

Slowly, almost shyly, the heavy man got to his feet, recovered his staff, which lay on the ground a few feet away, and walked toward Orris. The mage was breathing hard, and when Anizir settled to his shoulder, he stroked her chin and checked her to make certain that she was uninjured.

The stranger stopped in front of him and held out a hand. After a moment Orris took it and chanced a smile. "Thanks," he said. "I'd be dead if it wasn't for you."

The older man frowned slightly. He had a pleasant round face that reminded Orris in many ways of Hawk-Mage Radomil. Indeed, with his round belly and bald head this man would have looked just like Radomil if only he had a goatee and mustache. But apparently the stranger hadn't understood a word of what Orris had said.

"I don't speak your language," Orris told him. And then, remembering his exchange with Baram on the Isthmus, he shook his head and added, "No Lonmir."

The portly man smiled ruefully and shook his head as well, saying something that ended with the word "Tobynmir."

"Great," Orris mumbled. "We've managed to communicate to each other that we can't communicate."

Somehow the man seemed to understand what Orris had said, because he began to chuckle softly and shake his head again.

And in that moment, Orris decided that he liked this man, notwithstanding their inability to talk. It helped of course that the stranger had saved his life.

The portly man said something else and reached tentatively for Anizir. Orris nodded and then communicated to his bird that she should let the stranger touch her. She stretched out her neck and the man caressed her chin.

Then he looked at Orris again, said something, and motioned for Orris to follow him toward the avenue. "Gwilym," the man said as they stepped onto the main road and began to walk due west. It sounded like a name.

"Orris," the mage replied, holding out his hand again.

Gwilym took it and grinned.

Orris smiled as well. Perhaps with time they would be able to communicate after all. And for now, he and Anizir weren't alone anymore.

16

I have tried again and again to find some way to make sense of Baram's descriptions of the advanced goods and tools that are used in his land, but they are so far beyond anything that we have here in Tobyn-Ser that I find our language inadequate to the task. To say that this ability they have to mimic nature touches every aspect of their lives, that indeed it dominates their lives, fails to do justice to the impressions of life in Lon-Ser that I have gained from my conversations with the outlander. . . .

. . . Given all that I have learned from Baram, it seems to me that the most compelling question is not "How does this ability shape their lives?" but rather "How do they cope with the limits set by nature that lie beyond their control?" If their plains and farmland are gone, how do they grow food? If they have befouled their water, what do they drink? If they have used up their forests, how do they continue to produce items containing wood? In answering these questions we begin to understand our enemies as a people. And perhaps with time, doing this will allow us to see them as something other than just our enemies.

—From Section Five of "The Report of Owl-Master Baden on his Interrogation of the Outlander Baram," Submitted to the 1,014th Gathering of the Order of the Mages and Masters. Spring, Gods' Year 4625.

It had never happened to Melyor before. Never. Certainly she had recurring dreams now and then, nightmares that intruded upon her sleep again and again. She had relived the day of her father's assassination more times than she cared to count. But those were simply dreams. Never before had a true Seeing come to her more than once.

Until tonight. She had dreamed of the sorcerer again, which was strange enough, since he should have been dead by now. But not only had she envisioned him again, this Seeing had been identical to the one that had come to her several weeks before. Every detail and nuance had been the same. As soon as she awoke, sweaty and breathless as she always was after a Seeing, she knew what it meant. Jibb had failed. She tried to feel angry, but she found instead that she was vaguely relieved. Idiot! she growled at herself. This threatens everything! And yet . . .

She shook her head and glanced at the clock. It was still early enough. Barely, to be sure, but it could be done. She jumped out of bed, threw on some clothes, and crept to the door of her room. She had learned to master the electronic locking system within a day of her arrival at Cedrych's training center, and slipping past the guards who were ostensibly keeping Melyor and her crew within the confines of the center had proved laughably easy the last time she went to see Jibb. The main problem lay in defeating the alarm and surveillance devices that guarded the doors leading into and out of the center itself. Last time she had done it, but only after wasting far too much time on the effort. She didn't have that luxury tonight. She had also sensed something strange in her interaction with Cedrych the following morning, and she had been forced to acknowledge that her secret excursion into the Nal may not have gone unnoticed after all.

So tonight she decided to try something new. Just as she had last time, Melyor made her way through the brightly lit corridors to the lifter and she pressed the button for the level of the building that housed the combat grounds. Once she reached the grounds, and after she had convinced herself that the lifter was gone, she overrode the protections on the doors to the lifter shaft and climbed down the maintenance ladder. This time, however, rather than stopping at the main floor, she continued all the way down to the second subfloor. There she again overrode the door protections. From subfloor two, as she had expected, it was a small matter to sneak out of the center through an air purifier vent.

Hastening to the nearest alley, and from there into the underground tunnels, Melyor soon reached the small carrier that she kept stowed on a little-used byway a couple of quads from the center. An hour later, she was at Jibb's flat, defeating his lock as if it were a child's toy.

As it turned out though, she might as well have knocked. The break-law was awake already—or perhaps still—slumped on a sofa in his common room, his round features etched with fatigue, his dark curls even more unruly than usual. He wore an ugly red gash over his left eye, and dried blood still covered his face.

"If I didn't know better I'd say that you were waiting up for me," Melyor remarked as she closed his door behind her and dropped herself into a large, soft chair.

Jibb's expression didn't change. "I have been."

She stared at him. "What?"

"I have been waiting for you," he repeated. "I knew you'd be coming to find out what happened."

"I don't understand," she said, forcing the words out. Her mouth was suddenly dry, and her heart hammered within her chest. "I came to hear about the sorcerer; I assumed that you'd found and killed him by now."

"Stop playing games with me, Melyor!" Jibb spat, propelling himself off the sofa. He thrust his hands into the pockets of his overcoat and began to pace the length of the room. "You know that I failed, and you want to know why!"

"Jibb—"

"Don't!" he warned, halting his pacing and pointing a rigid finger at her. "You knew that he'd be coming; you knew what he'd look like; you probably even knew where he'd be. And somehow you knew that I failed."

Melyor shook her head. "No. I just—"

He stopped her again, this time with a raised hand. "It happened tonight, Melyor. Just a few hours ago. And here you are. Explain that."

For several moments she said nothing. Then she gave him the only answer she could, which, as it happened, was true, although not the way she intended him to take it. "I can't," she said softly. "I wish I could, but I can't."

Jibb started to say something, but stopped himself and began his pacing again instead.

"Why don't you tell me what happened tonight," she coaxed gently. "I need to know, and I haven't much time."

He said nothing for several moments as he continued to stride back and forth across the room. "There was a second man there," he finally told her, "another sorcerer I think."

"What?" she breathed. "Are you sure?"

"Of course," he answered, his expression hurt. "You think I'd lie to cover my ass?"

Melyor shook her head. "That's not what I meant, Jibb. Are you sure it was another sorcerer?"

"Who else could it have been?"

"Possibly . . ." She faltered. I don't have time for this, she told herself impatiently. "It doesn't matter. What happened?" she demanded, trying to keep the anxiety from her voice.

Jibb gave a small shrug. "Darel had been tracking the sorcerer for several hours, and he noticed a definite pattern to his movements. He stuck to the small roads and he traveled consistently to the northwest. So we set an ambush for him in an alley in the Twenty-First. Southeast quad ten. Chev and Darel were at the byway end; I was the cap man. The sorcerer came into the alley just an hour or two after dusk, just as we expected him to. We were about ready to spring the trap when this other man jumps out into the alley screaming a warning to the sorcerer."

"And why do you think that this man was a sorcerer too?"

The break-law shrugged for a second time. "He carried a stick with a glowing stone on it, just like the sorcerer. And he had on a green robe beneath his overcoat."

Melyor frowned. "He had an overcoat?"

"Yes."

"How about a bird?"

Jibb raised a hand to his injured brow, as if reminded of the wound by Melyor's question. "No," he answered after seeming to consider the matter for a moment. "He only had the stick and the robe. No bird."

Melyor sat forward, her eyes narrowing. "When he shouted to the sorcerer, did you understand him?"

"Yes," Jibb replied with a nod. "He said something about a trap and told the sorcerer to protect himself."

Melyor sat back again, her mind struggling to cope with the implications of what Jibb had seen. "A Bearer," she muttered to herself. "He must have been a Bearer."

Jibb stared at her. "A what?"

"You've heard of the Gildriites, right?" she asked him.

His eyes flicked away nervously. "Of course," he said, his voice sounding strange all of a sudden.

She knew what he was thinking, what he had been thinking since her arrival at his flat. She fought desperately to control the fear that she felt rising within her chest. "The leaders of the Gildriite settlements in the Dhaalmar are called Bearers of the Stone," she explained, pleased to hear how steady her voice sounded. "According to legend, they still carry the stones originally brought to Lon-Ser by Gildri and his followers. This second man you saw must have been a Bearer."

Jibb looked at her again. "How can you know that?" he asked almost petulantly.

"It makes sense, Jibb," she told him, allowing a note of impatience to creep into her voice. "He spoke our language, so he probably wasn't from Tobyn-Ser. He carried a staff but no bird. And from the way you've described what happened, it sounds to me like he wasn't traveling with the sorcerer."

After several moments, almost reluctantly, the break-law nodded.

Melyor glanced at the clock on Jibb's wall. "Tell me the rest of it," she urged, her voice gentle again. "I have to get back."

The break-law returned to the sofa and sat down heavily. "Once the sorcerer knew we were there, we didn't have a chance. He was able to use his magic as both a shield and a weapon. He killed Darel and Chev." He pointed to his brow. "I got this from his bird."

Melyor grinned for just an instant. "I figured."

"So what happens now?"

Melyor shook her head. "I really don't know. If a Bearer managed to get all the way to the Twenty-First without your knowing about it, he must have had help."

"The Network?"

"Probably. In which case the sorcerer could be anywhere by now."

Jibb let out a long breath and looked down at his hands. "I'm sorry, Nal-Lord."

She felt another surge of relief and she thrust it away violently. "It's not your fault, Jibb. None of us has much experience dealing with sorcery. And it sounds like there was nothing you could have done. We can't foresee these things," she added, regretting her choice of words immediately.

Jibb looked at her sharply, and Melyor braced herself for the questions that she knew would be coming. But as he had so many times in their four years together, the break-law surprised her. "If you want to find someone to replace me as interim Nal-Lord, I'll understand."

Melyor scowled at him. "Why would I want to do that?" she asked testily.

"I failed you," the big man said simply. "You gave me what was obviously a very important assignment, and I didn't complete it."

"I don't want to replace you Jibb." *You're my best friend.* "I have complete faith in you." She paused, her eyes meeting his. "The question is, do you want to find another employer?"

He shifted uncomfortably. "No. Why would I?"

Melyor smiled. "Any number of reasons," she said carefully.

The break-law looked away. "I can't think of any good ones."

Melyor stood and started for the door. "Good," she said. "I'm very glad to hear that."

"Melyor," she heard him say as she reached for the door handle. She turned once more, waiting. He was looking at her intently, and she could see him struggling with something. But once more she was caught off guard by his restraint. "Be careful," he finally murmured looking away again. "Cedrych isn't likely to be understanding."

She nodded. "I always have been." It was an admission of sorts, but this was Jibb, and suddenly she didn't mind if he knew.

Without another word she left the flat, jumped into her carrier and sped back to the center. She would be there before dawn, but not by much.

As she raced along the Upper, she found once more that she felt oddly comforted by the fact that the sorcerer had survived Jibb's ambush. The conflict she had felt within her mind the night she decided to have the sorcerer killed had been resolved; in a sense, her mother and father weren't fighting anymore. True, the problems that the break-law's failure would create promised to be numerous and complicated, but Melyor was not thinking of those. She had dreamed of the sorcerer again—she had seen once more the image of herself, fighting side by side with this strange man and his beautiful hawk, as if she and he were allies in some great cause. But even more than that, Jibb had seen a Bearer. The sorcerer was already allied with the Gildriites of Lon-Ser. Had the sorcerer come to end a thousand years of Gildriite oppression? Was that why she would eventually find herself fighting beside him? Was that why the Bearer had come?

Perhaps because she was so preoccupied, the trip back to the center seemed far quicker than the journey to Jibb's flat. Returning the carrier to its stowing place near the center, Melyor sprinted through the tunnels and alleys until she was back at the air vent. From there she retraced her clandestine route through the center, making certain to stop at the combat grounds before taking the lifter back to her room.

Despite her precautions, however, she knew as soon as she reached her room that she was in trouble. For one thing, her speak-screen was beeping. Arick knew how long ago the call had come in. And it came as no surprise to her when she finally got the machine switched on with trembling hands and saw that the message was from Cedrych.

It simply said, "See me."

She didn't need for it to say "immediately." Nonetheless, before going to see the Overlord she jumped into the shower, because she needed to, and because it was what Cedrych would have expected her to do if she really had spent an entire night on the combat grounds. It was a game, or more precisely, the continuation of a game that they had been playing for years. If Cedrych knew that she had left her room, which seemed likely given how strangely he had behaved after her last visit with Jibb, then the first thing he would have done was check the combat grounds for her. And if he had, of course, he would know that she hadn't been there. But on the off chance that her ruse had worked, she had to see it through all the way.

When she reached the door to Cedrych's training center office, which was three floors above her room, a stoic, muscular guard took her thrower, blade, and boots, and used a hand searcher to check her for other weapons. Even here, in his training center, Cedrych was taking no chances.

Melyor entered the room and found Cedrych in a familiar pose, standing at his window contemplating the Nal. This temporary office bore little resemblance to the office in his living quarters. The floors, like those in her room, were carpeted, and the furnishings, though sparse, were adequate. But overall, these accommodations were far less opulent than those in which she was used to seeing the Overlord.

"Sit down," he said without looking at her.

Melyor felt herself growing cold, and as she obeyed his command she strove to check the acceleration of her pulse.

"We have a problem," the Overlord told her as he continued to survey the Nal. "One that must be dealt with quickly, but with great caution."

"You've piqued my curiosity," Melyor replied, still fighting her nerves.

Cedrych turned, impaling her with the glare of his one good eye. Melyor held his gaze for as long as she could, but after several moments she looked away and swallowed. Glancing back at him an instant later, she saw a smile flit across his scarred features. He knows, she said to herself. This is all a game; he knows everything.

"There is a sorcerer in Bragor-Nal," he said at last. "He arrived three or four nights ago."

"A sorcerer?" she answered, trying to make herself look and sound surprised, just as she knew she was supposed to do. "You're sure?"

"I have men everywhere, Melyor. Little goes on in the Nal without my knowledge."

Melyor heard the warning in his words, but she forced herself to ignore this for the time being. "Where is he?" she asked, and immediately cringed at her slip. For just a second she wondered if he might have missed it, but this was Cedrych: he hadn't gotten this far by missing things of this sort.

"He?" the Overlord asked, pouncing on the word like a cat. He grinned. "Why would you think it was a man?"

Melyor felt herself blanch. "I just assumed," she managed to say.

Again the grin stretched across Cedrych's face, insidious and predatory. "Assumed?" he repeated, raising an eyebrow. "You of all people." He stared at her for another moment and then turned back toward the window. "As it happens, you're correct: it is a man. And to answer your question, I'm not sure. He had been in the Twenty-First—Wildon's Dominion—but my informants lost track of him last night. He could be anywhere by now," he concluded, much as she herself had in her conversation with Jibb.

Melyor watched the Overlord expectantly but said nothing. Finally he glanced back over his shoulder at her. "Wouldn't you like to know how he got away?"

"I figured you'd tell me when you were ready," she said, with slightly more asperity than she had intended.

"Indeed," he said, his expression revealing nothing. "Apparently the sorcerer was ambushed by a group of break-laws."

"And he survived?" Melyor asked innocently.

Cedrych pressed his lips into a thin smile. "So it would seem. We found the bodies of two men—marred beyond recognition, I might add—and blood from a third. But there was nothing to indicate that the sorcerer had been killed. In the confusion that followed the firefight, he must have slipped away."

Melyor sat waiting for more, wondering if Cedrych knew of the Bearer. For his part, the Overlord stared back at her, as if he too were waiting for something. "Well?" he finally said.

She cocked her head slightly. "Well, what, Overlord?"

He faced the window once more, but she could see the muscles in his neck tightening. She was treading on very dangerous ground. "Don't you find it strange that he should be ambushed so quickly after his arrival in the Nal?"

Melyor shrugged. "I just thought that since you knew of his arrival, you had ordered the ambush yourself."

"Well, I didn't!" he snapped, whirling to face her.

Melyor flinched back against her chair. "Perhaps it was a chance encounter," she blurted out, her heart suddenly pounding.

"It was a trap!" he flung back at her. "They were waiting for him in an alley! The two who died were the deep men; the cap man got away."

"Maybe Wildon ordered it," she suggested, still recovering from the shock of Cedrych's outburst. "You said it was in his Dominion."

The Overlord dismissed the idea with an impatient gesture and gripped the back of his desk chair with rigid fingers. "Wildon wouldn't know a sorcerer from a Gildriite," he remarked contemptuously, sending a shiver through Melyor's body. Fortunately, he was staring at his desk as he spoke. "He might have given the order to have the stranger killed, but he and his men wouldn't have known enough to send three break-laws after him." He shook his head. "It had to be someone else." He looked up at her again, the single blue eye blazing. "Where did you go last night, Melyor?"

So much for playing games, she thought, taken aback by the directness of the question. There was no sense in lying. "I went to see Jibb," she told him candidly.

"Why?"

"Because I'm finding it very hard to give up control of my Realm."

He narrowed his eye. "What?"

"Last night wasn't the first time I went to see him," she admitted. "I've gone twice now. I trust Jibb, but I can't seem to—"

"Wait a minute," he said shaking his head again and stepping around his desk to stand directly in front of her. "You're telling me that you snuck out of this center twice because you wanted to check on the operation of your Realm?"

Melyor suppressed a smirk. What she was saying was preposterous, she knew. So preposterous that Cedrych appeared to believe her. "Yes." She took a breath and allowed herself a grin. "And because I wanted to see if I could to it."

He stared at her for another minute, saying nothing, his features stony. Then he began to nod slowly. "That last I had figured," he said.

"Then you knew," she remarked.

"That you had left the center? Yes." He actually smiled at her. "But don't be disappointed. Getting out of here without setting off the security system or alerting my guards is no small feat."

She returned his smile, but only briefly. The Overlord was holding something back. She sensed it in his voice and manner. She might have distracted him briefly with her confession, but she was merely delaying the inevitable.

"So how were things in your Realm?" Cedrych asked, sitting back down in his chair and reclining comfortably.

"Fine. Turns out I had no need for concern."

"Jibb is well?"

Melyor shifted slightly in her seat. She didn't like the turn their conversation had taken. "Yes, he is."

"Good. I know how important he is to you."

She stared at him, wondering if the vague threat she heard in his words had been intended. Knowing Cedrych as she did, she had little doubt. *Leave him out of it, you bastard. If you want something, come after me, but leave him out of it.* "He's a good man," she said, careful to keep her tone neutral.

"And a busy one."

Too late, she realized that she had been ambushed herself. "What do you mean?" she asked, knowing already what he would say.

"Just that, in addition to what I heard about the sorcerer, I also received a report that Jibb ventured into the Twenty-First yesterday. There he met two of your men—pardon me, *his* men—and disappeared into one of the tunnels." He paused, pressing his fingertips together, his eye never leaving her face. "It seems something of a coincidence, don't you think, that Jibb and two of his men should be in the same Realm as the sorcerer just hours before the ambush?"

Melyor sat utterly still, her mind racing to weigh her options. She really only had two, and neither was very attractive. She could claim that Jibb had acted without her knowledge—knowing the break-law, he would have accepted sole responsibility for allowing the sorcerer to get away rather than betray her—or she could admit that she ordered her man to kill the sorcerer and accept responsibility for the stranger's escape herself. It was the right thing to do; she owed that much to Jibb. But this choice led inescapably to the question she could not answer: how did she know the sorcerer was in Bragor-Nal?

"What is it that you want, Cedrych?" she finally demanded, hoping to confuse the Overlord with her candor a second time.

Once again, it appeared to work. "Do you know where the sorcerer is?" he asked eagerly, sitting forward suddenly.

Melyor shook her head. "No. I assume he's with the Network, but I don't know where."

"I agree," Cedrych said. "He must be with the Network. How else could he have gotten away so quickly?" He stood again and stepped to the window. "I want to speak with him, Melyor," he told her, staring out at the buildings and quads. "I don't care how you do it, but I want you to arrange a meeting between us. We need to know why he's here, and how much he knows about the Initiative."

"What about training?" she asked, standing up as well, as if she might will their encounter to end.

"Don't worry about that. I'll keep them working. You just concentrate on finding the sorcerer."

"Am I allowed to leave the center?"

Cedrych turned. There was a smile on his lips, although it failed to reach his eye. "This is a strange time to start worrying about that." Melyor blushed and Cedrych faced the window again. "Yes, you may leave the center," he answered at length. "Use Jibb and his men and whatever other resources are necessary. Just bring me that sorcerer."

Melyor stood waiting, expecting more.

"That's all, Melyor," the Overlord finally said pivoting slightly to glance at her. "You can go."

She turned and took a step toward the door.

"Melyor," he called, stopping her. She sensed that he had turned again, that he was watching her, but she didn't look back. "Don't fail me."

She nodded once and then walked quickly to the door and out into the corridor. She retrieved her weapons and boots from Cedrych's guard and hurried to the lifter. Only when she was inside and the twin doors had slid shut did she allow herself the luxury of a deep breath and a moment to close her eyes and gather herself. Somehow she had gotten out of the Overlord's office without facing any questions about her ancestry. She wasn't at all certain how she had managed it. It had to have been luck; a rare oversight on Cedrych's part, one that he was not likely to repeat. Her reprieve would last only until their next conversation.

She opened her eyes again, realizing that the lifter wasn't moving, and pressed the button for the ground floor. She had to find the sorcerer, not just for Cedrych, but also for herself. She suddenly sensed that she had little future here in the Nal—it was just a matter of time before Cedrych learned of her secret. And learning of it, he would either kill her, or see her Sight as a talent that he might harness, one that would offset the advantages enjoyed by the sorcerers he was trying to defeat in Tobyn-Ser, in which case she would still be leaving for that land with the arrival of warm weather. In either case, she now knew, the sorcerer was the key to her future, regardless of whether her destiny lay in the land across Arick's Sea, or, as her recurring vision implied, by the stranger's side, fighting with him against some unseen enemy.

Reaching the ground floor, she crossed to the heavily manned guard station that blocked the main entrance to the center. As she expected, Cedrych had already informed the guards that she was to be allowed out of the structure.

"Your carrier is waiting, Nal-Lord," one of the burly men told her as she approached.

For a disorienting moment she could only picture the small carrier that she had stowed a few quads away, and she wondered how this man knew of it. Then she realized that he was referring to a personal, chauffeured carrier. I'm a Nal-Lord again, she thought, finding the notion both comforting and awkward after an entire winter of training and relative isolation. "Yes," she said after a moment's hesitation. "Thank you."

The man nodded and signalled to one of his colleagues with a sharp gesture. The gates and fortified glass doors of the security post swung open, allowing Melyor to step out into the grey, cold mist that was falling on the Nal.

A large black carrier waited for her in front of the center. She climbed into the back and glanced at the driver. He was one of Cedrych's men, one she didn't recognize, although that didn't mean she hadn't seen him before. They had all started to look the same to her: brawny, clean-shaven, vaguely handsome in a cold, unattractive way, and dressed impeccably in black.

"Where can I take you, Nal-Lord?" he asked her.

"Jibb's," she said without thinking. "I need to see Jibb."

"Of course, Nal-Lord," he said uncertainly, "but where . . . ?"

Melyor shook her head. I need to start thinking clearly, she told herself impatiently. There's too much at stake. "Fourth Realm," she said crisply. "I'll direct you once we're there."

"Very good, Nal-Lord," the man answered as the carrier pulled forward.

She stared out the window briefly as the carrier drove along the perimeter of the center to the road that would take them to the Upper. Then she sat back against the soft leather seat and began to wrack her brain for every scrap of information she had ever gathered about Bragor-Nal's Network of Gildriites.

17

I have tried to learn as much as possible about the Gildriites, but Baram's knowledge of their history and customs is quite limited. They are a people shrouded in mystery, and, as I have noted elsewhere, Baram is no historian. For these reasons, it would be dangerous to infer too much from the few details he has been able to offer. Nonetheless, I feel confident in drawing a few general conclusions.

The Gildriites have some power, although I am unable to determine the extent of their abilities. Certainly they have the Sight—indeed, they are often referred to as "Oracles"—but they carry no staffs and do not bind to any creatures. Largely due to their powers, limited as they may be, the Gildriites are outcasts. Many have fled the Nals for the remote mountains of northern Lon-Ser. Those who remain must conceal their heritage for fear of persecution. From what the outlander has told me, I believe that their status in Lon-Ser has remained largely unchanged for centuries. If they were ever revered or even tolerated by the people of Lon-Ser, it would have been in the distant past.

And yet, I find myself encouraged by their mere existence. For if the gods still favor them with powers that even remotely resemble the Mage-Craft, then perhaps the differences between Lon-Ser and Tobyn-Ser do not run so very deep.

—From Section Five of "The Report of Owl-Master Baden on his Interrogation of the Outlander Baram," Submitted to the 1,014th Gathering of the Order of Mages and Masters. Spring, Gods' Year 4625.

Cedrych continued to gaze at the door long after Melyor left his office, as if he could see her slender, curving figure moving beneath the loose fitting clothes. Just once, he would have liked to touch the flesh that he saw so vividly in his mind's eye, to cup his hands around her firm breasts, to feel himself enter her and drive himself into her as far as he could. Just once, before he killed her.

That she was dangerous went without saying: no one became Nal-Lord without achieving a certain level of skill with a blade and a thrower. Those who looked at her and saw merely a beautiful woman, or who underestimated the power and swiftness of her slight frame—Savil was the most recent—usually paid a steep price. Cedrych was wise enough to appreciate her ruthlessness and capacity for violence. And still, even he had been shocked by what he had read in the coroner's report on Savil's death and what he had seen in the still-shots of the Nal-Lord's body. *Prior to his death,* the examiner had written, *which resulted from a single burst of thrower fire to the chest, the deceased suffered a shattered larynx and a ruptured kidney. Given the severity of the injuries, I must conclude that he was already incapacitated when he received the killing injury.* There had been no cuts on him, no blood. This was Savil, arguably the most feared Nal-Lord in the entire Nal. And Melyor had defeated him without a blade.

After that, Cedrych knew, he would never misjudge her prowess as a fighter again. But in a sense, that wasn't the issue; it never had been. Cedrych was too confident in his own abilities to fear anyone else. What had begun to alarm him about Melyor, what had finally convinced him that she had to die, was his recognition of how clever she was, and his growing realization of another thing, so unexpected and disturbing, that he could scarcely comprehend it.

He was accustomed to controlling the conversations in which he took part. It didn't matter who he was talking to—break-laws, Nal-Lords, other Overlords, even the Sovereign himself—Cedrych decided where the discussion went and when it ended. Which made what Melyor had done today so astounding. For years the two of them had engaged in an ongoing contest of will and cunning. Each one of their encounters had become a battle of sorts, and, much to Cedrych's satisfaction, Melyor had presented more and more of a challenge each time. But today, for the first time, she had beaten him, which was another thing entirely, and utterly unacceptable. He had wanted to ask her how she knew about the sorcerer. How was it possible that she had sent Jibb and his men to kill the man when Cedrych had heard nothing about the stranger's arrival in the Nal until yesterday, just hours before the ambush? He needed to know. Certainly he had never intended to allow her to leave without demanding and receiving an explanation. Yet she was gone, and he still hadn't even asked her. With her guile and her charm, and her judicious use of the truth, she had evaded the issue entirely.

And she had done so intentionally. He had no doubt about that. She hadn't wanted to face that question. Which begged the question: why? Ever since her installation as Nal-Lord, Cedrych had marvelled at Melyor's foresight: her uncanny ability to anticipate the lapses of her foes, or to position herself to take advantage of seemingly unforeseeable opportunities. It had marked her as special long before she emerged as one of his best Nal-Lords, but he had never questioned its source. But this latest instance involving the sorcerer was too extraordinary to be explained simply by Melyor's obvious intelligence or to be attributed to plain dumb luck. There had to be another explanation.

It was possible that she possessed an intelligence network that rivaled his own, but Cedrych doubted it. If such a thing existed, he would have heard of it long before now. Which left two possibilities. She might have communicated with the sorcerer or someone else in Tobyn-Ser, who told her of the man's impending arrival in the Nal, in which case she had betrayed the Initiative and Cedrych himself. There were, however, several problems with such a theory. How could anyone in Tobyn-Ser have communicated with her, given that land's lack of any sort of advanced technology? If they had gotten hold of a communication device, perhaps from Calbyr or one of his men, why would they contact a Nal-Lord? Why not an Overlord, or, even more appropriately, one of the Sovereigns? And if, for some reason, they had contacted Melyor, why had the training center's security sensors not picked up the transmission? Too many questions, Cedrych told himself, shaking his head as he looked out at the grey sky hanging heavy over the grey buildings of the Nal. It's impossible.

So once more, with reluctance and just a bit of trepidation, Cedrych considered the other explanation, the only one that remained: Melyor had learned of the sorcerer's arrival through . . . supernatural means. It made a good deal of sense, far more than did the notion of Melyor betraying the Initiative or having the resources to create an intelligence organization that covered the entire Nal. Indeed, it offered answers for so much that had gone on in Cedrych's Dominion over the past four years that the Overlord was surprised that it hadn't occurred to him earlier.

Melyor was a Gildriite. Of course. And as such, she was both the most valuable subordinate he had and the most dangerous. For the time being at least, her usefulness outweighed the risks of allowing her to live. He needed her help in determining why the sorcerer had come and how much of a threat the stranger represented to the Initiative. And Cedrych could hardly afford to take the time to break in a new gang leader for the mission to Tobyn-Ser. But eventually he would have to kill her. If the Initiative succeeded she would no longer be a subordinate. She would be a rival, the only one he could imagine who might actually be able to thwart his ambitions.

He shuddered. He was not a man ordinarily given to irrational fears, but the ancient powers that enabled Gildriites like Melyor to divine the future made him uneasy. It was one thing to send a group of break-laws across Arick's Sea to do battle with sorcerers. It was quite another to work side by side with a woman who carried magic in her blood, or, he thought as he remembered the errand on which he had sent her, to invite one of these magicians into his office for a chat. Just last night, the sorcerer had killed two of Jibb's men. *Marred beyond recognition,* he had said in his conversation with Melyor just a short while ago. It had been easy, looking at the still shots of the two bodies, to accept that they had died in a firefight with the sorcerer. But only now did Cedrych stop to consider what that meant. The man himself was a weapon. He wielded a power that was older than any road or building in Bragor-Nal. He could conjure flame out of the air.

The Overlord shook his head. "I should have just told her to kill him," he said aloud. "What was I thinking?"

Orris had been below ground in the dark, rank passageways for what felt to be the better part of two days, guided through a bewildering maze of turns and forks by men and women who appeared and disappeared in the shadows like unsettled spirits. They had fed him and allowed him to sleep when he needed,

and though the food tasted bland and strange, and the pallets which they provided for his rest were uncomfortable, he had no cause for complaint. But he
could not stand to be confined in this meandering stone cage for much longer.
He needed to see light of day. Occasionally, when the darkness got to be too
much, he brightened his ceryll, illuminating the passageways with amber light
and drawing disapproving stares from his guides. But mage-light was a poor
substitute for sunshine, and it only solved part of the problem. For though he
longed to be above ground again, he knew that he could survive down here as
long as necessary. Anizir could not. Ever since they had descended into the tunnels she had seemed uneasy, crying out repeatedly and nuzzling him frequently
as if seeking reassurance. She was a wild creature; this was even harder on her
than it was on him. But more than that, she needed to fly and hunt.

Orris tried to communicate this to Gwilym as they followed yet another
guide, a short, stocky man with shaggy brown hair, through the dim passageways. Gwilym had not strayed far from Orris's side since their initial meeting
two nights before. It almost seemed to Orris that the portly man had assumed
responsibility for Orris's well-being, and, the mage had to admit, he found
Gwilym's presence reassuring. Now he placed his hand on the man's shoulder
stopping him. Gwilym turned to face him, calling something to the guide as he
did. The guide stopped and waited.

Orris pointed to his falcon. "Anizir," he said, "needs to eat." He mimed
putting food in his mouth.

After a moment Gwilym nodded. Then he held out his hands in a questioning gesture. *What does she eat?* he seemed to be asking.

Orris took a breath, and smiling self-consciously, he flapped his arms as if
they were wings and pointed up.

Gwilym exhaled through his teeth, nodded again, and then spoke to the
guide. Judging from the other man's reaction, Gwilym had understood well
enough. The guide shook his head vehemently and he and Gwilym began to argue. The discussion lasted but a few moments, and, when Gwilym faced Orris
again and nodded, the mage knew the outcome.

The three of them made their way to a dark flight of stairs that led to one of
the above-ground alleys. When they reached the doorway leading outside,
however, Gwilym placed a hand on Orris's arm. He pointed to Anizir and nodded; then he pointed to the mage and shook his head. *Your bird can go out,* the
gesture appeared to say, *but you can't.*

Orris nodded his agreement. Gwilym said something to the guide, who
opened the door. Orris conveyed an image of a grey dove to his familiar and she
leaped from his shoulder and soared out the door into the grey daylight. The
guide started to close the door again, but Orris stopped him with a sharp
word and a shake of his head. Again the man argued with Gwilym, and again
Orris's friend prevailed: the door remained open. Shaking his head in disap-
proval the guide descended the steps again, leaving Orris and Gwilym alone in
the doorway.

Orris had so many questions that he wished to ask the man that, even had
they been able to communicate, he wouldn't know where to begin. Had their

meeting been by chance, or had Gwilym known where Orris would be and that he would need help, and if so, how? Where were they going now? Who were these people who were helping them? Who were the men who had tried to kill them? Where had Gwilym gotten his cloak and staff? Orris smiled inwardly—this last was probably the least important of his questions, and yet it was also the easiest to ask, and, in many ways, the most intriguing.

Catching the man's eye, Orris pointed to his staff, with its glowing brown stone. Gwilym held it out to Orris, as if offering it to him. Orris held out his own as well, and the two men exchanged staves. Gwilym's staff felt remarkably light in Orris's hand, as if it was ancient, and the wood had been worn to an almost glasslike smoothness. Even the crystal looked old, its angles and edges rounded. Orris could tell that there had been runes carved into the staff, but in most places they had been worn away. But near the bottom of the staff, some of the carvings remained, partially obscured by years of use, but still visible. Looking at these more closely, Orris was shocked by what he saw. The runes were from Mi-rel, Tobyn-Ser's ancient language.

He looked up at Gwilym in amazement, and found that the portly man was already watching him keenly with his dark brown eyes, as though he was waiting for Orris's reaction to what was written on the staff.

"This comes from Tobyn-Ser," Orris whispered.

Gwilym nodded, seeming to understand.

"But how?"

Gwilym said something. It took Orris several moments to realize that he had spoken a name.

"What?"

"Gildri," the man repeated.

Orris shook his head. "Gildri? Who in Arick's n—" He stopped himself. There had been a Gildri in the Order once, in the earliest days of the Mage-Craft. He had been an ardent supporter of Theron, when the First Owl-Master struggled with Amarid for leadership of the Order. As the long friendship that Amarid and Theron shared deteriorated into a feud over the Mage-Craft's proper role in Tobyn-Ser, their conflict divided their followers and threatened to sunder the newly formed Order. This struggle came to a climax when Theron was put on trial for the death of a man in the Owl-Master's home village of Rholde. Led by Amarid, a majority of the mages voted in favor of Theron's execution. Theron responded by casting the dark curse that condemns those mages who die unbound to an eternity of unrest, and then by taking his own life and becoming the first of the Unsettled. And in the aftermath of this tragedy, a small group of Theron's most loyal adherents, led by a man named Gildri, left the Order and, eventually it is believed, Tobyn-Ser as well. History lost track of Gildri and his followers—no one in Tobyn-Ser ever learned what happened to them or where they went.

But here was Gwilym, standing in a doorway in the middle of this vast, befouled metropolis in Lon-Ser, apparently claiming that he carried Gildri's staff. And given the appearance of the wood and crystal he held in his hands, Orris could not help but believe him.

"How is this possible?" he asked, still gazing at his new friend.

Gwilym frowned. "Gildri," he said again.

"Gildri. Yes, I know!" Orris replied, his frustration mounting at their inability to communicate. "But how did you get it?"

The heavy man's frown deepened and after several moments he opened his hands in resignation and shook his head.

Orris forced a smile. "It's all right," he said gently. He handed the staff back to his companion and took back his own. But he continued to stare at Gwilym's glowing ceryll wondering how, if indeed it had belonged to the Gildri who knew Theron, it had ended up in this man's possession. He also noticed once again the robe that Gwilym wore beneath his dark overcoat. It was simpler than his own cloak, but in all other respects it resembled it closely. Had Gildri developed a following here in Lon-Ser all those centuries ago? Did the Mage-Craft or some semblance of it still exist here today? During their battle with the three men in the alley, Gwilym had shown no sign of wielding any power at all, but neither did he carry a hawk. Was he simply unbound at the moment? Did that explain his lack of power, or had whatever power Gildri brought with him faded over the last thousand years? Orris wanted desperately to ask Gwilym about these things, and he stood leaning against the stone doorway, cursing Baram for not teaching him Lon-Ser's language.

After a few more minutes, Anizir returned clutching a plump dove in her talons. Landing in the alley, just outside the doorway, she began to tear at the dead bird with such fervor that Orris actually laughed out loud. She finished her meal in just a few minutes and immediately flew off again in search of more food.

Gwilym glanced at Orris and offered a small smile. Orris grinned in return, and was surprised by the look of relief that flashed across the other man's round face. Apparently he had mistaken Orris's frustration at their language barrier for anger at him. The mage shook his head with regret. It wasn't the first time his temper and moodiness had put off a potential friend. Alayna and Jaryd had told him on several occasions that he was a difficult person to get to know, although, they were always quick to add, his friendship was worth the effort.

"I'm sorry," he said to Gwilym. His companion cocked his head slightly, obviously not understanding. Orris grinned again, drawing another smile from the portly man. *That will have to do for now,* Orris told himself. *It's all we've got.*

Anizir returned a short while later and ate her second dove nearly as quickly as she had eaten the first one. Then she flew to Orris's shoulder, seeming contented as she began to preen. Orris and Gwilym descended into the passageways again and found the guide waiting for them at the base of the stairs. He said something angrily to Gwilym, who merely shrugged in response, and then the guide spun away and began leading them through the corridors again.

They walked for what felt to Orris like several hours, pausing briefly to eat a light meal that had been left for them in a small chamber that sat just off one of the tunnels, before continuing their journey. While Orris had no idea in what direction they were going he did get the definite sense that they had a specific destination. The twists and turns of the passages, and the choices made by the guide when they reached forks and intersections no longer struck him as quite so random. And though completely ignorant of the Nal, the mage found this vaguely comforting. He didn't particularly like this guide, but neither did he doubt the man's motives. Certainly Gwilym appeared to trust him and, for now, that was enough for Orris.

They walked for another hour or so before coming upon a tall, dark-skinned man who stood in the middle of the corridor as if he had been waiting for them. Gwilym's brown eyes betrayed his concern, but Orris could tell that the guide knew this man, although he was as surprised as Gwilym to see him there. The guide and the stranger spoke for several minutes, and then the guide walked back to where Gwilym stood with Orris and spoke to the heavy man. Gwilym grew increasingly agitated as they talked, so much so that the stranger soon walked over and joined their discussion. He didn't appear to have any more success in allaying Gwilym's fears, but whatever he told the portly man did eventually convince him of something, for he abruptly pulled off his carry sack and sat down on the cold, stone floor. The guide and his friend did the same and Orris followed their example, sitting down beside Gwilym.

He glanced at his friend as he sat, hoping to read in his expression something that might explain what was going on, but Gwilym merely offered a thin smile that did little to allay Orris's growing fears. A moment later, the man looked away, and the four of them sat there in the dim corridor, saying nothing. They waited there for some time, until finally Orris heard voices approaching, faint at first but growing stronger by the moment. Soon he could hear footsteps as well, and a few minutes later, two people came into view. Both were women. One of them was of medium height and build. Like the stranger who had been waiting for Orris, Gwilym, and the guide, she had dark skin. Her eyes were hazel, and she wore her black hair pulled back tightly from her angular face.

But it was the other woman who drew Orris's attention. She was slender and not very tall, but despite the loose fitting trousers and tunic that she wore, Orris could tell that she was agile and strong. She wore a weapon strapped to her thigh, and, though he didn't see it, Orris knew that she also carried a blade, hidden somewhere, but accessible. And he was sure that she knew how to use it. She had amber hair that would have fallen to her shoulders had it not been for the wide black cloth that was tied around her head so as to cover her eyes.

The stranger and the guide stood, as did Gwilym and Orris, and the stranger spoke briefly with the dark-skinned woman. They then said something to Gwilym, whose face suddenly looked pale in the ceryll light. He seemed to hesitate before nodding his agreement to whatever they had told him. A moment later, much to Orris's surprise, the guide, the stranger, and the dark-skinned woman walked away, leaving Orris and Gwilym alone with the second woman.

Gwilym took a deep breath. Then he removed the weapon from the strap on the woman's thigh and handed it to Orris, and untied the cloth that covered her eyes. She glanced at him and said something, smiling briefly. Then she turned to Orris and regarded him with unconcealed curiosity. She was quite beautiful, Orris realized, with delicate flawless features, bright green eyes, and a full, sensuous mouth. But as he returned her gaze, Orris found himself vaguely unsettled by what he saw in her. There was something cold and uncompromising about her beauty, something that told him she was as deadly as she was alluring.

"I have been looking forward to meeting you," she told him. She glanced at Anizir. "And to seeing your bird."

Orris stared at her in disbelief.

She grinned. "Yes, I speak your language. This surprises you?" Her accent was strange, but Orris had no trouble understanding her.

"A bit yes," he said at last. "You're the first person I've met who does."

"I am not surprised," she replied. "My people usually are not welcoming of strangers." She extended a hand. "My name is Melyor."

"Orris," the mage replied, taking her hand and feeling her powerful grip. He saw that she had two parallel scars on the back of her hand. They looked like they came from a knife.

Noticing the direction of his gaze, Melyor pulled her hand away. "Your bird is beautiful," she said smoothly.

"Thank you. You can stroke her feathers if you'd like. She won't mind."

Melyor shook her head, suddenly seeming uncomfortable. "Thank you, no." She looked over at Gwilym. "How did you meet the Bearer?"

"What did you call him?" Orris asked.

"The Bearer. His full title is Bearer of the Stone."

He stepped closer to her, his eyes fixed on hers. "What do you know about his stone?" he demanded.

She smiled. "A great deal, and I will be more than glad to tell you all that you want to know. But this is not the time." She beckoned Gwilym closer with a gesture, before facing Orris again. "I came here to deliver a message. I have a friend, an important man in Bragor-Nal, who wants very much to speak with you."

The mage narrowed his eyes. "Why? Who is he?"

"His name is Cedrych. He has been interested in Tobyn-Ser and its sorcerers for a long time, particularly in the power you wield and the birds you carry. He sent me to arrange a meeting—he will speak with you any time you want."

Orris felt himself grow cold suddenly, as if a winter wind had swept through the corridors beneath the Nal. *He's been interested in Tobyn-Ser* . . . . "He sounds like someone I should meet," Orris agreed.

"I am glad you think so." She turned to Gwilym and said something to him. The Bearer shook his head, but Melyor repeated what she had told him and indicated Orris with a nod of her head. They spoke a short while longer. "Your friend does not want you to meet with him," Melyor said, turning to Orris. "He fears for your life."

"Should he?"

She hesitated. "I understand why he feels that way."

"That's not what I asked," Orris persisted. "How do I know that your friend—what's his name? Cedrych? How do I know that Cedrych won't try to kill me?"

"You have my word on it," Melyor told him.

Orris shook his head. "I don't know you any better than I know Cedrych. Why should I trust you?"

Melyor stared at him for several moments, saying nothing. Then she turned to Gwilym and spoke to him for several moments. At one point, the Bearer's eyes widened with shock and he asked her a question in a tight voice. She nodded and said a few words more before looking at Orris again.

"I believe your friend trusts me now," she said.

Orris looked at Gwilym, who nodded slowly, his eyes still wide. "How did you manage that?" the mage asked her.

She shrugged slightly. "I told him a secret that could get me killed if anyone else found out about it."

"Sounds interesting. Care to tell me?"

A smile flitted across her face. "I do not think you would understand right now. It is enough to say that your friend and I share a special bond that has something to do with that stone he carries."

"I see," Orris said. "Would I be wrong in thinking then that you and I share a bond of sorts as well?"

The color abruptly vanished from Melyor's cheeks and she gazed at the mage for a long time. "No," she finally answered in a small voice. "You would not be wrong at all."

18

The first of the outlanders' attacks on Tobyn-Ser took place just over five years ago at a small town on the Lower Horn called Valani. Like most of the early incidents that would follow, it seemed rather innocuous—a few homes were vandalized, some fishing nets were cut, and two small boats were set ablaze. Still, though it gave little warning of the horrors that would come later, this minor mischief represented the beginning of our strange conflict with the people of Lon-Ser. Over the year, the ferocity of the attacks increased steadily. At Woodsrest in Tobyn's Wood, a bit more than a half-year after Valani, the first homes were destroyed. A half-year after that, in the village of Sern, a man and his young son became the first of our people to die at the hands of invaders in over four hundred years. At Taima, only a few weeks later, an entire village square was razed, and, of course, with the brutal attacks on Kaera and Watersbend, the violence of the outlanders' campaign reached its most appalling level.

Fortunately, Watersbend also marked the end of their attacks—there is no telling how much more devastating the next incidents might have been, although it is hard to imagine them being much worse. Still, though the attacks ended over four years ago, the scars that they left on our land remain fresh and painful. . . . It remains to be seen whether our grief and anger can become positive forces for change and renewed vigilance, or whether we will merely allow these emotions to fester and grow into something as dark as the violence that provoked them.

—From Section Two of "The Report of Owl-Master Baden on his Interrogation of the Outlander Baram," Submitted to the 1,014th Gathering of the Order of Mages and Masters. Spring, Gods' Year 4625.

The summons came sometime during the night or early morning. Having slept late, Baden couldn't really be sure. He only knew that the glow of his ceryll had been constant late the previous evening when he returned to the inn from his nightly communication with the others, and that this morning, when he awoke, the orange crystal had been pulsating with the steady rhythm of a general summons. Sonel had used the Summoning Stone to call for an unplanned Gathering of the Order. Something must have happened. Immediately his thoughts turned to Orris, as they always seemed to these days. Surely the mage had reached Lon-Ser by now, if he was still alive. Baden shook his head; such worries did him no good. Especially now: it appeared that he had a long journey ahead of him.

The Owl-Master washed and dressed hurriedly and, assembling what few belongings he had, called Golivas to his shoulder and left the small, comfortable room that had been his home for the past several months. He stopped in the kitchen, where he found Peritte, the wizened innkeeper who had cooked his breakfasts and cleaned his room every day since autumn. She was standing by the large wood stove, stirring a fragrant pot of stew.

"Good morrow, Owl-Master," she said with a toothless grin, glancing at him. "Will you be wanting—" She stopped at the sight of his ceryll, her expression turning sober. "I guess you'll be leaving us, won't you?"

"I'm afraid so," Baden answered, struggling with a sudden surge of apprehension. *What did Sonel's summons mean?*

The woman regarded him keenly. "It's not those outlanders again, I hope."

The Owl-Master shook his head and made himself smile. "I'm sure it's not," he told her.

"Well, good," the woman said testily. "If you ask me, that man should have been killed a long time ago. Who was it wanted to keep him as a prisoner, anyway? It just encourages others to come and get him out."

"I should be leaving right away," Baden said, ignoring her commentary. "I do want to thank you for your hospitality, and to ask you if you know of anyone from whom I might be able to acquire a horse."

She frowned at him and made a clicking noise with her tongue. "You may not agree with me, Owl-Master," she said sourly. "But I'm not the only one around here who feels that way. Keeping that outlander alive was just plain foolish."

"A horse, Peritte?" he asked again.

She shrugged slightly. "Maybe Colton, the blacksmith at the end of town," she said at last. "But it won't be a beast you can push too hard."

"That should be fine," the Owl-Master replied. "Thank you again, Peritte."

She nodded. "You can take some food if you like," she said, turning back to the stove. "There's sweet bread on the table and some dried fruit and smoked meat in the cupboard."

Baden smiled. "That's kind of you; I think I will."

He quickly filled two of the leather pouches he carried in the pockets of his cloak with fruit and meat, and, with Peritte's permission, he filled his wine skin as well. Pausing briefly to take a large piece of the innkeeper's soft sweet bread, which he bit into immediately, he hastened from the inn and down the main street of the village to Colton's smithy.

As it turned out, the blacksmith had no interest in parting with his horse, but he directed Baden to a farmer who had several old plow horses for sale. Hurrying on to the farm, the Owl-Master soon found a grey and white gelding with a regal black mane that looked fit enough to carry him across Tobyn-Ser. The journey wouldn't be a swift one, but he would make better time on horseback than he would on foot. The farmer also offered Baden a tattered but serviceable saddle that the Owl-Master gladly accepted. In return, Baden used the Mage-Craft to mend several wooden fences and to heal a burn that the farmer had suffered two nights before. It seemed a fair trade, and Baden was on his way in less than an hour.

Before setting out for Amarid, he returned once more to the rocky shore from which he had reached with his mind for his friends in order to forge the psychic link. A thick fog hung over the shoreline, darkening the sky. But the air felt warm and carried the subtle scent of spring. The rains had ended less than a fortnight ago, and already the swollen buds of the maples and oaks that grew by the coast had begun to open. Riding to the edge of the sea, Baden dismounted and sat on a rocky outcropping. And as he had so many times before, he stretched his consciousness to the north and south, toward the Upper Horn, where Mered had been since the previous summer, and toward Jaryd and Alayna's home on the shores of South Shelter. Not surprisingly, the Owl-Master found nothing to the north; Mered was already on his way to Amarid. Jaryd, however, was still to the south, just where Baden had expected to find him.

You're waiting for Alayna? Baden asked his nephew.

Yes, the young mage sent back. *She should be here by tomorrow night. We'll be on our way the following morning. It's hard to wait though. Every time I look at my ceryll I feel this need to just mount up and start riding.*

Baden grinned. It still struck him as funny that Jaryd should seem so undisturbed by the notion of riding a horse across the land. At his first Gathering, nearly five years ago, Jaryd had been more intimidated by the notion of riding a horse than by the prospect of facing the unsettled spirit of Theron. *A day or two won't make too much difference*, Baden sent. *I'm sure you'll get there before I do.*

Are you going on foot? Jaryd asked.

No. I'll be riding too, but he's not much of a horse.

Don't let Trahn hear you talking that way, Jaryd sent. Baden sensed the young mage's laughter. *He'd tell you you're an ingrate.*

He'd call me worse than that, Baden agreed.

An instant later, the tone of Jaryd's thoughts turned serious. *Do you have any idea what's happened, Baden?*

None. I expect Sonel to contact me with the merging this morning. That's why I came back to the coast. This is where she usually tries to find me.

I think it's Orris, Jaryd told him. *I think someone's figured out that he's taken Baram.*

Baden shrugged. *Maybe. Probably*, he amended with resignation. *I guess we'll find out soon enough.* The Owl-Master sighed deeply. If his nephew was right, this Gathering would be even more contentious than recent ones had been. It was not an appealing thought. *Ride safely, Jaryd*, Baden finally conveyed.

And you, Baden. We'll see you soon.

A moment later Jaryd was gone from his mind and Baden was alone again in the thinning mist by Arick's Sea. The day was brightening as the sun struggled to burn through the fog. It would be a warm afternoon. He continued to sit on the jutting rock, listening to the waves crashing below and staring at his ceryll, waiting for the signal he knew would come: the momentary flicker of Sonel's green light within the continual flashing of his orange. He didn't have to wait long.

I've been waiting for you, he told her as he reached back to complete the connection that she had initiated. For someone who had never liked communicating by the Ceryll-Var because of how taxing it was for both his familiar and himself, Baden had used it quite often over the past year or two.

I figured you would be, she replied, the tone of her thoughts reserved and distant, much as it had been since that night late in the fall when he told her of Orris's departure for Lon-Ser. It still hurt to sense this aloofness from her. He missed their intimacy almost as much as he had missed Anla before his binding to Golivas. *I would have contacted you earlier*, she went on, *but Erland has been here for much of the morning. He only left a few minutes ago.*

Is he the reason for the summons?

You could say that, yes, she told him. *He tried to organize a vigil at the prison two days ago as a protest against our failure to execute Baram. When the guards there told him that Baram was gone, he came to me demanding to know why I had allowed the outlander to be moved back to the Great Hall.*

So Jaryd was right, Baden thought to himself. *Did you tell him the truth?* he asked.

Sonel hesitated.

It's all right, Baden sent. *I would have, if I had been in your position.*

I tried to keep it from him as long as I could, she admitted at last. *But he kept insisting on seeing Baram. "I want to look the butcher in the eye," he said over and over again. In the end, I had no choice but to tell him.*

Baden tried to imagine the scene, but he couldn't. *What did he say?* the Owl-Master asked with genuine curiosity.

He was speechless, Sonel answered, *probably for the first time in his life!*

Baden laughed, and he sensed Sonel's laughter as well. It was the easiest moment they had shared in months. Baden found it ironic that it should come now, in the midst of all this.

Once he recovered from the initial shock, however, Sonel sent, bringing them back to the grave realities of the situation, *he had a great deal to say. He formally demanded that I convene a Gathering so that the Order might determine how such a thing could be allowed to happen. He wants to charge Orris with treason and have him arrested and tried if he ever returns to Tobyn-Ser. And he spoke of the need to root out Orris's fellow conspirators.*

"Conspirators!" Baden repeated. *Was that his word?*

Yes, the Owl-Sage sent. *He said that he suspected Orris "of conspiring with others to subvert the will of the Order and betray the land." And he went out of his way to remind me that treason was punishable by death.*

Baden shook his head slowly. Undoubtedly this was just the opening Erland had been waiting for the past five years.

He didn't mention your name, Baden, Sonel told him, echoing his thoughts, *but I'm sure he suspects you.*

Oh, I'm certain of that, the Owl-Master sent back. *Frankly, I'm more concerned about Jaryd than I am about myself.*

About Jaryd? Why?

He's the one who told me that Orris had gone. They spoke just before Orris went to get Baram released. Again Baden shook his head. *Jaryd won't hesitate to defend Orris, and he won't back down in a confrontation with Erland. He's got too much of his father in him.*

And his uncle, Sonel added gently.

Baden grinned. *Yes, and his uncle.*

They shared a brief silence, which Sonel eventually broke. *Well, maintaining this link is only going to tire us out, and you've got a lot of traveling to do.*

Yes, Baden agreed. *But it's nice to be with you. I've missed this.*

Me, too, the Owl-Sage confessed after a moment. *Be well, Baden. Get here as quickly as you can. Please.*

Again he smiled. *I will.*

They broke the connection, and once again Baden found himself alone on his perch above the sea. He was tired from maintaining his connections with Jaryd and Sonel, brief as they had been. I'm getting old, he thought, climbing stiffly to his feet and mounting the docile farm horse.

They didn't cover much ground that first day. Baden was fatigued, and it took some time for the Owl-Master and the beast he was riding to find a rhythm that felt comfortable to both of them. In the days that followed, however, as they entered the foothills of the Seaside Range and then the lofty mountains themselves, their pace actually increased. They made fairly good time through the Seasides, despite the snow that still covered not only the peaks, but also the meadows that lay below, and they descended into the Emerald Hills after just over a fortnight in the mountains.

It took them several days more to make their way through the hills to the valley of the Sapphire River. Spring had not yet reached the hills, though even in winter they had a subtle, haunting beauty. The trees of their dense forests stood leafless and grey, like skeletons, their bare limbs reaching toward the sky. The same was true of Tobyn's Wood, but in the nine days it took Baden to cross through the vast forest, the air began to grow warmer, and the buds on the God's trees began to swell with life.

This first portion of his journey proved to be rather routine. He met few people along the trails he followed, and those he did meet were reserved though respectful, much as the people of Tobyn-Ser had been toward all members of the Order since the outlanders' attacks. He avoided villages and towns—something, he thought with regret, that he never would have done a few years ago—and he ate what the forest and Golivas provided. His days were quiet, and just a bit lonely, and his nights were times for little more than contemplation and sleep.

His last night in Tobyn's Wood, however, all of this changed. He had reached the foothills of the Parneshome Range late in the afternoon and, rather than pushing the gelding any farther, had halted for the day. It was just past dusk, and he was sitting in the firelight, finishing the hare that his owl had killed for him, when he noticed out of the corner of his eye a strange irregularity in the rhythmic flashing of his stone. It was very brief, lasting but a fraction of a second, and it was so subtle that as he stared at his stone, watching for it again, he began to think that perhaps he had imagined it. The wood he had found that night was dry and the fire was crackling and burning quite brightly. It would have been easy to mistake a reflection from the fire for something else. But just he was ready to dismiss what he had seen as no more than an illusion, he saw it again.

And he gasped with disbelief. Within the flashing orange of his stone, terribly faint, but unmistakable, he discerned the briefest flicker of another color. Orris's amber. Baden couldn't even imagine the effort it must have taken the Hawk-Mage to cast his awareness out all the way across Arick's Sea and half of Tobyn-Ser so that he could search for Baden's ceryll. When Baden had been on the shores of the sea, Sonel had reached for him from Amarid, which lay three hundred leagues to the northeast, and she had known just where to look for him. And still, their connection had required a tremendous effort on both their parts. Assuming he was in Lon-Ser, Orris was nearly seven hundred leagues away, and he hadn't known where Baden could be found. It was remarkable that Orris had found him at all.

Baden immediately stretched his consciousness westward, preparing himself as he did for what he expected would be a demanding connection. He was surprised when he found Orris's consciousness almost instantly, as if the mage had been hovering just above the treetops waiting for him.

Orris! By the gods! Are you well?

Yes, the mage answered, his reply clouded somewhat by the strain of what he was doing. He wouldn't be able to maintain the link for very long. Baden poured more of his power into their connection, allowing Orris to ease his own efforts slightly. *Thank you,* the burly mage sent a moment later, sounding less burdened.

Are you in Lon-Ser? Baden asked.

Yes. I'm in Bragor-Nal.

Is Baram still with you?

No, the mage sent. He seemed to be laughing, although Baden sensed that there was a bitter edge to his mirth. *Baram and I parted company almost as soon as we reached the Nal.*

So you're alone?

Actually no. I've been befriended by a group of people who seem to have some ancient connection to the Order.

The Gildriites! You've found them! I was hoping you would.

Orris's astonishment was manifest in his thoughts. *You know of them?*

Did you even read my report? Baden demanded irritably.

Some of it, the mage replied, an admission in the thought.

Baden shook his head ruefully.

I can just imagine your expression, Baden.

Good. Then I don't have to say anything.

Orris laughed again. *Anyway,* he went on, *one of them saved my life, and he led me to the others. They're feeding me and guiding me through the Nal, but they don't speak our language, and Baram taught me nothing of theirs during our time together.*

Your travels with him were difficult. Baden offered it as a statement.

Yes, but that's not important now. It can wait until I get back to Tobyn-Ser. Once again, Baden sensed that Orris was beginning to feel the strain of their connection. Baden felt it as well. *I contacted you because I need some information.*

Anything, Baden sent. *Just ask.*

In your conversations with Baram, did he ever mention a man named Cedrych?

Baden thought for a long time, sifting through his memories of his interrogations of the outlander. The name did not strike him as being familiar. *No,* he finally answered. *At least not that I remember. He spoke often of a man named Calbyr, but he was the leader of the group that came to Tobyn-Ser. He mentioned few names from his life back in Lon-Ser.* He paused. *I do know that Calbyr was what Baram called a Nal-Lord,* he began again a few seconds later, *and that he answered to an Overlord who, in turn, answered to a Sovereign. Does that help at all?*

It may, Orris told him, clearly disappointed with Baden's response. *I don't know Cedrych's title.*

How did you meet him?

I haven't yet. I was contacted by a woman who seems to work for him. She's the only person I've met here who speaks our language.

Baden felt the hairs on the back of his neck stand up. *What's her name?* he asked, trying to keep the tension from his thoughts.

Melyor.

The Owl-Master shook his head in frustration. That name wasn't familiar either. *How did she know where to find you?*

A good question. I think she got in touch with these Gildriites somehow. They brought her to me. She claims to have some connection to them, but they clearly don't trust her.

Do you?

Baden sensed Orris's uncertainty. He could almost see the burly man shrugging. *I'm not sure. That's why I contacted you. She said that Cedrych had "been interested in Tobyn-Ser and its sorcerers for a long time," particularly, she said, in the power we wield and the birds we carry.*

Baden shivered, though he could feel the warmth of the fire on his face. *What do you think she meant?* he asked, trying once again to mask his fear.

It was hard to tell, but I reacted the same way you just did: as if I knew somehow that this was the man who sent the outlanders to Tobyn-Ser.

You said you haven't met him yet, Baden sent. *Does that mean you're going to?*

I'm supposed to meet with him tomorrow, Orris answered.

Baden exhaled through his teeth. *You understand that if he is the one who sent Baram and his friends, he'll have no compunction about killing you. That may be why he sent this woman to find you.*

I know, Orris told him. Baden sensed that the mage was grinning. He sometimes wondered if Orris actually enjoyed being in danger. *I don't see that I have much choice, though. It's kind of like when you argued for sending the delegation to Theron's Grove: there's an inevitability to this that outweighs the risks. If he's the one who sent the outlanders, then I'll probably have to face him eventually. And if he's not the one, he may know who is. Melyor knows our language, and since no one else seems to, I feel that my best hope for learning something about our enemies lies with her. The Gildriites have been kind to me, but until I can communicate with them, they're not going to be able to help me.*

Baden sighed. *What you say makes sense, although I feel obliged to remind you that you spoke against going to Theron's Grove, and you were right. I hope your meeting with Cedrych turns out better.*

So do I.

Baden felt their connection growing weaker. He was tiring quickly, and Orris was working harder than he was. *Is there anything else I can do for you, Orris?*

No. Just tell the others that I'm thinking of them. Have you detected anything with the link?

No, nothing.

Orris seemed to sense something in Baden's tone. *Is everything else all right?*

Baden hesitated, though only for an instant.

What is it, Baden? Then he seemed to remember something. *When I finally found your ceryll with my mind it was flashing, wasn't it? Has something happened to Sonel?*

Sonel's fine. But everything's not all right. It was best just to say it and have it in the open. *Erland has finally learned of what you did, and he's demanded that Sonel convene a Gathering. He's convinced that you were acting as part of a conspiracy, and he intends to have you charged with treason.*

For a long time Orris offered no response, and when he finally did, he surprised Baden with the direction his thoughts had taken. *You're going to have to defend Jaryd, Baden. You and the others. He'll admit that he saw me leave, and he won't apologize for letting me go.*

In spite of everything, Baden smiled. *I know. I conveyed a similar thought to Sonel. Don't worry: we'll take care of him.*

Take care of yourself, too. Erland will go after you with even more venom than he will Jaryd or me. Their link had grown weak. Orris's voice in the Owl-Master's mind seemed now to be coming from a great distance.

Thanks, I will. Arick guard you, Orris. Come back to us soon.

Why? Orris sent with characteristic jocularity. *So that I can be tried as a traitor again?*

An instant later the Hawk-Mage ended their connection. Baden opened his eyes. The firelight seemed exceedingly bright, and his head was spinning with the strain of what he and Orris had just done. He glanced at white Golivas on his shoulder and smiled wanly as he stroked her chin. He felt her fatigue as much as he did his own.

"Thank you," he told her, his voice sounding thin and tired to his own ears. He sat for a few minutes, but he still felt dizzy. He was sorely tempted to mount his horse and continue the journey to Amarid immediately, but he knew that he needed rest. Reluctantly, he lay down beside the fire and instantly felt himself slipping into a deep slumber. He would wake early in the morning, he promised himself for his own peace of mind, and he would cross the mountains as swiftly as the farm horse would tolerate. They still had a good distance to cover, and there suddenly seemed to be so much at stake.

19

As I have noted elsewhere in this report, commerce in Bragor-Nal, and the advanced goods that are so much a part of this commerce, are far beyond our experience, making it difficult even to find words to describe them. Nowhere is this more evident than with respect to Lon-Ser's agriculture.

Lon-Ser's farmland was covered over by the enormous Nals long ago. Yet Lon-Ser's people must, of course, still eat. According to Baram, the food in Bragor-Nal comes from a large section of the city known, appropriately enough, as "the Farm." The Farm consists of several tremendous structures

*that house forests, grain fields, livestock pastures, orchards, vineyards, and
more. When Baram first told me of this, I thought he was joking. How, I
asked, could wheat and timber and fruit be grown within a house in quan-
tities large enough to feed all of his people? How could the natural elements
required for successful agriculture—sunshine, rain, suitable temperatures—
be created in a building? Unfortunately, the differences in our two languages made his reply almost incomprehensible. He did assure me, however,
that this was no joke.*

—From Section Five of "The Report of
Owl-Master Baden on his Interrogation
of the Outlander Baram," Submitted to
the 1,014th Gathering of the Order of
Mages and Masters. Spring, Gods' Year
4625.

Orris and Gwilym woke early and, led by still another new guide,
made their way to a nearby alleyway where they were to meet Melyor
so that she could take them to Cedrych. Waiting at the top of a darkened stairway for her knock on the small door, Orris realized that he was still a bit fatigued from his communication with Baden the day before. He had never
reached so far for anyone, and he hoped never to do so again. It had taken far
too much effort to learn far too little. Fortunately, Anizir appeared to have recovered fully.

Despite his disappointment with how little Baden knew about Melyor or
Cedrych, Orris had found their exchange oddly comforting. Baden's response
to Melyor's comments about Cedrych had mirrored his own precisely. And
while the fear he had sensed in the lean Owl-Master's thoughts had reinforced
his apprehension about today's meeting, it had also confirmed for Orris that,
even here, far from his home and friends, his instincts were still sound. He still
knew nothing about Melyor or Cedrych, but at least he felt sure of himself.

A single emphatic knock on the door made Orris jump and set his heart racing. Perhaps sensing this, Gwilym placed a reassuring hand on Orris's shoulder
before opening the door. Meylor stood in the alley, dressed in dark loose-fitting
breeches and an ivory tunic, just as when he first met her two days before. Her
amber hair fell to her shoulders in flowing waves that stirred in the light wind.
Her weapon was still strapped to her thigh.

She smiled and said something to Gwilym, who nodded once. Then she
turned to Orris. "Good morning."

"Good morning," Orris replied, as he and the Bearer stepped out into the alley.

She gestured toward one of the wheeled objects that he had been seeing
ever since his arrival in Bragor-Nal. It was black and large, and it emitted
a low humming noise and a constant stream of foul smelling grey vapor.
"Come on," she said casually, in her strangely accented voice. "Cedrych waits
for you."

She started toward the object and Gwilym followed her.

Orris didn't move. "We're going in that?" he asked.

Melyor stopped and looked back at him, an amused expression on her delicate features. "Even on the Upper it is over four hundred quads. Did you think we would walk?"

A quad Orris remembered from Baden's report, was roughly equivalent to one of Tobyn-Ser's miles. Which meant that . . . "How many days will it take us to get there?"

Melyor stared at him for a moment and then burst out laughing. Gwilym asked her something, and then he began to laugh in response to what she told him. Orris felt his face reddening.

"Traveling in this carrier," Melyor finally explained, as her laughter subsided, "we should be there within four or five hours."

Orris shook his head. "That's impossible."

For a second time, Melyor gestured for him to follow her. "In Tobyn-Ser, perhaps. But not here. Come with me and I will explain."

Reluctantly, the mage walked after her to the black object.

"This is called a carrier," Melyor said, opening a door on the side of it and indicating with a hand that Gwilym and Orris should climb inside. "It allows us to travel great distances in a very short amount of time."

"But four hundred quads—"

"I have gone twice that far in a day."

Orris blinked. Eight hundred quads in a day! Perhaps there were some advantages to this land's advanced goods after all. He gazed at the carrier, unable to conceal his admiration. "That is remarkable," he breathed.

Melyor gave him a smile that seemed genuine. "Get in. You are about to see a lot of remarkable things."

Gwilym climbed into one of the seats in the back half of the carrier and, at the Bearer's urging, Orris took a seat in front and pulled the door closed. Because the ceiling of the carrier was so low, Anizir hopped down to Orris's leg and ruffled her feathers defensively. Melyor opened a door on the other side and sat beside Orris and behind a large semicircular handle. She pushed a lever that rested on the floor between Orris and her, and the carrier started forward smoothly, almost the way a dugout moved on a swift stream. Anizir dug her talons into Orris's thigh to keep herself steady, and she made the frightened, soft mewing sound that Orris had heard from her so often over the past few days.

"Is your bird all right?" Melyor asked, glancing anxiously at the slate-colored falcon.

"She's fine," Orris answered, closely watching everything Melyor was doing with her hands, and, he soon realized, her feet as well. "How does this work?" he finally asked.

"Do you mean what makes it run, or how does one drive it?"

Orris grinned. "Both."

"It is difficult to explain to someone who knows nothing of our . . ." She paused, seeming to search for the correct word. They had emerged from the alley onto a large thoroughfare. "Of our advanced goods," she finally said. "The carrier burns blocks of fuel, which power a series of mechanisms inside of it, which makes the wheels turn." She glanced at him, as she turned the carrier onto a new street. "Do you understand?"

"Not really, but go on."

She gestured toward the semicircle, which she was holding with one hand. "This allows me to steer the carrier. I use the lever between us to stop or slow us down, and I use the foot pedals to control how fast we go—the right one lets us go forward, the left one is for reverse."

Orris nodded despite his uncertainty. A horse struck him as much simpler. But to cover over one hundred leagues in four hours . . .

"What does it eat?"

Orris looked at Melyor quizzically. "What?"

"Your bird. What does it eat?"

"Her name is Anizir," Orris told her. "And for the most part she eats other birds: ducks, quail, pheasant. Since we reached this place, she's been eating the grey and white doves. They seem to be the only birds that live here."

"Anizir," Melyor repeated. "That is pretty. What does it mean?"

"I'm not certain."

"I see. Did you name her that after someone you know?"

Orris shook his head. "You misunderstand. I didn't name her."

"Then who did?" Melyor asked, glancing at him.

"No one."

"But you just said—"

"Her name is Anizir, yes," Orris interrupted. "But no one named her that. That's just her name."

"But how do you know that if you did not name her?"

Orris smiled. "She told me."

Melyor laughed, and Orris gazed at her placidly. After several moments her mirth faded. "You are telling a joke, right?"

"No," Orris said, the smile lingering on his lips. "I'm not very good at jokes."

"You mean she speaks?"

This time it was Orris's turn to laugh. "No," he said at last, still laughing. "A mage and his familiar are linked to each other. We share each other's thoughts."

Melyor stared at him again, her mouth falling open. "How?" she managed to ask before facing forward once more.

"That I don't know. It's been this way since the time of Amarid."

Melyor shook her had. "Amarid," she repeated awkwardly. "This was a bird?"

"No. A man. A very great man. He was the first to bind to a hawk. He discovered the Mage-Craft, which is what we call the power we wield."

She said nothing for some time, as she turned the carrier onto a steeply inclined road that carried them toward a white avenue that appeared to float above the Nal. Abruptly Orris remembered standing with Baram in the great swamp south of the Nal looking at the great city and noticing the thin white ribbon of road that had arced above it. Now it seemed that he was about to experience that road.

"This is called the Upper," Melyor told him as the carrier leveled off and accelerated. "It allows us to bypass the guards below and take a more direct route to Cedrych's Dominion."

The Upper was enormous. It was wide enough to accommodate twenty distinct parallel paths, ten of them for carriers going in the same direction as Melyor's carrier, and ten for vehicles traveling in the other direction. And, Orris soon realized, the Upper was not a single road, but rather a web of roads that crossed over and beneath each other above every part of the Nal. He could not image how one could even conceive of such a thing, much less build it.

And then, of course, there was the Nal itself. Orris had been overwhelmed by the size of the city since his approach to its outer wall a few days earlier. But only now, speeding above it on the Upper, did he truly begin to appreciate just how vast it was. It sprawled beneath them, stretching to the horizon in every direction like an ocean, or a mountain range. There seemed to be no end to it, no relief from the terrible monotony of the identical buildings laid out in the identical patterns of the quads. Granted, the horizon seemed closer here because of the omnipresent brown haze that obscured the more distant buildings, but that only served to heighten the powerful effect that the vista had on him. Suddenly, his entire mission seemed hopeless. The people who had built such a city could not be reasoned with. They had done away with everything their land had given them for the sake of this Nal. Tobyn-Ser would mean nothing to them. And all the magic in the world would not be able to stand against them forever. Orris felt ill suddenly, as if he had been kicked in the groin.

Somehow, Gwilym seemed to understand. The Bearer leaned forward and placed a hand on the mage's shoulder. Orris looked back at him and tried to smile, but he knew from Gwilym's expression that he failed to do so. It was only then, however, that he finally realized what Melyor had said to him. "Where did you say we were going?" the mage asked, turning toward the woman.

"Cedrych's Dominion. He controls the northeast section of the Nal."

Orris narrowed his eyes. "What is his title?"

Melyor looked at him with interest. "Do you know that much of our system of government that his title would mean something to you?"

The mage felt his color rising. He had given too much away. "I just want to know how to address him," he told her. "You indicated the day we met that he's a man of some importance. I wouldn't want to offend him."

Melyor turned her gaze back to the road. "No you would not," she said, as much to herself as to Orris. "Cedrych is an Overlord," she told him after a brief pause. "One of three Overlords in Bragor-Nal, and by far the most powerful."

An Overlord. According to Baden, the man who had led Baram's band of invaders had answered to an Overlord. "Do you have a title as well?"

"Yes. I am a Nal-Lord."

"I hope I haven't offended you by calling you Melyor."

"Not at all. How are you known in Tobyn-Ser?"

Orris shrugged. "I'm a Hawk-Mage. Some people call us Children of Amarid. But mostly people just use my name."

Melyor accepted this with a silent nod, and for a long time none of the three of them spoke. Orris stared out the large side window of the carrier, looking at the buildings and noting with detached amusement the surprise registering on the faces of passengers in other carriers as they caught sight of him or his bird. After a while, Gwilym began to snore loudly, and Orris and Melyor shared a brief smile, but still they did not speak. Some time later though, Orris saw what appeared to be an abrupt break in the monotony of the buildings looming far in the distance. Standing like an island in the continuing sea of quad buildings was a large cluster of structures made entirely of glass. They were no taller than the rest of the Nal's buildings; indeed, several of them were considerably shorter. But they were far broader, and there appeared to be a great many of them.

"What are those?" Orris asked in a whisper, pointing to the glass structures.

A small smile touched Melyor's lips and then was gone. "We call that the Farm," she said quietly. "There we grow our crops and raise our livestock."

"Within the buildings?"

She glanced at him briefly. "Yes." She leaned forward and arched her back slightly, as if she had grown stiff from sitting too long. "We will reach Cedrych soon. We stop before the Farm."

Orris nodded and continued to gaze at the buildings of the Farm. Far behind them, he now noticed, barely visible through the dingy haze, stood a row of tall mountains. So there is an end to the Nal after all, he thought to himself.

Less than a half hour later, Melyor steered the carrier off the Upper and down a steep ramp to the streets of the Nal. After a quick succession of turns she stopped in front of a tall marble and glass building in the center of yet another quad. Immediately, six large muscular men, dressed entirely in black and wearing large weapons prominently on their belts, hurried out of the structure toward the carrier.

"Cedrych's guards," Melyor said quietly.

Orris nodded once. "Impressive."

"They are not as good as they think they are," she replied, not bothering to mask the disdain in her voice.

Orris looked at her keenly, but said nothing. In the next moment, the door to the building opened inward for a second time and several more of the brawny guards came out, followed by a bald man who appeared slight by comparison. He wore a loose-fitting black shirt and trousers, with a weapon like Melyor's strapped to his thigh. He walked with a distinct limp, yet there was an elegance and economy to his movement that seemed to defy whatever injury or deformity had affected his gait. As he drew closer to the carrier, Orris saw that his face was deeply scarred on the right side, and that there was only damaged, discolored skin where his right eye should have been.

"That's Cedrych," Melyor said, somewhat unnecessarily. Orris heard the sudden tension in her voice and he felt his own apprehensions rush back.

The Nal-Lord opened her door and stepped out of the carrier. Orris followed her lead.

"Good afternoon, Overlord," she called. Though he had only known her a short while, Orris could see that the smile she offered Cedrych was forced.

"Hello, Melyor," the bald man returned in a warm, clear voice. It took Orris a moment to realize that they were speaking his language.

"Hawk-Mage Orris, of Tobyn-Ser," Melyor said formally, "this is Cedrych i Vran, Overlord of Bragor-Nal's First Dominion."

The Overlord stopped in front to Orris and extended a strong though delicate hand. "Hawk-Mage, this is indeed an honor." He smiled broadly, his one, bright blue eye gleaming eagerly. "May I call you Orris?"

"Yes, Overlord, you may."

"Call me Cedrych, please." He turned his gaze toward Anizir. "What a magnificent creature." He reached a finger toward her throat, then stopped himself. "May I?"

Orris shrugged. "If it's all right with her, it's all right with me."

Anizir regarded the Overlord warily, but she allowed him to stroke her chin.

"Thank you," Cedrych said. He glanced at the bird. "Both of you." He turned to Gwilym, and though Orris did not understand what Cedrych said, he could tell that the Overlord greeted the Bearer with the same disarming courtesy that he had just shown Orris.

"I'm looking forward to speaking with you in private, Orris," the Overlord said, turning back to the mage. His facility with Tobyn-Ser's language was even greater than Melyor's "But I thought we might begin with a brief tour of this part of the Nal."

Orris nodded. "I'd like that. I'd be particularly interested in seeing the Farm."

"The Farm!" Cedrych repeated with genuine surprise. "What a splendid idea! Melyor, will you pilot us there, please?"

"Yes, Overlord."

They climbed back into the carrier, Orris joining Gwilym in the rear seat and Cedrych taking Orris's place up front. A second carrier, bearing four of Cedrych's guards pulled up behind their vehicle and followed as Melyor steered them though the streets of the Nal to the Farm. It was a journey of perhaps half an hour to the boundary separating the Farm from the rest of the Nal.

The entrance to the Farm was heavily guarded by men in light blue uniforms who carried huge weapons and wore dour expressions. They recognized Cedrych immediately, however, and waved the two carriers through the heavily fortified gates. Still, Orris and the others remained in the carrier for a while longer, moving slowly among the various buildings.

"As you can tell from the precautions that our Sovereign has taken," Cedrych explained, "the Farm is the most important and sensitive section of Bragor-Nal. This is where we cultivate our food, our timber, our livestock; everything we need to survive."

"I'm interested to know how you manage to do all of this within these structures," Orris said gazing out the carrier window.

"Actually, it's not very difficult. Take your next right, Melyor," Cedrych commanded. "We'll stop at the first timber house."

The Nal-Lord did as she was told, stopping the carrier in front of an enormous, cylindrical glass structure. It was extremely tall, and Orris could not even begin to gauge it's diameter.

"How big . . . ?" the mage whispered.

"I don't think you'd understand our units of measure," Cedrych told him, "but it would easily cover eight quads. And there are dozens more just like it throughout the Farm."

Orris had not been sure what to expect, but nothing that his mind conjured up could have prepared him for what he actually found within the building. It was raining when they walked in. Not hard, but more than a drizzle. Drops of water tapped lightly on the leaves of the oaks and maples that towered overhead. A woodpecker drummed in the distance and a flock of jays appeared overhead scolding loudly, alarmed, it seemed, by Anizir's presence. Orris's falcon stared at the birds avidly, and she conveyed an image to Orris that would have sent the jays scurrying for cover had they only known.

No, love, he sent back soothingly. *You can't hunt in here.*

She gave a soft cry in response.

"Is something wrong?" Cedrych asked, looking at Anizir.

"No," Orris answered. "She's just hungry. I'll let her hunt when we go back outside."

"She's welcome to hunt in here. The other hawks do."

"There are hawks in here?" the mage asked in amazement, gazing up at the trees and wiping the rain from his brow.

"Hawks, owls, foxes, even a pair of wildcats. This forest is as alive as any woodland of Tobyn-Ser."

Orris looked sharply at the Overlord, who smiled at him enigmatically.

"Please," Cedrych insisted. "Let her hunt. I'd like to see her fly; I'm sure it's quite a sight."

"All right," the mage agreed with a shrug. He sent an image to Anizir, who leaped off his shoulder, scattering the jays in all directions, and then disappeared among the trees. They all stared after her for a moment in silence.

"Let's walk," Cedrych said, indicating a path that led through the trees. "This rain shouldn't last long."

Orris fell in beside the Overlord, and Melyor and Gwilym walked behind them, speaking quietly in Lon-Ser's language. For some time, Orris and Cedrych said nothing. The mage knew that the bald man was watching him closely with his one blue eye, but Orris was too amazed by what he saw around him to care. He was within a building, strolling through a forest. Ferns and mosses grew on the forest floor. Oak and maple saplings intermingled with sassafras and hobblebush to form a dense layer of undergrowth, and the parent trees grew taller and straighter than Orris would have believed possible. Squirrels and chipmunks darted in and out of view among the tree trunks and shrubs, and thrushes sang from hidden perches.

"This could be any forest in Tobyn-Ser, couldn't it?" Cedrych asked as they came across a small, swift brook.

"Have you been to Tobyn-Ser?" Orris asked, meeting the Overlord's gaze. "Or are you just guessing?"

"Neither really," Cedrych replied amiably. "I've never been, but I've heard a good deal from Abboriji merchants and others who have."

Orris looked at the man for a while longer before glancing once again at the trees and shrubs growing all around him, their leaves glistening in the soft rain. It was easy to forget that this was not a true forest. Too easy. "Yes, I suppose it does look like Tobyn-Ser. Is it meant to?"

"No. It's meant to look like the forests it replaced here in Lon-Ser."

"And does it?"

Cedrych straightened, his mouth set in a thin line. "I wouldn't know," he said at last. "I never saw them."

They walked in silence for several minutes. Orris noticed that Melyor and Gwilym had stopped talking. He felt Anizir touch his mind and, an instant later, he heard her wing beats as she approached. She alighted on his arm, took her familiar position on his shoulder, and began to preen. Her light breast feathers were speckled with droplets of fresh blood and there was a small tuft of down stuck to her sharply hooked beak.

"I take it she was successful," Cedrych commented, a frosty smile on his lips.

"It looks that way," Orris said.

The rain abruptly ceased, and it suddenly seemed to Orris that the sun was trying to break through the cloud cover. Once again he had to remind himself that this was all an illusion created by people. The mage indicated the sky with a gesture. "What's happening?"

The Overlord grinned again. It appeared genuine this time. "What does it look like? The sun is coming out; the storm has moved on."

"But that's impossible."

"Is it?"

The two men stared at each other for some time. And then Orris closed his eyes and conveyed an image to Anizir. She soared off his shoulder again, circling above their heads once before flying up over the trees. As she soared above, Orris reached deeper for their connection so that he could see through her eyes. And doing so, he beheld things that he only vaguely understood. At the far end of the building there was an enormous round frame, covered with a fine grate. Within it was a slowly turning object comprised of four broad blades. Above where Anizir was soaring, held in place by hundreds of metal threads that stretched down from the transparent ceiling of the structure, hung a lattice of polished metal rods from which water still dripped. And above the metal lattice, which covered the entire forest, were a set of lights that shone so brilliantly that they seemed to sear Orris's mind when Anizir gazed up at them. Examining these strange things with Anizir's eyes, Orris could not even begin to imagine how they worked, or what else they were capable of doing. But somehow he knew what they were, or rather, what they were supposed to be: wind, rain, and sun.

He called Anizir back to him and opened his eyes again. "Remarkable," he breathed, looking at Cedrych and then at Melyor.

Cedrych narrowed his eye. "You saw?" he asked, his voice tinged with both fear and wonder.

"Yes."

"How is that possible?"

Orris tipped his head toward Anizir as she flew back to his shoulder. "My bird and I share a very special connection. She reads my thoughts and I read hers. And occasionally, when I need to, I can use her eyes to see."

The Overlord nodded slowly. "That too is remarkable."

"The things I saw," Orris said, pointing upward, "can they make snow, too?"

It took Cedrych a few moments to answer. He appeared preoccupied with what Orris had told him. "Snow? Yes," he finally said. "We can make snow, sleet, ice storms, wind storms. We have the timber houses on seasonal rhythms. We find that the forests grow more efficiently that way. For most of the other buildings—livestock, grain, fruits; things of that sort—we keep the temperature moderate."

They began to walk again, the path still leading them away from the building's entrance. After another hundred yards or so, the maples and oaks gave way far too abruptly to a stand of cedars and firs. It was, Orris realized, the first evidence he had seen with his own eyes that this was not a natural forest.

"We have need of a large variety of woods," Cedrych explained almost apologetically, as if he had read Orris's thoughts. "We can't always make the transitions as smooth as we'd like."

They soon reached a fork in the path and rather than continuing deeper into the forest, they looped back toward the entrance to the building. "There are other things I'd like you to see," Cedrych offered by way of explanation.

Returning to the carrier, they made their way to another building just a few minutes from the timber house. Like the structure containing the forest, this building was constructed of glass, and it covered an enormous area. But rather than stretching far up into the dingy brown sky of the Nal, this one was relatively low; only slightly taller than the Great Hall of Amarid. Within it, Orris found a vast golden expanse of wheat that swayed and danced in a wind created by several of the spinning, bladed objects he had seen in the timber house. A metal lattice, very much like the one in the taller building, hung overhead, dormant for now, and bright lights shone down warmly upon the grain like hundreds of tiny suns.

"There are thirty more levels in this building," the Overlord said. "All of them beneath us."

"All of them containing fields of grain?"

Cedrych shrugged. "We have many people to feed."

Orris took a long breath and nodded. It was fascinating and imposing and frightening all at the same time. And yet the mage was bothered much less by what he was seeing than he was by the very fact that he was being allowed to see it.

"Why are you showing me this?" the mage finally asked, turning toward Cedrych. "From everything I've learned of Lon-Ser, you people go to great lengths to conceal the secrets behind your advanced goods. And yet here you are showing me what you yourself have said is the most important part of Bragor-Nal. I don't understand."

Cedrych shrugged. "You're a guest here," he said disarmingly. "Were I to visit your land, I'd expect you to show me its greatest sites."

"No," Orris replied with a shake of his head. "I don't believe you. There's got to be more to it than that."

The smile faded from the Overlord's face, and the look in his sapphire eye hardened. "Why are you here? Why have you come to Bragor-Nal?"

Neither Orris nor Cedrych had moved, but the Hawk-Mage suddenly felt as though they had drawn their blades and were circling each other, looking for some kind of opening. He sensed that Melyor was watching them, and that she was holding her breath. Even Gwilym seemed to be paying strict attention, though as far as Orris knew, the Bearer did not understand a word of what they were saying.

"What does one thing have to do with the other?" Orris demanded at last, his eyes locked on the Overlord's face.

"Nothing at all. And everything. Are you here as an envoy of peace, or as a conqueror?"

Orris laughed. "A conqueror?" he asked incredulously. "I'm one man against a land that has tools and weapons that I can barely fathom, and more people than I can imagine. And you ask me if I'm a conqueror?"

"You may be one man, sorcerer, but I've seen what you can do, you and that bird of yours."

"*Seen?*" Orris asked, narrowing his eyes. "What have you seen?"

Cedrych pulled two pieces of paper out of his pocket and handed them to Orris. They appeared to be miniature portraits, although they were far clearer and more precise than any work of art the mage had ever seen. And they depicted figures so grisly that Orris only glanced at them before handing them back to the bald man.

"Those still-shots show what's left of the two men you killed in the Twenty-First Realm," Cedrych told him accusingly. "Certainly this isn't the work of a man seeking peace."

"They attacked me!" Orris fired back.

"I believe you, but that's not the point. You say that you don't understand our advanced goods. Well, we know even less about your powers."

Orris doubted that this was true, but he let it pass for the time being.

"To answer the question you asked before," Cedrych continued, "perhaps I'm showing you these things so that you'll take this as a gesture of trust and, in turn, tell me more about the magic of the Children of Amarid."

Orris looked sharply at Melyor. Earlier in the day, she had acted as though she had never heard of Amarid. But if Cedrych knew of the First Mage, wouldn't she as well? Orris read the answer plainly in the way she averted her eyes rather than meet his gaze, her attractive features turning pale. And Cedrych was speaking of trust?

"Perhaps," Orris said coldly. "Whatever your purpose, I've seen enough. Let's go someplace where we can talk."

By the time they returned to the building where Orris had first met Cedrych, night had fallen. Rather than stopping in front of the marble structure as they had earlier, they took a narrow road to a large underground chamber that contained dozens of carriers just like the one they were in. As soon as the vehicle came to a halt, several guards approached it and opened the doors. As Orris emerged from the carrier with Anizir perched on one arm and his staff with its glowing stone in his hands, the guard nearest to him backed away, his eyes wide.

Cedrych gave a sharp command in Lon-Ser's language and the guard started, his face turning scarlet.

"This way," the Overlord called, indicating a nearby chamber with one hand and gesturing with the other for Melyor, Gwilym, and Orris to follow. Escorted by two of the guards, the four of them entered the chamber, which appeared larger than it was due in large part to its mirrored back wall. The side walls were made of dark polished wood and the entire chamber was trimmed elegantly with burnished brass. When everyone was in the chamber, one of the guards touched a red circle situated atop a brass wall plate. Instantly, a door materialized out of one of the side walls and slid closed, as if guided by an unseen hand. A moment later, Orris felt his stomach drop as the chamber began to move upward. He and Gwilym shared an anxious look.

"We call it a lifter," Cedrych explained as the chamber continued to climb. "It allows us to reach the highest levels of our buildings without having to use stairs."

After several seconds more the lifter stopped, and Orris's stomach heaved upward uncomfortably. "It's a bit unsettling," he said, as the door slid open.

They stepped out of the small chamber and Cedrych led them down a long corridor toward a strange looking device that looked to be another lifter, although Orris sensed that it had a darker purpose. Cedrych spoke briefly to the guards standing in front of the strange object and then waved Melyor through it.

"The Bearer will have to remain out here," the Overlord said, just as Orris was stepping into the dark device.

"Why?"

Cedrych hesitated. "We may be discussing matters of some . . . delicacy. It seems appropriate that we should do so in private."

"But Melyor—"

"Melyor may have something of value to add to our conversation."

Orris shook his head. "This is ridiculous. He doesn't even speak my language."

Cedrych smiled thinly. "Nonetheless, I must insist."

Orris let out a slow breath. "Fine," he said impatiently. "Explain it to him."

Cedrych turned to the Bearer and spoke to him for several moments. Orris could see Gwilym growing increasingly agitated, and when Cedrych finished, the portly man turned to Orris and began speaking to him very quickly, and somewhat desperately in Lon-Ser's language.

Orris turned to Melyor, who was watching all this from the far side of the device. "What's he saying?" the mage asked her.

She swallowed and stepped back through to their side. She glanced briefly at Cedrych, who nodded once. "He is concerned for your safety, and his own. He says that he does not trust the Overlord and he thinks the two of you should leave right away."

Orris faced the Bearer and gave him what the mage hoped would be a confident smile. "I'll be all right." He gestured toward Anizir. "*We'll* be all right," he added. "We can take care of ourselves." He glanced at Melyor. "Tell him that." She looked at the Overlord again. "Don't ask him!" Orris snapped before Cedrych could give her any indication of what she should do. "Just tell Gwilym what I said!"

She said something to the Bearer—Orris could only assume that she had relayed his message accurately.

The mage faced Cedrych. "Now it's your turn. Tell your man that the Bearer is to be treated well. I'm not a conqueror, but if anything happens to Gwilym, I'll bring down this building, and you with it. Do you understand?"

Cedrych eyed him closely and then, for a second time, he nodded once. Never taking his eye off Orris, the Overlord gave a command to his guards.

When he was done, Orris placed a hand on Gwilym's shoulder. "Is that all right?" he asked. Melyor translated, and, after a moment, the Bearer gave a reluctant nod.

The mage smiled. "Good." He squeezed the portly man's shoulder. "I'm ready," he said, looking at Cedrych again.

Once more, Cedrych gestured for Melyor and Orris to step through the device and, when they had, he pushed open a door and led them through. The door to Cedrych's home opened onto what Orris guessed was the common room. Its pale grey floor covering and perfectly matching furniture were immaculate and luxurious-looking, but Orris only noticed these things in passing. He was drawn at once to the huge window on the far side of the room. Through it he could see what seemed to be the entire Nal, its buildings and avenues illuminated so brilliantly that it seemed to Orris for one dizzying moment that the world had been turned upside down, and that Leora's stars had been scattered at his feet.

In the next instant the sensation was gone and Melyor was beside him, drinking in the view as well.

"This is one of the best views of the Nal I have ever seen," she said quietly.

Orris nodded, but said nothing.

"Dinner will be here shortly," the Overlord called from the far end of the room. "In the meantime, Orris, can I pour you some wine?"

"Yes, thank you," the mage replied over his shoulder.

"I apologize for not being honest with you earlier today," Melyor said in a voice that was barely more than a whisper. Orris wondered if she really didn't want Cedrych to hear, or if this was still part of an elaborate ruse.

"So you had heard of Amarid." He offered it as a statement.

"Yes."

"Why did you pretend you hadn't?"

"I do not know. I suppose . . ." She trailed off, shaking her head. "I do not know," she said again.

Orris looked at her. She was watching him, an alluring vulnerability in her lovely green eyes. I'm alone with two strangers, he thought in that moment, and I really don't know which one of them is more dangerous. "I wish I knew whether to believe you," he told her, turning away and walking back to the center of the room.

Cedrych was waiting for him there with a glass of pale wine. "Please sit," the Overlord invited, handing him the wine. Orris inclined his head slightly in thanks and lowered himself into a large, comfortable-looking chair. Cedrych sat on a long couch located against the wall on the other side of the low glass table, and Melyor joined them, sitting in another chair that was identical to Orris's.

The mage sipped his wine, which was light and dry, and, he had to admit, very good.

"Do you like it?" Cedrych asked.

"Yes, it's excellent."

The Overlord grinned. "Most of what our vineyards produce is swill, but there are a few that do a very nice job. And there's one in particular," he added, indicating his own glass with a delicate hand, "that makes some truly exceptional wines. Every year on the Day of Lon I send a dozen bottles to the Sovereign."

"What can you tell me about the Sovereign?" Orris asked, hoping he sounded casual.

"Durell?" Cedrych said with a shrug. "He's a decent man, a competent leader."

"That's hardly a ringing endorsement."

Cedrych regarded him for several seconds with his lone eye. "If you're expecting me to say that he's the wisest and strongest Sovereign the Nal has ever had," he finally said with surprising candor, "I'm afraid I can't. He carries out his duties with satisfactory efficiency and he's done nothing to undermine Bragor-Nal's preeminent position in Lon-Ser. For now, that suits the purposes of his Overlords. But I wouldn't want to predict how long his tenure will last."

Orris took another sip of wine. "Is the length of his tenure something you determine?"

"Possibly," Cedrych answered, smiling inscrutably, and drinking from his glass in turn.

The three of them sat in silence for some time, sipping occasionally, and avoiding each other's eyes, until finally Cedrych's guards arrived with dinner and they moved to a large dining room. Like the common room, this chamber had silver-grey carpeting and a magnificent view of the Nal. The table and chairs were made of a dark, finely grained wood. Anizir settled on the back of an empty chair beside Orris and immediately closed her eyes and went to sleep.

The meal consisted of roasted meat, a pleasant though slightly bitter-tasting leafy green that Orris did not recognize, and a boiled root that reminded him of the mountain-root commonly served back in Tobyn-Ser.

"So tell me Orris," Cedrych said between mouthfuls, "now that we're speaking civilly again, why have you come to Bragor-Nal?"

Orris had been raising a forkful of meat to his mouth, and he paused now, placing the fork on his plate. Perhaps sensing his sudden tension, Anizir awoke and hopped to his shoulder. "I've come here as a representative of my people," he began cautiously, "seeking answers to some questions we have about recent incidents in Tobyn-Ser."

Cedrych nodded thoughtfully. "I see. Perhaps Melyor and I can help you."

Orris forced a smile. "That's kind of you, but I wish to take these questions to the Council of Sovereigns."

The Overlord spoke briefly to Melyor in their language. Watching them, not comprehending what passed between them, Orris suddenly realized why the Overlord had wanted to keep Gwilym out of the room. After a few seconds, Cedrych looked at Orris again. "The Council is always very busy. It would take weeks, perhaps months to get you an audience with them."

"I understand that," Orris replied. And then, acting on an impulse he did not fully understand, the mage added, "But the leader of my Order has already corresponded with the Council about this matter. I think they'll find time to see me."

Cedrych stopped chewing what was in his mouth and swallowed. "Say that again."

"The leader of the Order of Mages and Masters has written to your Council and has received a reply. I expect that when I present myself to the Sovereigns, they'll want to speak with me." Orris was bluffing, of course. The Council's letter had been peremptory in its dismissal of the matter, but he was gambling that Cedrych wouldn't know this.

"Do you know what these messages said?" the Overlord demanded, not bothering to conceal his interest.

Orris smiled. "Yes, of course."

Cedrych stared at him expectantly for several moments, and when he finally realized that Orris was not going to volunteer the information his face reddened and the expression in his bright blue eye grew icy. "You'll find, sorcerer," the Overlord said, clearly irritated, "that I don't take well to game-playing."

"On the contrary, Cedrych," Orris returned, sensing that he had the upper hand, "I'd guess from what I've seen thus far that you enjoy playing games a great deal. It's losing you dislike." Cedrych glared at him silently, and Orris allowed himself a small smile. "There is a gambling game we play in Tobyn-Ser called Ren-drah. Its primary object is to fool your opponent into thinking you have a more powerful set of cards than you actually do. I expect you'd be quite good at it."

"I take it you play this game."

"Yes, I do. Very well." The mage glanced at Melyor and found that she was watching him, a hint of a smile touching her lips.

Cedrych seemed to notice this as well. "Leave us, Melyor," he commanded coldly. "I want to speak with Orris alone."

Melyor stood but she continued to watch the mage, a look of concern creeping into her emerald eyes. Once more, Orris found himself unsure of whether to trust what he saw in her.

But again, Cedrych appeared to see it also. "Now, Melyor," he said sternly.

The Nal-Lord left the table, and, a few seconds later, Orris heard the door to Cedrych's home open and close. The Overlord continued to stare at her empty chair for some time after she had gone, his expression unreadable. "You seem to have made an impression on her," he said at last, his tone making it clear that this did not please him. He looked at Orris. "Perhaps she's made one on you as well?" Orris said nothing, and the bald man grinned. "Don't be embarrassed," he said with condescension. "You're certainly not the first. But before you do anything foolish, you might want to find out who sent the men who ambushed you in that alley the other day."

Orris felt a sudden tightening in his stomach. He put his fork down on his plate.

Cedrych's smile deepened. "So you've come to speak with our Council of Sovereigns," he went on smoothly. "Perhaps to sue for peace?"

"Perhaps," Orris answered, trying to force his mind past what Cedrych had said a moment before. *You might want to find out who sent the men who ambushed you. . . . Melyor?*

"And what if they can't help you?"

Orris stared at him blankly.

"Ah," Cedrych said, "this never occurred to you. You assume that the Council can help you simply because it is the land's highest authority." He shook his head. "Lon-Ser is a vast land, Orris; such a land doesn't lend itself well to centralized governance. The Council doesn't control everything that happens here. Sometimes, its members aren't even aware of what happens here." He paused, taking a forkful of meat and washing it down with a sip of wine. "This may be difficult for you to understand, coming from a land such as yours, where people outside of your Order are unlikely to have the power or reach to affect the world around them. But here, one doesn't have to be a Sovereign to have influence and resources."

The Hawk-Mage raised his glass to drink and was gratified to see that his hand remained steady. "You seem to know a great deal about my world, Cedrych," he said. "Why is that?"

The Overlord shrugged. "As I said, one doesn't have to be a Sovereign to have resources."

"I didn't ask 'how,' I asked 'why.' "

"Yes, I know," Cedrych said with relish.

"Well, if what you say about the Council is true," Orris began again after a brief lull, "what would you suggest that I do?"

Cedrych opened his hands slightly. "You've told me so little about why you're here. It's difficult for me to say. Perhaps, if you told me more. . . ."

Orris grinned darkly and shook his head. "I don't think so. I'll take my chances with the Council."

Cedrych's face seemed abruptly to turn to stone. "You're welcome to try," he said through clenched teeth. "But keep in mind that Bragor-Nal can be a dangerous place. Particularly for strangers."

Orris reached up and gently stroked Anizir's chin, his eyes never leaving the Overlord's scarred face. "Are you threatening me, Cedrych?"

"I'm merely saying that before you reject an offer of friendship, you should weigh the risks, not only to you, but to those who depend on you."

It took a moment, for Orris to figure out who the Overlord meant: Gwilym. He leveled a rigid finger at the bald man's heart as if it was his staff. "If anything happens to him, anything at all, I swear in Arick's name that I'll kill you!"

"I don't know what you're getting upset about, Orris. And I don't know who you're referring to. I was just saying that—"

"I know exactly what you were saying!" Orris said, standing abruptly and grabbing his staff, which was leaning against the wall beside him. "And I'm telling you that if you hurt the Bearer, if you even try to hurt him, I'll destroy you! I don't care if I have to tear this entire building apart, I'll destroy you!"

The mage spun away from the table and started toward the door, but before he reached it he heard Cedrych begin to laugh.

"When you walk through that door, sorcerer, you'll be all alone. There won't be anyone to help you, and there won't be anywhere you can hide where I can't find you."

Orris stopped, his hand on the door handle. "I guess you don't know as much about Tobyn-Ser as you thought, Cedrych," he called, conscious suddenly of Anizir's talons gripping his shoulder. "A mage is never alone." And with that, he pulled the door open and left.

20

As I have pointed out previously, the governing structure of Bragor-Nal is founded upon the systematic use of violence and the fear it evokes. The problem with such a system, however, is that those who use violence to gain power will only enjoy the status they have won as long as they remain the strongest and the most fearsome. Just as there will always be another wave rolling in off Duclea's Ocean, there will always be another who will be more powerful, more cunning, or more skilled with a weapon. It is just a matter of time. Hence, though violence gives the system whatever stability it might have, violence also threatens constantly to plunge the system into chaos. This paradox gives rise to the two central truths of life in the Nal. First, no one can be trusted. And second, no matter how good or bad one's standing is today, to-morrow is uncertain.

—From Section Five of "The Report of Owl-Master Baden on his Interrogation of the Outlander Baram," Submitted to the 1,014th Gathering of the Order of Mages and Masters. Spring, Gods' Year 4625.

For some time Cedrych did not leave the table. He drank his wine and finished the fowl and greens that were on his plate. Only then did he stand and make his way to his office and the speak-screen there.

He had hoped that his day with the sorcerer would go better than this, that he would learn more about what Orris and his colleagues knew of the Initiative before he had Orris killed. Cedrych shrugged. Sometimes things didn't go according to plan. That didn't change the fact that the sorcerer had to die; indeed it made it all the more important that the assassination be carried out swiftly.

He switched on the speak-screen and punched in the code he used on such occasions. After a few seconds, the familiar angular face appeared on the screen.

"Yes, Overlord. How may I serve you?"

"It's time, Blade," Cedrych told the man. "I want it done soon, and I want it done discreetly."

"Of course, Overlord. Just the two, as we agreed?"

Cedrych thought for a moment, rubbing a delicate hand across his smooth brow. "No," he finally answered. "There's a third as well. A woman."

Blade nodded. "Very well. That will be extra, naturally."

"Naturally."

"What's the woman's name?"

Cedrych took a breath. He was being rash, he knew. This would set back the timetable for the Initiative by months. But after what he had seen today, he didn't really have much of a choice. "Melyor i Lakin."

The man's pale eyes widened. "That will be quite a bit extra!" he said.

"I don't care," Cedrych told him. "Just make certain that you take care of all three of them."

The assassin exhaled through his teeth. "Yes, Overlord."

"And remember," Cedrych added, "I want you to take twice the usual contingent. The sorcerer is dangerous."

"So you've told me," Blade replied sourly. "Frankly, I can't imagine that I'd need eight men to take care of him, but given that he's traveling with Melyor, I'll do as you say."

"Good. Let me know when it's done." Cedrych pressed a red button at the top of his screen and the assassin's face disappeared. The Overlord remained at his desk; he had a second call to make. Clicking on the pad that sat in front of his screen, Cedrych brought up a listing of all the break-laws in his dominion and their screen codes. Running his finger down the list as he searched, he soon found the code he wanted and he punched it in.

The screen beeped several times with no answer. Cedrych cursed under his breath and reached to break off the connection. But just as he did, the break-law's face appeared on the screen. He had dark, unkempt hair that fell to his shoulders and partially obscured his blue eyes. His chin was square and unshaven, and he had a straight, aristocratic nose. He was naked from the waist up, and Cedrych assumed that there was an uestra girl somewhere in his flat.

"Overlord!" the man gasped, seeing Cedrych's face on his screen. "I'm sorry! I was . . ." He swallowed. "How can I serve you, Overlord?"

Despite his misgivings at what he was doing, Cedrych smiled. "Good evening, Dob," he said. "Is this a bad time?"

The break-law glanced back over his shoulder uncomfortably. "No, Overlord," he answered, facing the screen again, and forcing himself to smile. "Of course not."

"Good. I have some matters to discuss with you."

She was trembling violently as she left the Overlord's quarters. She could barely walk. Stepping gingerly through the weapons chamber, she saw the Bearer hurrying toward her, his brow furrowed with worry, and she tried to wave him away with a quivering hand.

"Is everything all right?" he asked a little desperately as he stopped in front of her.

"Fine," she managed. "Everything's fine." She turned away from him. She had no desire to talk right now.

"But the sorcerer!" he persisted. "He's still in there! He's alone!"

"He's fine!" she snapped.

Gwilym stared at her for a moment, his face reddening. Then he turned abruptly and walked away.

Melyor took a long breath. He didn't deserve that, she thought. She briefly considered going to him with an apology, but she remained where she was. There really was nothing she could say to him. Indeed, she didn't even have the right to give him the one assurance she had offered. She couldn't be certain that the sorcerer was fine. For all she knew Cedrych had sent her from the room because he intended to kill Orris himself.

In the next instant, however, she shook her head. Orris, she had realized during the course of this day, was more than capable of taking care of himself. And besides, that wasn't the way Cedrych worked. She closed her eyes, hoping this realization would calm her, but she knew better. She wasn't trembling for fear that Orris would be killed.

Nor was she afraid of what she had seen in Cedrych's eyes just before he dismissed her, although she knew she should have been. He was furious with her, enough to have her killed. But even that did not explain her racing pulse and the chills running through her body.

She was trembling because somehow, in the scant moments she had spent in Cedrych's quarters listening to the Overlord and the sorcerer wage their verbal battle, she had come to recognize something so startling, so overwhelming, that she feared she might become physically ill. And yet she knew it to be true, just as she knew her name was Melyor i Lakin.

She wanted the sorcerer to succeed. If it was peace he wanted, then she wanted it as well. If he had come to destroy all of Bragor-Nal, she would help him do it.

It made no sense. She had spent years in pursuit of the riches and power that the Tobyn-Ser Initiative would bring her, risking her life and taking the lives of others more times than she cared to count. She was going to be Overlord someday, perhaps Sovereign as well. This had been her dream, the single guiding ambition of her entire life.

But sitting at the table with Orris and Cedrych, it had been the memory of another dream that occupied her mind. She and the sorcerer were destined to be allies. She had Seen it. Since her vision she had assumed that something would happen to make that alliance a necessity. It had never occurred to her that she would actually choose to cast her lot with the mage.

I'm a Nal-Lord! she raged silently. I'm going to conquer Tobyn-Ser!

And as if in answer, she heard another voice within her mind, one that might have been her mother's. *You're a Gildriite*, this voice said. *it's time you acknowledged that.*

She had used her Sight for years, depending upon it to further her career just as she did her skill with a thrower or blade. Only a few days ago, she had used the fact of her ancestry to win the Bearer's trust. And ever since her encounter with Mink, she had shared her secret with every one of her victims just before they died. Acknowledge it? she wanted to argue. I've acknowledged it for years.

Somehow though, she knew that this was different. It was one thing to use her abilities. It was quite another to think of herself as a Gildriite. But tonight, watching Orris handle the Overlord's questions and threats with such ease, she had felt an inexplicable pride, as if his triumph were hers as well. And in a sense, she had realized at the time, it was. Just by standing up to Cedrych, by refusing to be intimidated by this man who had managed to intimidate every person in Bragor-Nal, Orris was striking a blow for all who carried Gildri's blood in their veins. For the first time she could remember, Melyor found that she was seeing herself as something more than a Nal-Lord. She was a Gildriite, and she wanted Orris to know it. She wanted the sorcerer to understand that she had, in that moment, taken up his cause as her own. So she smiled at him, hoping it would convey all she intended.

She wasn't certain if Orris understood, but clearly Cedrych had. And it seemed equally clear that in allying herself with the sorcerer, she had made an enemy of the Overlord. But she knew one other thing as well: Orris was probably the one person in Bragor-Nal capable of protecting her.

She took another breath, and felt herself growing calmer at last. Her life had just grown infinitely more complicated, but she had made her choice, and in an odd way, she felt better for having done so.

She walked over to where the Bearer was standing, his eyes fixed on his glowing brown stone, and she placed a hand on his arm.

"I'm sorry, Bearer," she said. "I didn't mean to be short with you."

He looked up from his stone and regarded her silently for several moments. Finally, he nodded once. "It's all right." He glanced over at the guards and then beyond them, toward the door to Cedrych's quarters. "I'll just feel better once we're out of here."

"So will I," Melyor breathed.

He gave her a curious look, but he said nothing more, and the two of them remained there, standing together, waiting for Orris.

The sorcerer emerged from Cedrych's quarters a short time later, striding past the guards as if they weren't even there, his dark eyes staring straight ahead and his yellow beard bristling menacingly. On his shoulder sat his falcon, surveying the corridor imperiously, as if daring anyone to approach them. Orris did not speak or stop when he reached Melyor and the Bearer, so the two of them fell in behind him and together they walked wordlessly to the lifter. It was not until the door slid shut, and the chamber began its descent that Gwilym finally broke the tense silence.

"Ask him what happened," he said to Melyor. It had taken her some time to get used to his strange dialect, but it was getting easier now. "Ask him what happened!" he repeated impatiently.

"What's he saying?" Orris asked in Tobynmir.

"He would like to know what went on between you and Cedrych," she answered in his language. "I would as well."

The mage looked at Gwilym and gave a small, reassuring smile. "Tell him that the Overlord and I didn't get along very well, and that I doubt we'll be seeing him again."

Melyor pressed her lips together for a moment. Cedrych, she knew, had a way of surprising people. If he decided that he wanted to see Orris again, there would probably be little the sorcerer could do to prevent another meeting. Nonetheless, she turned to the Bearer and translated what the sorcerer had said.

"Good," Gwilym said approvingly "I got a bad feeling from him."

When Melyor told Orris what Gwilym had said, the sorcerer nodded in agreement. "So did I." He looked at Melyor for a moment, seeming to consider something. "Ask him if he still trusts you," he instructed at last.

Melyor stared back at him, saying nothing. She had been ready to tell him of her dream. She wanted to desperately. We're meant to be allies! she wanted to say. I've Seen it! But the sorcerer's words stopped her cold. She was ready to throw away her life's ambition—as far as she knew she already had. Who knew what Cedrych had in mind for her now? And Orris didn't even know if he could trust her. I'm an idiot, she thought. And I'm going to get myself killed.

The lifter stopped and the door opened. The three of them stepped out of the chamber and, escorted by several guards, quickly left the building. Melyor's carrier was waiting for them at the base of the marble stairs, and the guards opened its doors as they reached it. Gwilym climbed into the back again, and Melyor and Orris sat up front.

"Ask him if he still trusts you," Orris said again, as Melyor started the carrier forward.

She shook her head. "No. I am not your interpreter, and I am not your attendant. Ask him yourself."

Orris smiled grimly. "You're afraid of the answer, aren't you?"

She spat a curse in Bragory. "The sorcerer wants to know if you still trust me," she said angrily, glancing back at the Bearer. "I get the feeling he doesn't."

Gwilym hesitated, looking from Melyor to Orris. "Tell him I'm not sure," he answered at last, his voice subdued.

"Fuck you both," she said, feeling a twisting in her heart, and cursing the tears welling in her eyes.

"What did he say?" Orris demanded in Tobynmir.

"He said he cannot say for sure," she admitted, stopping the carrier in an alley off one of the quads. "Which is fine with me. Get out. The two of you can rot for all I care."

Orris just sat in his seat, saying nothing and regarding her appraisingly.

"Go on, get out!" she said again, her voice rising.

"Not until I get some answers," Orris replied cooly. "Why did you have your men ambush me?"

Melyor felt her entire body go rigid, as if Orris had just laid the edge of a blade against her throat. "He told you!" she whispered.

"Actually, no," he said. "He just hinted. I didn't know for certain until now."

"What are you two talking about?" Gwilym asked.

"Why did you do it?" Orris demanded again.

"It was a mistake," she said, which was the truth, though she wasn't foolish enough to think that he'd understand.

"Because your men failed?"

"No. It was a mistake because I was trying to protect something that is no longer worth protecting."

"What do you mean?" Orris persisted. "What were you protecting?"

"What's going on?" Gwilym asked, leaning forward.

Orris raised a single finger, silencing the Bearer, though he never took his eyes off Melyor's face. "Tell me," he demanded.

The Nal-Lord took a long breath. I should have seen this coming, she said to herself. I should have known it wouldn't be so easy. "Cedrych is the one who sent the invaders to your land. When he heard nothing from the leader, he organized a second unit. I was to be in command."

"*What?*" Orris hissed, his dark eyes filled with loathing.

She stared out the front window at the alley; she couldn't bear to look at the sorcerer anymore. "If we succeeded, it would have put me in line to be the Overlord, maybe even Sovereign," she explained quietly. She licked her lips, which abruptly felt terribly dry. "I knew that you were coming to make peace; I could not allow that."

"So you tried to have me killed."

She nodded. "Yes."

They fell into a grave silence. After several moments, Gwilym cleared his throat.

"Explain it to him," the sorcerer instructed, not bothering to look at her. "All of it."

She nodded, and then told the Bearer everything she had just told Orris. When she finished, the heavy man sat back slowly and whistled through his teeth, staring out the side window.

After a few moments, however, he turned toward her again, his eyes meeting hers. "Tell the sorcerer I trust you now," he said.

Melyor blinked, wondering if she had heard him correctly.

Gwilym grinned. "Tell him."

"You may not believe this," she said, looking at Orris. "But Gwilym says he trusts me now."

Orris's eyes flew to the Bearer, and Gwilym nodded.

"Tell him that if you admit to these things, you must have no secrets left."

Melyor smiled and repeated what the Bearer had said.

"He has a point," Orris conceded.

"Does that mean you trust me, too?"

Orris looked out at the street again. "No. But it does mean that I'm willing to give you another chance."

Melyor stared at him for some time, though he wouldn't meet her gaze. Finally, she nodded. "Fair enough," she said, starting the carrier again, and pulling back onto the main avenue of the quad. "But we should get moving. Cedrych will be coming after us."

"I have news for you, Dob," Cedrych said, causing the break-law's heart to hammer against his ribs. "Some of it bad, I'm afraid, but some of it quite good."

Dob tried to swallow, but there was no trace of moisture in his mouth. He almost swallowed his tongue by accident. How long had he been waiting for some word as to who would replace Savil as Nal-Lord of the Second? Over half a year? It seemed like more. At first, in the immediate aftermath of that unbelievable night when the Nal-Lord was killed, there had been six of them warring for supremacy. But the contest had quickly narrowed to just two: Dob and a wiry, dark-skinned man named Bowen.

Dob had met Bowen two or three times prior to Savil's death and had even seen him fight once. He liked the man well enough; certainly he respected him. Bowen was keenly intelligent and not at all shy about sharing his opinions with others. He was also good with a blade, compensating for his lack of brute strength with quickness and cunning. The fight Dob had seen was a mismatch from the start, despite the fact that Bowen's opponent was brawnier and taller, and enjoyed a significant advantage in reach. It ended swiftly, with the larger man lying dead in a growing pool of his own blood.

But Dob's respect for his rival had not diminished the fervor with which he battled against him. Whichever one of them became Nal-Lord would enjoy status and wealth beyond the reckoning of all but the most successful break-laws. And so they sent assassins after one another; each sent men into the other's territory in order to provoke firefights; and they sent bribes and inducements to the other break-laws vying for control of the Second as they fell by the wayside, hoping to win their support and their manpower. Throughout the autumn and winter, and into the spring their struggle went on. Again and again, one or the other would appear to gain the upper hand, only to see that advantage slip away. As recently as a few weeks ago, Dob had convinced himself that he had the contest won, but a series of setbacks, culminating in a night of coordinated ambushes and strikes that left eleven of his men dead, had left him weakened and on the defensive. In recent days he had fought back, inflicting some casualties on Bowen's forces, but he was just trying to draw even at this point, and he wasn't there yet.

All of which made Cedrych's unexpected appearance on his speak-screen that much more unnerving.

"As you know, Dob," the Overlord was saying solemnly, "I've been keeping a close watch on the Second Realm. I spite of your excesses, you and Bowen have demonstrated resourcefulness, ingenuity, and tenacity, all of which are qualities I look for in my Nal-Lords. Either of you would do a fine job; I have no doubts about that."

Dob nodded attentively and tried to keep his temper in check. But he knew exactly what was coming. Or so he thought.

"I'm afraid, however," Cedrych went on, "that I've decided to give the Second to Bowen. You've both lost a lot of men, and I don't want to see you lose any more. Continuing your conflict could be . . . counterproductive. And as of right now, I'm sure you'll concede that Bowen has the upper hand."

"Not by much!" Dob argued. "If you'd give me just another week, Overlord, I'm sure—"

"I'm sure, too, Dob," the one-eyed man broke in. "But I want this to end now. And besides, I've got another job in mind for you."

Dob looked at the screen skeptically. "Another job?" he asked in a dull voice.

"Yes. This is the good news I mentioned before." The Overlord paused, allowing himself a smile. "Dob, how would you like to run the Fourth Realm?"

For several moments Dob said nothing. He just stared at the screen as if Cedrych had suddenly started speaking to him in some alien language.

"Dob?" Cedrych said at last. "You still with me?"

"Y-yes, Overlord," he stammered. "Of course."

"Do you have an answer for me?"

"The Fourth is Melyor's Realm."

"Thank you, Dob," the Overlord replied testily. "I never would have known without you to tell me."

"I'm sorry," the break-law managed, feeling flustered. "I just . . . I had heard that she was . . . I had heard that Jibb was running the Fourth now."

"And you heard this from someone who you believe to be more reliable than me?"

Dob closed his eyes and ran a hand through the dark tangle of his hair. He wasn't handling this very well. "No, of course not," he answered, opening his eyes again. "I'm sorry, Overlord. I'm just confused."

"There's nothing to be confused about!" Cedrych said impatiently. "I'm offering you the Fourth Realm! Do you want it, or don't you?"

He still didn't understand what was happening, but for now at least, that seemed to be beside the point. "Yes, I want it."

"Good," Cedrych said in a voice that made him sound sorry that he had even asked. "You'll have to move quickly to get your men in there. You're right in thinking that Melyor left Jibb in charge, and he doesn't know yet that I'm making a change."

"I understand."

"Do you, Dob?" Cedrych asked doubtfully. "Do you really?"

"Yes, Overlord, I do!" he replied, allowing his anger to show. True, this was Cedrych he was talking to, but he did have some pride. "What you're saying is that Jibb will see my arrival in the Fourth as a raid. So either I go in with enough fire power to subdue his forces, or I have him killed first and seize power during the ensuing confusion."

Cedrych sat back and smiled. "Very good, Dob. That's precisely what I was saying."

"The problem, Overlord, is that I'm short on men. This fight with Bowen has been costly."

"Yes, Dob, I know," Cedrych replied. He reached for some papers on his desk, as if already preparing himself for his next speak-screen communication. "I'll be sending you men, weapons, and cash; more than enough of each to take care of this matter. Is that what you wanted to hear?"

"Yes, Overlord!" Dob said. "Thank you, Overlord!"

"I expect you to move quickly on this, Dob," Cedrych said, no longer even bothering to look at his screen. "Tomorrow, ideally. No later than the day after. Understood?"

"Yes, Overlord." Dob saw Cedrych reach for the keypad button that would terminate their connection. "Overlord?" he said stopping Cedrych's hand.

"What is it, Dob?" Cedrych demanded, sounding annoyed.

The break-law hesitated.

"Well?"

Dob shook his head and tried to smile. "Never mind. Thank you, Overlord."

Cedrych frowned and nodded. An instant later his disfigured features disappeared from Dob's screen.

The break-law fell back against his chair and took a shuddering breath. He had never spoken with Cedrych before, but he had heard others describe it as a harrowing experience. Now he understood. He felt drained, as if he had just been in lengthy knife fight, and he sat for a long time with his eyes closed, rest-ing. After some time he opened his eyes again. It seemed quite dark in the flat, although there was a faint glimmer of residual light emanating from Dob's screen. Belatedly Dob remembered that he hadn't switched it off yet. Still he didn't move. He just stared at the screen trying to make sense of what had just happened to his life. The girl in his bed—he had forgotten her name—had called for him twice soon after his conversation with the Overlord ended, but he had not responded. He assumed that she had fallen asleep by now. Not that it mattered. He had lost all interest in her as soon as he saw Cedrych's face.

It was ironic in a way that Cedrych should offer him Melyor's Realm, since she had been the one to kill Savil. Dob still blamed himself for Savil's death. It had been Melyor in the bar that night; he was sure of it. She had been dressed as an uestra, her hair and eye color altered, and she had called herself Kellyn. But he knew now that it had been Melyor. Dob and the others had see Kellyn and Savil leave together, and that had been the last time anyone saw Savil alive. It was common knowledge that Melyor had killed him. Hence, he had con-cluded long ago, Kellyn had to be Melyor.

"I should have killed her when I had the chance," Dob muttered under his breath, as he had so many times in the past few months. And as he had each time before, he smiled at his vanity. *When I had the chance.* Such vanity. This was Melyor i Lakin he was talking about. He had *never* had the chance. He still remembered his utter shock at seeing her dagger pressed menacingly against his britches, and the humiliation he had felt at having to release her in front of his men. In a sense, learning that this had been Melyor and that she had bested Savil just a short time later had been a welcome balm for his wounded pride. But it did nothing to mitigate the chaos that she brought into his life that night.

He had been at war with Bowen ever since. And now, it appeared, he had lost. Cedrych, he realized abruptly, had saved his life tonight. Those who lost protracted battles for a Realm rarely survived the victor's consolidation of power. The Nal was too dangerous a place to allow new Nal-Lords to show mercy to their rivals. As soon as Bowen heard of Cedrych's decision he would dispatch assassins to take care of Dob and all his men. Dob had no future in the Second. In truth, he wasn't all that convinced that he had much future in the Fourth either. Even if he managed to have Jibb killed—no small feat given Jibb's well-earned reputation as the most formidable break-law in Cedrych's Dominion—there were at least half a dozen others in the Fourth who would have a more legitimate claim to the Realm and would deeply resent an outsider taking control. Even with the men and resources Cedrych had promised, Dob's chances for survival were only slightly better than even.

Cedrych must have known this; he must have realized that by sending Dob to the Fourth, he would be plunging the Realm into a protracted period of vio-lence and upheaval. Dob shrugged. He didn't understand it, but that wasn't really important. The Fourth was his to lose, and, risky as it was, it had more to offer him than the Second.

Unfortunately, he still had one piece of unfinished business here in the Second. He had thought about discussing it with Cedrych at the end of their conversation, but the Overlord had seemed impatient to be done with him. And anyway, it probably wasn't important enough to warrant bothering Cedrych. Why would the Overlord care about the capture of a crazed man, in strange, ragged clothes, who claimed to be a break-law and an escapee from a Tobyn-Ser prison. Dob would never have even thought to bring it up with Cedrych except that the man kept going on and on about a sorcerer who had allegedly come to Bragor-Nal, and, while Dob had no reason to believe him, he had heard from a number of sources that Cedrych had, in recent years, taken an interest in the sorcerers of Tobyn-Ser. *Perhaps I'll bring it up with the Overlord the next time I speak with him,* Dob told himself. *Certainly there's no rush.*

He heard sheets rustling in the bedroom, and a moment later the uestra stood before him, sleepy-eyed and naked, her red hair falling in tangled waves to the small of her back.

"Are you coming to bed or what?" she asked, with a yawn. "I charge anyway you know. You're paying for my time, regardless of what you do or don't do with the rest of me." She shrugged. "Sorry, honey. That's my policy for everybody. I wouldn't care if you were Nal-Lord; it'd still be the same."

Dob smiled and stood, feeling a stirring in his groin.

The uestra stepped around to the side of his desk, taking his arm with one hand and rubbing his chest with the other. "Come on," she coaxed gently. "I'm more fun than anything on that silly desk, aren't I?"

"I suppose," he said with a grin, fondling one of her breasts and trying to kiss her. She bit his lip, and then, giggling, pulled him back toward the bed. He followed, although not before remembering to switch off his speak-screen.

21

As I look over the intelligence reports I have on Tobyn-Ser I am painfully aware of their age and the possibility that they are, by now, obsolete. I regret having ceased our intelligence gathering activities after Calbyr's departure, but at the time I viewed it as a necessary precaution. And, to be honest, I was confident that the mission would succeed. Too confident, as it turns out.

Still, in all that I have read and heard of Tobyn-Ser in the past several years, one theme recurs most prominently: this is a land to which change comes quite slowly. The people and institutions of our eastern neighbor, including its Order of Mages and Masters, are bound by myriad traditions and thus are reluctant to embrace anything new. It is open to debate whether this trait will work to our advantaage or disadvantage when it comes to dis-

crediting the Order, but it does serve to allay somewhat my concerns regarding the continued value of our intelligence information.

> Personal journal of Cedrych i Vran, Overlord of the First Dominion of Bragor-Nal, Day 2, Week 3, Spring, Year 3060.

Jaryd and Alayna had never made the trip across Tobyn-Ser so quickly. In just under three fortnights they had ridden from their small home by the shores of South Shelter to the eastern edge of the Parneshome Mountains. Tomorrow they would be in Amarid, and as they sat together beside their low-burning fire, gazing up at the stars, Jaryd found himself frightened of what they might find there. He remained convinced that Sonel's unexpected summons indicated that someone had finally learned of what Orris had done. He even had an idea as to who is was, although that really didn't matter. Soon everyone in the Order would know, and the reaction would be fierce, perhaps even violent.

He still remembered vividly the response of those with whom he shared the link the night he finally explained to them why Orris would no longer be adding his consciousness to the protective net they cast over the western edge of the land. Alayna and Baden, of course, had already known, and Trahn reacted to the news with his usual equanimity. But the others were far less composed. Mered had been outraged, and had even come close to abandoning the link when he learned that Jaryd, Alayna, and Baden had known from the start, and had made no effort to stop Orris and make him return Baram to the prison.

Defying the Order to create this link is one thing! he had sent to them all with so much anger that it actually made his words difficult to understand. *But taking Baram is something else entirely! It comes dangerously close to treason!*

I agree, Ursel had chimed in, surprising them all. *I rarely disagree with Orris, and I consider him a good friend. But this is inexcusable!*

Even Radomil had been livid, something Jaryd had never seen in all the years he had known the bald mage, who had served Jaryd's home village of Accalia since before Jaryd was born. *I don't know what he could have been thinking! What he's done is just wrong! And frankly, Jaryd, Baden, I think the two of you were wrong as well for not trying to stop him.*

Jaryd and his uncle had spent most of that night defending Orris, and though they did not convince the others, they did at least manage to preserve the link. Alayna remained silent throughout the lengthy discussion and only later, as she and Jaryd lay together in their bed, did she reveal to him that she too disapproved of what their friend had done. "I hope it works," she had added hastily, "and knowing Orris as I do, I don't think that there's anything you or Baden could have said to stop him, but I do think that he went too far in taking Baram."

Jaryd had said nothing. Alayna's comments, and those of Mered, Ursel, and Radomil, mirrored his own private doubts too closely for him to argue with her. But remembering that night now, several months later, as he sat with Alayna in the mountains above Amarid staring up at the stars, he could not help but be frightened by the prospect of this Gathering. If Orris's closest friends felt this way, how would the rest of the mages and masters react? Orris had alienated many of them at one time or another over the years with his gruff manner and arrogance. They weren't inclined to like him anyway, especially the older Owl-Masters. By taking the outlander, Orris might have given them just the excuse they needed to expel him from the Order, or worse.

"Are you even listening to me?" Alayna asked, poking him gently with her elbow.

"No, I'm not," Jaryd answered, leaning over and kissing the top of her head. "I'm sorry. What were you saying?"

"It doesn't matter. I save all the important stuff for when our minds are linked. At least then I know that you have to listen."

Jaryd laughed and took Alayna's hand. "I was thinking about Orris," he explained after a brief silence.

"You still think that's what this is about?" she asked glancing at their cerylls, which lay side by side on the ground in front of them.

"Yes. I dreamed of him again last night. That's seven times since we left home."

Alayna let out a slow breath. "Was this one a Seeing?"

"No," he admitted. "It was just like the rest of them."

"So we can't know for certain."

"I guess not," he said. She was right of course. None of his dreams had been Seeings, so he couldn't really assign much significance to them. But though none of his visions had carried the weight of prophecy, he knew himself and his power too well to dismiss them as random images. This Gathering would be about Orris.

"Do you think he's all right?" she asked quietly.

"I don't know," he said. "I want to say 'yes,' but I just don't know. He's so far away, and it's such an alien place." He took a breath, and Alayna laid her head on his shoulder. "If anyone can make it to Lon-Ser and back, it's Orris," he told her. "He's as strong and courageous as anyone I've ever known."

"You're right," she answered quietly. "I just hope that counts for something over there."

They awoke the next morning as the first glimmer of daylight touched the eastern sky and the songs of thrushes and wrens began to filter up to them from the forests below. They rose quickly, ate a light meal, and within half an hour, had climbed onto their mounts and started the final leg of their long journey to Amarid.

By midday, they were steering their mounts through Hawksfind Wood, passing not too far from where Jaryd bound to Ishalla nearly five years earlier. It was clear from the images the grey hawk sent to him that Ishalla recognized her home. She glided above him, surveying the forest keenly, and wheeling and darting from side to side, as if too overjoyed by this homecoming to fly in a straight line.

Jaryd was pleased to see his familiar so happy, but he found it impossible to share her delight. Once again his sleep the previous night had been troubled by images of Orris and of the dark, alien land to which the burly mage had travelled. And with every mile he and Alayna covered this morning, Jaryd's apprehension about this Gathering grew.

It was not until he and Alayna reached the city of Amarid, however, that Jaryd realized just how grave the situation was. It was early in the afternoon when they arrived. The sky, which had been clear all morning, was beginning to cloud over, and a cutting wind was beginning to whistle among the homes and shops of the old town commons. After leaving their mounts in the stables of a blacksmith who had agreed several years ago to house their animals in return for whatever services he might require—healing, wood-mending, even once, during a particularly damp summer, help with getting his fire started—the mages made their way through the streets and alleyways to the Aerie, the inn at which they now stayed every time they visited the First Mage's city. Entering the inn, with its familiar smells of roasting meat, pipe smoke, and wine, the two young mages were greeted immediately by Trahn, who had been sitting alone at a small table by the door.

The dark mage grinned as he embraced them, but the smile did not reach his vivid green eyes. "I'm glad to see you both," he said warmly, resting one hand on Jaryd's shoulder and the other on Alayna's. "The link keeps me from missing you too much when we're apart, but it's not a substitute for actually being with you."

Jaryd nodded and shared a look with Alayna. They of all people knew about the limitations of the link.

"It's good to see you, too, Trahn," Alayna answered. "And Reivlad as well," she added, indicating the mage's dark chestnut hawk with a nod of her head.

Trahn stroked the bird's chin thoughtfully. "I'm glad she was able to make this journey one last time," he said softly. "She's been a good familiar."

Jaryd looked at his friend searchingly. "Is she sick?"

"No. She's just old. To be honest I don't expect that she'll make it to Midsummer." He shook his head. "It's the only good thing to come out of this: at least Reivlad and I were able to attend one last Gathering together."

" 'The only good thing?' " Alayna repeated. "Do you know why Sonel sent for us?"

Trahn looked around them, his dark features hardening. "Yes," he finally said. He gestured toward the back of the inn. "We should discuss this in private."

The three of them started toward an empty table in a far back corner of the large, dimly lit room, but before they had gotten very far, they heard the booming voice of Maimun, the Aerie's owner, calling to them from behind the bar.

"Hawk-Mage Jaryd! Hawk-Mage Alayna!," he bellowed, coming out to greet them, his massive, hairy arms open, and a smile on his broad face. "How are my favorite love-birds? Love-birds!" he said a second time, laughing at his own joke, and glancing at Trahn for a reaction. It was a line he had used many times before.

"We're fine, Maimun. Thank you," Jaryd answered. He actually liked Maimun, despite his overbearing manner. It was not a sentiment that Alayna shared. Nor, Jaryd knew, did Baden. Indeed, though Baden still came to the Aerie every year, his distaste for the hulking innkeeper had only increased with time.

"I've set aside a room for you," Maimun went on. "Best in the house." He winked at Alayna, who smiled thinly in return. "Will Master Baden be joining you?"

"Not in our room," Jaryd answered, "but I do expect him to be staying here, yes."

The innkeeper laughed uproariously, slapping Jaryd across the back with such force that the young mage almost fell over and Ishalla had to raise her wings to maintain her balance on his shoulder.

"If you don't mind, Maimun," Jaryd began gently, once the large man's laughter had subsided, "we were just on our way to a back table to discuss some matters in private. Can we have our meals brought there please?"

Maimun nodded, eager as always to please the mages who frequented his establishment. "Of course, Hawk-Mage Jaryd," he said. "Right away."

The man hurried off, and the three mages walked to the empty table they had spotted a few moments before.

"Erland has discovered that Baram is gone," Trahn announced without preamble as they sat down.

Alayna winced slightly and Jaryd exhaled through his teeth. "I had a feeling it was something like that," he said. "How did he find out?"

"He attempted to organize some kind of public demonstration at the prison."

Alayna nodded. "That figures. So what does he want to do? Expel Orris from the Order?"

Trahn looked at her grimly. "I wish that was all." The dark mage paused as a serving girl arrived with a platter of roasted fowl, some dark bread, and a bowl of steamed greens. A second server arrived soon after with three tankards of Amari Ale. It took some time for all the food to find its way onto the table and for the servers to depart.

"So Erland wants to do more than kick Orris out of the Order?" Alayna prompted once the three of them were alone again.

Trahn nodded. "He wants to have Orris tried as a traitor."

"A traitor!" Jaryd exploded. Trahn looked at him sharply and then glanced around the bar. Jaryd did the same, suddenly conscious of how loudly he had spoken. Maimun and one of the serving girls were staring in their direction from the bar, but as far as Jaryd could tell, no one else had paid heed to his outburst. "He can't really believe that will work," the young mage continued in a quieter voice. "Orris may have defied the Order's will, but he's just doing what he thinks is best for the land."

"The three of us know that to be true, and Baden and a few others as well,"

Trahn agreed. "I even believe that Sonel knows it, although she's not in a position to acknowledge it publicly." The mage paused and took a sip of ale. "But Erland and his allies, as well as Arslan and his, are a different matter. They can't see beyond the fact that Orris has freed Baram, a proven enemy of Tobyn-Ser. And technically, according to the laws of the land, that is treason."

Alayna leaned forward in her chair. "So you're saying that Arslan and Erland are in agreement on this?"

Trahn shrugged. "I don't know anything for certain," he replied guardedly. "I'm just saying it's possible."

Jaryd picked absently at his food, considering this. If Erland, the leader of the older Owl-Masters, and Arslan, one of the most outspoken of the younger Hawk-Mages, were united against Orris, the burly mage was in real danger.

"There's something you're not telling us, isn't there, Trahn?" Alayna asked, looking closely at the dark mage.

Trahn hesitated for a moment. "Again, it's nothing that I know for certain," he finally admitted. "I've merely heard people in the Great Hall talking."

"About what?" Alayna persisted.

"Apparently, Erland suspects that Orris is part of a larger conspiracy. He's mentioned Baden's name as someone who probably knew about Orris's plans prior to his departure, and he's hinted at others as well, including the three of us."

Jaryd stared at his friend, unable to believe what he had heard. Five years ago, Baden, Trahn, and Orris were falsely accused of treason and tried before the Order. But that had been different. Their accuser, Sartol, was a traitor himself, and his allegations were part of his elaborate scheme to win control of the Order and rule all of Tobyn-Ser through his mastery of the Summoning Stone.

But from everything that Jaryd knew, there was no sinister plot at work here. He had no reason to believe that Erland had betrayed the land. The Owl-Master just genuinely feared a conspiracy. Which, in a way, was far more frightening.

"So what do we do?" Alayna asked in a tight voice, running a rigid hand through her dark hair.

"I'm not sure," Trahn answered. "Erland is impatient to begin the Gathering, and he's been pushing the Owl-Sage to open the proceedings immediately. Sonel has insisted, however, that at least three quarters of the Order be in attendance before any formal discussions begin. The should give us close to a week to learn what Erland plans to do."

Jaryd pushed his food away. Suddenly he didn't feel very hungry. "Have you heard anything from Baden?" he asked Trahn.

"No, nothing. I expect he'll be here soon."

"I hope so. He and I linked briefly before Alayna and I left South Shelter. He was concerned about the journey; he wasn't very enamored of his horse."

Trahn chuckled. "He never is." He tore off a piece of bread and put it in his mouth. "I'm sure Baden will have some ideas of how we should defend ourselves from Erland's charges should they come. Certainly I hope he will, because I'm not very good at this sort of thing. But in the meantime, I'd suggest that we watch what we say to anyone, even those mages whom we'd normally trust."

Alayna and Jaryd both nodded.

Alayna took Jaryd's hand, as if seeking reassurance, even as she continued to gaze at Trahn. "Have you spoken with Ursel, Mered, or Radomil about this?"

"Only with Ursel," the dark mage told her. "Mered and Radomil have never been . . . comfortable with what Orris did. It didn't seem wise to bring it up with them."

Jaryd shook his head slowly. "He's not a traitor," he said softly. "What he's doing takes a remarkable amount of courage."

"That doesn't mean it's not wrong," Trahn answered, his voice lowered as well.

Jaryd recoiled as if his friend had struck him. "You too?" he breathed.

"I don't know how I feel, Jaryd. I've had doubts about it ever since you told us where he had gone." He started to say more, but them stopped himself. "I just don't know," he repeated.

Jaryd didn't reply—there seemed to be nothing to say—and the three of them finished their meal in silence.

Baden arrived in Amarid three days later, and, joining the others at the Aerie, immediately informed them of his startling communication with Orris.

"He actually found the Gildriites?" Trahn asked in amazement, when Baden had finished.

Jayrd looked from Baden to Trahn. "Who are the Gildriites?"

His uncle frowned and glanced at Alayna, a question in his blue eyes. She shrugged. "Didn't any of you read my report?" the Owl-Master demanded, his voice rising.

Jaryd and Alayna shared a look, both of them trying not to laugh.

"I shouldn't even tell you," Baden growled. "I should make you read it." He looked at Trahn, who averted his eyes and started to chuckle. "You're a great help. You'll remember from the story of Theron's Curse," the Owl-Master began, turning back to the young Hawk-Mages, "that after Theron died a small group of Theron's followers left the Order."

"They were the ones Amarid was worried about when he created the first psychic link, right?" Jaryd broke in.

Baden nodded. "Yes. They were led by a man named Gildri."

"Of course," Alayna whispered. For years, first as a child, and later as a Mage-Attend to Sartol, she had studied the old texts that related the history of Theron's Curse and Amarid's Laws. It was one of the reasons she was included in the delegation that journeyed to Theron's Grove. "I should have recognized the name."

"The descendants of Gildri and his followers still live in Lon-Ser," Baden went on. "According to Baram, they're known to some as the Oracles, suggesting that they still have the Sight, even if they no longer wield the same powers that we do."

"And they're helping Orris?" Jaryd asked.

Baden made an ambiguous gesture with his hands. "As much as they can.

They don't know our language any more than Orris knows theirs, and they've been persecuted over the years so they don't have any influence in Lon-Ser. But they are sheltering and feeding him, which is something."

Alayna pushed back her hair. "Do you think that he's in danger from this man he was asking you about?"

"From Cedrych? I guess I do, yes. I don't recognize the name, but I just have a bad feeling about him."

"Apparently Orris does as well," Trahn added, "or else he wouldn't have contacted you."

"You may be right, but he was planning to meet with Cedrych anyway." The Owl-Master pressed his lips into a thin line and rubbed a finger across them nervously.

"Well, there's nothing we can do to keep Orris out of trouble in Lon-Ser," Trahn observed. "But maybe we can help him with his troubles here."

Over the next three days, while they waited for the rest of the Order to reach Amarid, Jaryd, Alayna, Trahn, and Baden spent much of their time at the Great Hall, discussing the upcoming Gathering with other mages and gauging their opinions. And each night in the Aerie, as they ate dinner and sipped ale, they shared with each other all that they had learned.

Jaryd soon realized though that he didn't care about the opinions of the gathered mages as much as his friends did, or as much as they seemed to think he should. Nothing he learned in these conversations would affect his actions during the upcoming Gathering. He wouldn't lie to anyone, or tailor his views to protect himself; he wouldn't deny that he had seen Orris leave, or that on some level he approved of what the burly mage was doing. He owed Orris that much; all of them did really, but he and Baden were the only ones who seemed to realize it.

Indeed, the more he heard others equating Orris's actions with treason, the more Jaryd defended the mage. Several times during the course of those three days leading up to the official commencement of the Gathering, Jaryd found himself arguing with large groups of mages, young and old, defending Orris with far more fervor than he would have thought possible considering the doubts he had harbored just a short while ago. It was almost as if a part of him was trying to be contrary, as if he was merely reacting to the self-righteousness of so many of his colleagues.

On the third day, Sonel finally informed all the mages who had arrived in Amarid that the Gathering would begin the following morning. That night, as Jaryd and Alayna sat on their bed in the Aerie, talking about what they expected to happen during the next few days, Alayna expressed her concern about his growing combativeness and its possible repercussions. "If you antagonize enough of them," she told him, her tone betraying both annoyance and worry, "they'll turn on you with just as much vengeance as they have on Orris!"

"Maybe," Jaryd agreed evenly. "But someone has to defend him. Otherwise it's just too easy for them."

She narrowed her eyes. "Too easy? I don't understand."

Jaryd shook his head. "I'm not sure I can explain it. What Orris did was a reaction to the complacency of the Order, right?" She nodded. "Then allowing them to condemn him as a traitor also allows them to defend that complacency. We're all responsible for the fact that Baram was here in the first place. We all allowed Sartol's plot to go as far as it did; we all allowed the outlanders to do so much damage. Our complacency did that, too. But Orris is trying to make some good come out of it, by using Baram to spur Lon-Ser's leaders to take action. If Erland and the others convict Orris of treason, it absolves them of that responsibility. It allows them to continue to pretend that the Order wasn't at fault, and it punishes Orris for his courage." He shrugged. "He's my friend. I can't allow them to do that. And I won't let them hide behind their laziness and their cowardice."

Alayna stared at him for a long time. Finally, she leaned forward and kissed him gently on the lips.

"What was that for?" Jaryd asked her, allowing himself a brief smile.

It was her turn to shrug. "For your passion, and your loyalty, and your ability to see things in ways that others don't."

"Does that mean you agree with me?"

"It means," she said, putting her arms around him, "that I love you, and I'll defend you with all my might, even if I don't agree with you."

The two of them awoke the next morning to the tolling of the Great Hall's bells. They found Baden and Trahn waiting for them on the ground floor of the inn, and together the four mages hurried to the Gathering Chamber. They were among the last to arrive, and just moments after they took their seats at the council table, Sonel opened the Gathering. There was no ceremony or fanfare of any kind. She merely announced that the proceedings had formally begun and immediately recognized Erland, inviting him to address the Order.

"We're here at your request, Owl-Master," she said. "Perhaps you'd like to explain why."

"Thank you, Owl-Sage," the white-haired man began, rising from his chair and running a hand over his trim, silver beard. "I regret that I had to make the request to which the Sage alluded. I would rather be home tending my gardens and serving the people of Hawksfind Wood. But a matter has come to my attention that is so disturbing in its implications, that I felt it demanded our immediate attention." He paused. "The outlander is gone, and I have reason to believe that one of our colleagues has taken him."

A few whispered conversations greeted his announcement, but if Erland had been expecting an eruption of outrage and shock he would have been disappointed with the Order's response. By now, this was old news.

"How did you discover that Orris had taken him, Erland?" one of the younger mages asked.

"A large group of us had gone to the prison for a vigil, as a way of demonstrating our opposition to the leniency that we had shown this cold-hearted killer."

Alayna leaned over toward Jaryd. "So much for tending his gardens," she whispered.

Jaryd snickered under his breath, but quickly turned his attention back to what Erland was saying.

"When we arrived there, however, the guards informed us that the outlander had been moved back to the Great Hall, so that the Sage herself could continue his interrogations. According to the guards, it was Orris who took him away." Erland swept the chamber with his dark blue eyes. "My guess is that he's taken the outlander back to Lon-Ser, in spite of the fact that this body explicitly rejected the idea. As I say though, that's only a guess." He swung his gaze toward Baden. "I expect that others in this hall can tell us for certain."

It was time, Jaryd knew. Baden would take all the blame if Jaryd didn't speak up first, and Jaryd couldn't allow that. Baden hadn't approved of Orris's plan either, at least not in the beginning.

"Yes, Erland," Baden admitted, standing to meet the white-haired man's challenge. "I know where Orris has taken the outlander."

"Baden, don't!" Jaryd broke in.

"It's all right, Jaryd!" Baden answered. "I know where Orris is because he reached for me with the Ceryll-Var not long ago."

Of course, Jaryd realized, as the shocked silence that followed Baden's revelation quickly gave way to a flurry of shouted questions. This approach might give them a way around the conspiracy charges. He looked at Erland and saw that the Owl-Master hadn't moved. He was glaring at Baden as if he had been utterly unprepared for what Baden had said. No doubt, that was what Baden had been counting on.

"Why would he contact you?" Erland finally demanded harshly, plunging the Gathering Chamber into an abrupt silence.

All eyes were on Baden.

"He had just made contact with a man in Lon-Ser whom he suspected of being connected in some way with the plot against our land," the lean Owl-Master explained. "He wanted to know if I recognized this man's name from my conversations with Baram."

"And did you?"

"As it happens, no."

"So," Erland snarled contemptuously, "Orris casts his awareness across the sea so that he can ask you a question to which you have no answer, and you want us to believe that this is the only reason you know of Orris's plans?" He shook his head and bared his teeth in a malicious grin. "I don't think so."

Baden's pale eyes flashed dangerously, but his voice when he spoke remained surprisingly even. "You were speculating that someone in this Hall might know where Orris had taken the outlander. I was merely telling you what I learned from Orris himself. As to the rest of it, I really don't care whether you believe me or not."

"Was he still with the outlander when you communicated with him?" Arslan asked.

Baden hesitated, although only briefly. "No. He didn't explain what happened, but I gather that Baram slipped away from him once they reached Lon-Ser."

"Fist of the God!" Arslan spat. "So he's free now, and back in his homeland!" He slammed his hand down on the council table. "Orris will be made to pay!"

Several other mages shouted their agreement.

"Orris's time will come!" Erland called out over the rising din. "But there are others in this chamber who are equally deserving of punishment!" He spun toward Baden again leveling an accusing finger at him. "Beginning with you, Baden!" He grinned again, his eyes gleaming triumphantly. "I neglected to mention one important detail from my visit to the prison," he said, looking around the chamber and raising his voice so that all could hear. "One of the guards was surprised that I hadn't known the outlander was gone. It seems that Baden went to the prison the day after Orris took the prisoner away. According to this guard, Baden claimed to have known about the orders to move the out-lander back to the Great Hall." He glared at Baden once more. Everyone else in the room was looking at the lean Owl-Master as well. "Was the guard lying, Baden?" Erland asked in a mocking tone.

Baden took a long breath and shook his head. "No," he said quietly. "I did tell him that I knew."

"Then you were lying!" Jaryd called out, getting to his feet. "Baden lied to the guard to protect Orris. He didn't know anything about Orris's intentions."

"How do you know this?" Arslan asked skeptically.

"Because I was the one who told Baden what Orris was doing."

Arslan leaped to his feet. *"You knew?"*

"Yes. I spoke with Orris before he left."

"And did you try to stop him?" Erland demanded.

"No. Actually I encouraged him to go."

"What?" Arslan and Erland cried out in unison. Several other mages jumped out of their chairs and began shouting at Jaryd, calling him a traitor and worse. He glanced down at Alayna, who was already looking at him, the expression in her dark eyes bleak.

"Why would you do that, Jaryd?" Sonel asked, her words cutting through the clamor, though she hadn't spoken loudly. Immediately the others fell silent.

He could feel their eyes upon him, but Jaryd kept his gaze fixed on the Sage. She was watching him with avid interest and, he thought, the ghost of a smile on her lips, as if she knew what he would say. "When Alayna and I spoke with Theron, he told us that the Order would have to adapt if it was to defeat this enemy. And he warned us that unless we were willing to look beyond our shores, we were doomed to failure. 'The world has changed,' " Jaryd recited, hearing the Owl-Master's voice thundering in his mind as he spoke the words aloud, " 'even if Tobyn-Ser has not. You ignore these changes at your own risk.' " He paused, allowing the memory of his encounter with Theron to wash over him like a summer rain. It seemed so long ago. "I believe that Theron would approve of what Orris is doing," he went on after a moment. "In fact, I think it's very much the type of thing that the Owl-Master had in mind. And before Orris left, I told him as much."

For some time no one said anything, as was often the case after he or Alayna spoke of their encounter with Theron's unsettled spirit. Even after nearly five years, their two nights in the grove and the staff Jaryd carried as a token of the Owl-Master's good will continued to set them apart. Jaryd had never invoked Theron's name gratuitously just to add weight to an argument or enhance his own stature. But, not for the first time, he was pleased to see the effect his words had on Erland, Arslan, and the others.

"None of us questions the Owl-Master's wisdom," Erland began at last. "Nor have we forgotten the debt we owe you and Alayna for what you accomplished during your encounter with him. But I refuse to accept that anything Theron told you could justify what Orris has done, or, for that matter, what you have done in allowing him to go. You have subverted the will of the Order, which, as we all know, is grounds for expulsion from this body."

"As I recall, Owl-Sage," Trahn called out, "there was never a formal debate and vote on whether or not the outlander should be taken back to Lon-Ser. The discussion was terminated before any action was taken. There was no express will of the Order to contradict."

"I remember it that way as well," Radomil added.

"That's true only in the strictest sense!" Arslan argued. "The Sage ended the debate after a majority of us made clear that we would never allow the outlander to leave prison!"

"No, Trahn," Erland broke in, shaking his head gravely. "You cannot absolve yourself or your friends with a technicality. We are dealing with a matter far more serious than merely defying the Order." He raised his voice, glancing once more around the hall. "As I started to say before, Orris will be dealt with when and if he returns, but there are others here right now whose actions must be addressed. If Orris has betrayed us, then so have those who helped him, even if helping him meant no more than understanding his intentions and refusing to stop him. That's what Baden did, and, though it pains me to say it, Jaryd as well."

"What are you suggesting, Erland?" Trahn asked in a severe voice. "That Baden and Jaryd are traitors?"

The Owl-Master took a breath and tugged at his silver beard. "Yes, I'm afraid so."

"That's ridiculous!" Trahn shot back. "I don't know anyone who cares more about this land than they do!"

Erland nodded. "I'd expect you to say such a thing, Trahn. You and Baden are quite close aren't you. I find it hard to believe that he'd keep a matter of this importance from you."

"I suppose that means that you suspect me as well, Erland," Alayna said, her delicate features pale, though her voice remained strong. "If Trahn's friendship with Baden makes him guilty, then surely my marriage to Jaryd must implicate me."

"Yes, it does," Erland told her matter-of-factly.

"So where does it stop?" Alayna asked. She indicated the woman sitting next to her at the table. "Neysa is my friend. Does that mean that she's guilty as well? Is anybody who disagrees with you on this matter a traitor, or must they be friends with one of us as well?"

"I haven't passed judgement on anyone!" the Owl-Master snapped.

"You've accused Jaryd and Baden of treason!" Alayna shot back with equal vehemence.

"They admitted that they helped Orris! I have no doubt of their guilt! As to the rest of you, only a thorough inquiry will determine whether you are traitors or not!"

"None of us are traitors!" Jaryd insisted. "And that includes Orris! Don't you see? He's trying to save Tobyn-Ser, not destroy it!" He looked around the chamber, searching desperately for a sympathetic face. "It could work," he said, the words coming out as a plea.

"He's already failed!" Erland roared. "According to Baden the outlander is gone! He's free again! He'll be of no help to Orris!"

Jaryd started to reply, but then stopped himself. There was little that he could say. Orris might still succeed, but Erland was right: he'd have to do so without Baram. It wasn't treason, but perhaps freeing the outlander had been a mistake.

"Owl-Master Erland," Sonel broke in, her voice sounding weary, "how would you like us to proceed? You've made some very serious allegations, and I'm not entirely certain that I agree with the notion that Orris or anyone else has betrayed the land. But you are entitled under the rules governing this body to request a formal inquiry into any matter of importance. Clearly, this qualifies."

"An inquiry is not enough!" Erland answered. "I demand that Jaryd and Baden be formally charged with treason!"

Trahn stood abruptly, his fists clenched. "You have no evidence to back up such a demand!"

"They admit that they knew of Orris's plans and neglected to stop him! Jaryd claims that he encouraged him! That's evidence enough!" The Owl-Master glared defiantly at Sonel. "You've heard my demand, Owl-Sage. Will you present the charges?"

Sonel took a breath. "No, Erland, I won't."

"*You must!*" the white-haired Owl-Master raged. "They allowed an enemy of Tobyn-Ser to escape! They have betrayed the land!"

"You have not produced sufficient evidence to support your allegations!" Sonel fired back. "Until you do, I will not present your charges for formal consideration!"

Erland remained silent for several moments. His normally ruddy face appeared dangerously flushed, and he was breathing hard. "I had hoped it would not come to this, Owl-Sage," he finally said, his tone bitter. "But I do not believe that you are fit to make such a decision. I must demand that you step aside for the remainder of this discussion and allow First of the Sage Toinan to preside."

Sonel stared at him in disbelief. "What?"

Arslan shook his head. "Now you've gone too far, Erland."

"Have I?" the Owl-Master asked glancing at the red-haired mage. "She's just shown us all that she can't be objective in this matter. And I believe I know why: our Owl-Sage has as much interest as Baden in concealing the truth."

"What are you talking about?" Radomil asked.

Erland grinned darkly. "The Sage was the person who first told me what Orris had done. I'd like to know how she knew." He faced Sonel again. "That, it seems to me, is a legitimate question, one among many that a thorough investigation of this matter should seek to answer."

"Now we know what you're up to, Erland," Baden said, a stony expression on his lean features. "This is an attempt to gain power and nothing more. The Sage has done nothing wrong and you know it!"

"Then how did she know?" Erland replied, biting off each word. He looked sharply at Sonel. "Did Orris discuss it with you first, Owl-Sage, or was this just information you picked up in your bed?"

Suddenly Sonel was on her feet, her chair toppling over behind her as her owl leapt into the air. Her face was scarlet with rage. *"How dare you!"* she hissed. She looked around the table, her green eyes blazing with fury. "Is this what we've become?" she demanded bitterly. "Have we grown so distrustful of each other, that everyone is an enemy, and every piece of information is a weapon?"

For some time no one spoke, and all the mages in the chamber appeared to avoid meeting Sonel's wrathful glare.

"Erland was out of line, Owl-Sage," Arslan said at last. "But I must say that I share his concern. If you were aware of Orris's actions, we have a right to know how you came by this knowledge and why you kept it to yourself. As long as those questions remain unanswered, it would be most appropriate for First of the Sage Toinan to preside over this discussion."

Sonel stood beside her overturned chair, holding herself perfectly still save for her eyes which scanned the room. "Very well," she finally said, her voice tight, as if she were struggling to keep her emotions under control. "I will step aside in favor of Toinan."

She turned toward the First and nodded once. Toinan stared back at her for a moment and then rose.

"I see no need for further discussion," the grey-haired woman said matter-of-factly. "We have debated enough. We shall vote." She glanced at Sonel again. "With your permission, Owl-Sage, I would like to decide this question by private ballot."

Sonel seemed to consider this for a moment. "That's probably best," she said at last, picking up the crystal bell that sat on the table in front of her and ringing it once.

Instantly, the blue-robed attendants of the Great Hall appeared in the Gathering Chamber carrying slips of paper and dozens of writing leads.

"The question before us," the First announced, "is whether Baden and Jaryd should be formally charged with treason." She looked at Jaryd and then at his uncle. "I'm afraid you're both prohibited from voting."

An eerie silence descended on the hall as the gathered mages took their seats once more, marked their ballots, and then dropped them into one of the two large crystal bowls that two of the hall's stewards carried around the table. Jaryd had never seen a private ballot before, much less been the subject of one. It was emblematic, he thought, of the degree to which the Order was divided.

When all the mages had voted, the stewards brought the bowls to Toinan, who began to tally the results. It took her several moments, during which no one spoke. The only sounds in the hall were the rustling of the slips of paper in the First's hand, and the ruffling of feathers as a few of the birds preened themselves. At one point Alayna took Jaryd's hand, and they shared an anxious look.

"The motion has failed," Toinan announced abruptly, looking up from the papers. "Twenty-four votes 'yea,' twenty-nine votes 'nay.' "

"Fist of the God!" Erland whispered. He glanced around the chamber, shaking his head in dismay. "It's more than a conspiracy, isn't it? You have forsaken your vows to serve the land!"

"That's not fair, Erland!" Mered answered angrily. "Just because we disagree with you on this doesn't mean that we endorse what Orris has done!"

Erland opened his arms wide. "It might as well! If Jaryd and Baden did nothing wrong, then Orris must be innocent as well!" He faced Sonel again. "I must insist again that Jaryd and Baden be formally charged, if not with treason then at least with subverting the will of the Order. That's the only way to get at the truth of what's happened!"

Sonel shook her head. "I've already told you that there will be no charges presented until we have more evidence!"

"And that's your final word on the matter?" the Owl-Master asked solemnly."

"It is."

Erland took a breath. "Then you leave me no choice." He stood and raised his arm for his brown, round-headed owl, who flew to him and hopped up to his shoulder. He looked around the room, and it seemed to Jaryd that there was an expression of genuine sadness in his dark eyes. "When I became a member of this Order," he said, his voice surprisingly subdued, "I swore an oath to serve the people of Tobyn-Ser and to uphold the laws established for us by Amarid. I've come to the conclusion that I can no longer be a member of this body and be true to those oaths." Without another word, he turned away from the council table with a swirl of his green cloak and left the Great Hall.

For a moment, no one in the Gathering Chamber moved. Then, as if prompted by some hidden cue, four more Owl-Masters stood simultaneously, summoned their birds to their shoulders, and followed Erland out into the streets of Amarid.

Still, none of the remaining mages spoke. They all seemed to be waiting, as if they knew that the exodus was not finished and they were afraid to see who would be next.

Arslan, as it turned out. One moment he was staring at his hands and clenching the muscles in his jaw, and the next moment he was on his feet, his large brown hawk on his shoulder, and his brown eyes peering out nervously from beneath his wild red hair.

"Arslan, please!" Alayna called to him as he began to walk away from the table.

He stopped, although he did not look back at her. "I'm sorry, Alayna," he said softly. "I have to."

"Do you remember last summer when I wanted to leave, and you urged me to stay? 'If even one of us leaves,' you said, 'the damage might be irrevocable.' That hasn't changed. Don't you see what you'll be doing to the Order if you go?"

At that he did turn, the expression on his young face hard and bitter. "The damage has been done already. Orris did it, and Jaryd and Baden, too. For all I know, you're just as guilty as they are." He looked away. "Maybe I should have let you go after all."

He started toward the door again, and before he reached it, seven more Hawk-Mages had left the table to join him. And still it was not over. In the few minutes that followed, six more Owl-Masters departed, including First of the Sage Toinan. All told, eleven Owl-Masters and eight Hawk-Mages had left the Gathering, and perhaps the Order as well. It wasn't all the mages who had been on the losing side of the vote, but it was close.

For what seemed an eternity, those who remained sat without speaking, as if unable to comprehend what had just transpired beneath the portrait of Amarid that adorned the Great Hall's ceiling.

"What do we do now?" Ursel finally asked, breaking the painfully long silence.

Sonel shrugged slightly and turned to Baden, as if she expected him to have an answer.

But Baden merely shook his head, a haunted look in his pale eyes. "I don't know," he whispered. "I just don't know."

22

Looking back through these pages I find that I have too often used the terms "Bragor-Nal" and "Lon-Ser" interchangeably. This is misleading, for there are two other Nals as well—Oerella-Nal and Stib-Nal—and while Bragor-Nal is the largest of them, it is not necessarily typical of them. The fact of the matter is that Baram's knowledge of the other two, and therefore our knowledge of them, is limited. This, it seems, is a product of Lon-Ser's peculiar governmental structure. The three Nals are economic and political rivals. They do not share their knowledge of advanced goods; there is little social or cultural exchange among them. Indeed even travel among them is restricted and strictly monitored by each Nal's constable.

Still, from what Baram has told me I have reached a few rudimentary conclusions. The three Nals, the three survivors of the so-called "Consolidation" (about which I have written elsewhere) are separated by natural

barriers, mostly mountain ranges. Stib-Nal, from what I have learned, is the
smallest of the three and is of little consequence. But Oerella-Nal, located to
the northwest of Bragor-Nal and ruled by an ancestral matriarchy, is a
powerful force and Bragor-Nal's chief nemesis.

> —From Section Five of "The Report of
> Owl-Master Baden on his Interrogation
> of the Outlander Baram," Submitted to
> the 1,014th Gathering of the Order of
> Mages and Masters. Spring, Gods' Year
> 4625.

Tracking them was easy, even after Melyor abandoned the large black carrier in favor of her smaller, less obtrusive white one. It was not just that the Bearer and the sorcerer stood out like uestra girls in one of Lon's sanctuaries. Melyor appeared to have no idea that she was being followed. She was being cautious, but not the way she would have had she known that the Blade was after her. Had she known that, she would have done more than just switch carriers and occasionally exit the Upper to weave through alleys and byways before returning to the elevated roadway. Fear of the Blade would have elicited a stronger response than that, even from Melyor i Lakin.

He had gone by the alias for so long that no one still alive knew him by any other name. This suited him fine; he had always liked it, and given what he did for a living it seemed entirely appropriate, even though his weapon of choice was not a knife, but rather an oversized hand thrower. Recently, as flecks of grey had begun to appear in his black hair, his men had taken to calling him the Silver Blade. At first he had ordered them to stop, thinking it disrespectful. The last thing an assassin needed was for people to think that he was growing old. But he soon realized that it was a term of deference, a comment on his ability to survive in a profession that wasn't conducive to longevity. The Silver Blade. In the end, he decided that he had earned the distinction. He was a survivor. And his success had been based upon one simple principle: never take a job that you can't handle.

This one was borderline. When Cedrych first told him who his third target would be, Blade had been tempted to abandon the whole thing. Dealing with Gildriites and sorcerers was bad enough. There were too many unknown risks. He wasn't a man to give much credence to tales of prophetic dreams and magic. Personally, he believed that the centuries-long persecution of the Gildriites had been based upon myth and superstition. But that didn't mean that he wanted to have anything to do with them. As long as he avoided the Oracles, the question of their abilities or lack thereof was moot. But now he not only had to kill a Bearer and one of Tobyn-Ser's sorcerers, of whose power he knew little, he also had to take on the most skilled street fighter among all of Cedrych's Nal-Lords. Blade shook his head. This job was getting way too complicated. It was going to cost the Overlord a great deal of gold.

He caught up with them midway through the morning following his late-night conversation with Cedrych, although he had learned of their where-abouts several hours earlier. As soon as he finished speaking with the Overlord, Blade had sent out men to keep watch on Melyor's flat, Cedrych's office, Cedrych's training center, and as an afterthought, the flat of Melyor's security chief, Jibb. This last, as it turned out, was where Melyor, the Bearer, and the sorcerer passed the night. Learning of this, Blade had been concerned that Jibb might join them, further complicating his task. But, according to Blade's watcher, when they left early this morning it was still just the three of them, without the Nal-Lord's talented bodyguard. Blade's men followed them onto the Upper, where an hour or two later, Blade, with his contingent of eight as-sassins riding in two carriers, took over the pursuit.

Melyor did almost lose them when she switched carriers, but Blade had been doing this for too long to allow such a rudimentary tactic to fool him. Soon he was within sight of her again, hanging back far enough to keep her comfort-able, but not so far that he couldn't react quickly should she suddenly realize that she was being hunted. That had been nearly two hours ago.

"How do you want to handle this, Blade?" Ulbin asked, his normally deep voice sounding thin over the communication device that linked his carrier to Blade's.

Blade considered the question for a moment. "Her pattern seems pretty clear at this point," he said at last. "Northwest on the Upper for an hour or so—"

"And then she goes due east below for four or five quads," Ulbin broke in, completing Blade's thought. "I've noticed that, too. It's an interesting varia-tion on a standard evasion pattern." Blade could almost see his friend nodding with admiration at Melyor's guile. He and Ulbin had worked together for a long time. "You want to take them below?"

Again Blade weighed his options. Normally it wouldn't have mattered. Acci-dents occurred on the Upper all the time; it would be very easy to take them here without drawing too much attention to themselves. But Cedrych had made a point of ordering him to be discreet. And Cedrych was the one with the gold. "Yes, below," he said. "If she's doing four or five quads, we should take her in the middle of the third. Basic carrier cap and strike. You take the deep end, I'll cap."

"Sounds good," Ulbin replied. Again Blade could imagine him nodding, that deep, satisfied nod he gave when he was pleased with a plan or a recently completed job. "You must want to use throwers."

"Throwers to pin them down," Blade answered, "but I want to finish them with explosives."

"Boomers!" Ulbin said with surprise. "You sure?"

"Yes. We're not taking any chances with this one. The less that's left of them the better. I want SovSec to spend a few days just figuring out who they were, much less who did them."

The men in Blade's carrier laughed, as did Ulbin. "Blade, this is Melyor i Lakin you're about to kill. Everybody's going to know that you did it. You're the only hunter with balls enough to try."

Blade smiled in spite of himself. "Well that's all the more reason to be thorough. The longer it takes them to figure out it's Melyor, the longer we can keep our names out of this."

"I don't see what the problem is," Ulbin said. "It's just one more piece of the legend of the Blade. Besides, after this we'll get any price we want for a job." The men in Blade's carrier murmured in agreement.

"Maybe," Blade told him, "but Cedrych wants us to do this quietly." Ulbin and the other men abruptly grew quiet. They were good at what they did, and they knew it. But all of them were afraid of the Overlord. Blade would have been too, had he been in their position. But Blade couldn't afford to fear anyone, not even Cedrych. Not in his line of work; not in the Nal. It was quite possible that sometime in the not too distant future, someone would hire him to kill the Overlord. It wouldn't do for Bragor-Nal's finest assassin to be afraid of his target.

Several carriers ahead of them, Melyor's vehicle began to shift lane by lane toward the right edge of the Upper. There was a downramp a few quads ahead, and it had been nearly a full hour since her last descent into Nal. It was almost time.

Blade felt his pulse quicken slightly, as he always did just before he killed. Not so much that it diminished his skills, but enough to give him the sharpness and clarity upon which he depended at such moments. "Keep an eye on her," he ordered, addressing all of them. "It won't be long now."

Gwilym stared out the carrier window at the buildings of the Nal and the distant mountains, feeling the awkwardness of the silence that lay between Orris and Melyor. He was growing frustrated and a little desperate. He was still certain that the sorcerer offered the last best hope to end the persecution of his people. And in the past few days he had come to believe that this strange, beautiful woman had a place in the future of the Gildriites as well. He had no idea what role she might play, but he was a Bearer and he had come to trust his instincts in such matters. But regardless of how his two companions fit into the Gildriite redemption in which he had placed his faith, and for which he had given up his old life and the woman he loved, he knew that all would be lost if they could not work together.

Much to the Bearer's dismay, he had seen little to suggest that they could. Every time Gwilym thought that the sorcerer and Nal-Lord were on the verge of reaching some sort of accommodation, something happened to drive them apart again. After their conversation in the carrier the night before, when Melyor admitted that she had been part of a plot to conquer Tobyn-Ser, Gwilym was certain that they had finally gotten all the secrets out into the open. If the two of them could continue to speak to each other after that revelation, he thought, surely there was nothing left that could further damage their relationship.

But he had been wrong. And he knew it as soon as they entered the home of Melyor's bodyguard and realized who this Jibb she had been speaking of was.

Orris recognized Jibb immediately as the leader of the men who had attacked them in the alley. It was clear from the flash of anger in the sorcerer's dark eyes and the way he instantly dropped into a fighter's crouch, his staff aimed at the bodyguard's heart with its amber stone glowing threateningly. Even the sorcerer's bird seemed to know who Jibb was, judging from the harsh cry she gave when she spotted him.

Watching as Orris and Jibb stared at each other warily, hearing the beseeching tone of Melyor's voice as she spoke to the sorcerer in his language, Gwilym could not decide which of the two of them was more of a fool. Considering all that Melyor had confessed just a short while before, it should not have come as a surprise to Orris that she should know and trust the men who had tried to kill him. But by the same token, in light of how difficult it had been for Melyor to win the sorcerer's trust, she should have known better than to bring him to Jibb's home at that particular time. At that moment, Gwilym had been tempted to just throw up his hands and give up. The two of them were beyond help. Yet, he needed them, every bit as much as they needed him. So he had taken the first step toward establishing some semblance of peace in the bodyguard's common room. He had approached Jibb and offered a hand in friendship.

After a moment's hesitation, and a quick look to Melyor, as if for reassurance, Jibb had taken his hand and smiled. Reluctantly, Orris had followed Gwilym's lead, but the sorcerer had refused to speak to Melyor for the rest of the evening, except to tell her to convey an occasional message to Gwilym. The tension between them had persisted through this morning, even after they left Jibb's home and switched carriers. The three of them were, Gwilym gathered, headed for the mountains that loomed to the north, just barely visible through the brown haze of the Nal. Somehow Orris and Melyor had managed to agree on that much. But otherwise they had said little to each other, and Gwilym was left to deal with their sullen silence as best he could, sitting alone in the back seat of the carrier.

"Where are we going?" the Bearer finally asked, though he thought he knew the answer. Anything to get them talking.

Orris glanced back at him and then looked expectantly at Melyor. The Nal-Lord said something in his language—a translation of the question, Gwilym guessed—and then she looked briefly over her shoulder at the Bearer.

"Orris came here—to Lon-Ser, I mean—so that he could address the Council of Sovereigns and convince them to prevent future attacks on his land," she explained. "I've explained to him that Cedrych was the one who initiated the attacks and that he did so without the Council's knowledge. In fact I'm not even sure that Durell knew."

Gwilym shook his head. "Durell?"

"Durell is Sovereign of Bragor-Nal."

"I see. Please, go on."

Melyor shrugged. "Well, I told Orris this, but he doesn't seem to care. He says that since the Council rules Lon-Ser it should be able to keep Cedrych from attacking Tobyn-Ser again."

"And isn't he right?"

"In an ideal world perhaps," Melyor said sounding frustrated, "but given the political realities of the Council, it's just not that simple."

Gwilym smiled sadly. "Forgive me, but I don't understand these political realities any more than Orris does."

She sighed and ran a hand through her amber hair. "I know you don't," she said, obviously trying to keep the impatience from her voice. "The Council consists of the Sovereigns of the three Nals. You know that much, right?" Gwilym nodded and she continued. "Technically, each Nal has an equal vote, but in fact, on most issues, Bragor-Nal has two—Stib-Nal's and it's own—and Oerella-Nal has one."

Gwilym narrowed his eyes. "How can this be?"

"It's a long story, dating back to the Consolidation, but the easiest way to explain it is that Stib-Nal's Sovereigns have, for hundreds of years, exchanged their votes in the Council for the continued independence of their Nal. Stib-Nal is too weak and too small to risk defying Bragor-Nal, so they follow our lead on just about everything."

"So," the Bearer broke in, "you're saying that if Durell does know of Cedrych's plot, the Council will do nothing to stop him."

The Nal-Lord nodded. "That's right, and even if Durell doesn't know right now, he'll figure out that Cedrych's behind this soon enough, and he'll still refuse to stop him."

"How would he figure it out?"

She smiled ruefully. "This plan—the Initiative, we call it—has all the features of one of Cedrych's schemes. Anyone who knows him as well as Durell does will recognize them as such. Besides, there aren't many people in Lon-Ser with both the resources and the audacity to try it."

Gwilym considered this, and Melyor slowed the carrier and began to move it lane by lane toward the right side of the elevated roadway. Apparently she was getting ready to take them down into the Nal again. Gwilym didn't quite understand the logic behind these brief forays into the alleyways of the quads, but Melyor said that they made it more difficult for the Sovereign's security squads to follow them. In light of all he had heard about Bragor-Nal's security force from the people of the Network, Gwilym was not about to argue.

"So have you told Orris what you just told me?" Gwilym finally asked, returning to their discussion.

"Yes, last night, on our way to Jibb's."

"And was he convinced?"

She nodded. "I think so."

Gwilym grinned. "Well then I'm back to my original question: where are we going?"

Melyor gave a small laugh. She was remarkably beautiful when she smiled. "We're going to Oerella-Nal to see if we can meet with Sovereign Shivohn. If we can convince her that Cedrych's plan represents a threat to her Nal, maybe she'll help us find a way to stop him."

"Do you really think there's much chance of that?"

"I'm not sure," she admitted. "It's a gamble. But after last night, I don't think we have much to gain from staying in Bragor-Nal."

Gwilym felt the hairs on the back of his neck stand up, and he had a sudden foreboding of danger. "You think Cedrych will try something," he said, offering it as a statement.

"I'd be surprised if he didn't," she answered, a sudden tightness in her voice. "Orris is a threat to everything Cedrych's been working for, and Cedrych knows now that Orris can't be intimidated. So the only way to stop him is to kill him."

Gwilym nodded as if he understood. In a way he did, and that scared him. The ruthlessness and violence of life in the Nal was completely alien to the world he had left behind in the Dhaalmar. But he was so far from his home, and he had been for so long, that the Nal and its ways had begun to make a certain sense to him. Suddenly he felt unclean, and he longed for the cold clear streams of the mountains near his settlement.

Melyor steered the carrier onto a downramp that led them off the Upper and into the congestion and noise of the quads. Upon reaching street level, she immediately turned into the nearest byway and began once more to wind her way through the narrow alleys.

The sorcerer said something to her and she stared at him for several seconds as if she couldn't believe what she had heard. Then she shook her head and spoke back to him in a hard voice. Orris replied angrily, seeming to repeat what he had said a moment before, and again Melyor shook her head.

"What's going on?" Gwilym demanded wearily, his patience for their bickering gone.

"He wants us to stop so his bird can hunt," Melyor said, glancing at Gwilym over her shoulder with an expression that made it clear that she thought the sorcerer insane.

"She has to eat," Gwilym countered, "just like we do."

"We don't have time for this!" the Nal-Lord argued. "It can eat later."

"He knows her better than we do," the Bearer told her, trying to sound reasonable despite the fact that he shared Melyor's fears and her desire to keep moving. "From what I understand of Tobyn-Ser's magic, I believe it comes from the hawk. It's possible that if she's weakened from being hungry, his power isn't as strong. And we might need his magic before all of this is through."

Melyor spat a curse and brought the carrier to a sudden, jerking halt. "We don't have time for this," she mumbled petulantly, as Orris stepped out of the vehicle and sent his bird in search of food.

For several minutes the three of them said nothing. Gwilym got out to stand with the sorcerer, but Melyor remained in her seat, muttering to herself, and sending an occasional smoldering look Orris's way. The sorcerer's falcon returned several minutes later clutching a grey dove in her talons. Alighting on a pile of scrap metal a few feet away from where Gwilym and Orris stood, she tore hungrily at the carcass, making quick work of it. When she finished, she wiped her sharp beak on her perch and then flew to Orris's shoulder.

Gwilym returned to the rear seat of the carrier, and then Orris climbed back into his seat, saying something to Melyor with a smug expression on his bearded face. She said nothing in return, but before he had even closed his door, she started the vehicle forward with such abruptness that the sorcerer was tossed back against his seat like a child's doll.

He glowered at her, and she allowed herself a brief, satisfied grin. For some time the three travelers sat in silence as Melyor navigated the alleyways. But just as they came to the end of the second set of turns and prepared to cross a large avenue into the third, Melyor slowed the carrier and leaned forward, peering out the front window at a strange scene unfolding before them. A long black carrier stood at the near end of the alley, blocking the entrance. One of its doors was open, and a tall man stood beside it. He had black and silver hair and he wore a large weapon on his belt. He was shouting to another man, this one with short yellow hair, who was standing beside another black carrier parked at the far end of the alley. The second man's arms were spread wide and he was shaking his head, and he held a weapon in one hand.

"What are they doing?" Melyor asked quietly, more to herself it seemed than to Gwilym or Orris.

In that moment, before Gwilym could say anything, the yellow haired man saw them. He hollered at the dark-haired man and pointed directly at Melyor's carrier. The first man spun around to look, revealing a predatory, angular face, with cold, pale eyes.

"Oh shit!" Melyor hissed. "It's Blade!"

"Who's Blade?" Gwilym asked as the carrier leaped backwards.

The dark haired man pulled out his weapon and aimed it at their carrier, shouting something to his companions as he did. Red flame spurted from the weapon.

"Duck!" Melyor shouted, pulling Orris down as she took her own advice.

Gwilym dove down to the carrier floor in front of his seat just in time. In the next instant, crimson fire smashed through the front and rear windows, sizzling like raindrops falling on a fire, and scattering a shower of glass shards over the entire interior of the carrier.

Melyor sat up swiftly, her weapon already in her hand, and prepared to fire back. But Gwilym grabbed her shoulder with one hand and reached for her thrower with the other.

"Get us out of here!" he barked. "I'll worry about them!"

Orris yelled something in his language. Looking quickly at the dark-haired man, Gwilym realized that their attacker had fired again. The Bearer tried to throw himself down again, but he was partially blocked from doing so by the carrier's front seat, on which he had been leaning. The point of red fire was headed directly at him, and he closed his eyes, tasting his own death. But rather than the explosion of pain and fire that he had anticipated, he heard another kind of detonation and felt the entire carrier rock with the impact. Opening his eyes again, he saw the sorcerer holding his staff out before him, and Melyor staring at Orris as if he had just transformed himself into some sort of monster, or perhaps a god.

She stammered something in the sorcerer's language and he grinned fiercely.

"Get us out of here!" Gwilym shouted again, seeing the dark-haired man jump into his carrier, which started forward with a screech of its wheels and a puff of grey smoke.

The alley they were in was far too narrow for Melyor to turn them around, so she drove the carrier backwards as fast she could, scraping the vehicle against the sides of the buildings occasionally and smashing through piles of garbage and scrap metal.

Looking forward again the Bearer saw the attacker's black carrier barrelling toward them across the avenue. Just before it reached the entrance to the alley, however, Orris leveled his staff at the vehicle and unleashed a bolt of amber fire. The large carrier swerved in time to avoid the sorcerer's volley, but it crashed into the corner of one of the buildings. It backed away from the structure almost immediately and started down the alley after them, its front left corner mangled and crushed. By this time Melyor had reached the end of the byway, and backing into the alley adjoining this one, she got them going forward again, back the way they had come. Gwilym could hear the dark-haired man's carrier pursuing them, and a moment later it came into view, careening off the side of a building with a burst of white sparks as it made the turn.

"Who are they?" Gwilym called to Melyor over the roar of her carrier and the howling of the wind as it swept through the vehicle's broken windows.

"Assassins!" Melyor answered, her hands white-knuckled as they gripped the steering device. "Apparently Cedrych wants all three of us dead!"

"Why would he want to kill you?"

"Maybe he's figured out that I'm a Gildriite, or that I've decided to help Orris."

Gwilym nodded, surprised once more by his ability to understand the workings of the Nal mind. He glanced back at the pursuing carrier. Melyor hadn't gotten away from the assassins yet, but she hadn't allowed them to pull any closer either. A shaft of red fire hissed passed their carrier and hit against the wall of a building just in front of them.

"That was close!" Melyor called. "Give them something to think about, will you?"

"What?" Gwilym asked, shaking his head.

"Shoot the weapon at them!"

"Oh! Of course!" He turned and began firing the weapon at their pursuers. At first though his salvos flew wildly into the sides of the buildings or over the black carrier. The weapon was terribly difficult to control, particularly with Melyor's carrier moving so quickly and veering to avoid mounds of refuse. In addition, every time Gwilym pressed his finger on the fire button the thrower recoiled unpredictably. But after several attempts, the Bearer began to feel more comfortable with it. And with one blast he actually hit his target, destroying the black carrier's front window, much as the dark-haired assassin had destroyed theirs.

He turned toward Melyor to tell her what he had managed to do, but just as he did, the second black carrier appeared in front of them, stopping suddenly to block their escape. Swearing impressively, Melyor halted their vehicle as well, and as she shouted for Gwilym to take cover four men jumped out of the second vehicle and started battering Melyor's carrier with thrower fire.

Orris raised a shimmering shield of amber to block their attack, but even as he did, Blade's vehicle stopped behind them, and the dark-haired man and his companions began their own assault. Gwilym tried to fire back, but he was ill-suited to such battles, and he soon found himself cowering on the floor of the carrier listening to the streams of flame hammer at the shell of the vehicle. After several moments the concussions suddenly grew less severe. Looking up, Gwilym saw that Orris had blanketed the entire carrier with a shield of magic.

Melyor asked the sorcerer a question and Gwilym heard Orris reply.

"We have to get out of here," Melyor called to the Bearer. "Orris says that he can only maintain this shield for a few minutes before he and his bird grow too tired."

"Won't the carrier protect us?" Gwilym called back to her.

"Have you ever seen what happens when a thrower blast hits a carrier's fuel box?"

"No."

"It makes a hand boomer look like a pop toy."

"What?" Gwilym asked, wondering if Melyor had suddenly slipped into Orris's language.

"An explosion!" Melyor growled. "It makes a big explosion!"

The Bearer nodded. That he understood. "So how do we get out of here? Can we use the carrier?"

"I don't think so. They've got the alley blocked at both ends."

Orris called to Melyor, his voice sounding strained. Lifting his head to look at the sorcerer, Gwilym saw that his face was bathed with sweat. He was holding his staff out before him with both hands, and the muscles in his burly arms were quivering with the effort he was putting into the magic shield. Even his beautiful falcon seemed to be wilting under the strain of what they were doing. Her eyes were closed, and she sat hunched on the carrier seat next to Orris, trembling, her beak open as if she were panting. The assassins' thrower blasts continued to be absorbed by the amber casing Orris and the bird had created around the carrier, but the glow of the shield had grown dimmer. They hadn't much time left.

Looking out the side window of the vehicle through the shimmering amber light, Gwilym spotted one of the small doorways leading to the underground passages.

"Melyor," he said, drawing her attention and pointing to the door.

She stared at it for a moment and then looked at Gwilym. "What? You want to go underground? You must be insane. They'll follow us. With your stone and the sorcerer's showing them the way, they'll have no trouble tracking us. Besides, we need a carrier. It'll take us too long to get to Oerella-Nal without one."

"Leave that to me," he said, amazed at his own self-assurance.

"To you?"

"The Network will get us a carrier. We just have to get to the Network."

"The Network," Melyor breathed. Obviously, she hadn't even considered that possibility. "You think they'll help us?"

Gwilym shrugged. "I'm here, aren't I?"

A deafening explosion rocked the carrier so violently that for an instant Gwilym feared that the assassins had broken through Orris's shield. The sorcerer let out an inarticulate roar of rage or pain or just sheer exertion. Whichever it was, though, and regardless of what had hit the carrier, the shelter of amber power appeared to have held.

"That was a boomer," Melyor said, looking with concern at Orris. She asked him a question, and he shook his head vehemently in response. "I still don't like the idea of going underground," she said a moment later, looking at Gwilym again. "But I don't think we have any choice." She nodded toward the thrower that Gwilym still held in his hands. "Give me that," she commanded.

He handed her the weapon. Melyor placed a hand on Orris's shoulder and whispered to him. When she finished, he nodded. She said something else and he actually gave a small smile and opened his eyes long enough to look at her and nod a second time.

"What did you say to him?" Gwilym asked.

"I told him what we're going to try to do," she answered, her eyes never leaving the sorcerer's face. "And I asked him if he had enough energy left to send a couple of shots of magic at the carrier in front of us." She paused allowing herself a small grin of her own. "Then I told him that even though he's arrogant and abrasive, he can be convenient to have around."

Gwilym smiled. Maybe this will do it, he thought to himself. Maybe this will bring them together.

"Orris and I will try to keep them busy," the Nal-Lord went on, looking at Gwilym. "Your job is to get the door open as quickly as possible."

"I can do that," the Bearer said with a nod.

"Good." She looked at Orris again and said a single word. "Get ready to open the door, Bearer. On my signal Orris will stop shielding us. Then we move."

She looked at Orris once more. The sorcerer looked pale and spent, and Gwilym wondered where he would find the strength to run, much less throw his power at the assassins.

"Go!" Melyor hollered.

An instant later the amber shield vanished, and with it went all the stray thoughts in Gwilym's head. All he could think about was getting the carrier door open, which he did with little trouble, and getting to the doorway that led underground. The distance had not seemed great a few moments earlier, but as the Bearer scrambled out of the vehicle, nearly stumbling in the process, it suddenly felt like a very long way indeed. He heard rather than saw the bolts of fire leap from Orris's crystal and Melyor's weapon. And though he also never saw any of the assassins' fire, he felt the heat of one salvo as it hissed just inches behind his neck. Reaching the entrance to the passageways, he turned the handle and threw his weight against the door as hard as he could. Nothing happened. He tried a second time and a third, before remembering that all the previous doors of this sort that he had encountered opened outward.

"*What are you doing?*" Melyor screamed at him, as she and the sorcerer continued to trade volleys with their attackers.

Gwilym yanked the door open and dove inside just as a red bolt of fire tore a hole in the sheet metal just above the door handle. "Come on!" he shouted, waving them toward the doorway, terrified that his delay might cost them their lives.

Melyor pushed Orris toward the entrance and then came running close behind him, sending streams of red flame to the left and right as she did. Orris's bird came last, gliding low to the ground and avoiding two beams of red that came at her from either direction. When she was certain that they were all safely through the doorway, Melyor hid herself behind the door, closed it almost all the way, and aimed her thrower at her carrier. She fired twice with no result. But with her third blast the vehicle erupted with a thunderous roar and a brilliant flash of yellow light. Melyor slammed the door shut, and the three of them scrambled down the stairs into the passageways.

"Go on!" Melyor called. "I'll catch up with you."

"Which way?" Gwilym asked.

"North," she said, and then, anticipating his next question, she added, "To the right."

Gwilym started down the tunnels, supporting Orris with one arm, and holding his stone out before him to light their way with its golden brown glow. He heard several small blasts behind him and then a sudden rumbling sound that reminded him oddly of a Dhaalmar avalanche. A few moments later Melyor caught up with them, breathless but smiling.

"I destroyed the entrance way and the stairs," she explained, falling into step with them and returning her weapon to the strap on her thigh. "By the time they get past the flames from my carrier and the rubble that's blocking the doorway, we should be far enough from here to keep them from tracking us."

"Do you know where to find the Network?" Gwilym asked.

"You said I should leave that to you!" she threw back at him.

"Once we find the Network, I'll handle everything," the Bearer assured her. "They'll help us. I promise you. But I don't know where to find them."

Melyor rubbed her hand across her brow. "Neither do I. That's why they're the Network." She glanced around the corridor. "I'm not even sure what Realm we're in. I think it's the Twenty-Third, but I wouldn't swear to it. Finding the Network up here's going to be next to impossible."

"But you contacted them," Gwilym reminded her. "You got them to help you find Orris and me."

"Yes, but that was in the Fourth, my Realm! We're hundreds of quads from there! This isn't even Cedrych's Dominion! Besides, even in the Fourth, the Network contacts always insisted on meeting me in a public place, taking me to a carrier, and then blindfolding me." She shook her head. "I should never have let them do that."

"I doubt you had much choice," Gwilym said gently. "In my experience, they're not a very flexible group."

Melyor gave a small, rueful laugh.

The three travelers came to a fork in the tunnel and with barely a moment's hesitation Melyor led them to the left.

The Bearer looked at her quizzically. "Where are we going?"

"North," she said matter-of-factly. "We'll look for the Network along the way, but we might as well keep going toward Oerella-Nal."

They walked for what seemed like a long time, saying nothing, taking an occasional turn, and generally keeping to the left when the corridors split. But they encountered no one. Melyor was walking in the lead and setting a brisk pace; Gwilym sensed that she was growing impatient. In truth, he couldn't blame her. He didn't relish the idea of walking underground all the way to the end of Bragor-Nal either. He had little sense of the distance involved, but he remembered how far off the mountains had appeared from the Upper. It would probably take them several days. Maybe longer.

"This is ridiculous!" the Nal-Lord railed, breaking the lengthy silence. "We don't have time for this!" She glanced back at the Bearer and Orris. "These aren't just any assassins we're dealing with!" she said. "That was the Blade and his men. These tunnels won't protect us for long." She faced forward again. "We won't even be safe in Oerella-Nal," she grumbled, speaking more to herself now. "That is if we ever get there."

Listening to her, it occurred to Gwilym that in the course of less than a day she had gone from a position of power within the Nal hierarchy to being an exile of sorts, a target for the violent culture of which she had so recently been a part. True, she had chosen this fate by casting her lot with the sorcerer, just as Gwilym had chosen to leave Hertha and his home. But Gwilym, if he survived, could always go back to the Dhaalmar. He sensed that Melyor would have a much harder time reclaiming her status in the Nal. It seemed to the Bearer that she had lost everything with breathtaking swiftness. Recognizing this, Gwilym felt his own growing impatience with her ranting sluicing away, leaving him feeling angry with himself, and sad for Melyor.

He glanced sidelong at Orris and saw that the sorcerer was already watching him. The burly man inclined his head discreetly toward the Nal-Lord and grimaced slightly. Melyor had spoken in Lonmir, but clearly Orris had understood the tone of her voice. Gwilym nodded and then shrugged, as if to say that he didn't know what to do for her. Orris returned the gesture and then briefly gripped Gwilym's shoulder before looking forward again. The Bearer grinned inwardly. It seemed that they understood each other fairly well, in spite of their inability to converse.

The three of them soon came to a stairway leading back up to street level. Melyor walked past it, but then halted and stood motionless in the middle of the corridor as if considering something.

"Wait here," she finally told Gwilym, bounding up the stairs and out into the waning daylight.

Gwilym and the sorcerer glanced at each other, and again Orris shrugged. Then he seemed to get an idea and he started up the stairs with the Bearer close behind him.

As it turned out, Orris had decided to use this opportunity to let his bird hunt again, and as soon as they emerged onto the street, the falcon soared off eagerly in search of food. Gwilym and Orris stood together by the doorway watching for the hawk's return, and making certain that they were not seen from the nearby avenue.

They were still waiting for the bird when a dull grey carrier, larger than Melyor's white one, but smaller than the long black one they had ridden in the day before, pulled into the alley and stopped just in front of them. Melyor climbed out and gaped at them, her face reddening.

"Are you two crazy?" she demanded. "Do you want to get us all killed? I told you to wait—" She stopped herself and frowned. "It's the hawk again, isn't it?" she said to Gwilym. "That's why you're out here."

Just then, as if sent by the gods to confirm what Melyor had said, Orris's falcon glided into view bearing a plump grey dove.

"Where did you find a carrier?" Gwilym asked, as the bird began to eat.

Melyor grinned enigmatically. "It was easy. They're everywhere, you know."

It took a moment. "You mean you stole this?" Gwilym asked incredulously, feeling himself go pale.

The Nal-Lord laughed. "Of course. Where did you think I was going when I left you in the tunnel?"

"I—I didn't know!" he stammered. "I suppose . . ." He trailed off, staring at the carrier and shaking his head. "This isn't right," he said at last. "I won't do this."

"You don't have much choice," Melyor told him, her expression hardening.

"Of course I do! I won't ride in a pilfered carrier."

Melyor threw her hands in the air. "You've got to be joking with me! You're willing to risk getting all of us killed because your morals won't allow you to ride in a stolen carrier?"

Gwilym hesitated, and Orris asked Melyor a question.

She gazed at the sorcerer for a moment saying nothing. Then she faced Gwilym again. "Let's ask Orris what he thinks," she suggested. "If he has a problem with it too, I'll find another way to get us moving. But if he agrees with me, you leave your morals in this alley."

Gwilym swallowed. "Agreed," he replied.

Melyor looked at Orris again and spoke to him for several moments, gesturing spiritedly at the carrier and at Gwilym.

Orris held himself very still, offering no reaction to whatever it was that the Nal-Lord was saying. When she finished, he walked over to the carrier and circled it once, looking at it appraisingly. Then he asked Melyor a question and, quite unexpectedly, she burst out laughing.

"What?" Gwilym demanded. "What did he say?"

Melyor turned to him, still chuckling. "He wants to know why I couldn't find one in a better color."

Gwilym looked from Melyor to Orris, shaking his head again. "So I take it he agrees with you."

"He hasn't said yet," Melyor answered with a shrug.

She spoke to Orris again, and the sorcerer walked over to Gwilym and placed a hand on the Bearer's shoulder.

He said something to Melyor, although he continued to look Gwilym in the eye.

"He says he understands your feelings," Melyor translated. "And normally he'd share them. But he agrees that we have little choice in this instance."

Orris said more, and, even after he finished, Melyor continued to look at him, as if surprised by his words. After a few seconds, the sorcerer glanced at her and nodded, saying a single word.

"He also says" she began again, her voice subdued, "that considering how much I've lost in the last day, you should both do everything possible to make things easy for me."

Gwilym nodded slowly, his eyes meeting those of the sorcerer. "Tell him he's right," the Bearer said softly. He turned his gaze to Melyor. "And please accept my apology."

She looked away, but managed to acknowledge his words with a single nod. "Let's go," she said, walking to the far side of the carrier and climbing in.

Orris called his falcon to his shoulder, and soon they were on their way again, winding through alleyways and narrow roads until they reached a ramp to the Upper. Melyor said nothing, and Orris and Gwilym sat without speaking as well, staring out the windows of the carrier. It grew dark, and they continued to race toward the mountains, which loomed closer now, huge and black against the lights of the Nal and the unearthly glow they gave to the brown haze that hung over the giant city.

"Bearer," Melyor said, abruptly breaking the silence that had enveloped the carrier for so long, "did you travel through the Median Range when you came to Bragor-Nal?"

"Yes," Gwilym answered, his voice sounding loud to his own ears, even above the rumble of the carrier.

"And did the Network guide you through?"

"They told me the way," Gwilym explained, "but I crossed alone."

"You were met on this side though, right?" Melyor persisted.

"Yes."

"Where?"

Gwilym closed his eyes for a moment trying to remember. "It was by an old tree stump just past a sharp bend in the river."

"Which river?"

He closed his eyes again, wracking his brain, but the name wouldn't come. "I don't remember," he admitted at last.

"Was it Three Nals or—"

"Yes!" he said, almost shouting it as he leaned forward. "Three Nals River."

Melyor nodded. "Good, that helps. But there are several forks of the river leading out of the mountains. Do you know which one you were following?"

Gwilym fell back against his seat, deflated. "No," he said, his voice flat. "I have no idea."

"Do you remember anything about the river? Do you remember it joining other tributaries."

He thought for a minute. "Yes, it did once."

"Was this before it reached the Nal?"

"Yes."

"Good," she said again. "From which direction did the tributary approach?"

"North," Gwilym told her after a brief pause. "It came from the north."

"And you followed the river all the way to the Nal?"

"Yes."

"Very good, Bearer. I know exactly where to go."

The Bearer smiled, and Melyor, glancing back at him, grinned as well.

"You'll have to speak for us," Melyor continued after a moment. "The Network will be more inclined to help you than me."

"Do you think they'll recognize you?"

"It's possible," she replied. "We're a long way from my Realm, but I'm pretty well known."

"I'm sure they'll help us anyway," Gwilym told her. "Especially when they learn that you're one of us as well."

Melyor spun around, her mouth open. But then she clamped it shut and faced forward again.

"I'm sorry, Melyor," he said quietly. "They don't need to know."

The Nal-Lord shrugged ambivalently. "It probably doesn't matter any more." She looked as if she might say more, but she didn't.

A few moments later, Orris pointed at something out the front window and asked Melyor a question, and the two of them began to talk. Gwilym settled back in his seat once more and soon fell asleep listening to the voices of his two companions. He awoke once when Melyor, preparing to stop for fuel, had both Orris and the Bearer lie down on the floor in front of the rear seat. But they were on their way again quickly, and Gwilym soon fell back into a deep slumber.

When he rose again it was early morning, and the dirty sky had a dim grey cast to it. The carrier had stopped, and as Gwilym sat up and looked out his window, he realized that they were down off the Upper in yet another alleyway.

"We've reached the edge of the Nal, Bearer," Melyor said softly.

There were dark rings under her bright green eyes, and her delicate features were pale with fatigue. But she was smiling, and Gwilym wondered briefly what she and the sorcerer had spoken about during the night. And with the thought, he realized that Orris was not in the carrier.

"He's with his bird," Melyor said, as if reading his mind. "It was time for her to hunt again."

Her, Gwilym repeated to himself. Not *it*.

She held out a piece of soft bread and some of the processed fruit with which he had become so familiar in recent weeks. "I thought you might be hungry, too," she said.

"Thank you."

"The next part of this journey is going to be a little tricky," she told him, as he took the food from her and bit into the bread. "In order to leave the Nal, we need to get past SovSec. Normally, they'd let me go without a problem. My name used to carry some weight with them. It still might, but I can't be sure anymore. It depends upon whether they know that I've fallen out of favor with Cedrych."

"But it's not a gamble you care to take," Gwilym said, guessing at where all this was leading.

"No, it's not." Melyor looked away. Her expression revealed little about what she was thinking, but in that moment Gwilym thought that she appeared terribly young to be bearing such great burdens. "I'm not afraid of many people," she finally said. "But all of a sudden it feels like I'm being hunted down by every one of them: Cedrych, the Blade, SovSec." She shook her head and stared out the window at Orris. After some time she faced Gwilym again. "The point is, I'm not sure that I can get us out. I've done as much as I can. It's your turn now."

The Bearer swallowed a mouthful of bread. "But I don't know where to find the Network. I thought you could get us to the bend in the river I told you about last night."

"We're near the river." She pointed out the left window. "It's just on the far side of these buildings. And the boundary of the Nal is less than a quad away. But this is as much as I can do."

The Bearer took a long breath and rubbed his eyes. He was still half asleep, and even at his best he wasn't at all sure that he could do what Melyor was asking. And yet, after depending upon others for so long—the Network, Melyor, Orris—Gwilym found that he wanted to try. In the Dhaalmar he was a leader; he had been accustomed to having others turn to him. He missed that. And Melyor was offering him a chance to be in that position again. Yes, he would be turning to the Network once more, but he would be doing it on his companions' behalf.

"All right," he said at last. "Let me finish eating and we'll be on our way."

He was surprised by the relief he saw in her eyes as she smiled at him. "Thank you."

When Gwilym and Orris's hawk had finished their meals, the travelers returned to the underground passages through a small doorway near the stolen carrier. Immediately upon entering the tunnels, Gwilym could smell the river, or rather the dampness in the stone corridors that came from the river. It was a scent he remembered from his arrival in Bragor-Nal.

"There was an entrance to the tunnels outside the walls," the Bearer said quietly. "It was about fifty yards west of the river."

"This way then," Melyor said, starting down the corridor.

Orris followed and Gwilym walked behind the two of them shaking his head. He did not enjoy traveling underground. Already he had lost his bearings; he would have taken them in the opposite direction.

They hadn't gone very far, when they heard voices in front of them.

Melyor's weapon was in her hand instantly, and Orris had lowered himself into a crouch, his staff held out before him.

"It could be the Network," the Bearer whispered.

Melyor nodded. "Or it could be security goons," she answered, whispering as well. "Or break-laws."

"How do we find out?"

Melyor whispered to Orris, who nodded and closed his eyes. Almost immediately his falcon leaped from his shoulder, and glided forward close to the floor of the tunnel. The sorcerer said something. Melyor asked him a question and he gave a one word reply.

"Well they don't seem to be goons," Melyor said. "At least they're not in uniform." She asked the sorcerer another question and, after a brief pause, he gave the same terse response. The Nal-Lord looked intently at Gwilym. "They're not carrying weapons either."

"Few of the Network members I met did."

Once more Melyor spoke to Orris. The sorcerer nodded again and a few seconds later his falcon glided noiselessly back to his shoulder.

"What should we do?" Melyor asked, as the voices drew nearer.

"I trust you and Orris to fight our way through any trouble we encounter," Gwilym told her. "So I think we should declare ourselves and hope it's the Network."

She shrugged. "All right. That's what we'll do."

"Tell Orris to conceal his stone until they get close," Gwilym said, covering his own crystal. "I don't want them to flee before we've had a chance to tell them who we are. When I call to him, he should pull out his stone and brighten it."

Melyor relayed his instructions to the sorcerer, who signalled his agreement with a single nod.

The three of them waited as the voices continued their approach. There seemed to be only two, both of them men, and though their voices had carried from some distance, they were not speaking loudly. They came into view a short while later, although they appeared as only dark shadows in the dim corridor. Gwilym wouldn't have seen them had he not been looking for them, just as they did not appear to see the Bearer and his companions.

Still Gwilym said nothing, until they were just a few paces away. Then he pulled out his own stone and called to Orris to do the same. Despite the fact that Gwilym spoke in Lon-Ser's language, Orris seemed to understand. He uncovered his amber crystal and summoned from it a dazzling light that brightened the corridor like sunshine, revealing two young men, both of them fair-skinned with dark hair.

They each let out a gasp and turned to run.

"Wait!" the Bearer called out. "I am Gwilym, Bearer of the Stone! We need your help!"

Neither man broke stride. They had almost reached the end of the corridor when a single beam of red fire streaked between them, hitting the stone wall in front of them. They stopped immediately, whirling around to look back at Gwilym and his friends, breathless and wide-eyed.

"That's better," Gwilym said with a smile. "As I was saying, I'm Gwilym, Bearer of the Stone. I've come here from the Dhaalmar. With me are Orris, a sorcerer from Tobyn-Ser, and . . ." He faltered, looking at Melyor.

"Kellyn," the Nal-Lord said with a thin smile.

"Kellyn," Gwilym repeated. "She is a Gildriite, like me." He walked toward the two men, who appeared incapable of moving. "I'm guessing that the two of you are with the Network."

They nodded simultaneously.

"Splendid!" the Bearer said, his smile broadening. "We need to get to Oerella-Nal and contact the Network there as quickly as possible. Can you help us?"

"O-of course, Bearer," one of the men finally managed. "We had heard of a Bearer in the Nal, and of the sorcerer as well. But we never dreamed that we'd actually find you. Forgive us for running. You frightened us."

"I understand, and I'm sorry for startling you. We didn't want to drive you off, but we also didn't want to reveal ourselves too soon, just in case you were . . . someone else."

Both men grinned, and Gwilym got the distinct impression that they were brothers, perhaps even twins. "This way, Bearer," one of them said, sounding calmer now and gesturing in the direction he and his brother had started to run. "We can take you beyond the walls and tell you how to find our contacts in Oerella-Nal, but you should remain below until nightfall."

Gwilym glanced at Melyor, who nodded in agreement. "Very well," he said, looking at their new guides once more. "Lead the way."

They remained underground with the brothers for the entire day, receiving instructions on how to proceed across the Median Range, and filling Gwilym's pack with food and drink. Melyor, the Bearer noticed, grew increasingly quiet as the day went on. She appeared uncomfortable with the notion of leaving the Nal for the mountains, and though the two guides accepted her as another Gildriite, she seemed ill at ease with them. Just before dusk, when one of the brothers suddenly left them, heading back through the tunnels to the Nal, Melyor stared after him with manifest suspicion.

"Where's he going?" she demanded of the guide who remained.

The young man, who had been helping Gwilym on with his loaded pack looked after his brother with a blank expression. "I don't know," he answered after a brief pause. He shrugged. "We're supposed to patrol the tunnels under the northern edge of the Twenty-Third Realm. He's probably going to make our rounds."

Melyor looked off again in the direction the man had gone. "All right," she said, though obviously still skeptical.

Gwilym stepped closer to her. "What's the matter?" he asked in a whisper.

"I'm not sure," she replied softly, still staring down the corridor. "Nothing probably. I just got a strange feeling from him."

"They're difficult people to figure out," Gwilym agreed, remembering his own early impressions of the members of Bragor-Nal's Network. "When I first arrived here, I didn't know what to make of them. They live every day of their lives with this enormous secret and the fear that someone will find out. It's almost as if they live in two worlds at the same time. I don't know how they do it." He smiled at her, hoping he sounded reassuring. "But they got me to the sorcerer, and they'll get us to Oerella-Nal."

Melyor looked at the Bearer and essayed a thin smile. "You're right. I'm sure everything's fine."

"It's time for us to go," the remaining guide said, gesturing for the three travelers to follow. "Late twilight is best; it's dark enough to keep the security goons from seeing very well, but still light enough to make their search lights ineffective."

The Bearer adjusted his pack slightly, trying to get used to the weight; it had been some time since the pack had been so full. Then he started down the corridor after the guide. Melyor and Orris followed as well, although, Gwilym noticed, not before the Nal-Lord glanced back once last time, as if trying to catch a glimpse of the other guide.

It would be a brief conversation. They always were with the Overlord. The difficult part for Jeron was getting far enough away from his brother and the travelers to have the conversation in private. His brother, of course would never have understood. Lovel was a decent man and Jeron loved him. They had no one in this world except each other. But Lovel was hopelessly naive and just a little bit stupid. He never questioned where Jeron had gotten the money for their new carrier, or how they had managed to move to the nicest flat in the quad on what they earned together as workers in the Farm. For that matter, Lovel had never questioned how they had managed, with no connections and no experience, to get the highly coveted jobs at the Farm in the first place. He had just accepted it.

It was a good thing, too. How would Jeron have explained? He couldn't just say, "We've gotten all these things—the jobs, the money, the flat—because I betrayed the Network to work for Cedrych." Better to keep his secret—how many secrets could one man have? he sometimes wondered—and let Lovel believe that the world wasn't such a bad place, even for a couple of Gildriites.

From the beginning, Jeron had made his cooperation contingent on the Overlord's promise that no harm would come to Lovel. Not that he had fooled himself into believing that Cedrych's word was worth anything, or that he had the leverage to hold the Overlord to anything he said. But it had made the initial act of crossing over a bit easier to swallow. And, as it happened, Cedrych had never seemed interested in hurting any Gildriites. As he put it, he just felt better knowing where the Network was, and what it was doing. Always. Probably it made him feel safer, Jeron thought. Strange as it seemed to Jeron considering Cedrych's reputation, rumor had it that the Overlord was overly cautious when it came to matters of personal safety.

Jeron had also heard that Cedrych bore scars from a nearly successful attempt on his life. He didn't know for certain; the two of them had never met. Jeron's recruitment had been accomplished through intermediaries, and all their conversations had taken place using the hand-held communications device that he carried in the folds of his trouser leg.

Usually they spoke once a week, with Jeron calling the Overlord at a pre-arranged time. But two nights ago, Cedrych had buzzed him and told him to listen for word of the Bearer, the sorcerer, and a companion, a woman of some import, Jeron gathered.

"I want to know if you hear anything at all, Jeron," Cedrych had said. "Don't disappoint me again."

Jeron had winced at the reminder. Cedrych had been furious with him for not conveying news of the Bearer's arrival in Bragor-Nal. Jeron had tried to explain to the Overlord that he hadn't even heard of it until days after the fact, and then he had assumed that it was of little import. What threat could a Bearer pose to Cedrych or anyone else in Bragor-Nal? He had made the mistake of giving voice to his thoughts while still in contact with the Overlord, and had been rebuked with such vehemence that he had actually sat down on the speaking device to muffle the sound so that Lovel, asleep in the next room, wouldn't hear.

All of which made this conversation that much more important. It wouldn't do to make Cedrych angry a second time.

"Yes, Jeron," came the Overlord's voice after only one buzz. "You'd better have news for me."

"I do, Overlord," Jeron answered, trying with little success to keep his voice steady.

"You know where they are?"

"I've just been with them. Even now, my brother is seeing them off."

"Seeing them off?" Cedrych demanded, his voice rising dangerously.

"Yes, Overlord," Jeron said in a small voice. "They plan to make their way through the Medians to Oerella-Nal. Do you want me to stop them? I can make something up about the Sovereign's security—"

"No," Cedrych broke in. The Overlord said nothing more for a long time, until Jeron began to wonder if they were still connected. "No," he finally repeated thoughtfully. "This actually works very nicely. I wanted discretion. What could be more discreet than having it done in another Nal?"

Jeron cleared his throat. "I'm sorry, Overlord?"

"Never mind, Jeron," Cedrych said, his voice suddenly crisp again. "Well done. Let's speak again next week at the normal time."

A sharp click in the speaker indicated to Jeron that Cedrych had broken their connection. The young man sunk to the stone floor of the tunnel, closing his eyes and taking several deep breaths. *How else can we afford the flat and the carrier?* he asked himself, as he had so many times before. *How else could we be assured of our jobs at the Farm? I do it for Lovel.*

23

Equally troubling is the notion, propagated both in Baden's report and during recent debates within the Great Hall, that somehow we might find potential allies living among Lon-Ser's murderers and outlaws; like-minded people who will help us fight off the sort of villains who invaded our land four years ago. This seems to me utter folly and the worst kind of wishful thinking. It is based wholly upon conjecture and it runs counter to all the substantive evidence we have. One need only examine the weapons we took from the outlanders to know that they came from a cruel, harsh land. No one Nal is safer or kinder or friendlier than another and every citizen of Lon-Ser is, potentially, an enemy of our land. We would be naive and foolish to send envoys across Arick's Sea in search of friends. There are none in Lon-Ser to be found.

—From "A Response to the Report of Owl-Master Baden on his Interrogation of the Outlander Baram," Submitted by Owl-Master Erland, Autumn, God's Year 4625.

He knew that he did not belong in the Nal. Ever since his arrival there he had felt the weight of the ponderous, towering buildings as if he was carrying them on his back. He had winced at the sight of the brown haze that stained the sky like a disease, and had tried with little success to block out the constant noise that even seemed to reach him beneath the streets, in the oppressive stench and darkness of the tunnels where he had spent so much of his time. But conscious as he was of all that he hated about this alien place, Orris had not realized just how much he missed his home until he was outside the giant city, climbing into the impressive chain of mountains that Melyor called the Median Range.

He could still catch glimpses of the Nal if he looked back. When the cool winds blowing south down the steep, rocky slopes died down, he could still smell it. And though the sky had started to shade back toward a more natural blue, the mage could still see traces of the brown haze lingering above him. But there was dirt and rock beneath his feet. Aspens and firs grew overhead, in the sun and wind where they belonged. He could hear birds singing and he had seen several herds of deer. Every time he inhaled he felt as though he was being cleansed.

And yet Orris's relief at being out of the Nal was nothing compared with Anizir's. The thoughts she conveyed to him had been shaded by a constant shrinking fear for so many days—since her first glimpse of the Nal from the swamp that she and Orris had crossed with Baram—that Orris had almost forgotten what their bond had been like before they reached Lon-Ser. Now though, as Orris, Gwilym, and Melyor walked along a narrow path that carried them higher and higher into the mountains, the dark falcon soared overhead, wheeling and stooping in the sunlight with such abandon that even Melyor laughed aloud at the sight of her. The bird had already eaten three times since waking with the sunrise, and it was just barely midday. She and Orris were still a long way from Tobyn-Ser, but on this, their first morning outside of Bragor-Nal, the distance did not seem quite so great.

They maintained a good pace throughout the morning and into the afternoon, pausing briefly to eat in the middle of the morning and again early in the afternoon. Given Gwilym's girth, and the fact that the Bearer was by far the oldest of the three travelers, Orris had expected him to tire first. But Gwilym traveled the rough path and bore his heavy carry sack with an ease and deceptive grace that indicated to Orris that he was accustomed to life in the mountains. Melyor, on the other hand, seemed out of place on the trail. Her black boots, with their sharply honed tips, were ill-suited to the mountain terrain, and though she never complained, and she managed to keep up with Orris and the Bearer, she was already flushed and out of breath by midday.

They finally stopped for the day late in the afternoon, as sunlight angled steeply across the trail, illuminating the trees and stones with a brilliant golden light. Immediately, Melyor flopped down on the ground and lay on her back, her eyes closed as she muttered sullenly under her breath.

"Are you all right?" Orris asked her, sitting on the ground beside her and offering her some dry bread.

She opened one eye and squinted at him. After a moment, she took a piece of bread and popped it into her mouth. "You ask if I am all right," she said in her strange accent, sitting up and facing him. "You tell me what you think." She reached down and gingerly removed one of her boots, wincing as she did. The white hose she wore beneath the boot was torn in several places and stained with blood. When she pulled off what remained of the hose, Orris saw that her foot was covered with bloody blisters and torn skin. It was remarkable that she had walked as far as she had. She removed her boot and hose from her other foot, and Orris saw that it was even worse off.

He whistled through his teeth. "I can help with that," he told her, reaching for the closer foot.

She pulled away from him, wincing again.

"It's all right," he said soothingly. "I can heal you."

"No!" she said, shaking her head so vehemently that her amber hair fell over her face.

"But you don't have to be in pain."

"No," she said again, though more calmly this time.

The mage shrugged and climbed to his feet. "It's your choice," he told her, turning to walk away.

"Wait!" she called, stopping him before he could get very far.

Orris faced her again, suppressing a smile.

"When you say that you can heal me," she said tentatively, her green eyes sparkling in the sun, "do you mean with . . . ? Would you use . . . ?" Faltering, she pointed up at Anizir, who was still circling above them.

Orris nodded. "I'd use magic. Yes."

"And that would work?" Melyor asked.

The mage laughed. "It always has." He regarded her placidly. "Would you like me to try?"

She blushed slightly before looking away, and it occurred to Orris in that moment that she was probably the most beautiful woman he had ever known. She was even more beautiful than Alayna, which he had not believed possible. But none of that changed the fact that he still did not quite trust her. He knew that she had sacrificed a great deal by casting her lot with Gwilym and him. He had no doubt that the assassins in the two carriers had been trying to kill all three of them. Whatever status she had enjoyed in Bragor-Nal as one of Cedrych's subordinates was gone now. He understood as well that Gwilym trusted her, that by revealing to the Bearer that she was a Gildriite, she had forged a bond with him. Orris knew all this; he had more than enough reasons to place his faith in her as well. And yet the mage still found it hard to forget that she had tried to have him killed, or that she had been planning to conquer Tobyn-Ser up until his arrival in Lon-Ser. Despite all they had been through together in the past few days, Orris could not bring himself to see beyond who she had been when he first met her.

"Yes," she finally answered, meeting his gaze again. "I would like you to heal me. Please," she added, smiling at him.

He nodded and then gently laid his hands on one of her feet. Reaching for his connection with Anizir, he felt the power begin to move through him like a warm breeze on Tobyn's Plain, flowing through his hands into Melyor's skin. And, after a few seconds, he also felt her wounds beginning to heal beneath his touch. For several minutes he did not move, and it seemed to Orris that he was floating midway between Melyor and Anizir, anchored to the ground by the texture of her skin, and yet simultaneously drawn upward by the touch of his hawk's consciousness. *I miss this,* he thought. *A mage should use his power for other things besides combat.*

When he finally lifted his hands from her foot, the blisters had closed, leaving only discolored spots where the raw wounds had been. He heard Gwilym gasp behind him, and Melyor looked from her foot to Orris's face a number of times, wonder in her eyes.

"The dark spots will vanish in a few days," Orris told her.

"It does not hurt anymore," Melyor breathed. "Not at all." She looked up at Gwilym and spoke to him in the same awestruck voice. The Bearer murmured something in reply. "Thank you," Melyor said, her eyes meeting Orris's again.

The most beautiful woman he had ever known. . . . "Let me heal your other foot," the mage said, looking away and shifting his position so he could reach it.

When Orris finished tending to Melyor's wounds, the three travelers set about making camp for the night. Orris sent Anizir in search of game, and while Gwilym gathered some roots to go with their meal, Melyor and the mage collected wood for a fire. By the time night fell and stars began to emerge in a sky of deepest blue, the two quail killed for them by Orris's bird were roasting on spits.

They ate their meal wordlessly. Melyor seemed tired and preoccupied, as Orris might have expected. But to his surprise, Gwilym appeared withdrawn as well. From what the mage had gathered from his conversations with Melyor, the Bearer lived in another range of mountains farther to the north, and Orris had expected that Gwilym would be pleased to be out of the Nal and back in terrain that was at least somewhat familiar. Judging by the bald man's demeanor, however, the opposite was true. Being in the mountains appeared to be causing him pain, and Orris found himself curious about the life Gwilym had left behind.

"Do you have family?" Orris asked him abruptly. "A wife? children?"

Gwilym stared at him briefly and then faced Melyor, who translated the question. Looking at Orris again, the Bearer nodded and spoke softly. Orris thought he saw a single tear in the corner of Gwilym's eye reflected in the firelight.

"Two children," Melyor said, still looking at the Bearer. "And his wife, of course." She asked Gwilym something and again he nodded. "I thought so," she commented in response. She turned to Orris. "He is a Bearer," she explained, "which means that he is also the leader of his community. He gave up a great deal to come here."

Orris shook his head. "Why did you leave?" he asked Gwilym.

The mage waited while Melyor conveyed the question and then listened to the Bearer's response. "He was brought here by a dream," she finally said. "A dream of you."

Orris stared at her and then at Gwilym. "What?"

She smiled, although there was sadness in her eyes. "We Gildriites have a bit of power ourselves. We call it the Sight."

Orris nodded. "Yes, mages have it, too."

"Naturally," she said cryptically. "Gwilym had a vision of you being attacked by the men I sent, and he came to Bragor-Nal to save your life."

"But why?"

Again, Orris listened as Melyor and Gwilym spoke for several minutes. He was beginning to understand some of what he heard. Not a lot, but there were similarities between Lon-Ser's language and his own, which was not surprising given the common ancient history of the two lands. He recognized the Lonmir words for stone, land, and death, and he thought he heard something that sounded like the word "life" in his own language. But he could not make sense of what Gwilym said.

When the Bearer stopped speaking, Melyor took a deep breath and faced Orris again. "Your question is not easily answered," she began in her peculiar accent. "There is much history that you do not know." She frowned. "I am not certain that I can make it clear to you. We have the Sight, and for that, in the past, our people have been valued and sought out by the leaders of the Nals who thought that our knowledge of the future would bring them wealth and power. But we have been feared as well, and that fear has led to oppression and persecution. Eventually, as the civil wars fought among the various Nals grew bloodier, many of the Gildriites fled and the Nals for the mountains in the most remote part of our land, the Dhaalmar. Those who chose to stay in the Nals were forced to hide their ancestry and their ability to see the future or risk imprisonment and execution.

"Gwilym says that when he dreamed of you he saw more than just a sorcerer in need of help. He saw a man with the power to change Lon-Ser forever, a man who could end the persecution of the Gildriites."

"But I'm just one man," Orris protested. "I'm not even sure I can keep my own land from being attacked again. How am I supposed to change Lon-Ser?"

Melyor shrugged. "I do not know," she said quietly. "But maybe if you do what you came here to do the rest will take care of itself."

Orris gazed at her, weighing what she had said. After several moments he began to nod. "Maybe." He inclined his head slightly toward Gwilym. "Ask him where he got his stone."

"That I can tell you myself," Melyor replied, smiling again. "Legend tells us that when Gildri and his followers came to Lon-Ser from Tobyn-Ser they bore staffs and birds and cloaks like yours. The birds, of course, died, and the cloaks did not survive the centuries. But several of the staffs, complete with their stones, remain. They are kept by the Bearers who lead the Gildriite communities of the Dhaalmar."

"Has his stone always been that color?"

Melyor asked Gwilym, who shook his head and said something in response. "He says that when the stone belonged to his father it was green. When he took it, it turned to brown."

"So he's bound to the stone!" Orris said, his voice barely more than a whisper.

The woman shook her head. "I do not understand."

"As a mage, I'm linked to my ceryll as much as I am to my bird," Orris told her. "The ceryll allows me to focus my power, to control it. It's tuned to me; no one else can use it in that way." She stared back at him blankly and he rubbed a hand across his brow. "When I found my stone it was clear, like glass. Only when I held it in my hand did it turn amber. If another mage had picked it up, it would have turned a different color. As long as I live this stone will be amber and it will be tuned to my power."

Melyor narrowed her eyes. "Do you mean that Bearers have magic?"

"Not exactly. But there's obviously some residue of Gildri's power running through Gwilym's blood. Otherwise his stone wouldn't glow like that." He gazed at her in silence for a moment, and he could tell from the look on her flawless features that she was thinking the same thing he was. "That power is in your blood, too," he finally said.

She nodded. "I know."

Gwilym asked her a question and they spoke in Lonmir for some time.

"He wanted to know what we were saying," she explained. "In the Dhaalmar they say that he is joined with his stone, and they are aware that the joining is a legacy from Gildri and the others."

Orris looked at Gwilym and nodded. The bald man gazed back at him intently, but did not move.

"He also has a question for you," Melyor went on. "He wants to know what place Gildri has in your land's history."

The mage exhaled slowly through his teeth. He had been dreading this question since he first realized that Gwilym's people were tied to Gildri. "It's not an easy tale," he warned. "He might not like what I have to say."

Melyor conveyed this to Gwilym who responded tersely in a solemn voice. "He does not care. He wants to know."

"Very well," the mage said. And sitting beneath a night sky filled with stars that were both familiar and different from his own, Orris told his companions the story of Amarid and Theron: of how they met as little more than boys who had been exiled from their respective homes because of the strange, dark magic they had discovered, and of how the friendship they forged out of shared loneliness and the double-edged gift they had been given by the gods deepened over the years. He spoke of how, as Amarid and Theron wandered the land, they began to meet others who had bound to hawks, and of how the two young friends brought these other mages together and founded the Order. And Orris told Melyor and the Bearer of the deterioration of Amarid and Theron's friendship, which began with Amarid's marriage to Dacia and grew worse with their repeated clashes over the future of the Order and the role it should play in the governance of Tobyn-Ser. Finally, Orris told them of Theron's crime against a rival suitor, his trial, and the curse he cast in defiance of the Order's judgement that he should die for what he had done.

Orris related his tale a few sentences at a time, stopping frequently to allow Melyor to translate for Gwilym. And the alternating sound of their voices lent a strange, compelling cadence to the ancient story that seemed to still the air around them, as if the mountains themselves were listening.

"In the aftermath of Theron's trial and death," the mage concluded, as the glowing red coals of the fire sent a thin trail of smoke into the night sky, "several of his followers, led by Gildri, renounced their membership in the Order and left the Gathering. To be honest, Tobyn-Ser's history loses track of them after that. I only learned what became of them when I met the Bearer."

Melyor conveyed this to Gwilym, and then fell silent. The Bearer sat very still, staring into what was left of the fire and seeming to absorb all that he had heard. It was a long time before he finally spoke, and when he did, it was in a voice low and forlorn. His dark eyes never left the glowing embers.

Melyor regarded the Bearer with a pained expression as he spoke, and when he was done she reached out and squeezed his arm.

"What did he say?" Orris asked her.

"That he had often wondered if Gildri and his followers had discovered the Magic of the Hawk and had been banished from your land because of that. He had never thought of them as exiles from the other sorcerers."

Orris shook his head. "Don't think of him that way," he told the Bearer.

"He left Tobyn-Ser as a matter of conscience. It would have been far easier for him to stay, but his integrity wouldn't allow it. And," the mage added, smiling kindly, "judging from the Gildriites I've met, I'd say that he left an admirable legacy to his adopted land."

Melyor translated and Gwilym looked up at the mage. They held each other's gaze for several moments, and Orris saw both gratitude and disappointment in the bald man's expression. Then the Bearer rose and walked off into the night.

"Thank you," Melyor said quietly.

"What for?" Orris asked.

She looked at the fire. "For what you just said to him. In time I think it will help him. I think it will help me as well."

"I hope you're right," the mage answered.

She smiled suddenly, and even in the flickering light of the fire he could see that she was blushing. "Gwilym was not the only one to have a vision of you," she said.

"What do you mean?"

Her smile deepened. "I did as well. I saw us fighting together. I saw our battle with Blade."

He stared at her, not bothering to mask his surprise. "When did you see this?"

She looked away, her face reddening again. "Some time ago."

He heard the evasion in her reply and he considered pressing the matter. But then he thought better of it. They had finally reached an understanding of sorts and he had no desire to resume their bickering. In the end he merely nodded.

They sat without speaking for some time, listening to the coals settle. Their eyes never met, but Orris found that he was acutely conscious of her every move and sound. An owl called from farther up the mountain, and Anizir, perched on the ground beside Orris, stared avidly into the darkness.

"Do you know what she thinks about?" Melyor asked, indicating Orris's falcon with a nod of her head.

"Yes, although it's less a matter of what she thinks than how."

"I do not understand."

"Hawks are very intelligent—more so than many people I know—but their minds don't work the same way ours do. We form our thoughts with language; they convey ideas through images and sensations."

"So when she heard that bird call a moment ago, what did she think?"

Orris smiled. "Many things. There was an image of an owl, one that lives in Tobyn-Ser and has a similar call. Then she remembered a fight she had once had with such a bird before our binding. And then she remembered seeing a similar owl at the Gatherings of our Order."

"How long did it take her to tell you those things?"

"A second or two."

Melyor's eyes widened. "All of that in a second or two?"

The mage nodded.

"But how do you understand it all?" she asked.

"After a while it becomes a part of how you think, a part of your consciousness," he explained. "I was unbound once for several months—"

"Unbound?"

"After my first hawk died and before I bound to Anizir I was without a familiar. That's what it means to be unbound."

Melyor nodded.

"During that time," Orris went on, "I found it harder to keep my own thoughts clear than I had when I was bound. You just get used to having two sets of thoughts in your head. To me it's as natural as breathing."

"And does she perceive your thoughts as well?"

"Yes."

Melyor looked at him skeptically.

The mage grinned. "You don't believe me."

"You yourself said that birds do not use language as we do. I have been trying to live with two different languages for the past several days and it is very hard to translate everything in one's mind. It would be harder still to do what you suggest she does."

"You may be right," Orris countered. "But she does it nonetheless. She has shown me images of my own memories. She responds to my thoughts as if they were words: I can instruct her to do things, I can calm her when she's upset."

"But how is that possible?" Melyor persisted.

"I don't know," he conceded. "Maybe it's because our thoughts begin as emotions or images or desires that we then translate into language." He shrugged. "I don't know," he repeated. "But my thoughts are as much a part of her awareness as hers are of mine. I'm certain of that."

Melyor opened her mouth to say more, but at that moment Gwilym returned to the fire and spoke to her briefly, his voice taut though quiet. When he finished, she asked him several questions, her voice suddenly tense as well.

"What is it?' Orris demanded.

Melyor and the Bearer talked for several moments more before the woman faced Orris again. Her features looked pale in the dim light cast by the dying fire and the two glowing crystals. "Gwilym thinks someone might be following us. He walked to an overlook not far from here and thought he saw light from a small campfire at the base of the mountain."

"It could be anyone though, right?"

"Not really," Melyor told him. "Very few people venture out of the Nal. I asked the Bearer if it might be the Gildriites who helped us escape, but he says the Gildriites who met him when he first came to Bragor-Nal made no fires for fear of being discovered by SovSec. And there would not be any miners this far to the east." She paused, staring mournfully at her bare feet. "The Bearer thinks we should leave here now and get as far from them as we can."

"What do you think?" Orris asked.

She chewed her lip for a few seconds. "I am tired of running," she said. "We should fight them here. We have the advantage. They are below us."

"Did you tell the Bearer that?"

"Yes."

"And what did he say?"

"He does not want to fight. He says that we cannot know how many of them there are."

"He's right," Orris told her, trying to keep his tone mild. "Your weapon and my magic might not be enough."

Orris could see the uncertainty in her eyes and once more it struck him how difficult all this must have been for her. Just a few days ago she had been a Nal-Lord. And now she was being pursued through the mountains like an animal. He wanted to offer her some comfort, but he wasn't sure how. Despite the progress they had made, their relationship remained awkward.

"It is too dark," she said at last. "We cannot travel this path at night. We have no pocket lights."

With no effort at all, Orris summoned a brilliant glow from his amber stone, although he held the ceryll close to his body so that their pursuers would not see it. "That's not a problem," he said, grinning roguishly. "As long as I keep the stone close to the ground I should be able to light our way without attracting their attention."

Gwilym grinned as well, and nodded vigorously at what Orris had done with his stone.

Melyor looked from one of them to the other, her expression bleak. "Fine," she finally said, grimly reaching for her boots and hose. "We will go." She started to pull on the torn, bloody hose but then thought better of it. Instead she threw them on the fire and slipped the boots onto her bare feet. "You can heal me again, right?" she asked Orris, holding out a hand to him so that he could pull her up.

"As many times as you need," he answered.

The three travelers hastily gathered the few items they had taken out of Gwilym's carry sack, and in a few moments they were on their way again. They walked in a tight cluster, with Gwilym in front, holding his glowing brown stone out before him, and Orris just behind, carrying his staff upside down so that the bright ceryll would light their path.

They walked through much of the night, stopping just before dawn to rest for a short while, before continuing for several more hours. They reached the top of the ridge at midday, halting briefly so that Orris could heal Melyor's feet again, and the three of them could eat a light meal. Then they continued on, following the ridge for a few miles before cutting down through a small valley to begin their assault on the next line of mountains. They stopped for the day just before dusk, exhausted and hungry, but satisfied that they had put some distance between themselves and whomever might have been following them. After eating just enough to curb their hunger, Melyor and the Bearer lay down to sleep, while Orris and Anizir kept watch. After a few hours, the mage woke Gwilym, as they had agreed earlier, and Orris took his turn sleeping.

So it went for the next several days. They rose early, pushed themselves as hard as they could for as long as they could, and slept in shifts. Orris had to tend to Melyor's blisters a number of times for the first few days, until her skin began to callus, but otherwise they encountered few problems along the way. The travelers saw no further sign that they were being pursued, but they acted on the assumption that they were. Even Orris, who had been reluctant to believe it at first, came to accept that someone had followed them out of the Nal. It made sense really. According to Melyor, Cedrych had staked his reputation, his ambitions, and most of his resources on his effort to conquer Tobyn-Ser. He wasn't about to let Orris, Gwilym, and Melyor ruin his plans, even if they had managed to slip out of Bragor-Nal.

Late in the afternoon of the eighth day they spotted Oerella-Nal from a stony crag that also offered them a view of the dry foothills they still needed to cross. At the sight of the giant city, Orris felt his heart clench itself like a fist. Like Bragor-Nal, Oerella-Nal was blanketed by an ugly brown vapor, and its buildings stretched as far as Orris could see, huge and numbingly monotonous. Staring at the Nal, Anizir let out a soft cry, just as she had so many times during their journey through Bragor-Nal. Orris tried to soothe her by stroking her feathers and speaking to her in a gentle voice, but he shared her apprehension.

Gwilym pointed down into the foothills and said something to Melyor.

"He thinks we can follow that stream down the slope and through a low pass to the Nal," she told Orris, pushing her amber hair back from her brow. "He says there is a barren plain between the foothills and the Nal wall. We must cross it at night."

Orris gave a curt nod. "Fine," he said, his voice tight. "Let's just go."

Melyor looked at him with concern. "Are you well?"

"Yes, I'm fine," the mage said impatiently.

"I am sorry for asking!" she snapped, turning away and starting back toward the mountain path.

Orris closed his eyes and took a breath. "I'm sorry," he called, stopping her. "I just don't like being in the Nals very much. I'm not looking forward to this."

Melyor regarded him briefly, her mouth set in a thin line. "I know what you mean," she said levelly. "I feel the same way about the mountains." With that, she turned again and made her way to the trail.

The mage sighed heavily and glanced at Gwilym, who offered a sympathetic smile.

"It was my fault," Orris said.

Gwilym frowned in confusion.

Orris shook his head. "Never mind." He indicated with a gesture that they should go, and he and the Bearer followed Melyor back to the trail.

They made camp that night in the foothills, conscious of the fact that whoever was following them might be looking down on them now from the higher reaches of the mountains. They did not build a fire, and Orris and Gwilym were careful to keep their stones covered at all times. They ate a scant meal, nearly finishing the rations that Gwilym carried in his pack, and then took turns sleeping.

They rose at first light, broke camp without eating, and resumed their journey through the foothills. The path was more level here than in the mountains, and for the most part it carried them downward toward the plain Gwilym had mentioned. But the trail was dry and dusty and littered with loose rocks, making the footing treacherous and forcing them to go slower than Orris would have liked.

"We're kicking up a lot of dust," Orris said late in the morning, not bothering to keep the concern from his voice. "It's going to make us easy to spot from the mountains."

"Is there anything we can do about it?" Melyor asked from several feet behind him.

The mage glanced around him. Even off the trail, among the junipers and scrub pines, the ground was dry. They'd face the same problem if they strayed from the trail, and they risked slowing their progress even more.

"I don't think so," he answered at last.

"Then stop worrying about it."

He glanced back over his shoulder and nearly laughed aloud at the smirk of her face. He faced forward again, shaking his head.

"What?" she demanded.

"Nothing," he called back to her. "Nothing at all."

"Tell me!" she insisted, hurrying forward to catch up with him.

"You're funny," he said as she fell in beside him.

She looked at him sidelong, the smirk returning. "What do you mean by that?"

"Just that you're funny. Can't a person say something and just mean what he says?"

"Not in the Nal," she said. "Besides I understand your language well enough to know that what you said can mean different things. Were you saying that I am amusing or strange?"

"Do I have to choose?"

She looked away, although she couldn't quite hide the smile that touched her lips. "Now you are being funny."

"I just meant," Orris began, "that it's not always easy to know when you're really angry and when you're just playing."

"That is because I do not want it to be easy," Melyor told him. "I am a Nal-Lord and I am good at it." She gave a small laugh. "At least I was," she corrected. "And one does not do as well as I did by letting other people know what is on one's mind all the time. One cannot afford to be honest in the Nal. It is too dangerous a place."

"There must be someone there who you can be honest with. Don't you have any family?"

Melyor shook her head. "My mother was killed when I was a child, by an explosion that was intended to kill my father. And my father was assassinated when I was eleven. I have no brothers or sisters. I have an aunt who let me live with her after my father died but I left her home when I was fifteen. I have not spoken to her since."

Orris looked at her intently. She said it all so impassively, and yet it sounded like such a hard way to grow up. "What about friends?" he asked.

"I have one friend: Jibb, who you met." She grinned. "The one who tried to kill you."

"And that's all?"

Melyor looked surprised. "I am very fortunate to have him. He is the one person who has the most to gain from my death, and yet every day I trust him with my life. Not many people in my position are so lucky."

"You live in a strange land," Orris said quietly, as he tried to make sense of what she had told him. "I'm not sure that I could survive there very long."

She shrugged. "Actually I think you would do well there."

This time it was Orris's turn to be surprised. "You do?"

"Yes. You handled Cedrych. You revealed little about what you know of his plans, and yet you learned a good deal about him. Few people take so much from their encounters with him while giving so little."

He considered this. "Thank you," he said at last. "As a member of my Order I often find myself negotiating with other mages on contentious issues. One can't help but learn something of human nature in such a setting. I suppose over the years I've become somewhat adept at dealing with those I don't fully trust."

They walked in silence for some time, and once more Orris found that even without looking at her, he was aware of Melyor's every gesture and glance.

"So what about you?" she asked abruptly, squinting up at the sky for a moment as if judging the position of the sun.

"What about me?"

"Do you have a family? A wife? Children?"

He shook his head. "No. I'm like you in that way. I was an only child. My father became ill and died when I was just a baby and my mother died several years ago, also after getting sick."

"No wife?"

"No."

"Friends?"

"A few," he said, thinking of Jaryd, Alayna, Trahn, and, oddly, Baden as well.

"So," she ventured, "perhaps our lands are not so different after all."

"No," Orris replied. "Our lands are very different. It's you and I who are similar."

The three travelers rested briefly early in the afternoon, finishing the rest of their food before returning to the trail. They reached the bottom of the foothills a few hours later, stopping at the fringe of a vast, barren plain that was littered with low clumps of tangled dry grasses and pockets of wiry bushes. The sun hung low in the western sky, huge and orange, though partially obscured by the brown haze, and the Nal loomed before them, towering above a large metal wall that surrounded it. As Gwilym had warned, the last leg of their journey would require that they travel with no cover at all. They would have to wait until nightfall.

Seeing Oerella-Nal from this distance, rather than from the mountains, Orris realized that it was less like Bragor-Nal than he had thought initially. Yes, the air was foul, but not as foul. He had never seen sunlight penetrate the haze that hung over Bragor-Nal, but here light from the setting sun gleamed off the shining steel and glass of the buildings, giving the enormous city a lustrous quality that Bragor-Nal lacked. Like Bragor-Nal, this city had an elevated roadway, but this one shone in the sunshine, as white as bone. Above the roadway, Orris saw an object moving swiftly across the sky. It resembled Melyor's carrier, except that it had arms, like a person, and at the ends, where the hands should have been, there were blades spinning so rapidly that they appeared blurred. The object was red and it reflected the sunlight like a polished mirror. Like everything else Orris saw, it looked clean and well-maintained. Perhaps this Nal would be better than Bragor-Nal.

If Orris was at all relieved by what he saw, however, Anizir was not. Once more she let out a forlorn cry, and she sent Orris an image of their binding place near the rocky shores of the Lower Horn, just as she had several times over the past few days as she sensed their time in the mountains coming to an end.

Be easy, he sent. *This is why we came. We have to do this.*

The mage heard Gwilym speak in a quiet voice to Melyor and a moment later the woman placed a gentle hand on Orris's shoulder.

"The Bearer says not to worry," she said. "This place is not as bad as Bragor-Nal. And he remembers seeing birds here. Grey ones like she ate in Bragor-Nal."

"Thank you," Orris answered. And then looking at Gwilym, he thanked the bald man in Lonmir, drawing smiles from both of his companions.

They had nothing left to eat, so the travelers merely sat among the last low trees of the foothills, concealing themselves from whoever might have been watching the plain, and waiting for dusk. They said little, and, despite Gwilym's reassurances about Oerella-Nal, Orris sensed that all three of them were growing anxious. If they were unable to enlist the aid of Oerella-Nal's Sovereign, there would be little else left for them to try. Even if they could return to Bragor-Nal in safety, they would have little hope of stopping Cedrych without some backing from the Council of Sovereigns. In all likelihood, Orris was forced to conclude, this was his last chance to prevent a new assault on Tobyn-Ser. And though he didn't know what it would take to end the oppression of Gwilym's people or restore some semblance of normality to Melyor's life, he believed that the Bearer and the Nal-Lord had come to see his success as essential to their own.

It seemed to take a long time, but at last the sun dipped below the western horizon and stars began to appear through the haze. Gwilym and Orris covered their stones, and the three travelers left the shelter of the foothills and started across the plain. They could do nothing to camouflage themselves, so they did all they could to cross the open space as quickly as possible.

According to Melyor, Gwilym could not recall precisely where he and his guide had slipped through the wall surrounding the Nal, but he did believe that he could get them close enough to make finding the precise spot fairly easy. Striding quickly across the dry soil, however, Orris wondered if Gwilym was deluding himself. The wall surrounding Oerella-Nal, while not nearly as imposing as the one surrounding Bragor-Nal, appeared to have no markings on it at all. One section of it looked exactly like another.

It took less than an hour to reach the wall. Though Orris and the Bearer kept their stones hidden, the residual glow of the Nal reflecting off the haze that hung overhead provided them with ample light. As they approached it Gwilym slowed and glanced from side to side with apparent uncertainty. Orris cast a look Melyor's way and she shrugged but said nothing. After a moment, Gwilym started making his way slowly to the left, closely examining the wall as he went. Orris followed reluctantly, his doubts growing with each passing minute. But much to his surprise, they soon came to section of wall that had been broken loose in one corner. From the looks of the metal, it had been bent back and then forced back into place countless times.

Gwilym was beaming, and he spoke to Melyor with so much enthusiasm that the Nal-Lord actually had to raise a finger to her lips indicating that he should lower his voice.

"He says this is the place," she told Orris, somewhat needlessly.

"Give him my thanks," Orris answered.

Melyor looked around cautiously. "I will, later," she said. "But we should get into the Nal and find the Network first. I do not like being out in the open like this."

Orris pulled back the section of wall as far as it would go and ushered his companions through. Then, with a reassuring thought for Anizir, he entered Oerella-Nal.

Straightening on the other side of the wall, Orris found himself on a dirty, wide road that could easily have been in Bragor-Nal. The Upper curved overhead, the roar from the carriers echoing off nearby buildings. Led by Gwilym, the three travelers crossed the road to a small door, much like those that led to the underground tunnels in the other city. Without hesitating, Gwilym opened the door and hurried down the stairs to the dark corridors. They were not as rank as the tunnels of Bragor-Nal, but they felt just as confining, and Anizir shifted on his shoulder, so that she could nuzzle him for comfort.

Gwilym uncovered his stone, and Orris did the same. The corridor was empty.

Gwilym said something, his concern manifest on his round face.

"He says this is where he met the guide who led him to the mountains," Melyor told Orris. "He knows that the Network uses this corridor, but he does not know how often."

"Then perhaps we should wait here," Orris suggested.

"I am not certain how wise that would be," the Nal-Lord replied, not bothering to translate for the Bearer. "We cannot know who else might use this corridor. Sovereign Shivohn has a security force, too. They may not be as dangerous as SovSec, but we would still be better off avoiding them."

"Why?" Orris demanded. "We came here to see Shivohn. Who better to take us to her than her own security people?"

Melyor regarded him for a moment. "An interesting point," she finally conceded. She spoke to Gwilym, all the while keeping her eyes on Orris. When she finished, Gwilym nodded, as if considering what she had said. At length, he gave a brief reply.

Melyor gave a wry smile. "He agrees with you."

"And that bothers you?" Orris asked.

She shrugged. "No. But it does not surprise me either."

As it turned out, they did not have to wait for very long. They had only been in the corridor for a few minutes when they heard the voices of several men and saw beams of light hitting the corridor wall opposite a tunnel. Thinking of the two brothers they had met just before leaving Bragor-Nal, Orris assumed that the approaching men were Gildriites.

But when six uniformed men turned the corner and shined their lights on the travelers he realized his mistake. The men immediately drew their hand weapons and one of them shouted at Orris and his companions. Melyor said something back to them, but the guard merely repeated himself, the tone of his voice even more strident this time. Melyor nodded, removed her weapon from the strap on her thigh, and dropped it to the stone floor.

Once more the guard barked a command at them. Reluctantly, his hands trembling slightly, Gwilym placed his staff on the floor, and at the same time Melyor placed a hand on Orris's arm.

"They want you to put down your stone," she said quietly, although with an edge to her voice. "They are arresting us."

24

In seeking to defeat the intentions of our enemies in Lon-Ser, we would, in my opinion, be served best by following their example. In other words, just as they sought to undermine the Order and then exploit the mistrust sown among our land's people, we should seek ways to exploit weaknesses endemic to Lon-Ser's social structure, economy, or system of government. The problem of course, as I have noted elsewhere, is that our knowledge of these things is so terribly limited. We do not even know for certain who is responsible for sending the outlanders to Tobyn-Ser. Still, based on what I have learned thus far from Baram, I believe our best hope for influencing events within Lon-Ser will be tied to our ability to exploit one or more of the following: the violent instability of the Nal authority structure, the continued deterioration of liv-

ing conditions within the Nals, or the rivalries and suspicions that divide one Nal from another.

—From Section Nine of "The Report of Owl-Master Baden on his Interrogation of the Outlander Baram," Submitted to the 1,014th Gathering of the Order of Mages and Masters. Spring, Gods' Year 4625.

In all her years as a break-law and Nal-Lord in Bragor-Nal, Melyor had never been in prison, not even on an overnight carousal charge, not even during her time as an independent, when break-laws were most apt to be taken in by the security goons. But she knew plenty of people who had, men and women. And she knew from all that she had heard, that Bragor-Nal's prisons were wretched, foul places where male prisoners were as likely to die from disease as from the beatings they regularly endured at the hands of the guards, and where women prisoners were routinely raped. Some were worse than others of course, but none was good.

Certainly none was like the prison to which she had been taken by Oerella-Nal's security force. Examining the thick steel bars and heavy stone walls, she had no illusions as to her ability to escape; she would be here as long as they chose to keep her. But she had never imagined that a jail could be so clean and well-lit. The bars were polished, the stones immaculate. The solid steel pallet on which she was lying was hard and cold, but clean. The guard who brought her meal had not touched her, though he had looked her up and down hungrily. Even the meal itself, while relatively tasteless, had been ample and balanced. For a prison, it was remarkably comfortable. For a prison.

Gwilym and Orris, of course, had been taken to the men's side, which was fine with Melyor. She didn't really want to have anything to do with the two of them right now. If it weren't for them, they'd all still be free, making their way to Shivohn's palace through the tunnels beneath Oerella-Nal.

"I should never have listened to them," she mumbled under her breath. It took her a few moments to realize that she had spoken in the sorcerer's language.

It was almost morning. She could see the first silver-grey light of dawn seeping through the barred window at the top of her cell. She had been lying down for five or six hours, but she had been too agitated to sleep. She knew that Blade, if he was still following them, would be unable to reach them in the prison, but if he learned that they had been arrested it would make finding them very easy. And if they were released there was no guarantee that she would get her thrower or dagger back or that the Bearer and Orris would be given their staffs. In which case they would be easy prey for the assassins.

Once more, as they had for the past several days, thoughts of Blade and his men, carried with them fears for Jibb's safety. She knew Cedrych; she knew how he did things. If he had sent the assassins after her—and who else would have done such a thing?—he would have gone after Jibb as well. Having her killed and allowing the break-law to live carried too many risks. Was Jibb dead? she wondered, staring up at the small window. Had he been driven from the Fourth? She shook her head. She could do nothing for him, of course. She wasn't even sure that she could help herself or her companions. But that was what she should have been worrying about. She forced an image of Jibb's face from her mind and tried to concentrate instead on her own situation.

She needed to find some way to convince the guards here that she and her companions needed to see Shivohn, or at least one of the Sovereign's underlings—Legates, they were called in Oerella-Nal. But she hadn't even seen a guard for most of the night, not since the one heavyset man had brought her the meal. And that had been only moments after the security men first put her in the cell. She had heard steel doors opening and closing now and then, and she had heard the sobbing of one woman—a prisoner, Melyor guessed—and the retching of another. But those sounds had come from some distance. As far as she could tell, she was alone in this sector of the jail.

Melyor lay on the pallet for another hour or two watching the day brighten outside the cell's lone window. Then she heard the opening of a nearby steel door and the approach of two sets of footsteps.

Breakfast, she thought, sitting up.

As it turned out they were not prison guards, but rather members of Shivohn's security force in their neat crimson uniforms, and they bore no food.

"We need you," one of them said, the words hard to understand at first because of the man's Oerellan accent.

Melyor regarded him warily. "What for?"

"We can't understand one of your friends; the one with the vicious bird."

Melyor had been looking from one of the men to the other, paying little attention to their appearances. In truth, they both looked like the brawny, clean-cut guards she had seen so often at Cedrych's headquarters. But when the one man mentioned Orris's falcon she realized that he had an ugly, fresh gash on his temple. She fought an urge to laugh.

"He doesn't seem to understand us either," the security man continued, "and we want him to control his bird or we'll have to kill it."

Melyor stood. "You can't do that."

The second man narrowed his eyes. "Why not?"

"Because he's a sorcerer from Tobyn-Ser," she told them. "And," she went on, knowing that she was taking a huge risk, "because he's here as a guest of Sovereign Shivohn. We all are."

They looked at her skeptically. "If you're guests of the Sovereign, what were you doing hiding in the tunnels?" the second man demanded.

"We slipped out of Bragor-Nal and crossed the mountains to get here, but we think we were followed by assassins. We were hiding from them."

"I don't believe you," the first one said.

Melyor swallowed. She wouldn't have believed it either, but she knew a bit about dealing with men in their position. "I don't blame you," she said candidly. "But can you afford to be wrong about this?"

The security men looked at each other. "Maybe we should discuss this with the Legate," the first one said quietly.

"Yes, do," Melyor said. "But in the meantime let me see my friends. I can calm the sorcerer down for you." She still wanted nothing to do with them, but she also realized that if she wanted to win their release, she would need Orris's help.

The two men shared another look, but said nothing. She had put some doubt in their minds, perhaps some fear too, if she was lucky. "I'm not sure," one of them said.

"We'll still be in your jail," she coaxed. "You have them in adjacent cells, right?" The first man nodded. "So put me in the next one over."

"But they're on the men's side."

Melyor gave an exasperated sigh. "They're in prison cells! We all will be!" She grinned suggestively. "I'm good, but I'm not that good."

The second man colored all the way to the tops of his ears, but the first one just stared at her. "You think you can control the sorcerer?" he asked.

"I can quiet him down," she answered, growing serious. "I don't think anyone can control him." She thought about saying more but then stopped herself. It would be better to give them too little information than too much. At some point, she reasoned, it might help to have the guards and security men afraid of Orris's magic.

For a third time the security men looked at each other, this time for several moments. Finally the first man shrugged slightly. "It's worth a try," he said. "I don't want to tangle with that crazy bird again."

The second man nodded his agreement. They pressed a button on the wall outside her cell and a section of the steel bars slid open, allowing Melyor to step out into the corridor.

"This way," the first man instructed, gesturing with a calloused hand. They led her through several hallways and doors until they had crossed over into the men's side of the prison. The cells here were only slightly less clean than those on the women's side, but they were far more crowded. Almost all of them were full, and several had two or even three men in them.

As Melyor walked past the prisoners began to whistle and whoop at her. Many of them shouted obscenities. Melyor had endured much of it before, but not in many years; not since she had become a Nal-Lord. In recent years she had killed men for saying such things to her. Instinctively she reached a hand down to her thigh, but of course her thrower was gone, as was the blade that she usually carried in her boot, its handle resting against her calf. She felt naked without them.

"This might not have been such a good idea," the second guard whispered as the reaction to Melyor grew increasingly raucous.

"Shut up and keep walking," the first guard shot back. "Once we get to the back sector everything will be fine."

They passed a cluster of prison guards who smirked at the disquiet manifest on the faces of the security men, but did nothing to help quiet the prisoners.

A few minutes later—though it seemed longer—the two guards led Melyor through a large steel door, and, as the first man had predicted, the whistles and shouts suddenly ceased. This section of the men's prison was just like the others Melyor had seen, except that it was almost entirely empty, as the women's side had been. Only the last two cells were occupied, and they held her friends.

Notwithstanding her anger at Orris and Gwilym for allowing the security force to arrest them, Melyor found that she was relieved to see them.

"I hear you have been causing problems for our hosts," she said to the sorcerer in Tobynmir.

Orris grinned at her, though there was a fierce look in his dark eyes. "I've been doing my best. Is that why you're here? To tame me?"

"Something like that, yes." She turned to Gwilym. He looked somewhat paler than usual, but otherwise he appeared to be holding up well. "Hello, Bearer," she said in her own language. "Are you all right?"

He nodded. "I'm fine, thank you. But I was afraid for the sorcerer; I thought they were going to hurt him." He managed a smile. "I'm glad to see you, Melyor. I think Orris is, too."

She returned his smile. "Thanks. I'm glad to see you as well."

The first security man opened the door to an adjacent cell and motioned Melyor inside. "Keep them in line," he warned sternly, closing the door again. "We need to speak with our Legate."

Melyor nodded and the two guards departed.

"You almost got your bird killed," she told Orris. "Did you know that?"

She was gratified to see the color drain from his handsome face.

"No," he said quietly. "I knew they were angry, but I didn't think they'd kill her."

Melyor pushed her hair back from her face. "It surprises me that they did not. Whoever they answer to must have told them not to harm us."

"Why would they do that?"

"Curiosity, probably," she answered. "I cannot imagine that it is every day that a Bearer, a sorcerer, and a woman from Bragor-Nal show up in their tunnels."

"So what do we do now?"

"We wait," Melyor said, lying down on the pallet in her new cell. "I told them that we are here as guests of the Sovereign. Perhaps that will get someone's attention."

For some time it did not. The three of them spent the entire day and another full night in the prison. Orris, heeding Melyor's warnings, gave the guards no more trouble, but all three of them also refused to answer any of the guards' questions.

"We are guests of the Sovereign," was all Melyor would say, and she repeated the phrase a number of times. But as the hours dragged by she grew increasingly anxious. If her ruse did not work, there was no telling how long they might remain in the jail.

Finally, late the following morning, the two crimson uniformed guards returned with four of their comrades and a tall woman in a long black robe and matching black headpiece. A few wisps of golden hair stood out from beneath the cloth that covered her head, framing a square face that was attractive though severe, with blue eyes and a wide mouth.

She stood without speaking for several moments gazing appraisingly at Melyor and her friends. "I am Legate Wiercia. I've come to take you to the Sovereign."

Melyor stood, scarcely believing what she had heard. "You have?"

The Legate faced her, a disdainful smirk on her lips. "That is what you wanted isn't it?"

"Yes," Melyor answered, trying to recover from her initial surprise, "but I . . ." She trailed off, uncertain as to how much she should say.

The woman's smile deepened, although there was nothing warm or welcoming about the expression in her eyes. "But you didn't expect that we'd honor your request."

Melyor felt her own features harden. "I didn't know what to expect. The treatment we've received thus far has done nothing to give us confidence in the Sovereign or her . . . servants."

"I'd imagine," Wiercia returned without hesitation, "that the treatment you've received thus far is quite a bit better than what I might expect as a guest of *your* Sovereign's . . . servants."

Melyor glared back at the woman from behind the polished steel bars, but she said nothing. What could she say?

"What's happening?" Orris demanded in Tobynmir.

"They are taking us to the Sovereign," Melyor told him.

"Just like that?" Orris asked distrustfully. "Do you trust her?"

It struck her as a fair question, although not one she could answer. "Do you think it would be better for us to stay here?" she replied with more acerbity than she had intended.

"That's not an answer."

"I know," she conceded, hoping that he heard the apology in her tone. "But it is the only one I have."

Orris grinned. "That's all you had to say."

"So this is the sorcerer," Wiercia said, stepping closer to Orris's cell.

"I guess the bird gave it away, huh?" Melyor commented with heavy sarcasm, indicating the falcon on Orris's shoulder with a nod of her head.

The Legate offered no response other than to smile coldly and order the guards to let Melyor and her companions out of their cells. The tall woman then led the guards and the prisoners out of the jail by way of an alternate route that allowed them to avoid the crowded cells of the male prison.

They emerged from the prison in a large underground chamber where two black carriers were waiting for them. One of them was long and sleek, and clearly intended for the legate. The other was large enough for the six guards and Melyor, Gwilym, and Orris. As soon as they were all inside, the carriers started forward, taking them out of the chamber, onto the streets of the Nal, and then up onto Oerella-Nal's gleaming white Upper.

They travelled the Upper for some time, heading north, away from the Medians. From the elevated road, Melyor thought, Oerella-Nal looked much like

her home. The buildings shone more with the light of the sun, but in most respects the quads here appeared similar to those in Bragor-Nal. It was only when
the carrier returned to street level that she began to realize how wrong she had
been. Trees bearing young, bright green leaves lined the streets of every quad.
There was no refuse in sight. The crowded walkways were trimmed with colored tiles of blue, gold, and red. They reached a great lake, its deep blue waters
rippled by the wind and shimmering in the morning sun, and began to make
their way around it. Large shade trees and open expanses of green grasses surrounded the lake, and beyond its shores to the north, stood an immense palace
of unadorned white marble.

Melyor glanced at Orris to see if he was looking, but the sorcerer had his
eyes closed, as if in meditation. She looked at Gwilym next and saw that the
Bearer was also looking out the window, though he did not seem pleased by
what he was seeing. His face was pale again, as it had been in the prison, and his
hands were trembling.

"Is something wrong, Bearer?" she asked with concern.

He shook his head and tried to smile, although he maintained his silence,
and after another moment, Melyor turned her gaze back to the lake.

They were drawing near the palace, which, Melyor guessed, was Shivohn's
residence. It was actually, despite its size, a relatively modest structure, far less
ornate than the Gold Palace that housed Bragor-Nal's Sovereign. Its white
marble facade was plain, save for a simple carved pattern around doors and
large windows. It was surrounded, however, by extensive gardens that contained a greater variety of flowers than Melyor had even known existed.

The carriers pulled into a circular driveway and stopped just in front of the
main door of the palace. Melyor and the others were ordered to get out of
the carrier, and when they did, they were greeted by a large contingent of guards,
all of them wearing the crimson uniforms of Sovereign Shivohn's security force.
A group of six led the prisoners into the palace and made them wait in a huge
foyer with high, carved ceilings and dozens of portraits lining the walls. Melyor guessed that the paintings were of previous Sovereigns, since all of them
wore long robes of red that matched perfectly the color of the security men's
uniforms.

They waited in the foyer for several minutes until finally Legate Wiercia
emerged at the far end of the chamber and approached Melyor and her companions. "The Sovereign will see you," she announced solemnly. She turned
with a swirl of black cloth and motioned for them to follow. "This way."

She led them back the way she had just come, through a set of tall, white
doors into another large chamber. The opposite wall of this new room was almost entirely glass and it afforded a magnificent view of more gardens and, beyond them, the shining skyline of Oerella-Nal. The floors were made of dark
wood with a thin, straight grain, and intricate tapestries, the finest Melyor had
ever seen, hung on the side walls. There were several chairs, sofas, and tables arrayed around the room, and in the middle of the room, on a simple wooden
chair, sat a woman in a crimson robe.

Melyor had been hearing tales of Shivohn, Sovereign of Oerella-Nal, for over a decade. She was said to be a woman of iron will and keen intelligence, a tough negotiator who had little patience for foolishness and little mercy for enemies. And yet she sat before them now, a stout, round-faced woman wearing a mild expression. Her eyes were large and brown and her hair was so blonde it might have been white. She was pretty in a plain sort of way, and she looked like a kindly aunt or maybe someone's grandmother. But she certainly didn't look like the leader of a powerful Nal.

The Sovereign studied her visitors for a few moments, the look in her eyes revealing little. Then she glanced at the Legate and her guards. "You may go, Wiercia," she said in a low, slightly gravelly voice. "And take the guards with you."

The Legate bowed at the waist. "Yes, Sovereign." She motioned the guards out the door and then followed, leaving the three travelers alone with Shivohn.

For some time none of them spoke. Shivohn remained in her chair, looking from one of her guests to the next, her round face still wearing that same serene expression.

"Tell her who we are," Orris finally said in an urgent whisper. "Tell her we've come to her for help."

Shivohn turned her gaze toward Orris for a moment, before looking at Melyor expectantly.

Melyor cleared her throat and made an awkward attempt to mimic Wiercia's bow. "Greetings, Sovereign. You honor us with this audience. My friend wants me—"

"I know what he said," Shivohn interrupted, speaking in Lonmir.

Melyor felt her jaw drop. "You understand their language?" she breathed.

"Yes. I speak it, too. You seem surprised."

Melyor shrugged. "I . . . I guess I am."

"My second husband was an Abboriji merchant," the Sovereign explained, idly tracing a stubby finger along the arm of her chair. "He taught me Tobynmir as well as Abboriji. Besides," she went on, her eyes suddenly boring into Melyor's, "I'm a Sovereign; I should have such knowledge. It strikes me as much more unusual that a Bragory Nal-Lord should speak Tobynmir. Don't you agree, Melyor? Perhaps you can explain to me how you learned it."

Melyor opened her mouth to speak, but nothing came out. Her lips were dry and her heart was racing. How could she possibly answer? It was astonishing how swiftly the Sovereign had put her on the defensive. Shivohn still hadn't moved from her chair.

The Sovereign smiled coldly. "Those matters can wait," she told Melyor. She turned to face Orris. "Your bird is beautiful," she told him in flawless Tobynmir. "What's her name?"

"Thank you, Sovereign," he answered matter-of-factly. If the sorcerer was surprised by Shivohn's ability to communicate with him he showed no sign of it. "Her name is Anizir."

"And yours?"

"I am Hawk-Mage Orris."

The Sovereign looked him up and down for a moment, much the way a street fighter might scrutinize an opponent before drawing her blade. "Why have you come here, Orris?" she demanded.

The sorcerer smiled thinly. "I think you know."

Shivohn nodded. "Ah, yes. The missive from your Owl-Sage. You did not believe us when we told you that we knew nothing of the events she described?"

"No," he said bluntly. "These men used weapons that our land had never seen before. They carried mechanical birds that no artisans in Tobyn-Ser could possibly have made. Where else could they have come from but Lon-Ser?"

"I don't know," the Sovereign replied with equal candor. "But that is not proof that they came from here."

"We captured one of the outlanders," Orris went on. "He was from Lon-Ser. He told us a great deal about your land. I brought him with me, but he escaped once we entered Bragor-Nal."

"*What?*" Melyor broke in. "You told me nothing of this!"

Orris grinned at her maddeningly, but then he faced the Sovereign again without saying a word.

"The Owl-Sage's note mentioned only that all but one of the invaders had been killed," Shivohn told him, her tone grave. "I did not know that you had a prisoner, and I certainly did not know that he was from Lon-Ser." She paused, but only briefly. "Still, that does not prove that he was sent by anyone from our land. Many of our people fight as mercenaries. Just ask the Potentates of Abborij."

"He was sent by my Overlord," Melyor heard herself say in Lonmir. "A man named Cedrych."

Shivohn looked at her with unconcealed curiosity. "You know this for a fact?" she asked.

"Yes."

"How?" the Sovereign demanded.

Melyor took a long breath. "Their mission failed. I was to lead the next one."

Shivohn's eyes widened. After a moment she began to nod. "Hence your facility with his language."

Melyor said nothing.

"Why are you doing this?" the Sovereign asked her. "Why are you helping the sorcerer?" She indicated Gwilym with a gesture. "I think I understand why the Bearer is here. But why you? Why would Melyor i Lakin give up so much for something that promised her so little?"

"Whatever you think you know about me," Melyor returned evenly, "it's not everything. Maybe you have security files on me, and that's how you know who I am. And maybe every word in those files is true. But that still doesn't mean you know me."

Shivohn appeared to consider this. "You may be right," she finally said, her eyes meeting Melyor's. "But I ask you again: why are you doing this?"

It didn't matter anymore, Melyor decided. With everything else she had done since Orris's arrival in Bragor-Nal, it didn't matter who knew. "I'm a

Gildriite," she said, and she was pleased to see the genuine shock that registered on the Sovereign's features for just a moment before the stout woman managed to mask her emotions again.

"Are you convinced yet, Sovereign?" Orris asked impatiently.

"About the invasions of your land, you mean?" Shivohn replied, shifting easily to Tobynmir.

Orris nodded.

Shivohn chewed on her lip for several moments, the mannerism seeming out of place on someone who was arguably the second most powerful person in all of Lon-Ser. "In light of what you and Melyor have told me," she replied at last, "I don't see that I have much choice. I wish I had known all of this when the Owl-Sage's message arrived."

"Would it have changed your response?" the sorcerer demanded.

Shivohn rose and stepped to the large window looking out over the gardens. "A difficult question," she admitted. "What I believe and what the Council of Sovereigns does are two very different things." She faced the room again. "Had I known these things—had all of us in the Council known—it probably would have changed very little. I might have advocated sending your Owl-Sage a more sympathetic response, but Durell would have opposed me, and Marar would have done whatever Durell wanted."

"Yes," Orris said, looking sidelong at Melyor for a moment. "I've heard about the way your Council works."

"Then you will understand when I tell you that I cannot do anything to help you."

"But you know I'm telling the truth!" Orris insisted. "You can at least try to convince the other Sovereigns."

The Sovereign made a helpless gesture with her hands. "To what end?"

"Cedrych has to be stopped!" Orris told her, his voice rising.

"For all we know, Cedrych was acting on Durell's orders!" Shivohn fired back at him.

"No," Melyor broke in, "he was not. That much I do know. Cedrych has not told him about this at all."

Shivohn hesitated, but only for an instant. "It still doesn't matter," she argued. "Even if Durell didn't know before, he won't allow the Council to do anything to undermine what Cedrych is doing. He has everything to gain from it and very little to lose. Going to the Council with this will accomplish nothing," she concluded. "I'm sorry."

"You could at least try," Orris urged. "You have nothing to lose."

"On the contrary," the Sovereign told him, returning to her chair. "I have a great deal to lose. If Melyor has explained the politics of the Council to you, then you know that Oerella-Nal has to fight for everything it needs. If I expend all my leverage on matters in which I have no chance of success, particularly those that may prove embarrassing to Durell, I leave myself in a poor position to fight for things my people really need. My responsibilities to Oerella-Nal come first."

From another leader such statements might have sounded fatuous and self-serving. But for some reason, Melyor was inclined to take the Sovereign at her word in this instance.

"I'm sorry," Shivohn said again. "Truly. I harbor no ill-will toward you or your people. Actually, I've always been intrigued by the magic you wield. But I have no compelling reason to help you, and many not to. I know that sounds harsh, but it's the truth."

Orris nodded slowly, as if weighing the Sovereign's words. But Melyor could see from the expression in his dark eyes that he was already working on his next gambit.

"What you're telling me," the sorcerer began, "is that our conflict is with Bragor-Nal, not with the Council. Right?"

Shivohn's face brightened. "Yes!" she said. "Yes, precisely! I'm so glad you understand!"

"So in a sense," he went on, "my people and yours share a common enemy."

"Well—"

"If Bragor-Nal succeeds in conquering Tobyn-Ser it would give them a tremendous advantage in their competition with your Nal, wouldn't it? It would give them more resources."

Melyor nodded, seeing the shrewdness of Orris's argument and thinking back to their conversation a few days before, when the sorcerer had admitted to being "somewhat adept" in the art of politics. She realized now that he had been overly modest. "It would do more than that," she added. "It would ease our overcrowding. It would allow us to escape from the air and water we have fouled. In fact, it would allow us to move our people to Tobyn-Ser and use the Nal exclusively for manufacturing goods. I imagine that eventually the filth in our air would seep over the mountains and reach you. Certainly the fouling of our water would affect Stib-Nal."

Shivohn shook her head and smiled sadly. "You're very clever," she told Orris. "Both of you are," she amended, glancing at Melyor.

"There's nothing clever about it," Orris said solemnly. "It's just a matter of logic. By helping me, you deny your rival a victory and the spoils that it would bring. And perhaps you can profit instead."

"What do you mean?" the Sovereign asked, narrowing her eyes.

"I've only seen a small portion of your Nal," he said, "but it seems clear to me that it differs greatly from Bragor-Nal."

"We take great pride in that."

"I think my people would be interested to know that the Nals of Lon-Ser are not all foul and violent. In the past, we've believed that advanced goods bring misery and little else. But with time, we might be convinced otherwise. It's possible that your help in this matter would facilitate the establishment of relations between your people and mine, and perhaps—again, with time—trade as well."

"You think that's possible?" Shivohn asked, not bothering to hide her eagerness.

"I do. It would require patience on your part. My people don't like strangers, and our recent encounter with Lon-Ser hasn't helped. But I do think it could happen eventually."

The Sovereign regarded him for some time. Her initial enthusiasm had subsided, and her features were now as neutral as they had been when Melyor and the others first entered the chamber. After some time though, she smiled and shook her head. "It is an interesting proposition," she said. "And I concede the logic of your point: Bragor-Nal's gain is our loss."

Orris looked at her grimly. "But?"

"But there's still nothing I can do. You admit yourself that your fight is with Bragor-Nal, actually with one Overlord within Bragor-Nal. It's beyond my control. I can't presume to tell Durell how to run his Nal and control his subordinates anymore than I would tolerate him doing the same to me. Legally that can only be done by the Council, and as I've already explained that's not about to happen."

"Don't you think that Marar would be disturbed to learn of what Cedrych's doing?" Melyor asked. "It affects his people, too."

"Marar is a coward and a fool," Shivohn said with contempt. "But he's smart enough to know that it's safer to allow Bragor-Nal to conquer Tobyn-Ser than it is to provoke Durell into conquering Stib-Nal. I'm afraid you'll get no help from him." She shook her head again. "I'm sorry," she said once more.

A strained silence fell over the chamber, to be broken, surprisingly, by the Bearer, who had said nothing since they entered the Sovereign's palace. "Excuse me, Sovereign," he began respectfully. "I've understood little of what the three of you have said, but it seems clear to me that you have, for whatever reason, declined to help us."

The Sovereign nodded. "Yes, Bearer. I'm afraid I have."

"Then why did you invite us here?" Gwilym demanded. "Why have we just wasted your time and ours?"

Shivohn, glared at him, and for a moment Melyor thought that he had angered her. But then she smiled albeit sadly. "I received reports from a trusted Legate that her men had captured three strangers in the tunnels on the edge of the Nal. One was a Bearer; another appeared to be a sorcerer from Tobyn-Ser. And the third was a Bragory woman who bore a striking resemblance to one of Bragor-Nal's most notorious Nal-Lords. How could I not meet with you?" She shrugged. "I know that's not much of an answer, but it is the truth."

"And what are you going to do with us now?" the Bearer asked.

"I don't understand."

"All three of us entered your Nal illegally. Melyor, as you say, is a notorious lord from a Nal that you consider an enemy. She's also a Gildriite, as am I, and Oerella-Nal, while not as bad as its neighbor, has never been very kind to my people. And Orris is an outlander in a land that has traditionally shown little tolerance for strangers. So I ask you again: what are you going to do with us?"

"I'm going to treat you as I would any honored guests of the Matriarchy," the Sovereign answered without hesitation. "You are welcome to remain in Oerella-Nal for as long as you wish. I'll have rooms made up for you here in the palace. And you are free to go anywhere you'd like."

"You should know that assassins may have followed us here," Melyor told her. "An attempt was made on our lives just before we left Bragor-Nal, and we believe that we were pursued over the mountains."

Shivohn nodded. "I had heard something of this from Wiercia. You mentioned it to her guards I believe," she added, raising an eyebrow, "just after you declared yourselves to be guests of the Sovereign."

Melyor felt herself blush. "My apologies, Sovereign. It seemed necessary at the time."

Shivohn allowed herself a smirk as she walked to a small desk in the far corner of the chamber and pressed a button that was mounted on the wall. "I will assign one of my bodyguards to you, along with a security detail. You should be safe with them."

"May we have our weapons back as well? My thrower and blade? Orris's blade, their staffs?"

Shivohn made no reply. There was a knock on a small door by the desk and a young man with dark hair and a lean, muscular build stepped into the room.

"You called, Sovereign?" he asked, bowing to her.

"Yes, Iwan. I'd like you to take care of my guests for me. See to their needs, escort them wherever they choose to go. Take a security detail with you: we have reason to believe that they may have been followed from Bragor-Nal."

"Yes, Sovereign."

Shivohn glanced at Melyor, her expression grim. "And bring their weapons, Iwan. They may need them."

"Very good, Sovereign." An instant later the man was gone.

"Normally I would not allow it, Melyor. Not with your reputation. But under the circumstances I'll accede to you wishes."

Melyor nodded. "I understand, Sovereign. Thank you."

"You should know, however," Shivohn went on sternly, as if she hadn't heard Melyor speak, "that the security men will be there to watch you as well as to protect you."

Melyor grinned. "Security men haven't had much success controlling me in the past, Sovereign. But you needn't worry."

"I hope not," Shivohn said sourly. "I hope not."

25

One question that has troubled me since our confrontation with the out-landers at Phelan Spur, is why their attack came when it did, and why they chose such a subtle tactic. They have the ability to construct weapons of enormous power and the problems that prompted the attacks in the first place have plagued their land for decades....

To some extent the unsettled spirit of Theron addressed this question in his conversations with Hawk-Mage Jaryd and Hawk-Mage Alayna, maintaining that the outlanders knew they could not defeat the Mage-Craft directly and thus sought to undermine the strength of the Order.

Baram, however, offers a different explanation. The three Nals of Lon-Ser fear each other more than they do any foreign enemy. They do not share their knowledge of advanced goods, and indeed they go to great lengths to keep such goods from falling into each others hands. They also struggle to maintain what Baram refers to as "Balance," by which he appears to mean the stability maintained by the near equality of the militaries of Bragor-Nal and Oerella-Nal. An overt attack on our land by any of the Nals would have endangered this "Balance" as well as the secrecy that they value so highly.

—From Section Two of "The Report of Owl-Master Baden on his Interrogation of the Outlander Baram," Submitted to the 1,014th Gathering of the Order of Mages and Masters. Spring, Gods' Year 4625.

He hadn't stopped trembling since their carrier left the Upper and wound its way through the shining streets of Oerella-Nal to the Sovereign's palace. Nothing he had heard in Shivohn's chamber while the Sovereign spoke with Orris and Melyor had reassured him. It wasn't his friends' fault, nor was it the Sovereign's. The three of them had their own concerns, and though Gwilym hoped that Orris and Melyor would find a way to end Cedrych's campaign against Tobyn-Ser, and perhaps even begin the process of redeeming his own people, the Bearer realized now that neither of those things mattered to him any more. All that mattered, he suddenly understood, was his home in the Dhaalmar and the people he loved there. All he wanted was to be back in the mountains, holding Hertha and walking among his people. He had saved Orris's life. That was why he had come, and he had succeeded. It was time to go home.

"No heroics," Hertha had said. "Do whatever it is that you have to do and then come home to me." Wise woman.

These other issues—Cedrych's Initiative, the politics of the Nal, even Melyor's fate—were beyond his control. They had nothing to do with him. Certainly they had nothing to do with the cold, primal fear that had gripped him a short while before. And no resolution of these matters would make the fear go away.

The return of his stone and Orris's, along with Melyor's weapons, did not help either. Nor did Iwan's presence and the contingent of well-armed guards who accompanied them off the palace grounds and back into what the bodyguard called the Lake Quarter, the unique section of Oerella-Nal that surrounded Shivohn's home. Indeed, despite the low, attractive buildings that

Gwilym and his companions found in the Quarter, their return to the Nal only served to heighten the sense of dread that had tightened Gwilym's stomach into a fist and made the blood in his veins feel like melting snow running off the mountain near his settlement. How could it be any other way?

For this tree-lined avenue on which they were strolling, its walkways adorned with colored tiles and crowded with Oerellan men and women, was the place he had envisioned in the dream that came to him in the dry foothills of the Median Range, just after he left Oerella-Nal for Bragor-Nal so many weeks ago. He still remembered the dream with unnerving clarity: the way the giant buildings of the distant quads gleamed in the midday sunlight—just as they did now; the feeling as he drove his staff into the street and the sight of his stone changing from brown to scarlet as he did; and finally, most strangely and frighteningly, the indifference with which he walked away from his staff as it still vibrated with the force of the blow that had sent it into the avenue.

At the time he had tried to dismiss the dream as a disturbing vision and nothing more, but he had known better. Even though his parents had not appeared before him, as they did in all his true Seeings, he had sensed that this dream carried the weight of truth, a perception that had been confirmed for him this morning when he first saw the avenue from the carrier. He wasn't sure what it meant; he still hadn't figured out the meaning of his dream. But the dark foreboding that accompanied his memory of the vision had him shivering as if he had just stepped naked into a chill Dhaalmar wind.

The Bearer heard Orris speak and a moment later Melyor placed a hand on his arm. "Is something wrong, Bearer?" she asked quietly. "Are you ill? Orris is concerned. He says you look pale and you haven't spoken much." She hesitated. "I'm concerned, too," she finally added.

He placed his hand over hers and gave a gentle squeeze. "I'm not ill," he answered, choosing his words carefully. "I'm . . . frightened."

"Of what?"

"This place," he said, indicating the avenue with an open hand. "I've dreamed of it." He saw the color drain from Melyor's face. She's a Gildriite, he reminded himself. She understands the power of dreams.

"What did you see?" she asked, her voice barely more than a whisper.

He smiled thinly. "Nothing that made any sense," he told her. "I can't even say if it was a true Seeing."

"But we're here," she said, completing his thought, "and you recognize this place."

After a moment he nodded.

She turned and spoke to Orris. Gwilym guessed that Melyor was explaining all this to him. When she finished, Orris looked over at the Bearer, his expression grave and the look in his dark eyes thoughtful. Apparently the sorcerer knew something about visions as well. Orris said something in a low voice and Melyor nodded as if in agreement.

"He says if you want to go back to the palace, it's fine with him," the Nal-Lord translated. "It's all right with me also."

Gwilym let out a slow breath. "No. I think you both know that won't work. If the gods have determined that my fate rests here, returning to the palace will only delay the inevitable. We Gildriites can't run away from the Sight or what it shows us."

Melyor conveyed this to Orris, who nodded and smiled grimly as he said something back to her.

"He says that being a Gildriite is much like being a sorcerer." Melyor looked at Iwan, who had been waiting patiently as the three of them spoke. "We have reason to believe that we may be in some danger here," Melyor told the courtier. "We'd appreciate it if you and your guards would be especially watchful for anything out of the ordinary."

Iwan inclined his head slightly. "Of course, Mistress. Would you prefer to return to the grounds of the Sovereign's home?"

"No," Melyor said simply.

"Very well." Iwan spoke briefly with the captain of the guards, who, in turn, issued orders to his men. In response, the six burly men, who had been walking on either side of the travelers, moved into a tighter, diamond-shaped formation, with the captain in front, two men to either side, and the sixth man walking behind them.

Iwan drew his thrower, but continued to walk beside Melyor, relating to her and the others the history of the Lake Quarter, which was, as it turned out, one of the oldest parts of the Nal, predating even the oldest of the quads. The lake itself, officially known as the Lake of the Matrons, had been constructed under the supervision of Sovereign Oerella herself. Oerella-Nal's founder had grown up by the Bay of Storms, and had been torn late in life between her desire to spend her last years near the sounds and scents of the water and her belief that a Sovereign should live in the midst of her people.

Gwilym tried to listen to the bodyguard's tale, but as Iwan moved beyond Sovereign Oerella to stories of her successors, the Bearer found it increasingly difficult to concentrate. Even with the guards clustered tightly around them, even having seen Melyor's skill with a thrower and all that Orris could do with the power he wielded, the Bearer felt vulnerable. And yet, he felt his initial fear ebbing away, being replaced by a sense of dark anticipation. There was an inevitability to all this he was starting to realize. *Something* was going to happen. He knew that now; there was nothing to be gained by trying to prevent it. Rather, it was a matter of controlling events: of being prepared for what was coming, of not allowing himself to be surprised by whatever form it took.

And so, in a strange way, he was ready when the beam of red fire appeared out of nowhere, catching the captain of the guard full in the chest and sending him sprawling onto his back, the front of his uniform blackened and bloody and still smoking. An instant later shafts of thrower fire were everywhere, cutting through the warm air with a sizzling sound that reminded Gwilym of meat roasting on a fire. One more guard died in the assassins' first volley, falling at Gwilym's feet with a circle of flame burning his crimson uniform around the edges of the wound that had killed him. Stray volleys also struck several of the people walking along the avenue who had nothing to do with Gwilym and his companions, plunging the Lake Quarter into chaos as the panicked survivors fled screaming in all directions.

Iwan hollered for the four surviving guards to fire back, but they didn't seem to have any more of an idea of where the blasts had come from than Gwilym did. And even if they had, they were too busy diving for cover behind trees and parked carriers to use their weapons. Melyor and Orris had ducked down as well, using a long black carrier as a shield. Gwilym rushed to join them, and together the three companions peered cautiously through the windows of the vehicle, hoping to catch a glimpse of their attackers.

Iwan began to shout to his men a second time, but another round of fire cut him off with brutal abruptness. Gwilym could not see what had happened to the bodyguard, but he assumed the man was dead.

"Spread out!" Melyor called to the remaining guards. "Draw their fire if you have to! We need to figure out where they are!"

None of the guards moved. Instead they just looked at each other, as if gauging whether they ought to obey her commands.

"*Do it!*" Melyor exploded, waving her weapon at them. "Or I'll kill you myself!"

The four uniformed men stared at her for a moment as if she were crazy, and then, apparently deciding that she just might be, they did as she said. As soon as the four men began to shift positions, however, the assassins opened fire again.

"There!" Melyor hissed, pointing to a pair of alleyways on either side of a low building on the far side of the avenue. "They're by the blue building!" she shouted so the guards could hear. "In the alleys!"

The Sovereign's guardsmen may not have been comfortable taking orders from Melyor, but there could be no disputing their skill and efficiency. It almost appeared to Gwilym that they were pouring the fire from their weapons into the alleys before Melyor had finished speaking. The Nal-Lord blasted her thrower into the alleys as well, and Orris sent torrents of amber power in the same direction.

In fact, all of them were so intent on the assassins across the avenue, that none of them noticed the four men charging at them from either side, weaving through the mass of panicked people, their bodies held low, and their blades drawn. None of them, that is, except Gwilym who shouted a warning.

Two of the assassins jumped on guards before the Sovereign's men could react. The other two came straight at Gwilym and his friends.

The Bearer had no thrower, and even if he had, he could not have fired at the approaching assassins without risking the lives of innocent men and women. He did not carry a blade, either. But he had his staff, and he had used it in the past, albeit as a younger, leaner man, to ward off wild cats and bears in the Dhaalmar. And holding the ancient wood out before him with both hands, he rose now to meet the two killers rushing toward him. He sensed that someone was beside him, and glancing over just for an instant, he saw the sorcerer, his staff held before him as well. Orris flashed him a fierce grin, and then the two of them crouched in unison to meet their attackers. A moment later Gwilym lost track of his friend, and of everything else except the tall, muscular man with dark hair, who was bearing down on him.

As the assassin drew near he raised his blade over his head, as if intending to bury it in Gwilym's neck. Instinctively the Bearer lifted his staff to block the blow. And doing so, he left himself open to the vicious kick that the man delivered to his stomach.

Gwilym fell to the pavement, gasping for breath, and it was only by sheerest good luck that he happened to roll onto his back just as the man dropped down on him, slashing at his throat with the large knife. Gwilym managed to block the assassin's arm with a desperate thrust of his staff, and then he swung his stone upward in an attempt to smash his attacker's face. But the assassin was too quick and he rolled out of the way of Gwilym's blow.

Still fighting to catch his breath from the kick to his midriff, the Bearer scrambled to his feet and faced his attacker again. The man wasn't even breathing hard, and he was grinning savagely, much the way Orris had a few moments before. They circled each other for a few seconds, Gwilym holding his staff in front of him, and the assassin shifting his blade smoothly from hand to hand. The Bearer could hear the hiss of thrower blasts behind him, but he did not dare take his eyes off the man in front of him. He just had to hope that his friends were all right, and that none of the streams of fire hit him in the back.

The assassin lunged at him, his right arm, which held the blade, swinging in a wide arc toward Gwilym's chest. Again, the Bearer raised his staff to meet the blow, only to leave himself open to another unforeseen attack, this one from the man's left fist, which crashed into his kidney, sending him to his knees once more. Before Gwilym could move, the assassin swiped at his head with the knife, slicing through the top of the Bearer's ear. A warm river of blood gushed down the side of Gwilym's neck and jaw, soaking into his cloak. Still on his knees, the Bearer swung his staff at the big man's legs, but the assassin jumped away easily, grinning again at the sight of Gwilym's blood.

Slowly, painfully, Gwilym climbed to his feet, gripping his staff like a club and eyeing his opponent grimly.

He heard Hertha's voice in his head again. *No heroics.* He almost laughed out loud. No need to worry about that, he thought. There's nothing heroic about the way I'm fighting this battle.

Somewhere to his side and slightly behind him, Gwilym heard the sound of Orris's staff striking flesh. At least the sorcerer was fighting well.

"You're going to die, fat man," the assassin said, his teeth bared in a cruel smile. "Why don't you just let me finish you?"

Gwilym said nothing. He merely crouched down again and began to circle.

The assassin laughed and nodded, and then he too resumed their deadly dance.

The Bearer's ear was throbbing, and he was still out of breath. Perhaps sensing this, the tall man wasted little time before attacking again. He leapt forward, his blade glinting in the sunlight as he thrust it toward the Bearer's chest.

Gwilym started to react to the strike, but this time he fought his instincts and so saw the hidden blow before it landed. It was a kick again, aimed at his side. He swung his staff downward to block the man's leg and in the same motion, with more agility than he had ever imagined he possessed, he delivered a kick of his own, to the side of the knee of the assassin's planted leg.

With a snarl of rage and shock, the big man toppled onto his back. He tried to turn over, but before he could, Gwilym sprang forward and, without even thinking about what he was doing, drove the butt of his staff into the man's chest with all his might. The assassin let out an appalling, animalistic shriek, that echoed eerily off the buildings of the avenue and died away. His body convulsed several times, like a fish thrown onto dry land, and then he lay still, his eyes and mouth open and his back arched.

Gwilym did not move. He just stared at what he had done. His staff stuck out of the assassin's chest slightly aslant, vibrating still with the force of his blow. This was his vision, he realized, terrified and overwhelmed by the implications of it all. This was just what he had dreamed. Except that the staff was in a man he had killed, rather than in the street, and the color of his stone had not changed from its glowing brown.

It took him a moment to understand that the rest of the battle was not yet over. He still heard thrower fire, and after another few seconds it occurred to him that someone was calling his name. He turned and saw Orris still struggling with an assassin. For just an instant Gwilym wondered if he had been fighting the same man the whole time, but then he saw that two other men lay dead at Orris's feet.

Still someone was calling his name. He pivoted again and spotted Melyor, still crouched behind the carrier, firing her weapon toward the alley. One of the Sovereign's guardsmen was firing at the assassins as well. The others were dead: two from knife wounds, the rest with thrower burns on their uniforms.

"Get down!" Melyor shouted at him. Apparently she was the one who had been calling to him. "Get down before you get killed!"

The Bearer nodded vaguely, but instead of following her instructions, he hurried over to where Orris was fighting intending to help him. Just as he got there, however, one of the carriers near Melyor exploded with a bright orange flash, sending a cloud of billowing black smoke into the sky. The force of the blast threw the Nal-Lord and the guardsman backward several yards, knocked Gwilym onto his back, and drove Orris and his assailant to the ground. Fortunately, the sorcerer landed on top of the man he was fighting, and wasting no time, he pierced the assassin's throat with his dagger.

Melyor and the guard appeared too stunned to move, but Orris leaped to his feet and immediately was forced to block two shafts of thrower fire with a rippling shield of amber power. Gwilym stood as well and saw that two men were coming at them from across the avenue, both of them carrying large hand weapons. After a moment he recognized them as the two men he had seen from Melyor's carrier in Bragor-Nal. One of them was a large man with short yellow hair, but it was the other one, a lean man with sharp features and black and silver hair, whom Gwilym remembered most clearly. Melyor had called him the Blade, and looking at the man at the time, Gwilym had been struck by the cold cruelty of his pale eyes. The eyes of an assassin, he thought now, watching the man lope across the avenue like a wolf, his weapon poised to fire again.

Orris raised his staff and threw a ball of fire at the two men, but they both managed to avoid the blast, diving out of the way and rolling to safety on the far side of the same carriers Melyor had used for protection a short time ago.

Seeing them do this, Gwilym was struck with an idea. He rushed to Melyor's side, grabbed her thrower and began firing into the vehicles. The two men peered over the top of the carriers and raised their weapons, but before they could shoot, Orris forced them back down with a forked stream of power that just barely missed their heads. Gwilym continued to fire into the carriers so rapidly that he actually felt the weapon growing hot in his hands. The assassins stood and prepared to fire again, but just as they did, the Bearer finally set off an explosion. A big one. It tossed the two men into the air like rag dolls, and sent flames so high into the air that they ignited the crown of one of the trees lining the avenue. The blond man landed awkwardly on his back in the middle of the street and lay still. But Blade landed smoothly, rolled, and came up firing, despite the fact that the sleeve of his overcoat was ablaze.

Orris was ready though. Once again he blocked the assassin's bolt of red fire, and in the next instant he sent his own torrent of flame at Blade. The assassin had no time to react. The blow hit him square in the chest, lifting him off his feet with its force and dropping him to the ground in a vortex of fire.

The sorcerer sighed deeply, and his bird, which had been circling overhead during the fighting, settled to his shoulder and nuzzled him gently. Gwilym let out a long breath as well, and he walked over to Orris and placed a hand on the burly man's shoulder.

"Well done," he said.

The sorcerer appeared to understand. He nodded and smiled and then, with an effort, speaking Lonmir in a heavily accented voice, he said, "Thank you."

The two of them walked over to Melyor and helped her to her feet. She still appeared dazed, although she grinned at Gwilym and the sorcerer as they pulled her up. Her eyebrows and bits of her hair had been singed by the explosion that knocked her to the ground, and she had a cut on her forehead that Gwilym assumed had come from a piece of broken glass.

"That was some nice shooting, Bearer," she said.

"Thanks," he replied, smiling sheepishly and handing her back her thrower. "I find it's easier to hit a carrier that isn't moving."

Melyor laughed and turned to say something to Orris. Gwilym heard voices calling to them from the direction of the palace and looking that way he saw a large number of the Sovereign's guards hurrying toward them. He raised his hand in greeting and opened his mouth to call out to them, but in that moment he felt a sudden explosion of white hot pain at the base of his skull and heard a sound like a mountain avalanche within his mind.

He realized that he was lying on the ground, face down. He didn't remember falling. He felt himself being turned over and saw Orris and Melyor kneeling over him, their faces pale. Melyor's lips were trembling and the sorcerer had tears on his cheeks.

The yellow-haired man, Gwilym thought to himself. Blade's friend. He did this to me.

With an effort that nearly blinded him with agony, Gwilym turned his head to look at the man he had killed. His staff was still there, as it had been in his dream, standing just a bit askew. But the stone still glowed brown. I'm not dead, he told himself. Not yet.

And then he knew. He understood his dream and what had to be done. The stone wouldn't be going back to the Dhaalmar after all.

He looked at Melyor again, the effort tearing a gasp from his chest. "Is he dead?" he managed to croak out, hoping the Nal-Lord would know who he meant.

She nodded, a river a tears flowing over her face. She was so lovely.

He forced himself to speak again. "There's something you must do." He closed his eyes. There was so much pain.

"Anything," he heard her sob. It seemed to come from a great distance. The avalanche still thundered through his head.

"My stone."

He waited, finally opening his eyes again. Orris was gone, but Melyor was still just kneeling there.

"My stone," he said again, more insistently this time.

"Orris is getting it."

Gwilym swallowed and nodded. He didn't have the energy to apologize. Once more, he hoped she understood.

Orris returned a few moments later with Gwilym's staff and he tried to place it in the Bearer's hands. But Gwilym shook his head—there was more pain than he could bear—and looked at Melyor.

"Yours," he whispered.

She stared at him in disbelief. "No," she said. "No. This belongs with you. With your people."

"Yours," he repeated. He tried to push it toward her, but his hands didn't seem to work anymore.

Orris understood though, and gently he held it out to her and nodded. Reluctantly, her tears still flowing, Melyor reached for it. As soon as her hands touched the staff, the stone blazed with a bright white light. And when the white faded, the crystal was no longer brown. It was scarlet. Just as Gwilym had known it would be. Just as he had seen in his dream.

"Yours," he said one last time.

Then, he closed his eyes and summoned an image of Hertha. And it seemed almost that the waves of pain parted to let her through. She came to him in the meadow near the settlement, her hair shifting in a light breeze, that inscrutable smile on her soft, round features, and love in her dark eyes. And clinging to that image as if it were everything in the world, the Bearer allowed the darkness to take him.

* * *

The staff felt strange in Melyor's hands. Light and perfectly balanced. And alive, as if it were breathing; as if there was blood running through it. Which of course there was. Gwilym's blood, and hers, and her mother's, and the blood of every other Gildriite who had ever lived in Lon-Ser. Even Gildri's blood, the blood that tied her to the sorcerer standing beside her, flowed in this piece of wood. So it was fitting that the stone atop the staff, the multifaceted crystal to which her eyes were drawn again and again, should glow with the color of blood.

She remembered hearing once from Cedrych that the first group of men sent to Tobyn-Ser with Calbyr had carried red stones. No doubt they had looked much like this stone—her stone—looked now. There could be no doubt that this staff had been meant for her. It struck her as impossible, and yet it seemed in that moment as if the gods had decreed that it should be so.

Melyor shook her head. Such thoughts would have been so alien to her just a few days before.

Orris placed a hand gently on her arm.

Looking up at him she saw that there were still tears on his face, though he offered her a kind smile.

"What am I supposed to do with this?" she asked him in Tobynmir. "Do I take it back to the Dhaalmar? Do I carry it around the Nal? Why would he have given this to me?"

The sorcerer nodded at the crystal, as if it were answer enough. "He knew it was yours."

"But it is not mine."

"The stone says otherwise."

She opened her mouth to argue but then stopped herself, feeling her own tears start to fall again. "I have spent my whole life pretending I am not a Gildriite," she finally said. "I do not deserve to be a Bearer."

The sorcerer hesitated and Melyor held her breath, uncertain of what she wanted to hear him say.

"I believe that the gods decide such things," Orris told her after a brief pause, "and that they do so for their own purposes. I know many men and women in Tobyn-Ser—good people, all of them—who want more than anything to be mages. And yet, the gods pass them over. And I've also known some—actually one man in particular, who was chosen, and who proved himself capable of such cruelty and treachery and deception that it makes me wonder what the gods were thinking when they gave him this gift." He shook his head, as if trying to rid himself of a bad memory. "My point is," he went on, "asking yourself why the gods chose you to take Gwilym's place is futile. Just accept that they have, and do your best to carry on as he would have. Perhaps, given the history of his—" He smiled. "Given the history of your people, it may be time for a Gildriite with your skills to be seen in Bragor-Nal. Perhaps, that will prove to be the path to redemption for which Gwilym had been looking."

Melyor felt something loosen in her chest, and she actually managed a smile.

"Perhaps," she said. "Thank you." She turned to the Sovereign's guards, who were standing together surveying the carnage on the avenue: eight assassins and five guardsmen dead; Iwan with half his head blown away; and Gwilym. "Take us to Sovereign Shivohn," she offered in Lonmir. "She'll want to see us."

One of the guards nodded, and while several remained behind to see to it that the bodies of Gwilym, Iwan, and the guardsmen were returned to the palace, a small contingent of uniformed men escorted Melyor and the sorcerer back past the Lake of the Matrons and into Shivohn's residence.

When they entered her chamber, they found the Sovereign pacing before the great windows that looked out on the gardens.

As soon as Shivohn saw them she came forward, her movements sharp and tense. "What happened?" she demanded immediately in Lonmir. "Where's Iwan?"

"We were attacked by assassins," Melyor answered in Orris's language. "Your bodyguard was killed, as was the Bearer and all but one of your guards."

The color drained from the Sovereign's face and she slumped forward suddenly, as if she had been punched in the stomach. "Fist of the God," she whispered. She leaned on her chair for support and then dropped herself into it. "Who were they?" she asked in a flat voice, her eyes fixed on the floor. She, too, had shifted to Tobynmir.

"Assassins from Bragor-Nal," the Nal-Lord said, "led by a man known as the Blade. As I told you earlier, they tried to kill us once before, and we suspected that they had followed us across the mountains."

"Yes, I remember," Shivohn said, nodding vaguely. "Who sent them?"

"I cannot say for certain, but I assume it was Cedrych."

The Sovereign said nothing for a long time. She just sat there, shaking her head and staring at the floor.

Finally, Orris cleared his throat, drawing Shivohn's attention. "It seems we have a common enemy now, Sovereign. If Cedrych will send invaders to Tobyn-Ser and assassins to the gates of your palace, what else might he do? Now is your chance to go to the Council and end this threat for good."

The Sovereign glared at him, a bright red spot appearing high on each of her cheeks. "I've just lost a young man who was very dear to me, Hawk-Mage!" she said imperiously. "And you dare to speak to me of common enemies and Council politics?"

Orris straightened, his short beard bristling. "Do you know how many people died in Tobyn-Ser as a result of Cedrych's actions, Sovereign?" he fired back. "Hundreds. Entire towns were destroyed. Men and women and children were slaughtered in the streets. Several members of my Order were killed. I'm sorry that Iwan died, and I grieve for the Bearer. But they're just two men among the horde that Cedrych has sent to the gods. And unless you and I do something now, there will be more. I promise you."

"Orris is right," Melyor said. "I think you know that, Sovereign."

Shivohn continued to glare at them for several moments, before taking a slow breath and looking away. "Yes, I do," she conceded. She propelled herself out of her chair and began to pace again. "There may be an opportunity in this," she said, as if weighing their options. "The Council has not agreed on much over the years, but it has been consistent in upholding the law that prohibits the citizens of one Nal from engaging in any attacks upon the citizens of another." She glanced at Melyor. "You're certain that this Blade of whom you spoke was responsible?"

"Yes," Melyor said with a nod.

"And you're confident that he was working for Cedrych?"

Melyor nodded again, although she felt a bit less sure of herself on this question.

Apparently Shivohn sensed her uncertainty. She stopped pacing just in front of Melyor and gazed purposefully into the Nal-Lord's eyes. "I need you to be certain about this, Melyor. Is it possible Blade did this on his own accord or on behalf of someone else?"

The Nal-Lord shook her head. "Blade was a hunter; he did nothing on his own. Someone had to be paying him and there are not that many people in Bragor-Nal who could afford him: Cedrych, Newell, Wildon, Durell, and maybe a handful of Nal-Lords. And of all of them, Cedrych was the only one with much to gain from sending him after us."

Shivohn regarded her doubtfully.

"I promise you, Sovereign," Melyor insisted. "Blade was working for Cedrych."

The diminutive woman said nothing for several moments more. Then she frowned. "I suppose I haven't much choice but to believe you." She started pacing once more. "If you're right, Bragor-Nal is guilty of a rather serious offense. I'll demand that Cedrych be punished and that Bragor-Nal pay restitution to the people of Oerella-Nal. If he refuses, I'll move to have the Council impose sanctions."

"What about Marar?" Melyor asked her. "Why would Stib-Nal support you in this when they support Bragor-Nal in everything else?"

Shivohn grinned. "Because Durell will tell him to."

Melyor stared at the Sovereign dumbfounded. "That makes no sense at all. Why would Durell tell Marar to support you?"

"Council politics are rather strange, my dear," Shivohn said, as if this explained everything. "Durell may deny responsibility publicly, for the benefit of his other Overlords, but he'll do as I demand if I can show him that the assassins' weapons came from Bragor-Nal." She paused. "I can show him that, can't I?" Melyor nodded. "Good," the Sovereign went on. "The Nals have fought wars over matters of less significance than this, and though Durell's Nal is powerful, he's not ready to fight me. Not yet at least. So he might make a show of fighting my demands—he may even go so far as to force me to call for sanctions—but in the end he'll have Marar vote with me. That way I'm happy, his Overlords are satisfied, and everything goes back to being the way it was before, which is just how Durell likes it."

"So what should we do until you've met with Durell?" Orris asked the Sovereign.

"I made you guests of the Matriarchy," Shivohn said matter-of-factly. "Nothing has happened to change that. I'd suggest that you remain here until it's safe for the Nal-Lord to return to her home."

The sorcerer gave a small bow. "Thank you, Sovereign."

Shivohn nodded and walked to her small desk in the corner of the chamber and pressed the button on the wall, just as she had done to summon Iwan earlier that day.

Melyor wanted to ask the Sovereign how it would ever be possible for her to return to Bragor-Nal. *Don't you understand that Durell can't control Cedrych?* she wanted to say. *Don't you see that the Tobyn-Ser Initiative and Gwilym's death prove that.* But in a sense she knew that this was not Shivohn's problem. The Sovereign would do what she could, but ultimately it would fall to Melyor to take care of Cedrych. And if she was lucky, Orris would be at her side.

26

Considering the entirety of Baden's report, one cannot help but be struck by its myriad inconsistencies. Baram is a mercenary, capable of the most revolting acts of violence, yet he is also little more than a boy, still scarred by the early loss of his parents. Bragor-Nal is a place ruled by violence and vendetta, but still we must attempt to understand its people so that we might come "to see them as something other than just our enemies." In making their lethal weapons and terrifying "advanced goods" the people of Lon-Ser have destroyed their land and air and water, things which the people of Tobyn-Ser would never allow to happen here. Nonetheless, we are told, our people have so much in common with their people that peaceful relations with them are not only possible, they are inevitable.

It almost seems that our friend is at war with himself, vainly attempting to reconcile two contradictory impulses. On the one hand, the Baden we have come to respect for his years of service to the land, the man of wisdom and erudition, is offering us an informative assessment of Lon-Ser's culture and politics. The cogency of this Baden's presentation, however, is being undermined by the polemics of the other Baden, the one who has made himself an object of resentment and ridicule in recent years with his uncompromising advocacy of extreme and unreasonable positions.

—From "A Response to the Report of Owl-Master Baden on his Interrogation of the Outlander Baram," Submitted by Owl-Master Erland, Autumn, God's Year 4625.

Every time he came to the Gold Palace and saw its glittering carved facade, every time he saw the Sovereign's men, in their trim blue uniforms, standing at attention by the huge golden doors, Cedrych felt himself grow giddy with the knowledge that one day this would all be his. And every time the guards escorted him inside, forcing his own men to wait outside, and seating him in the vast, garishly decorated sitting room just outside Durell's office, the Overlord seethed at the fact that his day had not yet come. Never mind the ignominy of having to wait like this for a man of Durell's limited capacity—that he understood. It was all a part of Durell's office. It was important that the Sovereign assert his power from the outset in dealing with subordinates, particularly someone like Cedrych, who had never bothered to hide his ambition. And what better way to establish that power than by forcing a visitor to wait interminably in a room whose glorious history and tremendous scale could be so intimidating.

What bothered Cedrych was that Durell had ruined this room. He had changed it from a place that inspired awe to one that invited ridicule. Cedrych had seen still shots of the West Sitting Room of the Gold Palace as it appeared before Durell's tenure began. Its walls had been covered by brilliant portraits of former Sovereigns, painted by the greatest artists in Lon-Ser's history. The doors and windows had been framed by exquisitely carved light woods that complemented perfectly the intricate grain of the ancient oak floors. And, of course, there had been the famous mantel over the hearth on the far wall. Timur's Mantel it had been called, for the Nal's second Sovereign, Bragor's son, who had the palace constructed to commemorate his father's accomplishments. Carved from a single remarkable piece of rose-colored crystal, the mantel had been the most renowned feature of the palace for literally thousands of years. Every Sovereign since Timur had been invested before the mantel. Dalrek had accepted Einar's surrender in this room, officially ending the Consolidation. From all that Cedrych had read and heard, it seemed that no one who stepped into the sitting room could help but be overwhelmed by its beauty, elegance, and power.

That is, until Durell became Sovereign. Out of vanity, or perhaps insecurity, Durell had all the portraits replaced with paintings of himself and his family done by an artist of mediocre talent, whose sole qualification appeared to be his knack for seeing beyond the Sovereign's physical shortcomings. Durell had the carved wood around the doors and windows painted gold—"This is, after all, the Gold Palace," he was heard to say at the time. And most inexcusably, he had Timur's Mantel mounted with a series of tiny, solid gold carvings of nude women in various titillating poses, a process which involved drilling holes in the crystal.

Cedrych found that he couldn't even enter the sitting room without grinding his teeth in frustration and anger. The various times he had spent waiting here for Durell were excruciating for him; each time he happened to even glance at the mantel, he felt as though the drill that had been used on the stone were boring through his skull. His first act as Sovereign, long before he did anything with respect to the Nal itself, would be to have this room restored to its original splendor. The gold paint would be removed, the portraits of the Sovereigns would be put back in their rightful places. And Timur's Mantel would be repaired. He had spoken to a sculptor he knew; it could be done.

Other parts of the palace needed work as well, including Durell's study, the walls of which were currently painted a lugubrious dark maroon. But the sitting room came first.

A door at the end of the room opened and a guard motioned for Cedrych to follow him. "Sovereign Durell will hear you now," the man said solemnly.

Hear me? Cedrych thought with amusement. He summoned me. He suppressed a smile. It was, he knew, what the guard said to all Durell's visitors. He walked after the guard, his hand wandering, by force of habit, to the strap of his thigh where he normally carried his thrower. The guards, however, had taken his weapon before allowing him into the palace. Durell had a weapons chamber, too.

When Cedrych entered the office, the Sovereign was standing at his desk, looking over some papers. He didn't even bother to look up. But the Overlord could see that he didn't look well. His paunch seemed larger than Cedrych remembered. His red and silver hair was disheveled, and his face was puffy and wan from lack of sleep. You look old, Durell, Cedrych thought with satisfaction. Perhaps the stress of your position is getting to be too much for you. Perhaps it's time for a younger man to take your place.

"Sit down, Cedrych," Durell commanded in a flat voice, interrupting the Overlord's thoughts. It struck Cedrych as an uncharacteristically brusque greeting. He had assumed that his conversation with the Sovereign would be routine; he hadn't even bothered to wonder what it might be about. But apparently he had been mistaken. He felt himself growing curious. Wordlessly he lowered himself into an opulent chair near the desk.

For some time, the Sovereign continued to read whatever it was he held in his hand. When at last he faced Cedrych, the look in his grey eyes betokened an anger the Overlord had only seen in him one or two times before.

"This note I've been reading is from Shivohn," he said.

"Really," Cedrych answered flippantly. "How is the Dwarf Queen?"

"She is a Sovereign!" Durell shot back. "Just as I am! I expect you to show both of us the respect we deserve!"

"Of course, Sovereign," Cedrych said placidly. "My apologies."

Durell glowered at him, the muscles in his jaw working.

"You have news from Shivohn, Sovereign?" Cedrych prodded gently.

"You do understand that, don't you, Cedrych?" Durell went on as if he hadn't heard, his voice rising. "You do realize that I'm the Sovereign, and you're the Overlord. Just one of three, I might add."

"Of course, Sovereign," Cedrych assured Durell. He indicated the room they were in with a gesture. "One cannot be in this palace and forget," he added, choosing his words carefully. "Your imprint on the place is . . . unmistakable."

The Sovereign nodded once. "I'm glad to hear you say so," he said churlishly.

Once more, Cedrych suppressed a grin. Irony was simply lost on the man.

"I wish, however," Durell continued, "that you would show me the same courtesy with your actions that you do with your words."

"Oh, I assure you I do, Sovereign," Cedrych broke in, unable to resist.

"Don't lie to me, Cedrych!" the Sovereign snapped. "I'm not the fool you think I am! Don't you think I know about your precious Initiative?"

Cedrych merely stared back at him. His conversation with the sorcerer had prepared him for this. "Yes, Sovereign. I assumed you knew of it. Little goes on in the Nal that escapes the notice of SovSec."

The Sovereign sat down in his desk chair, his eyes never leaving Cedrych's face. "If you've assumed I knew, why haven't you spoken to me about it?"

"For the same reason you never asked me about it," Cedrych replied, the lie coming to him easily. "So that if the Initiative fails, the blame will fall on me alone."

"And if it succeeds?"

"I won't bother being coy with you, Sovereign. It's no secret that I hope to live in the Gold Palace some day, just as Newell and Wildon do. When the Initiative succeeds, all of Bragor-Nal will benefit—"

"But you most of all."

Cedrych smiled coldly. "It seems only fair. I conceived of it, I provided the resources to see it through. I deserve to profit from it. And I don't want very much. All I'm asking is that you designate me as your successor when you step down. That's reasonable, isn't it?"

Durell nodded. "Very. A couple of days ago I would have agreed to those terms without hesitation."

A couple of days ago. . . . Cedrych felt a strange pressure in his chest, as if someone had taken hold of his heart. "I don't understand," he said, trying to keep his temper in check. "What's changed?"

Durell held up the letter from Shivohn. "It seems your Initiative isn't the only venture with which you've been involved recently."

"What are you talking about?"

The Sovereign scanned the note again. "Isn't Melyor i Lakin one of your Nal-Lords?"

Cedrych grabbed at the letter, but Durell kept it out of his reach. "Yes," the Overlord growled. "She's one of mine."

"And were the assassins who attacked her in Oerella-Nal in your employ?" Cedrych hesitated and the Sovereign shook his head. "Of course they were," Durell said, answering his own question. "There aren't many others in Bragor-Nal who can afford the Blade's services."

"How do you know he was hired by someone in Bragor-Nal?" Cedrych asked halfheartedly, already knowing what the Sovereign would say.

"Come now, Cedrych!" Durell snapped. "Why would someone in Oerella-Nal hire a Bragory assassin to kill a Bragory Nal-Lord?"

The Overlord said nothing for some time. He just sat in his chair rubbing a hand over his scar-ravaged face. "Is Melyor dead?" he asked at last.

Durell's jaw dropped. "What?" he demanded incredulously. "You're asking about Melyor? Do you have any idea how much trouble you've made for me?"

"No, Sovereign, I don't," he replied with disdain. "But I'm certain you're going to tell me. I just want to know first if Melyor is dead."

Durell stared at the Overlord and shook his head. "No," he finally told him. "Melyor is alive, as is her sorcerer. Blade and his men are all dead, and so is the Bearer, one of Shivohn's bodyguards, and several of her security men."

"Fist of the God!" Cedrych mumbled under his breath.

"Believe me, Cedrych: Melyor is the least of your problems."

"Meaning what?"

"Meaning that by sending assassins into Oerella-Nal you violated several provisions of the Green Area Proclamation!"

"Don't be ridiculous!" Cedrych scoffed. "The Proclamation allows each Nal to police its own people, even if that means straying into the other Nals to enforce the law. Melyor is a renegade Nal-Lord. She's violated countless laws in my Dominion and I was just trying to bring her into custody."

"*With assassins?*" Durell asked, his voice rising. "That will never satisfy Shivohn! The fugitive section of the Proclamation is very specific: you have to send in security men, and it must be done with the approval of the Nal's Sovereign."

"A technicality!" Cedrych said, waving his hand dismissively.

The Sovereign shook his head. "No, Cedrych. We can't justify this under the provisions of the Proclamation."

"Then accuse Melyor of being a spy and tell Shivohn that the assassination attempt was justified by her own sponsorship of espionage. It'll be your word against hers. The Council will have to settle the matter, and we both know whose side Marar will take."

Durell shook his head a second time. "That approach carries too many risks. Shivohn is threatening war, Cedrych, and I'm not ready to go that far. Not over this."

"Then what do you think we should do?"

"I think in this case," the Sovereign began, standing and stepping to the window nearest his desk, "the most prudent course would be to accept her demands."

"Which were?" Cedrych asked warily.

Durell shrugged. "The usual. A formal apology, restitution, and punishment for those responsible." He turned to face Cedrych again. "In this case, of course, that would be you."

"*What?*" the Overlord hissed. Somehow he was on his feet. "You can't be serious! You're going to let the Matriarchy tell you how to run Bragor-Nal?"

"Of course not!" Durell replied impatiently. "At least not in the long term. I just think it would be best if you were to step down as Overlord temporarily, perhaps until autumn, when things will have calmed down a bit."

"*Never!*" Cedrych shot back, livid at the very thought of it. "Do you know what Newell and Wildon would do to my Dominion in that amount of time?"

Durell shrugged again, with infuriating equanimity. "You'll have to choose your replacement carefully. Think of it as practice for when you finally become Sovereign and have to select a permanent successor."

"I won't allow you to do this!"

The Sovereign's flaccid features hardened. "You don't have much choice in the matter, Cedrych!" he said in a steely voice. It seemed the old man still had some nerve left in him after all. "Perhaps next time you'll think twice before overreaching like this!"

"Better to overreach, than to cower at the threats of an old woman!"

"That's enough, Overlord!"

They both held themselves very still, their eyes locked on each other, as if each was waiting for the other to make the next move. As the moments stretched on, Cedrych saw the resolution in the Sovereign's grey eyes begin to waver, and he allowed himself a smile.

"I think you'd better leave, Cedrych," Durell said, his voice trembling just slightly.

"This isn't over," Cedrych said quietly.

The Sovereign walked to his desk and pressed a small red button at the base of his speak screen, never once allowing his eyes to leave Cedrych's face. Just a few seconds later, three guards appeared at the door.

"You called us, Sovereign?" one of them asked.

"Yes," Durell said, a hollow grin on his lips. "The Overlord was just leaving. Would you see him out please?"

"Of course, Sovereign."

The three man came forward, their stiff blue uniforms rustling softly. The one who had spoken pointed toward the door. "This way, Overlord."

Durell and Cedrych continued to look at each other. The Sovereign's grin had vanished, and he looked old again; pale and tired. Durell had been right about one thing: he wasn't ready for a war. Too bad he had just started one.

"It's a shame you took down all those portraits, Durell," Cedrych said in a low voice. "They were the only real leaders this palace has seen in years."

He turned and began to leave, but just as he reached the door, Durell called to him. "You have three days, Cedrych! I'll do you the courtesy of allowing you to pick your successor, but if you try to stall, or you defy me in any way, I'll be forced to take control of your dominion myself and divide it between Newell and Wildon. Do I make myself clear?"

Cedrych had stopped on the threshold of the sitting room, and he glanced back over his shoulder now and smiled coldly at the older man. "Perfectly, Sovereign. Three days."

Without another word, he left, walking swiftly through the sitting room. But as he passed Timur's Mantel, he slowed, briefly examining the crystal and the gold abominations that had been mounted on it.

"Please keep moving, Overlord," one of the guards said sternly.

"Of course," Cedrych answered absently, lingering by the mantel a moment longer. Then he looked at the guard and grinned. "That can be restored you know."

The Nal-Lord is behind him as they enter Cedrych's quarters, and Baram feels his presence as if the man were a thrower pressed against his back. He's sorry now that he allowed himself to be caught, but it had seemed like the right thing to do at the time. He is a break-law, after all. Yes, he's been away, but he was a break-law before he left. He's been a break-law longer than he's been anything else in his life. Even longer than he's been a prisoner.

But the Nal has changed since he left all those years ago with Calbyr, Keegan, and the others. The Nal-Lords he knew have all been replaced. The streets look strange to him. Nothing seems to fit the way it used to. Even the tunic and britches given to him by Dob just before they left the Nal-Lord's flat to come here don't feel right, though he remembers wearing such clothes in the past. He misses the woolen overshirt he has worn since leaving Tobyn-Ser with the mage. The only thing that has remained the same, it seems, is that Cedrych still runs this part of the Nal. Baram remembers Cedrych very well. Or more precisely, he remembers all that he has heard about Cedrych. And he has no idea why Cedrych would want to see him.

"Sit here," Dob says gruffly, pointing to a long, plush silver couch. "Overlord?" he calls, after making certain that Baram has obeyed his command.

"Just a minute," comes the reply from another room.

Dob looks at him sidelong and then rolls his eyes and shakes his head. Baram wonders briefly if the Nal-Lord has brought him here to be killed. He feels surprisingly calm.

A few seconds later Cedrych enters the room and Dob motions desperately for Baram to stand up again. Climbing to his feet once more, Baram turns to look at the Overlord.

He has heard of the assassination attempt that left the Overlord scarred and lame, but he is not prepared for what he sees. The entire right side of the bald man's face is pitted and lined with dead skin, as if it has been mauled by a wild animal. Baram tries not to stare.

"You're late," Cedrych tells Dob, the one blue eye regarding the Nal-Lord coldly.

Dob nods. "I'm sorry, Overlord." He points to Baram. "He was . . . He needed to be cleaned up and changed."

"A Nal-Lord doesn't blame others for his screw-ups, Dob," Cedrych says. "At least my Nal-Lords don't."

Dob's eyes flick to Baram; only briefly, but long enough for Baram to see that the Nal-Lord hates him. "Yes, Overlord," he answers.

Cedrych looks Baram over for a moment before talking to Dob again. "Tell me again how you found him."

"I didn't, Overlord. One of my men did. He was just wandering the streets, dressed in strange clothing and ranting about sorcerers and Tobyn-Ser prisons. My break-law brought him to me and I thought I should let you know." Dob smiles. "I've heard that you have a special interest in Tobyn-Ser," he adds in a confidential tone.

Cedrych looks bored. "This was in the Fourth?"

"No, Overlord. The Second."

"The Second?" Cedrych repeats, frowning. "So you found him before our conversation about Melyor's Realm? And you didn't tell me?"

"I—I'm sorry, Overlord," Dob stammers. "Our conversation was over before I had the chance to say anything about it. And I've been busy ever since, trying to secure the Fourth, just as you told me to."

"Yes, of course," Cedrych says with disdain. "Have you found Jibb yet?"

"No, Overlord, not yet. But we will, I assure you." Dob hesitates, but only for an instant. "Perhaps if you were to return your men to the Fourth, just for a bit longer—"

The bald man gives a small, mirthless laugh. "If you haven't found him yet, you're not going to. I could give you my entire army and it probably wouldn't make a difference. Not at this point. If I were you, I'd watch my back."

Dob swallows nervously, but says nothing.

"Leave us," Cedrych commands, gesturing vaguely toward the door. "I want to speak with him alone. Go back to the Fourth. You'll hear from me if I need you."

"Yes, Overlord," the Nal-Lord says with a nod. He casts one more spiteful look at Baram and turns to go. "Good night, Overlord."

"The man's an idiot," Cedrych comments after Dob is gone, as much to himself as to Baram. "It's amazing he's lived this long." He indicates the couch with a hand that is surprisingly delicate for a man of his size and reputation. "Please sit down. Can I get you anything?" Baram shakes his head, and Cedrych lowers himself smoothly into a large, chair. "What's your name?" the Overlord asks, smiling warmly.

"Baram," he replies, his voice sounding awkward to his own ears. He still is not used to conversing in Lonmir.

"Were you one of Calbyr's men?"

Baram nods. He tries to keep himself looking at Cedrych's one blue eye, but his gaze continually slides back to the ravaged socket where the other one should be, as if the Overlord's face is sloped downward to that one spot.

"What happened, Baram? What happened to Calbyr and the rest?"

He hesitates. It's been so long, and it's a difficult tale to tell. "We were defeated by a ghost," he finally says.

The Overlord leans forward, a quizzical expression on his face. "A ghost?"

"Two really. A man and a wolf. The mages carried us all to the ghost, and when the ghost arrived we tried to kill him but we couldn't, and the mages defeated us."

"So the mages defeated you with their magic," Cedrych says, his brow furrowing.

Baram nods. "Yes. And with the ghost." He knows that he's not making himself clear, but the empty eye is distracting him.

Cedrych takes a long breath. "What happened after that? Were you captured?"

He nods.

"And put in prison?"

He nods once more.

"For how long?"

Baram thinks. He remembers counting the days for the first several months of his captivity, but after that he lost track. And then he started counting stones instead. "I don't know. Years, I think. A long time."

Cedrych grimaces sympathetically. The look in his one eye is kind, and strangely familiar. Baram finds himself wondering if he has met the Overlord before and forgotten. "That must have been awful," Cedrych says. "Did you grow to hate them very much?"

Baram shrugs and looks away. He has never met the Overlord before, he realizes. He is remembering Baden's eyes which were the same color.

"It's all right if you didn't," Cedrych says. "Did you tell them much about why you were in Tobyn-Ser?"

Baram holds himself very still. He says nothing.

Cedrych reaches over and pats Baram's leg compassionately. "That's all right, too," he says. He leans back in his chair again. "How did you get back here?"

"The mage brought me!" Baram answers quickly. "There's a mage in Bragor-Nal!"

Cedrych nods, surprising him. "Yes, I know. Did he tell you why he wanted to come here?"

"He says he wants to make peace," Baram answers warily. "He needed me as a guide to get him to the Nal."

"Do you believe he really wants peace?"

"I don't know."

"Do you like the mage, Baram? Is he a friend?"

He shakes his head slowly. "No. As soon as we reached the Nal, I got away from him. I tried to tell people he was here. I tried to tell the Nal-Lord."

Cedrych narrows his eyes. "The Nal-Lord," he repeats. "Do you mean Dob?"

Baram nods, and Cedrych looks disappointed.

"Yes, Dob," Baram says. "I tried to tell him, but he wouldn't listen. He's very strong."

"The mage you mean."

"Yes. He has powers that are . . ." He shakes his head, searching for the right word. Eventually he gives up. "He's very strong," he says again.

"Are all the mages as strong as this one?"

"Yes," he says quickly. Then he falters. "I think so. Sartol might have been even stronger."

"Who was Sartol?" the Overlord asks with obvious interest.

"He was a mage who helped us. He and Calbyr worked together, although I don't think they liked each other."

"*You found a traitor in the Order?*" Cedrych asks with astonishment.

Baram nods, briefly afraid that he has said the wrong thing. The Overlord looks at him keenly, as if he suddenly sees in Baram something that he has missed previously, and he leans forward again. "How much do you remember about Tobyn-Ser, Baram?"

He shrugs nervously and chews his lip. "I remember what it looks like," he offers in a quiet voice. "I remember its language and the way mages are supposed to act."

"Do you still know your way around? Do you remember where the major towns and rivers are?"

Baram looks at his hands and thinks. He knows from Cedrych's tone that this is an important question. "Maybe," he responds after several moments. "I think so."

Cedrych stands and begins to wander around the room, glancing out the large window that looks out over the lights of the Nal, and straightening pictures that are already hanging straight. "It might interest you to hear, Baram, that I'm sending another group to Tobyn-Ser. I'm hoping that they can finish the work that you and Calbyr and the others started." He pauses, glancing over at Baram. "Did you know that?"

"No."

"Do you think they can succeed?"

Baram considers this. "Maybe. If they stay away from ghosts. Baden says that some people don't trust the Order anymore. He says it's because of what we did."

"Who's Baden?"

Once more, Baram looks away.

Cedrych returns to his chair and sits on the edge of it. "It's all right, Baram," he says. "Was Baden a friend?"

Baram nods.

"And was he also a mage?"

"Yes. He spoke to me while I was in the prison."

"Do you miss him?"

Baram meets the Overlord's gaze. "I don't miss the prison," he says.

"That's not really what I asked."

"Yes, it is."

Cedrych nods and a smile spreads across his scarred features. "I think I understand." He stands again. "Baram, would you be willing to help me? I've just lost the leader for this new group that I've mentioned. And I need help preparing her replacement. Your knowledge of Tobyn-Ser could be enormously useful."

Baram hesitates. He's just gotten back to the Nal after being away for so long. "I don't want to leave again," he says, looking away. "I want to stay in the Nal."

Cedrych laughs, although gently, not like Dob and his friends. "I have no intention of sending you back, Baram," he says. "But if you help us—if you tell us what you remember about Tobyn-Ser—I can give you a place to stay, and food to eat, until you're . . . until you're ready to be on your own again. And I can pay you a great deal of money." Cedrych comes closer, a question in his eye. "Does that sound good to you? Does that sound fair?"

It sounds almost too good, and Baram regards the Overlord dubiously.

"Ah," Cedrych says with a knowing smile. "You don't trust me, do you?" He doesn't wait for Baram to answer. "I wouldn't either if I were you, after all you've probably heard about me in the quads. Especially not after all you've been through, never knowing who was your friend and who wasn't." He reaches into his pocket, pulling out several gold pieces and a few silvers, and he holds them out to Baram. "Take these. Consider them a gesture of my good will."

Baram takes the money, but he says nothing.

"You're free to go, Baram. Think for a few days about what I've offered you. You're welcome to stay in the First Realm, or you can go elsewhere if you care to. Whatever you want to do. If you decide that my offer is fair, come back. The guards downstairs will let you in and I'll be glad to see you."

"What if I say 'no'?"

Cedrych shrugs, the smile lingering on his lips. "I'll be disappointed, but that's all. You keep the money, regardless."

Baram hesitates. Nobody has given him this much choice in years. Not even Baden, whose eyes are the same color as Cedrych's.

"You can go," Cedrych says again, and this time Baram hears a dismissal in the words.

He stands up abruptly.

"I'm sorry, Baram. I don't mean to rush you out, but I have some arrangements to take care of. I have a big day planned for tomorrow."

Baram nods. "Thank you, Overlord."

"Think about what I've said," Cedrych tells him as he places an arm around his shoulders and guides him to the door. "Let me know what you think." The door opens and there are several guards standing on the other side. "Get Baram some food and then lead him down to the quads," Cedrych says to the closest guard. "Whatever he needs or wants, give it to him."

The guard looks Baram up and down quickly and then nods. "Yes, Overlord."

Cedrych gives Baram a quick smile and steps back into his quarters. An instant later the door closes and Baram is alone with the guards.

"This way," the guard who spoke with Cedrych says. He walks through the weapons chamber and down the corridor, and Baram follows obediently.

But just as they reach the lifter, Baram turns and gazes back at the door to Cedrych's suite. He feels as if he has just allowed something precious to slip through his fingers.

27

I have always said that when the time comes for me to assume my rightful place in the Gold Palace, no one will stand in my way. I have worked too hard and endured too much to allow one person, or even a hundred people, or a thousand, to keep me from my dream.

More recently, I have come to understand that this time will be of my own choosing. I would prefer to wait until the Initiative has succeeded, assuring

Bragor-Nal of permanent preeminence in Lon-Ser. As Sovereign, with the Council constantly looking over my shoulder, I would find it difficult to devote myself to the Initiative, and I am reluctant to entrust the project to anyone else.

But if Durell should die before the mission is completed, or if other circumstances arise making it necessary for me to take the Palace before then, I will do so. Wildon and Newell are nothing; Durell is a mere figurehead. The Palace is mine when I want it.

I have often pictured myself standing before Timur's Mantel, surrounded by the blue uniforms of SovSec, holding in my hand the letter from the Council of Sovereigns conferring upon me the title of Sovereign of Bragor-Nal. I am no Gildriite, but I know prophecy when I see it.

> —Personal journal of Cedrych i Vran, Overlord of the First Dominion of Bragor-Nal, Day 1, Week 6, Spring, Year 3060.

There were nine of them, all of them men, although Melyor might have become one of them if her business sense hadn't been so good. They were highly proficient with both blade and thrower, and though none of them would have made a very good Nal-Lord, each was quite intelligent. Cedrych didn't call on them very often. Usually they just served as guardsmen, offering no hint to their comrades of the additional responsibilities they had assumed. But occasionally, when the need arose, the Overlord would call them into his office and from there, lead them on one of the assignments for which they had been specially trained in more secret late-night sessions than Cedrych cared to count.

Once more, the need had arisen.

The day began early, with a lengthy trip by carrier to the Twenty-Second Realm in Trestor-Proper. There Cedrych and five of his men slipped silently into an exceedingly well-guarded building, placed a small, but powerful bomb in a carrier, and left the building as stealthily as they had entered it. The bomb was one of Cedrych's own creations. Most carrier devices exploded when the carrier was started, killing drivers and destroying underground vehicle stowing areas, but usually missing their intended targets. Cedrych's bomb, however, was pressure sensitive, and when installed beneath the rear seat of a carrier could be counted on not to detonate until passengers climbed into the vehicle. Given what he knew of Newell's schedule, Cedrych figured that he and his men would already be three hundred quads away when the bomb went off, killing his rival Overlord.

It was several hours later when they finally reached their second destination. This one was in the Twelfth Realm, south of the Farm, in the southern reaches of Bragor-Proper. Here, Cedrych had something a bit more elaborate in mind, for he had an old vendetta to settle with Wildon.

They stowed their carrier half a quad from Wildon's headquarters and stole through alleyways to the rear entrance of the building. Even this doorway was heavily guarded, just as Cedrych had expected it would be. He and Wildon were really quite similar in many ways.

But like his own headquarters, Wildon's defensive systems were designed to prevent a subtle attack, not an overt one. Cedrych and his unit took out no less than ten guards with their first volley of hand boomers. The second volley killed five more. And when Cedrych and his soldiers rushed the building, their throwers blasting through a haze of smoke and dust, Wildon's guards had no choice but to give ground. Two more bombs took out a security post on the ground floor, and by the time Cedrych and two of his men reached the lifter, most of Wildon's guardsmen lay dead or wounded in the rubble.

A pair of boomers destroyed the lifter chamber, giving them access to the shaft's steel maintenance ladder. Immediately Cedrych and his two companions began to climb. The rest of his men were working the stairs. They were a feint of sorts. Like Cedrych's headquarters, Wildon's building had security scanners in the stairwells and the lifter. Seeing the fighting in the former, and knowing that the latter had been destroyed, Wildon would, Cedrych hoped, mass his forces at the stairway doors, ignoring the lifter shaft. Cedrych and his men had created so much smoke in their initial assault on the building that Wildon would have no way of knowing precisely how many men had attacked. Cedrych's men would keep to the stairwells for as long as they could, hopefully giving Cedrych enough time to reach Wildon's office.

So far, the assault was going just as he had anticipated. The building had proven to be quite vulnerable to this type of attack, although, the Overlord knew, no more so than his own headquarters would have been. Indeed, he had planned this raid in his building, by considering how an enemy might go about trying to assassinate him. Even with his weapons chamber, he was only as safe as the security systems on his ground floor allowed him to be. It was lucky for him that no one else in Bragor-Nal had balls enough to attempt such an audacious attack.

It was a long climb, especially for Cedrych, with his maimed right leg. Though he was enjoying himself immensely—he rarely got to do this sort of thing any more—he was tiring, and the day's work was not even half done yet. He was forced to rest several times on the way up. Fortunately, his men were not only skilled, they were also discreet: they said nothing at all about the slow pace or frequent stops. They merely rested when Cedrych rested, and climbed when he climbed. But the Overlord was suddenly acutely aware of his limitations. He was getting too old for this. It seemed that he was making his move just in time.

When they finally reached the level of Wildon's office they forced open the doors separating the lifter shaft from the corridors and were immediately greeted with a barrage of thrower fire. It took Cedrych several moments to realize that it was actually just two of Wildon's guards firing their weapons rapidly and continuously. The shaft made for awkward cover, since it forced Cedrych and his men to hold the ladder with one hand and fire with the other.

But despite his fatigue and the old injuries, the Overlord could still use a hand weapon. He climbed a bit higher, giving his companions access to the door as well. And within minutes the three of them had killed Wildon's two men. They swung themselves into the corridor and made their way noiselessly to its end. At that first corner, however, they encountered more substantial resistance.

There were easily twenty guards standing between them and Wildon's weapons chamber, all of them armed. The hallway was cramped, neutralizing their enemies' advantage in numbers to some extent. But it was clear to Cedrych that he and his men could not prevail in a firefight. So while Cedrych's men returned the guards' thrower fire, the Overlord activated two boomers and tossed them down the hallway, shouting for his companions to take cover as he did. The three of them dove back into the first corridor and an instant later the building trembled with the force of the explosions. Cedrych and his men lay still, allowing the smoke to clear before they renewed their assault, but Cedrych knew that the guards were all dead.

After a minute or two, the three of them rose and peered cautiously around the corner. No one fired at them. They started forward, picking their way past debris and bodies. One of Wildon's guards stirred, only to have Cedrych's men finish him with simultaneous blasts of thrower fire to the chest. The two men grinned at each other.

Wildon's weapons chamber had survived the explosions, but Cedrych disabled it with a couple of well-placed streams of red fire. He then destroyed the locking device on the door to Wildon's office and had his men kick the door open.

"Wait here," he commanded as he stepped past them and through the doorway. "I'll only be a minute."

Wildon's office was tastefully decorated in pale blue, with natural wood furniture and well-let glass sculptures. It was a design Cedrych might have chosen himself, and once more the Overlord remarked to himself how similar he and his rival were.

Which perhaps explains how he knew to look to the side at that very moment, just barely in time. He dropped to the floor like a stone, avoiding the thrower blast that Wildon had aimed at his head. He landed awkwardly, but managed to roll out of the way of a second salvo, firing his weapon wildly and catching Wildon in the leg with one of his shots. The lanky man gasped with pain and fell to one knee. He raised his weapon to fire again, but by then Cedrych had regained his balance. He got off his own blast before Wildon could, hitting his rival near the shoulder of his firing arm. Wildon fell heavily onto his back, and his thrower clattered across the floor to a far corner of the room.

"Shit!" Wildon hissed, wincing at the pain and breathing heavily. He had his eyes closed, and there was a sheen of sweat on his bearded face. "Shit," he repeated.

"Does it hurt much?" Cedrych asked with a smile.

"Yes, you bastard, it hurts like a son of a bitch!"

"Good."

"So you're reaching for the palace, eh Cedrych?" Wildon said through clenched teeth, ignoring Cedrych's last comment.

Cedrych pulled a chair over and sat down. "So it would seem," he said. "Newell?"

"He should be dead by now. Bomb in the carrier."

"How original," Wildon said drily.

"Yes, I know. But I was in a rush to get here. I wanted to do something a little more personal for you."

Wildon opened one eye. "I'm flattered."

Cedrych grinned. "I thought you would be."

The wounded Overlord closed his eye again. "What about Durell?"

"The Sovereign is meeting with the Council today. I'll be paying him a visit this evening."

"You know I've always hated you, Cedrych," Wildon said. "But I hate Durell even more. I'm glad to know he'll be dead soon."

Cedrych chuckled quietly. He and Wildon were so very much alike. For even as the lanky man was saying these things, he was reaching surreptitiously with his uninjured arm for the throwing dagger he wore on his belt.

Cedrych let him get his hand on the hilt of his blade before firing a short blast into the man's good shoulder.

"*Shit!*" Wildon spat, writhing on the floor. "Just end this already, would you?"

"No," Cedrych said, grinning again. "Not yet at least."

"What do you want?"

"Just a simple answer: I always believed that Vanniver had help, that he couldn't have come up with his plan to kill me alone. Were you the one he turned to?"

Wildon stopped writhing and opened his eyes. But he offered no reply.

Cedrych fired his weapon again, this time hitting Wildon in his uninjured leg.

The wounded Overlord screamed in pain. "All right!" he snarled. "All right! Yes, it was me!"

"I always thought so," Cedrych said calmly, lowering his weapon for a moment.

"So why wait until now to kill me?"

Cedrych shrugged. "I could never be sure; there was never any way to prove it."

"I'll take that as a compliment."

"Take it any way you wish."

Cedrych heard a boomer go off in the distance, and he thought of his men fighting in the stairwells.

"I should be going, Wildon," he said, standing up and stretching his legs.

"One day you'll be where I am, Cedrych," Wildon managed through labored breaths. "Someday, someone's going to get past your guards and your weapons chamber, and they're going to kill you."

"Perhaps," Cedrych said solemnly. "But it won't be you." He raised his weapon again, aiming it at Wildon's heart. But then, at the last moment, he thought better of it, and adjusted his line of fire slightly. And when he pressed the fire button on his thrower, a stream of red flame smashed through Wildon's right eye.

She stood on the balcony gazing out at the sea, listening to the waves lapping at the rocky beach below and feeling the warmth of the afternoon sun on her back and shoulders. Gulls cried overhead as they fought for a morsel of food, and a warm wind whistled through the carved stone supports of the railing on which she was leaning. Occasionally she heard Marar's footsteps as his pacing carried him past the doorway that led out to the terrace, but otherwise no human sounds reached Shivohn at all.

Usually she found Durell's habitual tardiness irritating, which was why he did it, she knew. But today she didn't mind waiting. Peace and solitude were luxuries that she had done without for too long. She took a deep breath, savoring the clarity of the air and the fresh scent of brine that it carried, and she turned to face the great house.

Once, hundreds of years ago, this structure had been home to Lon-Ser's monarchs and the cape on which it sat had been known as Lon's Promontory. But with the abolition of the monarchy and the ensuing violence of the Consolidation, the Monarch's residence had been abandoned as a relic of a bygone era and left exposed to the depredations of thieves and vandals. Only in the aftermath of the Consolidation did the surviving Sovereigns reclaim the house and establish it as the meeting place for the Council. And in their vanity they renamed the God's promontory Point of the Sovereigns.

From outside, it was a home of simple magnificence: a monument to a time when Lon-Ser's architects were less heavy-handed and their creations tended to blend with their natural settings. It was constructed entirely of stone and perched, it seemed, on the very edge of the world. And yet, despite its proximity to the sea, the house had survived, intact, since its construction nearly three thousand years ago.

Inside, however, the structure was almost bare. There was a modern kitchen where the original stone ovens once had been, six of the seventeen bedrooms were furnished, and the council chamber contained modest but comfortable wood furniture. But the rest of the residence might as well have been a catacomb. It made sense really: the Sovereigns and their attendants were the only ones who ever used it, and recently the Council had met no more than seven or eight times a year. But Shivohn could not help but feel that the place was being wasted.

She turned once more to look out at Arick's Sea. A small flock of cormorants flew past, their black bodies standing out against the pale green water. Maybe he won't show at all, she thought. Maybe I can stay out here all day.

And of course, as if on cue, Shivohn heard Durell's voice from inside the chamber. He's always late, she thought, shaking her head. And yet he always arrives too soon for my taste.

She heard footsteps at the door to the balcony. "He's here," Marar told her.

She pivoted to respond, but Stib-Nal's Sovereign was already gone. She shrugged and remained where she was. The two of them would need a few minutes alone anyway. Durell had to give Marar his instructions. She smiled to herself, although sadly. This was no way to govern.

She actually had a shorter wait than she had expected. Only a few moments later Durell stepped out onto the terrace, a condescending smile on his lips. His face appeared fatter than usual and his skin was blotchy in the bright sunlight. He did not look well.

"Hello, Shivohn," he said, taking one of her hands in both of his. "I want you to know how sorry I am about what happened. I had no idea that my Overlord was doing such things. I promise you it will never happen again."

"Save it, Durell," she answered coldly, pulling her hand away. "You're only sorry because he got caught."

Durell's grin vanished. "What do you want, Shivohn? I've punished Cedrych—I've stripped him of his power. I'll pay restitution as the law demands, and I've already apologized. Don't reach for too much, Sovereign. I still control this Council, and I still command the strongest forces in Lon-Ser."

Shivohn smiled. "Of course you do. But I don't think you want this matter going that far." Seeing the doubt in Durell's grey eyes, she felt her smile deepen.

"What do you want, Shivohn?" he demanded again, but in a different tone of voice.

She walked past him toward the house. "Come along. We can discuss it with Marar."

They found Stib-Nal's Sovereign already seated at the large, dark table around which their debates usually took place, his hunched, narrow shoulders and thin, bony face making him appear even more inconsequential than he actually was. The Council secretary sat at the table as well, but as usual none of the Sovereigns took note of him.

"Whatever you brought us here to discuss had better be important," Marar said petulantly to Shivohn as she and Durell took their seats. "It doesn't take much for the two of you to get here, but I have to travel quite a distance."

"Shut up, Marar," Durell said with quiet intensity.

Marar looked at him with a wounded expression, but he fell into silence.

"I called you here," Shivohn began, "because of an attack on citizens of my Nal by assassins hired by one of Durell's Overlords. I'm demanding restitution, formal apology, and punishment for the man in question, as is my right under the Green Area Proclamation."

Durell gave an exaggerated nod. "And as I've already said, I will acquiesce to all those demands. That should end the matter."

"Not quite," Shivohn replied, shaking her head. "The intended target of these assassins was a Bragory Nal-Lord named Melyor i Lakin. Melyor claims to be involved with an effort, initiated by this same Overlord, to conquer Tobyn-Ser for the purpose of facilitating Bragor-Nal's expansion into that land."

"*What?*" Marar said with genuine dismay. He stared at Durell. "Is this true?"

"Melyor is a renegade Nal-Lord," Durell told Shivohn calmly, ignoring Marar's outburst. "Cedrych should never have sent the assassins to Oerella-

Nal, and that's why I'm willing to do whatever is necessary to put this matter to rest. But this woman is a murderer and a habitual liar. You can't expect this Council simply to believe everything she says, particularly when her claims are so outlandish."

Shivohn glanced at Marar, who had paled noticeably and was flicking his eyes back and forth between Shivohn and Durell.

"Her claims don't seem outlandish to me" Shivohn said. "They're entirely consistent with the message we received early last year from Tobyn-Ser's Owl-Sage. And they're supported by conversations I've had with Melyor's companion, a sorcerer from Tobyn-Ser named Orris."

"You've spoken with a sorcerer?" Marar asked in a whisper.

"Yes, I have. He and Melyor came to me asking for my help in thwarting this plot."

"That makes no sense at all!" Durell broke in with a chuckle. "Why would Melyor, who claims to be involved with this effort, wish to have you stop it?"

Shivohn hesitated, although only for a moment. She had considered the possibility that one of her fellow Sovereigns would raise this question. There really was only one believable answer, and though it might place Melyor in a difficult position sometime in the future, Shivohn felt that she had no choice but to offer it. "Melyor is a Gildriite. And when she met the sorcerer she found that she could no longer sanction what this Cedrych was attempting to do."

She was gratified to see the shock that registered on Durell's face. Clearly he hadn't been prepared for this. Marar looked surprised as well, although no more so than he had for the past several minutes.

"I believe Melyor's claims have merit," Shivohn concluded, pressing her advantage. "As you pointed out, Durell: she was a part of this plot. She stood to profit from it, and yet she has come forward because she sees that it's wrong. But beyond being wrong," she added, her voice hardening, "it threatens the delicate balance that has existed among our three Nals for several hundred years. I won't allow that to happen. As part of Bragor-Nal's expiation for the incident in Oerella-Nal's Lake Quarter, I formally demand that the Initiative against Tobyn-Ser be halted. If this demand isn't met, the Matriarchy of Oerella-Nal will consider it grounds for war."

Durell glared at her angrily, but for the moment at least, Shivohn was far more interested in Marar's reaction. While speaking with Melyor and Orris a few days earlier, Shivohn had said that though he was a coward and a fool, Stib-Nal's Sovereign was smart enough to allow Bragor-Nal to conquer Tobyn-Ser if it meant preserving Stib-Nal's sovereignty. Since then, however, Shivohn had come to understand that Marar actually faced a somewhat different choice, one between condoning Bragor-Nal's assault on Tobyn-Ser and preserving the status quo. The question in Shivohn's mind was whether Marar was intelligent enough to recognize what the success of the Tobyn-Ser Initiative would mean for his Nal's future. Stib-Nal only continued to exist because the rivalry between Oerella-Nal and Bragor-Nal demanded that Bragory leaders seek some advantage within the Council. If the Tobyn-Ser venture succeeded, and Bragor-Nal gained enough economic and military power to overwhelm Oerella-Nal,

Stib-Nal would become superfluous. And judging from the troubled expression on Marar's lean features, Shivohn guessed that he understood this.

Durell seemed to think so as well. "I want a recess to think about these matters," he said angrily, rising from his chair.

Shivohn shook her head. "No."

"What?"

Shivohn looked up at him and smiled thinly. "I said no. I don't want you to have any chance to bully Marar into following your lead. I want a vote on this matter right now."

Durell bared his teeth in a forced grin. "I don't know what you're talking about, Shivohn. Marar is free to vote however he chooses, as he is on all questions that come before this Council."

"Good. Then you'll have no objection to voting on this before your recess."

Durell clenched his jaw and stood over her silently for several moments before finally throwing himself back into his seat.

"Marar," Shivohn said, turning his way, "it's obvious how Durell and I intend to vote. What about you?"

The third Sovereign cleared his throat and cast a nervous look at Durell. "I should think," he began slowly, clearing his throat a second time, "that if these claims were true, all of us would be alarmed by them." He grimaced slightly. "That is to say, if a subordinate of mine had undertaken such a venture—without my knowledge," he added hastily, looking at Durell again. "If such a thing were to happen, I would be just as alarmed as I would expect my fellow Sovereigns to be. So if this is true, I would expect that, learning of such a thing, the responsible Sovereign—which is to say, the Sovereign who is responsible for the person who did this, because no Sovereign would authorize such an endeavor himself, or herself—the responsible Sovereign would want to stop this project before it went too far. If this is true, that is. We should, of course attempt to determine if this is true."

He stopped, mercifully. Shivohn fought to keep herself from laughing, and she looked at Durell for his reaction. Despite Marar's backtracking and tortured syntax he had at least hinted at the possibility that he would vote against Durell in this instance. But more importantly, he had given the Bragory Sovereign a way out. *If a subordinate of mine had undertaken such a venture without my knowledge . . .*

Now it was up to Durell, who was sitting perfectly still, staring straight ahead, his hands clasped together and resting on the table. At first he said nothing, and the three of them sat in an awkward, tense silence. Finally he looked at Shivohn, though he addressed himself to Stib-Nal's Sovereign. "I see your point, Marar. I certainly can understand how all this might be alarming to Bragor-Nal's neighbors." He exhaled slowly through his teeth. "It does seem possible that Melyor is telling the truth," he admitted at last, "and that the Owl-Sage's note was based in fact after all. Cedrych is a difficult man, and quite capable of doing something this outrageous completely on his own."

"That much is clear," Shivohn observed icily, refusing to give any ground. "The question is: what are you going to do about it?"

Durell's face reddened, and for just an instant Shivohn feared that she had pushed him too far. But when he spoke again, his tone was surprisingly mild. "Cedrych has been removed from power. Originally, I intended this as a temporary measure: one that would perhaps teach him some restraint. But in light of what I've learned today about this Tobyn-Ser Initiative, I see that the only reasonable thing to do is to make his dismissal permanent. Without the resources to which he has had access as an Overlord, he should be unable to follow through on his plans." He eyed Shivohn for a few seconds. "Will that be satisfactory, Sovereign?"

He was trying to deceive them, of course. It was obvious to Shivohn that he had known about the Initiative for some time. She found it impossible to believe that he hadn't. But she was willing to let him salvage this one small victory. "Yes, Sovereign," she replied. "That will be fine."

Durell pushed back abruptly from the table, propelled himself out of his chair, and started toward the door. "Good," he said curtly over his shoulder. "Then I'll be heading back to Bragor-Nal."

The next moment he was gone, and Shivohn and Marar were left alone at the council table. They looked at each other and Marar offered a wan smile.

"I think that went rather well," he said placidly. "Don't you?"

Shivohn actually laughed aloud, and she regarded the slight Sovereign with newfound respect. Perhaps he was more adept at this game than she had thought.

It was nearly dark by the time his entourage returned to the Gold Palace, and Durell was exhausted. Council meetings, he had noticed recently, had this effect on him. It wasn't just the travel, although that part of it was bad enough, even using the air-carriers that shortened the trip so. Shivohn seemed more defiant than ever these days, and Marar had been annoyingly independent in recent months. And today Bragor-Nal had actually lost a vote. True, the official minutes of the meeting wouldn't reflect that. No formal vote was ever taken. Whether intentionally or not, Shivohn had spared him that humiliation. But the three Sovereigns would always know the truth: if it had come to a recorded vote, Durell would have lost.

And somehow Durell had to tell Cedrych that he would never be Overlord again, and that the Initiative was to be terminated. The Sovereign shuddered at the thought of it. He was afraid of Cedrych. He would never have admitted it to anyone, of course, although it seemed clear to him that Cedrych knew. Who could blame him? The man was brilliant, fearless, and crazy, an extremely dangerous combination. And Shivohn had forced Durell to remove him from power. He'll kill me, the Sovereign thought, climbing the palace stairs to his bedchamber.

To which a voice in his head answered, *Not if you have him killed first.* He stopped for an instant, his foot poised above the next step as he considered this. Of course. Even with Blade dead, there were still dozens of hunters in Bragor-Nal, and any one of them would be delighted to be employed by the Sovereign.

Certainly he had the resources to hire them. He could even put a gold bounty on Cedrych's life and make it a contest: first one to kill the Overlord gets it all. Smiling, to himself, Durell continued up the stairs. He felt much better.

It was only when he entered his bedchamber, closing the door behind him, that he realized he had not seen a single guard since his arrival back at the palace. Cold with panic, he whirled around and grabbed the door handle, shouting for the captain of the guard.

But when he pulled the door open Cedrych was there, his thrower aimed at the Sovereign's head.

"Hello, Durell," the one-eyed man said evenly. He stepped into the room, forcing the Sovereign to back away. "How did your meeting with the Council go?"

"How did you get in here?" Durell demanded. "Where are my guards?"

"It's a funny thing," the Overlord commented, his voice infuriatingly calm. "One would expect the Sovereign's guards to be exceptionally skilled. Certainly one wouldn't expect the army of a mere Overlord to have any chance against them. And yet . . ."

He left the thought unfinished and smiled.

"All of them?" the Sovereign asked in a whisper. "You killed all of them?"

"Apparently their training was far too lax," Cedrych observed mildly. "I'll need to make it more rigorous when I become Sovereign."

Durell stared at him wordlessly.

"Sit down, Durell," Cedrych commanded, waving his weapon toward a chair by the large bed. "Tell me about your meeting."

Durell lowered himself slowly into the chair, but he still said nothing.

"Did you agree to Shivohn's demands?" the Overlord asked. "Have you promised to remove me from power?"

"Only temporarily," Durell lied. "Just until autumn."

Cedrych raised his eyebrow skeptically. "And she accepted this? Come now, Durell."

"What does it matter?" the Sovereign asked eagerly. "As you were saying the other day: she doesn't run Bragor-Nal."

Cedrych grinned, although the expression in his single blue eye was shockingly cold. "Yes, I remember saying that. I believe it was just before you had me removed from the palace."

"Y-yes. Well—"

"I wouldn't bring up our last conversation again," Cedrych warned. "It wasn't one of our best."

"What do you want, Cedrych? Do you want me to step down as Sovereign, and have you installed in my place? Fine. I'll do it. Gladly."

"Of course you will," the Overlord said, his scarred face still wearing the frosty smile. "And then you'll hire someone to kill me so that you can reclaim your position.

"Well what do you think Newell and Wildon are going to do if you just kill me and take over?" Durell asked testily. "Simply accept it and go about their business?" He shook his head. "Not a chance! But with my endorsement, it won't matter what they do."

Cedrych chuckled in a way that made the hairs on the back of Durell's neck stand on end. "Newell and Wildon aren't going to do anything," he said with such assurance that the Sovereign understood immediately that the other two Overlords were dead.

"My best guards weren't here when you arrived," Durell said, desperation creeping into his voice. "They were with me. But they're here now. And they'll never let you do this." It wasn't much of a threat, he knew, but it was all he had left.

Cedrych shook his head with amusement. "You know as well as I that SovSec works for the Sovereign, whoever he might be. When I declare myself the rightful leader of Bragor-Nal, your guards will accept me as such."

"Shivohn knows about the Initiative!" the Sovereign blurted out. "She's willing to go to war over it if she has to! But she and I have a rapport! I can talk to her on your behalf; I can get her to back down!"

"You see, Durell, that's the difference between us," Cedrych said with that same maddening serenity. "You're afraid of war with the Matriarchy. I'm not. It might be costly, and it might take some time. But it's a war we can win. And to me, winning is all that matters." The bald man had allowed the hand holding his weapon to fall to his side, but now he raised it again, pointing it at Durell's face.

The Sovereign flinched away and threw up an arm to guard himself. "No, Cedrych! Please!"

"That's another of our differences. Given the choice, I'd rather live than die. But I'm not afraid of death."

From another man, it would have been an empty boast. But looking now at Cedrych's face—the scars, the icy blue of his remaining eye, the dispassionate expression on his features as he spoke of killing and war and dying—Durell found that he believed him. The two of them *were* different. And that, as much as anything, explained why Cedrych was about to become Sovereign, and why Durell was about to perish.

And that may also be why the Sovereign, in the final moments of his life, was moved to help his killer. "Marar is showing signs of assertiveness," he said matter-of-factly. "Before you go after Shivohn you should take steps to control Stib-Nal."

Cedrych regarded him with genuine surprise, and even lowered his weapon for a moment. "Thank you, Sovereign," he said. "I'll do that. And for that, I'll make this as swift and painless as I can."

The Overlord raised his weapon again and the last thing Durell saw was the subtle movement of Cedrych's thumb as it depressed the firing button on his thrower.

"In the end," Shivohn said in Tobynmir, concluding her summary of the previous day's Council meeting, "Durell had no choice but to give in to my demands."

She was standing before the large windows in her chamber that looked out on the palace gardens. She seemed pleased with herself, and far more at ease than Orris remembered from the first day they met.

Melyor shook her head in disbelief. "Marar really sided with you?" she asked in her heavy accent. "I never expected that he would stand up to Durell like that."

Shivohn smiled. "It wasn't the most forceful assertion of Nal sovereignty I've ever seen, but in his own way he made it clear to Durell that Bragor-Nal had overstepped its bounds."

"So you believe that Cedrych no longer poses a threat to Tobyn-Ser?" Orris asked, seeking reassurance, and almost afraid to let himself believe that this could be true.

The Sovereign turned to him, the expression on her round features growing sober. "I'd like to tell you that I'm certain, Hawk-Mage, but Durell has lied to me too many times before. I will say this: he seemed sincere, and I think that Marar's actions gave him some indication of how seriously the people of Stib-Nal and Oerella-Nal take this matter. I'm afraid though, that it will take some time before we know how much his promises are worth. I wish I could be more reassuring."

The mage nodded. "I understand. Whatever happens, I'm grateful for what you've done for my people." And then, before she could protest, he added, "Even though I realize you were doing it all for your people, not mine."

She grinned. "Perhaps not all," she said quietly. She faced Melyor again. "I'm sorry to have to tell you, Nal-Lord, that I was forced to inform Durell and Marar of your heritage. It was the only way I could think of to convince them that you were telling the truth about the Initiative. My apologies."

Melyor gave a small shrug and glanced self-consciously at the glowing red stone mounted atop the staff she now carried. "You do not need to apologize," she replied, smiling sadly. "I have this staff now, so it will be difficult to keep it a secret anyway."

"Then you've decided to keep the staff?" Orris asked gently.

She met his gaze, and there seemed to be tears in her green eyes. "It was Gwilym's decision, I think. Who am I to argue with him?"

"Then I owe you another apology," Shivohn said solemnly. "I called you 'Nal-Lord' when I should have addressed you as 'Bearer.'"

Melyor flushed deeply. "I will have to get used to that."

"You will in time," Shivohn told her, smiling again. She turned back to Orris and cleared her throat awkwardly. "I was hoping, Hawk-Mage, that we might discuss the trade possibilities you mentioned at our first meeting. I found your offer intriguing."

The mage grinned. He like Shivohn, he had decided. She had been candid with him from the start, even when she was denying his requests for help. He appreciated that. The Order needed a few people like her. "I'd be happy to discuss it, Sovereign," he said. "You must realize though that I'm just one mage, with no authority to speak for the people of Tobyn-Ser. Personally, I believe it's time that we looked beyond our land's shores, in commerce and other matters as well. But few in my Order would agree with me, and my people have been frightened by their recent encounter with outlanders. Still, I'll try; I owe you that much."

The Sovereign opened her mouth to reply. But before she could, there was a knock on the door to her chamber. "Enter!" Shivohn called. Then, smiling, she called again, this time in Lonmir.

A young courtier walked in, looking hesitant and, Orris thought, a bit frightened. He held a small, folded piece of paper in a trembling hand.

The Sovereign spoke reassuringly to him in her language and beckoned him forward. He stepped to her quickly and handed her the note before retreating to stand by the door again. Shivohn seemed amused by his diffidence, and she grinned at him briefly before unfolding the paper.

As soon as she began to read, however, her bearing changed entirely. She leaned heavily on her small desk, all the color draining from her face, and her eyes widening with alarm. She looked up at Melyor and Orris, and then appeared to read what was on the paper a second time, as if hoping that somehow the words had changed in that single moment.

"What is it, Sovereign?" Orris heard himself ask, although somehow he already knew. New as he was to the Nals and their peculiar ways, he knew.

"Durell is dead," Shivohn said in a flat voice. "So are two of Bragor-Nal's three Overlords."

Melyor was nodding as if she had expected this all along. "Of course," she said. "Newell and Wildon. There was no sense in killing Durell if he wasn't going to kill them, too."

"What does this mean?" Orris asked. But he knew.

Melyor stared at him, looking more frightened than he had ever seen her. "It means that Cedrych is Bragor-Nal's new Sovereign."

28

We who have formed this League have done so reluctantly. All of us would have preferred to continue as members of the Order of Mages and Masters so that we might reform that body from within. Indeed, we made efforts to that end, only to have them rebuffed. And so, with regret, we concluded that we could not in good conscience continue to wear our green cloaks. We are resolved that Tobyn-Ser should be served by the Mage-Craft as Amarid envisioned: without regard to personal glory or status or influence. . . .

Every new member of this League shall pledge to abide by Amarid's Laws—save the Third Law which shall be amended as indicated in Article Two—for this body is the one true inheritor of the First Mage's legacy and its members are the true Children of Amarid. The League exists solely to serve the people of Tobyn-Ser, to protect and heal them, and mediate their disputes, just as Amarid intended. It does not seek to rule them, nor does it intend to lead them blindly into foolish ventures beyond the land's borders. That is not what Tobyn-Ser's people want, nor does it conform to Amarid's vision of what the Mage-Craft should be.

—From Article One of "The Charter and Bylaws of the League of Amarid," drafted at the 1st Annual Conclave of the League of Amarid, Spring, Gods' Year 4626.

Marcran wheeled overhead, the bright midday sun lighting the russet feathers on his back as if Leora herself had laid her hand upon them. He hovered above Cailin for several moments and then suddenly tucked his wings close to his body and dove toward the ground.

Seeing him dive, Cailin closed her eyes and reached for the deep connection with him she had first learned to forge last winter, when the Owl-Sage visited her. It came to her easily now; she had done this many times. Abruptly she was no longer a young girl. She was a falcon, hurtling toward the earth, her talons outstretched as she pounced on a small green snake. She tore with her beak at the base of the creature's head, killing it. Or, rather, Marcran did. At times like these Cailin found it hard to tell where she ended and he began. Then they rose from the ground again, laboring to carry the snake to a dead snag at the far edge of the clearing. As soon as they landed they began to rip at it with their beak, even as the creature continued to writhe in their grip.

It seemed to Cailin that warm, sweet blood filled her mouth, and she broke the connection, as she always did at that point. It was not that the killing bothered her, nor the taste of blood. Once they had, at first. But that had passed long ago. In fact, the opposite was true. As always, she felt exhilarated by Marcran's hunting. She was breathless and flushed. And just a little bit ashamed. It was wrong—it had to be wrong. And yet, every time she saw him stoop to kill, she could not resist the urge to join her mind with his.

She opened her eyes and started toward her hawk. But she had only taken a step or two when she heard the sound of clapping coming from behind her. She whirled around, feeling her cheeks shade toward crimson and fearing that they would give her away.

"Splendid!" came a man's voice from just outside the clearing.

It took Cailin a moment to spot him, and only when he stepped out from among the trees and into the clearing could she see what he looked like. He was tall and solidly built, and his hair and short beard were as white as snow. He carried a large, round-headed owl on his shoulder and in his hand he bore a staff that was crowned with a glowing grey stone. Cailin was fairly certain that he was an Owl-Master. And yet his cloak, rather than being forest green like those worn by members of the Order, was as blue as the sky, with intricate black embroidery on the cuffs and around the hood.

"Splendid!" he said again, grinning broadly and still clapping. "He's a beautiful bird and a fine hunter."

"Who are you?" Cailin asked warily, trying to slow her pulse and begging Arick to let the blood leave her flushed cheeks.

"My name is Erland," the man said, coming forward, the smile still on his lips. "And you must be Cailin. I've heard a great deal about you."

Of course you have, she wanted to say. Everyone has. That's the way it sometimes seemed. Every adult she met said pretty much the same thing to her. *You must be Cailin, the little girl with the hawk. I've heard so much about you.* People had said this to her—or something like it—so many times she had lost count. It was an improvement, she supposed, on how the adults had treated her before she bound to Marcran, when everyone had known her as the orphan from Kaera, but it still bothered her.

"Why does your cloak look like that?" she asked, not bothering to respond to his last comment. If it's so obvious, there's no need for me to tell you you're right, she said within her mind.

He smiled at her mysteriously. "A good question. But before I answer it, I have some questions for you. What do you think of the Order, Cailin?"

"Are you the new Owl-Sage?" she asked, still scrutinizing his blue and black cloak.

His smile deepened. "Tell me what you think of the Order," he insisted.

She glanced briefly at Marcran, wishing this man would go away and leave the two of them to fly and hunt. "I'm never going to join!" she said, not bothering to hide her bitterness. "I hate the Order! No one can ever make me take the oath!" If he wanted to know what she thought of the Order, then by the gods she'd tell him.

"Why do you hate the Order so much?" he asked calmly

She stared at him in disbelief. Didn't he know who she was? Hadn't he heard about what she had been through? "They let my parents die!" she told him as if he were simple. "They let my home and my entire town be destroyed! And they had promised to protect us!" She looked at his cloak again, wondering why she was saying "they" instead of "you." "Who are you?" she demanded hotly. "What do you want from me?"

"I told you: my name is Erland," the man said mildly, stroking his owl's chin.

"That's not what I meant! Why are you wearing that cloak?"

"You know what I think, Cailin? I think that one of the reasons you hate the Order so much—beyond what they did to Kaera—is that because you can't bring yourself to join the Order, you're forced to be all alone as a mage." He held up a placating hand and shook his head. "Don't get me wrong: no one blames you for not wanting to take the oath. But I imagine that it's very lonely for you at times, not being around others who share your gift."

Cailin stared down at her feet, unwilling just then to look Erland in the eye. She still wasn't sure what to make of this man, and she certainly wasn't ready to confide in him. And yet . . . "A woman came during the winter and spoke to me," she said quietly. "Owl-Sage Sonel." She glanced at the white-haired man briefly to see how he reacted to hearing the Sage's name. But he merely continued to smile at her. "She told me that she'd talk to me about being a mage any time I wanted."

"I don't doubt it," he said. "But why do you think she did that?"

Cailin shrugged, still not meeting the Owl-Master's gaze. "I guess because she wanted me to join the Order." She didn't want to believe that. She had tried to convince herself in the weeks and months since Sonel's visit that the green-eyed woman had really wanted to be her friend. But if that was true, why hadn't Sonel visited since? There could be only one explanation.

Erland nodded knowingly. "They haven't been very fair with you, Cailin. They've tried to use you and control you, but they haven't been nice to you. And do you know why?"

Cailin shook her head.

"Because they're afraid of you. They don't like the fact that you're a mage who won't join them. But really that's the least of it. You're a very famous young woman, Cailin. People throughout the land know who you are, and they see you as more than just a child, more even than just a survivor of the outlanders' attacks. To many, you're a living symbol of the Order's failure to protect the land. That's why the Order is afraid of you, particularly now that you're a mage yourself."

She just stared at him, shocked that any adult would say these things to her, especially a mage. No one had ever been so honest with her. Not her parents, not Linnea or the other Children of the Gods, and definitely not Sonel. "Who—"

He held a finger to his lips, stopping her. "One more question, Cailin, and then I'll tell you everything you want to know."

She gazed at him for a moment and then nodded slowly. But suddenly she knew who he was and why he had come. Her dream. Abruptly she was reliving the dream she had had so many months ago, even before she had bound to Marcran. She was fighting off Kaera's attackers with her deadly golden fire. And she was wearing a blue cloak, exactly like the one Erland wore. She fell silent, as he had told her to, and she waited. But she already knew what he was going to say. In a sense, she had known for a long time.

"What would you think?" the mage asked, "if someone told you that you could be a part of a group of mages that had nothing to do with the Order? Nothing at all."

"That's why your cloak is blue," Cailin said, her voice barely more than a whisper.

"Yes," he said, a wondrous smile spreading across his ruddy face. "A group of mages has left the Order and formed what we call the League of Amarid. There are currently twenty-three of us, Hawk-Mages and Owl-Masters. And our numbers are still growing. We abide by Amarid's Laws, but we're not only here to serve the land. We also intend to keep watch on the Order; to make sure that they keep their oaths and to stop them from engaging in the type of mischief that's caused so much trouble over the past several years."

"Are you the League of Amarid's Owl-Sage?"

"I'm First Master of the League, yes." He paused, taking a step toward her.

"I've come to ask you if you'll join us, Cailin. We'll all understand if you don't want to. Given all you've been through, no one will question you, no matter what decision you make." He took another step and placed a hand gently on her shoulder. "But we're not the Order. We'd want you to take an oath to abide by Amarid's Laws, but that's the only similarity. The League is something new, and I'm confident that it will replace the Order someday to become the sole caretaker of the Mage-Craft in Tobyn-Ser."

Cailin chewed her lip for several moments, staring off to the side and considering Erland's offer. "If I joined," she asked, looking at him again, "would I have to leave the Temple?"

The Owl-Master shook his head. "No. Linnea and I have spoken about this. Neither of us has any objection to you remaining here."

She fell silent again. Marcran reached for her suddenly, and in the next instant he alighted on her shoulder, his talons causing her to wince despite the padding that one of the Temple's seamstresses had sown into the shoulders of her blouse.

"You'd get a cloak," Erland added with a gentle grin. "And the shoulders are reinforced with leather."

Cailin laughed and scratched Marcran's head lightly. Then she grew serious again, thinking about his invitation. She liked the Children of the Gods, but they seemed uncomfortable with her and her magic. It would be nice to have friends who were mages, too; who understood her relationship with Marcran, and who could teach her more about the Mage-Craft. And then, of course, there was her dream. She took a deep breath. "All right," she said. "I'll join."

Erland smiled broadly, his blue eyes appearing to sparkle with sunlight and ceryll-glow. "I'm very glad," he said. "Delighted, in fact. And the others will be, too."

She blushed slightly, pleased by his reaction.

"Actually," he went on, "there's more that I'd like to ask of you." He seemed embarrassed suddenly. "Again, no one will blame you for refusing, but the others wanted me to ask." He hesitated, but only for a moment. "In light of all that's happened to you and because of your extraordinary achievement— binding at such a young age—we would like you to serve as First Mage of the League."

Cailin gaped at him, wide-eyed with amazement. "First Mage?"

"Yes," he said casually. "Only if you're interested, of course."

Interested? She was overwhelmed. The people of Tobyn-Ser called Amarid the First Mage, and now here was the leader of Amarid's League asking her to accept the same title. It seemed impossible. It was too much. And yet, it was so tempting. "What would I have to do?" she asked, feeling intimidated by the prospect of it.

"Not much really. Your duties wouldn't involve anything that we weren't all confident you could handle. You'd lead our processions, and call our Conclaves to order. And during our discussions, you'd sit with Second Master Toinin and me at the head of the meeting table."

Cailin smiled. "That's all?"

"That's all."

"That sounds easy."

Erland smiled. "It should be, for you." His expression grew serious. "That doesn't mean it's not important, though," he told her. "First Mage is a position of great symbolic significance. This is a tremendous honor the League is offering you."

Cailin nodded. "I know!"

He raised a white eyebrow. "So are you interested?"

"Yes," she answered after weighing his offer briefly. "I'll do it."

"Good," the Owl-Master said with a nod. "The other members will be pleased." He looked her up and down for a few seconds. "We'll have to have a cloak made for you and somehow we need to get you a ceryll."

"Don't I need to go to Ceryllon for that?"

"It worked that way once," Erland told her. "Few mages make the trip there anymore. Most get their stones from merchants who have made the trip, or occasionally from older mages who have acquired extra stones over the years." He grinned at her slyly. "As I have."

"You have an extra ceryll?" Cailin asked eagerly.

In response, the Owl-Master reached a hand into his cloak and pulled out a crystal that was easily the size of Cailin's fist. It was clear as a mountain stream and it sparkled in the sunlight, casting rainbows on the grass at their feet.

"It's beautiful," Cailin said breathlessly.

"Would you like it?"

She tore her eyes from the stone and looked at Erland to see if he was teasing. He was grinning at her, but kindly, giving no indication that he was mocking her. She gazed at the ceryll again, too astonished to speak.

"It's all right," he said quietly. "As you can see, I already have a ceryll. This one is just gathering dust in my home."

"I don't have a staff for it," Cailin said, feeling embarrassed.

"Neither did I when I first got mine. But you know how to shape wood don't you?"

Cailin nodded. "But I'm not very good at it yet."

"What better way to practice. Take it," he urged, holding it out to her. "Please."

Still Cailin hesitated. It struck her as an extraordinary gift—almost too extraordinary. She wished that there was someone she could ask, someone who could tell her if it was all right for her to accept it. But she didn't think that the Children of the Gods would understand. This was a matter relating to the Mage-Craft. Her mother and father would have known what to do, she thought with sudden heartache. And thinking of them, trying to weather the brief but intense anguish that always came with the memory of their faces, she made her decision.

"All right," she said, reaching for it. "Thank—"

As soon as her fingers touched the stone it appeared to burst into flame.

Golden light poured from it as if a piece of the sun had fallen from the sky and landed in the Owl-Master's hand. In the next instant the light ebbed, but it did not disappear entirely. Where once the crystal had been perfectly clear and colorless, it now glowed with a deep golden fire.

Cailin had snatched back her hand as soon as the light appeared and now Erland extended his hand, offering it to her again.

"Congratulations, Cailin. You've bound to your ceryll, just as you once bound to your falcon. As long as you live, this stone will glow with your ceryll-hue and no other mage will be able to use it."

Tentatively, as if expecting it to burn her hand, Cailin picked up the ceryll. It was heavier than she expected, and despite its fiery appearance it felt cool to the touch. She lifted it close to her face and turned it over and over in her hands, examining every facet, wondering how anything could be so exquisite.

"You now possess everything you need to be a Hawk-Mage: the power that you carry within you, your familiar, and your stone. These are the three elements of the Mage-Craft."

"How does it work?" Cailin asked, still staring at the golden crystal. "What do I do?"

"You use your power just as you always have, except that you channel it through your crystal."

She looked at him quizzically. "Huh?"

Erland smiled. "Let's try it this way. What do you do when you want to light a fire?"

Cailin thought for a moment. "I reach for Marcran, and I form an image of fire in my mind."

"And then what?"

She shrugged. "It's hard to describe. I kind of push my power at the wood and it lights."

"Has your power ever gotten away from you when you did that?"

Cailin looked away, blushing as she remembered the tree she had burned the previous autumn.

"It's all right if it has, Cailin," the Owl-Master said soothingly. "It's happened to all of us at one time or another." He pointed to her crystal. "But if you use that ceryll, it's not likely to happen again. When you 'push' your power, as you put it, send it through the stone. You'll find that the ceryll amplifies and focuses your power, just as a lens can focus sunlight and make it burn. Do you understand?"

"I think so," Cailin said, nodding.

Erland reached out and gave her shoulder a gentle squeeze. "Good. I'll let you practice. I have to be going anyway." He turned to leave the clearing.

"Wait!" Cailin called after him, taking a step forward. "What am I supposed to do now. . . ." *Now that I'm First-Mage of the League,* she wanted to say. But she couldn't make herself speak the words. She could hardly believe all that had happened to her on this day.

Fortunately, Erland appeared to understand. He faced her again, smiling indulgently. "I'll send for you. Our Conclave should begin in a few weeks, around the time of Amarid's birthday. I'll sent a message to the Eldest and she'll see to it that you're escorted to our meeting place."

"Where is the Conclave held?"

"This first year it will be at my home in Pinehaven. That's a small town a bit north of the Temple. Hopefully by this time next year the Hall of the League will have been constructed in the city of Amarid." He was still smiling at her, although Cailin sensed that he was anxious to be leaving. "Farewell, Cailin. Arick guard you."

"And you, Owl-Master."

He nodded and turned again.

"Thank you, Owl-Master!" she called to him as he stepped out of the clearing. "For everything."

"My pleasure, child," he replied over his shoulder.

She watched him until she lost sight of him among the trees. Then, gently stroking Marcran's chin, she turned her attention back to the magnificent stone she held in her hand. *You now possess everything you need to be a Hawk-Mage.*

"Not quite," she said aloud. And giddy with excitement, she began to search the edge of the clearing for a piece of wood long and straight enough to be a mage's staff.

The Eldest had been watching for him from the entrance of the Temple for over half an hour when he finally came into view. Catching a glimpse of his blue cloak through the trees, she immediately slipped back inside, unwilling to let the Owl-Master see how interested she was. She waited a few seconds in the shadows, until she could hear the sound of his footsteps. Then she walked out of the Temple as if on her way somewhere.

"Owl-Master!" she said, smiling and feigning surprise. "I didn't expect you back so soon. Did you find her?"

He looked at her skeptically. "No, Eldest," he said with sarcasm. "I've spent the better part of the last hour conversing with the trees." He stopped in front of her. "And with the establishment of the League, I'm properly addressed as First Master Erland."

"Of course you are," she said, a little too sweetly. "How did your conversation with Cailin go?"

"Very well, actually. You're right: she's a very impressive girl.

"Has she agreed to join your League?"

Erland smiled triumphantly, his dark blue eyes gleaming. "Of course. How could she refuse? I offered her a chance to interact with other mages and I made her First Mage of the League."

"First Mage?" Linnea asked with concern. "What does that mean? You realize that she's just—"

"Relax, Eldest," he said, laughing. "It means very little. She'll have a few ceremonial duties. Nothing more. But it will allow us to put her at the head of our processions and at a place of honor at our meeting table."

"In other words it's an excuse to put her on display, as if she were a trophy of some sort."

The Owl-Master's smile faded abruptly. "That's a cruel way to characterize what we consider a bestowal of honor."

"Perhaps," Linnea conceded coldly. "But is it accurate?"

Erland pressed his lips into a thin line, saying nothing.

"I see," Linnea murmured.

"No harm will come to her," the Owl-Master assured her. "You may not approve of our motives, but we're not going to mistreat her in any way."

"Oh, I know that," the Eldest answered quickly. "If I thought even for a moment that you would, I never would have allowed you to speak with her."

"Well then you know that she has nothing to fear from the League."

Linnea shook her head. "I didn't say that. She's just a child, and I don't like the idea of her being thrown into the middle of your quarrel with Sonel."

"It's much more than a quarrel, Eldest," Erland said petulantly. "You shouldn't underestimate the League's significance. For the first time in a thousand years, a group of people has challenged the Order's authority to control the Mage-Craft. The ramifications of what we've done could be enormous. Everyone in Tobyn-Ser will be affected. Even Arick's Children," he added, looking at her intently.

Linnea met his gaze steadily. "All the more reason not to involve a child."

Erland let out an exasperated breath and walked a few steps away. He was silent for several moments, before turning to face her again. "You and I have a good deal in common, Linnea," he said earnestly. It was a familiarity she would not normally have tolerated, but she let it go. "We're both leaders; we both have a deep love and keen understanding of our land and its people. But most significantly, we share a common enemy: the Order. We should be cooperating with each other. Frankly, I'm surprised and disappointed by your failure to recognize that."

"Pardon me if I don't embrace you as an ally immediately, Erland," she replied, "but until quite recently you were a part of the Order. You can't win the Temple's trust simply by declaring yourself an enemy of the Order. If you want an alliance with the Keepers you're going to have to earn it."

"Fine," he said. "How?"

"You can start by making it clear to your followers and to the people of Tobyn-Ser, that the League is not interested in ruling the land, and that it recognizes the Temple as an equal partner in its efforts to serve and protect Tobyn-Ser's citizens."

The Owl-Master smiled. "That's already a part of our charter."

"It is?" Linnea asked with genuine surprise.

"We've never been interested in governing Tobyn-Ser, Eldest. That's one of the reasons we left the Order. We believe that Sonel and her followers, particularly a man named Baden, are intent upon making the Order into some kind of omnipotent ruling council and then using that power to involve us in dangerous ventures beyond Tobyn-Ser's borders. The League wants none of that. We certainly don't wish to rule Tobyn-Ser. We want the Mage-Craft to fulfill its original objectives, those intended by Amarid when he first discovered Leora's Gift a thousand years ago."

"And they are?"

"To serve the people of the land," he answered. "To be the arbiter of disputes. To use our powers to give aid and comfort in times of need."

Even Linnea recognized the litany: Amarid's Law. Almost word for word. "Erland," she said with a smirk. "Are you a zealot?"

"I am a mage," the Owl-Master said, his expression remaining solemn.

Linnea shivered. She crossed her arms over her chest, hiding her hands, which were trembling, within the ample sleeves of her silver-grey robe.

"Cailin's membership in the League is absolutely crucial to its success as an alternative to the Order," Erland went on a moment later. "There is no greater symbol in this land of the Order's failure to uphold its pledge to serve Tobyn-Ser's people. When her parents died and her town was destroyed, she became your responsibility. But when she bound to that falcon she became mine as well."

"Yours or Sonel's," Linnea told him, not quite believing that she could say such a thing.

"What?" Erland hissed. "You can't mean that!"

She wasn't sure what she meant. Neither alternative seemed terribly attractive at the moment. She didn't know if she could bring herself to involve the Order in Cailin's upbringing, but Erland struck her as unbalanced and dangerous. Linnea could keep Cailin in the Temple for a while longer, but at some point, she understood, as Cailin's powers developed, she would have to choose.

"I do mean it," she said, trying to muster as much resolve as she could. "Cailin is still my charge. I, and I alone, will determine what's best for her."

"Well you'd better hurry," Erland fired back at her. "She's a mage, and she's going to grow stronger every day. Especially now that she has a ceryll."

Linnea felt the blood drain from her face. "You gave her a ceryll?"

"Yes. If she's going to be First Mage, she needs to have a ceryll and staff. I assumed she didn't have a stone yet, so I purchased one from an Abboriji merchant before I came."

The Eldest swallowed. "Sonel told me that she wasn't ready yet. She said that a child her age needed to learn to control her powers first."

"That's ridiculous," the white-haired man said, with a dismissive gesture. "She can't learn to control her power without some means to focus it. That's what the ceryll does." He shook his head angrily. "You see? This is just what I mean. Sonel and Baden are already trying to control her, just as they want to control everything in Tobyn-Ser." He took a step toward her, and Linnea had to force herself to stand her ground. "They have to be stopped, Linnea. The Order can't be allowed to continue down this path. Together, the League and the Temple can do it. Given time, I know that I can draw enough support from the Order to make it obsolete. But I need Cailin. She's the key to everything."

Linnea felt as though he was kneeling on her chest. She could barely breathe. Cailin had a ceryll. Whatever time Linnea had thought she and the other keepers had to make this decision was gone. Suddenly. Without any warning at all. Because Cailin had a ceryll. She wondered briefly if Erland had planned this; if he had given the ceryll to Cailin in order to force Linnea to go along with his scheme. She wouldn't have put it past him. But it didn't matter. Whatever his reasons, he had done it.

"You can accompany her to the Conclave," he offered. He was smiling now. No doubt, he could read his victory in her face. "You'll have to leave during the session itself, of course. But you can travel with her, and you can take care of her when we're not meeting."

She couldn't say a thing. She just stared past him into the woods, imagining Cailin in her clearing. She could see the girl's hair stirring in the wind, her blue eyes sparkling in the sunshine. Linnea might even have smiled at the image.

"I know how much you care about her, Eldest," Erland said gently. "I'm glad you love her so much. I'm sure that as I get to know her, I'll come to feel the same way. Perhaps that will be the foundation on which you and I can build an alliance."

"Perhaps," Linnea whispered, still gazing into the trees.

"Then you'll let her join the League?"

She looked at the Owl-Master. "You've already told her she can join," she replied in a cold voice. "You've already made her First Mage. You've even given her a ceryll. Do I really have a choice?"

Erland smiled. And Linnea saw just a hint of malice in his dark blue eyes. "No," he said. "I don't suppose you do."

They had decided to not to return to western Tobyn-Ser until summer. It was the logical choice, really. Even on horseback, by the time they reached their home on the shores of South Shelter it would be time for them to turn around and cross the land again, in order to be back in Amarid for the Midsummer Gathering. Mered, Radomil, and Ursel had all done the same thing. Baden, who had been chosen by Sonel to replace Toinan as First of the Sage, had not yet decided what he was going to do. And Trahn had returned to the Great Desert, explaining that even a short stay with his wife and children was better than none at all. Thinking about it rationally, Jaryd knew that he had no reason to question the choice that he and Alayna had made. But it bothered him. By the time they returned home after the Gathering, an entire season would have passed. What if something happened? A freak storm, or a fire, or even a land tremor? Who would take care of the people of the Shelter and the Lower Horn?

Alayna, of course, shared his concern. And so they did the one thing they could. For the remainder of the spring, they decided, they would become migrants rather than nesters. They would travel throughout Hawksfind Wood and over the mountains to Tobyn's Wood—perhaps they would even ride southward to the upper reaches of the God's plain. And they would offer their services in the towns and villages that they found along the way. In this way they hoped to find a satisfying substitute for the lifestyle they had left behind on Tobyn-Ser's western shores. Jaryd knew that it would not entirely assuage the regret he felt at leaving his neighbors in western Tobyn-Ser without immediate access to the Mage-Craft, but he thought it might help.

And for the first few weeks it did. They rode through the lower half of Hawksfind Wood, and then into Tobyn's Wood, healing minor wounds and mending broken tools and fences. And though the people they met were somewhat reserved in their gratitude, Jaryd was satisfied in knowing that he was helping someone. But as the spring progressed, warming the air and deepening the shadows of the God's forest, he and Alayna noticed that the people they encountered were growing increasingly wary of them. At first the young mages merely assumed that word had reached the villagers of the split in the Order's ranks. They soon realized, however, that there was more to it than that.

They were in a small village along the banks of Fourfalls River in Tobyn's Wood when they first heard of Erland's new League of Amarid. A traveling peddler, on his way from Amarid to the towns near Duclea's Tears, told them of the League's new charter and its assertion that this new body was the one true steward of the Mage-Craft.

"Erland can't really believe that his League will replace the Order," Alayna commented to Jaryd, as the peddler watched them with manifest curiosity, apparently trying to gauge their response to the news he had offered.

Jaryd shrugged. "I don't see that he has much choice. I can't imagine him coming back to the Order, at least not yet. And he and his followers are better off organizing themselves than they are wandering the land on their own."

"Personally, I think it's a shrewd move," the peddler volunteered. Both mages looked at him. "With the outlanders and all that's happened, people don't trust the Order so much anymore. But we still want mages doing things for us. In fact," the man went on, growing bolder as he spoke, "it wouldn't surprise me if the League replaces the Order within just a few years." He took a breath to say more, but then stopped himself, his face reddening, as if he suddenly remembered that he was speaking to members of the Order. "I'm sorry, Hawk-Mage," he said to Alayna self-consciously. "I didn't mean any disrespect."

"I know," Alayna said. "It's all right." She smiled at the man reassuringly, but Jaryd saw that the expression in her dark eyes was troubled.

Over the next several days it seemed to Jaryd that everywhere they went, they heard people talking about the League. At first the townsfolk they met talked of Erland and his followers openly, but as the days went on, the people grew more furtive. Animated conversations ceased abruptly when the speakers noticed Jaryd and Alayna approaching. The few who would talk to them about the League did so not in confidence, but in voices that carried a note of defiance, as if by offering information they were telling the young mages where their loyalties now lay.

"It's about time you mages in the Order were given something to think about," one outspoken woman told them in another town in Tobyn's Wood, this one a short distance from the Riversmeet Traverse. "Maybe now you'll start to do the things we want you to do, rather than watching out for yourselves all the time."

"What would you like us to do that we haven't done?" Alayna asked gently, her features looking pale and fragile.

"Well, I don't know," the woman said uncomfortably. "I suppose you could start by punishing that outlander the way he ought to be punished."

Jaryd and Alayna shared a look, and he saw his own thought mirrored in her eyes. *At least they don't know about Orris yet.*

Later in the same day, they caught up with a group of musicians along the trail they were following. There were six of them in all: four men carrying instruments, and two women who, the mages learned, did most of the singing. They appeared to be more sympathetic to the Order than the villagers had been, but only slightly, and they bore disturbing news. Erland had begun to tell people what Orris had done, and he had spoken openly of what he claimed was a conspiracy of traitors within the Order. The lute player, an older man who seemed to be the leader of the group, said that the people who had told him of Erland's actions were more than willing to believe the worst about the Order.

"What he told you about Orris is true," Jaryd admitted. "But those of us who support him don't consider what he's done treason. He's trying to save Tobyn-Ser, not destroy it."

"I'm inclined to believe you," the bard replied. "But I'm in the minority, even among my friends here."

Jaryd glanced at the other performers and saw that the three younger men and the younger of the two women were eyeing him doubtfully.

"I don't know what happened in the Great Hall, of course," the older man went on. "But at this point most people don't care who's telling the truth. Erland is offering Tobyn-Ser an alternative to the Order, and that's something a lot of folks have been wanting for several years now."

Since the outlanders. The musician didn't have to say it. Jaryd and Alayna both knew what he meant. After the mages rode on, and were out of earshot of the bards, Jaryd gave voice to a thought that had been bothering him for several days. "It almost doesn't matter whether Orris succeeds or not," he said. "The outlanders have accomplished what they wanted. If this keeps up, the Order will be gone in no time. Whoever sent the last contingent won't even need to send another."

Alayna looked at him gravely. "I had been thinking the same thing," she said. "And then it occurred to me that Erland may have been right all along."

"What? I don't understand."

"Think about it," she answered. "The outlanders tried to eliminate the Mage-Craft as a threat, and they decided that the best way to do that would be to destroy the Order. But they were wrong. The Mage-Craft is much bigger than the Order. The fact that so many people are willing to support the League proves that. Even if the League takes the Order's place, Tobyn-Ser will still be protected, and the outlanders will be no better off than they were before."

"What you're saying may be true," Jaryd admitted, "but that doesn't mean that Erland's right."

"Doesn't it?" She took a breath and shook her head. "Erland's arrogant and pompous, and he sees conspiracies everywhere he looks. I know all that. But at least he understood that the Order and it's members are less important than Amarid's Laws and the Mage-Craft. We serve the land, and we have to respect its laws. We've all been so concerned about protecting Orris from Erland's charges that we've lost sight of that."

"But Orris of all people understands just what you're talking about. By taking Baram, he risked everything to save the land, even though it meant going against the will of the Order."

Alayna nodded. "You're right. I guess he and Erland have more in common than either one of them suspects."

"We'll have to tell him that when he gets back," Jaryd said. "He'll find it amusing." They shared a brief smile. "So what do you think we should do?" he asked her a moment later.

"About the League you mean?"

Jaryd nodded.

"I don't think there's anything we can do. We just have to continue serving the land. And we need to hope that eventually we can restore the Order to the way it was: regardless of what we think of Erland, we're stronger—the land's stronger—when we're united."

Jaryd knew that she was right, but with each day that passed, it became harder for them to do even that much. Two days after their encounter with the musicians, the young mages came to the edge of Tobyn's Plain and steered their mounts into a relatively large farming village within sight of the Emerald Hills. As they reached the town common, they found a sizable group of villagers speaking excitedly with a slight, grey-haired man who wore a long silver-grey robe that marked him as the Keeper of Arick's Temple in the town.

Seeing the mages approach, the townspeople fell into an awkward silence.

"Greetings!" Alayna called to them, casting a wary glance in Jaryd's direction as she did. "I'm Hawk-Mage Alayna and this is Hawk-Mage Jaryd. We've come to offer our service to your town."

None of the villagers spoke, and Jaryd noticed that the Keeper wore a small, satisfied grin.

"I hope we haven't come at an inopportune time," Alayna added after several moments of silence.

"This is a fine time," the Keeper finally said, his icy tone belying his words. "You're not familiar to us though. In the past, a woman named Neysa has served us. Isn't she still a member of your Order?"

"Yes, she is," Alayna answered, ignoring the taunt in his words. "But she's elsewhere right now. I'd imagine she's in the hills," she added, pointing to the west.

"Well," the grey-haired man said with unconvincing civility, "I'm certain that any service we might require can wait until she returns."

Jaryd looked at Alayna and after a moment she nodded to him. There was no sense in remaining. There were other towns.

"Then we'll be going," Alayna told the Keeper, forcing a smile. She and Jaryd turned their mounts to leave.

"Don't you want to know what we were discussing when you arrived?" the Keeper called after them.

Jaryd and Alayna faced him again. He was grinning broadly, not bothering to conceal how much he was enjoying this. The villagers watched the two mages expectantly, and some of them were grinning as well.

"You stopped speaking when we arrived," Jaryd said, trying to sound pleasant. "We assumed that it was none of our affair."

"On the contrary," the Keeper said. "This should interest you a great deal."

Jaryd held himself very still and waited, bracing himself for whatever was coming. With all that had happened since Sonel had first summoned the mages back to Amarid, he wondered if anything could surprise him anymore.

"Do you remember Cailin, the little girl left orphaned and without a home by the Kaera massacre?"

"Of course," Jaryd answered cautiously. "What about her?"

"She has bound to hawk. She, of all people, is a mage."

"Yes, we've heard that," Jaryd said, nodding and feeling something loosen in his chest. If this was all—

"Erland has convinced her to join the League."

It was as though Jaryd had been kicked in the stomach. He felt nauseated and he could barely breathe. With Cailin in the League, the Order would lose even more support than it had already. He suddenly heard the words of the peddlar he and Alayna had met several days earlier, repeating themselves in his head. *It wouldn't surprise me if the League replaces the Order within just a few years.* It might not even take that long, Jaryd thought to himself.

Seeing the mage's reaction, and Alayna's as well, the Keeper actually laughed out loud. "Judging from the look on your faces, I'd guess that you hadn't heard about this."

"No," Jaryd managed in a voice that was barely more than a whisper. "We had no idea."

"It's not true," Alayna said a little desperately. "It can't be true. Cailin wouldn't join any organization of mages."

The Keeper pulled a rolled piece of parchment out of his robe. "This is a message from Eldest Linnea herself, telling me and my brothers and sisters of the Temple of Cailin's decision. She says that Erland visited the Eldest's Temple just a few days ago hoping to persuade the child to join. He was, it would seem, very convincing." He grinned and held the parchment out to Alayna. "Would you care to read it yourself?"

She shook her head and passed a rigid hand through her long dark hair.

The grey-haired man turned to Jaryd and offered him the parchment as well, the smile lingering on his lips.

"No," Jaryd said. He needed no proof. Notwithstanding Alayna's denials,

Cailin's decision made perfect sense to him. What better way for her to take her vengeance on the Order for its failure to protect Kaera.

"With Cailin in the League, the Order's days are numbered!" one of the townspeople called out. The others nodded their agreement.

"I would have to concur," the Keeper told Jaryd affably.

"As long as the mages of the Order continue to serve the land," Jaryd replied, "most people will accept them as legitimate stewards of the Mage-Craft."

"Not necessarily," the Keeper said, his expression hardening. "What if we won't accept their service?"

Jaryd felt as though a chill wind had suddenly scythed through his cloak.

"What do you mean?" Alayna demanded.

"What if no one in this town accepts any form of service from a mage of the Order? What if we only welcome League mages into our homes and businesses? What will the Order do then?"

Jaryd and Alayna looked at each other bleakly, but neither of them spoke. Alayna's grey hawk sat on her shoulder like a statue, and Jaryd was suddenly aware of Ishalla's talons gripping his own shoulder through the padding of his cloak.

"As far as we're concerned," the Keeper went on, "Sonel and her followers have betrayed the land's trust. We've felt this way for several years, but up until now, we've had no recourse. We need the Mage-Craft and the Order has controlled it for a long time." He grinned, although the look in his eyes had grown fierce, like the gleam in the eyes of a hunting bird. "But with the formation of the League we have a choice. And this town chooses the League!" The townsfolk roared their approval. "Erland is a man we can trust," the Keeper added a moment later. "He's a leader, like Amarid was."

"What about Neysa?" Alayna asked the townsfolk. "What about all she's done for you over the past several years? Hasn't she earned your trust as well?"

"That's up to her," the Keeper said solemnly. "If she wishes to keep our trust and to continue to serve our town, then she must forsake the Order and join the League of Amarid."

"And if she refuses?" Alayna asked.

"Then she will not be welcome here anymore." The Keeper held Alayna's gaze for several moments and then looked at Jaryd. "Pay attention to what we're telling you, Mages," he warned. "We may be talking about Neysa, but I assure you: this is your future as well."

Once again, Jaryd shared a look with Alayna, and he saw from the despair written across her features and in the depths of her eyes, that she recognized the truth in the Keeper's words, just as he did.

29

The untimely death of Sovereign Durell has left all of Bragor-Nal shocked and saddened. So, too, have the unfortunate incidents that claimed the lives of two of Bragory's most beloved leaders. As a result of these tragedies, we find ourselves with no one to guide us through these troubled times. Where just yesterday we enjoyed the stability and assurance that comes with strong, reliable leadership, today we have nothing.

Someone must step forward to fill this void, to reassure Bragor-Nal's people, as well as her neighbors to the north and south. Though it is not a responsibility I relish, I understand that as the Nal's sole remaining Overlord, it falls to me to shoulder this burden. I do so reluctantly, but resolved that Bragor-Nal shall not relinquish its position as the most powerful and influential Nal in Lon-Ser. . . .

Therefore, in accordance with the procedures established by the Cape of Stars Treaty of 2802, I hereby formally petition Lon-Ser's Council of Sovereigns to recognize my claim to the position of Sovereign of Bragor-Nal by admitting me to its ranks.

—Formal petition for admission to the Council of Sovereigns, submitted by Cedrych i Vran, Overlord of the First Dominion of Bragor-Nal, Day 4, Week 10, Spring, Year 3061.

It was just a few hours past dusk when it began. The attack came so suddenly, with such precision and savagery, that Jibb and his men were on the defensive almost instantly. Caught off guard, outnumbered and outmaneuvered, he lost two of his twelve units in the first hour of fighting. Forced to abandon Melyor's flat and the buildings surrounding it, Jibb fell back and tried to organize a counter-assault. It failed miserably, and eleven more of his men died. The rest managed to get away, scattering into the tunnels below the Realm, just as they were supposed to in the event of this kind of debacle. But the damage had already been done. Coming so soon after the loss of Chev and Darel, whom he'd yet to replace, his encounter with Dob's men left him with only seven full units and another with only five men instead of six. Forty-seven men in all, barely enough to offer any hope of recapturing the Realm. It wasn't even morning yet.

It seemed to Jibb that there was nothing left to do but run. So that's what he did. Leading his men into the relative safety of the tunnels, he started southward, ranging as far as the Fifth Realm. But Dob's men nearly caught him there two nights later. So for the next several days—Jibb wasn't sure how many; it was easy to lose track in the tunnels, especially when you were being hunted—he doubled back, taking his men northward and then to the west. He avoided the passageways under the Farm, which were always heavily guarded by SovSec, and skirted the western edge of Bragory Wood.

At one point, he convinced himself that he had lost his pursuers, but they found him again in the Third Realm. There Jibb tried to rally his units for a firefight, but they were still outnumbered. Dob's men forced them to fall back toward the northwest corner of the Third, obviously hoping to corner them by the Gold Inlet, where the tunnels ended. In the end, Jibb and his men escaped, but they had to retreat into the Twenty-Second. Dob had driven them out of Cedrych's Dominion entirely.

It was then that Jibb became convinced of what he had suspected from the start: Dob was getting help, probably from Cedrych, although Jibb was unwilling to rule out the possibility that SovSec was involved. Whoever it was, though, they were the reason for Dob's success. Dob was capable and the men he commanded were fairly well-trained. But even at full strength, they should have been no match for Jibb's forces. And Dob wasn't at full strength, not after all the time he had spent fighting Bowen for control of the Second. Yet the break-law had shown up suddenly in the Fourth with more manpower and weaponry than even a well-established Nal-Lord should have had.

No one within the Fourth would have helped him, which was not to say that no one in the Fourth wanted Jibb dead. There were many break-laws who resented his close relationship with Melyor and who were no doubt incensed by his unexpected installation as Nal-Lord. But none of them would have helped an outsider like Dob. They might have united behind one break-law from the Fourth, but even that seemed unlikely.

Besides, the fighters Jibb and his men encountered were too disciplined and methodical for ordinary break-laws. They were highly trained, like security goons, or Cedrych's guards. With his forces depleted and exhausted, Jibb had no chance against an army of this caliber.

That at least is what Jibb told himself as he and the contingent of men who remained with him fled through the concrete passageways of Newell's Dominion. Bewildered by what had happened, and feeling sorry for himself, Jibb almost gave up.

I can start over, he thought. *I can look for work in Trestor-Proper; sign on with Bren or one of Newell's other Nal-Lords. There's plenty of work to be found in this part of the Nal.*

It didn't take him long to abandon that notion, however. It wasn't his Realm they had taken. It was Melyor's. And though he and his men had done the fighting, Jibb realized that the attack itself had been aimed at her, not at him. Which probably meant that it was Cedrych who had been helping Dob. Whatever dangerous game Melyor had been playing with the scarred Overlord had ended with Dob's takeover of the Fourth. And Jibb had let it happen. Indeed, he might have been responsible for it. Perhaps if he had succeeded in killing the sorcerer, none of this would have happened. True, Melyor and the sorcerer appeared to have come to some sort of an understanding, but that didn't change the fact that at one time she had been so desperate to have the stranger killed that she had all but admitted to Jibb that she was a Gildriite.

So rather than retreating into the anonymity of a new life in a new Dominion, Jibb allowed his men to rest in the Twenty-Second for a couple of days and then began to lead them back toward the Fourth, formulating plans to retake Melyor's Realm as he did. He came up with little at first. His resolve had returned, but he still commanded a depleted force, and he faced a powerful enemy that was, by this time, well entrenched in the Realm. His one hope lay in the possibility that after helping Dob drive Jibb and his men from the Fourth, Cedrych had pulled back his guards for some other assignment. Against Cedrych's forces Jibb had little chance. But against Dob alone, he felt reasonably certain that he could prevail. The trick lay in determining which was the case. If he guessed wrong and launched an assault on Cedrych's guards, he and the rest of his men would probably die.

His answer came a few days after he and his men slipped back into Cedrych's Dominion, while he was still making his way back across the Third toward Melyor's Realm. One of the patrols he had sent to scout the tunnels ahead, returned with news that the Sovereign had been murdered in the Gold Palace several days earlier, and that Newell and Wildon had been assassinated as well. Apparently Cedrych had been busy with much more than just the Fourth Realm. Jibb knew that there was no way the Overlord would have undertaken such a venture without a full contingent of guards protecting his own headquarters. He had deliberately plunged all of Bragor-Nal into chaos. All three Dominions were without Overlords. Nal-Lords throughout the Nal would be battling each other for supremacy for weeks to come, and break-laws in every Realm would be vying to replace those Nal-Lords who became Overlords, as well as those who died trying.

It was a brilliant strategy. While the rest of the Nal descended into civil war, Cedrych would consolidate his power, offer aid to those Nal-Lords and break-laws he believed he could trust, and thus assure himself of a long and comfortable tenure as Sovereign. But as ingenious as Cedrych's gambit was, it was also fraught with dangers. As a young boy, Jibb had been fascinated by the Consolidation and had read as much as he could about its heroes, villains, and battles. One could not be a student of that era of Lon-Ser's history without gaining a healthy respect for the turbulence and unpredictability of internecine warfare. If Cedrych managed to control the course of events, nothing would stop him from becoming the most dominant Sovereign Bragor-Nal had seen since Dalrek, who ruled the Nal at the end of the Consolidation. But the Overlord would need every resource at his disposal to keep himself from being sucked down into the vortex of violence that he himself had created.

Which meant that Dob was on his own.

It also mean that Jibb and his men could afford to be a bit less cautious in the passageways and concentrate instead on getting back to the Fourth as quickly as possible. Without Cedrych helping him Dob would not have enough manpower to patrol the tunnels much less continue his search for Jibb. And with every Nal-Lord and break-law in the area on the move, Jibb and his men would be far less conspicuous. The hazards were just as great as they had been the day before, perhaps more so. Every person they encountered now was a potential enemy. But at least they weren't being hunted anymore.

It was another day and a half before they reached the western edge of the Fourth, and an additional day after that before they drew near Melyor's flat. By that time, Jibb guessed, Dob had already begun to position himself for his run at becoming Overlord. He certainly wouldn't be expecting to see Jibb again so soon. Standing near a three-way fork in the tunnel that would lead them to Melyor's old home, waiting for one of his patrols to return, Jibb shook his head. It would have been much smarter for Dob to strengthen his hold on the Fourth. He was too new to his power and he was still weak from his battle with Bowen. He wouldn't have a chance against the more established Nal-Lords of Cedrych's Dominion. But though Jibb didn't know Dob very well, he understood the man's thinking well enough to know that, like most break-laws, Dob was incapable of such restraint. He'd make his play for the Dominion, and he'd leave himself open to whatever attack Jibb came up with.

Actually, Jibb realized, chuckling and shaking his head a second time in the dim light, Dob probably had as good a chance as anyone. With Savil dead and Melyor nowhere to be found, there were no truly formidable Nal-Lords left in Cedrych's old territory. Had she still been around, Melyor would have been the clear favorite to succeed the one-eyed Overlord, but without her, it was an open contest among equally mediocre rivals. It didn't seem right, Jibb thought. Melyor deserved this more than any of them. Once more, for what felt like the thousandth time since that last night he saw her with the Bearer and the Sorcerer, Jibb wondered where Melyor was and if she was even still alive.

He heard footsteps behind him and turning, he saw Premel come into view leading the rest of his unit. A couple of weeks ago, the sound of approaching footsteps would have sent Jibb's pulse racing. After spending so much time on the run, however, he seemed to have developed something of a sixth sense. He found that he could anticipate trouble before it arrived, and he no longer panicked unnecessarily.

"Report," Jibb commanded, as Premel stopped in front of him, his normally shaved head covered now with short, dark hair that stood straight on end.

"We didn't see anything unusual," the break-law answered, an eager look in is pale eyes. "But we have news from above." He paused as if for impact. Premel was a good man, but he was prone to theatrics.

"Out with it, Premel."

"It seems Bowen has chosen to stay out of the fight for Overlord. He's throwing his support behind Enrek, and according to my sources, Enrek has promised in return to unite the Second and Fourth under Bowen's command once he becomes Overlord."

Jibb nodded slowly, weighing what the break-law had told him. It made sense. By himself, Enrek was no more formidable than any of the other Nal-Lords. Indeed, as leader of the Sixth Realm, he was surrounded by enemies and in a poor position strategically. But with Bowen behind him, he had a significant advantage. And Bowen was doing exactly what he should: he was biding him time, consolidating his power, and, in the process, making himself the obvious choice to succeed Enrek as Overlord should their plan work.

"Did you get any sense of what Dob is doing?" Jibb asked after several moments.

The break-law grinned, revealing sharp, yellow teeth. "He's getting ready for a fight of course. Now that he's taken the Fourth he thinks he's invincible." The other men in the tunnel murmured their agreement.

"Who's he going after?"

Premel's grin deepened. "Everyone, just as you'd expect." The others laughed.

"Good. We'll stay underground for a while longer. I want two units positioned in each of the quads surrounding Melyor's flat by midnight. I'll take northeast quad four with the depleted unit. The rest of you can deploy as you like, but do it quickly. I want to be finished with this before dawn. Understood?"

Premel nodded, his eyes gleaming hungrily, the large gold hoop in his ear glinting like a blade in the dim light of the tunnel. "I'm glad we're not running anymore," he said.

Jibb gave a grin of his own. "So am I. We've been—" He froze, his heart suddenly pounding in his chest so hard that he could actually feel his body move with each beat. Premel was utterly still as well, although his eyes were wide with astonishment. The sound had been so soft that Jibb would probably have missed it two or three weeks before. But tuned as he was to the tunnels after so many days of hiding in them, Jibb knew precisely what he had heard.

A footfall, close by. He was fairly certain that it had come from the fork that ran off to the left.

"I thought you checked the tunnels!" Jibb mouthed to his break-law, allowing his anger to show on his face.

Premel shrugged defensively and shook his head in confusion.

They drew their throwers simultaneously, and the five men standing behind Premel followed their example. None of them made a sound.

"Your men are well trained," came a familiar but utterly unexpected voice, echoing through the passageways. "Not that I find that surprising. But I wonder how you managed to let us get so close to you. You could have been killed you know."

Jibb opened his mouth to speak, but found that he couldn't. He actually thought for a moment that he might cry, he was so happy.

A moment later, Melyor stepped out of the shadows, her amber hair falling loose around her shoulders, and a crooked smile on her flawless features. The sorcerer was behind her, still concealing the top of his staff within the folds of his robe. His imposing dark hawk sat on his shoulder, peering cautiously at Jibb and his men with its dark eyes.

Jibb took a step toward Melyor, intending to throw his arms around her. But then he saw something that stopped him in his tracks. It seemed from the sudden flurry of whispered conversations that filled the passageway that his men noticed it at the same time. Jibb looked Melyor in the eye for a moment, but her expression remained neutral and an instant later—he could hardly help it—his gaze returned to the thing she held in her hand: an ancient wooden staff that was crowned with a glowing red stone. It took him some time to figure out where she had gotten it.

"The Bearer?" he asked, his eyes meeting hers again.

"Killed in Oerella-Nal," she answered in a flat voice.

"But wasn't his stone—?"

"It's my stone now," she said, as if that explained why the crystal was red instead of brown.

Jibb swallowed. He still found it hard to accept that she was a Gildriite. And his men, he realized with a start, had known nothing of this until now. Premel and the others in his unit were regarding the Nal-Lord with varying degrees of awe, fear, and distaste.

"Our Nal-Lord has returned!" Jibb announced pointedly, thrusting away his own doubts as he looked from one man to the next. "Once again we serve Melyor i Lakin!"

None of the men spoke, until finally, in a low, uncertain voice, Premel said, "But look at what she's holding. She's a Gildriite!"

Jibb started to respond, but Melyor stepped forward and gave his arm a gentle squeeze.

"Yes, Premel," she said matter-of-factly, "I'm a Gildriite. I always have been, even when I was also your Nal-Lord. I carry this stone now, which means that I'm properly addressed as Bearer."

"But . . . but you never told us," the break-law stammered.

"It was none of your business," she continued in the same tone. "It was my secret to keep, just as it's now my story to tell."

"It changes nothing!" Jibb broke in hotly. "She's still the same person and we still work for her! And any one of you who refuses will answer to me!"

Melyor turned to face him, a sad smile on her lips. Jibb thought that she had never looked so beautiful. "I'm afraid you're wrong, my friend," she said gently. "I'm not the same person I was, and my carrying this staff changes a great deal. Gildriites have been persecuted in this land for hundreds of years. You can't expect that to change overnight." She looked at Premel and the others. "I need your help desperately, but I won't force any of you to fight for me. It's your decision to make." She faced Jibb again. "I'll understand if you don't want to work for me either. I know how you feel about Gildriites."

"Gildriites aren't all that bad." He grinned at her. "I guess you're right: you carrying that staff has changed things some."

She smiled, and a look of profound relief flashed across her features. An instant later though, it was gone, and her brow furrowed with concern. "What's happened?" she demanded. "Why are you in the tunnels?"

"You've heard about Durell?"

She nodded. "Yes. And Wildon and Newell, too."

"Well, before Cedrych went after them, he helped a break-law named Dob take the Fourth."

Melyor stared at him in disbelief and a short, high laugh escaped her. "Dob? You've got to be kidding me!"

Jibb narrowed his eyes. "You know him?"

"I ran into him in the Second, the night I went looking for Savil."

"Of course," Jibb said quietly. "I had forgotten about that."

She smiled self-consciously. "Dob and I had a bit of a run-in."

"Do you think that's why Cedrych chose him?"

"Maybe," Melyor said with a shrug. "That's just the type of thing he'd do. You say that Cedrych helped him," she went on, her expression growing serious again. "What do you mean?"

"He gave him men, weapons, he probably helped him plan the assault."

"Are you sure?"

Jibb laughed. "You've met the man: do you think he could have beaten me otherwise?"

Melyor laughed as well. "No, I guess not." She glanced at Premel and his unit. "I take it you have more men left than just these."

Jibb felt his smile fade. "Don't joke. I lost almost four whole units the first night."

The color drained from Melyor's cheeks, leaving her looking surprisingly fragile. "Fist of the God," she whispered. She stared at her crystal for several moments, as if she could see Jibb's battle with Dob repeating itself within the scarlet light. "It's my fault," she finally said, her voice faint. "I defied him, and then I ran away." She looked at Jibb again. "I'm sorry."

Jibb wasn't certain what to say. He had never known her to get so upset about the loss of her break-laws before. No Nal-Lord, or break-law for that matter, enjoyed losing the men he or she commanded. But it was part of life in the Nal. It was unavoidable. She was different, he realized, and he didn't know what to make of the transformations he saw in her.

Fortunately, a moment later he saw her features harden in a way he remembered quite well. "As I said a moment before," she said, turning to Premel and the others and raising her voice so that it echoed through the tunnels, "I won't force any of you to fight for me. But I need you, not only to reclaim the Fourth, but also to strike back at Cedrych!"

"At Cedrych?" Jibb asked incredulously. "You can't be serious!"

She pivoted to face him once more. "You said yourself that he took the Fourth from us! He also sent Blade after us while we were in Oerella-Nal, and as a result, the Bearer died!"

"But even at full strength," Premel protested, "we wouldn't stand a chance against Cedrych's men!"

Melyor grinned fiercely, and seeing it, Jibb couldn't help but smile himself. She wasn't so different after all. "I may be a Bearer now, Premel. But I'm not stupid."

"No, Nal-Lord," the break-law said hastily. "Of course not."

"I don't intend to attempt a full assault on Cedrych's headquarters."

"Then what do you have in mind?" Jibb asked.

"Orris and I have come up with a plan that we think might work."

Jibb glanced at the sorcerer, who had remained in the background since he and Melyor first arrived. Jibb wasn't sure how much the burly man understood of what had been said in the past few minutes, but the sorcerer was watching everything and everyone with obvious interest. Seeing Jibb look his way, the man gave slight nod. Jibb returned the gesture, but found himself thinking back to the battle they had waged against each other in an alley in the Twenty-First Realm. It seemed a very long time ago.

"Can you tell me anything about this plan?" he asked Melyor.

"In time," she said. "But first I need to know how much help I'm going to have." She looked expectantly at Jibb's men. "You've all seen me fight," she said evenly. "And you know that I never begin anything that I don't intend to finish. That hasn't changed. I understand that you know nothing about the sorcerer, but believe me when I tell you that he has more reason than any of us to hate Cedrych, and that the power he wields is more formidable than even the Overlord realizes. All we need is your help getting us into Cedrych's headquarters; Orris and I will do the rest. But we do need you."

Jibb held his breath. His men knew how he felt, and if that were the only factor, they would have followed him without question. But these were Premel's men as well. If he refused the others would be torn. And if this unit wouldn't follow Melyor, the others probably wouldn't either. Strange as it seemed, everything suddenly rested on Premel's decision.

It seemed that Melyor recognized this as well. "I remember the first time we met, Premel," she said, taking a step toward him. "It was in that disgusting bar on the border between the Fourth and the Second. Jibb and I saw you best two men with nothing more than your boot tips and a single blade, and I knew immediately that I wanted you working for me." She gestured toward Jibb. "He actually needed to be convinced: he said your technique was too unconventional, that it wouldn't blend well with the other men he was training. But I convinced him."

Jibb smiled to himself. He remembered it as well.

"I never regretted doing that," Melyor went on, "and I never will, regardless of what you decide. But I'm asking you to put your faith in me now, just as I did for you then. I need you, Premel."

The break-law flushed slightly. The others were watching him, and he appeared to know it. A moment passed. And another. Still he said nothing, though he took a long breath. "All right," he said at last, his eyes meeting Jibb's for just a second before flicking away. "All right."

Melyor smiled broadly. "Thank you." She looked beyond Premel to the other break-laws. "And the rest of you?"

One by one, they voiced their willingness to serve her. Two of them did so with obvious reluctance, but Jibb knew them both well. They were competent and dependable. When the time came, they would do whatever Melyor or he asked of them.

"So what now?" Jibb asked, feeling a sudden wave of giddiness pass over him. Dob still held the Fourth, and Melyor seemed intent upon going after arguably the most dangerous man in Lon-Ser. But he and the Nal-Lord were to-gether again, just as they were supposed to be.

"Our first priority should be getting the Fourth back," Melyor answered crisply.

Jibb nodded. "Of course."

"You said that Cedrych helped Dob take the Realm. Is he helping him run it, too?"

"I assume he's not," Jibb replied. "Given what he started when he killed Durell, Wildon, and Newell, I'd assume that he's got all of his men with him."

"You're probably right," she agreed. "In the long run Cedrych probably couldn't care less whether Dob survives or not. He already accomplished what he wanted to."

"Taking the Fourth from you, you mean."

Melyor regarded him with genuine surprise. "Is that really what you think?"

Jibb blinked, then shrugged. "Yes. Why else would he have done it?"

"You underestimate yourself, Jibb."

"What?"

Melyor grinned. "How long ago did Dob attack?"

The break-law thought for a moment. "It was about three weeks ago."

"Which was around the same time Cedrych sent Blade after me. He wasn't taking the Realm from me; he assumed that I'd be dead. He was afraid of you, of what you might try to do if word got back to the Fourth that Cedrych had had me killed. He probably figured that even if Dob didn't succeed in killing you, he'd keep you occupied for a while."

Jibb shook his head. "Cedrych was afraid of me?"

"Well, to the extent that he's afraid of anyone."

He shook his head a second time, and they stood for a moment without speaking.

Premel cleared his throat. "Nal— Uh . . . I mean, Jibb."

Jibb looked at the break-law and gave a sympathetic smile. None of this could be easy for his men. Up until a few minutes ago they had all been calling him Nal-Lord. Now Melyor was back; they couldn't help but be confused. "What is it, Premel?"

"Well, I know that you and . . ." he glanced at Melyor and swallowed. "I know that the two of you have a lot to talk about, but shouldn't we get going? The other patrols will be waiting for us at the next fork."

Jibb and Melyor exchanged a look. Premel was right, of course.

"Thank you, Premel, Melyor answered, as was appropriate. "You're ab-solutely right. Lead the way."

The break-law grinned. "Yes, Nal-Lord," he replied, seemingly without thinking.

Premel and his men started down the passageway and Melyor and Jibb fell in behind them. It took Jibb several moments to realize that the sorcerer was with them as well, a few steps behind, his bird still on his shoulder, and his amber stone exposed now and casting a dim light on the walls of the tunnel.

"Do you have any idea what Dob is up to?" Melyor asked after they had walked a short distance.

"According to Premel, the word in the quads is that he's preparing to make a run at Overlord."

"Overlord?" Melyor said with a laugh. "Talk about overreaching." She shook her head, and then looked sidelong at Jibb. "I hope you don't pick up any bad ideas from watching him."

"Don't worry," Jibb told her. "I'll be more like Bowen."

"Who's Bowen?"

"The break-law who beat out Dob for Savil's Realm. He's pledged his support to Enrek in return for control of the Second and the Fourth if Enrek takes the Dominion."

Melyor raised an eyebrow. "Are you worried?"

He smiled at her. "Not anymore."

Jibb heard the sorcerer call Melyor's name in his strangely accented voice, and, when she glanced back at him, the burly man spoke to her briefly. Melyor gave a short response in Orris's language and the sorcerer nodded. A moment later Melyor faced forward again.

Jibb wanted to ask what they had talked about, but he found that he couldn't speak. He was suddenly and quite unexpectedly grappling with the realization that he was jealous. He had no reason to believe that Melyor and the sorcerer were lovers, and certainly he had no claim on Melyor. Indeed, he knew that she had been with several men in the time he had worked for her. But abruptly none of that seemed to matter. Listening to them talk to each other, he couldn't help but envision them together, and the very notion of it made his chest ache, as if he had been blasted in the heart with a thrower.

"Are you all right?" Melyor asked him after they had walked some distance down the passageway.

"Sure," he said, fighting a wave of nausea and trying to force a smile. "I was just trying to figure out what you two were saying."

She looked at him as if he were crazy. "It would probably be easier if you just asked me."

He tried to laugh. "You're right. What were you talking about?"

"None of your business."

He stared at her, wondering if he had heard her correctly and she began to laugh.

"I'm kidding, Jibb!" she said, shaking her head. "You lose a Realm and suddenly your sense of humor is gone." He said nothing, and a moment later she continued, although not before she shook her head again. "In order for the plan Orris and I devised to work we need outside help from someone who Cedrych will trust. Originally I told him that you might have an idea of who we could go to, and he was reminding me to ask you. But as I just told him, I'm not sure anymore that we need to go looking for an ally."

"You're not?"

She flashed him that wonderful, inscrutable smile. "No. I think we have him already, or at least we will shortly."

Jibb stared at her, not understanding. *We will shortly.* They were on their way to join the rest of his men. Did she mean one of them?

"You don't know who I'm talking about, do you?"

He gave a half-hearted shrug. "No. I—" He stopped, the realization coming to him so abruptly that he actually halted in mid-stride, almost causing the sorcerer to walk into him. "You must be joking!" he said, but he was already beginning to see the sense in it. *Someone who Cedrych will trust.* And, she might have added, someone who would be as afraid of saying 'no' to them as he would be of lying to the scarred Overlord.

"You see the logic in it, don't you?" she asked, her eyes sparkling with the scarlet light given off by her stone.

He nodded, unable to tear his gaze from hers. She was brilliant and beautiful, and he loved her. Whatever there might be between the sorcerer and her, he loved her. And there was nothing he could do about it. "Yes," he finally managed. "I see the logic."

"The hard part will be convincing Dob that he's better off working with us than he is remaining loyal to Cedrych."

"No," Jibb corrected. "The hard part will be keeping my men from killing him."

30

Once more, I find myself thinking of the Gold Palace. It is irresponsible of me, I know. I should be concentrating on the Initiative and the maintenance of my Dominion. Those are the foundations for all I expect to accomplish in the future. Yet, here I sit planning for the day when I am finally ready to make my move. I must have a strategy, not only for taking the Palace but for keeping it. And already, one is forming in my mind. . . .

I am reminded of an old saying that I believe has its origins in the Consolidation. "Chaos," this saying goes, "is like fire. Woe to the enemies of he who can control it. And woe to he who can't."

> Personal journal of Cedrych i Vran, Overlord of the First Dominion of Bragor-Nal, Day 6, Week 7, Spring, Year 3060.

The waiting was the worst part. He would have preferred to be out there himself, joining in the firefights and tossing the occasional hand boomer into an alleyway. But he had so many units in so many different quads, that he could hardly afford to be away from his headquarters for very long. Besides, manpower wasn't a problem anymore. Ever since he had become a Nal-Lord, independents had been practically lining up to work for him. As good as he was with a blade and a thrower, his men didn't need him in the streets. They needed him just where he was: in Melyor's old flat, coordinating their activities. And it was driving him crazy.

Even as he spent every waking moment trying to win control of the Dominion, Dob wondered if he was really cut out to be an Overlord. He liked fighting. He liked drinking with his men after a good fight. And he liked bedding uestras after he finished drinking. Coordinating units from an empty flat, and looking over his shoulder every other minute, waiting for the next assassination attempt were not his idea of a good time. He hadn't been with a woman since that night Cedrych called him to offer him the Fourth, and he hadn't had a decent night's sleep either. Where was the justice in that? He'd have been happy to trade one for the other on any given night, but to go without both. . . .

Pacing the floor of Melyor's flat, he shook his head. It didn't help that his prospects already looked so bleak. It had only been a week or so since Wildon, Newell, and the Sovereign were killed, but that had been long enough for Dob to discover just how ill-prepared he was to make his run for Overlord. He would have quit and accepted his losses in manpower and resources as the price of a hard lesson, but then Enrek had to go and offer Bowen the Fourth, leaving Dob no choice but to fight. At this point, he wasn't even fighting for his own advancement. He was just trying to keep Bowen and Enrek from winning. He had sent a couple of units south to harass Enrek's men in the Sixth and to support the Nal-Lords Enrek was attacking in the Eighth and Tenth, but most of his units were in the Second right now, keeping Bowen occupied so that the wiry Nal-Lord could offer little help to Enrek. It seemed the best strategy. The Second was closer than Enrek's Sixth, and his men knew the territory well.

He had only one unit here guarding the flat, which he knew was a bit unwise. But that was one of the few advantages of being in such a weak position: none of the other Nal-Lords cared about him anymore. He wasn't worth the attention and effort that sending another band of assassins would have required. True, there was still Jibb to worry about. Dob could still hear Cedrych's words blaring like a security alarm in his head. *If you haven't found him yet, you're not going to. . . . If I were you, I'd watch my back.* The memory of the Overlord's warning had haunted his sleep for days, and yet he had still seen no sign of Melyor's bodyguard. No one had, not since he had evaded them all in the tunnels and fled into Newell's Dominion. With every day that passed, Dob became increasingly convinced that Jibb was gone for good. Perhaps he was dead, killed by his men for leading them into such a predicament. Or perhaps he decided that life in Trestor-Proper would be easier than retaking the Fourth. Whatever the explanation, Dob didn't need to worry about Jibb anymore.

This, at least, is what he wanted to believe. He stopped pacing and peered out the window into the night, as if he might spot Jibb and his men approaching the flat. Then, shaking his head at his own foolishness, he resumed his pacing. Even without Cedrych's words repeating themselves in his mind again and again, Dob would have had his doubts. Jibb's reputation was enough to frighten anyone. His men wouldn't have turned on him: their loyalty to both him and Melyor was almost legendary. And he wouldn't have just given up: a streetfighter of his skill and tenacity would never shy away from a good fight. Dob hadn't left himself vulnerable because he honestly believed that he had rid himself of Jibb. He had done it because right now, under these particular circumstances, Bowen and Enrek represented more of a threat.

Three quick beeping sounds pulled him out of his thoughts and self-pity and sent him scurrying to his desk, where he switched on his speak-screen, his heart pounding in his chest. Only when the beeps repeated themselves did he realize that it was his hand communicator making the sound, not the speak-screen. He pulled the device out of his pocket, and fumbled with it for a moment until he found the small button on the side. He hated these things, but he couldn't exactly send his men into the quads carrying speak-screens, could he?

"What is it?" he barked into the communicator. "Report!"

"We've been driven back, Nal-Lord!" came a tinny voice in reply. Dob could hear voices calling out in the background and the occasional hiss of thrower fire.

"Who is this?" he demanded. "Where are you?"

"This is Honid, Nal-Lord! Unit eleven! I'm in the Second with units nine and ten! But Bowen's men have cut my unit off from the others!"

Dob exhaled heavily. Honid was a competent fighter. Nothing special really: he had courage, and he was fairly good with a thrower, as all Dob's men were, but he lacked creativity. Send him back in and he'd probably get himself and the rest of his unit killed.

"Are nine and ten in trouble?" he asked the break-law.

"I . . . I don't know!" Honid answered, a note of panic creeping into his voice.

"All right," Dob said with a sigh. "Get out of there. I could use a bit more security back here anyway."

"Yes, Nal-Lord!" Honid answered with obvious relief. "Right away!"

Dob switched off the hand communicator and tossed it onto his desk with disgust. What did he need security for? The Fourth wouldn't be his for much longer anyway.

"Sounds like you're having a rough day."

Dob whirled at the sound of the voice, knowing immediately whose it was, and reaching desperately for his thrower.

"Don't do it, Dob," Melyor i Lakin commanded calmly.

He halted in mid-turn, his left hand on his weapon, which was still strapped to his thigh.

"Jibb here is just itching for an excuse to kill you, Dob," Melyor cautioned, "as are the fifty men we brought with us. I'd suggest you don't give them one."

Dob nodded once, but otherwise he didn't move.

"Pull out the thrower with your right hand, drop it on the floor, and kick it away."

Slowly, he did as she instructed and then turned to face her. He had only seen her once before and of course she had been disguised as an uestra. Kellyn she had called herself. He had thought her lovely then, but seeing her, he now realized that the eye lenses and colored hair had actually diminished her beauty that night. She stood before him now in britches and a loose tunic, with a thrower strapped to her thigh. Her eyes were bright green and her amber hair tumbled to her shoulders in waves rather than ringlets. She was, he thought in that moment, something out of a break-law's dream: bold, exquisite, and deadly. And he was surprised by the first thought that came to him: *Savil never had a chance.*

Looking more closely, Dob saw something else as well. She was carrying a long wooden stick that had a glowing red stone mounted at the top. And behind her, with Jibb and several of the bodyguard's men, stood a stranger whose mere presence here in the Nal caused Dob's world to shift abruptly in ways he had never thought possible. The man carried a stick much like Melyor's, although his stone shone with a rich yellow-brown color, and he wore a dark green hooded robe. But these things Dob noticed only in passing, for his eyes were drawn to the creature that sat on the man's shoulder. It was a magnificent dark bird, larger than any he had ever seen before, and with a look of intelligence and ferocity that seemed almost unworldly. A sorcerer, Dob thought with awe and just a touch of fear. Apparently the crazy man he had found in the Second and taken to Cedrych hadn't been so crazy after all. But what was this man doing with Melyor, and why was she carrying that stick? He thought about asking, but thought better of it. Besides, he had other concerns.

"What did you do to my men?" he demanded, inwardly cursing the flutter in his voice.

A smile sprung to Melyor's lips, indulgent and just slightly mocking. He remembered that smile from the night Savil died. "I like that," she said, in a tone seemingly free of irony. "Your first thought is for you men. Perhaps you have some future as a leader after all."

Dob felt himself blush, and, as he had several times over the past half year, he wished that he had found a way to kill her when he had the opportunity. He glared at her, but said nothing.

"Your men are fine, Dob," Melyor finally answered. "We took their weapons and locked them in the storage area under the flat." She smiled again. "Frankly though, you ought to be more concerned about yourself."

Dob shrugged, trying to feign indifference, but he was trembling. "I attacked Jibb. I stole the Fourth from you. I figure I'm a corpse no matter what I do."

Melyor stepped casually to his desk—or rather, her desk—and sat down. "That's certainly one way we could go," she said, looking up at him placidly. "Normally there would be no question, but as you know, these aren't normal times."

He almost didn't believe his ears. He had assumed his life was over as soon as he saw Melyor and Jibb standing in the flat, and he had been trying to determine how he might take the two of them and a few of their men with him when he died. Yet now she seemed to be holding out some small hope for him. "What do you want?" he asked quickly, not bothering to mask his eagerness.

"First, some answers," she said. "Do you know if Cedrych has moved his headquarters yet?"

"I want to know what we're talking about here," Dob countered. "Amnesty? Or are you offering more than that?"

Melyor's eyes flashed angrily and she sat forward. "I'm not offering anything yet!" she told him in a voice like a beam of thrower fire. "And I'd be more than happy just to kill you and find someone else who can tell me what I want to know!" She nodded once to Jibb, who came forward, grabbed Dob by the hair, and pressed a thrower against Dob's temple. "Now, are you ready to answer some questions?" Melyor asked.

Dob nodded.

"Good," she said, smiling once more and leaning back in her chair. "Has Cedrych moved his headquarters?"

"No," Dob said hoarsely. "He's still in the First."

"Why?"

He held out his hands. "I only know what I hear out of the quads. I swear, I haven't spoken to Cedrych in days."

Melyor rolled her eyes impatiently. "I believe you, Dob. What have you heard?"

He licked his lips nervously. "Some say that he's waiting for the Council to respond to his petition for entry. I've also heard that he's renovating the Gold Palace and doesn't want to move in until the work is finished."

Melyor smirked. "That I'd believe," she said as much to herself as to anyone in the flat. "Is he still helping you?" she asked a moment later.

In spite of everything, Dob started to laugh, although even he could hear the brittleness of it. "What do you think?" he replied, gesturing vaguely at the disheveled flat. "If I was getting help from Cedrych do you think you would have been able to walk in here so easily?"

Jibb tightened his grip on Dob's hair and pressed the nose of his thrower even harder into Dob's head. "Answer the question!" the bodyguard growled.

"It's all right, Jibb," Melyor said. "He's right: it was a stupid question."

Jibb relaxed his hold on Dob slightly.

"He hasn't given me anything since a couple of days before Durell was killed," Dob volunteered.

"Whose idea was it for you to take the Fourth?"

"His," Dob said quickly.

"I'll bet," Jibb commented with bitter sarcasm.

Dob closed his eyes for a moment, swallowed, then looked at Melyor again. "I swear to you on everything I have left in this world, it was his idea. I was fighting for the Second at the time. I assumed that the Fourth was Jibb's. Cedrych called me, told me that he was going to give Bowen the Second, and offered me the Fourth." He shrugged. "What was I supposed to do? Say 'no' and let Bowen kill me or drive me out of the Realm?"

"Did he tell you why he was doing this?" Melyor asked, ignoring his question.

"No."

"So," Melyor said, smiling thinly, "you've been a Nal-Lord for a week and you're already trying to become Overlord, is that right?"

He could see the mockery in her eyes again and he looked away. She already knew the answer, and she seemed to have a pretty good idea of how things were going for him. "That's how it began," he said in a low voice. "At this point I'm just trying to keep Bowen and Enrek from taking the Realm."

"The Realm Cedrych gave you," she goaded.

"Look!" Dob shot back, ignoring Jibb's tightening grip. "I admit that I couldn't have taken it without Cedrych's help, but it's not like we planned this out together! Given what he had in mind for the entire Nal, I don't even know why he bothered with me and the Fourth! All I know is, he didn't do me any favors by putting me here!"

Melyor raised an eyebrow and began to nod slowly. "I'm glad to hear you say that, Dob." She grinned. "Very glad." She stood and walked to the front of the desk, just a few feet from where he and Jibb were standing. "We need your help, Dob," she said. "We intend to take the Nal from Cedrych and we need your help."

At first he thought she was kidding and he started to laugh. But no one else in the flat even cracked a smile, and Dob felt his mirth sluice away leaving him almost too weak to stand. "Do you know what you're saying?" He looked beseechingly at the others in the flat, but he saw from their expressions that he'd get no help there. "Are you all insane? Don't you know who you're talking about?"

"Of course I do," Melyor responded serenely. "I daresay I know him even better than you do."

"Then you know how crazy that is!" He started to laugh again, hoping that the others would join him. "This is Cedrych! You don't just take the Nal from him, like he's some spent old independent!" He narrowed his eyes. "I know that you killed Savil, and that's impressive. But Cedrych is something else entirely. He's got an army of the best trained men in the Nal." He glanced sidelong at Jibb. "I know your men are good, Jibb, but you've seen Cedrych's men, and you've seen how many of them he has. You can't think that you can take him."

Jibb returned his gaze. "Talk to her," he said. "I agree with you."

Dob stared at Melyor again. "Even if you can get into the First Realm, which I doubt, you couldn't get near his headquarters. And if you somehow managed to get that far, you'd have his weapons chamber to deal with." He tried to shake his head, but Jibb still held him by the hair. "It can't be done," he concluded.

"That's why we need you, Dob. You're the one person who can get us into Cedrych's office."

"Me?" Dob asked with disbelief.

"Yes," Melyor said in that same calm tone. "All you need to do is claim that you captured us trying to sneak back into the Fourth. The sorcerer and I will do the rest."

"You expect me to go into Cedrych's office with you? Do you remember what he did to the guards who were on duty the day of the bombing?"

"Dob—"

"I won't do it!" Dob insisted. "There's no way I'm going in there with you!"

"I promise you," she said. "Our plan will work. You have nothing to worry about."

"I don't believe you! And I'm not going to help you! Not against Cedrych!"

"Fine!" Melyor snapped abruptly. "Then you'll die right here!" She nodded once at Jibb and without another word started toward the door.

"Do I have to do it quickly?" Jibb asked her, baring his teeth in a cruel grin.

"I don't care," Melyor said over her shoulder. "Take your time if you want to; Orris and I have a lot to talk about."

Jibb laughed, and as Melyor and the sorcerer closed the door behind them, the bodyguard shoved Dob to the ground. Immediately three of Jibb's men grabbed him, hoisted him to his feet again and turned him around. Jibb was coming toward him, the grin still on his face. He had put his thrower away and he was playing idly with a long-bladed dagger. Dob struggled to get free, but the three men had his arms and legs locked. There was nothing he could do.

"You should have helped her, Dob," Jibb said.

"Against Cedrych?" Dob said, breathing hard and staring at Jibb's blade. "I'm not crazy!"

"Maybe not," Jibb replied, his tone low and dangerous, "but nothing Cedrych would do to you could be any worse than what I have in mind."

"Wait!" Dob pleaded. "I can pay you whatever you want!"

"You mean out of what you've stolen from my Realm?" Jibb said, stopping right in front of him and bringing his face very close to Dob's. "That's not a very good offer." And with a motion so swift that Dob saw little more than a blur of silver out of the corner of his eye, Jibb flicked the dagger at Dob's cheek.

There was a brief, sharp pain, and then, a moment later, Dob felt blood trickling down along the line of his jaw. "You're crazy!" he whispered, his eyes widening with fear.

"That's not a nice thing to say," Jibb replied, cutting Dob on the other cheek as well.

"I have gold of my own!" Dob said desperately. "I'll give you all of it! I swear!"

Jibb said nothing, but he flicked his blade a third time, slicing off a piece of Dob's ear.

"All right!" Dob yelped. "All right! Call Melyor back! Maybe we can work something out!"

Jibb smiled. "Too late." He raised the blade to the corner of Dob's eye and began to laugh.

Dob twisted his head away, but Jibb's men grabbed him by the hair and chin and forced him to look forward again. He squeezed his eyes shut. "Whatever you want!" he gasped. "I'll do whatever you want!"

"Good," Melyor said, her voice coming from right beside him. "Here's what we have in mind."

He is in an alley just off the main street of a quad, leaning against the cool, smooth stone wall of a building, his eyes closed, his head tilted up toward the sky. Water drips on his face from a narrow overhang, the last remnants of an early morning rain. And for just a moment, he imagines that he is back in his cell in Tobyn-Ser, enjoying a midsummer thunderstorm beneath his small steel-grated window. These walls are not as rough, and there's too much light, but if he tries hard enough he can convince himself.

Until a mass carrier rolls by, its loud hum and acrid smell shattering the illusion. He opens his eyes in time to see the frightened faces peering out through the carrier windows, as if every passenger expects a thrower blast to shatter the glass in the next instant. The Nal is at war with itself, and the people on the carrier just wish to survive another day.

Like Baram.

He knows that the Sovereign is dead, and two of the Overlords as well. He has heard enough to know that Cedrych is still alive, and he still understands the workings of the Nal well enough to know what that means: Cedrych killed them all, or at the very least had them killed. And he remembers enough to know that, had all this happened several years ago, he would have been in one of those gangs that roams the streets at night, looking for firefights.

Instead, he runs from them, traveling the alleys and huddling in the small stairwells that lead underground. He would like to go back underground. It would be safer there, easier to hide. But he's already tried that once, when the fighting first began. He shudders at the memory. He has vague recollections of running the tunnels as an independent many years ago; of using the vast labyrinth to escape SovSec. And yet this time, when he tried to do the same to escape the fighting, he got lost. For hours, perhaps days—he really has no idea how much time passed—he groped through the dim corridors searching for something familiar, or just a way out. Finally, mercifully, he stumbled across a stairway that took him back to quad level, and since then he has kept to the streets.

He shudders for a second time. Merely thinking about his time underground brings on the panic again, welling up within him like rain in a clogged gutter. His clothing still reeks from when he soiled himself, though he has tried to clean his trousers several times since.

His stomach rumbles noisily and he realizes that he has yet to eat today. He pushes himself away from the wall and starts to shamble toward the main road. As he walks, he hears the silvers and gold pieces that Cedrych gave him jangling in his pocket. He should have spent them, he knows. He should have bought new clothes. But all he's done is buy a morsel or two of food and one glass of ale. The rest of the coins he's kept. *Consider them a gesture of my good will,* the Overlord said. Perhaps they'll keep him from getting killed.

He still has not gone back to see the Overlord again, but he remains in the

First Realm and has since their conversation. Except of course for the hours he spent underground; he could have been anywhere then. In recent days he's wondered if Cedrych would still hire him. They spoke a while ago, and a great deal has happened since. But as long as he can hear the coins in his trouser pocket, he believes that the opportunity still exists. And as time goes on he finds himself increasingly drawn to the idea of working for Cedrych.

It frightens him still. Cedrych is not a man who accepts failure, and it's been a long time since Baram succeeded at anything. But perhaps he's ready to try now. The night before a band of break-laws tracked him through the alleys and cornered him against a building only to lower their throwers, laughing and pointing when they saw him more clearly. He has no future in the quads, at least not without help.

The coins ring like bells.

He crosses the avenue and winds his way through another set of alleys emerging into the next quad just as it begins to rain again. Looking up into the rain he catches a glimpse of a quad sign, and reading the street code, he realizes that he is only a quad or two from Cedrych's headquarters. He surveys the quad and sees dozens of the Overlord's guardsmen, their stiff black uniforms spotted with raindrops.

Baram approaches one of them, a tall muscular man with dark skin and pale green eyes. "I want to talk with Cedrych," Baram says.

The guard looks him up and down and then, wrinkling his nose, makes a sour face. "You stink!" he replies, taking a step back and waving his hand in front of his face.

"I want to see Cedrych," Baram says again. "He told me that I could come and see him and he'd give me a job."

"Did you smell like that at the time?" the guard asks, starting to laugh.

Baram opens him mouth to answer, but then closes it again, realizing that it wasn't a serious question.

"Hey, come here!" the guard calls out to his friends, beckoning them over with a gesture.

Several other guards approach, all of them dressed in black, all of them large and powerfully built. Baram feels like a child beside them. *Sixteen deep, twenty across. Sixteen deep, twenty across.*

"Whew!" one of them exclaims, fanning the air in front of his face as the first guard had done a moment before. "What did you find, Odell?"

"If you ask me," another adds, "it smells like a pile of shit." All of them laugh.

"Listen to this!" Odell tells them. "Listen to what he's saying." Odell faces Baram again. "Go ahead. Tell them what you told me."

Baram stares down at the street. He has his hands in his pockets now, and his right hand fingers the coins Cedrych gave him, although he's very careful not to let them make a sound. "I want to see Cedrych," he repeats.

The other guards chuckle, but it's obviously not the reaction Odell is looking for. "Tell them the rest!" he commands, his tone harsh now.

Baram chews his lip for a moment. "He told me he'd give me a job," he says, his voice almost a whisper.

This time the men laugh heartily, and Baram looks up for just an instant, long enough to see Odell grin broadly, pleased to have been vindicated.

"When'd he do that?" one of the guards asks, poking Baram in the chest with a rigid finger. "Before or after you started smelling like a sewer?"

More laughter.

"Before," Baram answers, but he's not even sure that they can hear him anymore. Or that they care. He tries to walk out of the circle they've formed around him, but they won't let him. *Sixteen deep, twenty across.*

"Not so fast, Shit-Man," another one says, pushing him back. "We have orders to lock up derelicts like you."

"Yeah," Odell agrees. "But what jail would take him?"

"Wait!" one of the men shouts. "I know! We can take him to the Farm and use him as fertilizer!"

The guards laugh uproariously.

An instant later though, a new voice cuts through their laughter. "What's going on here?"

The guards abruptly fall silent. Baram looks up again and sees an older man who is also dressed in a black uniform. He is solidly built and muscular, though not as large as the younger guards. But the look in his dark eyes seems more than a match for the brawn of the others. "I asked a question," he tells the others, impatience seeping into his voice. "What's going on here?" He indicates Baram with a nod. "Who is this man?"

"A derelict, Commander," Odell finally responds. "We were just taking him into custody."

"Five of you?" the commander asks skeptically. "Funny, he doesn't strike me as that much of a threat."

Odell says nothing and the guards stand in awkward silence, avoiding the commander's gaze.

"Well?" the older man demands.

"He claims to know the Overlord, Commander," Odell tells him at last. "He says the Overlord offered him a job. But look at him!"

The commander does just that, stepping closer to Baram. An expression of distaste appears momentarily on his face, but it passes, and the man examines Baram closely, squinting slightly as his eyes come to rest on Baram's face. Then he starts to nod. "I remember him." He glances at Odell. "He does know the Overlord. I don't know about any job, but the Overlord did say to give him whatever he wants."

"I want to see Cedrych," Baram says to the commander. He refuses to look at any of the others.

The commander takes a long, slow breath and quickly surveys the quad. "All right," he says, his gaze coming back to Baram. "I'll take you to him. Odell you're with me." He looks at the other guards. "The rest of you return to your positions," he commands.

The other guards disperse quickly, appearing all too eager to be far from Baram and the trouble he has nearly caused them.

Odell and the commander lead Baram to a black carrier and put him in the back seat before taking their places up front. Odell makes a point of opening his window, and though the commander looks at the guard disapprovingly, he then does the same.

The trip to Cedrych's headquarters takes only a few minutes, and the two men quickly lead Baram into the building and to the security station near the main entrance. There they have one of the guards call up to the Overlord.

The speaker buzzes several times before the Overlord finally answers. "What is it?" he asks impatiently.

Baram flinches at the sound of Cedrych's voice. The Overlord sounds angry. Looking toward the door, Baram wonders if it's too late to leave.

"There's someone here to see you, Overlord," the guard says meekly.

"Who is it?"

The guard looks at the commander, who turns to Baram. "What's your name?" the commander asks.

"Baram."

"He says his name is Baram, Overlord," the guard says to the speaker.

There is a long silence, so long in fact, that Baram starts to wonder if the speaker is broken. The guards look at each other.

But then Cedrych's voice comes over the speaker again, sounding much calmer than it had before. "Send him up."

Odell and the commander take Baram to the lifter and the three of them ride up to the top floor of the building. The lifter doors slide open and they walk down the broad corridor to the weapons chamber. Baram's companions leave their throwers with the chamber guards and then they all step through the device to the door to Cedrych's office. The commander knocks once, and a few moments later the door opens revealing the Overlord. He is dressed just as he was the last time Baram saw him: black pants, a loose black tunic, and a thrower on his thigh. And as before, Baram finds that he cannot tear his gaze from the empty, scarred space where Cedrych's right eye should be.

The Overlord motions the three of them inside. "I'm glad to see you again, Baram," he says with a thin smile, closing the door behind them. "Your timing is perfect."

Baram looks at him quizzically and then realizes that there are others in the room as well. One of them is a woman he does not know. She's very beautiful, and she regards him with a strange mix of surprise and fright, as if the very fact of his arrival has altered her entire world. Dob, who he remembers all too well, is there also, regarding him venomously. But it is the third person who draws all of Baram's attention, for he never expected to see this man again. He feels himself begin to tremble with fear and rage.

"Hello, Baram," the sorcerer says, trying without success to smile.

31

As I continue to review in my mind all that might have gone wrong with Calbyr's mission, I am forced once more to question the Nal-Lord's judgement, and my own. Just as I should have insisted that he take more sophisticated communications equipment, I should never have acquiesced to his demand that all of his men be given stones of the same color. Granted, it might have allowed the men of his crew to recognize each other and thus avoid potentially fatal errors, but all that I have learned of Tobyn-Ser's mages indicates that the color of a sorcerer's stone is unique. It seems quite possible that the appearance in Tobyn-Ser of so many identical crimson stones doomed the mission by alerting the true mages to the presence of impostors in their land.

I can understand how Calbyr could have made such an error. Despite his considerable talents, he was not one to pay heed to such small details. He was a formidable street fighter, a clever strategist, and a good leader. But he was not a man of overwhelming intellect. I, on the other hand, should have known better.

—Personal journal of Cedrych i Vran, Overlord of the First Dominion of Bragor-Nal, Day 7, Week 11, Winter, Year 3059.

They had understood from the outset that their chances for success were slim. There were so many factors working against them, and so many risks they had to take to give themselves even the slightest hope of defeating the Overlord, that the odds were impossible to ignore. Knowing how wary Cedrych was bound to be of both her and Orris, Melyor expected that he would only meet with them in his office, where he could be sure, thanks to the weapons chamber, that he was the only one of them carrying a thrower or a blade.

More than that, though, Melyor knew from her own experience how hard it was to lie to Cedrych even once. He had a keen mind and a disturbing talent for divining the thoughts of others. It still amazed her that she had managed to keep her ancestry a secret from him as long as she had. And yet, the success of the plan she and Orris had developed hinged not on one lie, or even two, but rather layer after layer of deception. That they were forced to rely on Dob's cooperation, coerced as it was, only served to deepen Melyor's uncertainty.

Jibb warned her repeatedly against trusting the dark-haired break-law, as did Orris, who seemed to have an instinct for such things. And Melyor herself knew that there was nothing they could do to keep Dob from betraying them as soon as they reached Cedrych's office. Indeed, Melyor admitted to Orris that Cedrych would probably reward Dob for such a betrayal with wealth and status beyond the break-law's wildest imagination.

"Do you think Dob understands that?" the sorcerer had asked her early in the morning, as a heavy rain fell on the Nal and splattered drops of water against the window of her flat.

"He would have to be a fool not to."

"Which makes us even greater fools for trusting him, doesn't it?"

"Perhaps," she had answered with a grin, hoping that she conveyed more confidence than she felt. "We need to impress upon Dob that if he does betray us, you will spend your last breath making certain that he pays with his life."

Orris had grinned in return. "I can do that."

Not withstanding their bravado, however, both of them would have gladly abandoned this plan for almost any alternative. But neither of them could think of one. And Orris appeared to understand as well as she that they could not afford any delay. Once Cedrych moved into the Gold Palace and fully integrated SovSec into his already formidable army, he would be virtually invulnerable to any attack at all. They had to go after Cedrych now, and, thus, they had do it this way.

Which was why they were standing now in the common room of the Overlord's flat, with Dob beside them looking pale and anxious.

"You captured them on your own?" Cedrych was asking Dob, his skepticism manifest in his stance and his scarred features.

"Yes, Overlord," Dob answered. "Me and my men."

The Overlord smiled thinly. "And where did you get those cuts on your cheeks?"

Dob flushed deep red, but said nothing. Cedrych shook his head slightly.

Melyor wouldn't have believed Dob either. If he really had captured Melyor i Lakin and a sorcerer, he would have been strutting around the room like an independent after his first kill. Instead, he looked a frightened school boy caught in a lie. This was never going to work. She glanced sidelong at Orris, but he was oblivious to what was happening around him. She understood why, and it only served to heighten her concern.

"I find it hard to believe that you could be captured so easily," the Overlord commented, looking now at Melyor. "Unless I overestimated you for all these years."

"I had only a handful of men," she replied in a low voice. "I was counting on the sorcerer's power to offset Dob's advantage. But one of his men got off a lucky shot and killed Orris's bird."

"Ah, yes," Cedrych said, nodding sagely. He turned to Orris. "How does it feel to lose your hawk, Mage?" he asked in Tobynmir.

Orris didn't respond, and his eyes maintained the strange, distant look they had taken on almost as soon as they reached Cedrych's headquarters.

"Mage?" the Overlord persisted.

"What?" Orris said, shaking his head and focusing his gaze on Cedrych's scarred face.

"I asked you how it felt to lose your hawk."

Orris glared at him with unfeigned enmity. "I've been unbound before," he answered. "That's part of being a mage."

Cedrych nodded, eyeing him closely for another moment. Then he stepped to a table near the common room's large window and began to examine the two staffs that rested on it, one of them bearing a glowing red stone and the other an amber stone.

"So you're a Bearer now," he commented, speaking in Lonmir once more and picking up the more ancient of the two staffs. "Is that right, Melyor?"

Melyor shot another glance toward Orris. This time he was already looking at her and they shared a quick smile. She opened her mouth to reply to Cedrych's question, but in that instant she heard the buzz of a speaker from the Overlord's office.

"Fist of the God!" Cedrych spat. He looked at the staff for another few seconds before putting it back on the table and stepping into his office. The speaker continued to buzz intermittently for several moments more, until finally Melyor heard the Overlord respond. She couldn't make out what he said, however, and a minute or two later he returned to the common room, an enigmatic grin on his lips.

"This day is getting more interesting by the moment," he said drily. He returned to the table without explaining his remark, and resumed his inspection of the two staffs. "I'm curious, my dear," he began in Lonmir, not bothering to look at her, "how long have you known that you were a Gildriite?"

"Years," she answered, relieved in a way to be telling him.

He looked at her, and she was pleased to see the look of surprise in his one blue eye. "Did you know before you became a Nal-Lord?"

She allowed herself a grin. "I knew when I was still a little girl, although I didn't admit it to myself until I was fifteen."

He nodded and then turned his attention to the staffs once more. It was clear that something about them had caught his attention, but it was equally clear that he had yet to figure out what it was. The longer it took him, the better.

Early this morning, before they left Melyor's flat, Melyor had made Orris switch the stones, placing his amber crystal on the ancient staff that Gwilym had given to her, and her scarlet stone on the staff Orris had carried from Tobyn-Ser. At the time, the mage hadn't seen the point of doing this, but Melyor had insisted.

"He's seen me with my ceryll," Orris had reminded her. "Remember? The day we went to the Farm. He knows what color I carry."

"He saw two stones that day," she replied. "Yours and Gwilym's. The colors were almost identical then, and now one of them has changed. The fact that I am a Bearer is going to disturb him. It will take him some time to accept that, and longer still to remember which stone was which color. We do not need to fool him for very long. Just for a few minutes. Just long enough for you to kill him."

Melyor knew now that she had been right. Cedrych was confused, and though he obviously was skeptical of the claim that Dob had captured them, he appeared to believe that Orris's hawk was dead. Otherwise he surely would have destroyed the two stones by now. Instead, he was hovering over them, indulging his obsessive fascination with anything that pertained to the Initiative and the magic of Tobyn-Ser's mages. Just as Melyor had known he would. Everything was going according to their plan.

Except that Orris's hawk wasn't here yet. She glanced at the mage and saw that he had turned his gaze inward again. He had warned her about this ahead of time so that she wouldn't worry. He was reaching for his bird, searching for their connection. But the hawk wasn't close enough yet. If she had been, Cedrych would have been dead by now.

In order to maintain the illusion that the falcon was dead, they had released her when they reached the boundary between Melyor's Realm and Cedrych's, pulling off the Upper and into a narrow alleyway to do so. Orris had wanted to delay doing this for several quads more, but Melyor feared that once they were in Cedrych's Realm they might run into SovSec or the Overlord's men. She didn't want to have to explain anything out of the ordinary.

Still, she knew that releasing Anizir so far from their destination complicated things. Orris had to convey to the bird how to find Cedrych's headquarters, but the sorcerer was terribly unfamiliar with the Nal and its layout. Even after listening to Melyor's detailed description of where the Overlord's office was located and imparting the instructions to his familiar, Orris worried that the hawk might have trouble finding them.

"Even if she has no trouble," he had told Melyor, as Dob steered the carrier back onto the Upper, "we'll be there well before she is. She can't fly this fast."

To which Melyor had replied in Tobynmir, with a flippant tone she now regretted, "Then we will stall."

At this point, however, they had used up whatever time they had. With each passing moment, it became increasingly likely that Cedrych would figure out which stone was Orris's. And when he did, he would probably destroy it, eliminating the one chance they had to defeat him.

No one spoke for several moments. Cedrych continued to look over the staffs, and his three guests stood silently in the common room, Orris reaching for his bird, Dob fidgeting nervously, and Melyor eyeing the Overlord carefully, trying to gauge his reaction to the stones. She nearly jumped out of her skin when a sudden loud knock on the door broke the stillness.

"Ah, there we are," Cedrych said with a smile, pivoting away from the table and walking to the door. He paused as he reached for the door handle and gazed back into the common room, an amused smile on his face. "What a wonderful coincidence this all is," he murmured quietly. Then he turned again and opened the door.

She couldn't see who had come, nor could she hear what Cedrych said to them. But when the two guards and the bedraggled, foul-smelling man they were escorting stepped into the common room, Melyor felt as though someone had slipped a dagger through her heart. The last thing they needed were more complications, particularly in the form of Cedrych's imposing guardsmen. It took her several moments to understand that the two muscular men were the least of their worries.

The third man had long, stringy hair and a filthy tangled beard. His clothes were stained and torn, and he smelled like he had fouled himself. His eyes were pale and round, and there was a wildness to them that she found unsettling. An instant later, he gazed directly at her and their eyes met. It lasted but a single second; his eyes flicked away almost immediately. But that single look was enough. He's insane, Melyor told herself, the realization coming to her with frightening clarity. She wondered if Cedrych knew.

Whatever the Overlord's link with the man, it was apparent that Dob and the stranger had some history. There was loathing in the break-law's eyes as he regarded the man, and the stranger appeared to flinch slightly as he returned Dob's stare. Curious as to whether Orris had noticed this as well, she glanced at the sorcerer, and was horrified by the expression she saw on his rugged features. It was as if Orris were looking at a ghost. His face was pale, and his dark eyes appeared almost as wide and wild as the stranger's. For his part, the filthy man seemed as agitated as Orris. His hands were shaking and he bared his teeth at the sorcerer as if in a silent growl. But it was only when Orris greeted the stranger by name, that Melyor begin to grasp just how much of a threat the newcomer represented.

"Baram," she repeated to herself after Orris had spoken. She didn't realize that she had spoken aloud until the stranger looked at her.

"Yes," Cedrych said. "This is Baram. He's a friend of mine. Baram, this is Melyor. I believe you know Dob and Orris."

Baram's eyes darted toward her a second time, but just long enough to show that he had heard Cedrych. He seemed reluctant to take his eyes off Orris for even an instant.

Of course, Melyor thought to herself. Baram. Orris had only mentioned his name once, but she recognized the stranger from the sorcerer's description. This was the prisoner Orris had brought back to Lon-Ser to serve as a guide and as proof of what Cedrych had done to his land. Somehow Cedrych had befriended him. And somehow, by some trick of fate or whim of the gods, Baram had ended up in the Overlord's flat at the same time as Orris. "A wonderful coincidence," Cedrych had called it a few moments before. Hardly, Melyor thought with bitterness. And yet, she found some comfort in the Overlord's comment, although admittedly not much: at least Cedrych hadn't planned this. At least he hadn't known enough to have Baram here waiting for them. In the end, he had beaten them with sheer dumb luck.

Cedrych crossed the room to the table again, and Melyor cast a look at Orris. The sorcerer was already watching her and he shook his head grimly. They both knew what was coming.

"Come her for a moment, Baram," the Overlord said, beckoning the man over with a gesture. "I'd like you to look at something."

Baram remained perfectly still, his eyes never leaving Orris's face.

Cedrych looked up and gave a soft chuckle. "It's all right, Baram. I promise you he's not going anywhere."

Baram continued to glare at the sorcerer for several moments more before finally tearing himself from the place he had been standing with an effort that actually appeared to cause him pain. He shuffled to the table where Cedrych was standing, glancing over his shoulder several times as if to reassure himself that Orris was not attempting to escape.

"Do you recognize either of these?" the Overlord asked, indicating the staffs and their glowing stones.

Baram immediately started to point at one of them, but then stopped himself and bent over the table to take a closer look. For several minutes he said nothing at all, although he continually interrupted his scrutiny of the staffs in order to check on Orris.

"I know this stone," he finally said, pointing to the amber one and turning to glare fiercely at Orris, "but it doesn't belong on this stick."

Cedrych grinned triumphantly. "Thank you, Baram. That was what I thought, but I'm glad to have you confirm it for me." He looked past the bedraggled man to Orris and Melyor, holding up Gwilym's ancient staff so that Orris's stone shone over his head like an amber star. "An interesting ruse," he commented in Tobynmir, so the sorcerer would understand. "But I'm forced to wonder why you would go to such lengths to fool me if Orris's bird really is dead." His grin abruptly vanished, and his one eye flashed angrily at Melyor and then Orris. "Where is it?" he demanded harshly. "Where's your bird?"

"She's not here," Orris answered defiantly. "If she were, I'd have killed you by now."

"Is she dead?"

Orris hesitated, drawing another grin from the Overlord.

"No, she's not!" Cedrych said, answering his own question. "Your uncertainty gives you away, Mage!"

Still Orris said nothing. And looking at the sorcerer closely, Melyor understood why. He sensed his hawk. She was coming, and even now he was reaching for her, and for the stone that the Overlord still held. Cedrych seemed to understand that something was wrong as well. He narrowed his eye and, taking a step forward, placed a hand on the grip of his thrower.

"Look!" cried one of the guards who had arrived with Baram, pointing out the window.

Melyor spun in the direction the man had indicated, her eyes scanning the sky for Orris's falcon. At first she saw nothing, but then she spotted the bird as well. She was flying straight toward the window, her sleek, dark wings outstretched and her beak opened as if she were screaming.

Melyor whirled back toward Orris. "Do it!" she shouted. *"Kill him!"*

The sorcerer's eyes were closed, and a brilliant light had begun to brighten the room.

Melyor heard an inarticulate roar torn from Cedrych's throat, and she turned in time to see the Overlord, his shirt sleeve ablaze, swing the staff with all his might and hurl it along with its shining amber stone at the large window. A bolt of power burst from the crystal just as it hit the glass, causing the window to explode into thousands of tiny fragments. But the bolt of fire Orris had conjured from the stone slammed harmlessly into the wall, leaving little more than an enormous black mark. Cedrych dropped to the floor immediately and rolled over twice, extinguishing the flames that had begun to consume his shirt.

And Orris's stone disappeared from sight, as the staff that held it fell end over end toward the avenue that lay sixty stories below.

When Cedrych sprang to his feet again he held his weapon in his hand. He was breathing hard, and Orris could see that his right arm was blistered and blackened from his wrist to his elbow. But he was still very much alive, and there was a look of barely checked rage in his icy blue eye.

"You just earned yourself an excruciating death, Mage!" the Overlord told him, leveling his weapon at Orris's chest. He nodded toward Melyor and Dob. "And you've assured your friends here of the same!"

Orris didn't respond. Instead he conveyed an image to Anizir, who was hovering outside the window, crying out repeatedly.

"First though," Cedrych went on, "I'm going to kill that hawk if yours."

The one-eyed man turned to the window, but by then Anizir had already tucked in her wings and begun to stoop toward him with dizzying speed, her talons outstretched. Cedrych threw up his uninjured arm to block the blow and was partially successful. One of the falcon's claws only tore through his shirt sleeve. The other, however, found its target, leaving three parallel gashes on the top of the Overlord's head that immediately started to bleed profusely.

The Overlord spat a curse, whirled, and fired his weapon at the bird, missing her narrowly. Orris tried to rush at him, to keep him from firing again, but before he could take a step, someone grabbed him from behind and threw him to the ground, landing heavily on top of him. The mage tried to roll away, but his attacker—no doubt one of the guards who had escorted Baram—had him pinned to the floor. Orris felt a knee grinding into the small of his back and powerful hands wrapping themselves around his throat. He tried to reach behind to get at his attacker, but all he could find were the guard's powerful forearms, which he could not move. The man's fingers began to gouge into his larynx.

He could hear the sound of Cedrych's weapon discharging and from what Anizir conveyed to him, Orris knew that his hawk was keeping the Overlord occupied. He could hear Melyor and Dob as well, struggling with Cedrych's other guard, and Orris guessed that the older and smaller of the two guards was the one who had attacked him. It was small consolation really, considering what the man was doing to him.

He had only one chance. He sensed that Anizir was tiring already, which was not surprising; she had flown a long way just to get here. Her cries were growing increasingly urgent, and he sensed mounting desperation in her thoughts. Without his ceryll, they couldn't accomplish much together, so she was better off fleeing before one of the streams of fire pouring from Cedrych's weapon found its mark. But there was one thing they could do before she flew away.

He was starting to grow desperate himself. His lungs were burning from lack of air and the guard was dangerously close to crushing his throat. He closed his eyes, formed an image in his mind, and reached for Anizir.

The heat surprised Orris with its intensity, and opening his eyes he saw that the fire had materialized much closer to where he lay then he had intended. It had the desired effect, however. His attacker jumped off of him, allowing Orris to roll onto his back and kick upward with all his strength. He was barefoot—Cedrych's guards had required that Melyor, Dob, and he all remove their shoes before entering the Overlord's quarters—but he caught the guard full in the groin.

The man doubled over and then dropped to his knees. Orris tried to kick him again, this time in the head, but the guard was ready for him. He blocked the mage's blow and then drove his fist into Orris's kidney. Gasping for breath, Orris tried to scramble to his feet, but the guard lunged forward, knocking Orris to the floor again, and then started buffeting Orris's head and face with his fists. The mage was able to block most of the man's punches, but he could do little else. He could feel the flames just beside him, licking at his clothing and skin, but if the guard noticed he showed no sign of it.

Finally, Orris succeeded in grabbing hold of the man's wrists. The guard tried to yank his hands out of Orris's grasp, but the mage maintained his grip. The guard growled in frustration, and then drove his head downward, as if to smash it into Orris's face. Orris twisted his head to the side at the last moment, and the guard's head hit solidly into the floor. The man lifted his head quickly, but he was clearly dazed. Sensing his opportunity, Orris twisted himself into his side with an abrupt wrenching motion, throwing the guard off of him into the fire. The man yelped in pain and immediately dove back out of the flames. His shirt was on fire, as was one leg of his trousers. But still he came at Orris again, seemingly intent on pummeling the mage into submission.

By now, however, Orris was on his feet, and when the guard rushed at him, the mage ducked under the man's wild swing and hammered his fist into the guard's stomach. Again the guard doubled over, and this time Orris was able to drive his knee upward into the man's face with an impact that felt and sounded sickeningly solid. The guard crashed to the floor and lay perfectly still.

Looking up from the guard's prone body, Orris saw that the flames had spread quickly across the floor, effectively cutting Cedrych and Baram off from the others. Anizir was still diving at the Overlord, but her tail feathers were singed and smoking. She hadn't much time left.

Anizir, fly! Orris sent. *Get away quickly!* The bird gave one last cry, but then did as he had instructed, flying out the broken window and then slicing sharply upward and to the side. Cedrych twisted and sent two more shafts of red flame at her, but both missed.

Orris glanced to the side and saw that Melyor and Dob had subdued the second guard, leaving him in the middle of the floor, where the fire had now claimed his body. His nostrils filling with the smell of charred flesh and oppressive acrid smoke given off by the material that covered Cedrych's floor, Orris turned his gaze back to the Overlord.

And had just barely enough time to dive to the floor in order to avoid a blast from Cedrych's weapon. As soon as he landed, he had to roll to the side to dodge another beam of red fire that bored through the rising flames. Keeping low and using the fire he had started to screen his movements from Cedrych, Orris took cover behind a large, heavy chair. He peered over to where Dob and Melyor had been standing and saw that they too had been forced to duck down behind the Overlord's furniture.

Cedrych continued to fire his weapon, the bursts coming with growing frequency. It seemed to Orris that there was no coherent strategy to the Overlord's aim; Cedrych was just firing randomly through the flames, hoping to hit Orris and his companions. The mage nodded to himself. Had he been in the Overlord's position he would have done the same thing. The bald man was trapped on the far side of his quarters by the fire, with no way out save the window. There was little that he could do except fire his weapon out of desperation and fury.

Or so the mage thought. For in the next moment, small doors in the ceiling slid open—Orris hadn't even noticed them before—and metal objects appeared that began to spray water into the chamber. The fire had spread rapidly, and had begun to scorch the ceiling, but even so the water's effect was immediate. The flames started to recede, slowly to be sure, but there could be no mistaking the trend.

Somewhere beyond the fire, Cedrych laughed, although he continued to fire his weapon.

"Soon, Mage!" the Overlord called out. "You can't hide forever, particularly once your fire is gone!"

Orris glanced to the side and saw that Melyor was watching him, her hair damp and her eyes filled with despair.

"What will you do then, Mage?" Cedrych goaded, his voice rising. "What will you do without your fire?"

The scarred man fired his weapon several times more. One of the blasts hit the chair Orris was using as a shield, slicing through it like a knife through flesh and just barely missing Orris's head.

"I'll tell you what you'll do!" Cedrych said, laughing again. "You'll die!"

32

As the only surviving outlander, Baram has become a symbol for the people of Tobyn-Ser. He is the embodiment of the razing of Taima and the massacres at Watersbend and Kaera. As such, he is probably the most reviled man in the history of our land, surpassing even Theron. Indeed, with so much hatred directed at Baram, many have overlooked the treachery of Owl-Master Sartol, whose crimes, I believe, were far more heinous. Still, though I have fought to prevent the outlander's execution, I do understand why so many have come to hate him so much.

To me, however, Baram is more than our enemy, more than just "the outlander." He is the only living person who has spent significant lengths of time living in both Lon-Ser and Tobyn-Ser. He is, in a sense, a bridge between our two lands and I have hoped that he might, at some point in the future, help us resolve our dispute with Lon-Ser. I fear though, that if he remains in prison for much longer, he will not be of much value to us when that time finally comes. A man cannot be imprisoned for an extended period without it affecting his mind.

—From Section Four of "The Report of Owl-Master Baden on his Interrogation of the Outlander Baram," Submitted to the 1,014th Gathering of the Order of Mages and Masters. Spring, Gods' Year 4625.

There was no way out for them. Cedrych knew that. Yes, they were near the door. But with the sorcerer's stone lying on the street below and his bird gone, they were no match for the dozens of guardsmen who stood in the corridor beyond it. In essence, they were as doomed as Cedrych by the fire that Orris had somehow managed to conjure. The only difference was that Cedrych had a weapon and they didn't, at least not anymore.

But none of this mattered if the fire system didn't work. And as the flames climbed higher and higher and spread across the carpeting, driving Cedrych closer to the shattered window, the Overlord found himself wondering, with surprising detachment, when he had last had the system checked. He was so concerned with assassination attempts—with good reason, to be sure—that he had given no thought to the other protection systems in years. Fires, land tremors, whirlwinds: these things all occurred in the Nal with some regularity. Yet Cedrych had ignored them, as if daring the gods to come after him.

It had never occurred to him that someone would deliberately burn his flat as a way of killing him. It was brilliant, albeit foolhardy. Cedrych couldn't do anything to save himself. He could fire his weapon blindly through the fire, gambling that before he died he might kill Orris, Melyor, and Dob as well. And he could hope for the fire system to turn on. But otherwise he was helpless. It wasn't a feeling to which he was accustomed.

So when, at last, the ceiling compartments opened and the water dispersers switched on, Cedrych could barely contain his glee. Without the fire to contend with he would have no trouble finishing off the sorcerer and his friends. That was the beauty of the weapons chamber. That was why he had spent so much having it designed and constructed.

Cedrych wasn't usually one to taunt, but then again, he didn't usually come so close to dying in his own headquarters. And the throbbing pain from his burned arm offered an undeniable reminder of just how close Orris had come to killing him. He couldn't be blamed for celebrating his victory over the mage.

Orris, however, did not respond to any of Cedrych's comments. At first the Overlord assumed that Orris simply refused to say anything in return. But soon the Overlord found himself wondering if he had already killed the sorcerer with a thrower blast. "Are you going to beg for your life, Mage?" he called in Tobynmir, peering through the diminishing flames, hoping to catch a glimpse of Orris or Melyor. "Or perhaps for the lives of your friends." He didn't see any of them. "I might be willing to spare them, you know. I always cared for Melyor, and Dob has served me well in the past."

Nothing. The flames were dying down under the steady spray of water, and Cedrych edged closer to the fire, still searching for some sign of them. Was it possible that he had managed to kill all three of them with his random thrower blasts? A blackened body lay in the middle of the charred portion of the floor, but Cedrych was fairly certain that it belonged to one of his guards. He could see the other guard as well, lying utterly motionless beyond the fire, his face covered with drying blood. But where were Orris, Melyor, and Dob?

He heard a gasp from behind him and turned to see Baram cowering against the wall beside the window and staring out at something in the sky. Following the line of his gaze, Cedrych saw Orris's falcon hovering just outside the window. The Overlord raised his weapon and fired quickly, but the bird darted out of the way. Then she began to hover again, higher this time, so that he could just barely see her tail. Cedrych took two steps toward the window and fired a second time. Once more she dodged his blast and resumed her hovering still higher. He took another step, and then suddenly halted, realizing what he had done. Or rather, what the detestable creature had tricked him into doing.

He spun back around as fast as his maimed right leg would let him, but it was already too late. Orris was charging at him, his forearms raised, and his teeth gritted against the flames that reached for his hair and clothing as he dashed through the fire. Cedrych didn't have enough time to level his thrower at the mage, and he had turned too swiftly to be in position to brace himself for the impact. There was nothing he could do.

Orris crashed into his chest so hard that Cedrych actually felt his feet leave the floor as he flew backwards toward the window. The Overlord's thrower slipped from his fingers and he clawed frantically at the mage. His hair, his face, his arms, his clothing. Anything he might grab onto to keep himself from falling, or, at the very least, to make certain that Orris fell with him. He landed awkwardly on his upper back and slid a foot or two on the water-soaked carpet, which was covered with fragments of glass. He came to a stop with his shoulder blades on the metal frame where the giant window had been.

Orris had landed a few feet short of there, and the mage immediate tried to get to his feet. Cedrych kicked at him with his good leg, catching the mage in the temple and sending him sprawling back to the floor. The Overlord scrambled to his feet. But as he did, he felt a sharp raking pain across his back. He whirled and saw the falcon veering away, its talons red with his blood. And before he could turn back again he felt someone crash into his back.

He staggered forward, flailing with his arms in a frenzied attempt to keep his balance. But he was falling. He twisted his body, reaching back with his uninjured arm. And he saw Melyor swing the staff that bore her red stone. He felt an explosion of white pain on the side of his head and then he was aware of nothing except the whistling of the air as it whipped past his ears and through his clothes. Faster and faster. He saw the pavement rushing to meet him and he closed his eyes to scream.

The water is falling on him like rain in a summer storm, and the wind blowing in through the shattered window makes him shiver. The woman and the mage are standing at the edge staring down at Cedrych's body, which lies on the pavement below, its limbs protruding at odd angles.

But Baram's eyes are focused on something else, something much nearer and more precious. He has been lost for so long. He has been beaten and bound; forced to wander through the mountains of Tobyn-Ser and the jungles of the isthmus; thrown back into the disorienting familiarity of this Nal that was once his home, but is no more; ridiculed and abused by break-laws and guards. All since the mage entered his life and dragged him from the peace and safety of his cell.

But finally, just a few feet from where he stands, his back pressed against the wall of Cedrych's flat, he sees the means to rid himself of the mage forever. On the floor by the window ledge, surrounded by tiny shards of glass that glitter like gems, lies Cedrych's thrower. It is so close, closer by far to him than it is to the mage or the woman.

Slowly, so as not to draw their attention, he takes a step away from the wall, crouches, and grabs the weapon. He is standing with the thrower aimed at them before they even realize what he has done.

Seeing their eyes widen with shock, seeing the relief that Cedrych's death has brought them give way to fear of him and the thing he holds in his hand, Baram laughs out loud.

"Baram, don't do this," the mage says. "Please. There's no need."

"I want you dead!" Baram answers in the mage's language. "I want you gone forever!"

The mage nods. "I know, and you can have that." He gestures toward the window. "Cedrych's dead. I have no reason to remain here. I'll be leaving, and you won't have to see me ever again."

"Cedrych was going to give me a job," Baram tells him. "And you killed him."

"I can give you a job," the woman says in Lonmir. "I'm going to need to hire lots of people."

"You're a Gildriite," Baram says with disgust. "How can you give me a job?"

"I may be a Gildriite," she replies, "but I'm also Melyor i Lakin. If I say I can hire you, it's true."

Melyor i Lakin, he repeats to himself. He knows the name from before he left for Tobyn-Ser. She is a Nal-Lord—perhaps more than that by now. He starts to ask what kind of job she can give him, but then he shakes his head. It doesn't matter. Nothing matters as long as the mage is alive.

Without realizing it he has lowered his weapon. But now he raises it again, intending to kill the mage.

Before he can fire, however, something large and heavy smashes into his shoulder, staggering him. A chair. Dob has thrown a chair at him. He tries to right himself, but before he can, the break-law crashes into him, sending him sprawling toward the edge. He slips, drops the thrower, and tumbles out of the flat, just barely managing to grab the ledge with one hand to keep from plummeting to the street below.

The mage is there above him almost immediately, reaching for him. The woman is there as well.

"Take my hand!" the mage shouts over the sound of the wind.

Baram shakes his head. "I will not let you kill me!" he shouts back.

"I'm not trying to kill you, I'm trying to save you!" the mage tells him. "Now take my hand! I'll pull you back in!"

"No!"

"Don't be a fool, Outlander!" the mage yells. *"Take my hand!"*

Baram smiles at him. "I am called Baram," he says. And then he lets go of the ledge and begins to fall.

Despite the fact that Cedrych was dead, Melyor did not want to face his guardsmen unarmed. Fortunately, thanks to years of experience with the Overlord, she knew that they didn't have to. He kept a spare thrower fastened to the bottom of the middle drawer of his desk, and after the flames died down, she slipped into Cedrych's office and retrieved it.

When she returned to the common room she found Dob and Orris standing face to face in silence. Dob was regarding the mage appraisingly, as if to determine if he could beat Orris in a fight. The mage just looked angry. His falcon had returned to her usual place on his shoulder.

"Tell him I didn't want Baram to die," Orris said. "There was no need to throw that chair."

"He says thanks for saving our lives," Melyor told the break-law.

Dob glanced at her skeptically. "That didn't sound like a thank you."

She shrugged. "Tobynmir's a strange language."

She retrieved her stone and started toward the door, with Orris following close behind her. "You didn't tell him what I said," he complained. "I know the Lonmir word for thank you."

She stopped so suddenly that he almost ran into her. "Well you should have been thanking him!" she replied angrily in his language. "Baram was about to kill you!"

"I could have talked him out of it."

"No!" she said shaking her head vehemently. "He was insane, and he hated you! Nothing you could have said would have stopped him!" She took a long breath. "I understand that you wanted to help him. And I would not blame you for feeling responsible for him in some way. But what Dob did was necessary." She held his gaze for several moments until at last he nodded.

He looked back briefly at the break-law. She could see the welt on his temple where Cedrych had kicked him. "Thanks," he muttered.

After a few seconds Dob gave a small nod, as if he had understood.

Melyor continued to the door and opened it without hesitating.

"What's happened?" one of the guards asked immediately. "Where's the Overlord?"

"Cedrych is dead," she declared. "My name is Melyor i Lakin and I'm Overlord now."

The guard blinked, but said nothing. Several of the others standing behind him in the corridor began to whisper among themselves.

"Any of you who wish to remain here and work for me are welcome to do so," Melyor went on. "If you choose to leave, I'll allow that as well. I ask only that you return whatever weapons Cedrych issued to you." She paused for effect. "If any of you try to stop me, I'll kill you."

She stood there a moment longer and then walked past the guards toward the lifter with Orris and Dob following.

"What did you say to them?" Orris asked after the lifter doors had closed.

"I told them that I am their Overlord now," she explained in Tobynmir. "I offered them the choice of leaving, working for me, or dying."

The mage raised an eyebrow. "Your name must carry some weight around here."

She grinned. "A bit, yes."

"What do you think they'll do?"

"I expect most will stay. Many of them will have qualms about working for a Gildriite, but given what Cedrych has done to the Nal, this is no time to be giving up good jobs."

"Will any of them challenge your right to take Cedrych's place?"

She smiled grimly. "As far as they're concerned I killed him. That gives me a legitimate claim on his Dominion."

Orris did not respond, but after several seconds he gave a single nod. And in that moment Melyor found herself achingly aware of the chasm that separated the mage's world from her own. No doubt he would be leaving the Nal very soon.

They rode the rest of the way to the ground floor in silence. When the lifter doors opened, revealing another large contingent of Cedrych's men, Melyor stepped forward and told them much the same thing she had told the men outside the Overlord's flat. Then she and her two companions walked out into the street.

Cedrych lay in the middle of the avenue, his eyes staring sightlessly at the dirty sky, his legs and arms protruding from his shattered body at impossible angles, and a river of blood flowing slowly from his head. Baram was nearby, his body and limbs broken and contorted as well. But the ragged man's eyes were closed, and his face wore an expression that Melyor could only describe as serene.

Between Cedrych and Baram, lay Gwilym's ancient staff and Orris's crystal. Or rather, what was left of them. The stone had fractured into thousands of tiny, sparklng pieces. And the staff had split down its entire length and was held together by a few scant fibers of wood. There was a deep depression in the pavement where the stone had hit, and thin jagged cracks radiated from the spot in all directions.

Melyor and Orris stood motionless, staring wordlessly at the crystal fragments and the splintered staff. After some time, the mage's bird gave a soft cry and Orris scratched her chin gently.

"I am sorry for your stone," Melyor said at last, unsure of how losing the crystal affected his ability to wield magic.

Orris nodded, but still said nothing.

"Will you be able to find another one?"

He nodded a second time. "I know an Abboriji merchant who sometimes has them to sell. Or, if I have to, I can always go back to the Ceryll Cavern."

Melyor looked at her scarlet stone. "Will your next stone be the same color as your first?"

"I don't know," Orris answered. "Mages lose their familiars several times during the course of their lives, but they rarely lose their cerylls. I don't know what to expect."

She bent down and picked up the broken stave. "I had wanted to return the stone to the Bearer's staff," she said shaking her head. "They belong together."

"We still can," Orris told her.

"Even without your stone?"

He nodded. "It'll be a bit more difficult, and it might not look perfect, but I can do it."

She smiled at him. "It would make me very happy."

She handed him both Gwilym's staff and his own, which still bore her stone. He walked off a short distance before sitting down on the edge of the street and laying the broken wood across his lap. Anizir hopped off his shoulder and sat beside him, and the mage laid his hands on the staff and closed his eyes.

"What's he doing?" Dob asked.

"Fixing my staff."

The break-law narrowed his eyes. "With what?"

Melyor laughed. "He's a sorcerer," she told him.

It seemed to take Dob several moments to understand what she was telling him and Melyor smiled sympathetically. There was little room in the Nal for magic, she knew, particularly for men like Dob. Indeed, an instant later he appeared to remember that she was a Gildriite, and he backed away from her.

"Is that how you beat me that night?" he asked. "With magic?" The word sounded funny coming out of his mouth.

"Gildriites don't have magic," she said, laughing again. "We sometimes have dreams that foresee the future."

He waited for more. "That's it?" he finally asked.

She nodded. "That's it. And for that, the Gildriites have been persecuted for hundreds of years." She paused allowing that bit of information to sink in. "To answer your question," she continued a few moments later, "I beat you that night because I'm smarter than you are and I'm better with a blade." And then, to soften the blow, she added, "That's why I beat Savil, too."

Dob stared at her for some time with a wounded expression. Then he looked away and swallowed. He might even have nodded. "So I guess with you as Overlord, and Jibb back in the Fourth, I'm out of luck."

"Not necessarily."

He met her gaze again, and there was an eager look in his blue eyes.

"Orris had hopes of helping Baram," she said in a confidential tone as she indicated the mage with a gesture. "But I don't think there was anything he could have done. Baram wanted to kill us and I'm convinced that you saved our lives today by throwing that chair at him. Of course, before today, you had attacked Jibb and stolen my Realm." She paused briefly, as if considering something. "I guess the two balance each other. So let's call it even."

His eyes widened. "You'd do that?"

"Yes, provided Jibb is willing to go along. He might want you to compensate him in some way. Perhaps a few months of free work before he starts paying you."

"So you're saying you'd let me stay in your Dominion as one of Jibb's breaklaws?" You'd have thought from the man's tone that she had just given him an entire Realm. Which, as it happened, was precisely what she had in mind.

She grinned. "You're aiming too low, Jibb."

He looked at her with a puzzled expression and shook his head. "I don't understand."

"Let me put it this way: I don't expect to be Overlord for more than a day or two."

"Why not?"

"Because I expect to be admitted to the Council of Sovereigns."

It took him a moment. He really wasn't very sharp. But he had been loyal to Savil, and with what she was about to give him, she could expect that he would be loyal to her, too, which would be important, given what she had in mind for Bragor-Nal. "So if you're Sovereign, then Jibb will become Overlord, and I . . ." He smiled at her, looking for all his muscles and rugged good looks like a little boy on the Day of Lon. "You're giving me the Fourth, aren't you?" he asked in amazement. "After everything that's happened, I'm going to get the Fourth!" He threw his head back and laughed. "Wait until Bowen sees what I have in store for him now!"

"No!" she said severely, wiping his grin from his face. "There will be none of that! This Nal has been destroying itself for too long! Things are about to change: I won't tolerate any more assassinations or warfare! As far as I'm concerned that all died with Cedrych! And if you can't abide by the rules I set, then you'll be stripped of your Realm and banished to Stib-Nal! Understand?"

He stared at her for several moments. And then he nodded. "Yes, Overlord. I understand." He nodded again. "That's probably for the best," he added in a quiet voice.

Melyor regarded him closely, looking for some sign that he was humoring her. But his agreement seemed genuine, and she was forced to wonder if perhaps there was more to him than she had thought.

Dob inclined his head slightly toward the far side of the street. "Here comes your friend."

Melyor turned and saw Orris walking toward them. He held his own staff in one hand and the ancient staff in the other. It appeared whole again, and once more it held her glowing scarlet stone.

"You fixed it!" she said in Tobynmir, flashing the mage a broad smile. "Thank you!"

"You're welcome," Orris replied. "But you should take a closer look before you get too excited. I wasn't able to fix it entirely."

As he drew nearer she saw what he meant. There was a thin dark line running down the length of the staff where it had been split and there were small cracks around the seam between the wood and the crystal.

She sensed that the mage was watching her closely as she examined his work. "I'm sorry," he said. "But I did warn you."

After several moments she looked up from the staff, took his hand in hers, and gave it a gentle squeeze. "You do not have to apologize," she told him. "It looks wonderful." She released his hand and traced a finger along the thin line in the ancient wood. "This will always remind me of you."

The mage's face reddened and he looked away. "What have you two been talking about?" he asked, trying to sound casual.

"I have been telling Dob of my plans to become Sovereign."

Orris gaped at her. "Are you serious?"

"Why?" she demanded with feigned indignation. "Are you saying I would be a bad Sovereign?"

"No!" the mage answered quickly. "That's not—"

She began to laugh and Orris shook his head.

"You'll be great," he said in a tone that made her blush. "But do you think the people of Bragor-Nal are ready to have a Gildriite as their Sovereign?"

She shrugged. "They had better be."

33

Even if, after due consideration, we as a people decide not to engage the leaders of Lon-Ser in a dialogue about our lands' futures, and even if, despite the troubles Lon-Ser continues to face, our enemies there do not launch another invasion against Tobyn-Ser, we must acknowledge the enormous impact this episode has had, and will continue to have upon our land. I refer to more than merely the violence and indignities we have suffered, and the shock, after so many centuries of peace, of having to fight off invaders once more, although certainly these things have left wounds upon our land that will take years to heal. I refer, however, to something less obvious, but perhaps more insidious. Our people have witnessed the might and cruelty of Lon-Ser's advanced goods. They have seen strange, terrible weapons destroy their homes and kill their loved ones. They have come face to face with a force that both mimics nature and defies it. Having seen this power, having learned of its existence, our people will never again view the world in the same way. Even if we never experience it again, we will never be the same for having witnessed its devastating potential.

> —From Section Nine of "The Report of Owl-Master Baden on his Interrogation of the Outlander Baram," Submitted to the 1,014th Gathering of the Order of Mages and Masters. Spring, Gods' Year 4625.

Notwithstanding the bluster with which she spoke to Orris and Dob of becoming Sovereign, Melyor harbored doubts. In truth, Orris had asked her the wrong question. It mattered much less what the people thought of having a Gildriite Sovereign than it did what the leaders of SovSec and the surviving Nal-Lords thought of it. And she had a pretty good idea what they would think.

As she told the mage, it did help that they had killed Cedrych themselves. Just as the one-eyed man had made himself the natural choice to succeed Durell by killing the Sovereign, so Melyor had made herself Cedrych's heir apparent by killing him. It also helped that her reputation had travelled far beyond the Fourth, even beyond the bounds of Cedrych's Dominion. Every lord and break-law in the Nal knew of Melyor i Lakin. She was cunning, deadly with both blade and thrower, and a shrewd Nal-Lord who had run one of Cedrych's most profitable Realms. True, word had already begun to spread that, in addition to all this, she was a Gildriite and a Bearer of the Stone, but she hoped that she would be admitted to the Council long before word of this reached Trestor or Merne-Proper.

As she had anticipated, most of Cedrych's men remained with her, enough certainly, when combined with Jibb's forces, to give her a formidable army. SovSec and the other Nal-Lords remained a problem though. Or so she thought. The day after Cedrych's death, as Melyor sorted through the Overlord's papers and saw to the repair of what was, for the time being, her headquarters, the speak screen on Cedrych's desk beeped unexpectedly.

Glancing briefly at Jibb and Orris who were with her in the office, and giving a small shrug, she switched on the screen. The face that appeared before her a moment later was one she had seen in still shots many times before, although she had never seen it in person. He had aged considerably since the last of those shots had been taken. His hair was now the color of steel, and his cheeks were lined and hollow giving him a cadaverous appearance. The look in his dark eyes though, which made no concessions to old age, bespoke a finely honed intelligence and supreme self-confidence. And wearing the trim blue uniform of the Sovereign's security force, which he commanded, the man was still a formidable presence, even on the screen. Melyor blinked once, fighting to check the sudden acceleration of her pulse.

"Good day, Overlord," the man said with a smile that gave him a ghoulish look.

"Good day, General Slevin," Melyor replied steadily. "What can I do for you?"

"Actually, I contacted you so that I could ask you the same."

Melyor's jaw nearly dropped open and she wasn't entirely certain if she had heard correctly. "I—I'm afraid I don't understand."

"Do you mean to tell me that you don't intend to petition the Council?" he asked, though the tone of his voice made it clear that he knew better.

Certainly there was no sense in denying it. "I expect to send the petition tomorrow," she told him frankly.

"As I expected," he said, grinning again.

Of course he expected it, she thought. He had been running SovSec for years. She wondered when he had last been surprised by something that happened in the Nal, and then, looking up at Orris briefly, she realized that it probably hadn't been that long ago. It also occurred to her in that moment that SovSec might have surveillance systems in Cedrych's office. The idea of it both amused and alarmed her.

"I just wanted you to know, Overlord," Slevin went on, "that the security force will be at your disposal as soon as your petition is accepted."

"Thank you, Slevin. That's good to know."

"In the meantime," the lean man added, "if you need anything taken care of—anything at all—I'll be happy to assist you. In an unofficial capacity, of course."

He was full of surprises. "Of course, Slevin. Again, thank you."

Slevin nodded and a moment later he disappeared from Melyor's screen. She switched off the device and stared at Jibb, an amazed smile on her lips.

"What was that all about?" she asked.

The big man shrugged. "You're the most powerful person in the Nal. You can't really be that surprised. This is how people are going to treat you from now on."

She made a dismissive gesture. "Break-laws and Nal-Lords, maybe. But SovSec? This is Slevin we're talking about!"

"And you're Melyor i Lakin," he countered. "Plus you're a Bearer."

"What's that got to do with it," she demanded, narrowing her eyes.

"People are afraid of you, Melyor. They don't know what it means that you're a Gildriite. They only know that you killed Cedrych." He nodded toward Orris. "And you did it with the help of a sorcerer. People like Slevin and Bren and Enrek don't understand what that means. All they know is, they don't want to take any chances on making you angry. I guarantee you that Slevin won't be the last to offer you his support. In fact, I wouldn't be surprised if no one challenges your claim to the Gold Palace." He paused, as if considering something. "But I'll guarantee you this as well: every person who promises to help you will be trying to figure out a way to kill you at the same time. Including Slevin."

Melyor continued to stare at him for sometime after he finished. He was right, as usual. She had been looking on her ancestry as a handicap, and in many ways it was. It made her a target. But in the short term, in ways she hadn't anticipated, it might also give her an advantage.

She gave Jibb a small smile. "I guess that means I'll need Overlords I can trust," she said pointedly.

"Yes, you will. But I don't want to be one of them."

She couldn't believe what she was hearing. "*What?* Of course you do!"

He shook his head soberly. "I've been giving this some thought. I can't do my job if I'm your Overlord."

"Your job?"

"Taking care of you."

She started to laugh, but then, seeing that he was serious, she stopped. "So what are you suggesting?"

"Slevin was calling today because he's worried about his job. And he should be. New Sovereigns usually bring in their own person to run SovSec. That's what I want."

It shouldn't have come as a surprise. If she had given it any thought at all she would have anticipated this. "I'll give you any position you want, Jibb," she told him. "You know that." She made a sour face. "But do you really want SovSec?"

He laughed. "It's the perfect position for me," he said. "Security is what I do best. And besides, it will put me where I can keep an eye on you."

Something about the way he said that last sentence made her pause. But just for an instant. Had it been any other man, she might have wondered if he was telling her the truth about why he wanted SovSec, but not Jibb.

"If that's what you want," she said, "it's yours."

Jibb nodded. "Thank you." He glanced at the sorcerer, who was staring out the window with his hawk on his shoulder, ignoring their conversation. "I guess I should be going," the bodyguard said, though he sounded reluctant, as if he suddenly didn't trust Orris. "Premel has been trying to teach our security system to Cedrych's men, but they're a bit resistant."

"Go ahead," she told him. "We'll be fine."

He nodded again and gave Orris another look. Then, without another word, he left Cedrych's flat.

Melyor walked over to where the sorcerer was standing and glanced out at the Nal as well. "What are you looking at?" she asked him in Tobynmir.

"Nothing really," he answered without moving. "It all looks the same to me. It's like staring into fog: I try to find some detail on which to focus, but my eye just keeps moving from one thing to the next."

She swallowed, not wanting to ask the next question, but knowing that she had no choice. "When do you think you will leave?"

At that he looked at her, his dark brown eyes meeting hers for just a moment before he turned his gaze back to the Nal. "Tomorrow, I think. Perhaps the next day. It's a long journey, and I have a great deal to tell my people."

She cleared her throat awkwardly. "Once the Council accepts my petition I plan to leave the Nal for a short while. I want to find Gwilym's settlement and tell his wife what happened to him." She looked sidelong at him and licked her lips, which abruptly felt dry. "I was hoping you would come with me."

Orris took a long breath. "I'd like that," he said. "But I'm anxious to be home."

Melyor nodded. She had known what he would say, but she had to try.

"There's a part of me that wants to stay, Melyor," he went on, surprising her. "I hope you know that." He made a small, helpless gesture that looked strange coming from such a powerfully built man. "But this place . . ." He shook his head. "It's just too different." He reached up and stroked the feathers on his falcon's back. "And Anizir could never survive here for very long."

"True," Melyor agreed. "The way she eats we would run out of doves very soon."

The humor felt hollow, but they both laughed.

"Will you at least allow me to take you to the isthmus in my air-carrier?" she asked him.

He hesitated. He didn't even like riding in street carriers, she knew.

"Please," she persisted. "It is the least I can do for you, and it will shorten your trip back. Besides, use of the air-carrier is one of the privileges of being Sovereign. And I want to give it a try."

He took another breath, then smiled. "All right."

"There is another matter I wish to discuss with you," Melyor continued, stepping away from the window and forcing herself to regard the sorcerer as a business associate. "When we visited Shivohn, you discussed with her the establishment of trade relations between your land and Oerella-Nal."

"I told her that it was a possibility," Orris corrected quickly. "And I tried to make it clear that it would take several years. My people will be opposed to this.

It will take a long time before they'll even consider it. I certainly didn't promise her anything."

"I understand that," Melyor said, smiling. "I just want to know if the same possibility exists for Bragor-Nal."

"I don't know, Melyor. After what Cedrych did to our land, I can't promise anything."

"You can promise to try."

Orris said nothing for several moments, although he continued to stare at her. Finally, he nodded. "I promise," he said. "I'll try."

"Thank you," Melyor murmured.

They stood without speaking for what seemed a long·time, before Orris turned back to the window, and Melyor returned to Cedrych's old desk and resumed her perusal of the Overlord's papers.

As Jibb had anticipated, Melyor was contacted by several others during the course of the day, including six Nal-Lords and a number of Bragor-Nal's more successful break-laws. All of them offered their service and support, and Melyor realized as she listened to them that none of them meant it. The threat of assassination had always been a part of her life. Any Nal-Lord who failed to recognize that was a fool or a corpse. But Melyor was beginning to see that as Sovereign she would have to take that threat far more seriously than she ever had before. She took great comfort in the knowledge that Jibb would continue to be her security chief.

At the same time, however, she also found herself in the familiar position of chafing at the limitations Jibb tried to place on her activities. He argued vehemently against her plans to visit Gwilym's settlement, pointing out that traveling on foot, through unfamiliar and treacherous terrain, she would be vulnerable to a wide variety of attacks.

"You don't even know where the settlements are!"

"No," she argued, "but I have contacts in the Network who do." He started to say more, but she cut him off. "I'm going to do this, Jibb!" She lifted her staff and gestured sharply at the shining red stone it bore. "I have to do this!"

"Well at least let me come with you!" he insisted. "We'll take five or six units of my best—"

"No," she told him. "I need you here. There's no one else I can trust to take care of the Nal while I'm gone."

"Fine!" Jibb countered. "Then Premel can lead the units, or one of the others!"

Melyor shook her head in frustration. "I refuse to take an army with me into the mountains. Don't you think that will attract some attention? Wouldn't it be safer to let me go alone? Nobody would notice that."

Jibb opened his mouth to argue again, but then he hesitated. "That's an interesting point," he conceded after a moment. "A small group of guards might make more sense."

"And no guards would be even better," she pressed.

"That's not an option."

"Not an option!" she repeated. "You seem to be forgetting that I'm the one who's going to be Sovereign! You work for me!" She regretted it as soon as the words left her mouth. She had never said such a thing to him before.

"I know that,' he said quietly, looking hurt. "But either you let me do my job as head of your security, or you find someone else for the position."

That pretty much ended the argument. Melyor agreed to an escort of Jibb's three best men and she sent a message to Shivohn requesting that her air-carrier be allowed to fly the four of them over Oerella-Nal to the edge of the Dhaal-mar Mountains. But even after Melyor apologized for what she had said, and Jibb assured her that he wasn't hurt, she sensed a sudden awkwardness in their friendship that she had never imagined possible.

She was still thinking about it the next day, as she and Orris flew southward over the Nal toward the LonTobyn Isthmus. She tried to convince herself that everything would be fine once she returned to the Nal from Gwilym's settle-ment, but she could not rid herself of the nagging feeling that she had altered their relationship forever.

"You're very quiet," Orris observed as they sped over the buildings and quads, the twin blades on either side of the carrier humming softly.

She glanced at the sorcerer and tried to smile, but it was no use. First she had alienated her best friend, and now Orris was leaving her. She wasn't certain which was worse. By his very existence, this man had forced her to embrace her Gildriite ancestry. He had changed her life forever, and in the process he had helped her realize her greatest ambition. Because of him, she was about to be-come Bragor-Nal's Sovereign. And yet none of that mattered nearly as much as the fact that he was about to leave. She had never been in love before, so she couldn't be certain, but "in love" seemed as good a description as any for what she felt.

"Jibb and I had a fight last night," she explained, hoping he would accept that this was all that was bothering her. "I said something to him that I regret."

"What was the fight about?"

"He does not want me going into the mountains alone."

Orris nodded and glanced out at the Nal. "Jibb is a wise man."

She exhaled heavily and looked away. "I should have kept my mouth shut," she said with annoyance.

"You have very little experience in the mountains, Melyor," the sorcerer per-sisted. "And no one should undertake such a journey alone."

She shot him a look. "You do all the time!"

He grinned and scratched his falcon's chin with his forefinger. "A mage is never alone."

She gazed at him for several seconds and then nodded. A few weeks ago she wouldn't have understood, but she had learned much since then. It struck her as ironic. As leader of the Initiative she would literally have killed for the knowl-edge she now possessed of Tobyn-Ser and the magic Orris and his kind wielded. Yet, in gaining that knowledge, she had deliberately destroyed the Ini-tiative and killed its creator. All because of Orris. He had changed everything. She looked at her staff with its glowing scarlet crystal and took a long breath.

"Jibb is trying to take care of you," Orris told her. "and that can't be easy."

In spite of everything she laughed. "No. I do not think it is. I just wish he would take his job less seriously."

"His job has nothing to do with it."

"What do you mean?" she demanded. "Of course it does."

A strange smile touched his lips. "You really don't see it, do you?"

"See what?"

"Jibb is in love with you."

She stared at him, saying nothing. A few weeks ago she might have laughed, but in light of Jibb's odd behavior over the past few days, what the sorcerer said made sense. "What should I do?" she asked him.

Orris shrugged. "Follow your heart."

She shook her head and looked away. "If I follow my heart I will end up in Tobyn-Ser." She caught her breath. The words had slipped out before she could stop them. Idiot! she raged at herself. Twice now in less than a day she had spoken without thinking. At least this time she hadn't hurt anyone with her foolishness.

"I don't belong here, Melyor," Orris said gently. "Any more than you belong in my land."

She nodded, still not willing to look at him.

They were drawing nearer to the Guardian Swamp. It wouldn't be long now. Melyor began to tremble.

"Will you ever come back here?" she asked him impulsively, swiveling in her seat to face him.

"I don't know." He indicated the Nal with a gesture. "This place is . . . difficult. I don't belong here," he said again.

"It will change," she told him with conviction. "I am going to change it."

His eyes met hers, and this time Melyor forced herself not to look away. After several moments, he nodded. "I believe you."

She almost asked him if that meant he would return, but she stopped herself. She didn't really want to know the answer.

The pilot landed the carrier on the southern edge of the swamp, within a few hundred yards of the Southern Timber Stand. Melyor and the sorcerer stepped out of the vehicle and were immediately beset by mosquitoes and biting flies. At least this will be quick, Melyor thought.

"Be well, Melyor," Orris said, taking her hand. "I'll never forget you." He hesitated, and then gave a rueful smile. "And for what it's worth, Jibb isn't the only one who loves you."

It was remarkable how a single phrase could hurt her so much and at the same time bring a smile to her lips. There was nothing she could say. She stepped forward, kissed him lightly on the lips, and then tried to pull away.

She wanted to retreat to the safety of the air-carrier, but Orris would not release her hand. Reluctantly, she turned to face him again. His expression had grown grave. "Tell Gwilym's family that I'm sorry, and that I was proud to call the Bearer my friend."

She nodded. "I will."

He let go of her hand, turned, and walked away, the sleek falcon on his shoulder, his carry sack, bulging with the food she had given him, strapped to his back, and the stoneless staff in his hand. Melyor watched him until he reached the trees. Then she climbed into the carrier and ordered the pilot to take her back to her headquarters.

Melyor and her escort reached the first of the Gildriite settlements four weeks later. The people there regarded her and Jibb's men with both alarm and fascination, but none of them questioned the authenticity of her stone and staff. They were reluctant, however, to direct her to Gwilym's settlement. The leader of the village, a tall, white-haired man named Oswin, who carried a stone of pale blue, asked her many questions about Gwilym and what had happened to him. She answered honestly, hoping to overcome his suspicions, but he and the villagers who were listening to their exchange gave no indication that they were willing to trust her. Centuries of persecution had taken their toll on the Gildri-ites, even up here in the Dhaalmar.

"So you have come to return his stone to his village?" Oswin asked after some time.

"No," Melyor told him. "I intend to keep the stone. It changed color when Gwilym gave it to me. I believe that means it's mine now."

The white-haired man conceded the point with a nod. "Then why have you come?" he asked.

"I want to see Gwilym's family. I want to tell them what happened, and that I'm sorry I couldn't save the Bearer's life."

"I will tell them for you."

Exhausted from her journey, and frustrated by Oswin's intransigence, Melyor turned away, exhaling loudly through her teeth. She turned to argue with him again, but doing so, she saw a large, muscular man standing among the other villagers. He looked strangely out of place in the settlement and Melyor stared at him for several moments.

Oswin turned to look in that direction as well, and then he began to nod. He beckoned the man forward. "Come here, Kham. Perhaps you can help us. Kham used to live in your Nal," Oswin explained, as the crowd parted, allow-ing the big man to come forward. A moment later the muscular man stopped before them. She noticed that his right hand had been maimed. "Do you know this woman, Kham?" the Bearer asked.

The man pushed his long blond hair back from his face and looked closely at Melyor. "I'm not sure."

"Perhaps you know my name," she said. "I'm Melyor i Lakin."

Kham's eyes widened.

"Do you know her?" Oswin asked again.

"Yes," the big man said in a hushed voice. "She is a Nal-Lord from Bragor-Nal."

"Actually, I'm Sovereign now."

"Sovereign?" Kham whispered. He glanced at Oswin. "I don't know what to tell you, Bearer," he said. "She has a reputation as one of the most danger-ous lords in the Nal. But if what she says is true, if she is both Sovereign and a Gildriite, then things in the Nal are far different from what they were when I left. I can't help you."

"Your friend is right," Melyor said. "About a number of things. I've always been good with a blade and thrower; I've done my share of killing. But I've changed in the time I've had this stone, and as Sovereign, I plan to change the Nal as well."

Oswin stared at Melyor for a long time, as if weighing her words. Then he appeared to make a decision. "I will tell you how to reach Gwilym's settlement under one condition."

"Name it."

"You will leave your weapon and your companions here. Kham will guide you."

"Sovereign, no!" one of Jibb's men pleaded.

But Melyor ignored him. "That's acceptable. Thank you, Bearer."

Gwilym's settlement proved to be only a day's walk away. Melyor and Kham entered the small valley just before sunset, and were surrounded immediately by a knot of curious villagers. Then one of them recognized Melyor's staff, and abruptly the crowd fell silent.

At the same time a woman stepped forward to stand directly in front of Melyor. She was a stout woman with deep brown eyes and soft features. Her hair was brown with thin streaks of grey, and her clothes were plain, much like those of every other person in the settlement. Indeed, there was really nothing that set the woman apart. And yet Melyor knew that this was Gwilym's wife.

"My husband is dead," she said in a low voice.

"Yes."

"And his stone is yours now."

A number of the villagers began to object, but the woman silenced them with a glare.

"He told me it was, just before he died."

The woman nodded, a single tear rolling down her cheek. "So be it," she said. She placed an arm around Melyor's shoulders and led her toward a cloth shelter near the top of the valley. "My name is Hertha," she said. "I dreamed you would come."

34

All members of the League of Amarid shall, at the time of their initiation, take an oath to obey and uphold the Bylaws enumerated in these pages. They shall also pledge themselves to abide by Amarid's Laws as written by Amarid himself, save for the following exception.

Amarid's Third Law states: "Mages shall never use their powers against one another. Disputes among mages shall be judged by the Order." We hereby amend the Third Law to read as follows: *"Mages of the League shall never use their powers against one another. Disputes among mages of the League shall be judged by those members of the League who are not party to the dispute."*

In addition, we hereby amend Amarid's Laws by adding a Fifth provision which reads as follows: "Mages of the League shall, whenever possible, avoid using their powers against other mages. When, in the course of fulfilling their oaths to guard the land, mages of the League find that they must act against other mages, they shall do so with restraint and in a manner that poses as little risk to Tobyn-Ser's people as possible."

> —From Article Two of "The Charter and Bylaws of the League of Amarid," drafted at the 1st Annual Conclave of the League of Amarid, Spring, Gods' Year 4626.

The weather remained mild and predictable throughout their journey across the isthmus, allowing Orris and Anizir to maintain a good pace. The heavy afternoon rain showers provided the travelers with all the water they needed and brought cooler air, but still Orris chose to follow the contours of the land bridge's meandering northern coast rather than brave the jungles in the heat of summer.

Despite the distance this added, and Orris's eagerness to reach Tobyn-Ser, the mage and his falcon enjoyed their journey. Freed from the oppressive shadows and rank air of the Nal, Orris savored the scent of Arick's Sea and the feel of the bright sun on his skin. Anizir hunted and soared with a fervor that Orris had never seen in her before, and while the mage did eat some of the bland Nal food that Melyor had given him, he and his bird usually made meals of the ducks and other fowl that Anizir brought back from her frequent forays into the jungle or over the water.

At night, as he sat beside the low driftwood fires, the mage thought of Melyor, wondering whether she had found Gwilym's settlement and trying to imagine what it meant to be Sovereign of the entire Nal. He did not regret leaving Lon-Ser, but he knew that it would be some time before he would be able to look at another woman and not think of Melyor.

They reached the eastern edge of the isthmus in early autumn, just as a cool wind began to blow out of the north. Thrilled to be back in his homeland, the mage turned northward into the forests of Duclea's Tears and increased his pace. He was anxious now to find Jaryd, Alayna, and his other friends, and he was hungry for news of the Order.

Keeping to the western slope of the Seaside mountains, Orris traveled for two more days before he finally encountered a village. It was a small one, nestled beside a narrow stream, just at the base of the Lower Horn. As he approached the small wooden houses he could smell cooking fires riding the breeze. There was a clearing on the far side of the stream where the common garden was located, and he heard the ring of a blacksmith's hammer in the distance. Several people were milling about near the town center, but at first, no one noticed him. Orris smiled, quickening his steps. He was home. He didn't even know the name of the village, but he was home.

And yet, as he passed the first of the homes he noticed something that made him halt in the middle of the rough road leading into the village. A square, unmarked blue cloth hung on the door of each house, stirring slightly in the wind. Looking toward the center of the village, Orris spotted the Temple of Arick and saw that its tallest spire bore a cloth as well. It was the same color as the others and it was also square in shape, but this one was far larger than those on the houses.

Orris felt a sudden inexplicable clenching in his stomach, and, not for the first time since leaving Bragor-Nal, he wished he had a ceryll on his staff. Sensing his disquiet, Anizir let out a soft cry. Orris scratched her chin absently.

It's all right, he sent reflexively, although he was not at all convinced of that himself. He started forward again, but cautiously.

He had only taken a few steps when one of the villagers near the center of town saw him approaching and called out to the others. Almost instantly a crowd formed. A woman in a silver-grey robe emerged from the Temple and spoke briefly to the people gathered there before leading them toward Orris.

"This can't be good," the mage muttered to himself stopping in his tracks again. Anizir cried out a second time.

"Greetings, Keeper!" Orris called out, making himself smile as the mob drew nearer. "I am Hawk-Mage Orris. I've—"

"What do you want here?" the Keeper demanded in a severe voice, halting a few feet from where Orris now stood. She was a small woman with short brown hair and large, widely spaced brown eyes. She couldn't have been much older than Jaryd and Alayna.

"I've travelled a great distance," Orris explained, his smile fading. "I was hoping to get some food and ale. In exchange for my services, of course."

"This is a League town," the woman told him. "Don't you see the blue flags?"

Orris glanced at the houses again and nodded. "I see them, yes," he said. "But I don't understand what they mean. Perhaps you would be kind enough to—"

"This is a League town!" the Keeper repeated. She sounded angry, but there was fear in her eyes. "You must leave immediately!"

The mage closed his eyes briefly and took a long breath. He had never been a patient man. "I've been away from Tobyn-Ser for a long time," he told her. "I don't know what the League is, but perhaps I can help you."

"Your cloak is green," the woman said.

Orris stared at her for several moments. Had she lost her wits? Had they all?

Orris had heard of such things happening to entire villages. "Yes," he replied slowly. "My cloak is green."

"So you belong to the Order."

"Of course."

"And what I'm telling you," the woman continued, a note of impatience creeping into her voice, "is that this is a League town."

"What in Arick's name is the League?" Orris exploded.

She stared at him as if he was the one who had gone insane. They all did. "The League of Amarid," she said, as if this explained everything. "It was formed by First Master Erland and First-Mage Cailin."

The League of Amarid. First Master Erland. Of course. That made perfect sense. All of it did. Except Cailin. Orris thought for a moment, and then nodded. Actually that made sense, too. He felt sick.

"So there are League towns and Order towns?" he asked in a flat voice.

"Yes," the woman said. "You really knew nothing of this?"

That's what I was trying to tell you! he wanted to scream. But suddenly he didn't have the strength. He wasn't even sure he could walk. He would have liked to sit down—right there, in the middle of the road. But he was even more eager to leave the town. He just needed a bit more information.

"How long?" he managed. He swallowed. He was afraid he might throw up.

"Just since the end of spring," she answered. She looked at him closely. "The League is open to all mages. I'm sure First Master Erland would welcome you."

Just since the spring. Orris still remembered using the Ceryll-Var to contact Baden. That had been in the spring, too. "Erland has finally learned of what you did," the Owl-Master had said that day. "He's convinced that you were acting as part of a conspiracy, and he intends to have you charged with treason." Was that what all this was about? Orris knew Jaryd and Alayna would never have allowed Erland and his allies to charge him with treason. Which would have convinced Erland that they had betrayed the land as well. Orris shook his head. Had he done all of this? Was he responsible for the collapse of the Order?

"What about Cailin," he asked. "Has she been with the League long?"

The woman nodded. "Almost from the beginning, yes. Do you know her?"

He shook his head. "Not very well." He hadn't seen Cailin in years, not since she had left the Great Hall to live with the Keepers. But he could still envision her face, and he still remembered the night he learned of the attack on her town. He had been at Theron's Grove with Jessamyn and Peredur and the rest of the delegation. And he had blamed Baden.

"Thank you," he said to the woman. "I'll be leaving your village."

He turned to go.

"Wait!" the Keeper called.

Orris looked back at her.

"Are you going to join the League?"

The mage tried to smile. "I don't think they'd want me."

He left the village as quickly as he could and continued northward, driven still to find Jaryd and Alayna, but by a different kind of urgency.

He came within sight of the waters of South Shelter several days later and turned inland to follow the inlet's eastern shore. He had passed by several more towns since his conversation with the Keeper, but the homes in all of them had been displaying blue flags. He wondered if there were any Order towns left.

It was another day and a half before he reached the village nearest Jaryd and Alayna's home, and he was relieved to see that this town at least displayed flags of forest green. He hurried through the town, following a narrow lane through the woods that led to the home of his friends. In spite of everything, his heart was suddenly pounding with excitement at the thought of seeing them.

The house was just as he remembered: small, but homey, with a clear view of South Shelter and a small plume of pale grey smoke rising from the chimney. Orris stood for some time at the edge of Jaryd and Alayna's garden, just gazing at the house. *At last,* he sent to Anizir. *We're back at last.*

After some time, Alayna stepped out of the house carrying a bucket of dirty water. Her long dark hair was tied back, and the muscles in her thin arms were corded. Her magnificent grey hawk sat on her shoulder, and it was the bird who first spotted Orris.

Alayna saw him a moment later. She hastily set down the bucket, called for Jaryd, and ran into Orris's arms so quickly that both of their hawks had to leap into the air to keep from being crushed.

"By the Gods!" Alayna whispered, wrapping her arms around him. "By the Gods!"

Orris couldn't speak. He just held her.

"Alayna?" Jaryd called from within the house. "What's—"

Orris glanced over Alayna's shoulder and saw Jaryd standing frozen in the doorway, his hair long, and his face looking squarer and more mature than Orris remembered.

"I knew you'd make it back!" the young mage breathed. And an instant later he was there as well, throwing his long arms around Orris and Alayna both.

The three of them stood that way for a very long time, each of them seemingly unwilling to let go.

"What does a guest have to do to get fed around here?" Orris finally asked.

His friends laughed, and Alayna released him and stepped back. Her cheeks were damp with tears.

"We've eaten," she said, "but there's still plenty. Even for an appetite like yours."

They led him into the house and sat him down at the table. And as they placed bowls of food in front of him, they began to pepper him with questions about his journey. He answered as many as he could, giving them a very brief account of what had happened in Bragor-Nal and making it clear that the threat to Tobyn-Ser had died with Cedrych. But then he held up a hand, cutting Jaryd off in the middle of yet another question.

"You have to let me eat!" he said, drawing smirks from both of them. "I'll tell you more later, when I'm done!" He took a sip of wine. "In the meantime, why don't you tell me about the League."

Jaryd and Alayna exchanged a look, their smiles vanishing abruptly, and then they proceeded to relate what had happened at the Gathering convened by Sonel the previous spring. They took turns speaking, and both of them went out of their way to avoid saying the obvious. So, in the end, Orris was forced to say it himself.

"This happened because I took Baram, didn't it?"

The young mages glanced at each other uncomfortably.

"It had been coming for some time," Jaryd offered.

"I know. But that doesn't really answer my question."

"I think Erland had been wanting to do something like this for a while," Alayna said. "You just gave him the excuse he needed."

Orris considered this for several moments before giving a single nod. "How bad is it?" he asked.

Jaryd shrugged. "It's hard to say. Many of the towns are still sorting themselves out. At this point, there are more League towns than Order towns."

"That much even I could see," Orris said.

"You came up from Duclea's Tears?" Alayna asked.

Orris nodded.

"You can't judge just on what you saw between here and there. There are still places where the Order has a majority of the towns: the Northern Plain, the northern half of Tobyn's Wood, and most of the Great Desert. Jaryd's right: the League probably has a majority of the land's towns, but it's not nearly as one-sided as it seems around here."

"So what happens to mages who belong to the Order but serve areas dominated by the League?"

"It varies," Jaryd answered. "Those who want to remain in the Order usually find a new area to serve."

Orris raised an eyebrow. "And the others?"

"The others join the League."

He didn't want to ask, but he had to. "How many do we have left?"

Jaryd shook his head and said nothing.

"Twenty-five," Alayna told him. "Thirty at the most."

Orris let out a slow breath. "Twenty-five would be less than half."

Alayna nodded. "I know."

Orris rose and stepped to the doorway. It was dark out. Stars shone overhead and he could see Leora spinning in her endless dance. "I feel like I've destroyed the Order."

"From the little bit you've told us," Jaryd replied, "it sounds to me like you saved Tobyn-Ser."

Orris turned back to them. He wanted to believe them; he wanted to believe that he hadn't caused all this. But he knew better. It was his fault. Perhaps, on some level, Jaryd and Alayna knew this as well. But if they did, they were hiding it.

"Believe him," Alayna said, as if she had read Orris's thoughts. "You're not to blame."

Orris smiled in spite of himself. "I've missed the two of you."

Alayna grinned. "We've missed you, too."

He sighed heavily. He wanted to change the subject. "How are Baden and Trahn?"

"They're both fine," she said. "Actually, Trahn is expecting us to reach for him soon."

"You're still maintaining the link?"

Jaryd gave a small laugh. "If you can call it that. Without you and Baden, there are only six of us left. I'm not sure how effective we've been."

Alayna looked at the young mage. "I guess we're through with that though, aren't we?"

Jaryd returned her smile. "I guess we are."

"Wait," Orris broke in. "Baden's not helping with the link anymore?" He felt a sudden surge of apprehension. "Is he all right?"

Jaryd nodded. "He's fine. But he's Sonel's First now. He spends most of his time at the Great Hall."

"What happened to Toinan? When I left, she was the Sage's First."

"She's with the League now."

Orris shook his head. It came as a relief that Baden was well, but there seemed to be no end to the harm he had caused. "Can't you tell me anything good?" he asked them. "Are there any tidings that don't include the League or Erland?"

Again the young mages shared a look, and Orris felt his heart expand at what he saw pass between them.

"We have some news," Alayna said, a radiant smile lighting her face.

Orris knew instantly what she was going to say, and he found that he was grinning as well.

"We're going to have a baby."

He looked at Jaryd, who was smiling like an idiot. "That's wonderful," Orris said. He wanted to say more—he could see that they were expecting him to—but he couldn't think of anything else. Normally he would have made some comment about how their child was fated to be a mage, perhaps even Owl-Sage, but under the circumstances, that didn't seem appropriate. For all he knew, the Order would be gone by the time this child was old enough to master the Mage-Craft. He couldn't imagine Tobyn-Ser without the Order. It had never even occurred to him to try. Until now. Even this, Orris thought with both anger and heartache. I've even ruined this.

They were watching him, waiting. He had to say something. "That's wonderful," he repeated at last, hoping the words wouldn't sound as hollow to his friends as they felt to him.

35

Orris's report on his remarkably successful journey to Lon-Ser makes for such extraordinary reading that I felt the Keepers of Arick's Temple and the members of your League should have the opportunity to read it. Therefore I have taken the liberty of having extra copies scribed, and I hereby present the volume to you as a gesture of the Order's good will.

As you will see, despite dire predictions of what might happen as a result of Orris's impetuous but well-meaning actions, we have less to fear from Lon-Ser today than we have had at any time over the past decade. The man responsible for planning and supporting the attacks on our land has been killed. The new Sovereign of Bragor-Nal has vowed to address the problems that first led to the attacks on Tobyn-Ser. The Sovereigns of both Oerella-Nal and Bragor-Nal have professed their interest in peaceful relations with our land. And finally, Baram has died as well, and though I am saddened by this last development, I am willing to concede that it brings to a close a painful and divisive episode in our land's history.

In short, all the issues that have divided us over the past several years have been settled. I am hopeful that after you have read this report you will agree that the time has come to heal the rift between us.

—Letter from Owl-Master Baden, First of the Sage of the Order of Mages and Masters, to Owl-Master Erland, First Master of the League of Amarid, Spring, Gods' Year 4627.

The songs of wrens and finches floated through his house like dandelion seeds, calling him out to his garden. The spring rains had passed. The grasses and trees outside his home were bathed in the bright warmth of the sun. He should have been tending to his columbine and pruning his roses. But Erland could not stop staring at the traitor's report and the gloating letter from Baden that had accompanied it.

Notwithstanding Baden's claims to the contrary and his fatuous plea for some sort of reconciliation, Orris's alleged accomplishments changed nothing. The Hawk-Mage had defied the will of the Order. He had given aid to an enemy of the land. The outlander had earned his execution, and instead Orris had given him freedom and returned him to his home. That Baram died there did nothing to absolve Orris of his crime. At least this is what Erland told himself.

But a voice in the back of his mind, small but too insistent to be ignored, kept whispering, *This changes everything.*

The League had thirty-five members now, perhaps more; he'd know for certain at the next Conclave. But he was confident that the League's membership exceeded that of the Order by at least ten mages. And the gap was still growing. Erland believed that by midsummer the Order would be forced to abandon its pledge to serve the entire land. How could twenty mages—or, dare he hope it, even fewer—hope to serve so vast a land? It was impossible. Sonel and Baden would have to give up the western shores. Between Duclea's Tears and Leora's Forest fewer than ten villages remained loyal to the Order, in part because people on the coast felt particularly vulnerable to attacks from across Arick's Sea. And with more and more mages leaving the Order, Sonel and Baden could not afford to waste any of their meager membership on an area that offered them so little. True, the Order was still strong in the Great Desert, in parts of Tobyn's Wood, and on the Northern Plain, but once the western shores belonged to the League, the rest of Tobyn-Ser would follow. In another year there might not even be an Order. Or so he wanted to believe.

He shook his head, as if responding to something his owl had said. He found it hard to fathom how one mage in a land as alien as that described in Baden's ponderous report could effect such sweeping changes. How could Orris be so sure that this Melyor of whom he wrote would not revert to her old ways and renew the attacks on Tobyn-Ser? What assurances had she given him? And if the leader of Oerella-Nal—Sovereign Shivohn he called her—if she was as sympathetic to our concerns as the mage claimed, why hadn't she stopped the previous attacks? Erland didn't believe any of it. And even if he did, he refused to accept that there weren't others in Lon-Ser who were already plotting to take up Cedrych's cause as their own. They lived in cities so large that they covered the entire land. They had created weapons that could destroy entire villages in a matter of minutes. People like that couldn't be trusted. Anyone in their right mind understood that.

Surely, the people of Tobyn-Ser did. They wanted nothing to do with Nals and Sovereigns and advanced goods. That was why they had turned to the League in the first place. They knew that Tobyn-Ser was better off following the principles espoused by Amarid and defended with such valor by Fordel, Decla, and Glenyse. The First Mage and the land's three Eagle-Sages had devoted their lives to protecting Tobyn-Ser's sovereignty. But more than that, they had seen to it that no alien influences of any kind impinged upon the land's customs and culture.

The attacks by the outlanders had demonstrated the dangers of straying from these principles. And all of Baden's arguments could not obscure that essential truth. Tobyn-Ser's safest course was not to reach out across Arick's Sea to embrace these monsters as friends, but rather to guard its borders with renewed vigilance lest it fall victim to such atrocities again.

The people of Tobyn-Ser possessed a simple wisdom. They understood this, even if the Order did not. They had to. There was too much at stake. Lon-Ser, they knew, was peopled with brutes and governed by a system that bred cruelty and violence. This was why the League would prevail, why it had to prevail.

"The people are turning away from the Order," Erland said out loud, drawing a wide-eyed stare from his owl, who had been asleep on the mantel above the dormant hearth. "It may be able to survive for a short while, but in the end the League will be the sole guardian of Amarid's legacy."

He stared at his familiar, as if daring her to disagree with him. She returned his gaze for several moments before ruffling her feathers slightly and closing her eyes again.

The Owl-Master had to admit that Orris's successes might win back some of the Order's support. To many, the end of the Lon-Ser threat—if, in fact, Orris's report was to be believed—justified the mage's treachery. Indeed, it even seemed possible, perhaps even likely, that the League would lose some of its newer members, who had never been fully comfortable with their decision to leave the Order.

But for every mage who was willing to forgive Orris for what he had done, there would be another who wanted him dead. For every village in the land that might be willing to pledge its loyalty to the Order one last time, there would be another that would never again welcome a man or woman wearing a green cloak. The Order's very survival depended upon its ability to overcome the doubts and fears of Tobyn-Ser's people. The League needed only to feed those doubts and wait.

And Orris's report even gave Erland and his allies a place to begin. It was a minor point, buried in the final section of the report. But it had caught the Owl-Master's eye as if it were a weed growing among his peonies.

Opening Orris's report once more, Erland reread the passage.

"It also bears mentioning," Orris had written, "that I discussed with the Sovereigns of both Oerella-Nal and Bragor-Nal the possibility of establishing trade relations between Lon-Ser and Tobyn-Ser. I gave them no assurances, and I made it clear to them that such relations would be established well in the future, if at all. But I believe that at some point our land could benefit from commerce with the our western neighbor just as it has benefitted from our trade with Abborij."

It came as no surprise to Erland that Orris had the audacity to discuss such an arrangement with the Sovereigns. Clearly the man had no regard for authority or propriety. But that he should choose to mention this in his report struck the Owl-Master as either grossly arrogant or astonishingly foolish. Even the suggestion of trade with Lon-Ser, coming so soon after the outlanders' attacks, would only invite the scorn of every sane person in Tobyn-Ser. A truce was one thing, but commerce was quite another. The people would never stand for it. And if Baden, Orris, and the rest pushed too hard, it would only hasten the Order's demise.

This changes everything.

"Not this," Erland whispered. "Surely not this."

His owl opened one eye and then closed it again.

The Owl-Master shook his head, retrieved his pruning knife from the table, where it lay beside Orris's report, and stepped out into his garden.

He would think about the report again later, after he had seen to his flowers and herbs. There was an answer, he knew. There was a way to turn all of this to the League's advantage. He just needed some time to clear his mind. Feeling the sun on his face, he paused and closed his eyes. He inhaled deeply, trying to draw some comfort and peace from the warm air and the scent of his roses. He could still hear the wrens and finches calling from hidden perches all around him, and he found himself hoping that their songs would be loud enough to drown out the voice in his head.

About the Author

David B. Coe grew up just outside of New York City, the youngest of four children. He attended Brown University as an undergraduate and later received a Ph.D. in history from Stanford. He briefly considered a career as an academic, but wisely thought better of it.

He is now a freelance writer. He lives in Tennessee with his wife, Nancy J. Berner, their daughter, Alex, and, of course, Buddy, the wonder dog. *The Outlanders* is his second novel. He is currently working on *Eagle-Sage*, the final volume of the LonTobyn Chronicle.